PRAISE FOR THE CAS[illegible]

"In this Southern Gothic lo[illegible] w Orleans's storied past, Arden [illegible] and mystery . . . A thoroughly sat[illegible]ner and a strong debut."

—*Publishers Weekly*, Starred Review

"Debut author Arden offers readers a full plate of Southern Gothic atmospherics and sparkling teen romance in a patiently crafted tale that will best reward careful readers . . . Satisfying teen entertainment but also a cathartic, uncompromising tribute to New Orleans."

—*Kirkus Reviews*

"A slow-burning novel in the tradition of Anne Rice."

—*Rue Morgue Magazine*

"A smart story with a surprising amount of emotional dept . . . in the grand tradition of *Buffy* and *The Lost Boys*."

—*IndieReader*

"Nothing short of a stunner ."

—*Examiner.com*

"Eerie, magical, and gritty, getting into the grimy seams of New Orleans in the tradition of Anne Rice or Poppy Z Brite."

—*SP Reviews*

PRAISE FOR THE ROMEO CATCHERS

"Fans will be floored by *The Romeo Catchers*, the much-anticipated follow up to *The Casquette Girls*. An intense dreamscape of a read full of magic, menace, and mystery."

—Tonya Hurley, *New York Times* bestselling author of the ghostgirl series and the Blessed trilogy

"Arden continues to woo culture and history mavens, adding vivid New Orleans color (the funeral procession) and plenty of post-hurricane detail (such as Isaac's grim recovery work, so similar to that carried out after Katrina). Warm, carefully drawn characters are the story's main attraction. A meticulous blend of witchery, New Orleans lore, and teen angst."

—*Kirkus Reviews*

"This detailed and descriptive sequel is every bit as engrossing as the first, with deftly drawn character arcs and a captivating setting."

—*School Library Journal*

"Adele's supernatural roller-coaster ride continues at breakneck speed, with shocking revelations along the bloodstained way. Rich descriptions of post-storm New Orleans as well as a variety of vivid secondary characters create a lush background, allowing this extraordinary story to thrive. Readers will be enchanted and horrified in turn as Arden plunges them into a sudden, unpredictable cliffhanger that will leave them as stunned as her characters."

—*RT Book Reviews*

The Cities of Dead

ALSO BY ALYS ARDEN

The Casquette Girls Series

The Casquette Girls

The Romeo Catchers

The Cities of Dead

ALYS ARDEN

This is a work of fiction. Names, characters, organizations, places, events, and incidents are either products of the imagination or used fictitiously. Any resemblance to actual persons, living or dead, or actual events is purely coincidental.

Published by For the Art of It, New Orleans

www.alysarden.com

ISBN-13: 978-0-989757744

Cover illustration by Galen Dara

Cover design by Parajunkee

Map illustration by Mystic Blue Signs

Chapter heading designs by Christy Zolty

Printed in the United States of America

To the witches of New Orleans:
past, present, and future.

ARMSTRONG
CONGO SQUARE
RAMPART
CANAL
BIENVILLE
CONTI
TOULOUSE
ST. PETER
BURGUNDY
ORLEANS
ST. ANN
DUMAINE
ST PHILIP
URSULINES
GOV NICHOLLS
BARRACKS
ESPLANADE
DAUPHINE
VODOU
BOURBON ORLEANS HOTEL
ARCADIAN BOOKS
CLOVER GRILL
Cafe Orleans
Lafitte's BLACKSMITH SHOP
ROYAL
Bottom of the Cup
TEA ROOM
Le chat noir
CHARTRES
SAINT LOUIS CATHEDRAL
JACKSON SQUARE
URSULINES CONVENT
DECATUR
AMPHITHEATRE
Le VIEUX CARRÉ
MISSISSIPPI RIVER

PART I
THE AFTERMATH

Un seul être vous manque, et tout est dépeuplé !

Sometimes, only one person is missing, and the whole world seems depopulated.

Alphonse de Lamartine, L'isolement, Méditations Poétiques

CHAPTER 1

MAGICLESS

April 16th

Everything felt off.

The kitchen *looked* the same—the morning light shining through the delicate, unwashed lace curtains over the sink, the dull black-and-white tiled floor, the same old canisters on the counter that had protected saltine crackers and vanilla wafers from the humidity before the Storm. It was all so familiar yet now, it all felt wrong.

The scent of yesterday's coffee lingered, because nothing had disturbed the air since. We were out of cookable food. Our supply of oatmeal had once seemed endless, but yesterday I'd eaten it for breakfast, lunch, and dinner, just like I had the day before and the day before, and that was the end of it. The pot was still in the sink, full of tepid, gluey-looking water.

As I stood lifelessly staring at the stove, cold seeped from the floor tiles through the furry purple socks Mémé and Pépé had given me two Christmases earlier. Three of the burners were empty, and the fourth held a brass kettle my father had made ages ago. A trace of chemicals wafted down the hallway from his studio, just a faint stain in the air; he hadn't been spending much time in his workroom.

If I stilled my breath, I could hear a gentle wheeze through his bedroom door. His keys and wallet were on the island behind me. The contents of his pockets, and the snoring, were the only signs that I wasn't alone in the house. My gaze fixed on the front right burner and a shiver ran up my spine. My temperature seemed like it could never regulate—I was always too cold or too hot. The chill deepened the longer I stared. *Remember, Adele, when this was all you wanted to happen when you looked at the stove?*

Nothing. Just like any other non-magical girl.

I focused on the gap beneath the metal grate holding the kettle. A wave of shudders danced around my neck, leaving behind a feverish trace as I tried to feel anything. Warmth broke out across my hairline.

There was no tingling.

No supernatural sensation.

No magic.

My fire was gone.

Everything felt off.

My mother was dead.

A surge of anger ripped through my limbs, an impulsive need to kick the oven door in. Instead, I turned and opened the fridge, hoping by some miracle my father had refilled it when he got off work this morning. Or maybe refrigerator fairies or kitchen elves had scurried in overnight.

A lonely jar shone under the fluorescent bulb. Pickles. Not the giant kind you bought at a Jazz Fest tent nor the crinkle-cut kind good for po'boys, but the miniature kind that were standard in France. *Les cornichons.*

When I was little, the fridge was never without them, or the super seedy mustard that cost like eight dollars a jar because *il est importé de France.* My mother had said having them made her feel like a tiny piece of home was with her every day.

After she left, our fridge never saw another cornichon—and I'd all but forgotten about them—until I ended up in Paris after the Storm. To me, they didn't taste like France; they tasted like home. The one from my childhood. The one I'd shared with my mother and father. The one I'd jammed to the black-hole corner of my mind along with anything else I wanted to fade away with my adolescence: the taste of sour on my tongue that had made my four-year-old face squinch; the way my mother had slowly moved her lips until I pronounced "les cornichons" correctly; and the way my father had lovingly watched us when I announced that I liked yellow American mustard better than her Dijon.

I'd rediscovered my love for *les cornichons* while at a café in Montmartre with Émile. After that, he'd always made sure my dormitory refrigerator was stocked with them, saying they were from my mother. I'd never believed him, but now I wanted to think it was true. When he and Brigitte showed up in New Orleans last fall, a box of them had appeared on our doorstep, straight from Paris. We'd struggled to find basic necessities, but we were stocked with fancy pickles.

That was eight months ago. Now there was one jar left in the fridge, one last little gherkin floating in the vinegary water. If I ate it, the juice would be drained down the sink, the jar would be tossed in the trash, and the memories of our home would wash away with all the other long forgotten things.

My eyes stung. Brigitte and I never had a semblance of a relationship, and now we never would. I don't know why I ever thought I could save her.

My mother and I never stood a chance.

My gaze flicked to the only other item on the top shelf in the fridge: a stack of too-orange cheese slices that had coagulated into a plastic-looking brick. They were the remains of a months-old government handout: a crate half-filled with supplies—American cheese, bread, rice, soup, red beans, and cans of water—that had gone to the first wave of returnees post-Storm. That was, until they'd run out. I'd felt guilty when we'd received one of the crates, but over the past couple weeks when my dad stopped going to the store, I was glad that we still had most of it. Now there was nothing in the fridge but a jar of Mémé's mixed-fruit preserves that Jeanne had brought over to try to make me feel better, a bottle of Ren's moonshine to try to make my dad feel better, one fancy pickle, and a brick of plastic cheese.

Plastic cheese.

The image of Nicco walking into the living room to erase my father's memories slid into my mind, and I slammed the door.

It was stupid to be mad at Nicco. Mac had only known my secrets for a couple hours, so in theory we were just back to the way things had always been, but I still had a violent reaction whenever I thought about it. Maybe it was simply the death of my mother. Maybe it was the loss of my magic. Maybe it was because I felt completely alone without the coven. Maybe I just . . . wanted a reason to shut Nicco out.

Maybe I just wanted him to be here now?

Another shiver jutted up my spine.

We were back to the way things had always been, but it wasn't the same. Knowing definitively that my father would *never* know the truth about me, or about Brigitte, cut deep. My mother, in a moment of weakness, had once told my father everything—and then she'd wiped his memories for his own safety. Now I'd done the same, via Nicco, and I'd inadvertently driven a wedge between me and my father that I didn't know how to live with. I was beginning to see why Brigitte had needed an ocean of separation from him, from us. The same secrets felt heavier now. Like the magic had borne some of the weight, and now that my magic was gone, the secrets were crushing me.

I re-opened the fridge, grabbed the block of cheese, and chucked it into the trash. I hated that everything reminded me of Nicco—of his soapy scent and leather and *bellas*. I hated that every time I went to sleep, I was afraid our dreams would connect. I hated that every morning when I woke up, I was sad that they hadn't.

Even my power, as "vapid as dream magic," as Callis had called it, was gone. The chill returned.

As I hugged myself, the sleeve of Nicco's green-and-black checkered flannel shirt pushed to my elbow, revealing the mark on my arm: the thin black line of a triangle about the size of my fist. I'd tried to scrub it off fifty times. *What does a mundane need with the mark of the witch?* And yet, in the darkest times over the last couple months, it had been the only thing I had left to cling to: a tiny pulse of hope buried beneath an avalanche of depression. I should have been thanking Mother Nature for not letting the mark wash away.

My stomach gurgled, begging me to fill it with anything. I turned to my father's things on the counter and visualized myself picking up his wallet, opening the front door, stepping outside, walking down the street to Palermo's for groceries. Mr. Felix would greet me with hugs and tell me a cherished story about my mother. I'd do my best to hold in the tears, but I'd start crying while I picked over the selection of canned goods; and then Mrs. Rosaria would bring me straight back to the kitchen and force-feed me a PB&J.

I want ten PB&Js.

I sighed and trudged down the hallway toward the front door, my furry socks sliding against the wooden floor. Something was missing. I paused, listening. The foyer was too silent. No tick-tocking pendulum swings. The hands of the grandfather clock were frozen.

I considered winding it manually, but admitting that my magic was gone made my heart ache. I gazed at the front door, at the metal handle. It'd been so long since I'd used my keys, I didn't even know where they were. My hand slid to the staircase banister as I walked up to my bedroom instead.

I hadn't left the house in eleven weeks.

CHAPTER 2

HEARTLESS

Under the cover of my duvet, I dreamt of fire.

And I awoke to the distinct sounds of metal clanging in the kitchen —not something I'd have noticed months ago, but now I was so used to the silent solitude that any little sound echoed up to my room. I threw off the blanket and sprang from bed, but then groggily stumbled. I grabbed a pale pink cable-knit sweater from a pile on the floor and stretched it over my head as I went downstairs with visions of sandwiches and soup and cereal dancing in my head.

But when I entered the kitchen, there wasn't any evidence of grocery shopping. No empty bags on the floor, no boiling water or signs of food to come. My father finished drying the oatmeal pot and hung it back on the rack above his head. Empty beer bottles had been organized into a bag for recycling. We still didn't have collection service, but he dropped them off at the recycling center every couple weeks because it was next to the junkyard where he scavenged scrap metal.

"Good morning," he said, kissing my cheek.

I winced when his unshaven cheek scraped my skin. "It's four p.m."

"Well, I just woke up, and from the looks of it, you just woke up too."

I opened the nearest cabinet, closed it, and opened the next. There wasn't a grind of coffee or a single bud of chamomile, much less food. I knew we'd both taken a turn for the worse over the last couple months, but this level of absentee parenting was extreme even for his dark times.

"You know what most people do in the morning?" I asked. "Drink coffee, orange juice. Eat breakfast. Eat anything."

He frowned.

I nearly apologized for being snippy, but then my stomach rumbled. I grabbed a bottle of water from the pantry and glugged back a third of it, hoping it would stop the ache, but it only made me feel nauseous.

"Dad, we don't have *any* food."

"I left my wallet on the counter for you, sweetheart, just like I do every morning when I get home."

My finger pressed into my forehead, and I bit back a snarky response.

"You know . . ." he said, "you *could* still finish out the semester at Ursuline—"

"Dad, I'm not going back to that place!" I exploded. "We agreed!" We'd discussed this endlessly, but I'd thought it was over. "You said if I completed the correspondence classes— I finished everything. You can't make me go back!" Suddenly, I was there. Being tied up to the statue, my magic being used against me to kill Nicco and Brigitte.

"Sweetheart?"

Then I'm lying on the stone floor, seeing my mother loom over Codi, feeling the panic as I slice open my arm to get her away from him.

"Adele!" My father's eyes widened with worry.

I let go from clutching the counter behind me and glanced at my wrist. No scar, thanks to Nicco's blood. No hint that anything had even happened. Just memories and nightmares and regret. Just something that happened on the school grounds that I couldn't tell my father about.

"Breathe, baby."

I tried, but it felt impossible. I faked a big inhale by standing up taller.

"I'm not making you go," he said with reassurance. "I was just asking if you'd given going back to school any more thought. It might be nice to finish out the year with your friends."

"They said taking a grievance period doesn't affect your records."

"I'm not worried about your records, Adele. I'm worried about *you*."

"*Me*? You barely left your room for the first month. Just the bar and then straight to bed. Bar. Booze. Bed. Bar. Boo—"

"I know!" His gaze shuffled around the room. "I've been meaning to talk to you about that." A look hid behind his eyes that I hadn't seen in a while, but that had become prominent the closer I'd gotten to my teenage years. The one that said he knew he'd never be as good a parent as my mother would have been, that he didn't know how, and that he was sorry for it. Until now, I'd never said anything to make him feel that way, and now I hated myself even more.

His gaze finally landed back on me. "I should have been more available to you. I should have—"

"It's not your fault, Dad."

"I-I was in shock. Some days I'm still in shock. It's not an excuse. I'm sorry."

This is not your fault, Dad. It's my fault. I'm the one who trapped them in the attic in the first place and then led their sworn enemy straight there. I'm the one who told Annabelle about the convent. That traitorous little—

"I'm so, so sorry, baby. It's hard to explain—hard to admit—it was never real to me before. I always believed she was going to come home one day. Knowing she never will . . ."

Every sentence crushed me a little deeper into the ground. Each word was dirt spraying on my face, mud shoveling on top of my chest. My legs. My arms. My shoulders. Into my mouth and throat, choking me. *She didn't leave us; she died!*

I wanted to tell him how I'd tried to save her. *I tried, Dad!* A wheeze expelled from my throat, and my chest pinched as I tried to catch my breath. I couldn't tell him. He was a mundane. I was a witch. A witch without magic. My lungs locked.

Tighter. Tighter.

My father reached for the drawer just as quickly as he used to when I was a child. He pulled out my inhaler.

"I . . . don't . . . need it." I gripped the counter. *Calm down, Adele.* My thoughts flashed to the last time I'd had a major panic attack, in the attic after the Michels' funeral with Isaac—and suddenly I couldn't breathe at all.

"Adele!"

I snatched the inhaler from him, brought it to my lips, and

punched down on the plastic button with both hands. My lungs puffed, and I held in the blast of albuterol.

"Count to ten before letting it out."

My eyes slanted upward at him. *I know how to use the freakin' inhaler.*

By the seventh second, I could feel the relief kicking in, and by the ninth, my lungs felt like they were going to pop, desperate to exhale.

"We need to get back into our running routine," he said casually as the air puffed from my lips. My father knew that for some reason I always found this particularly humiliating.

"If you were worried about me"—I sucked in another quick puff for good measure, holding it in as I spoke—"you'd go grocery shopping." I dropped the plastic inhaler back into the drawer.

He pushed his wallet along the counter to me. "Not that you need cash. The Palermos will put anything you need on our store account."

As I exhaled the steroids, it suddenly all made sense. All this time I thought he was so far gone wallowing in grief that he'd forgotten essentials like feeding me, but really he was . . . "You're-you're trying to starve me out! What the *hell, Dad*?"

"Don't curse, Adele."

I scowled.

"Sweetheart, I know it feels impossible right now. Believe me, I know. But we're going to get through this. And . . . you have to leave the house. I'm sorry to do this to you. It doesn't have to be school, but you *have to leave the house.*"

"It's not like it's been that long!"

"It's been over two months. I was even thinking that you might want to visit Brooke. A little Los Angeles sunshine, ocean breeze?"

"Dad! I am *not* going to California. Christ, I'll go get groceries!" Panic flooded my veins. "I'm not leaving you!"

"Okay. Today, then. Promise me."

"I promise," I said through gritted teeth, unable to even look at him. I didn't know if I was more annoyed with myself for not realizing what he'd been doing or at him for actually doing it.

"One more thing, sweetheart. Your mentorship. I'm not just going to sign off on the paperwork. If you want your credit with NOSA, you have to get back into the metal shop."

"You haven't even been working in the studio."

"I know. It's the perfect excuse to get both of our butts back in gear." He kissed my head, pulled something out of his pocket, and slipped it into my hand before he walked out the door.

The round, foil-covered object was rough in my palm, and for a flash it reminded me of when Nicco had slipped me the metal note—right before he spun me around and tossed me out the attic window. *To save me from his family.* It's weird how I'd blocked it out after that night, but now I could remember it so clearly. I guess a near-death experience could do that to a person.

I opened my fingers.

A peppermint patty. It was warm from being in my father's pocket. Barely getting a look at it, I unwrapped the chocolate with more enthusiasm than Charlie and gobbled it down.

For a brief second, a sugar-induced endorphin rush flooded my heart.

It didn't last long.

I paced down the hallway to the front door.

Just thinking about leaving made anxiety spider in my chest, and the lingering chocolate taste on my tongue felt traitorous. But the longer I waited, the worse it would get. I'd start picturing all the horrible things that *could* happen if I went outside. Having to confront everything I'd been avoiding: the enemies I wanted to slay, the jealousy I'd been harboring against my best friends who still had their magic, the secrets I'd kept from the coven. And then of course there was Nicco. I didn't know how to re-integrate Nicco into my life. Wooziness washed over me. I thought about the pile of paper airplanes from Isaac still in their crash-landing places under the sill. I'd avoided that part of my life completely.

I knew if I didn't leave right that very second, I was going to run up the stairs, climb back into bed, and not wake up again until tomorrow.

I grabbed the front door handle, realizing only then that nothing but furry purple socks covered my feet. I stepped into the pair of shiny black rain boots lined up next to my father's industrial looking ones. It was April—I mean, it could rain today.

As I reached for my purse and the canvas shopping bags in the closet, I got a glimpse of myself in the hallway mirror. My hair was a ratty, oily, matted mess. The pale pink sweater engulfed me, falling off my left shoulder where my collarbone jutted out in a way it never had before. I pulled up the sweater to cover it. The circles under my eyes were so dark, my face looked hollow, almost like Callis's when I first met him, when he was . . . starving. My teeth clenched.

I pulled an elastic band from my wrist, wrapped my waves into a sloppy topknot, retrieved my sunglasses from my purse, and grabbed the doorknob. The sounds of the lock unclicking twisted my insides, but then . . . I was standing on the stoop, shielding my face from the sun.

I was outside of the house.

This is a bad idea.

Breathe.

My head remained down, focusing on my steps. The bright light was harsh even under the dark glasses. Was this how Nicco felt every time he stepped into the daylight? I concentrated on each little thing my feet passed as the distance between me and our Creole cottage became greater: cracks in the slate, a Pat O'Brien's plastic hurricane cup filled halfway with a questionably yellow liquid, a pile of garbage on the curb so huge its shadow engulfed me as I walked past. Someone must have recently returned home and begun the purge.

I turned the corner without looking up. I didn't need to; I'd walked to the corner delicatessen hundreds of times. Like Mémé et Pépé Michel, the Palermos had known me my whole life. *How well had they known my mother? How many people did my father tell about her death, and what details did he give?* I wasn't even sure how many details Nicco had given him. Just enough to keep him from asking questions, I suppose. Car accident. Brigitte had been on holiday in the South of France. The driver survived, but neither she nor her assistant made it. Their bodies were badly burned and, due to the poor post-Storm connectivity, she'd already been buried by the time we found out, so we had missed her funeral in France.

Lies.

All lies.

Except for the fact that she'd died.

Only, she'd died just a few blocks from our house, in my arms, with her fangs plunged into my neck. She'd pulled on my blood until her last dying breath. I hadn't a clue where her body was now, but it sure as hell wasn't in the Dupré family plot in Paris.

My autopilot feet stopped and I looked up. Only the letters ***P*** and ***A*** remained of the neon namesake sign high above the shop. After all the anguish, it had only taken six minutes.

I took a deep breath, pushed the sunglasses to the top of my head, and opened the door.

The smell was overwhelming as I walked into the store, like someone had painted the muggy, non-temperature-controlled air with Tabasco. The local NPR station chattered from a small speaker beside the register where Lucy, the Palermos' daughter, was sorting through paperwork. She was older than my dad, with short buzzed hair and a wide stance like she was always ready for a bar brawl. I'd rarely ever seen her here. She nodded hello. I did the same.

It had been weeks since I'd spoken to anyone other than my father. I'd even stopped charging my phone so I wouldn't have to see all of my unopened texts from Dee.

The mood in the shop seemed oddly somber. Maybe it was just the current state of the city—or just my current state. Mr. Felix, who hadn't noticed me yet, was sitting in the corner next to a propane tank and a giant crawfish boiling pot, the source of the potent smell. He was wearing the same suspenders and tweed pageboy hat he always wore regardless of the temperature. He leaned forward against the paddle, looking like he'd fallen asleep. My stomach gurgled. It was crawfish season, that was, if their habitats hadn't been destroyed in the Storm, but it didn't smell like a boil.

"Dad!" Lucy yelled over the radio-rant. "Adele's here!"

He shook awake and tried to pretend he hadn't dozed off. "Addie! Ya hungry?"

Hungry hardly described how the smell was making me feel. I wanted to shove my face into the twenty-five-gallon pot and suck it dry. I nodded rapidly, and he lifted the lid and moved the paddle, slowly stirring the biggest pot of gumbo I'd ever seen.

"It's not the best, but it's not the worst either," he said, scooping rice into an old margarine tub and ladling over a big helping.

"*Merci.*" I slurped it straight from the tub, not stopping when it scorched my tongue. It didn't taste quite right—nothing did post-Storm—but it tasted liked manna at the same time.

"When I was growing up, it was called the Depression." His voice sounded so much feebler than I remembered it. "You learned to get by with what you had."

I looked back to Lucy and her mountain of receipts. Mid-slurp, I asked, "Where's Mrs. Rosaria?"

They both looked to me, but neither immediately said anything.

When Lucy didn't respond, Mr. Felix said softly, "She's upstairs resting, Adele. Don't you worry her any mind."

I glanced back and forth between them. Something else was going on. Something bad, and they thought I was too fragile to handle it. I wanted to press them for answers, but Lucy went back to the receipts and Mr. Felix was stirring the pot again, gazing into the swirling roux. The sadness in his eyes made my pulse flicker. "Send her my love, *s'il vous plaît.*"

I scolded myself. For weeks, while I was holed up in my room, the world had felt frozen, as if time had stopped. I'd been so wrapped up in my own self-pity I hadn't given anyone else a proper thought.

And yet a part of me couldn't help but think, *At least she's led a full life.* Mrs. Rosaria was in her eighties; my mom had barely made it to forty.

I wasn't sure which of my thoughts made me feel more horrified. If I stopped thinking about my mother, I felt guilty; if I thought about her too much, I felt guilty. It was a lose-lose.

Carrying my gumbo, I walked down the aisle, surprised to find how many of the shelves were full compared to the last time I'd been here. Only now, instead of being full of food, they were full of cleaning supplies. There was an entire aisle of garbage bags and bleach, and another comprised entirely of duct tape, sponges, and steel-wool pads. The rest were lined with non-perishables. There was no milk, but an endless supply of Kool-Aid.

I opened the canvas bag on my arm and, between sipping straight from my gumbo bowl, began filling it with canned goods and bags of rice, pasta, and beans.

Most of the space on the walls where the refrigeration system had been was now filled with mops and brooms, but a single freezer was loaded with plastic bags of vegetables, pre-chopped and just waiting to be thawed out, cooked up, and in my belly. The frozen vegetables were now treasures, leagues above their canned counterparts. I filled my second bag with frozen fruit, and then even scored six fresh carrots and an onion from the produce shelves. I couldn't remember any fresh produce last time I was here. The fact that I'd been living solely off oatmeal for the last three days now made me feel like a child. I picked up a bag of potatoes, and my arms began trembling, which I hated. I guess that's what happened when you stayed in bed for most of winter.

Under the weight of the groceries, I could feel how much time had passed. *What else did I miss?*

"Take this to your daddy," Mr. Felix said from the front of the shop.

I hurried back, cans clanking, and he stuffed two frozen chickens into the bag on my left arm. I tried not to sink.

"Put one in the freezer when ya get home."

I put the totes on the counter so he could ring me up, but instead he added two margarine containers full of gumbo and a loaf of French bread, and waved the bags away. "Bread's probably stale by now. We're only getting one delivery a week. Come back Monday for a loaf hot off the Langensteins' truck. Anyhow, put it in the oven with a little olive oil and it'll be fine."

I nodded thanks. I felt foolish that it had taken me so long to step out of the house. There were so many others who weren't so fortunate, and I'd let myself go hungry when there was food just a couple blocks away.

Just as I stepped to the door, Mr. Felix called out, "Addie, we're so sorry about your mother."

I froze.

"We heard about the car crash."

I turned around, nodding awkwardly.

"If there's anything you and your pa need—"

"*Merci beaucoup.*" The words rushed out of my mouth as I ran out of the shop.

Seventeen cracks in the ground later, the spike of adrenaline leveled. I tried to keep up the pace, but two frozen chickens, a sack of potatoes, and two totes full of canned and frozen food made it impossible. I felt like a slug.

By the time I finished the first block and a half, my shoulders ached, and the bags were digging so deeply into my skin that they felt close to drawing blood. I readjusted them, nearly spilling the cans, trying not to think about how much lighter they'd be with a magical assist, but then I felt the sun on my face, and I registered that the winter chill was almost completely gone from the spring air. *When did the season change?*

After that, I couldn't help but pay special attention to everything. How much bluer the sky seemed, how much sweeter the chirps of the birds fluttering from roof to roof sounded, how many more parked cars were on the streets than the last time I'd been out of the house. Freshly potted annuals—purple pansies, pink geraniums, and multi-colored petunias—waved from baskets under the LaBordes' windows. Bright blue tarps hung on the roofs of at least half the buildings on the block, potted ferns graced the third-floor balcony of a neighboring townhouse, and even though I was still half a block away, I could smell incense billowing out of the Pharaoh's Cave, the Egyptian shop on the corner.

I was almost glad my father had forced me to leave the house. It was one of those perfect spring days. Winter was over, and the world had been moving on without me while I'd been lying in my bed staring at the ceiling for all those weeks.

Who else is back in town? What else has reopened?

Maybe I could visit Café Orléans to catch up on all the neighborhood happenings—if it was even still open. I decided that after I put away groceries, I'd go check it out. *And if it's closed, I'll open it back up.* A few café au laits with Ren would catch me up on all things recovery-related and gossip-related in one fell swoop.

First, you have to take a shower, Adele. I turned the corner at the side of our house and jerked to a stop.

My heart erupted violently, filling my limbs, hands, and feet with lava.

A guy was on our stoop, finishing a conversation with my father. He turned to leave, and I tried to leap back around the corner, but the bag of potatoes snagged the iron work that held open our shutters and ripped, spilling the spuds all over the sidewalk.

He saw me. He saw me. He saw me.

"Adele!" Isaac seemed as shocked to see me as I was to see him, which was ridiculous since he was at *my* house.

I mentally cursed everything and everyone as I scrambled for the potatoes, shoving them into the already full bags. I unzipped my purse, putting the smaller ones inside two at a time. Then his hands were in my sightline, picking them up too.

"I don't need help," I said, refusing to look up at him and grabbing another potato. There were so fucking many of them.

He placed one inside the canvas bag on my shoulder, his hand brushing my arm.

"Stop it!" I leapt away, but toppled. The skin on my palms scraped on the sidewalk as I landed hard.

"Adele!" He tried to help me up.

"Don't touch me!" The words came out louder and sharper than I'd intended.

He froze, shock chiseled on his face.

The lava flowing through my veins hardened like rock. We both just stared at each other, wide-eyed, him looming over me, looking utterly flustered, and me about to come unglued.

I steadied myself on my knees and resumed gathering the potatoes, this time slower, with more control, trying to regain some of my dignity. He just stood there, watching me, as if petrified of setting me off again. Petrified was not Isaac. *Isaac wasn't scared of anything. Not of hurricanes or vampires or succubus witches.* I couldn't look up—couldn't bear to see the hurt in his caramel-colored eyes, the flecks of gold that glistened when he tried to blink back pain. I wished there were a hundred more potatoes to pick up. A thousand. Infinity more potatoes so I never had to look up.

When I placed the last potato in my purse, I stood and lifted the bags to my shoulder, trying my best to exhibit not needing help.

"Adele—" His voice was choked. "I am *so sorry*."

My eyes watered, but all I could do was stand there as the lava hardened in my throat.

"I just need to know you're okay."

My gaze flicked to the gate handle behind him.

"Please, just say something."

I had to get inside, but he felt like a mountain I couldn't climb around.

"Anything," he pleaded.

I glanced up at him through the filmy tears threatening to spill. He looked even fitter than I remembered, and his hair, pulled back, no longer fell in his face.

"*Please*."

The longer I waited in silence, the glossier his eyes became. I couldn't handle seeing him tear up. When I opened my mouth, words tumbled out, but not the words I meant to say. "You killed my mother."

I didn't know who was more stunned. The bags fell off my shoulders as I rushed past him, letting the contents spill onto the sidewalk. I twisted the gate handle and leapt up the stoop. I needed to be on the other side.

The heavy wooden door slammed shut behind me and I prepared for the floodgate of tears, but they didn't come. I wrapped my arms tight around my stomach, twitching violently, and fell to my knees, my hand slapping the marble foyer floor as I puked, the fiery spices of the gumbo singeing my throat.

It hurt. Everything hurt.

Panting, I tried to sit up on my knees, but my stomach threw my frail body right back down, and I gagged again.

"Adele?" my father yelled from somewhere deeper in the house.

"Don't come in here!" I screamed, my face hot with tears I didn't remember shedding and the floor around me covered in vomit. Tremors ripped through me, paralyzing my body in the hunched-over position.

Footsteps pounded closer.

I groaned.

"Adele . . . ?"

"No, Dad!"

I heaved as he came into view and desperately clutched my stomach, trying to keep it in. He leapt for the umbrella bucket, dumped the contents, and slid down to the floor just in time. I retched into the bucket over and over again.

"It's okay," he said, one hand rubbing the small of my back. "It's going to be okay, I promise."

I dry-heaved as he stayed kneeling in my vomit, saying soothing things, until there was nothing left inside my stomach and the convulsions calmed into a series of feverish waves.

"Baby, what happened?" he asked.

Over the last eleven weeks, I'd ignored Isaac's calls and messages, and I'd let his paper airplanes pile on the floor, until I eventually shut the window. Then I had to close the curtain so I'd stop getting nervous every time a bird flew by. I sat back on my knees, shaking, grocery-less, completely humiliated, until my breathing slowed.

When my father asked again, and I still didn't speak, he stood and opened the door, as if he was going to find the answer outside, find some kind of monster lurking.

There was no one there, just the groceries, perfectly lined up on the stoop, including a pile of potatoes carefully stacked into a pyramid. The fresh air was cool on my fevered face.

"Did this have anything to do with that boy who just came by?"

I thought about the vial of Désirée's sleepytime potion in my nightstand—I'd been saving the last remaining drops for a really bad day. I looked at him through my wet lashes. "There's no boy. I told you I didn't want to leave the house."

CHAPTER 3

LOST BOY

April 18th

"Faster, Isaac . . ." Julie's wispy words melted into my ear as her ethereal form coiled around my waist and up my chest like an icy scarf. She knew I was distracted. And distracted was never good in a chase. She glided ahead to scope out the dark street, rustling the canopy of trees above.

Amid the lulls of the cicadas, the only other sounds disturbing the night were my sneakers' rubber soles hitting the pavement and the ghostly echoes of Stormy's toes clicking alongside me. The chill of Julie's touch lingered, reminding me that I was alive despite feeling like a hollow spectral form of myself, no different from her or Stormy. Adele's words hadn't left my mind for a single second over the last two days.

You killed my mother.

Not "my mother is dead," not "my mother tried to kill me," not "my mother was a vampire."

You killed my mother.

The words were scorched into every cell of my being, floating like ash in my head, clouding my other thoughts.

I took a sharp turn at the street corner and paused, gripped a wrought iron fence, and bent over my knees, struggling for breath. Stormy yelped, her back stiff and head alert, confused as to why we'd stopped at the decrepit antebellum house.

In a whoosh, Julie was back at my side. "What's wrong, *mon cher*?"

Stormy circled us then carefully took a few steps out in either direction before turning back to me like a practiced guard dog, as if she knew the vamps were back on the streets.

"Nothing, I'm fine." I straightened up and tried to even out my erratic breathing. I'm not sure why I bothered; her heightened senses picked up on the slightest emotional cues.

"What frightened you?" Her French accent thickened when she was worried. "Was it Emilio?"

The irony of a ghost asking me if I was frightened was not lost on me. "I'm fine. I just needed a second." What scared me had nothing to do with the predators still in town, even if Emilio Medici did want to revenge-kill me.

"It's not safe for you to linger on the street at night, *mon cher.* You need to keep moving."

I wiped sweat off my forehead with my arm, which was already damp from the thick air, and took off again, ramping up from a slow jog.

Staying on the main drag was safer, but the moon beaming through the rustling leaves created a nonstop fluttering of shadows, testing my nerves. Maybe I shouldn't have broken ahead from Dee and Codi.

We were on the fringe of the Lower Garden District, one of the wealthiest neighborhoods I'd ever seen, but this strip of Oretha Castle Haley was just one abandoned house and one looted shop after another. The curfew had been extended to midnight a few weeks ago, but the crime rate was still so high, people tended to stay inside after dark, which was good considering the five vampires lurking in town. Not too many Storm refugees had returned to Central City, judging by the shape of the neighborhood. The dark streets and lack of witnesses made it the perfect hunting ground for the Medici. Only Nicco and Emilio could come after me this far out of the Quarter, thanks to our ancestors' curse, but that didn't exactly bring comfort, considering they were the two who hated me the most. But what was I supposed to do, stay inside for the rest of my life? Now more than ever, the streets needed patrolling.

Ahead of us, a single functioning street lamp glowed dimly through the humid air. The homes were tall and old and the street was wide, like it had once been an important thoroughfare. Graffiti covered the bus stops, and every shop window looked like it'd had a date with a baseball bat. Vines crawled up the houses in tight chokeholds, and overgrown bushes crept out into the broken sidewalks. Nothing looked unlooted.

It was hard to tell whether the crime rate was so high because of the vamps, the desperate conditions in the city, or the Possessed—a repercussion of Callis's coven's feeding frenzy the night of the attack. His coven must have assaulted dozens of ghosts because people infected by the stray souls—the remnants of the spirits—had been popping up in the weeks since. We intercepted them where we could, but because they were possessing everyday, normal people like Ren, the only way to find them was after they deteriorated and became violent, committed crimes, or caused an unusual disturbance. Deciphering what was unusual and what was just New Orleans was almost impossible.

A shadow moved up ahead—more shifting light. The hairs on my arms rose. *He's here.* The harmonic shrill of cicadas hummed louder as if warning me of the pending danger. I didn't see anyone, but I didn't need to. I'd felt his presence half a mile back when we crossed over from the Warehouse District. Then, about six blocks ago, I'd seen a flash of movement behind a parked car. I focused on the air until my skin pricked again. The slightest twinge of supernatural sensation.

He's close.

Julie's icy swirl wrapped around me again. "Faster, Isaac." A hint of concern coated her voice.

She felt it too.

She broke ahead. Stormy raced after her. Ghosts seemed to have endless energy as long as they weren't being attacked by psychotic, spirit-sucking witches. Her long black hair and white dress fluttered behind as she gained half a block. Must be nice not needing functioning lungs.

Must be nice to be alive, I reminded myself.

The residential street forked in a V, with a grassy space separating the two sides—in New York, it would have been considered a small park. Metal crashed nearby, and I stopped so suddenly, I nearly stumbled. A hubcap spun out onto the street from a Storm-parked Chevy.

I scanned the road for a rat or squirrel, but my gaze landed on a lone figure standing perfectly still on the grassy median. He was just a silhouette, but some primal survival instinct told me we'd made eye contact. There is a precise moment when you know you're caught: a burst of adrenaline pops your nerves as you look for an escape route. Flashes pound your head, attempting to pinpoint the exact moment you screwed up. *A wrong turn? Too fast out the gate?* You start wondering if you can overpower your assailant, if it comes to it. My pulse climbed.

It was about to come to it.

It's now or never, Isaac.

We both took off at the same moment, weaving through cars and trees and telephone poles in the dark, deeper into the neighborhood.

"Come on, girl," I whispered to Stormy, dodging trash cans and piles of debris. I listened for his footsteps, zeroing in on all the tiny sounds striking the silent night: the gravel under his shoes, the indiscernible swearing as he skidded and then caught himself.

Just one more burst. That's all I needed.

I pushed myself into a sprint. Stormy followed suit with high-pitched yelps. She knew this was it: we were going for it.

Chain link rattled as he jumped over a short fence, stumbling on the landing. I cleared it easily and gained a couple steps as he bolted ahead. I launched myself into him, arms outstretched, and locked around his midsection. We both went down, skidding along the rough pavement. We rolled twice, thrashing and grunting as our shoulders and hipbones collided with the street. And then slammed to a halt when my back hit a drain grate at the curb. *Fuck.*

He'd landed on top, but I was still bear hugging his middle.

"Get the hell off me, you little prissy-ass-punk!" he yelled, slamming me into the metal bars.

The pain made me feel alive; I tightened my grip. He was shorter than me, but stout and unnaturally strong, and if he was possessed like I suspected, then he might not be in control of himself either. He dug his boot into my quad, pushing away. I swallowed a groan as my hands began to slip. He pressed harder and the pain deepened.

Stormy's deep-throated growls graduated to barks, and I couldn't help but grin. *Perfect timing.* My grip would only last another second.

He ripped away, scrambling up, but he didn't get far.

"Whur'd you come from?" he yelled as Codi emerged from the dark. His accent was more backwoods than anything I'd ever heard in

NOLA—the suspect was supposed to be a local. He snapped back at me: "Need y'ur boyfriend to come rescue you?"

I inched forward in a crouch, ready to take off whichever way he ran. Codi did the same on the opposite side. The guy's eyes darkened, and I could see him recall where he'd misstepped. A single working street lamp shone over us, and I finally got a good look. His description fit the vague police profile. About 5'7", dark skin, a tattoo on his right arm. "Landry Dempsey?"

His eyes lit up.

"Who the hell's asking?" he yelled, bobbing back and forth.

"You're not going anywhere this time," Codi said.

Landry's gaze flicked between us, as if debating who would be easier to bulldoze. "*Mysteries are the last thing you want in a fight,*" Johnny Lombardo, one of my oldest friends from back in Brooklyn, used to say. Codi and I were about the same height and build, but Landry had already collided with me. Codi was still a mystery to him.

I hunched, ready to block. *Come and get me.*

He turned back to Codi, whose stance widened, and then he spun my way.

Dominate, Isaac.

Landry came at me without fear in his eyes, his face wild and his arm thrust out—I caught the glint in his hand too late and lurched away. It ripped through my shirt, slicing deep. I knocked his legs out from under him with a gust of wind as I went down, clutching my side. "*Shit. Shit. Shit.*"

"Isaac!" Julie screamed.

Codi charged Landry, who was already scrambling up, the blade scraping the pavement.

"Knife!" I yelled just as the guy swiped at him.

I should have grabbed it off the ground. *Get your shit together, Isaac.* Wetness soaked my fingers where they pressed over the wound. I sucked in a sharp breath. Medic protocol raced through my head. *Don't freak out. It will only make it worse.* With one arm clutching my side, I pushed myself off the ground, doubling over as I stood.

The guy veered back my way, wildly slashing at me a second time—and then he froze. The knife clanked to the street as I hovered just out of his reach. I hadn't meant to, but my body had snapped into crow form as a defensive response.

Landry stumbled a few steps back. "What the—? Where'd you—?"

Codi grabbed him from behind.

"Devilspawn!" He leaned forward, trying to flip Codi over his back.

I flapped higher, pain rippling through my bird bones—and the full realization of what I'd done hit me: I'd turned in front of a mundane. Désirée was going to kill me. *Did this guy still count as a mundane?* Blood soaked my feathers; I started losing air. I fell back to the street and snapped into human form upon impact, groaning.

"Isaac!" Codi yelled.

"Don't let him go!" I grunted. "I'm fine."

But it was pointless; Codi was already coming my side, along with Julie.

"Just come back for me! It's only a scratch." I clutched my side harder as he tried to lift my shirt.

"Where do you think you're going?" a female voice punched through the dark.

Thank God. There was no way Désirée would let Landry get away. He stopped about ten feet away from her.

"*Y'ur* gonna stop me?" he scoffed. "I got a better idea." His rubbed his crotch, his pelvis tipped in her direction. "How about you come with me?"

Codi's eyes narrowed, and for a second I thought he might abandon me to rip the guy's head off. The more you dealt with the possessed, the harder it was to remember that someone else might be speaking for them.

"Classy," Désirée said. "But I'd rather take you home to meet my family."

Codi smirked, pressing back down on my wound. "He's dead."

"Pretty much."

Despite Codi and Dee having only recently become friends, his confidence in her matched mine. Granted, she did practically bring him back from the grave with her Spektral magic; if that didn't instill confidence in someone, I'm not sure what could.

"Pretty girl like you shouldn't be consortin' with these devil-worshipping fruitcakes," Landry said.

Codi's eyebrow raised to me and I snickered, the pain making me wince.

"Devil-worshipping?" she asked, twirling her hands in the air.

"*Heathens*. Probably did some kind of Voodoo shit on you."

"Probably." Her usual indifferent expression morphed into a sly smile.

He crept closer to her, and I tensed, but just beyond her, a long stretch of ivy was unwinding from the trunk of a live oak.

"I'll keep you safe from them," he said, and grabbed for her.

Désirée whipped her hand, and the ivy slapped the street like a crack of thunder.

"What the ever-lovin' hell?" He looked at Désirée and then back down at us. "*Freaks*." He took off running.

"I thought we were going to play?" Désirée asked, and with a motion of her hand, the vine whipped against the street.

Landry sped up as the vine cracked around him. Codi's gaze was fixed on Désirée as she showed off to the cicadas and oak trees and moonbeams that she was Queen of the Supernatural Rodeo. When she yanked the plant back, the guy came flying with it, landing hard at her feet. He had a least a buck-twenty on her; simple laws of physics rendered the move impossible, but the laws of the Natural World went out the window when magic was involved. As she walked him back to us, he spewed remarks about her ass that would have made even the surliest of New Yorkers blush, but Désirée just looked down at him and said, "You're going to want to calm down now."

"Devil-girl with y'ur devil-bird. Freaks all gonna burn."

"Wait, devil-*bird*?"

He pointed my way. "That freak of nature turned into a bird!"

"That's *preposterous*." Her face hardened on me.

"He stabbed me!"

She rolled her eyes and walked the guy back to us, wrapping the vine around her hand, shortening the leash.

"It was a reflex!" I clutched Codi's wrist as he let up on the pressure.

The guy looked back to Dee, suddenly concerned. "Who are you people? What are you going to do with me?" There was something different about his voice. He sounded more refined, and his good ol' boy accent faded. "Are you the Devil? You've come to take me to hell?" He sank down to his knees begging her. "I didn't mean it. I-I-I didn't mean to do it. I don't know what happened—?"

"You need to calm down before someone hears us." She slung her little leather backpack from her shoulder to her chest and dug into it with her free hand.

"Oh, God, oh, God. Are you going to kill me?" His eyes stayed fixed on the bag. "I didn't mean— I really haven't been feeling like myself. I'm going to hell. I know it. I deserve it." He attempted the sign of the cross, and then the expression on his face twisted into something dark, and his Dixie accent returned along with a chorus of swear words.

Désirée, unfazed, pulled out a jar and wedged it between her hip and elbow. Landry started to pace, jerking her vine-entwined hand back and forth. "Calm. *Down*," she repeated, unscrewing the lid with her other.

"Devil-whore—!"

She opened her palm and blew a puff of magenta-colored powder into his face.

His feet stilled, his voice lowered, and a look of confusion washed over him. A single four-letter c-word shook out of his mouth over and over again. We'd been after this guy for two days, and he was making it more and more difficult to think there was still someone left to save in there somewhere.

Désirée whispered something under her breath and then forcefully blew another cloud of powder into his face.

"Watch it," Codi said, leaning out of the way as the pink puff dissipated around us. He fanned the powder away from my head.

Landry aggressively shook back and forth, like he was trying to hold onto something—the memory most likely. Pink dust fell from his beard as his mutterings dissolved into a different repeated word: "*Bird. Bird. Bird.*"

"What bird?" Désirée asked with fake ignorance.

"Why 'er ya askin' about birds?" he shouted. "That guy just attacked me!"

The tension in her face eased as she re-screwed the lid and shoved the jar back into her bag. I stopped stressing over my witch-status being compromised—two breaths of Dee's memory powder and Landry seemed to have forgotten all about seeing a human morph into a giant black crow. She'd been working on the powder for months. If he was super resistant, he'd remember *something*, but likely chalk it up to a daydream or a drunken hallucination—not unusual for the French Quarter.

Désirée pulled Codi up, gave him the magic-soaked vine, and looked down at me with an expression that let me know she was about to let me have it. As she knelt, the anticipation made the pain pulse.

"You're an *idiot*!" she said, pulling my hand away.

I tried not to look down as the blood oozed, but I couldn't help myself. Blood didn't scare me, not since my early first responder days—which for me was junior high thanks to my pop dragging me around on work trips.

She pushed my clammy chest back down. "Lay back."

I squinted as Codi shone his bright phone light over us.

She shook her head. "You just *had* to break ahead of us. Go out on your own."

I groaned as her long, bony fingers prodded the depth of the cut.

"You *said* if we went out, we'd stick together. You shouldn't even be out here with Emilio still in town! Why am I the only person in our coven who can stick to a plan? Stick with the group? What the hell is the point of being bound together if we *never stick together*!?"

"I'm sorry." I doubled over, clutching her arm.

"We're not *all* bound together," Codi mumbled, reminding of us of his lone-witch status. We'd all agreed to wait for Adele to bind him in, but it didn't stop him from continually expressing his disappointment about not being official.

Désirée's eyes slipped shut and her fingers pulsed with magic. She began to tremble but didn't let go. "I'm starting to think you have a death wish. I'm going to start calling you Isaac Le Moyne." She clamped down on my side.

"Shit!" I gasped. *"That hurts worse than the knife!"* You'd think healing magic would feel like a dose of morphine, but it's more like electroshock therapy.

She gripped me tighter and I tensed, letting out a few more expletives of my own.

The pain passed from Roman-candle-explosion level to sparkler level, then it was just little electric pulses. She was shaking, and I couldn't tell if it was because of the strain the healing took on her magic or because she was still pissed.

I curled onto my side. "Jesus, Désirée, I was just stabbed. You think you could be a little gentler?"

She sat back on her knees. Sometimes she passed out after using her

Spektral power, which she *hated.* Codi squatted next to her in case there was recoil.

"You, too," she snapped, looking at him.

"What did I do?"

"You're both taking too many risks! Stop trying to outdo one another; this isn't football practice!"

"*Pfft.* Like either of us played football." Codi smiled, grabbed my hand and pulled me up to my feet.

She rolled her eyes.

"Relax, Dee." I fanned out my bloody shirt. "All that matters is that we got him."

"Got him? We don't even know if he's one of them! I assume that you weren't able to confirm his possession as you were rolling down the street in a death grip?"

I pulled the ball chain that hung around my neck from underneath my shirt. "Well, let's find out."

Désirée's gaze dropped to the silver feather hanging next to my grandpop's dog tags. She could hide her feelings better than any guy I knew, but I caught the flicker in her eyes when she saw it—the worry about Adele. Sometimes I think yelling at me was the only way she knew how to deal with it, which was fine. Désirée was angry that Adele was shutting us out, but I was worried that Adele didn't have anyone, and that the depression over losing her mother would swallow her up and she'd never come out of the house. That she'd hate me forever. That she'd blame me forever.

Most of all, I worried that when she finally let someone in, it would be Nicco.

I thumbed through the dog tags and feather for the third piece of metal dangling from the chain: the small magnifying glass whose lens I'd replaced with a mirror.

I circled around the guy and crouched down over his back. Every atom of Spektral magic in my body told me he was possessed; I could sense the ghostly creature inside of him.

"Wha-at are you doing?" he stuttered.

Codi and Dee peered over my shoulder, and Stormy scratched at my leg while I held the mirror in front of his face. All breath stilled at his reflection that stared back at us: instead of a youngish African-American guy, it was a middle-aged white guy with glasses that looked like they were from 1979 and a porn-stache from the same era.

"See," I said.

It never got easier to comprehend that someone else's soul was infecting another person, parasitically feeding off his spirit—his future ghost, slowly driving them insane.

A cool wave pressed into my back. "I wonder how long ago he was possessed?" Despite having felt her presence before Julie spoke, it didn't keep the chills from rippling up my spine. "The soul looks unhealthy."

"Agreed."

"Agreed with what?" Désirée asked.

"Sorry, Julie is worried about how long he's been possessed."

Désirée's eyes slanted my way, as if she might finally catch a glimpse of her. "So creepy."

"Says the girl with the houseful of bones and bat wings," Julie replied, unamused.

My chest shook, holding back a laugh. "For real."

Stormy continued to scratch at my leg. I bent down to pet her head, and her tail wagged. "I know, girl, that's enough excitement for one night. Let's go home."

When I looked back up, Dee, Codi, and the possessed guy were all staring at me.

"F-f-freaks," Landry muttered, twisting in his magical vines.

I smiled at him. "At least we aren't parasitic-soul-level freaks."

"Para-what?"

"Just wait until you start talking to yourself all day long," I said, thinking about Ren. "You're gonna wish you were talking to a ghost dog."

Dee twisted her finger in the air, and the vines unwound from around Landry's torso and slithered down his arms to form cuffs. "You're coming back with us to the French Quarter; my family is going to help you."

"If you're lucky," Codi mumbled.

Désirée shot him a cold look.

"What? It's not like you've successfully depossessed anyone yet. Ren's on the verge of a permanent trip to the nuthouse . . ."

She scoffed.

"I'm not going anywhere with you, devil-whore!"

Codi's face hardened, and he yanked the guy to his feet. "You know how you haven't been feeling like yourself lately?" Désirée stepped close and blew another puff of powder in his face. He guy coughed and tried to blow it away, but Codi held him in place. "It's because you're not *just yourself.* We're going to help you before you do something you'll regret for the rest of your life."

"If he hasn't already," I said, picking up his knife and wiping my own blood from it onto a patch of grass.

"I don't regret anything!"

Désirée tightened his restraints with a flick of her finger.

"I'm going to carve you up like a jack-o'-lantern, just like I did that other prissy girl."

A wave of shudders passed through me, and Codi took a permanent place in between him and Désirée. "That's exactly why you're coming with us," I said, shoving him forward.

He turned and spat in my face. I grabbed him by the back of the neck and gave him another shove. "You're coming with us because you're going to die if we don't get that extra soul out of you." I left out the details of the imprisonment. Up until that moment—having seen Ren trapped in the Borges guesthouse every day—I'd been uncomfortable with it, but this was exactly why Ritha was doing it, and she'd keep doing it until they figured out a way to extract the souls.

CHAPTER 4

LOST SOUL

The threat of death only silenced Landry for about a half mile. There were only two neighborhoods until we were back in the French Quarter, but his commentary made it feel like we were walking across the continent. Especially because we were all considerably more uneasy after his confession. *We didn't get to him fast enough.* I wondered if he'd be able to live with what he'd done, if and when he was exorcised.

The memory of throwing the stake into Brigitte flashed in my head. *That was different, Isaac.*

Codi grew tenser as the guy repeatedly called him derogatory names, many of which I'd never heard but which were all apparently synonymous with pansy.

"So much for your calming powder," he said through gritted teeth to Dee.

"Well, maybe if our would-be Aether coven member hadn't turned out to be a backstabbing, power-grabbing, two-faced *witch*, she could have persuaded him to be quiet, and I wouldn't have to use the powder."

Codi's jaw clenched tighter. No one was forgetting that Annabelle's crew had beat him so badly he'd nearly bled out at the convent.

Désirée's pace quickened, her steps punching through the tense air. I never saw her get so worked up as when Annabelle was mentioned.

Annabelle had tricked us all, but she'd been Désirée's best friend since kindergarten, so the resentment ran deep. I knew she felt responsible for Annabelle. We both did. Adele had tried to warn us, but we wouldn't listen, and she was the one who ended up suffering the most because of it.

My thumbs pressed down hard on my fingers, cracking my knuckles.

Annabelle was MIA. Dee had gone to her house looking, only to learn that she must have mind-melded her parents: Mrs. Drake told her that Annabelle had been accepted into an early admittance program at Vanderbilt for Storm kids and was in Tennessee for the semester.

All the Ghost Drinkers had vanished that night, including Callis. We didn't know whether Emilio had finished him off or whether he'd just fled, but it was hard to imagine anyone surviving that vampire attack. Emilio had practically ripped his throat out. We still didn't really know who Callis was. Of course, I was sure Nicco had all the answers. The only thing I knew for certain was that this all had to do with Niccolò Medici and his low-life family. A part of me wished I'd taken Callis straight to the convent when he'd asked about the Carter brothers. Not that I would have joined his ghost-sucking coven or anything like that, but they could have settled their business without us—without Adele getting into the middle of it. Without Adele's mother getting killed. *Her mother was a Medici vampire. What the fuck?*

"You killed my mother."

Adele is never going to speak to me again.

Landry had moved on to Dee with his commentary, but I barely heard it through the ashy haze of Adele's words. I hated that Adele was in pain. I hated that she'd lost her magic. I hated that her mother was dead . . . but *Adele* would be dead if I hadn't thrown that stake.

Dead.

Brigitte had tried to kill her *own daughter!*

That's how repugnant these monsters were.

"I should have known the Devil'd be a young black girl," the guy crowed, "with legs as lickable as licorice sticks."

Désirée flinched.

"*What* did you say?" I spun around and grabbed him by the throat.

"Don't tell me that you don't think about what her skin tastes like."

"You piece of shit."

"Isaac, don't!" Dee screamed.

My fist smashed into his face.

"Stop!"

I drew back to hit him again, but before I could land another punch, Codi was dragging me off. "Let it go, Isaac!"

I jerked away, but he held on. "All right!" I yelled.

The guy spat blood from his busted lip, half-wailing, half-cursing.

"Christ, Isaac," Désirée said, seething, as she knelt next to him.

"*What*? You think I'm going to let someone talk to you— Didn't you hear—?"

"Just shut up!" she snapped, the anger on her face melting into humiliation.

My mouth closed. Embarrassment was not a Désirée Borges trait.

She refused to look at either of us as she healed the scumbag. Her voice was weak when she finally spoke. "It's not anything I haven't been hearing my entire life . . ." Her voice sharpened. "From people who don't have the excuse of a parasitic soul."

Codi's eyes caught mine in a sobering exchange. I wasn't oblivious to the racist-sexist-homophobic shit still happening in the world, so I didn't know why I found this so shocking. I guess I just never thought about it happening to Désirée—not in her world of publicists and sophistication.

"I'm sor—"

"And I *don't* need some white boy to save me!"

"I— I know you don't!"

When she stood, she rocked a little, and I instinctually reached out for her elbow to steady her from the recoil, but then I froze, unsure if she wanted me to.

"Let's . . ." she started to say, but her eyes fluttered and her knees buckled.

Codi stepped in and caught her, holding her steady. "Don't worry, I'm multi everything: racial, mixed magic, and raised by gays in a tarot shop."

She smiled as her head bobbed.

His mouth turned into her ear, but I still heard him softly say, "Feel the ground through your feet."

I wondered if this recoil thing would always be an effect of her Spektral magic, or if she'd grow out of it as she became a stronger witch.

I did not like seeing her so vulnerable. Ritha had said she needed to lean more into the magic instead of transferring so much of her own healthy energy to others.

Her eyes popped open, looking straight at me. "Let's go."

Codi slung her bag over his shoulder, took the vine, and told Landry to get a move on. At the first sign of mumbles from Landry's lips, he pulled out a fistful of chamomile buds from Désirée's bag and blew them into his face. "No more talking. *Walk.*" They floated around his head, putting him in an instant state of relaxation.

We followed streetcar tracks that I'd yet to see function, falling into silent pairs, Dee and I behind Codi and Landry. Whenever I checked on her out of the corner of my eye, she was always looking straight ahead. Sweat broke across my hairline. Awkwardness wasn't something I was used to with her. At first impression, I'd thought she was a spoiled, privileged, over-entitled brat, but when we finally started hanging out, I'd realized that our lives weren't that different: both kids of men in government with positions of power. But the way that guy had spoken to her—in my entire life, no one had ever said anything like that to me. Not even close.

"I'm sorry," I said. I didn't know if I was apologizing for hitting the guy, or for what he'd said to her, or for how fucked up the world was.

She didn't say anything or glance my way, but the air between us began to feel lighter. By the time we cleared the Warehouse District, the tension had dissipated.

The buildings became taller and more modern as we crossed into New Orleans's central business district. It had a similar vibe to downtown Brooklyn: a mix of mini-skyscrapers and prewar buildings. The thoughts of home led to my most regular daydream, where I showed Adele all my favorite places in New York.

"*You killed my mother.*"

We passed by shutdown hotels and a ruined Starbucks and one closed restaurant after another, and then at some point things shifted—instead of me checking in on Désirée, I sensed little glances of concern coming from her.

"What?" I finally asked, gently, in a way that pleaded with her not to pry.

"What's *wrong*?" Of course, she pried.

I didn't say anything.

So she continued, "I'm usually the aggressive one, not you. You're the soft, sensitive artist guy. If I didn't know better, I'd think one of these parasites hooked *you.* Should I be holding a mirror up to your face? You're supposed to be the empathetic one."

I think you're confusing me with Adele.

"What's *wrong,* Isaac?"

"Well, my girlfriend was taken by a coven of Ghost Drinkers, robbed of her magic, and nearly killed in the process. Then she was bitten by her starved vampire mother, who I locked in an attic and then later killed."

"Yeah, besides all of that. I know something else happened. Stop trying to hide it from me."

My fingers tightened around my thumbs. I might not have been possessed by an extra soul, but the mix of anger and guilt and confusion swirling around inside me felt like something was eating me alive. The worst was the helplessness. I knew Adele wanted space, but there was a difference between space and isolation, and I was scared she'd crossed the line. Remembering how skinny she looked the other day gnawed the inside of my stomach.

"Isaac," she said sternly. "Did one of the Medici threaten you? If something happened and you aren't telling me, I'm going to kill you myself."

"I haven't had any vampire run-ins."

"Then what?"

My eyes stayed glued to the ground. I didn't want to tell her, to admit what had happened. But then I realized, she was gone. When I turned back, she was just standing there, feet planted, arms crossed.

Fuck. My hands laced on top of my head.

I paced a couple steps away, looking up at the dark buildings and oak tree branches, and the words gurgled out into the darkness: "I ran into Mac the other day."

And by ran into, I mean, I went to Adele's house, because I thought I might actually lose my mind if I didn't talk to her.

Everything behind me went perfectly silent. The wind rustled an old, torn flag hanging above us. I'd meant to tell them the whole truth; I don't know why I didn't.

When I turned back around, Julie was beside them and all three were looking back at me, wide-eyed.

"What! Why didn't you—?" Désirée couldn't get her questions out fast enough.

"Did you see Adele?" Codi asked, sharply. "Was she okay?"

"Are *you* okay?" she echoed.

I nodded. I'd never lied to them before, but I couldn't talk about how small and frail Adele had looked, or how she'd kept looking at the door handle and back to me, like I was a monster blocking her only escape route. I straightened my shoulders. "Mac had no idea who I was . . . None. When he answered the door, it was just like that first morning. He asked if I needed help, if I was lost." *I know this was Nicco's doing. I know he deleted Mac's memories.* "It's not like it matters. It's not like things would have gone back to the way they were. *I killed his wife!*"

Désirée threw her arms up in exasperation. "You saved his daughter from a vampire!"

"I killed Adele's mom!"

"Isaac, Adele's mother was going to *drain* her," Codi stammered. "I-I wish there'd been something I could have done."

"You were half-dead."

"She saved me that night. And you saved her. End of story."

Désirée looked at him. "Don't you mean *I* saved you that night?"

"I'd have been way past the point of saving when you arrived if Adele hadn't lured her mother away from me."

"What do you mean?" That night Codi had muttered something in his delirious, near-death state about Adele saving him from a vampire, but I'd just assumed he meant Nicco or Lisette or one of the others.

"At the convent . . . Adele's mom came at me first. Maybe she wouldn't even have come into the room if I hadn't been covered in blood. Adele was out cold after dragging me into the room to hide." He pinched his forehead. "I barely even remember getting from Callis's circle to inside, but I woke up to Mrs. Le Moyne leaning over me. I hadn't seen her since I was a kid, but I knew it was Adele's mom. She looked exactly the same, except her eyes were . . . savage, and so black. That's what I remember: those huge dilated eyes. I started begging her to remember me, and then Adele's voice came from the dark corner. She was trying to coax her mother away, but Brigitte just leaned closer and . . . that's when Adele did it."

"Did what?" I asked sharply.

He nodded to the necklace dangling against my chest. "That

feather. She slashed her arm open with it. I yelled at her to cover up the blood, but she wouldn't listen to me. You know how Adele is . . . And then her mother turned away from me and attacked her. I-I could barely move."

Désirée and I stared at him in horror. I thought we'd known everything about that night, at least everything he could tell us.

He turned to Dee. "Don't get me wrong. I'm totally appreciative of your phenom Spektral powers, but I'd have been dead on arrival if it weren't for Adele."

Of course Adele would sacrifice herself for someone she loved.

"Why didn't you tell us?" I asked.

"I don't know. It just seemed like something she might not want people knowing."

The idea that there might be things Adele wouldn't want us—me—to know was slicing. *Why didn't she just tell me about her mom?* The feeling of the freshly whittled cedar strapped tight against my ankle gave me a pretty good idea.

Codi looked me dead on. "You didn't kill her mother, Isaac. A vampire did, a long time ago. You saved Adele, and even if she doesn't see it now—"

"*I know*! And I'd do it all over again if I had to. I'd do it over a hundred times!" I kicked the metal grate of a trash can. *Calm down, Isaac.* But I didn't want to calm down. I wanted to break every window on the block and scream at Adele until she'd listen to me and stop trusting vampires. If you can't trust your own vampire mother not to kill you, how could you trust any of them?

Désirée walked over to me with an awkward look on her face. She spread her long, smooth arms over my shoulders and linked them behind my neck. They didn't cradle my shoulders, just kind of hovered, barely touching me.

"What are you doing?" I asked.

"I'm giving you a hug. Isn't this what people like you do?"

"You call this a hug?"

"You look like a flamingo practicing a ballet pose," Codi said.

Landry began murmuring. "An angel. An angel's coming to save me."

My gaze followed his to a dim glowing orb not too far from Désirée's head. I slid my arms around her, knowing her impulse would be to do the opposite of whatever I said. “Désirée. Do *not* move.”

“Wh-a-a?” Her spine stiffened. “Is it a roach? Get it off me!”

I held her tighter as she squirmed. “*Not* a roach.”

“Shit!” Codi said, staring at the bobbing light with awe.

“*What*?”

I tightened my grip, keeping us both as still as possible as the little ball of light hovered. One touch of a soul meant possession, and in the current state of things, possession meant death.

Codi slowly pointed to a dormant fountain about fifty yards away in a public square. He flashed three fingers.

Two.

One. The fountain sprang to life, arcs of water dancing through the air. I threw us to the ground, away from the glowing orb, trying not to land too hard on top of Désirée.

“What?” she yelled, then followed my gaze to Codi, who was running toward the fountain, the orb zooming behind him. “Codi, behind you!”

I ripped a gust of air toward the orb, trying to slow it down. Codi looked back and threw his arm over his shoulder. An arc of water from the fountain whizzed through the air like an iridescent chain. He spun around and stopped, weaving his hands through the air—the chain of droplets threaded itself together into a sparkling chain-link fence and planted itself into the ground as the soul zoomed straight to him.

Désirée screamed, but the orb bounced off the water and bobbed in the air. Codi peered at it through his Water magic.

“Jesus,” she gasped.

He carefully pushed his hands toward the liquid fence and then twisted them together. The water followed his command, circling the ball of light over and over, until it was completely encased.

I sensed Désirée’s breath halt as Codi cupped the air around the sphere. Fingers spread wide, he rocked his hands around the soul, careful not to touch the light, and the chain of water swayed back and forth with the motion of his hands until all the tiny droplets congealed, forming a single bubble around the glowing soul. There must have been oil mixed into the stagnant fountain water, because the bubble had a holographic sheen like the abalone shells I used to collect at the beach with my mom.

I moved closer, mesmerized by the whole thing, but Désirée hung back. Julie hung even farther back, near Landry, trying to keep Stormy, who definitely thought the ball of light was a new supernatural tennis ball, at bay.

"What's wrong?" Codi yelled to Désirée.

She peered at the bubble, and back to him.

"Hey," he snapped. "Just because I don't have my Maleficium yet doesn't mean there's anything wrong with my Elemental magic."

"I-I know. It's just . . . I've never been that close to one before."

Codi's Aunt Fiona and her three daughters had been the ones officially tasked with capturing lingering souls.

"Well, today's your lucky day." He walked over and took her hand. "Don't worry, my magic's got you."

Her eyes widened as he led her to the bubble. We all stood around it, and Codi swirled his hand, making the orb spin in the moonlight.

Désirée, no longer scared, was now totally enchanted by the glowing entity in front of her. "Who are you?" she whispered.

"*Heathens*." Landry hissed, writhing in Désirée's leash, trying to rip the vine from the lamppost.

She snapped her fingers, and a sapling, not more than two feet tall, sprang from a crack in the sidewalk. With a flick, it wrapped itself around Landry's head, stuffed itself into his jaw and muffled his words.

She walked over to him and leaned close to his face. "No. More. Talking."

Things were significantly more chill for the rest of the walk back to the Quarter. When we passed Bottom of the Cup, Codi peeled off with the soul, and Dee and I continued on to Vodou Pourvoyeur with Landry.

Because that's how the two magical families had divided the responsibilities of the current supernatural crisis: the Borges were trying to figure out how to exorcise the Possessed, and the Daures were trying to figure out what the hell to do with the loose souls.

CHAPTER 5

KILLING A WITCH

A redolence of enchantment clung to the air around witches, but the scent of magic transcended the olfactory. It was partly a scent and partly a sound—so faint you wouldn't catch it if you didn't know what to listen for, like the crackle of water as it frosts—but magic was mostly a feeling. It changed the very air around you as you breathed it in. Or maybe that was just the intoxication that came with a sense of something you once had and will never get back.

That hint of magic now imbued my senses.

Emilio stretched and clenched his fists. He'd picked it up too. We both moved faster down the street, our soundless steps in perfect sync.

A magical upbringing focused on the third eye, honing and mastering a witch's intuition as a first line of defense, elevating them above the mundane; but the predatory senses of a vampire were astronomical in comparison. I didn't need to see a mark. I could usually sense a witch with a couple of deep inhales.

Although, in New Orleans, it was a little trickier to track the supernatural. The jasmine-infused humidity cradled everything that traipsed through it, but tonight not even weather could hide this witch's scent. My family had searched every block of the French Quarter for Callisto's coven, and then Emilio and I had searched the Faubourgs Tréme and Marigny, and what was left of the Ninth Ward, on our own. Tonight, we'd widened our search to a more desolate part of the city. It was only fitting to be reduced to the two of us, given that we'd been entangled in this chase on and off for the last two hundred years. No matter how different were the lives we led, and how far away from each other we stayed, the Salazars always seemed to bring Emilio and me back to the same point on the globe. And Saint-Germain always brought us back to La Nouvelle-Orléans.

And suddenly it was the 1790s and 1840s and 1930s all over again, which was how we both knew with complete certainty that Callisto Salazar was *not* dead. The Animarum Praedators had escaped death so many times thanks to their peculiar Spektral power that I'd never believe they'd met final death until I touched their hollow, spiritless bodies with my own fingers. Not until I heard the silence coming from their chests.

The air crackled, and my fangs snapped to point. Emilio and I gave each other the exact same look. *This witch was foolish enough to use magic on the street.* The traces were woven through the air like an enchanted tapestry, and a loose thread was dangling right in front of us. Surely they knew we were hunting them? A part of me wondered if it was a trap. The other part of me was ready to rip my way out of it, if it meant unveiling Callisto. With hardly a signal to each other, we split off to opposite sides of the street.

Usually this particular cat-and-mouse chase brought a fire to Emilio's eyes, birthed in a time gone by when it wasn't entirely uncommon for a man to slay another in the street with his blade, and when war was an inevitable part of the male birthright. The glint was there now but overshadowed by a darkness I'd never seen in my brother. A darkness stirred by pain, loss masked by infuriation. Pain that condemned Callisto Salazar.

It had been ages since Emilio and I had so irrevocably agreed on something, but after the events at the convent, the Salazars needed to be eradicated. No more chase. No more feud.

The Salazars almost got Adele.

Because of my carelessness.

I sucked in a deep breath and moved faster, following the enchanted thread, tugging it, my desire for what we'd find on the other end becoming intemperate. I could imagine why Callis would be enthralled with this city—how he thought he was going to make it his own, build a castle where the supernatural dripped with the rain and bebopped alongside the pentatonic scales. A spiritual nexus that drew the willing and beguiled the mundane. It was no wonder descendants of so many of the Great European witching families had ended up here. New Orleans was a place you wanted to be born from and die in. Even I, who'd been drained of magic for centuries, could feel her alluring whisper begging me to stay.

As I moved quicker, an energy pummeled through my veins, making me feel alive in a way I'd forgotten. I didn't know what I was more thrilled by: being out of the attic, or the prospect of ripping Callisto Salazar's throat out, or . . . Warmth pinched my cheeks, and I brushed the thought away. *It's not that, Niccolò.*

The thread pulsed from a decrepit house on Emilio's side of the street that looked as rotten and feculent as I'd imagined the Animarum Praedators had been when they'd risen from their graves. I whipped across the street, rejoining my brother, and within seconds, we were both over the iron fence, pausing for a moment, feeling for the scent of magic. *Inside or out?*

Out.

Emilio tipped his head to the right, and I took off the other way, just in case it was a trap.

An entanglement of rosebushes had overgrown the path, their fragrance momentarily overpowering my senses, masking the enchanted bread crumbs. I stalked straight through them, thorns scraping my skin with scratches that would heal before I cleared the thicket.

My steps hastened. With Callisto, it was the same feud, the same enemy. Another city, another century. Everything was the same, but nothing was the same. This time, it wasn't just two Medici brothers fighting two Salazar siblings. This time, Callisto had a grimoire. The House of Salazar had gotten back their magic. The flip in power enthralled me.

For the first time in over four hundred years, his coven was bound.

I would never let him touch my family, and I would never let him touch *her*. I could still feel the thumps of her heartbeat from the other side of the attic door, the exultation I'd felt every time she'd drawn nearer.

After centuries of mundane generations, Adeline Saint-Germain finally had a magical heir.

We were so close. *No one,* not even Callisto Salazar, was going to stop me from taking back everything León had stolen from my family. *What the hell was I thinking, letting them step foot back in that attic?* The risk I'd taken was completely reckless.

I could hear Emilio crashing through from the other side of the house. He was reckless enough for all of us, but something in me—maybe it was foolish desperation—had just believed in her, Saint-Germain and all. The intuition had superseded all survival instincts, all reasonable thought, all reasonable sanity even. It was an intuition that had a pulse of magical heritage—a feeling I couldn't recall having since I was . . . *a witch.*

I took a deep, controlled breath to temper my creeping pulse. She'd protected me. She'd saved me. All of us. Even as Callisto was taking her magic.

Anger seethed rapidly through my bloodstream, almost reminding me of what it had been like to have my *magia Elementale*—those tiny pulses of electricity.

The enclave of roses led to a wooded, swampier area. Damp foliage covered the ground, so that when the twig snapped nearby, it was barely audible. I glanced over. It was just Emilio.

In silence, we took a beaten path through thickening fog, deeper into the property. I wondered if we were just tracking one witch or if this old abandoned monstrosity was where the coven had set up camp. Could we be so lucky? We passed a fountain bespattered in mire, and I imagined myself tying Callisto to it and leaving him there for scavengers to peck out his organs for the rest of eternity like Prometheus.

He'd nearly taken her from me—my only link to León. By blood and by magic. *He'd nearly killed her.*

Emilio looked over to me again. He was getting a read on my accelerating heartbeat; it was distracting him from the hunt. Still, I thought about him touching her. I thought about him demanding that she deliver me to his coven, and about her telling him *no.* Rage ripped through me.

The end of the thread led to tombstones, old and crumbling.

"Show yourself, witch," I sneered, twisting under the moonlight, searching.

He was wearing an invisibility cloak of some kind, and the false sense of protection it gave him would be his demise. The scent of magic was crackling, flaring up my sense of revenge, reminding me why we sat at the top of the food chain.

I punched through the magic and grabbed his throat. Fire burst from his hands, but his blood was already spilling into my mouth, my fangs sinking deeper into his flesh.

The flames in his palms brightened as he dug deeper for a last pull of magic.

My jaw locked, and I sucked harder, overwhelmed with the desire to hear his pulse slow to nothingness. This was where I always stopped feeding and altered their memories before letting them go. *Not this one. Not tonight.*

Not a Salazar.

The rush that came next nearly knocked me to the ground. It had been so long since I'd felt it: the jerk of the bloodlust.

Beneath the shadows, Emilio's face brightened. "Our Salazar years are some of my fondest with you, Niccolò. It's nice to see you being your true self."

I detached from the witch and, with one swirl of my tongue, licked the wound so it would heal—not that I had any intention of letting him live longer than he was useful to us, but there was no point in making a mess. "I'm always my true self."

He snickered. It was a lie. We both knew it.

With one shove, the witch was out of my arms and into Emilio's, who tore into his neck with a forcefulness that would startle anyone who didn't share his surname. He held the witch so tightly that his bones snapped. He cried out, and I let him, so he could feel the fear that no one was coming to his aid.

On another night, with any other person, I'd have demanded my brother be gentler, but this witch had sealed his fate when he helped steal Adele's magic—and almost her life.

My jaw tightened, and I went back for more, but I saw the rage in Emilio's eyes, and stepped back. The more my brother could work out his aggressions on the Animarum Praedators, the less I had to worry about him retaliating against Adele's coven. It would have been an exercise in futility to try to stop Emilio from killing in his current state of mourning. The more strategic choice was to try to guide his rage. The runs, the hunts, the kills, the feedings were all good for the greater safety of the town.

"*Silenzio*," I said to the witch as he writhed beneath Emilio's bite, and after that moment, he did not so much as whimper beneath the weight of my hypnotic thrall, not even when the blood spilled from Emilio's mouth as he sucked faster than he could swallow.

I could tell he was distracted. My brother might be maniacal, but he wasn't sloppy. He was simply belligerent over the loss of his child.

The fact that, Emilio, two-months-starved, had sunk his fangs into Callisto Salazar, and dropped him free, was a testament to his true feelings for Brigitte Dupré Le Moyne, which I'd always found perplexing. Never had I thought that either of us would make a child, not in our whole immortal lifetimes—for two entirely different reasons, of course.

Every vampire understood the pull *to* the Maker. If I thought about her long enough, I still longed for Séraphine, despite the hatred I'd harbored for her—that feeling would stay buried deep inside of me, locked within a box within a box within a box. Each with a code. Each with a key. Each made of impenetrable steel. But it was only in the last decade, seeing the way Emilio had changed when he was around Brigitte, that I began to understand the pull *on* the Maker. He may have bitten and turned her in a move of strategic warfare, but he loved her more than I'd ever seen him love anything, other than himself and battle. He hadn't loved anyone like that since Giovanna. Even though he'd hidden it well, he'd been truly devastated when we didn't find our dear sweet sister in the attic with Gabriel as we'd hoped. But I knew my brother; he couldn't hide from me.

And so, the fact that he could nurture anyone had stunned me. When he'd dropped Callisto to run to Brigitte's aid, he'd revealed a flicker of humanity I hadn't known existed in him, not as vampire nor as man.

The witch sank to the ground underneath my brother's pull. Now that we'd caught one of them, pleasure stirred inside me. This wasn't just for Emilio; this was about Medicean revenge.

I bent to the Ghost Drinker's face. "By the time my family is finished with you tonight, you will be begging the gods for your mortality."

A blood-high beamed from Emilio as he licked the witch's wounds clean. The punctures began closing instantly—if only I'd understood the medical benefits of vampire saliva back when León and I were in our lab and Séraphine was in our cage.

Emilio shoved his prey forward and told him to walk, but the witch slumped to the ground.

I grabbed him by the back of the collar and lifted him up. "Walk, unless you want to be dragged."

He miraculously found the strength.

As we followed behind, I continued to think about all that had happened over the last few months. Though partially cursed and without my sister, my family was back together. Adeline Saint-Germain finally had a magical descendant. León had an heir. And we were all here, tiptoeing through the *je ne sais quoi of La Louisanne.*

Perhaps the most intriguing part—what stirred my imagination and my fear most of all—was that Callisto had restored his Elemental magic. In my four hundred years of life, I'd never heard of such a thing, nor could I find any such tales in the histories of witchcraft. And not only that, but I'd put my faith in a Saint-Germain. I'd trusted my intuition, and in turn she had saved me from certain death from the oldest Medicean enemy to still roam the planet—one whose family had once been the greatest threat to the entire European witching world. A family whose darkness Adele could not yet comprehend, and who had utterly deserved to be stripped of their magic by our father all those years ago.

Adele was magical.

She made me feel magical.

"Niccolò . . . ?" Emilio asked.

"*Cosa*?"

"You're smiling."

"No, I'm not."

CHAPTER 6

ASYLUM

Désirée led the way through the shop, with Landry Dempsey between the two of us, still cuffed by her magical vine.

There weren't many things that made me anxious, but something always pricked my nerves when I crossed the threshold at Vodou Pourvoyeur. Maybe it had just been since Ritha Borges momentarily lost her gourd and thought *I* was the enemy attacking the local spirits. *Talk about the Fairy Ghost-Mother.* Or maybe it was just that every time I went to the shop, which was frequently these days, there was always something new in the bizarro category that I couldn't believe I'd previously missed: a dried tarantula, a jar of squid ink for writing incantations, a necklace with a raccoon's *penis bone* dangling from the center, for . . . I don't even want to know what.

The place was a living encyclopedia for witches. The more answers you discovered, the deeper you went; the deeper you went, the more questions it revealed to you. And *this*, I was starting to understand, was at the core of everything about being a witch: the more you knew, the more you realized you knew nothing.

That feeling engulfed me as we walked through the front room, the hall of Voodoo dolls, and into the apothecary. Désirée paused at the curtain on the back wall. I knew she was listening, trying to feel the energy in the rest of the house. I'd have offered to fly ahead and scope things out, but I didn't want to leave her alone with this psycho.

"Do you have a plan?" I asked.

"We don't need a plan. We just need a story: We were out for a run—not patrolling, not actively seeking out the Possessed—and we happened to come across this guy on the street. Your Spektral Spidey sense told you something was up. You and Codi gingerly tackled him just long enough for me to do the mirror test, confirming possession. We brought him in, no harm, no foul."

"Oy vey." *Gingerly tackled him?* "Any plan that involves lying to Ritha Borges just seems like a bad idea."

"It's not a plan. It's a story that we're sticking to." She removed the sapling from his mouth and put it in her bag.

Landry reached for Désirée's hip, making a slurping sound with his tongue. I grabbed his arm, no longer caring about the plan or the story. I was just glad this guy was off the street.

And through the curtain and up the staircase the three of us went.

On the second story, between the bedrooms and the taxidermy studio, there was a huge double-parlor where Ritha's coven held their circles. People—witches—flitted in and out, all carrying armfuls of ritual items: big palm branches, baskets of flower petals, and bottles that might have been water, might have been liquor. They jewelry jingled as they walked by.

Désirée kept her head straight forward, emitting a cool *nothing-to-see here-people* vibe as we looped around the staircase and continued on up to the third story camelback. No one glanced at us, or at least, not with any suspicion. They all seemed busy preparing for something, and Désirée was, after all, Ritha's granddaughter.

At the top of the stairs, Désirée turned back to me with one finger over her mouth, making me wonder how confident she really was with this plan—er, story.

There were only three rooms on the third floor. The first, and the eeriest, was where the exorcisms took place, and it was most likely where Ritha could be found. As we walked past the open doorway, I tried not to rubberneck, but it was impossible not to. A round window high in the center wall between the angled roof let the moonlight flood the room, which was simply decorated with an old claw-foot tub and a twin bed. An elderly woman with long white hair lay on the bed.

Instead of trying to pull the soul out of her, like usual, two middle-aged female witches were tending to her. One was rubbing her body with oil while the other braided her hair. Beside them, a man sat quietly slapping a tall drum. The woman on the bed looked like a corpse being prepped for a funeral. *Jesus, Isaac, morbid much?*

The man turned his head as if he could feel my presence, and our eyes locked as I cleared the doorway. I imagined him whispering to the others that we were here. When Désirée joined our coven instead of theirs, some of them saw her as a spoiled child in a rebellious phase, and some seemed bothered when we were around on Saturday nights. I was a clear outsider despite having my mark.

Désirée turned into the next room, which took up most of the floor and was divided by a thick black velvet curtain. On this side of the curtain, the décor was something between a hospital room and a witchy medical supply closet—basically the triage area for any Possessed who were brought in with injuries.

We strode through the room, past two hospital beds and a gurney, past shelves lined with regular first aid supplies, and then more cluttered ones, overloaded with huge quantities of oils, powders, bath salts, scraps of paper to scribble intentions for spellwork, and other supplies to aid with the exorcisms. Landry was in perfect health, which meant he skipped triage.

Désirée opened the curtain, and I nudged him into the parlor of reflections.

Black velvet curtains covered all the windows and doorways, making the lit candles seem extra bright in the darkness. Mirrors stood on the floor, leaning up against the walls, but it was the jagged glass shards hanging from the ceiling on invisible strings that made the room feel less like a fairy tale and more like a torture chamber.

Of course, it was neither. It was a holding tank for newly captured Possessed, where Ritha recorded their vitals and tried to figure out as much as she could about the entities inside them to help with their exorcisms. The mirrors helped her see the parasitic souls and identify them. She said, they disoriented the parasites while she examined them.

A girl sat on the couch, her head hanging to the side and eyes glossy, half-obscured by her strawberry blonde bob. She looked different from when we'd captured her last week, despite still wearing her medical student hospital scrubs. She appeared so innocent now, but last week she'd attacked Codi, ripping at his hair and clawing him like a rabid animal. Now she was tranquil, as if heavily sedated . . . or maybe in a trance.

"Make yourself cozy," Désirée said to Landry. "Given that it's Saturday night, you might be waiting a little while."

He mumbled incoherently and plopped down next to the girl.

I grabbed the back of his collar. "I don't think so." I shoved him into an adjacent armchair.

"*Pa deplase*," Désirée said, telling him to *stay* in Haitian Creole. The words were also the incantation that enchanted the furniture to bind its occupants. The Possessed hated it, but it was better than being bound with rope.

And there he'd remain until Ritha could see him. His dark brown eyes, filled with fear. Desperation. The true-self of the host shining through for a moment. I shook my head, my heart bleeding for whoever this poor guy was.

Landry tilted his head to the side, a smirk on his face, and then spat. I moved just in time to avoid a lugie to the eye, but it flew past and hit the girl on the cheek. When I looked back at Landry, I realized that had been his intention.

I grabbed the bandana still in my pocket from work that morning, strode over, twisted it into a rope, and secured it between his jaws.

"Savage," Désirée said.

I wasn't trying to be, but if it were me, I'd want to be tied up so the monster inside me couldn't hurt the girl on the sofa, or anyone else.

There was a hop to Désirée's step as we went down the stairs. I struggled to mimic her *oh-so-natural* behavior as we cruised through groups of her relatives in the hallway, through the taxidermy studio, and out the second story back door.

"Should we bounce to HQ?" I asked, following her across the balcony that bridged the upstairs of the shop to the second floor of the guesthouse. Witches bustled below us, all in flowy white garments.

"We're fine. As long as we stick to our story, we'll be fine." She walked faster.

Désirée's definition of "fine" clearly differed from mine when it came to the wrath of Ritha.

The guesthouse hallways were not for the faint of heart. They were lined with small rooms that made me wonder if it was once a slave quarters, but it always felt too weird of a thing to ask. Now the rooms contained the Possessed, twenty-three of them, locked with Earth-witch magic. They were taken out four times a day to stretch their legs in the courtyard and get some sunlight, but otherwise they slept, ate, and spent all their time imprisoned. Each room had a bed and a desk and a few personal effects, but nothing they could injure themselves or others with.

The prisoners' voices bled through the doorway cracks, yelling, hissing, and moaning. The only thing more heart-wrenching than the noises was the look on their faces after they'd been in the exorcism room, and their happiness to be back in the bedroom-cells.

We turned the corner and had nearly reached the master bedroom at the end of the hallway where Ren was, when an unmistakable voice rang out from the main house: "*Désirée Nanette Borges*!"

Désirée looked at me. "I guess Gran found Landry. We might as well just go and get it over with."

And as things often went at the Borges', the mood took a sudden shift to the dramatic.

When we walked back into the room of mirrors, Ritha was checking Landry's pupils. She stopped and turned to us, crossing her arms. "And how did this gentleman end up on my sofa?"

Désirée pulled out a little pot from her pocket, unscrewed the lid, and rubbed the ointment onto the red-haired girl's cracking lips, ignoring Ritha's question as if it were rhetorical.

"*Désirée*. Both of you," she snapped, looking at me. "I *told* you to leave the Possessed alone. It's too dangerous! We have it covered!"

"Clearly," Désirée said under her breath.

"Désirée, I will lock you in this house if you don't stop hunting down the Possessed!"

"I didn't even do anything! Isaac and Codi did *all* the dirty work. I just stood by with the memory powder, right?" She looked to me.

"Uh—"

"I don't know what's worse, Désirée, the disobedience, or that you expect me to believe you stood by while the boys took care of him!"

"She's a lying heathen!" Landry yelled. "She trapped me in her magical vines!"

Ritha's eyes widened. "You used magic on the street?"

"He killed someone!"

"That's exactly *why* you need to stay away from them!"

"Whore!" Landry shouted.

Ritha's finger snapped toward his mouth, and his words were muffled, lips pinned shut. *Holy shit.*

His eyes bulged as he tried to open his mouth.

"We had it under control, Gran. We even contained a loose soul!"

"What! Where?"

"Central City."

"What were you doing in Central City at night, Désirée!"

"If we hadn't gotten it, it could have infected someone else."

"It's too dangerous, child. You are done with this. If you two want to aid with the Possessed, there is plenty for you to do here at the house. Powders. Baths. Mojo bags." Ritha looked straight at me this time. "Do not think for a second I won't ground you, too."

"Yes, ma'am," I mumbled, really not wanting to get in the middle of this.

"It's fine!" Désirée said. "Landry doesn't even remember what happened thanks to my memory powder . . ."

"You mean, other than your magical vines? What else happened that he'd have to forget?"

I gulped.

A yelp came out of Landry's mouth, and we all turned his way. He was staring up at the glass shards, which were reflecting a face that wasn't his.

Ritha released the silencing spell, and he turned to her, frantic. "The girl's right. Bring me to jail, I beg you!" His face snarled and a deluge of racist filth spewed from his lips.

"Gran! Some Grand Wizard pervert is trapped inside this innocent black man!"

"Even more reason for you not to be chasing him down!"

"What's—what's happening to me?" he asked, his hand twitching.

"We have to help him!"

He snarled, kicking and thrusting up in the chair. "I know what you can do for me . . ." He licked his lips at Désirée, who shot him the bird.

"Goddess help me," Ritha said, rubbing her head.

A pink cloud puffed up from the counter into Désirée's face. I fanned it away without looking up.

She'd tried to smooth things over with Ritha by telling her about the memory powder she'd used on Landry, but her plan backfired when Ritha took an interest in it and asked her to make her a fresh batch. So Dee was at her cauldron behind the shop counter, and I was across from her with my sketchpad. Not that it really made a difference; if Ritha hadn't asked for it, we'd probably be doing the exact same thing, only at the brothel instead.

Drumming thumped from deeper in the house, and a spicy, smoky scent wafted from the same direction. I copied a symbol that had been drawn onto the wooden floor with chalk, or probably with something weirder like the powder of crushed sand dollars. I'd seen these symbols before: on the sidewalk outside, in the courtyard, and etched into the candles that filled the racks in the front room where the more touristy things were shelved.

It was formed by two long lines crossed at the heart, creating a quadrant embellished with pineapple-like shapes, starbursts, curlicues, and crosses. The juxtaposition of blunt lines and soft swirling edges made the symbol feel both primitive and queenly at the same time.

"It's a vèvè," Désirée said as if no further explanation was required. Her hair was still in the tight ponytail atop her head, but she'd changed out of her sporty Possessed-chaser clothes and into a baggy brick-colored dress that slouched off her shoulder and was cinched by a thin leather belt at her hips.

"And a vèvè is . . . ?" I slid the pen back behind my ear and closed the pad.

"Think of it as an astral invitation to the ritual that's about to happen upstairs."

"Like, to astral project your family's coven members who can't be there in person?"

"No," she laugh-snorted. "Here, the vèvès are invitations for the lwa to descend to the Natural World."

"And the lwa?"

"Are the intermediaries between the magical ones and the great Bon Dieu, the supreme creator."

"Like angels?"

"Er . . . kind of? Most lwa are syncretic with Catholic saints."

"Random."

"Not random. It's from, you know, the days of Catholicism being forced upon slaves."

"Uh . . . no, I don't know." Adeline's journal had revealed that Désirée's ancestor was a slave in Haiti before arriving in New Orleans, and it still sent a chill down my spine every time I thought about it. About anyone being enslaved. "So, the vèvès are portals for the lwa?"

"No, they're invitations. The lwa don't need mere humans to create portals for them to enter our world."

"Invitations that . . . conjure up the lwa?"

"As if. Lwa are not jinn in magical lamps. When witches call on them, it's usually to ask for something, so a formal invitation starts the process of appeasement. Along with a multitude of offerings, prayers, promises, and sacrifices, all specific to their individual desires." She nodded to the floor. "This vèvè is for Papa Legba." She said his name with endearment, as if he were a beloved grandfather.

I grabbed an apple from a basket on the counter. "You called to him in some of our rituals, like the night we bound our coven at the diner on Bourbon Street"—I took a bite—"and the night at the cemetery, during the séance when Marassa Makandal appeared to me."

"Someone was paying attention."

"So, who is he? Legba?" I bit off another hunk of apple.

"In Voodoo tradition, Legba is the keeper of the crossroads, the intermediary between the witches and the lwa. He speaks all the world's languages so he can communicate with anyone who needs him."

"So he's like a translator."

Her brow creased. "Yeah, actually. The translator between the mortal and the divine. He grants or denies permission to communicate with those in the Spirit World. For the Borges, Saturday nights are all about Papa Legba just as much as Monday nights are all about red beans 'n' rice."

"Why red beans and rice?"

She looked at me. "I have no idea, that's not a Voodoo thing; it's a New Orleans thing. Ask Adele, when she's back; I'm sure she knows."

The certainty in her voice that we could just ask Adele at some later date eased the persistent pang in my chest, for a little while at least. Désirée was completely confident that when Adele re-emerged, everything would be fine. We'd all be back together, better and stronger than before, sans Annabelle, plus Codi. I, on the other hand, wasn't so sure Adele was ever going to be in the same room as me again. Désirée didn't know what it felt like to hold your dead mother in your arms.

She nodded to the curtain on the back wall. "Gran's Saturday night circle is starting. Do you want to see for yourself?"

"Uh . . . yes?" Apple crunched between my teeth. *Was she really inviting me to Ritha's circle?*

I dropped the core into a trash can behind the counter and followed her behind the curtain. Her ponytail swung as she led me up to the second story. Someone had lit all the candles that lined the stairs.

The drumming became more resonant as we ascended.

Another vèvè was drawn on the floor in the second-story hallway, outside a closed door: a heart-shaped head atop a series of rectangles and triangles that formed a body and limbs. The heart-man had starburst feet and stick fingers that looked like Wolverine's claws.

"They're calling for Gran Bwa," Désirée said, glancing at the symbol. She very gently pressed her ear to the door. "The lwa of the sacred forest. For Earth witches, he's like, the end-all. Gran Bwa protects all the plants and animals."

"What do they need him for?"

"I don't know, but he's the greatest healer in the Voodoo pantheon; he knows all the magical secrets hidden in plants." Her face became serious. "They must be getting really desperate. The last time I heard them calling for Gran Bwa, my great-uncle was dying of colon cancer."

"He could heal someone with cancer?" My heart skipped.

"No. Maybe in a freak chance, although, I have a cousin who'd say yes. I think they were just trying to take away some of his pain so he could be more comfortable."

A nightmarish image of my mom in the hospital bed crept into my head. She'd always told me she wasn't in pain, but I knew she was lying.

Désirée looked back as she reached for the door. "Just don't be disruptive or Ritha will do a silencing spell on you, or turn you into a spider and put you in a jar, or something."

I laughed awkwardly, telling myself that she was just joking.

And then, as if sensing my hesitation, she took my arm and pulled me into the dim, hazy room.

CHAPTER 7

GRAN BWA

The door closed behind us on its own, and I immediately broke a sweat.

I tugged at the collar of my T-shirt; it had to be at least ten degrees warmer in here than the rest of the house. The low light made the drum beats and the chanting feel deeper.

Flames flickered all around the room, muted by the thick smoke coiling from herb bundles burning in oyster shells scattered throughout, and from the fat cigars wedged between the fingertips of witches. A few were actually smoking them, but others seemed only to be waving them around as they danced in a casual circle. All of the witches, a dozen or so, were dressed in assortments of white: linen shirts with matching pants, tank tops and flowing skirts. Some wore white headdresses, some wore layered necklaces of shells, fishbone, and fresh flowers. Both Papa Legba's and Gran Bwa's vèvès had been drawn in the circle they danced around.

A fragrant floral smell mixed with the smoke. The perimeter of the room was lined with fresh cuttings of elephant ears and banana tree leaves, and among the piles of foliage, haphazard groupings of candles in glass bottles melted wax down their sides. As the Earth witches moved in a fluid circle, bells jingled from their wrists and ankles. Their flowing garments drifted close to the flickering flames, but no one seemed concerned.

Exhilaration swept me. I fully expected Ritha to throw us out as soon as she saw me, so I tried to soak in as much as I could. The chant was filled with words I couldn't understand, but whatever their words, their intention pulsed throughout the room. The swaying hips, tribal beats, and foreign chanting around the flames felt unpredictable yet grounded, daunting and alluring at the same time. As they all performed the cacophonic rite, inclusion had never made me feel so much of an outsider.

"Do you see that woman?" Désirée whispered.

Through the cracks of dancing witches, in the center of the circle, the elderly woman I'd seen earlier was crumpled in the fetal position, her white hair now braided into crowns around her head. This time, I recognized her from the mirror-room—from the night Ritha had accused me of being a Ghost Drinker. She was possessed by the soul of the young blonde girl who'd drowned at my worksite, the one who'd used the mirror to try to warn me of the Animarum Praedators, and who I'd failed to help.

"What are they doing to her?" I asked, unable to temper the New Yorky accusation in my voice.

"They're trying to *help* her. But if they're calling on the lwa for assistance, things are grim."

"Help her how? Are they trying to remove the extra soul? Can Gran Bwa do that?"

"I doubt Gran Bwa would consider that his business, but he can make her healthier, which would give us more time to figure out how to exorcise the parasite."

The vision of the blonde girl in the pond rose in my mind: her hair so green with algae, her thin arms outstretched. Was her soul really now a parasite? Did it—did *she*—know what she'd become? Could she remember her old life? Her parents, her school friends, her dreams?

The thought made me shudder.

"Why can't *you* just heal her?"

"Don't even get me started. Gran said it would be too much of a strain on my magic and too risky while my Maleficium is so new." She rolled her eyes, but I knew she was thinking about her recoil. "What good is getting your Spektral power if you aren't allowed to use it?"

A burst of energy rushed around the room, fluttering the loose garments, and the chanting became so intense even the squarest of the mundane would have felt it. It was impossible not to creep closer to the circle. My pulse pounded deeper to the beat of the drum.

"Isaac," Dee gasped, brushing my arm.

I turned her way just as her knees buckled and caught her lanky body as she folded to the ground. "Désirée?" My voice was barely audible over the crowd. Her head fell forward. "Désirée!"

The bells and drums lulled, and the witches cooed, turning our way. Then the drums and chanting picked up again, and everyone began to dance a faster rhythm. Désirée convulsed in my arms, triggering me into immediate first-responder mode. *Seizures.*

Taking special care of her head, I tried to lay her on the ground so I could turn her on her side, but a young man and woman hurried over and grabbed Dee under the arms with far less care.

"Hey!" I cried.

"It's a sign," said the guy.

The pair looked so similar, they must have been siblings. Her hair hung in hundreds of tiny braids to her waist, while his was practically shaved, but they both had the same russet-colored eyes that flickered in the candlelight.

"She's supposed to be with us," the girl agreed.

They ignored me and carried her into the circle, her feet dragging along the floor. I tried to follow them, but the other witches closed the loop, barring my way and my view. They all raised their arms higher and swung their hips harder, ringing the bells and beating the drums.

"Désirée!" I yelled.

"Even the lwa are trying to drag her back to her blood-circle," said a man who I think was her uncle. The woman next to him smirked.

I tried to step through a gap between two of the dancing witches, but an invisible wave knocked me back and I fell to the wooden floor. And then, for the first time ever, I purposefully took crow form in front of people who were not my coven members. I needed to know that Dee was okay. I circled above the witches so I could get a better view.

The two witches were propping her up in the middle of the ring, directly in front of Ritha. I scanned the room for Désirée's mother. Ana Marie was beaming with joy, leaning forward as if in anticipation, hand clutched to her chest.

The dancing, drum beats, and jingles swelled to a peak, and my pulse rose with them. A large taxidermied fox was mounted to the rear wall to look like he was running through it. I swooped through the air and landed on his back.

Désirée's head slowly began to lift. The two witches let go of her arms and faded back into the circle.

Her eyes popped open.

They were huge and completely white, just like Ritha's had been the night I'd seen her in the courtyard talking to herself. *Désirée had said I'd interrupted Ritha talking with the lwa.*

A joyous round of whispers went around the room in a wave. Ritha raised her hand, and the room silenced.

At first it was hard to tell if Ritha was happy, upset, or just surprised. She stepped toward her white-eyed granddaughter with an air of caution. "*Byen venu, Gran Bwa.*" She spread her arms wide. "Welcome." Her sternness faded as she stared up at Dee, who'd grown a little taller than her. "I beg your pardon. I know we have spoken many times over the years, but seeing you choose Désirée . . . overwhelms my heart with love."

Gran Bwa? The lwa?

The room was so still and silent, it was as if no one even dared even to take a breath.

Désirée stretched her long, bare arms over her head, like a moth breaking out of a cocoon, and watched her own fingers fan out, as if seeing her body for the first time. She tilted her head back, stretching her neck one way and then the other, her ponytail swaying. A ripple of energy rolled up the line of her skeleton, rolling her hips, arching her spine, until she swooped up on the tips of her toes. There she stayed suspended, as if marionette cords were holding her up. She looked down and gasped, and the real Désirée's eyes momentarily showed through; but then her head tipped back and her eyes went white again. Her gangly arms floated up and out, waving through the air.

A man in the corner of the room who looked too old to physically participate slapped down on the animal hide drum once . . . and then again.

As Dee's body swayed, the loose-fitting dress slipped off her left shoulder. She glanced at herself, as if enthralled, then wiggled her other shoulder until the dress slipped down that arm too, exposing her bare chest. I hopped up the fox's back, hiding behind its head, trying to obstruct my view of her naked breasts. Her dress would have fallen off completely if there hadn't been a belt at her hips trapping the fabric. I peered out between the two fox ears. A smile rocked her mouth, as if she were happy to finally be free of the clothes.

I squinted, waiting for someone to cover her up—her mother, her grandmother—but no one approached her, and no one seemed fazed either. Dee shimmied her hips a couple times, as if trying to rid herself of the clothes completely, and I nearly fell off the fox trying to look away. Luckily, her belt stayed put.

The drum rippled with anticipation, and then Désirée's gaze landed straight on me. Her lips slowly pursed into a smile. "*Zwazo nwa.*" It was her voice, but the pitch was both lighter and higher, telling me the words belonged to someone else.

Every head in the room turned to me, as if waiting. Ritha sighed and held out her arm.

Is that an invitation?

Désirée's expression was childlike and gentle, which kind of made me nervous. "Gentle" was not a word I'd typically use to describe Dee.

Ritha gave me a look that asked, *What are you waiting for?*

I swooped down, praying Désirée had been right about Gran Bwa being protector of the forest and that Ritha wasn't in need of a sacrificial lamb—er, bird—for this ritual. I landed on her shoulder, directly in front of Dee-Gran Bwa, trying not to look at her tits. I'd sketched live nude models plenty of times, but this was *Dee*, one of my best friends. Too weird.

She began swaying to the left and the right, arching her back. I tried not to notice the motion of her waist, or shape of her nipples, or the line of her triceps as her arms bent behind her head. Still smiling, she pulled the elastic band from her ponytail and shook her long, straight hair free. It spilled down over her shoulders, covering her.

Thank Goddess, as she would say.

She still looked like Désirée, but that smile was someone else's. The way Gran Bwa moved Désirée's long, lanky limbs with such grace was otherworldly. She pressed her fingers together, cupping her hands like hooves, and extended a hoof-hand toward me.

I looked at Ritha, and when she gave me a slight nod, I fluttered off her shoulder and landed on Désirée's wrist. Despite the temperature in the room and the beads of sweat on her face, a wave of cold crept from her arm to my talons, pricking my feathers.

Gran Bwa's white eyes roamed past me to the witches standing in the circle around us. She fixated on a girl about our age. Her skin was a lighter brown than Dee's, highlighting a spatter of freckles on her nose, and her black hair was big and curly, tied with a white scarf like a headband. Dee-Gran Bwa took slow, measured steps toward her, using the full stride of Désirée's long legs.

The young witch bowed, whispering Creole words, and Dee-Gran Bwa gently dipped her head and held still. The girl took a flower chain of gardenias from her own neck and placed it around Dee-Gran Bwa's.

Dee-Gran Bwa smiled, and we moved on to the next person. Each witch offered something from their person, until Désirée's neck was so loaded with shell necklaces and flower chains that I no longer had to worry about catching sight of any side-boob or underboob or anything else through the strands of her hair.

As we completed the circle, Ana Marie put a wreath on Désirée's head and kissed her cheek. "*Mèsi,* Gran Bwa, for accepting our invitation and choosing my daughter. *Mèsi anpil.*"

Désirée's brown, sweaty skin glowed in the light of the flickering candles. She looked like a dewy forest nymph as she swept back to the center of the circle, where Ritha was cradling the head of the old woman on the floor, who appeared to be unconscious.

Dee-Gran Bwa stood over them, energy rippling through her, making her tremble. I fluttered off her wrist and circled tightly around them as she slowly raised both arms to the ceiling. When she couldn't reach any higher, she lifted her right knee in the air too, each motion holding everyone's breath. With a primal cry—part lioness, part hyena—she grabbed fists of air and wrenched down her hands, thrusting her leg to the floor with a stomp that seemed to shake the whole house; it sent everyone into a chant simultaneously, as if she'd commanded them.

Ce lan bwa fle yo ye
Ce lan bwa bwansh yo ye
Ce lan bwa fey yo ye
Mwen ce gran Bwa.

The drums resumed, and the dancing-stomps made it feel like the gods were coming down from Olympus, or wherever it was that the rest of the lwa lived. Caws sang from my throat as I swooped around the inside of the circle, the swirling energy making it impossible to not participate. As I watched Dee-Gran Bwa own the room, I better realized the magnitude of everything Désirée had given up to be a part of our coven. *No wonder she's so annoyed with the way things are shaking out.*

She floated back up to her tiptoes and held her hands over the possessed woman. Unlike every other time I'd seen her heal, this time she didn't touch the afflicted. Creole words that I was sure she didn't know rolled off her tongue, and her fingers began to curl, clutching the air. Liquid that was way too black to be blood slowly dripped from the corners of the woman's closed eyelids.

It's in the woods, the flowers are,
It's in the woods, the branches are,
It's in the woods, the leaves are,
I am Gran Bwa.

The witches chanted louder, Désirée's faced tensed, and the black liquid began oozing from the woman's nose and ears. The chanting and drumming and dancing escalated, until finally the woman's eyes bulged open and she screamed, spitting out globs of black goo. A gust of wind ripped around the room, and the necklaces exploded from Dee's neck, flowers and shells and bones and beads shooting off in every direction. Her hand reached for me as her knees buckled again, and she clutched me so tightly, I snapped back to human form. My feet hit the ground just in time for me to reach out and break her fall.

"Désirée . . . ?" Her head bobbed against my shoulder. I shook her limp body again. "Dee!"

The circle of witches enveloped us, but no one got too close.

Her fingers tensed on my back, clutching me, and only then did my pulse calm. "Désirée?"

The room roared. More stomping. Drumming. Shaking bells.

"Am I . . . *naked*?" She hugged me tight, using my body to cover herself.

"Um . . ." I awkwardly pulled up her dress until she could slip it back over her shoulders.

A tall man with long dreads looked right at me. "You might want to watch out."

Before I could ask him what he was talking about, a stream of black liquid projected from Désirée's mouth straight down my chest.

Everyone in the room howled with laughter as I lurched back, flicking the stuff off my hands. "*Gross*!"

Désirée stepped closer. "How many of my relatives just saw my tits?" she asked, wiping her mouth, unconcerned that she'd just doused me in some kind of mystical Voodoo juice.

"Um . . . it was pretty dark. Probably no one." I pinched the only piece of my shirt that seemed to be dry and held it away from my chest.

Ana Marie took her hand. "Only as many as changed your diapers and took baths with you when you were little, Désirée."

"*Not* the same thing, Mom," she said through gritted teeth, and I jumped back, scared that another round of Gran Bwa barf was coming.

"Possession-plasm," said the girl with the long braids.

"So powerful," echoed her brother.

"So gross," said the girl with the freckles

And they all continued to whisper: *"I never thought we'd see this day." "Maybe now she'll come to her senses and join us."*

My back stiffened. *There's no way. I can't lose Dee too.*

Ana Marie pulled her into a warm hug. "I'm so proud of you, baby. I'm going to go call your father."

It only took about .4 seconds before everyone descended onto Dee, hugging her, fawning, wiping the corners of their eyes. I inched away so I wouldn't be trampled, feeling like I'd gone back in time to junior high and was at one of the dozens of my classmates' Bar Mitzvahs I'd attended . . . except this room was filled with scattered flowers, tree branches, and the smoldering aroma of magic.

The witches made room for Ritha to approach her granddaughter. "I can't remember ever seeing a lwa ride a witch so young! You are destined for greatness, my child." Ritha pulled her into a hug, and Désirée groaned. "Now listen to me. Being a *cheval* to the lwa is an honor and a privilege."

"I know."

She held Désirée's jaw to keep her gaze. "And *not* something to be taken lightly. It's powerful and dangerous, and not to be practiced without the supervision of other powerful witches. Do you understand me?"

Dee's eyes tipped toward the ceiling. "Way to ruin the moment, Gran."

Ritha stroked her cheek. "Nothing could ruin this moment, my dear."

As I stood there, holding a pinch of my plasm-soaked shirt away from my skin, I wondered what my own mother would have thought about all this witch business. She was pretty liberal, but this shit was pretty weird. The matriarchal thoughts led me to the memory of plunging the stake into Adele's mother's back. *If I'd seen Brigitte's face, would I have known?* Would I have realized she wasn't Giovanna? *Would it have mattered, Isaac?* She was killing Adele.

My thoughts spiraled, sucking the energy out of the room like a black hole. I slowly backed away, through the smiles and sweaty hugs, and slipped out.

I wandered down the dark hall, through the taxidermy lab, and through the back door, gulping the fresh air as I hurried across the balcony over the courtyard to the guesthouse.

The flames flickering in the dark halls made it feel like I was going back in time. The witches used the old oil lamp sconces on the walls, saying the Possessed responded better to organic light. I tried my best to ignore the pleas of the Possessed slipping through the doorway cracks as I headed all the way to the back of the house, to the master bedroom.

My mind was imprinted with that proud smile Ana Marie had just given her daughter. Désirée liked to play it off like her family weren't close, but they were *so* tight-knit. I couldn't imagine what it would have been like growing up in a magical family. Their sense of togetherness drowned me with loneliness. I tried to imagine a version of tonight with Adele. With her here, it wouldn't feel so lonely and empty. We'd be happy for Dee and be celebrating, and we wouldn't feel like we were missing out by not having magical families. We'd have each other.

I tried not to think about how we'd sneak away to be alone.

I miss her. I miss her so fucking much.

My gross wet shirt made me shiver. I yanked it over my head and let it drop to the floor.

"Yankee?" a voice called into the darkness. "Is that you?"

I stopped outside a familiar open doorway and took a box of matches from the bookshelf just to the right of it. The pocket doors were opened wide, creating an illusion of freedom, but invisible, impenetrable magical bars, constructed by some combination of Borges-Daure magic, trapped him inside.

I struck a match and held it close to my face so he could see me. "Hey, Ren." And then I lit the lamp in the wall sconce. The scent of the sulfur lingered in the air after I blew out the match.

He was sitting on a twin bed, facing out in the dark, still in a white shirt that seemed like it was from another century and a black leather vest, but the pasty color of his skin was reaching a level that looked translucent, and the way he squinted at the light made him appear like a shadow of his former self.

"How goes it, on this fine eve?" he asked, loudly. You could hear the "actor" in his voice, as my mom would have called it. His tone was resonant and lively, like he was under the spotlight, but also overdone, like he was trying to push through something else.

"You know, same ole French Quarter," I said. *Avoiding the Carter brothers and the rest of their bloodsucking family.* "Hunting for souls with Julie and Stormy. Désirée just made contact with a lwa."

"Sounds like my kind of night!" He rose from the bed, and I could tell how much weight he'd lost by the loose fit of his clothes. "Have you come to spring me, Yankee?!"

The fact that I was shirtless and he wasn't making a crack about my abs really made me wonder which one of them I was talking to, but it was always the sign of a good day if he called me "Yankee"—it meant he was lucid. There'd been some days where Alessandro had completely taken over his mind, and others when it was unclear what was going on under that thick skull, but the worst days were the violent ones. Ren was such a peaceful person, so to see him tear around the room when he was in one of his fits was not only heartbreaking but also surreal, like he was just some giant goth character from WrestleMania and it was all just pretend.

"Ren, you know I can't let you out." I had once, thinking I could handle him. He'd promptly knocked me out and made a run for it. He went straight home and attacked Theis for letting the Borges hold him prisoner. Now Ritha was pumping magic through this house, into their rooms and into their food, to keep them calm—to keep the deranged side of them from taking over.

"Why so sad, sugarplum?" he asked. "You're not the bird trapped in the cage."

I looked up, and my problems seemed minuscule. At least I wasn't infected by a parasitic soul who was literally sucking my spirit out.

"Give me a report on the outside, kid," he said. "Who's keeping the politicians from sucking the FEMA funds dry? Who's keeping the vampires from sucking the neighborhood dry?"

"Huh?" I asked, pulse accelerating.

"Well, now that I'm not there, checking in on them with my nightly tours."

"Oh . . ."

"Come on, kid! Give me some dirt! How's Mac doing with the moonshine biz?"

"I-I don't know, Ren. I haven't been by the bar in a while." I wanted to puke out everything that had happened. "Adele and Mac hate me," I mumbled.

"*Qu'est-ce que*? Speak up, son!"

Before I could repeat myself, Désirée's voice came from down the hallway. "Isaac, he doesn't *hate* you. He just doesn't remember who you are."

She tossed me a folded purple T-shirt with the white letters K&B on it. "Sorry, it's one of my old nightshirts. It's all I could find that would fit you." She had two large mugs of tea in her other hand.

"Thanks." I stretched it over my head. "He might as well hate me."

"You won him over once. I'm sure you could do it again. The man treated you like his son. Stop whining and go re-meet him!"

I looked at her. I don't know why that had never occurred to me. I'd been so focused on wanting things to go back to the exact same way they were before the night at the convent, I hadn't really thought about starting over.

"I must be missing something here," Ren said. "Can someone bring me my flask?"

"Ritha said no more moonshine." She handed him the mug and promptly moved out of the way as he took a sip. "We don't need anything else messing with your head."

The spray of tea he spat through the invisible bars coated my face and neck, but I didn't even care; it was the first time I'd felt hopeful in weeks.

I'd had it all wrong. Wanting things to go back the way they were before now seemed so immature. Adele's mother was dead. She would never be the same. Hell, none of us would ever be the same. We'd all seen things we'd never forget; we'd all had some kind of brush with death.

I tugged the hem of the clean shirt up to wipe my face off, and the façade of perfection I'd smothered my memories with began to peel back.

Yes, Adele and I had been intimate in a way that now felt like oxygen, but it hadn't been perfect. I'd been so concerned about Nicco and the Medici that it had made me overly aggressive and suspicious. And now I knew that Adele had been keeping secrets about her mother too . . . She'd been lying to me the entire time we were together.

But none of that mattered. I believed in us. With everything out in the open, we could get past it. Get rid of the Medici and just live in peace, with each other and our magic and the coven. Even if Adele never got her magic back, I didn't care about any of it. *Not the magic, not my Air, not my flying.* I cared about Adele, and I'd give up my magic in a heartbeat for her.

"I heard you made contact with a lwa, young lady," Ren said, sipping his boozeless tea, pinky up, as if he hadn't just sprayed me with it.

Désirée shrugged as if it was no big deal and took a sip of her own tea.

"Dee, come on! That was the coolest thing I've ever seen."

She lifted the mug higher to her face, hiding her smile.

"Was it one of the Ghede?" Ren asked. "The Baron? Maman Brijit? I always said that if I could take a whirl with a lwa, it would be Ghede-Oussou. You know his name means *tipsy.* I think we'd get along."

"It wasn't a Ghede," said Désirée. "It was Gran Bwa."

"Keeper of the forest!" He jumped up and dramatically bowed down to her.

"Who are the Ghede?" I asked her.

"The family of lwa who rule the dead."

"Naturally," I said, wishing I could just go fly through Adele's bedroom window and curl around her, telling her about all the crazy things that happened today. In my dreams, she still always left her window open for me.

I made a pact with myself to stop looking backward and longing for what we had. I saw a version of us in the future that was even better, where there were no secrets and no vampires. One where there was art and family and bootlegged moonshine. College and humid summers in the South and snowy winters in New York. And Mac was the first step to it all.

Ren started going on about the Ghede and their raucous ways, and a place called Guinée.

"I'm going to the bar," I said, kissing Désirée on the cheek as I moved past her. "You're brilliant."

"FYI, you smell awful," she yelled after me.

CHAPTER 8

HOMELESS

My confidence dipped the closer I got to the bar. I was freshly showered, shaven, and had on the cleanest pair of jeans I could find, but I had no idea what I was going to say. The first time I'd met Mac, I'd been with my work crew in his then illegally operating bar. When I'd ordered a beer, he'd given me a stern eye and I'd thought he was going to deny me for being underage, but then he looked at the rest of my crew and served me anyway. There had been this mutual level of respect that I'd felt from the very beginning—something I never really had with my own father. Everything with my Pop was just his way or the highway. If it were up to him, I'd be heading back to NYC this summer to prep for freshman year at Columbia, with plans to enlist upon graduation. So I'd opted for the highway.

And now I'd lost almost everything I had here.

Don't mess this up, Isaac. You might only get one shot.

Just when I started to reconsider, telling myself I should come back with a more fully baked plan, Troy, the bouncer, called out, "Isaac, my man!"

No turning back now. I returned the greeting as he pulled me in for a half-hug, half-back slap.

"Haven't seen you around here in forever," he said, and then luckily kept talking without requiring an explanation. "Man, that's crazy about Mac's wife. How's Adele? My poor baby."

"Uh . . ." I really hadn't thought this through. I'd only thought about the Mac part of this equation, not the fact that *everyone else* would still know who I was. "She's about as good as can be expected."

He shook his head, kissed his knuckle, made the sign of the cross, and glanced at the sky. "You never know when it's your time to go."

I nodded, and he stepped aside to let me through. "You get Adele to come around when she's ready. We all miss her around here."

You and me both, buddy.

I stepped into the courtyard as three older guys who looked like they were all part of the same leather-vest motorcycle gang came out of a door to my left, all lighting their cigarettes one by one with the same match.

Mac's reopened the main floor of the bar.

I couldn't believe it'd been so long since I'd last been here. I'd pretty much avoided the place ever since the night of the attack, partly because it felt like the right thing to do considering Adele wasn't speaking to me and partly because I was worried how the whole thing would go down. I had no idea what Mac had been told about Brigitte, but I guessed there'd been some kind of cover-up.

I walked into the flood of music and voices, hoping the bartender would be someone unfamiliar to make this whole thing easier.

Mia's head popped up from behind the bar. "Isaac!"

So much for that.

"Long time no see!" she yelled over the music. Her glitter lips sparkled like a disco ball.

I pushed out a smile.

She grabbed a beer from a cooler and flipped off the top. "As if the past year hadn't already been bad enough," she said, shaking her head.

I nodded, wondering if every single person who saw me was immediately going to bring up the woman I'd killed. I took a long swig of the beer.

"It's killing me seeing Mac so broken-hearted," she continued. "It's like, I don't know, watching a sad koala or something."

I couldn't even muster another nod without feeling like a phony.

"Can you imagine dying like that?"

She knows the cover-up story. "Like what?"

"Like how Brigitte died."

"Yeah, that was . . . terrible." I wanted to ask her a hundred more questions, but I couldn't let on that I didn't know, especially as everyone here seemed to think Adele and I were hunky-dory.

"So terrible," she said, pouring herself a shot and slamming it back.

I scanned the room for Mac.

"He's up in the cabaret," she said, wiping her mouth. "Mac's keeping the makeshift bar open for, you know, *after* curfew." She rolled her eyes. Her opinions on the curfew that followed were peppered with profanity; Mia was originally from New Jersey.

I thanked her for the beer and retraced my steps back out to the courtyard, my anxiety growing as I hopped up the wooden stairs to the secret bar in the garçonnière. By the time I was through the dark hallway and parlor rooms, it felt like rats were gnawing at my stomach. I used to frequent this place every night with my crew, back before Adele even knew it existed. How could it feel so weird now?

Mac was behind the bar, alone. I hung back a few feet, holding my breath as the hipsters next to me puffed clouds of cigarette smoke into the air. A couple sat on the right side of the bar, pawing at each other drunkenly, and to the left—*shit.* It was Matthews, already looking like he'd had a few too many. This wasn't going to work with that jackass detective sitting at the bar. He knows that me and Adele are—*were?* —dating.

And then, as if someone was answering my thoughts, the man next to him, his partner, I think, got a bleep on his two-way, and they both got up and left.

My boots were suddenly made of lead, bolting me in place. It had taken me and Adele so long to get together in the first place, I was scared the Fates wouldn't be so generous a second time. What would I even talk to Mac about? *Get a grip. It's just Mac! Talk about the Saints, the Storm, art, anything.*

I chugged the beer back and set the empty bottle on the smoking hipsters' table. *There. Now you have a reason to approach.* I sucked in a big breath and stood up straight, but not too straight; I didn't want to come across as macho or aggressive. *Jesus Christ, Isaac.* I straightened my button-down shirt—one of several that I hadn't worn in months because they were all too tight now, and annoying—and I walked up to the bar, armed with a line about a sculpture in the city I knew he'd made. But when we made eye contact, my throat filled with a lump so huge that I couldn't speak. *I killed this man's wife. The love of his life.* I grabbed the edge of the bar, as casually as possible, to steady myself.

"What are you having?" He was looking directly at me, drying a tumbler with a towel. It had been so long since he'd asked me that. Once Adele and I started dating, he never asked me again, because he'd only let me drink beer, and never more than two.

"Um. Whatever you have on tap, or in a bottle—it doesn't matter. Can't be picky post-Storm, right?" I tried to smile, but instead a nervous laugh slipped out. Everything about this felt so unnatural.

"No beer at this bar, but they might have some downstairs. All we've got in the cabaret are cocktails."

I knew he kept a stash for himself here because he always used to share it with me. I tried not to wonder if we'd ever get back there. "Oh. Whatever you've got is fine."

He scooped ice into a tumbler, grabbed an unmarked bottle from a shelf lined with a bunch of other unmarked bottles, and poured in a generous shot. He topped it off with something clear that bubbled and swirled a twist of lemon peel around the rim before plopping it in. "That's about as good as it gets," he said. "But it's distilled locally, so it keeps the post-Storm prices down while we're gouged with everything else."

I accepted the drink, exhibiting the appropriate amount of understanding and frustration with the current economy, and then took a sip —and immediately coughed, choking it down.

He sputtered a laugh. "Sorry, should have warned you. It'll put hair on your chest." He offered the soda gun to dilute it.

I waved my hand. "It's fine." I took another sip to prove it, hiding the cringe as best I could.

Who had been helping him with the moonshine now that Ren was incapacitated? Maybe it was something he needed extra help with? We'd have to spend time together. He could get to know me again.

I suddenly wondered what Adele would think about all of this.

The thought of her hating it, and then me subsequently wondering if I should leave, only made me realize how much I actually missed Mac. He'd welcomed me into their home. I missed the studio and fixing things around his house.

"Hey, Isaac."

I looked up. *Shit.* Theis was setting down a case of bottles behind the bar. I wiped my sweaty palms on my pants and nodded hello. *What if he asks me something about Adele? Calm down. He just said hello.* I took a long sip of the drink, this time more prepared for the harsh taste. Theis tipped his head to Mac, and then was gone as fast as he'd arrived. I should've known he wouldn't hang around. Theis wasn't into small talk, the total opposite of Ren, who never missed the opportunity to hear his own voice.

As the fiery booze coursed through my chest, my fingers tapped the bar, and I heard the words coming out of my mouth as if someone else was saying them: "Do you guys need any help with the moonshine? I mean, I don't know much about distilling, but I'm a fast learner."

He looked at me crookedly. "What moonshine?"

"This stuff." I raised the glass before I caught myself. *Shit.* I wasn't supposed to know that *they* were the ones bootlegging it.

"I don't know who makes that stuff. I just buy it from a local distributor."

"Oh, sorry, I just thought . . . I was wrong . . . Never mind."

He leaned on the bar, peering at me. "Do I know you?"

The question revved my pulse. "I-um-I don't think so. I used to come in here a lot. After the Storm." I downed the rest of the drink.

He squinted, as if trying to place me. "No. It's not that. I've been in this business a long time. I never forget a face."

Sure you do. I was at your door the other day.

He snapped his fingers. "My daughter! You're that kid!"

My heart jackhammered against my ribcage. *Holy shit, he remembers.*

"You're the kid who punched that cocky P.O.S. photographer!"

I felt the color drain from my face.

"My daughter and I were in the crowd." He grabbed two shot glasses from the shelf behind him and filled them.

Fuck. I do not want to be known to Adele's dad as the guy who punched someone on the national news.

He handed me one of the shots and clanked the little glass with his own, which he tossed back with a tense forehead; I had no choice but to follow suit. My brain had to transcend my body in order to get the shot of moonshine down without gagging. I never thought I'd long for the days when he was yelling at me about staying out of trouble. I wasn't sure how much more I could handle of Mac treating me like a normal nobody bar customer.

This was a bad idea. I pulled my wallet from my back pocket.

He waved away my money. "Son, I know plenty of folks around here who'd love to buy you a drink or ten. You're welcome back anytime."

I smiled and shook his hand, playing it off, trying to hide my mortification. And then I hurried out, down the hall and past the rooms that had been destroyed by termites years back, the booze causing a fiery sensation all the way to my toes as I hopped down the steps into the courtyard.

Ugh. This blows. I wanted to know the Mac who gave me art lessons, not the Mac who poured me shots of unregulated liquor. I gently pushed through the crowds of people until I was through the courtyard and back walking on the street.

There were only two ways I could think of for Mac to have completely forgotten who I was: the first was that Adele had cast some kind of Memory spell on him, like the triplets had cast in the attic in 1728; and the second was that a vampire had done it. I'd put all my money on this being Medicean thrall rather than a Monvoisin spell. Nicco had been with Adele that morning to comfort her after her mother's death. With Mac too, in their house! *It should have been me!*

But you were the one who killed Brigitte, I reminded myself.

My fists balled as I hustled down the street. I wanted to fly, but I didn't know how well my smaller bird frame would handle the booze.

Something whipped down the street a couple blocks ahead, leaving a faint trail of supernatural disturbance in the glow of the gas lamps. My defenses skyrocketed. *A Medici.* I hated the way they roamed the streets with a mocking casualness, as if there was nothing any of us could do about it, even if we knew their murderous secrets. Predators living among us.

It's him. I know it.

Fuck it. It was a bad idea, but I took a running start, launched myself into the sky, and soared down the street to catch up.

When I dropped back to my feet, he was just up ahead. Aggression rippled through my limbs, and some animalistic instinct overcame any rational thought. "Nicco!" I yelled.

He came to an abrupt stop . . . and slowly turned around.

I eyed the street in both directions, making sure he was without siblings. That's when I knew I was drunk; the sober, rational version of myself would've made sure the street was void of other vampires *prior* to calling one out.

A look crept onto his face, like I was a petulant child he was going to have to deal with. His patronizing attitude, a family trait, was at the top of the list of things I hated about Niccolò Medici.

"*What*?" he asked, his tone polished with annoyance.

"I know it was you." Forming words wasn't as easy after shots of moonshine as it was after two beers. "You can't just erase me from her life."

His expression morphed to comprehension, like he'd known this moment had been bound to surface. "Oh, I'm sure you'll do a good enough job of that all on your own," he said, without lowering his voice, as if to warn me that he wasn't scared of the open public.

My jaw clinched. "You don't even bother to deny it."

He shrugged. "It could have been worse. She could have asked me to delete you from *her* memory."

"You're blaming her? She'd never ask you to erase anyone's—"

"I tried to talk her out of it . . . told her it was a bad idea and that she'd regret the request." He paused, letting that sink in.

I tried not to show that his words felt like bullets.

"Don't fret too much. She'll regret it soon enough and then you can swoop in, in her moment of vulnerability."

"*Me* take advantage of her vulnerability! You knew it was a bad idea, but you did it anyway!"

"She *insisted*."

"You're a vampire! She's a sixteen-year-old girl. And she was in total shock! You didn't have to do anything."

"She needed her sense of control back."

"You don't know what she needs. She needs all of you to get the hell out of her life." Without thinking, I stepped forward and slammed my palms into his chest. His form was so solid it was surreal. He barely wavered.

His smirk somehow became even more smug. "Is that what she needs? Or is that what you need?" His lack of retaliation pissed me off even more.

"I shouldn't have given your metal note back to her."

His nostrils flared.

"If she hadn't read it, she wouldn't have ended up in the convent that night. Callis wouldn't have captured her. She wouldn't have opened the attic to save you."

"I should have let my brother throw you off the balcony."

"And I should have burned the attic after we trapped you. Adele staked those shutters closed because she knows you should be locked away."

"I wish you had. Then you could have watched her rescue me from the flames."

His stare was like a lethal weapon. There was nothing I could say. We both knew it was true. I didn't want to believe it, and I sure as hell would never admit it to him, but I knew Adele and her heart of gold would have saved Nicco. And I fucking hated it.

"Codi and I are going to break the rest of the curse, so you can take Gabe and his vampire spawn and Emilio and get the hell out of New Orleans."

"Breaking the curse is advisable, but I'm not leaving. I'm not leaving her. At least not until she has her magic back and can protect herself."

"She doesn't need you to protect her! She has us!"

He put his hands in his pockets and rocked back on his feet, as if the statement was so ridiculous it was unworthy of a response.

Then he smiled. He *fucking smiled.*

"You should feel lucky she didn't ask me to wipe *your* memory as well." And with a slight nod that let me know he was done here, he turned and began walking away.

"And Isaac," he said, without looking back, "you already have one of my brothers after you; you really don't want Gabriel after you too. Don't forget, there's one other way to break a witch's curse."

"And Nicco," I called out, "don't forget there's one other way for Mac to get his memories back."

He paused. A slight shift of his shoulders instigated an immediate sense of fight or flight in me.

I knew I shouldn't provoke him any more, but the alcohol pushed confidence to my mouth. "And I have more stakes."

I didn't see him so much as flinch before his hands slammed against my chest, and I was hurling down the street, limbs flailing. I hit a garbage dumpster, the sound of banging metal ricocheting in my ears. Pain shot out in every direction—the back of my head, neck, and back.

The sound was still ringing in my head as two of them came my way. *Emilio, fuck.* I panicked for a split second before realizing I just had double vision.

He bent down so he could look into my eyes. "Never threaten me again."

I could barely hold myself up. My voice shook. "Please, don't let her blind trust in you be her demise, Nicco. We both know how that is going to end."

His eyes flared bright. "You have no idea how this is going to end. You don't even know what this *is*. But I can promise you, if you get in my way, you will not live to regret it."

He stood, towering over me for a second, then flashed out of sight, moving so quickly down the street, it was as if he'd just vanished into the thick NOLA air.

I collapsed back against the dumpster, and the surge of adrenaline plummeted, allowing the pain to erupt. Only then did I realize my shoulder was dislocated. I'd done it before, skateboarding, and I knew how to snap it back in place, but judging by how painful it was to breathe, I'd also cracked a rib. I sighed, cursing as I dug my phone out of my pocket and hit the redial button.

"I'm at the corner of Decatur and Barracks."

"Goddammit, Isaac," she said before I pressed END and everything went blurry.

In the darkness and silence, the pain intensified. I focused on taking shallow breaths, holding my chest with my good hand to minimize movement.

I tried to think about anything to distract myself. Sunshine. Ocean waves. Susannah Norwood Bowen on the Bermudian beaches, watercoloring in our grimoire.

Dandelions blowing in the breeze. A magical breeze.

Minutes went by.

Someone nudged my foot, and I cringed, opening my eyes to Désirée's special blend of sarcasm and concern hovering over me. And to pain. *So much effing pain* it was difficult to pinpoint the source.

"Passed out in the gutter? Are you *trying* to get killed by Emilio?"

"I'm not passed out. Shoulder." I sucked in a tight breath. "And I think I re-cracked a rib." Or three.

She put her foot on my right hip and picked up my left wrist. "What the hell happened?"

"I fell down some stair—"

She pressed into my hip and pulled my arm, jerking my shoulder.

"Shit!" The word exploded from my mouth and I kicked out involuntarily, knocking her over so she sat down hard on the pavement.

"Jesus!" she yelled.

"Sorry." My voice wavered; the sudden movement made my rib feel like I'd been chopped in half with a machete.

She looked at me without an ounce of sympathy, and when I didn't elaborate, she crossed her arms and stared.

My sigh came out more like a gasp. "I ran into Nicco."

"You picked a fight with a vampire?"

My voice raised. "Why do you assume that?"

"Because I know you. And I know him . . . kind of . . . Actually, I don't know him at all, but I know you! And you've been in a mood for days."

Under the weight of Désirée's stare, the embarrassment began to sink in. I'd envisioned everything boiling over between me and Nicco a thousand times, and not a single second of *this* was how I'd imagined it going down.

She placed her hands on my chest and then under my shirt. "So, I'm assuming things didn't go well with Mac?"

A burning sensation emanated from her palms. At first, it always felt like the warmth of something good to come, like hot apple pie, but we'd been through this enough for me to know that it wasn't going to last. I grabbed her wrists as her magic grew stronger and the cracked bones started moving. I yelped, a cry of pain and catharsis, and squeezed her arms as my bones snapped back into place.

When I looked up, her eyes were already fluttering. *Here comes the recoil.* And then, as if on cue, she collapsed onto my still sore chest. *Oof.*

"Get a room!" someone yelled, and I glanced over her shoulder.

Two girls were stumbling down the sidewalk, holding each other up, giggling. They shouldn't be alone on the streets drunk.

Désirée stirred and bolted upright to her knees. She was always a little disoriented when it happened, and she always tried to play it off.

"You don't normally pass out healing something so minor," I said.

"Well, it's been a long day, in case you've forgotten." She stood up too quickly and wobbled, reaching out.

I grabbed her hands to steady her. "I'm sorry. You shouldn't be wasting your healing energy on me . . . *again*."

She sighed. "It's not a waste." She pulled me up. "I just wish you'd be more careful."

"I will."

She gave me a look as we began to walk.

"I *promise.*"

When we got to the corner where we could have parted ways, I kept going with her, despite knowing she'd protest.

"I don't need you to walk me home, Isaac. It's two blocks."

"I'm not doing it for you. I'm doing it for me."

Her left eyebrow crooked up.

"Let's just say, on the freak chance that something happened to you —like a vampire was able to take down the legendary Désirée Borges— Codi would be so mad I didn't walk you, he'd kick my ass. And then you wouldn't be around to heal me, because you'd have been eaten by a vampire, so then I'd be out of commission too, and I wouldn't be able to hunt down the Possessed. Think of all the innocent people who'd get hurt after that, all because I didn't walk you home. See, I'm doing it for me and the unsuspecting citizens of New Orleans. Nothing to do with you, really."

She gently shook her head, and something that might have been considered a smile for a Borges slipped out. I knew the argument was over.

"Do you think Codi could kick your ass?" she asked.

"Uh . . . no. I mean, it would be close, but he couldn't *kick my ass*." When I looked over, she appeared to be contemplating it. "Wait, do you?"

This time it was a real smile. "Maybe."

I squinted at her, and she laughed.

Another few houses and we were in front of Vodou Pourvoyeur. I yawned as she unlocked the door.

"Isaac," She turned to me. "I'm turning off my phone and going to sleep. If you get into any more trouble tonight, you're going to have to call my gran."

"I won't." Désirée would never turn off her phone, but I got the hint.

"Dee . . . ?"

She looked over.

"Thanks." And I didn't just mean for tonight. I meant for everything over the last couple months.

She nodded. "Sure."

Just as I was about to turn away, her arms slid over my shoulders. It wasn't a flamingo hug; it was a genuine human hug. "Please don't pick any more fights with Nicco. She's not going to end up with him."

My heart raced. "How— How do you know?"

"Because. Adele is a good person. She's not going to end up with a monster." She said it with the same level of certainty with which she spoke about her own future. "Now, promise, no more fighting."

"Okay, I promise!"

She uncoiled from around me.

"Thanks," I said. "Goodnight."

"See you tomorrow."

Instead of turning to leave, I just stood there. My gaze moved past hers. "Dee, I didn't just run into Mac."

"What?"

My palms suddenly felt damp. Telling someone made the situation so much more real. "I ran into Adele."

"*What?* When? What happened?"

A million race horses galloped across my chest. "She looked right at me and said, 'You killed my mother.'"

Her eyes widened. "*She said that*?"

"Those exact words."

"That's bullshit! You saved her life!"

"I don't think she's really considering that, right now."

I remembered what it had been like right after my mother died. People had constantly told me, *At least she isn't suffering anymore.* In those days, I didn't care about her suffering. I just wanted her back with me and my pop. I couldn't think about anything else but wanting her back. It had completely consumed me. In the last few weeks, it felt fresh again, as if she'd just died. I still couldn't process the fact that Adele had lost her mother too, and that I was responsible for her death. Why hadn't Adele just told me?

"How was her magic?"

I gave Dee a hard look. *Like I gave a fuck about her magic?*

"What? It's a legitimate question about her state of being."

"I don't know. She was . . . horrified to see me."

"I-I'm sure she was just caught off guard," she stammered, as if thinking of more excuses for Adele, which wasn't her usual attitude on the situation. "You have the tendency to do that to people sometimes. Isaac, she's not going to hate you forever."

I didn't argue, but I couldn't look at her either. The soft tone in her voice, the sympathy in her eyes: Désirée wasn't supposed to look at me like that. Adele had the emotional, trepidatious looks. Désirée had two looks when it came to me: utter confidence and sibling rivalry. I couldn't deal with this from her.

Her fingers brushed my arm. "Isaac, just stay over." She made a weird face. "I mean, like, on the couch. Obviously. Or I can make up one of the guest rooms for you."

I appreciated what she was doing, but I wanted to be alone with my patheticness. "I'm fine. I just . . . wanted to tell you the whole truth."

She nodded, but didn't move either. "Sorry I called you just *some* white boy earlier."

I tried to smile, but I couldn't. "That guy—his parasite?—is an epic asshole."

She shrugged, and I hated how she was casually brushing it off, like she really did deal with racist, sexist shit all the time. *This is so effed.*

"Okay. Well . . ." Her thin lips crooked into a half smile. "I'm sorry I barfed on you."

"Anytime." I laughed. "And Dee, sorry I saw your tits."

Shock sprawled on her face. "Not anytime!"

"You have nothing to be ashamed of. They're very nice. Fit for a Voodoo Queen."

She slapped the same shoulder she'd just fixed. "I know they are!"

As I took off down the street, I could feel her still watching me, so I dove into the air and took crow form. I could practically hear her mentally cursing at me for turning in the middle of the street. Laughter vibrations rippled through my feathers.

I turned left on Royal so she could see me going in the direction of the pier where the S.S. *Hope* had been docked since the Storm, but as soon as I was out of her sightline, I made another turn and soared in a different direction.

The brothel.

The warmth from our shared laughter waned as I swooped through the broken transom on the top floor, and straight into Cosette's bedroom. Despite the warm weather outside and no matter how many fires I lit, a chill hung in the air. It was like all the warmth had been zapped from HQ along with Adele's powers. I'm sure the shift in energy was more likely due to the lack of magic being practiced, but I liked to imagine that the old bones of the house were waiting for her return.

I pulled pillows and bedding out of the closet where my army-grade duffel was and threw it all down on a patch of floor that was drenched in moonlight, so I could sketch for a while.

My pop had kicked me off the S.S. *Hope* after the stunt I'd pulled on the bridge: *"You're lucky I'm not sending you back to Brooklyn,"* he'd said. As if he had any choice in the matter; I was eighteen. What he meant was, I should be thankful he wasn't taking away my FEMA job and leaving me both homeless *and* penniless. But they were desperate for laborers, and even my asshole father wasn't going to take away aid from people in need just to teach me a lesson.

And so, I'd been on my own for the last few months. *The highway.* I uncapped a pen. The nights were the worst. Especially sleeping.

A full sketch of Onyx and Julie later, I tried to pass out, but I just ended up tossing and turning on the pallet.

The drowning nightmares had ceased after I'd rescued Jade's ghost at the convent. Now every time I shut my eyes, I saw Adele, which gave me a different kind of anxiety.

I flipped the pillow, pressing my face to the cooler side. I imagined her smooth skin and her soft lips pressing onto mine. I could smell the lavender scent of her hair. When I opened my eyes and she wasn't curled against me, the pain came back tenfold. It was always like this . . . somehow, every time I opened my eyes and saw nothing but darkness beside me, the pain was always worse than it had been before, and the cycle repeated itself over and over again.

My eyes pricked. *I did the right thing that night.* If I hadn't thrown that stake, Adele would be dead. I wished she could see what I'd seen: how horrifying it had been. I wished she could have heard her screams —seen her body limp beneath the monster spilling her blood.

Nicco tried to stop me. He'd known about Brigitte all along.

"I didn't kill her!" I yelled to no one. Emilio Medici had done that twelve years ago.

I staked a vampire who was killing her own daughter. That's what I told myself, but it didn't matter. I'd taken Adele's mother away from her. Now Adele haunted my dreams like the ghost of someone I used to know. Like Jade. Like my mother.

For a second, I reconsidered staying at the Borges', but that would feel too much like moving on. I needed to hold onto the image of Adele walking through that door. Coming back to me. And I needed to be here when she did.

I just . . . needed her.

Everything was different now.

Adele's mother was dead.

I killed Adele's *mother*.

CHAPTER 9

CIAO, BELLA

April 19th

The strawberry-shaped mug full of tea warmed my hands as I sat on the couch, watching Jeanne and Sébastien argue. Only a coffee table separated us, but I felt like I was in orbit a million miles away. The living room was drafty, and I just wanted to be curled up in my bed with my noise machine on, tuning out the world. At least they'd brought chamomile.

I'd barricaded myself inside the house for the last three days since my run-in with Isaac. After the first day of not leaving my bedroom, my father had coaxed me out with canned tomato soup and stale garlic (powder) bread. The twins were apparently his next tactic.

Jeanne had had a breakthrough in her lab this week, which Sébastien had not been there to witness, and she was *not happy about it*. How were they such highly productive people given how much loss they'd experienced: first their parents, then their grandparents? I guess they had each other. Growing up with them, I'd always wished I'd had a twin too. When I was little I used to pretend Codi was my twin brother.

Jeanne and Sébastien had each other. And they had science.

I wished I loved something that much, anything to pull me out of this hole. I hadn't sketched or so much as folded a piece of fabric since that night in the attic. Wasn't sadness supposed to fuel great periods of creativity? Maybe I wasn't destined to be an artist.

Deep down, I knew magic was something I could love as much as the twins loved science.

But none of that mattered now. It was gone.

I was a magicless witch.

Worthless.

I'd killed my mother.

I took a sip of chamomile.

"There are other ways to help—" Sébastien said.

"*Other ways to help?*" His sister's voice rose again. "How is having one of the most brilliant minds in the city fingerprinting corpses a way to help?"

I nearly choked on my tea.

"They're not corpses," said Sébastien. "They're people."

"No. *People* are alive."

"I'm sorry," I said. "Why are you fingerprinting cadavers?"

"Adele?" Jeanne said. "Come back from la-la land. They aren't cadavers. Sébastien quit school five weeks and three days ago."

"*What*?" I asked, spilling a few droplets of tea on my lap.

"I didn't *quit* school! Jeezum. I took a deferment." Sébastien looked at me. "I wanted to do something to help the city, so I got a new job. I'll go back to my lab next semester."

"He got a job at D-MORT, hence the suit," Jeanne explained. "He's processing Storm corpses for the FEMA—"

"It's more than *processing*—"

"Your research at school will help far more people in the long run—people who are still alive."

"It's one semester!"

She looked at me. "You can thank your boyfriend for this research-freeze on how natural killer cell receptors inhibit immune responses . . ."

My heart skipped a beat. "He's not my . . ."

They both looked at me with concern, and blood bloomed in my cheeks. *Was he?* "What does Isaac have to do with this?" My tongue seemed to tangle on his name.

"Ever since Isaac made the papers, Bastien has been on a mission to ruin his scientific career . . ."

Sébastien groaned and took off his glasses. He wiped away a smudge, glancing at me. "I talked to Isaac about joining his crew."

"You did?"

"He said that he was going to speak with the site boss, but then he ended up getting me an interview with the Head of the Victims Identification Laboratory at D-MORT. I guess he was unsure about what I could bring to the metaphorical table on a construction site."

My stomach soured, thinking about what I'd accused Isaac of. My speaking privileges should be permanently revoked.

"What are you doing at D-MORT?" I asked, trying to sound excited for him, suppressing the guilt that was unbottling inside my heart and slowly poisoning my bloodstream.

"My team uses all available scientific means to help identify the bodies of Storm victims before they are autopsied. It's really interesting work. I could see myself being a forensic specialist in another lifetime."

"Oh, now you believe in other lifetimes?" Jeanne huffed.

"It's *an expression.*" He gave me a questioning look.

I nodded to confirm that it was indeed an expression.

"We synthesize all of the antemortem and postmortem evidence, the location where the body was found, cause of death, fingerprints, DNA, dentistry, optometry, external or internal markings, and a host of other data points. Then algorithms match the profile against more databases than you could ever imagine. You'd be *scared* if you knew the ways facial recognition was being used today."

I thought about Sébastien being in a giant warehouse, surrounded by corpses, stacks and stacks and stacks of them—a giant puzzle for him to figure out. I wondered what conclusion he'd have come up with autopsying my mother.

"All those bodies," I said. "All of those people getting buried unidentified . . . It's horrible. Congrats on the new job."

"I'm sure they're incinerated," Jeanne piped in, "not buried."

"That's not the point," he said. "But I've heard there's a plan for a new cemetery to commemorate all of the unnamed dead."

"The powers that be will get around to that in 2050," Jeanne said, and we nodded in agreement.

They each kissed both of my cheeks and made promises to visit again soon.

"*À bientôt*," I said, locking the front door behind them.

I stacked the cups and saucers, carried them to the kitchen, rinsed them, dried them, and put them away, all the while fighting the urge to retreat to my bed. I looked at the door to my father's studio, recalling what he'd said about finishing my metal-shop work if I wanted my mentorship credit. I sighed. *Well, I'm already downstairs.*

Static broke through the voices on the scratchy radio speakers on a work table across the room as I manually twisted little rings into chainmaille. The process took about four times as long without my magic, which I tried not to dwell on. I focused on the tiny tuner knob, just like I already had seventeen times, and just like all the other times, I failed at twisting it telekinetically.

"*Eight months after the Storm, the latest records show that one hundred and thirty thousand people have returned to the city. That's only one-seventh of the city's pre-Storm population. Acting FEMA director Norwood Thompson held a press conference this morning with Mayor Borges to unveil a housing recovery plan for key areas of Mid-City.*"

The DJ spliced in a soundbite of Norwood: "*We're working together on the most comprehensive rebuilding plan in US history.*" Seconds later, a caller was lambasting the plan and both men's efforts on the housing crisis to date.

I snuck a glance at Isaac's empty seat. For more than two months, I'd buried everything. All of our memories. All of our kisses. I'd stripped all of his drawings from my walls. Kicked my sketchbook under my bed. And now I couldn't tell if it was heartache or magic-ache, but something made me grab my phone and plug it into the charger. Not because I was going to use it, but because that's what people did: normal, functioning people kept their phones charged. Anxiety pricked my nerves. *He killed my mother.*

Norwood Thompson's voice was spliced back in, this time talking about hospital infrastructure. I got up, manually snapped off the radio, and returned to my seat.

In the silence, Norwood's New York accent became Isaac's, and all I could hear was the pleading in his voice. I twisted the pliers harder, the metal pressing grooves into my fingers, the image of Isaac's eyes—the pain—scorching into my mind.

I knew there were so many people to blame for my mother's death before him. Emilio, for starters; Callis, for forcing me to let them out of the attic before I had a plan; Annabelle, for being a traitor; and most of all me. If I hadn't gotten drunk and confided all the things *I swore I wouldn't tell Annabelle*. . . If I'd been stronger. If I'd fought back harder. If I hadn't let Callis take my magic. If I'd dragged Codi away from the vampires, out of the convent.

She was going to kill him. I slammed the pliers down.

Even knowing all of this, every time I closed my eyes, all I saw was the stake releasing from Isaac's hand and flying at us—straight into her back.

My phone buzzed on the table, a string of vibrations as the deluge of texts and voicemails popped up on the screen. Anxiety swirled in my stomach, and I fluttered my eyelids, blurring my vision so I didn't accidentally read any of them. By not looking at anyone's messages, I somehow justified not answering any of Isaac's. But as I went back to the chainmaille, my eyes betrayed me and stole a glance at the last message flashing away. "*How are u? Can I see u*?"

Even though I hadn't opened any of the paper airplanes he'd flown through my window, or read any of his other messages, a tiny part of me hoped it was him.

I picked up the phone to check the sender and breathed a sigh of relief mixed with disappointment. Without thinking, I flicked the screen so I could read the whole thing.

> **Codi 5:41 p.m.** How are u? Can I see u? It's probably too much, but my parents would love to have you over for dinner. Maybe you could talk to them about the whole magic thing?

I mean, it's probably good that it wasn't Isaac. What would I even say to him? I twisted the phone in my hands, over and over. He'd probably never message me again after the other day.

Isaac killed your mother, Adele.

Knowing that the thought was ridiculous didn't make it any easier to live with. Any of it.

In my heart, I knew that I was the one who'd killed my father's ballerina.

The front doorbell chimed. My back stiffened. *What if it's Isaac?*

Panic flooded my bloodstream. And just like that I went from wishing a text message was from him to wanting to flick off the lights and hide under the table like a lunatic.

But then, as if some greater force was lifting me from the stool, I stood. I floated from the studio into the kitchen and down the hallway, feeling like I wasn't in control of my body at all. *It's probably not even him. I don't deserve him. I don't deserve my friends. I don't deserve my magic.*

A storm swirled in my chest. A few more steps, and the metal knob was cool in my hand, the door was cracking open.

"*Ciao, bella.*" His voice was soft.

Thump-thump.

Thump-thump.

I held on to the door as Nicco smiled at me from behind the gate. It wasn't his usual half-smile that turned my knees to jelly, or the patronizing smile of sympathy I'd gotten from everyone else over the last couple months. It was a gentle smile of sorrow and understanding—and perhaps hesitation—and it made me open the door wider. "*Ciao,*" I replied, barely able to get the word out.

I hadn't seen him since the morning I'd thrown him out. A part of me had convinced myself that he hadn't visited because he'd left town, but the part of me that was sure the sun was going to rise each day—that had trusted him since the moment we'd met—knew he couldn't possibly have left without saying goodbye. I went down the steps and opened the gate.

He shifted up close to me, and the stoop had never seemed so small.

"I wanted to give you some time," he said, gently.

My heart beat so hard, I was certain it must be punching out of my chest. All I could do was nod. I told myself it was just my lack of human interaction. *Nothing specifically to do with him.*

When I didn't say anything, he touched my fingertips. I'd been imagining this moment for weeks, him being here. Sometimes I swore I could hear his heartbeat from blocks away. His fingers wrapped around mine, and the light in his eyes shifted. His hands tightened.

He's going to tell me something bad.

No. I shouldn't have opened the door. *If something happened to my father, I'm going to die right here on these steps. Nicco promised he'd be safe if his memories were deleted!*

I started to shake.

"Adele, we're giving your mother a funeral."

"What?" I gasped.

"I've been stalling my brother so you'd have time to process everything, but I can't delay him any longer. He needs closure, or I fear for others in his path. You do too. It's time to bury Brigitte."

A trapped breath expelled from my lips as the guilt pummeled me in three giant waves—the first for not immediately thinking of my mother, then another because I wanted to collapse into Nicco's chest and feel his arms wrap around me, even though I knew it was wrong on ten different levels. The final wave of guilt—for killing my father's ballerina—was so big it nearly swept me off my feet and dragged me down the street.

"Tonight, after dark," Nicco said, studying my face, stealthily trying to assess my mental state.

I glanced behind him at the sky. That wasn't long from now; the sun was already starting to set.

"I understand your father's family has a plot in St. Louis No. 1?"

They're having a funeral for my mother, like she's one of them.

I nodded, and only then did I process what he'd said about *Emilio* needing closure. I wanted to retch. *She* was *one of them, Adele.*

"It will be simple and respectful."

I'll never know my mother.

"Adele, I want you to come with me."

"What?"

"We could go together—if you want."

I shook my head. "No. No way."

His forehead creased.

"I don't need to go. I barely knew her." The last words came out a whisper. We both knew they were the truth.

"I know it doesn't seem important now, *bella*, but you'll regret not going, I promise."

"How would you know?" I snapped, but I caught my tongue, remembering the dream—Nicco's memory of finding his parents in bed, mauled by Séraphine. "I'm sorry, I can't go. I can't. I *can't.*" I crossed my arms, trying to hide the shaking. *That vampire corpse was not my mother.*

He nodded understanding and stepped closer. His hand gently

cupped the side of my face and his lips pressed to my temple, and I'd never had to exert so much energy to remain standing. "If you change your mind, you know where we'll be. The cemetery will be locked, but call me and I'll let you in."

I nodded, and he hurried away in a blur, pulling away any breath left in my lungs.

I locked the gate, and every lock on the door, then I went to the kitchen and locked that door too. No one else was coming inside and giving me more distressing news.

I waited for the tears. When they didn't come, I turned to the stove where my Fire used to be. "I'm not going!" I thought about my mother on Halloween night—how she'd been so bound to Emilio she threw herself into my flames to protect him, and then how she'd held him at bay so I could escape. *How much had she really changed?* She'd protected us both that night.

My fingers went to my neck, touching the spot where she'd bitten me. "I'm not going," I said again.

But instead of retreating to the studio, I headed to the stairs, my pace quickening on the ascent, my hands pulling my shirt over my head, dropping it onto my bedroom floor.

"I'm not going," I repeated, turning on the hot water in the shower, convincing myself that I just needed to relax. I had another excuse when I washed my hair and shaved my legs for the first time in weeks, and another when I sat at my vanity, hair soaking in a towel, and slathered my mother's brand of lavender moisturizer all over my skin.

I poked at the dark circles under my eyes, and then grabbed a tube of concealer, and blended it in from muscle memory. Foundation. Powder. Before long, a face that looked more like my old self was staring back in the mirror, encouraging me to keep going. I dried my hair. Applied wing-tipped eyeliner and mascara. *See, I'm definitely not going. Who wears mascara to a funeral?*

I laid out a pair of black pantyhose on my bed and flipped through the hangers in my closet, giving as much attention to the colored garments as the black ones because I wasn't going to a cemetery. I landed on a dress that used to belong to my mother. It was a deep navy-blue velvet with long sleeves and a mock turtleneck. I pulled it out and laid it on my bed along with a pair of black pumps I hadn't worn since I was in Paris.

I thought about calling Désirée and telling her about the funeral. Maybe she would tell me to go. *Maybe I should go.*

I threw my phone back on the bed. They wouldn't understand why I'd want to go to my vampire-mother's funeral with her vampire family. "It doesn't matter; I'm not going."

I stretched the stockings over my legs, slipped on the dress, and fluffed my hair a couple of times. Heels. Translucent plum-colored lip gloss. I reached for my necklace, but then remembered it was gone, lost the night of the attack. I spritzed perfume in a cloud around me—also my mother's scent.

I'm just getting dressed. Because that's what normal, functioning people do. They make groceries and eat meals and charge their phones and wear clothes that aren't pajamas.

I looked out the window. It had been dark for a while. I pushed off the pumps and stepped into my boots, hastily tying them. I couldn't run in pumps. And I wasn't going to make it if I didn't run.

CHAPTER 10

LES CENDRES AUX CENDRES

I was panting by the time I got to the cemetery, which took up the better part of a city block and was as old as anything else in the Quarter. An eight-foot brick wall bordered the perimeter, protecting the dead from vandals, grave robbers, and public-urinating tourists. Flames flickered in old gas lanterns on either side of the wrought iron gate, which was crowned with a winged hourglass. The realization that we're all on borrowed time sank onto my shoulders.

You can still go home. No one would even know you came.

As I dug through my small blue bag for my phone, I noticed that the gate was slightly ajar. *They're here.* The Medici were so meticulous about covering their tracks, leaving the gate open seemed strange. Nicco must have left it open for me.

I pushed the iron bars open just enough to slip inside before I let the handle quietly click closed. I felt a rush of energy when my hand let go of the metal—not magic, per se, just that particular blend of spiritual and creepy that always lurked in cemeteries. A thick chain with a padlock was coiled in a pile on the ground, next to a statue of two cherubs.

Without the ability to conjure my orbs, I was forced to activate the light on my phone if I didn't want to trip over crumbling graves.

I took the path to the right, which led to our family plot. A mix of gravel and shells crunched under my feet, and I tried not to think of Ren's stories about decomposing bones being mixed in with the shells. I tried not to think of the news stories about Storm-breached coffins. I tried not to think about Lisette hurling Minette Monvoisin's skull at me on Halloween night.

Faint light began to glow through the mausoleums, and soft female voices singing a French requiem grew stronger as I neared. I peered around the corner of a dilapidated tomb, the bricks cool on the tips of my fingers.

Two candles flanked the entrance of a mausoleum chiseled with:

LE MOYNE

The Medici were all standing around a coffin covered in more flowers than I'd have believed could be found in post-Storm New Orleans. Buds and petals spilled onto the tufts of weeds and bricks beneath their feet. They were all clad in funeral garb: Lisette with a black cape and hood pulled over her white blonde hair, and Martine with a scalloped black shawl drawn over her head, covering the tops of her eyes. All together with the black and the lace and the flowers, with their European finesse, they looked like a Dolce & Gabbana editorial spread. Cold and deeply saturated and dramatic and perfect.

In the breath before the chorus, my boot crunched a dried magnolia pod, and Emilio's head snapped my way. "What is *she* doing here?" More words sputtered out in Italian.

My fingers curled into a fist, containing imaginary sparks, and Nicco hissed something at him in their native tongue. He quickly composed himself and hurried to me.

"We're glad you decided to join us." His hand lightly touched my lower back as he guided me over to the others.

Gabe was at the foot of the casket, with Martine and Lisette on either side. We stood at the head, directly across from Emilio, whose eyes looked red and sore against his pale skin, even in the dim light.

I looked down and choked. Brigitte had died over two months ago, but still, the lid was partially opened, just enough to see her from the torso up. She was so inhumanly pale despite someone having put rouge on the apples of her cheeks and her lips. She was beautiful even in death. I started to back away but bumped into Nicco; his hand slipped over my hip, grounding me. The simple touch gave me enough strength to look back at her. It was like looking into my future. It was her; it was me. My mother. Ballerina. Vampire.

The gentle French song drifting over to us made the air feel lighter, like I was floating, and like Brigitte was floating away from me. Where did vampires go upon death? Were they ghosts just like everyone else? Would Adeline be with her? Brigitte wasn't technically a Le Moyne, but I found myself praying that Adeline would help my mom. Tears stung beneath my eyelids.

My mother had left my father so long ago, I'd never thought about them being next to each other eternally. I pushed the thought away. I did not want to think about my father being dead.

Over the years, I'd always imagined myself going to my mother's funeral—but in France. We'd been estranged my whole life, so I would have attended out of morbid curiosity before donating her entire estate to charity. I never expected to feel anything looking at her corpse. I never expected to care. I never expected it to happen so soon, or for her to be so beautiful.

The flames flicked shadows on Emilio's face, and he stared at me with rage in his eyes, as if I was responsible for this.

The song faded into the quiet night, and Emilio began to speak in Latin—not Italian, which I could at least have understood a little of thanks to my French. *Of course.* He doesn't want me here. He doesn't want me to be able to participate.

But it didn't matter; in the darkness, Nicco leaned closer, whispering the translation in French.

The black lace, flower petals, and Latin phrases made her funeral feel cold and somber, melancholic. It was ceremonial and unceremonious at the same time when compared to the Michels' jazz funeral. No one was shaking my mother's casket or dancing in the street. No one was celebrating her life. We were just mourning her death. Emilio was mourning her death. Tension crept up my back like the invasive roots of a live oak, gripping my spine and neck and shoulders.

As the words floated from Nicco's lips into my ears, I couldn't take my eyes off Emilio. *What ironic, absurdist, Gothic hell is this?* Standing around my father's family's plot with a family of vampires: Gabriel pulling Martine and Lisette closer, somberly kissing their cheeks in a familial way, all of them taking turns to say kind things about

Brigitte, about how warm she'd been and how graceful, and how lovely her laugh was . . . all things I would never know. When they paused and looked at me, giving me a chance to speak, nothing but dead air came out of my throat. Her one and only daughter had nothing to say.

"Brigitte saw the world through artistic eyes," Nicco said, filling the void. "She was always able to find beauty in even the simplest and most mundane parts of life." He looked at me. "The only thing she loved more than art was her family. May she rest in a place of peace and tranquility for eternity."

I didn't look up at him. I couldn't, partly because it hurt too much that Nicco knew more about my own mother than I did, and partly because my eyes were locked on his brother. Nicco's words had made Emilio's jaw clench, and his breathing became heavier and more charged.

We each stepped aside as Nicco and Gabe slid the casket into the mausoleum. Now there were just a few steps of darkness between us.

Emilio became more distraught, panicked almost, as they closed the marble door. "No," he said. "*No. No. No.*" He ran his fingers through his hair just like Nicco often did.

The pain billowing off him mirrored my own. The emptiness and sadness I harbored turned to rage. I could not handle watching my mother's killer weeping at her grave. I imagined him killing the Michels. I imagined him attacking my mother, her begging for her life, her telling him to take her purse, her phone, even herself, but please not to kill her, that she had a little girl at home who needed her. But he bit her anyway. And drained her. And then that wasn't enough. He needed to keep her for eternity.

Well, I guess he didn't get her for eternity.

He caught me staring and sneered. "You will never understand our bond. Our love."

I sneered right back at him. "I may not have known my mother as well as some here, but I know she could have never loved a barbaric animal like you." If there was ever a moment to confirm that my Fire was gone, this was it, because I would have roasted him. "You took her from me!" I screamed, lunging for his throat.

He didn't fight back, just fell to the ground in defeat, murmuring, "I didn't protect her, I didn't protect her."

"Protect her?" His throat was cold and slender in my hands as I started to squeeze.

"Adele!" Nicco grabbed my waist and pulled me off. "He killed my mother!" I shrieked, my legs kicking the air.

Emilio stood, brushing off his clothes, eyes on me.

"You took her *life*," I spat.

Hostility overtook the sadness in Emilio's eyes. "I *gave* her life. Eternal life."

"You stole her away from the people she loved." Hot tears welled, but I refused to let them spill. "No one in their right mind would ever love you."

Emilio's nostrils flared, just like Nicco's did when he was angry, and his fingers curled like he was preparing to tear me apart.

Gabe and Lisette stepped closer, as if to intervene, but Emilio whirled away, gravel-dust kicking up where he'd been standing.

I ripped my arms away from Nicco. I hated his brother.

In the awkward silence that followed, Gabriel approached and softly kissed both of my cheeks. "*Sentite condoglianze.*"

Martine and Lisette did the same, offering condolences in French.

Nicco and I followed the trio through the rows of mausoleums, our footsteps crunching in the darkness. About twenty feet from the gate, I paused, watching Lisette's cape flutter as she passed over the wall.

Nicco turned inward to me and stroked my arm. "I'm so sorry, Adele. I wish I could go back in time to that night so things could have ended differently. I wish I could have gotten to you a minute sooner. I'm so sorry."

I looked straight past him, afraid the sympathy in his eyes would make my tears shed. I didn't want to be that blubbering girl in front of him.

"If it's any consolation . . . in their years together, Emilio really did love her. He worshiped Brigitte and cherished her in a way that I've never seen him with anyone since Giovanna."

Your sister, who he abandoned to a coven of witches to meet her final death? There was no way I'd ever believe Emilio had a redeeming quality.

I didn't feel closure. I felt translucent.

I looked up at his pale face in the moonlight. "Sometimes I can't breathe . . . and I keep thinking the feeling will go away, but it doesn't. I don't know what I'm supposed to think or do or feel. It's like I'm in a tiny boat by myself in the dark, bobbing in a black sea. And there are no stars and no moon, only blackness and fog, and I'm just waiting for the boat to tip so it will all be over."

His voice was soft and steady. "I'm not going to let the boat tip, Adele." When he touched my face, I shuddered. "You can feel whatever you need to feel for as long as you need to, and you don't have to worry —I won't let the boat tip."

I nodded.

He leaned so close his face brushed mine as he spoke. "I'm not going to let anyone else hurt you, Adele." Then it was like all sense of impulse control had been cast out of my body and I slid my arms around his neck. He pulled me close, and for those moments, all the pressure, all the sadness and darkness, lifted away because . . . I believed him.

"*Grazie*."

"For what, *bella*?"

"For saying that Brigitte would have found beauty in me, even though I'm mundane now."

"*Prego*." His hand slipped to my jaw so I'd look up at him. "But that's not what I meant. You are anything but mundane, Adele."

I laughed, tears shaking out. That I didn't believe. "Not anymore, Nicco. I'm not magical anymore."

"*Sì, bella*. You are." His hand ran down the length of my arm, and dipped into the velvet sleeve, his fingers curling around my wrist. "I can feel it inside you."

"I don't think that has anything to do with magic."

Color pinched the tops of his cheeks, and I couldn't believe I'd said it out loud.

"You are magical, *bella*. You don't have to believe it right now, but I believe in you enough for the both of us."

He pulled me closer, and I curled back into him. I wanted to believe him, about Emilio cherishing my mother, about my magic not being gone forever.

His fingertips traced the curve of my spine at the small of my back. The small movement simultaneously put me in a hypnotic state and enlivened every nerve in my body. And for just a moment I didn't allow myself to feel any guilt over my mother's death, or for my behavior over the last couple months, or for being here with him.

I pressed myself closer, wishing I could see her one more time so my last memory of her wasn't of the stake plunging into her back. I wished I could tell her goodbye. I wished I could see her one last time to tell her I loved her, and that I understood why she left us.

"You are magical, *bella,*" Nicco whispered again.

The wind caught the words and echoed them around us. Beneath the velvet dress, chills ripped over my spine and down my arms. It was like the temperature had suddenly dropped ten degrees.

A rush of darkness fluttered overhead, obstructing the stars and the moon.

Our necks craned, and Nicco's arms tightened. A flock of large black birds was soaring over the cemetery. One broke from the formation, circling back over us, and the others followed. They landed on the walls and spikes of the gate, all turning to face us. The original crow had landed on top of the winged hourglass. It stared directly at us.

My heart skipped and the guilt rushed back, but Nicco's grip didn't loosen. He knew it. I knew it.

It was Isaac.

Movement came from the ground all around us: lines of black, slithering and circling our feet without touching us. *Ants.* Millions of ants moving in perfect time like synchronized swimmers. More movement came from behind a mausoleum, something much bigger than an insect. A bird. A black . . . rooster? It pecked its way toward us, slowly and surely.

The wrought iron gate swayed in the wind.

Nicco's hand lowered to my waist. "Let's get out of here, *bella.*"

As the hairs on the back of my neck raised, I couldn't agree more.

We walked through the gate, and the air whooshed above us as all the birds took flight at once.

CHAPTER 11

OUT FOR BLOOD

I stomped my boot into the shovel, breaking up the ground around the old dead tree root. It was hard to aim—the sky was cloudy, muting the moonlight, and the fairy lights we'd strung up all around the brothel's back garden weren't exactly work lights.

The backyard was massive, but we'd been transforming it week by week, and slowly it was looking less like something from a Mary Shelley novel and more like Tolkien-Elven lands.

"Do you need my help with that?" Désirée asked me, kneeling over the flower bed she'd been digging.

"No, thanks." I swung the hoe harder, not telling her that I was imagining the root to be Nicco's head. I was still in shock after seeing Adele out of the house.

"Suit yourself." She shrugged and scooped out some seedlings she'd been germinating in an egg carton.

Codi wasn't too far away, examining a crepe myrtle in the back corner of the property, near an ancient pair of weeping willows. He started asking Dee questions about Gran Bwa. I wiped my face with my forearm, trying to let their voices drown out the questions racing through my head. *How long has Nicco been in touch with her?*

"But what did you *feel* during the possession?" he asked Désirée, inspecting a branch of a crepe myrtle covered in white fungus. He waved his hand toward the pond in the rear of the backyard, and a dozen baseball-sized water bubbles rose out and floated over to him. They glistened in the dark, catching the fairy lights and reminding me of Adele's fireballs.

"It's hard to describe," Désirée said. "I felt really light but at the same time very solid, grounded. *Really strong.* Like I-could-have-ripped-your-head-off-if-you-betrayed-me strong."

"*Nice.*" He twirled his finger, and the bubbles followed suit, forming a ring around the base of the tree.

"But also intensely emotional. I think Gran Bwa can feel everything of the living—the trees, the plants, the flowers, every blade of grass—like they're all his children. And I could feel it too."

"So insanely cool . . . I wish I could have been there." Codi snapped his fingers, and the ring of bubbles burst, watering the tree at the root.

Désirée walked over and ran her hand over the diseased crepe myrtle branch he was inspecting. As the branch soaked in the blend of Earth and Water magic, the white powdery fungus began to dissipate. In two or three places, tiny pink blossoms opened. "This one should be fine in a couple days."

Codi motioned again toward the pond, and another string of bubbles danced out, surrounding the tree like a crown. They all burst at once, spraying water everywhere. Désirée jumped out of the way, shrieking something about her hair.

"This place is going to be awesome by the time Adele's birthday rolls around," Codi said, directing more pond bubbles at a small grove of trees.

I nodded. I'd started working on the garden mostly to try to take my mind off things, but at some point I'd decided that I wanted to have the whole garden restored in time for Adele's birthday, and they began helping me. Codi had been scrubbing out the fountain for days. I liked him; he wasn't afraid to get his hands dirty.

"August nineteenth. Leo-Virgo cusp."

He said it as if that meant something very particular, and I wondered what it was like growing up eating off tables etched with the zodiac wheel.

"Isaac?" Désirée said, gesturing to the flower bed, a seedling in each of her palms.

I picked up a rusted gardening fork that must have been a century old and went over to help loosen up the soil.

"Don't step on those." She motioned to a line of plants with clusters of bright lemon ball-shaped florets. Even the stems and leaves had a yellow hue.

I carefully broke up the compacted soil where she directed.

"What are they called?" I asked, still looking at the flowers.

"Technically, helichrysums, but most witches know them as immortelle."

"Why?" I asked, my tone turning snarky at the mere mention of immortality. "Did they spring from the fountain of youth?"

Codi laughed.

"No—" She started to answer, but then he finished: "They retain their golden color even after death, making them still look alive."

Désirée acted like she wasn't impressed, but I could tell she was and it threw her for a loop; she was definitely used to being the teacher when it came to spellcasting.

As I jammed the fork deeper into the earth next to the immortal flowers, all I could think about was a certain immortal with his arms wrapped around my girlfriend. I didn't like him being there for her. Consoling her. *She doesn't need him. She has us.*

She has me.

A warm breeze blew through my hair, and I looked up to the third-floor balcony, the one Emilio had thrown me over. Something Nicco had said echoed in my head: *"I may be a monster, but I'll never be the one who killed her mother."* He was right, and this whole thing was so fucked. I wiped the sweat from my brow. "What if she never comes back to the coven? What if she joins them instead?"

"What do you mean, joins *them*?" Defensiveness rose in Codi's voice. "You think Adele would actually join Callis's coven?"

"What? No! She'd never join the enemy coven." I stuck the fork into the ground and let go. "The Medici clan."

Codi let his last bubble smash to the ground and crossed his arms over his chest. "Are you *kidding me?*"

"What? Her mother did."

Désirée's eyes widened. "That's dark, Isaac."

"Mrs. Le Moyne didn't *decide* to join the Medici. There's no way she *wanted* to leave her family and become a vampire!"

"How do you know?" I asked. "What were you, like, six when she disappeared?"

"Jesus Christ, Isaac," Désirée said. "Don't give up on her."

"Sorry." I pinched my forehead. "I'm not saying Adele's mom wanted it. But what if she was naïve and they lured her in? I just worry that sometimes Adele doesn't know who the enemy is."

Codi's tone became sharp. "Maybe you need something else to focus your energy on."

"For real." Désirée said. "I've been reading up on the purging properties of charcoal—maybe you could start testing how to incorporate it into our depossession techniques. Or we could work on channeling our energy together. The more strength we have—"

"Do you know what would make us stronger?" Codi asked.

Désirée raised an eyebrow.

"If you bound me into the coven."

She looked to me and blew air out of her mouth.

"You go get Adele," I said, "and we'll bind you into the coven." *You can probably find her at Nicco's.*

"She's your girlfriend."

"Do you think we should tell her about Ren?" Désirée asked, suddenly serious. "He's getting worse every day."

I pictured her at the cemetery, the sadness in her eyes. I shook my head. "Not yet. She's had too much tragedy to deal with."

"Agreed," Codi said.

Désirée's look became distant. "It's so weird to think about Alessandro's soul slowly chewing away at Ren like a swarm of termites."

Codi folded his arms. "Borges, that's sick."

"Well, that's what's happening, and he's going to be nothing but a bag of bones if we don't figure out a way to separate them."

Working on all those old houses with my crew, I'd seen the destruction termites could do. It was unbelievable that something so small and delicate, and practically invisible, could destroy something as strong as wood. Adele had mentioned that even the garçonnière at Le Chat Noir had termite damage.

"*Termites*," I whispered.

I had an idea. I wasn't giving up on her—or on Mac.

⚜

I padded down a dark hallway, detouring en route to the cabaret ballroom. Despite the number of times I'd been to the bar, I'd only been in the back once. It was closed off to the public because of the safety hazard, but on New Year's Eve, after Adele and I had rung in midnight and finished helping Mac serve champagne to the patrons, we'd snuck away with a bottle to one of these rooms for what started out as light kissing and turned into more of a next-step-in-our-relationship kind of make-out session. She'd said, "This is what garçonnières were for, back in the day." She was tipsy and I was tipsy, and I had no idea what she was talking about, but whatever it was, I liked it.

Jesus, Isaac, don't think about that right now.

I tried one of the hallway doors, expecting it to be locked. It creaked like it hadn't been opened in years. I stepped inside, the wood crunched like dried leaves, and my boot went through the floorboard. Total dry rot, as I'd suspected. I grabbed the industrial flashlight from my knapsack and shone it across the floor and up the wall to the crown molding. I'd bet all the other wooden detailing was ruined too. I'd salvage anything I could. It would be dirty, disgusting work, but not something I couldn't handle.

I wove in and out of a couple other rooms: all had suffered the same damage. I clicked off the flashlight. This was a solid plan.

The chatter, music, and scent of cigarettes grew as I neared the bar. In the secret cabaret, a woman in a red dress was singing jazz with a three-piece band. Mac was at the bar, but no one else I recognized. I got a few hellos on my way over but made it across with relative ease.

"Hurricane hooch?" Mac asked, recognizing me this time.

I grabbed a barstool. "Sure." I would have liked anything else, but apparently my response system only knew how to agree.

"How goes it?" he asked, simultaneously pouring the moonshine and spraying the soda gun into the glass.

"Still mourning the shortest winter ever."

"Blink and it's over." He squeezed a tiny piece of lemon into the drink and slid it across the bar.

"I heard it was still snowing in New York this week." I took a sip.

He grabbed a bottle of beer from his secret stash and flicked the cap into the trash like I'd seen him do dozens of times. "I think the last time it snowed here, my daughter was . . ."

My back stiffened.

"In second grade—she's nearly seventeen now. I still remember taking her out of school so she could see it." He removed his wallet from his back pocket and pulled out a picture: a mini-Adele bundled in a ridiculous amount of clothes, lying on the ground making a snow angel. It couldn't have been more than a couple inches, just enough to stick to the ground.

I laughed. "That's not snow."

"Don't tell her that. I don't think she's seen a single flake since."

Talking to Mac about his daughter filled me with warmth, but having to pretend like I didn't know her also made me feel gross. As he tucked the photo away, his gaze focused on something over my shoulder. I turned to look, eager to change the subject. On the other side of the room, in a corner near the stage, Gabe was sitting with his two blonde vamp-spawn, one of whom had nearly slit Adele's throat open with her claws when we locked them in the attic. They were all in black, sipping moonshine cocktails and listening to the singer belt out a slow jazzy song. This place always kinda felt like a time portal; they only exacerbated the feeling.

"You know them?" Mac asked.

"No." I turned back. "I mean, I've seen them around."

His gaze lingered, and he took another swig of the beer. Mac had good instincts; he knew they were trouble. I let another sip of the drink burn down my throat and then let the words spill out: "I was, um, looking for a bathroom and came across some rooms that look in pretty bad shape. Termites?"

He shook his head and cursed. I'd never heard him curse before.

"It was treated a while back. The whole place had to be tented. Cost an arm and a leg."

"I could work on it for you," I said, before I wussed out. "I mean, it would take a while, but I could go room by room."

He half-smiled. The look on his face told me he'd had this conversation before. "Thanks, son, but unfortunately, it's just not an option right now. With the economy so volatile, I have to save every penny."

"You wouldn't . . . I wouldn't . . ." I'd never dream of taking cash from Mac. "I don't need any money."

His face formed a questioning look.

"It would actually be helping me out if . . ."

"If?"

"If once a room is habitable, I could stay there while I worked on the others? I want to stay in New Orleans with my recovery crew, but the place I was staying kind of . . . expired. Rentals in the city are scarce and totally price-gouged. It's not really an option on FEMA pay."

Mac folded his arms and shook his head. I knew it wasn't at me but more at the general state of things. "Are you sure about this offer? It seems a bit unfair."

"Oh, well, I could help around the bar, or whatever else you need."

"I didn't mean unfair to me." He laughed. "I meant unfair to you."

"Oh." I felt my cheeks flush. "Don't worry about me."

He stared at me, as if giving me a chance to back out or change the terms. I didn't. "All right, kid, you've got yourself a deal."

He held out his hand, and for once I didn't have to be embarrassed by the calluses that covered my palms because his were just as rough.

"By the way, I'm Mac Le Moyne." He squeezed my hand.

"Isaac. Thompson." My pulse accelerated. "Nice to meet you, Mr. Le Moyne."

"Call me Mac."

He turned to a drawer behind the bar and procured a set of keys. It was difficult to temper my excitement as he placed them in my hand.

"You won't regret this, sir."

A two-way radio bleeped, and we both turned to look. A bunch of cops were sitting at a table nearby, shooting the shit. I missed the first bit of what the voice on the radio said and strained to hear the rest.

". . . David 430. 10-19 to the area of Iberville and Rampart for a subject acting erratically. Suspect is a Hispanic female, early twenties, long brown hair, ponytail, wearing blue jeans and a dark-colored tank top. Last seen heading towards Armstrong Park. Unknown if subject is armed. Multiple reports from citizens."

Groans came from around the table. Most of them looked like they'd already pulled an all-nighter or ten.

Something about the way the dispatcher had said "subject acting erratically" piqued my interest. The little mirror hanging underneath my shirt felt cool against my skin. If I flew, I could beat the cops . . .

I drained the drink, thanked Mac again, and headed for the door.

Even with a new potential victim of possession running around the park, this was the most optimism I'd felt in months. And I'd solved two of my biggest problems at once. I really did need a place to live.

I pulled out my phone and sent a message to Dee and Codi.

Isaac 22:03 Armstrong Park. Possible Possessed. Going to check it out before the cops get there.

We'd agreed to stop chasing the Possessed, but what was I supposed to do? This one just fell into my lap. *It's probably nothing, anyway.*

Désirée's message popped up immediately.

Dee 22:03 WAIT FOR ME AND CODI at the entrance.

I stuffed my phone in my knapsack, tightened the straps, and ran toward Royal Street, looking for a place to take flight. I ducked into an alley across the street from Bottom of the Cup where the shadows were dark.

The air felt cooler as it zipped through my feathers. I stopped at the shop's bay window just long enough to peck the pane of glass.

A head of long black hair flashed into view and Stormy barked. In a blink, Julie was at my side, and we were gliding down Orleans Avenue with the clicking of Stormy's nails against the street echoing up to the cathedral steeples.

I should've waited for Dee and Codi but the cops would be here in no time. I swooped under the arc of dead-lightbulb letters of the Broadway-esque **A-R-M-S-T-R-O-N-G** sign, unlit since the Storm. The park at night was like flying through an obstacle course the dark: dodging willow tree branches, modern art sculptures, and dormant fountains.

Chills pimpled my flesh, causing my feathers to rise.

"Do you feel that, *mon cher*?" Julie asked, her voice fearful.

I cawed. My intuition was right. This girl was definitely possessed. We needed to find her and haul her to the Borges' before the cops got here.

As I dipped lower, feeling for the supernatural sensation, two giant hands wrapped around my mid-section, and the whole world spun. I choked. Someone . . . was . . . *squeezing.*

"Isaac!" Julie screamed.

I exploded back to human form to avoid being crushed and tumbled to the earth, my attacker still clinging to my back. He slammed my head into the ground so aggressively that it felt like I'd hit concrete. Rolling over, I caught the exposed white teeth and gleam of wild eyes above me: *Emilio.*

His fangs sank into my neck, and the scream that came out of my mouth was as unrecognizable as the pain that ripped all the way up to my brain. I struggled underneath him, but he'd wrapped himself around me like a six-foot spider with iron appendages. The more I fought him, the more my own limbs began to feel full of lead.

It's the venom.

My head fell back and dizziness overcame me. Warmth pooled beneath my hair. He sucked harder, murmuring Brigitte's name under his breath. Blood gurgled out of his mouth, pouring down my neck like warm maple syrup, spreading like the paralysis moving through my body. I tried to yell; he didn't silence me, only smiled against my neck, pressing deeper. I focused on the Air, wrapping it around his torso and trying to tug him off me, but he clamped tighter, sucking harder. My magic began slipping away with my consciousness, the Air slowly releasing from my grip.

The trees rustled all around us. Wind. Leaves. Feathers. Chirping.

Spots of bright light pinched the darkness, like Adele's Fire orbs. They faded in and out.

But Adele wasn't here to save me.

A swirl of black enveloped us. Chirping, flapping, pecking. Little swallows descended from every direction, landing on his back, on his arms, pecking his neck, his head, any place they could land. Not just swallows but bluebirds, blackbirds, ravens. He murderously swatted them away, but more came, pecking. A talon ripped into his face, digging out a fleshy part of his cheek. It was the last thing I saw before my vision grayed, and screeches filled my ears. My muscles gave out, my arms flopping to the ground and my feet turning outward to a place of rest. All I could sense was his anger. I had killed his love, and now he was killing me.

Julie screamed my name.

Désirée was going to be so mad.

I should have waited for them.

I should have begged Adele harder to forgive me.

I couldn't feel anything anymore.

No more pain. No more vision. Just a sound: the frenetic thrashing of feathers. I remembered the whirl of air and sheet music that had cradled Adele and me the first time we kissed. I loved her.

I will always love her.

Everything went dark.

CHAPTER 12

BITTEN

Birds screeching.

Or are they screaming?

And darkness.

Darkness.

Screams.

Then silence.

Nothing . . .

but . . .

more darkness and . . . nihility.

Pressure caves in my chest.

Darkness.

A million pounds of pressure punching me.

Light.

I try to gasp but can't.

Paralysis.

"Come on, man, don't die on me! Isaac!" A voice I recognized. *Codi.*

His hands pressed into my chest as he counted. My lungs ballooned. My eyes cracked open, just long enough to see Désirée slumped into a pile on the ground next to him.

"Isaac, stay with me!"

He blurred into darkness.

Nothingness. Only the sounds of Stormy barking and Julie's panicked French.

Darkness.

Silence.

Nothing.

Nothing and everything.

Blackness. Bright white and rainbows.

And then I was weightless. Floating. On my back, bobbing. Light as a feather, stiff as a board. Just like we used to play at sleepaway camp. My hands were crossed on my chest. Voices talking. Voices I didn't know.

I was in the air. Not flying.

Floating.

Spots lit up the insides of my eyelids, reminding me of the racks of lights hanging in the Eugene O'Neill Theatre where my mom once starred in a production of *Our Town.* She'd told me the play was about "the transience of human life," which I think was a fancy way of referring to death. I wondered if she knew she'd die a year later—if she could sense the impending death like I could now.

"Why isn't my magic healing him?" Désirée screamed. "Why isn't *anything working*?" The words twisted together inside my ears like the taffy on the boardwalk at Coney Island.

I was so cold, wrapped in snow.

One day I'd show Adele what *real* snow was. We'd make real snow angels.

Angels.

Bright.

White.

Light . . .

"We've got to get his fever down," Ritha said, her soft, wrinkly hands pressing my face.

Ritha? This is bad.

Everything was shadows, but there were voices: men and women, Codi stuttering, explanations being demanded, crying. *Désirée's crying?*

A rush of panic filled my chest. Julie sat at the edge of the bed near my feet, stroking Stormy's head. I couldn't see anyone else. Just black silhouettes of frenetic energy, bustling around the room. Ideas. Suggestions. Disagreements.

Chanting and magic—pulling me, warming me, cooling me. More chanting and more magic and more shaking. Violent shaking.

Tears.

Witch tears forming pools of darkness that I wanted to sink into forever. I was too tired to swim. I wanted Adele.

I tried to fly out of the pool of darkness, but it wasn't water; it was black tar coating my feathers, pulling me back down.

Drowning.

Sinking.

Just like Jade had.

I should have saved Jade.

I wanted . . .

My mom.

CHAPTER 13

SECRET KEEPER

I held my breath under the warm water.

The lavender oil stung through the cracks of my eyelids.

My face broke the surface just enough to take a breath, and I plunged back under, feeling my hair float up. Nicco had been right about one thing: I don't know if it was screaming at Emilio, or seeing my mother's body safely tucked away for eternity, or letting him see me cry, but part of me felt lighter. Another part of me knew it wouldn't last.

Nicco had offered to stay with me after the funeral, but I'd opted for solitude.

Something pounded in the distance, muffled through the bubbly water.

A chime followed.

The doorbell?

I broke the surface again and peeked at my phone nesting on the pile of clothes on the floor. Nothing. If it was important there'd have been calls.

I relaxed back into the water. The warmth encased me, and the knocking went away.

My thoughts floated back to what Nicco had said about my magic . . . I wanted to believe him. I wanted him to be right.

Nicco was right about a lot of things, but he was wrong about this.

I focused on the hot-water faucet, trying to turn it on—something I could have done in my sleep a few months ago.

I remembered the time I'd unscrewed the lightbulb before I even knew about my magic or Adeline Saint-Germain or covens and Maleficiums, when it was just me and David Bowie and the Spiders from Mars and a cleaning rag. *Just twist, dammit!*

Nothing.

I dunked myself back into the water, bubbles blowing out of my mouth as I sighed in frustration.

An arm broke the surface of the bathwater with a splash. I screamed, inhaling a mouthful of water, as someone pulled me up. I frantically yanked away and fell back, sending a wave onto the bathroom floor. I gasped, choking up water, and scrambled to crisscross my hands over my boobs.

"*Get out,*" Désirée demanded, pulling my arm again.

"What are you doing?" I shrieked, coiling my arms around my knees, coughing.

"Adele, *get out!*" She grabbed a towel from the inset wall cabinet. "You have to come with me now."

I always knew there'd be a day that Désirée would end up at my front door, fed up with my behavior, but I didn't envision me being wet and naked when she tried to drag me out of the house to do a séance to talk to our ancestors or something. I hugged my knees tighter.

"Get—" Her breath became short. "We did everything we could."

"What . . . ?" Then I realized how terrible she looked. Her hair was in a messy low ponytail, she didn't have any makeup on, and her skin had an ashy hue.

"Désirée, what happened?"

Her puffy eyes watered. "E-e-everyone did everything they could," she choked. "I did everything. Gran's coven. The Daures. If you want to tell him goodbye, you have to come—"

I clutched the side of the tub. "*Who,* Désirée? Who are you talking about?!"

"Isaac!"

I scrambled out so quickly, I fell into her, banging my knee on the tub. She caught me with the towel.

"What happened?" I ripped the towel across my back and grabbed the velvet dress from the floor, pushing my arms through the long sleeves.

She yanked it down, the material clinging to my wet body, soaking up the bubbles from my skin while I squeezed my hair into the towel. "Emilio attacked him in Armstrong Park."

"What?" I rushed into my room, dropping the towel on the floor, and grabbed a ball of black socks from a basket of clean laundry. Hopping on one leg, I tried to yank one up the other foot.

"Emilio *bit* him." She retrieved a pair of panties from the basket and slapped them into my hand. "And it's *bad*."

"No. There's no way," I said, stepping into them. "Isaac is strong. And fast. And magical. He can *fly*, Désirée!" All I could picture was the rage in Emilio's eyes after I'd lunged at him in the cemetery earlier this evening.

"Not fast enough."

As soon as I'd slipped into my boots, she was pulling me along, not even giving me a chance to tie them. Her urgency chilled me to the marrow.

As we exited the front door, I looked both ways down the street. "Where's your car?"

"I didn't drive. I ran."

And then I was running too, faster than I knew I could, with Dee half a step behind me.

I'd called Emilio a monster. And now he'd shown us just how much of one he was.

As soon as we entered the candlelit bedroom, the somberness began to suffocate me like quicksand. Edgar, Chatham, and his sister Fiona were there with Codi. Next to Ritha and Ana Marie was a girl with long box braids and an old man sitting behind a drum, thumbing the hide-skin, his head bobbing as if he were in another world. Even Papa Olsin was there, leaning on his feather-adorned cane.

Their whispers stopped as I moved toward the large bed. No one said anything. Branches of palm leaves crunched under my feet.

A blanket had been pulled up to Isaac's chest, which barely moved.

His brow was drenched in sweat, and a poultice was tied around his neck, specks of blood seeping through the muslin.

"No . . ." Tears shook out of my eyes. He was so pale. Isaac was never pale; he was always working outside in the sun. Or running or flying. Isaac was strong and fit and a fighter.

I spun around, shouting, "Why isn't anyone doing anything?"

Chatham and Edgar both stepped toward me, their hands ready to caress me in a comforting way. "Sweetie."

"No!" I yelled, and everyone began talking at once, their voices reeling in my head: "*He's too far gone.*" "*His blood-toxicity levels are too high from the venom.*" "*Someone needs to call Norwood.*"

"No," I screeched. "No one is calling Mr. Thompson. Isaac is going to be fine!"

Codi stepped close. "I'm so sorry, Adele." He looked exhausted. "We found him too late."

A cool breeze whipped around the room, and a series of jars flew off a teacart and smashed into a wall, leaving iodine-colored splotches of potions dripping down to the shards of glass.

"Julie!" Chatham yelled. "We're doing everything we can! There's more magic lighting up this boy's body than a fire dancer's during Beltane!"

"It's the only thing keeping him alive," Désirée choked, tears filling her eyes as she looked at me. "The magic."

I shook my head, tears flinging.

Ritha's hands gently stroked my arms. "There's nothing more we can do, baby. We're going to give you some time alone with him."

"No. No. *No.* No time alone. I survived a vampire bite. Adeline survived a vampire bite. Isaac is *going to survive* a vampire bite."

Ritha sighed, her face hanging with sympathy.

"I refuse to accept this." I wiped away the tears and headed for the door.

Several of them stepped toward me, but I stormed past them as they called my name.

"I refuse to accept this," I mumbled, racing down the hallway and the stairs.

I heard footsteps following me, and the energy told me it was Désirée.

"Adele," she shouted. "You cannot leave him right now!"

"You shouldn't have waited so long to come and get me!" I screamed back over my shoulder.

Pain swelled in my chest. Me staying at Isaac's side—magicless and pathetic—wasn't going to save him.

My damp hair slapped against my back as I ran all the way to the Carter brothers' house.

The gate was unlocked. I pounded the old cedar door with my fist. Just as I opened my mouth to scream for Lisette, the door opened.

"Adele?" Nicco said, his expression morphing into deep concern.

I rushed past him into the foyer, which was no longer dusty and coated in cobwebs and raced up.

"Adele, what's wrong?" He was at my side, easily taking the steps two at a time.

"Where is Lisette?"

"What? Why?"

"Where is she?" I screamed.

He moved ahead of me to the top of the staircase. "What happened?"

The look on my face must have frightened him, because he didn't belabor the question. Instead, he turned and led me through parlor rooms, a ballroom, a dining room with a long table and floor-to-ceiling windows covered with thick curtains and into a hallway. He paused beside one of the doors and turned to me. "Adele, just tell me what happened so I can help you."

I pushed past him, reaching for the crystal knob.

"No! That's Emilio's." He started walking again. "Come on, I'll take you to Lisette."

Hearing his brother's name, knowing he was just behind this door, filled me with a blind rage.

"Adele!" Nicco shouted as I went in.

I slammed the door behind me and fumbled for the brass lock. His voice became muffled through the wood, and my heart pounded when I heard the metal click.

Locking myself in a room with a psychotic vampire: not my smartest move.

This is not the same as Halloween night, Adele. Now you're just a magicless girl.

I turned. Emilio was lying on his back on the bed, fully clothed, his hands beneath his head as he stared at the ceiling. Other than my chest rising and falling, the room was perfectly still.

"Emilio?"

He didn't so much as turn his head.

"Emilio!" His detachment enraged me. I had only two cards left to play, and I was ready to play like a Medici. No more doe-eyed Ingénue, no more little witchling. I stalked across the room and launched myself onto the bed, one leg swinging over his hip, my hands slamming down next to the sides of his face.

Even with my arms boxing him in, he didn't flinch.

Seeing him so perfectly calm, so perfectly at ease after what he'd done, electrified my blood, zapping it through my veins like live circuits. "You are *never* going to touch him again. Do you understand me?" My head hung directly over his, forcing him to drop his gaze from the ceiling to me, but otherwise not a muscle in his face moved. "*Comprenez-vous*?"

His eyebrow furled. "And *you* are going to stop me?" he asked in French.

"*Oui*." My teeth clenched.

"And how are you going to do that, *ma chérie*?"

I lowered my lips to his ear so as to not be heard by prying vampiric ears. "If you don't leave Isaac alone, I'm going to tell your brothers that when you escaped from the attic window with Giovanna"—his eyes lit up—"you ran like a rat, leaving her to die, surrounded by a coven of witches. You're not tough. You're not brave. You're not a legend. You killed your sister."

He lay perfectly still. I didn't blink, waiting for his reaction.

"*I* don't even have my memories from that night. How could *you* know that?"

"Because I know who drove a stake through her heart." My tone was threatening in a way I'd never heard it before—it was how I always imagined Adeline, or Cosette, or even Giovanna could sound. The sound of a witch protecting her family.

Isaac was my family.

The hint of uneasiness in his eyes told me what he was contemplating: whether or not he could have done such a thing. "No one is going to believe you."

"Would you like to test the theory?" I sat up. "*Nic—*!"

He jerked me down. "*Entendu*," he growled. "Fine."

"Adele!" Nicco banged on the door so hard, the hinges partially cracked away from the wood. One more bang and it would be flat on the floor.

"I'm okay, Nicco! Give me a minute!" I had no idea what Emilio Medici's word was worth, but I wanted to hear him say it. I glared at him. "Fine *what*?"

He peered up at me. "I won't touch your precious little witch-boy."

I sat back, stunned that he'd given in.

Emilio's expression softened. "It's incredible how much you look like your mother," he said gently in French.

"You're disgusting," I spat, trying not to imagine him touching my mother.

"*Incroyable*." His hand slid over my thigh, under my skirt, and I jerked up, feeling his erection between my legs. He tried to press me closer, but I jumped away so quickly I fell onto the floor.

"*Répugnant*." I scrambled away from the bed and back to my feet, the moment of power feeling drained. There weren't enough languages in the world for me to express how much so. I stumbled out through the door and slammed it behind me.

"What happened?" Nicco demanded. His gaze went to the door, as if he were wondering whether it would be easier getting answers out of him than me. "What did he do?"

"Where's Lisette?" I moved to the next door, prepared to open every one of them until I found her.

"Adele . . ." he pleaded as I quickly opened doors, revealing closets and studies, one with the strewn clothes of multiple people. *Where is she! I shouldn't have stopped.*

Nicco stepped in front of me, blocking me. "Adele, tell me what's going on, *now*."

"Isaac's nearly dead," I choked out. "Thanks to your brother!"

He cursed in Italian. "Where is he?" He pushed his hand through his hair.

"*Merci*, but I've got my own plan." *And it can't involve your fangs in Isaac's neck.*

"Adele, just take me to him."

I opened the next door, revealing the library. Lisette sat on a bench near the window. "Please trust me, Nicco."

He sighed as I closed the door on him again. This time I didn't lock it. I was probably being foolish and naïve; for some reason being alone with Lisette made me more nervous than being alone with Emilio.

She was drenched in moonlight, feet tucked beneath her dress, raising a crystal goblet to her lips and sipping something I was sure wasn't a vintage Merlot.

"I should have known that was you, *ma fifille*," she said without looking at me, "stampeding through the house like a wildebeest."

Lisette had once nearly slashed my throat open, but she'd also saved Annabelle the night of the attack at the convent. I knew her heart wasn't as petrified as she wanted people to think.

I approached with caution and sat on the bench beside her. I had no idea if my second card was as strong as my first, but the only way to find out was to lay it on the table. "*J'ai besoin de ton aide, Lise.*" I angled myself toward her and looked her straight in the eye. "My coven needs your help."

She scoffed.

"Emilio attacked Isaac. He's going to die if he isn't detoxified."

"*Hmph . . .* " She laughed in a mocking way.

If I'd had my magic, I'd have lit her hair on fire. "And you're going to help him," I said without sharpness, just matter-of-fact.

She opened her mouth to speak, but I was done with this; there was no more time. "You are going to help him, or you won't have to worry any longer about the Monvoisin memory spell holding."

Her fangs snapped out.

"I'll tell Gabe exactly how you ended up in the attic together, and why he killed you, and how much he hated you. I'll tell him that you were one of the witches who cursed him in the attic for *three hundred years* and who tried to lock away his entire family for eternity."

Her eyes hardened on me, and my pulse raced. She tilted her head slightly to the left, as if asking me if I was really doing this, if I was prepared to suffer the consequences for blackmailing a vampire. I didn't flinch.

Her pouty lips curled into a smile, and I knew she was going to help. I also sensed that she was imagining ten different ways of killing me.

She set the glass down on the window ledge and stood, smoothing her dress as if I was about to make her do something undignified.

“He’s at Vodou Pourvoyeur,” I said. “We need to run. There isn’t much time.”

She left the room in a blur.

I followed her. Nicco was still waiting outside.

“I’m sorry,” he said.

“It’s not your fault your brother is a monster.”

The look that hung in his eyes as I passed him told me that, even after all these centuries, he still believed that it was.

CHAPTER 14

BRIGHT LIGHT

Lisette hesitated outside Vodou Pourvoyeur's entrance, and I worried she was going to renege.

"Hurry," I said in French, opening the door.

"You really think I'm going to enter a house full of enemy witches?"

"You really think I won't tell Gabe that you used to *be one* of those enemy witches?"

Her eyes narrowed.

"Let's go," I said, inviting her in with a wave of my hand. The air warbled and the protection spell bent, allowing her passage.

We sprinted through the shop, past the curtain on the back wall, and up the stairs. *What if we're too late? What if I wasted too much time?*

When we entered the bedroom, everyone leaped out of their chairs, hands in magical defensive positions. Papa Olsin raised his cane in our direction, and Lisette hissed.

I extended an arm in front of her. "She's here to help."

The old man lowered his cane, but his eyes gave her a piercing stare.

"*Allons.*" I brought her to the bed.

The pangs in my chest deepened when I saw how much more gaunt and feverish Isaac already looked. I removed the poultice from his neck and choked back the tears. Instead of puncture marks like I'd imagined, there was a pair of gashes that looked like the result of a wild animal attack. Under his severely bruised skin, the veins all around the neck were visible, as dark as if they'd been filled with black ink.

I picked up a hand towel, wrung it out in the rose-water-filled basin on the nightstand, and dabbed the wound.

Lisette looked to me, concern in her eyes. Her voice was shaky when she whispered, "*I don't know how to do this.*"

"You better figure it out in the next ten seconds," I said in French.

Her expression told me she was never going to forget that I made her do this, but I didn't care. I didn't even care if she killed me; she just had to save Isaac.

"You were there," I said, trying to be gentler, "when Gabe saved Adeline. You saw him do it. You know what to do." I picked up a candle from the nightstand and switched places with her.

Everyone curled around the bed, curiosity clouding the room.

Désirée leaned over the mattress directly across from us and looked straight at Lisette. "If you hurt him, you will never make it out of here alive."

Lisette hissed again, but then pulled back the blanket. She looked over to Chatham and Edgar. "Hold him down."

They each took one of his legs.

I brought the candle closer.

She ran her left hand across Isaac's chest to his shoulder, both of which were covered in bruises, then pressed down, pinning him in place. She leaned in, her lips drawing close to his wound.

I rummaged under the blanket with my free hand, looking for his, so he had something to squeeze if the pain was too much to bear.

My fingers sank between his just as her fangs plunged into his neck.

But, as Lisette sucked, he didn't flinch. Tears streamed down my face. I was the one who needed something to squeeze.

She gagged and pulled back, spitting the bloody venom into the basin, and her eyes met mine, letting me know once again that she'd never forget this.

The water in the basin went from clear to pink to crimson; she must have taken his blood ten times. I squeezed and I squeezed. When worry crept onto her face, I wondered if I was killing him, stealing the last moments of his life and making him die with a vampire attached to his neck. I wondered if he had enough consciousness to know what was going on—that I was here and I'd brought a vampire—and if he hated me for it. I could barely breathe.

"Isaac," I whispered through tears so thick I could barely see. "I'm sorry." The lifelessness of his hand in mine made the pangs in my chest so unbearable, I had to sit on the bed.

Lisette spat in the basin and then plunged back into his neck. She no longer made faces at the taste of the venom, and her hand was no longer pinning his shoulder down but massaging it as she drank. Her head bobbed up and down, along with her body, pressing against his.

"That's enough," I said.

Her jaw clamped down and she looked up at me like she was enjoying it.

"That's enough!" I screamed.

Codi rushed up and put his hands over her shoulders. One slipped around her neck, and coaxed her away. I didn't like any part of his body being that close to her mouth.

As he pulled her away from the bed, I grabbed her wrist. She looked back at me, her lips and teeth stained red. "Give him your blood," I said.

Gasps went around the room. Her eyes pulsed wider, and I knew I was making an enemy for life, but I didn't care. "*Do it.* Give him your blood."

"Adele—" Désirée said.

"*Donnez-lui votre sang, maintenant,*" I repeated in French so there was no room for misinterpretation.

Lisette brought her wrist to her mouth and bit into her own flesh. When the blood began to trickle from her lips, she smiled at me. My gaze was unwavering.

She carefully lowered herself back down to the bed and slipped her free arm underneath Isaac's neck, cradling him. Her eyes darkened as she looked back at me, and she wedged her arm between his lips, just like Nicco had done to me, and like Gabe had done to Adeline, only both of us had been conscious. I kept waiting for Isaac to wake up and freak out over the vampire blood being forced down his throat, but he didn't.

He wasn't moving. I could barely tell if he was breathing.

"You do realize," she said in French, "that if he dies with my blood in him, he's going to start to transition?"

My heart pounded. Isaac would *never, ever* want to be a vampire. *He's not going to die, Adele. He's not going to die.* The room tipped and I felt lightheaded, as if I was the one giving blood. I sat back on the bed. *This can't be happening.*

"Stop," Désirée snapped at Lisette. "You're done here."

Lisette pulled her wrist away, blood still dripping over his lips. She dragged her tongue over the drops, sucking his bottom lip with another glance back to me. Part of me wanted to claw her eyes out. Another part of me wanted to melt into oblivion. Dissolve into a billion atoms and blow away in the wind. I'd never felt such a level of emptiness.

I hated myself for ever breaking the curse in the first place, for falling into Callis's trap. I hated myself for getting my mother killed and for deleting Isaac from Mac's memories. I'd deleted him from the world.

I hated myself.

Edgar walked Lisette out, thanking her for her service. Slowly the others left the room, glancing back at me with sympathetic looks. There was nothing left to do but wait. Finally it was just Ritha, Codi, and Dee left.

As Ritha made her way to the door, she paused beside Isaac's clothes and boots piled on the floor. She pulled something from the heap and handed it to Codi.

He nodded to her, pure terror in his eyes. I caught a glimpse of what was in his hand. *A stake.*

He clutched it tight.

"No." I shook my head at both of them. "He's still breathing." I kicked off my boots, slipped under the blanket, and splayed myself over Isaac's chest. "He's still breathing." Codi would have to drive that stake through my back to get to Isaac.

He moved to the side of the bed next to Désirée and sat in an old bucket chair, his back stiff, the stake in his hand, the stunned look still in his eyes.

Désirée crawled onto the bed on the other side of Isaac and stared at the ceiling, tears dripping down her face to the pillow.

My grip around him tightened. "I'm sorry, Isaac. I'm sorry. You can't die. *Please don't die.*" My whispers became moans and pain pierced my head and throat until it silenced me. Curling around him, I listened for his heartbeat, felt for the rising of his chest.

In a silent rhythm, waves of shudders passed through his body.

Fight it, Isaac.
Fight it.
You have to fight it.

When I woke, the room was completely dark except for the moonlight shining in over Codi, who still sat in the chair, gripping the stake. Désirée had moved to the chair beside him and was curled in a ball, sleeping. The candles had burned out, but a tinge of smoke lingered in the air, mixing with the aroma of rosewater and the metallic scent of blood. But it wasn't the smoke that had woken me; it was the *murmuring.*

I sat up quickly. Isaac's eyes were still closed, but his lips were moving. My ears strained to understand him. Something about bracelets?

I felt for his wrist, for the tangle of embroidered threads that had belonged to his dying mother, and was struck with a wave of panic.

"Pop's going to be so alone," he mumbled. "I don't want him to change any more than he already has. He's so bitter. Lonely."

"No! *No* talking to dead mothers." I hoisted myself closer to his face. "*No* ghosts helping you cross over. *No* bright light. You are not dying!" I cupped his jaw, tilting his head slightly to kiss his cheek. "You can't die, Isaac. I need you. I'm sorry for what I said. I didn't mean it. I never meant to hurt you." My arm slid around his shoulder, my face burrowing into his neck. My tears made his clammy skin even slicker. "Please don't take him," I pleaded with his dead mother. "It's all my fault. He can't die too. I love him."

The words caught me by surprise. "I love you, Isaac."

I knew my love wasn't worth anything, but I also knew I'd have cut out my own heart to save his.

The next time I woke, I was still lying on top of his chest, my face buried in the crook of his neck, but something was different . . . heavier.

His arms were wrapped around me.

He'd moved.

I sat up, peering into his face, feeling his forehead. His fever had broken. "You're going to be okay," I choked, pressing my lips to his cheek.

"Please don't let them call my dad," he wheezed, his eyes cracking open. "I really don't want to have to explain any of this to him." And then he smiled—or at least, tried to.

My chest shook with laughter and tears trailed from my eyes as I nodded.

His hand slipped around my wrist. "You're here."

Rendered mute with relief, all I could do was nod.

"Breathe," he said, cupping the side of my face.

More nodding and more hot tears streaming.

"I'm gonna be okay." His thumb rubbed my cheek.

I curled back into his chest, and his arms curled back around me. It wasn't long before his breathing indicated that he was sleeping again.

For the first time that night, Codi relaxed back in the chair, and the tension in the room deflated.

As everyone slept, I lay there in the darkness, Isaac's musky scent filling my lungs, my emotions swirling. I thought about everything that had happened over the last eight months, trying to figure out how we'd ended up here. *The Storm. Paris. The shutter. The curse.* My memories of the night at the convent with my mother and Isaac—and the stake, and Nicco closing her eyes—played over and over in my mind in an endless looping reel.

I wanted her back. I didn't want this.

I wanted my mother.

What would happen tomorrow morning when everyone woke up? Would they just expect everything to go back to the way it was? What was I going to say? Could I force myself to smile?

Knowing that Isaac was going to be okay, I suddenly found myself wishing I could teleport back to my own bed, under my blanket. Alone. I didn't know how to go back to the way things were before. My lungs tightened.

His fingers traipsed into my hair, gently stroking the nape of my neck, sending chills down my arm. "I love you," he whispered.

My eyes pinched shut.

I didn't know what else to do but pretend to be sleeping. My heart beat erratically against his chest and I worried he could feel it. Why couldn't I say it back? How would I ever slip back into this world? Everything felt off.

And it gave me a sickly feeling.

How could lying in this bed with him feel completely right and completely wrong at the same time? It's Isaac.

But I didn't belong here. I didn't have any magic and wasn't a witch.

I wished I'd never gotten my mark. That way, it would all go away and I wouldn't remember anything and they could move on without me. Anxiety stormed in my belly . . . and I hated myself because I knew what I was going to do.

I lay there in the darkness until his fingers stilled. Then I gently picked up each of his arms and slid out from underneath them and off the bed. With my boots in hand, I padded out of the room and into the dark hallway.

When I turned to the staircase, I saw a glimpse of movement from inside another bedroom. I craned my neck to peer into the shadows, and someone crept closer. A mop of white-blonde hair.

"Lisette?" I whispered. "How did you get back in here?"

She looked sheepish, as if she herself was unsure why she was still here. "How is he?" She just stood there, awkwardly waiting. I didn't know if it was genuine concern for Isaac's wellbeing or just curiosity over whether she'd unintentionally made a vampire-child or what.

I thought about everyone sleeping and all the death looks she'd given me earlier. My arms crossed. "You need to leave."

She nodded but still didn't move. "Is he okay?"

"What do you care? You wouldn't even help until I blackmailed you! What would Susannah say if she was here? She'd throw you out the window like she did Martine." I immediately felt bad, but I didn't apologize; it was all true.

Shame shadowed her gaze.

I sighed. "*Oui, il va bien se passer.*"

A look of relief—I think—washed over her face.

"He's going to be fine," I repeated, partly for her, partly for me.

She nodded and stepped out into the hall, turning to leave.

"And Lisette," I said.

She looked back.

"*Merci beaucoup.*"

"*Je vous en prie.*" And with that she was gone in a blur of white.

The exchange made me feel uneasy. I wasn't stupid—I knew that nothing good could ever come out of blackmailing a vampire. Blackmailing *two* vampires.

I hurried down to the first floor and through the shop, but halfway to the front door, footsteps thudded rapidly down the stairs.

"Adele!" Désirée called out.

I stopped and turned around.

"Where are you going?" With a few quick strides she was standing in front of me.

"I—I'm just going home," I said, hardly able to look at her.

"Why? *No.* You need to be here when he wakes up."

"He's going to be fine. His fever broke, and he was talking. He's lucid." I wondered if she'd heard any of our conversation.

"Adele! Do you even hear yourself?"

"I have to go."

"He needs you!"

"He has you, and everyone."

"This is bullshit."

She was right, but I didn't know how to fake it when he woke up—fake it to him or anyone. I couldn't tell her the truth—I knew how horrible it would sound—but staying and going through the motions seemed worse than just leaving.

"I have to go."

"What is *wrong* with you?"

"I don't know . . ." My voice cracked. "I don't know how to be with him right now. I can't."

"He doesn't need you to love him," she snapped. "He needs you to forgive him!"

Tears stung my eyes for the millionth time that night. I didn't know how to do that either. "I can't," I gasped. "I'm sorry." And I turned away.

"Adele!" she yelled.

"You're going to wake him up!" I hissed over my shoulder as I walked through the room of Voodoo dolls.

She stormed after me. "Stop acting like you care!"

"I care!"

"You have a funny way of showing it!"

I kept walking.

"Adele! If you walk out of that door . . . Don't come back."

My socked feet paused on the wooden floor like she'd zapped me with a stun gun. I'd heard Désirée say a lot of cold things over the months, but I'd never heard that tone from her.

I knew I should stay, that it was the right thing to do, but it would feel like a lie. And lying to Isaac hurt more than leaving him. *Waking up alone will be better for him than waking up next to me. He's going to be fine.*

I took a deep inhale and kept going, feeling Désirée's stare burning a hole straight through my spine, into my heart.

Then I was in the cooler nighttime air, and finally I could breathe again. I paused at the curb, blinking back the tears until they were gone.

I sensed someone watching me and looked up.

Across the street, sitting on the stoop of a turquoise Creole cottage with violet trim, Nicco waited patiently in the darkness.

I walked over and sat next to him on the cement step. His presence filled me with immediate relief. I dropped one boot on the ground and slipped on the other. "How is he?"

I tightened the laces. "Stable."

"Are you . . ." He turned to me. "Stable?"

I nodded. "*Merci.* I'm sorry I yelled at you earlier."

"*Je comprends.* I'm just glad he's okay."

I expected him to ask me about what had happened with his brother and with Lisette. If there was one thing I knew about Nicco, it was that he didn't like being in the dark; but he didn't press me.

"Do you want me to take you home?" he asked.

A few minutes ago, all I'd wanted was to be home, but as I pulled on my other boot and laced it up, I realized something had changed.

I shook my head. "I don't really want to be alone."

He nodded. "There's somewhere I want to show you."

He helped me up, and we walked down the street together.

I had no idea where we were going, but suddenly, I was eager to get there with Nicco.

CHAPTER 15

ROLLERCOASTER

I waited outside Nicco's house to avoid a run-in with Emilio or Lisette as he went in to "grab a flashlight." He quickly came back out with a duffel bag bigger than me. What was in it, whose car we got into, and our destination remained unknowns. I didn't ask. Nicco's mysteries were part of his allure.

He took the old highway that went through the Lower Ninth Ward and out to the Rigolets, further adding to the mystique of the journey.

Once we were past the broken residential streets, the road was clear because the National Guard had been using the highway to get in and out of the city ever since the Storm collapsed the bridges over Lake Pontchartrain. God only knew when they'd be reconstructed.

Nicco shifted the car into fifth gear; I clipped on my seatbelt.

There was no music and no talking, just us and the soft sound of the engine as we soared down the pitch-black strip of road. As I stared out into the darkness, I curled my knees into my chest and settled back into the seat, relaxing into the feeling that we were leaving the night's events behind us.

Soon we were out of the city limits, surrounded by more marsh than civilization—we could have been driving all the way to the Atlantic for all I cared. Beyond the illumination of the headlights, all I could see for miles were the silhouettes of cypress trees under the moonlight. A drawn-out howl came from somewhere in the distance—not a sound I'd ever heard before the Storm, but people weren't the only ones displaced by the hurricane.

Pre-Storm, there hadn't been much along HWY-90, but now, there was nothing.

I thought about the large duffel bag in the trunk and gave him an exaggerated eye-slant. "You're not taking me out to the swamp to dispose of my body, are you?"

He laughed. "No, *bella.* I wasn't planning on getting *that* dirty tonight."

I was unsuccessful in suppressing a smile. It was always a little strange to hear Nicco break from his stoicism to make a joke.

"Speaking of dead bodies," he said, looking out my window.

Beyond the trees, a huge sterile-looking warehouse was lit up with stadium-sized lights. The structure couldn't have been there pre-Storm, just based on the fact that it was still standing. It seemed to go on for half a mile.

"What is it?"

"That's D-MORT."

The Disaster Mortuary Operational Response Team facility . . . We passed it by, and I turned in my seat, watching it shrink in the distance behind us. I'd seen photos of the building in the paper, but it looked so much bigger in person.

I thought about Sébastien working in the lab and about the thousands of people who would never make it to their family cemeteries like my mother had.

"We've had enough death tonight," he said and floored the gas. We sped away, falling back into silence as we took the dark open highway to . . . somewhere?

When Nicco finally slowed down and turned onto a gravel road, I still didn't know where we were going. After a few more twists and turns through a desolate wooded area, we pulled into a mammoth parking lot.

In the flood of the car's bright lights, all I could see were white parking lines on pavement stretching into the darkness beyond.

He drove through slowly. "You still don't know where we are?"

The satisfaction in his voice made me grumble internally for not having figured it out.

He grinned and nodded to the windshield.

A behemoth unlit neon sign, all the colors of the rainbow, came into view as we rolled to a stop.

JAZZLAND

Dammit. I'd been to this amusement park at least once a summer with Brooke since we were kids. How had I not figured this out? We'd always taken I-10, of course, and we'd never arrived at night. I guess backroads and moonlight were the vampire way of life.

Nicco cut the engine, and I turned to him with a half-laugh. "What are we doing here?"

He shrugged. "Whatever we want."

He reached into the back and handed me a flashlight, his not-so-innocent smile returning.

I got out of the car, and instead of being greeted by the background sounds of giggling, sugar-rushed children and gaggles of teens screaming on the coasters as the metal roared over the tracks, it was a chorus of frogs and cicadas and other swamp life I'd rather remain clueless to. The eye of the Storm had torn through this area. All the people who'd lived in the neighboring suburbs were now all displaced. We were very—very—alone. I clicked on the flashlight and shined it at the sign as he fetched his bag from the trunk. Underneath the neon, in black plastic letters, was a message from management:

CL SED FOR STORM

"More like closed for good," I muttered.

I shined the light over the ticket booths in the distance. Vines twisted around the turnstiles, and foliage peeked out from every nook and cranny. The weeping willow tendrils almost entirely obscured the gates. It was amazing how overgrown the grounds had become in less than a year: it didn't look like a place to take kids; it looked like something from *Jurassic Park.*

"Are you ready?" Nicco asked.

I did my best to hide my enthusiasm and took off for the gate. The head start, of course, didn't matter; when I reached the entrance, he was already there, and I was the only one sucking in breaths.

He jerked the two gates apart, snapping the metal lock. He rarely exhibited such supernatural strength in front of me. My next thought—of how easy it would be for him to snap bones—made me realize why.

"So that's how you got into the cemetery?" I asked as he pulled away the thick chain.

"Hmm? We wouldn't desecrate a cemetery; we hopped the fence. Much less conspicuous."

"But then you broke the chain so I could get in."

"No. I assumed you used your magic to get in."

"*Nicco,* I don't have my magic anymore."

"You do."

"I don't."

"*Oui. Tu fais,*" he repeated in French, as if language was the mere problem here. He adjusted the duffel bag on his shoulder. "Wait here, *je reviens tout de suite.*"

Before I could respond, he whipped away, leaving behind a trail of *tinks* every few seconds until they, along with the whoosh of his footsteps, were masked by the hum of crickets.

His French was perfect. I wondered how many languages he'd known as a human. I wondered if as a vampire, he knew them all. I slowly swung the flashlight from side to side, telling myself that all the wildlife was asleep and there was no way alligators were lurking.

Before I could completely freak myself out with thoughts of swamp monsters, Nicco was back, trying not to smile, as if he was up to something. *When wasn't Nicco up to something?*

"I'm almost finished." He gave me the duffel, which now felt empty, and took off again.

I peered in the direction he'd gone, and a flicker of light appeared, not much bigger than a firefly. Then another, and another. I slung the bag over my shoulder and followed the glow along a brick path darkened with algae, bursting apart by weeds pushing through the crevices.

A few steps closer and I could see that it was a flame—on a tealight. I stuffed the flashlight in the bag and ran to the next one, following the trail of candles until I was standing in a little town square, a replica of the French Quarter. Or at least, what remained of it. The hodge-podge of French-Spanish-Haitian architecture looked just like the real thing, only more destroyed. The townhouse balconies had the same ironwork as my neighbors; some even had ferns and Mardi Gras beads dangling from them, waiting for actors in antebellum costumes to toss them down to the park-goers below. Only now, the ferns were dead and overgrown with weeds; and the purple, green, and gold metallic finishes on the pearls were faded from the sun. The actors would have been antebellum zombies.

This was what the French Quarter would have looked like had it been hit as hard by the Storm as this area. The buildings were covered in graffiti, the windows were broken, and the roofs were smashed in sections. Spray-painted messages caught my eye as I walked by:

WE'RE STILL DYING HERE
No one cares
ALL SHALL STAND BEFORE GOD

A somberness heavier than the destruction spiraled around me like thick fog, and everything suddenly felt surreal in a way that could only be brought on by thinking of victims of the Storm.

So much death. So much unnecessary death.

Eight months ago, I'd have been sure that things would have improved by now. Now I wasn't so naïve—it was only getting better for some. I hated how helpless it made me feel. I needed to be more like Isaac. He always found a way to help.

Rusty gates creaked in the breeze as I walked through rows of ghostly vendor booths. Red-and-white striped tarps, ripped and stained, half-covered broken cotton candy and popcorn machines. A smiling hotdog with arms and a black streak of mud across his eyebrows watched me as I passed. I walked faster, through piles of stuffed bears in prize booths that looked like they'd been mauled by real ones, and dunking tanks filled with swamp water. I stopped short when I got to the open area of the park, expelling the somberness with an exhale.

The candles no longer formed a simple trail. They were *everywhere.*

Every main attraction in the park had been outlined with the tiny flickering lights: the Mardi Gras Menagerie, an old-style merry-go-round; the Jester's triple loop; and the Eiffel Tower structure that went all the way up to the Observatory. But the *pièce de résistance* was the Mega Zeph, the old wooden coaster that now shone in twinkling loops and whorls. None of the dilapidated rides would have been visible in the pitch-black night, but now they flickered like constellations in the sky.

I hurried onward, toward the old carousel, but my boot splashed into mucky water. *Gross.* I stopped and clicked the flashlight back on. This entire area of the park was still flooded, and it looked like the water got even deeper further out, like Mother Nature was reclaiming the land. The merry-go-round was a decaying island of colored porcelain and brass in the middle of the black-sludge swamp, a haven for unicorns, white rabbits, and the rest of the menagerie still stuck on their metallic poles.

As I stood there, I noticed movement up on the iconic Ferris wheel, the Big Easy, which had been constructed to match the one from the 50s at the old Pontchartrain Beach. One by one, tiny flames lit up the sky where each of the seats hung. There was just enough moonlight to see Nicco's shadowy figure run across the beam of the spoke and leap down to the ground—it was just how I'd imagined Gabriel running across the mast on the S.S. *Gironde* when I'd read Adeline's diary.

A few moments later, he was back at my side, his eyes shining with barely repressed enthusiasm, and it was impossible not to be breathless. The whole thing was so magnificent, I didn't know what to say. Sharing in Nicco's secrets was like a drug I could never get enough of, especially when he looked at me like he was now, like a little of the loneliness, and the sadness, had lifted.

"So," I finally asked. "You were a Fire witch?"

He nodded.

I touched his arm where I knew his mark was hidden beneath his sleeve, regretting every time I'd tried to scrub mine off or wish it away. Magical or not, it was a part of me, and it made me feel closer to him.

He didn't even look down at his arm, just at me. He wasn't ready to talk about it—something I understood all too well. "Are you scared of heights?" he asked.

"No." I couldn't imagine fearing anything with him.

He hurried me along to the Eiffel Tower Observatory, which had been designed to mimic Paris's most famous attraction. Nothing could capture the real thing, but Nicco's flickering candle flames gave the tacky replica a certain *je ne sais quoi.*

At the base of one of the tower's metal feet, he took the bag from my shoulder and dropped it to the ground. I craned my neck up. The structure disappeared into the night, just dark shapes and darker shadows. "I'll be right behind you."

That was all I needed.

I jumped up, grabbing the first steel beam, and he boosted me higher. As soon as I got my footing, I grabbed the next bar on my own, and then the next and the next. His hands were never more than a foot from my ankles.

The wind blew my velvet dress open, and I tensed against the structure. I wanted to die a little with Nicco right there.

"Don't look down!" he yelled in a teasing voice.

And of course I did. That's when I realized we were at least five stories up. I clung to the bar as the wind ruffled my hair. I wasn't scared of heights—I could climb to the top of the bell tower at Notre Dame without any vertigo—but free-scaling the metal rigging of the observation tower took it to a whole new level.

A rung below me, he smiled, shaking his head. If he was concerned about me falling to certain death, he hid it masterfully. "Keep going!"

I took a deep breath and began climbing again, checking every handhold and never more thankful for my shit-kickers. The metal bars became cooler the higher up we went.

When we reached the viewing platform, I saw that the thick plexiglass safety barrier was long gone.

"Stay right there," Nicco said. "Hang on tight."

It was advice I did not take lightly. Every muscle in my arms and legs shook as I hugged the rail.

He quickly climbed around me and up over the edge with cat-like grace. Then he reached down and pulled me up onto the platform.

The view almost swept me away. I stepped to the ledge facing the park, taking in the full expanse of the destruction—it didn't look real. *How could anything so indestructible be so broken?* The black swampscape of flickering amusement park rides looked toy-sized under the blanket of stars and the perfect crescent moon.

I felt Nicco come up behind me, standing close. "It never really gets old."

My muscles ached like they'd been thrust out of a deep hibernation, but it felt like we'd transcended Earth and were nestled into the cosmos.

I gazed up at him, my head knocking his collar. "That was way better than taking the elevator."

"I'm glad you think so." He slid one arm around my waist, his smile becoming devilish. "Are you ready?"

"For what?"

He reached over my head and grabbed a handle.

The zipline.

"It's the only way across."

"Wha—?"

He pressed me firmly against his chest and jumped off the ledge, his jacket rippling open behind us and a scream ripping from my throat as we soared down the wire, across the broken, flooded park like bats. I felt invincible, tearing through the starry night with him.

The speed picked up and the rattling intensified. "Get ready!" he yelled, as if my mind could process instructions.

"What?"

Then . . . he let go of the bar. *Of me.*

I screamed again, only this time it was pure terror. My heart plummeted as I free-fell, no longer wrapped in the safety of his arm.

Down.

Down.

Down.

Just like Alice in the rabbit hole, only there were stars and firefly constellations flickering around us.

My back hit on something firm but stretchy. *The safety net.* I grasped for the ropes but the bounce sent me straight back up into the air. Nicco too, and then as quickly as his arms had left me, they were back around me, and we fell together, bouncing and tumbling across the net until we came to a halt. He landed directly over me so I wouldn't bounce away. He looked down into my eyes, and neither of us moved. We just lay there, bobbing together gently in the net. My breathing was so heavy I couldn't have spoken even if I had wanted to.

I ran the edge of my finger over his cheek, watching my hand like it was some other person's . . . because I would never be so bold. Not with Nicco.

Thump-thump.

But the way the moonlight framed his face and created shadows in his cheeks—I wanted to remember this moment forever.

My voice had the slightest tremor. "Does tearing through the air still give you the same thrill, being immortal and all?"

He gently shook his head. "But being here with you does."

Thump-thump. Thump-thump.

Breathe.

His lips were barely parted, but I could see his fangs. He wasn't trying to hide them from me anymore. *Was there really a need? They'd been inside my neck.* But still, I felt like he was testing me. Studying my every little reaction to him.

His arm slid under my back and he rolled us into the center of the creaking net, so that now I was squarely on top of him. For the first time in months, I felt like I was playing with Fire. Nicco felt more enchanting than anything else I'd ever touched. It couldn't be possible that his magic was gone forever.

His hands crossed over my lower back, anchoring me closer. A shudder ran up my spine and every urge for him I'd ever suppressed rushed me at once. But then I saw the slight shift in his eyes—the glossiness—a barely noticeable difference from their usual shimmer. My shoulders tensed.

"You should"—he blinked rapidly and then sucked in a breath —"probably get off me."

I nodded briskly.

He didn't move.

Warmth bloomed in my cheeks. "Nicco, you're still holding onto me."

"*Sì.*" He released my waist. "Sorry."

I rolled next to him so we were lying shoulder to shoulder, staring up at the midnight sky. Cicadas hummed in the background. I tried to temper my pulse, pulling air through my nose, feeling my lungs expand and then slowly release. He seemed hypnotized by the cosmos above, and I imagined him in Tuscany, hiding from his brothers with his poetry, staring up at the same moon.

"*Stella Polaris,*" he said, gazing at the brightest star. "It's the only thing that's remained constant in my life. Since I was a child. Since before . . ." His voice trailed off.

It was the most profoundly sad thing I'd ever heard anyone say. Lost for words, I turned my head to his, trying to comprehend how much he must have missed Gabe and Giovanna after they'd disappeared. The lengths he would have gone through to get them back. How much he must have hated Adeline for locking them up. *Had Emilio been the only person with him through all these years?* I looked back to the sky, trying to process the thought.

I felt like I'd known him forever, but I'd spent more time with him through his dreams than in real life . . . and yet I still didn't know how he really felt about our dreams connecting. There were *so* many things I still didn't know. I began, treading lightly. "So . . . was Galileo *really* your tutor?"

His lips curled into a smile. "When he discovered Jupiter's first four moons, he named them after me and my siblings." His head tilted to mine. "But later he fell out of fashion, and that *Marius* renamed them after Zeus's lovers." He rolled his eyes with playful exaggeration. I loved how he spoke about an obscure spat in astronomy as if it was common knowledge—maybe it had been at the time. Then he sighed. "It's kind of fitting, I suppose. My whole family was taken out, their legacy erased."

He got quiet, and I wondered if I shouldn't have brought up the past. "Nicco, you're still here. Your family's legacy lives on with you."

He rolled on his side, head propped on his elbow, but his gaze dropped in shyness.

"What?" I asked.

"That sounds exactly like something my father would have said."

"Well, clearly, he was a brilliant man."

He touched the fabric at the waist of my dress, as if studying it. And then his fingers roamed across my stomach to the curve of my waist. I wondered if he could feel how every inch of my skin reacted to his touch beneath the velvet. Another test, perhaps.

His thumb rubbed the soft fabric as his gaze found mine. "And then he would have said, 'And now go find León and *rip out his throat.*'" His eyes pulsed brighter.

I felt the blood drain from my face. I sat up on my elbows, the tone of his voice pricking the tips of my magicless fingers. "León loved you, Nicco. Do you really think he could have let Séraphine out of her cage?" I'd never mentioned something so private from his dreams. "Do you really think he could have done that to you?"

"And now you sound like Giovanna." He lay back down and I turned on my side toward him.

"I just don't think he'd have hurt her like that."

"I've had four hundred years to come to terms with it, *bella.* It's true, even if I still don't want to believe it either. León is a bastard who burrowed his way into my father's home and my sister's bed, and then into my laboratory, and finally . . . into my family's coven."

I knew he meant, *burrowed his way into my head and heart.*

"I should have listened to my intuition when I first met León." His tone softened. "I always knew there was something off about him. He was good at it, though . . . It wasn't totally uncommon back in the Old World for witches to rear children from birth as spies, but only a master could have won over my father and Gabriel. The only person who never trusted him was Emilio."

I had a hard time imagining Emilio being right about anything.

"With all my brother's faults, I must give him credit there. He was right all along about León *Medici.*"

"You were León's *world.* You, and your father, and Giovanna." I sounded ridiculous, speaking with so much conviction for a man I'd never even met, but something deep in my blood compelled me to defend Adeline's father. "He was your brother, if not in blood, in magic."

"No, he wasn't," he spat, sitting up on his elbows. "My brothers would never betray me like he did. León stole everything from us. He took my family's magic. He took *my* magic."

I wished I knew a way to comfort him.

He turned on his side, mirroring me. "Do you understand why he must die?"

"*Sì,*" I whispered because I knew it was what he needed to hear. "Nicco . . ." I proceeded with caution, knowing what kind of reaction her name usually elicited. "When Adeline locked your family away, she didn't know about any of this. She was just protecting herself and her friends and her father. *Her* family."

"Maybe. Or maybe she was trying to protect the Saint-Germain legacy, which was built on everything her father stole from us, including the Medici grimoire. Adeline was intelligent, magical, cunning . . . and extremely good at getting what she desired."

He spoke with so much conviction, it was like he needed it to be true.

"Nicco," I said softly, "I don't know where he is. I don't have anything he stole from you. All I inherited was Adeline's travel diary, a necklace, and some of her father's letters, which are nothing more than a father's loving sentiments to his daughter. If I had anything that belonged to your family, I'd give it to you. You have to believe me." The fear that gripped me caught me by surprise.

His finger dusted my cheek. "*Bella*, I do believe you. You are nothing like them. León and Adeline Saint-Germain took my family from me. You gave them back."

Thump-thump.

I was ready to stand at Nicco's side for whatever came next, but when he put it so simply, I couldn't help but feel a little bit like a traitor to the Saint-Germains, my own family.

"You broke Adeline's part of the curse—which I now suspect was cast by her coven. I wish you'd have told me that others—*your* coven—were responsible for the rest. I could have diverted my brother's rage better had I known."

"I would never put my friends in danger."

"I know." His fingers ran through my hair just above my ear. "I'm not going to let anyone else hurt you. *Io prometto, bella.*"

I nodded. "I know."

He leaned closer, and my gaze fixed on his lips. My heart pounded.

"And I'm not going to let anyone hurt you."

Then a feeling washed over me. Shame. It was like León and Adeline were there with us, watching me make promises that might betray our bloodline. Even still, I couldn't push him away. Maybe he sensed them too, he tilted his face to press his lips against my cheekbone. I shivered in a way that made me blush.

"I promise, Adele."

And I believed him because I trusted him more than I'd ever trusted anyone other than my father. I might not have known the truth about León or Adeline, but I knew in my heart that Niccolò Medici was on my side, just like I had known it the night in the attic—just as I knew in my blood that León Saint-Germain could not have killed his family.

"Adele, there is one thing I must ask that is of grave importance."

"*Hmm*?"

"Even if you don't believe that León took my family's grimoire, Callisto can *never* know that you may have any connection to it—not magically, and not through your bloodline."

My pulse whipped through my veins like an electrical current. "Callis is alive?"

He nodded. "Likely weakened from the fight and needing to focus all of his magic on sourcing sustenance, lest he starve. Adele, the Medici grimoire is the most comprehensive tome of magic ever known. From Constantinople, to Cairo, to Damascus, my family spared no expense on the quest for knowledge. If he thought there was even the slightest chance that the Medici grimoire still existed, he would stop at nothing to get—"

"I will *never* let Callisto Salazar take anything again. From me, from my coven, or from you."

His eyes held my gaze. "I know you won't, *bella*."

His utter confidence in me made me feel powerful.

Anger seethed through me. I wanted back everything he'd taken from me. "Where do Callis and Celestina fit into all of this insanity? What do they have to do with all of this?" My voice rose.

Nicco smiled. "Insanity is exactly the word I would use to describe the House of Salazar."

The House of Salazar?

"But that conversation can wait."

"For when? I have a *lot* of questions."

"And I will answer every single one of them, but first we have something much more important to do."

"Like *what*?"

"Ride the roller coaster. We *are* at an amusement park, Adele."

"There's no way it works!"

"Ye of little faith." He jumped up, bouncing me, and scooped me into arms.

I shrieked, arms tightening around his shoulders as we zipped down the path of flames.

He stopped on the platform at the Mega Zeph and lowered me into the rickety old coaster car, which wasn't much more than a rectangular box with a metal bar along the front. Then he turned away.

"Where are you going?" I asked, twisting around. I lurched as the car started moving. He was behind the coaster, arms braced against the car, *pushing* the beast with slow, steady steps forward. The old wooden track creaked, feeling the weight of the machine for the first time in close to a year.

As I watched him, I imagined the boy from my dreams of Italy, wearing fine clothes and studying medicine with León. The one who grew up in a Florentine palazzo, being tutored by legendary artists and astronomers, his father grooming him to one day take over their family coven, and now here he was pushing me up a roller coaster that looked like a relic from a zombie apocalypse. My chest shook with laughter at the absurdity of it all.

"What?" he asked, looking up.

I leaned over the edge of the car. "So, what was it like to basically be a magical Italian Renaissance prince?"

He laughed under his breath. "First of all, it wasn't *all of Italia*, just the Repubblica Fiorentina—"

"*Ooh*, excuse me! Just the *Repubblica Fiorentina*," I said, drawing out the last syllables to mimic his accent.

"And I wasn't a prince."

"Was there a palace?"

"*Sì*."

"And a royal guard?"

"*Sì*."

"And Michelangelo's statues, and Galileo's telescopes, and a secret lair for your ancient coven to practice?" I teased.

"*Sì. Sì. Sì*."

"Sounds like a magical kingdom to me!"

"It was technically a duchy. Two completely different things!"

I faced front, gazing out over the flickering outline of the park, and goosebumps pricked my arms. We were at the top of the tallest arc of the coaster. It was so dark, it was hard to tell where the candle flickers ended and the stars began. I grabbed hold of the bar as the cart slowly tipped forward.

"Do you know the difference?" he yelled, jumping over the back and sliding into the car with me.

"*Noooooooooo*!" I screamed as we dropped, his arms and legs hugging me tightly so I didn't fly away.

The old coaster shook and rattled as we roared over the curves, and the car bucked as if we might bounce off the rails completely—and yet I still felt safe, because I was with him. I closed my eyes and felt the wind blowing through my hair as we soared upward again, and then over the next peak. It was exhilarating. He was exhilarating.

On the next ascent, we began to lose momentum, and the cart didn't make it all the way up the arc. It slowed, halted a moment, and then sailed back down in reverse, gravity pulling me closer to him. We took several more dips, losing height with each one, until we slowed to a stop, the candles on the platform still flickering all around us.

I turned around in his lap. "Nicco?"

"*Sì?*"

I spoke softly, my voice raw from the screaming. "I'm sorry about what happened to your family. I'm sorry for what happened to you."

His eyes peered into mine. "*Grazie, bella.*"

"*Prego.*" I didn't even know if it was the right response in Italian, but it made him smile, and when Nicco smiled it made me feel like I'd produced alchemical gold. "Do you want to go again?" I asked, because I knew he did.

The second time, I raised both hands in the air, feeling the power of the wind and the wood and the metal of the machine. The power of his arms around me.

When we coasted to a stop and I started to stand, he didn't let go of me. There was something different . . . a neediness I'd never sensed from him before.

"What's wrong?" I asked, turning in his arms.

"Nothing's wrong."

"Then what?"

"*Grazie.*"

"For what?"

"For not letting them burn me at the stake."

Thump-thump.

As I moved the slightest bit closer, I could *feel* the rush of his heartbeat picking up speed, and it made me feel more powerful than the wind, the metal, and Mother Nature combined. I kissed his cheek—softly—but it felt like the boldest thing I'd ever done in my life. "Never."

His eyes shone like flickering flames.

Thump-thump.

"When I was on the other side of the door," he said, "lying in the dark, I could hear your heartbeat . . . It was the only thing that gave me hope."

"I can hear yours now."

"You can?"

I nodded, not having the words to explain the hope it was giving me—even without my mom. Or my magic. Or my coven.

I still felt like I was out on the little boat in the obsidian sea, under the obsidian sky, lost. But when I looked out into the darkness, now there was something different.

Now there were stars.

CHAPTER 16

HINT OF MAGIC

"Go ahead, ask me whatever you like," Nicco said, pulling me along to what used to be the Zydeco Zinger, a brass toadstool-shaped structure strung with single-seat metal swings and decorated in old-carnival style. When it was working and spinning fast enough, the seats flew out on their metal chains so that they were almost horizontal. But now each seat held one of Nicco's candles.

"I'll tell you everything you want to know about the Salazars," he said, "as long you do one thing for me."

"I thought the one thing was riding the roller coaster?"

"One more thing."

"What?"

He moved a candle from one of the swings and sat in it. "Push me."

"Uhhh, okay. You're really into this whole amusement park thing." I started to step behind him.

"*Mm-mm*," he murmured, pulling me around in front of him again. "With your magic."

"You know I can't."

"Just push the swing."

I crossed my arms.

"Adele, I realize Callisto took your *magia Elementale*, otherwise I'd have made you light every one of these candles around the park, but you are still magical. Even after the Salazars were excommunicated, even after their grimoire was burned and they were buried alive, they didn't lose *all* of their magic. Your Spektral magic is part of you, Adele. You've just buried it underneath shock and grief and guilt."

I wanted to believe him, but I'd already tried a million times to recover my magic.

"Magic must be believed in, *bella*, and it must be honed. Sometimes it comes easy, and other times it needs to be mastered. You've gotten a long way without much effort."

My face soured. He was right; I hadn't put in half the work the other members of my coven had.

"It's a *complimento*. You're a natural."

"Do you think that's why Callis was able to take it away?"

"No. I think he was able to take it because he is a four-hundred-year-old witch who had his entire coven with him." He rattled the swing. "Now, let's go."

Just talking about Callis ignited something inside me. I backed up about ten feet. Aside from the glass bulbs that would have lit up the Zinger, the entire ride, from swings to chains, was metal. I looked around the dark park . . . all the flames flickered shadows on steel and iron and brass. I was quite literally in my element.

"Focus, Adele."

This was his plan all along.

"Feel for your center."

I imagined the swing slowly moving toward me. My stomach fluttered as my fingers curled into the air. I felt for the positive space, pulling at the chair, the chains. And then I pulled harder. Grasping. Yanking. Ripping—*harder!* I screamed with frustration and fell forward, hands on my knees. Nothing.

"Again."

I stood, trying not to be embarrassed.

"Plant your feet and feel the earth . . ."

This *used* to be easy for me.

"Feel the energy pulling you to the ground, not letting you float off into the ether."

I shut my eyes and tuned out everything else until all I heard were the ambient hums of crickets and frogs in the distance.

And then there was just his voice. "Feel all of the emptiness inside of you."

I don't want to feel the emptiness. I want to feel my magic.

"Feel the darkness."

I pictured my little orbs floating around Callis, each of them enslaved, forced to obey his desires of arson.

"Push it aside and make room for your power!"

I pulled one more time, and an explosion punched me in the gut like an invisible cannonball. I went flying back, landing hard on my tailbone and skidding through the weeds.

"*Merda*!" Then Nicco was there, helping me up. "*Bella*!"

He was saying something else, but I wasn't paying attention. The area around us seemed . . . *darker.* All the candles on the Zinger had singed out. My jaw clenched.

"Are you okay? That was great!"

"What are you talking about? That wasn't my magic! I just destroyed all the Fire around us!"

I started to walk away, but before I could spiral further, Nicco's arms twisted around me. "It's going to be okay."

"I'm worse than non-magical, I'm *anti*-magical!"

He brushed my hair to my left shoulder and his breath swept my neck as he whispered, "You are very, very magical. *Lo promo, bella.*"

A tiny gasp slipped from my lips—suddenly, we weren't in the amusement park anymore. I was in the bell tower, moonlight pouring through the windows, feeling his presence so close against me. I arched my neck at the touch of his lips to the delicate skin. "*Do it, Nicco,*" I whispered.

His voice hummed against my skin. *"It will be quick. Lo promo, bella.*" I felt the graze of his teeth.

"Nicco, don't!" I ripped away, staggering into one of the swings.

"What's wrong?"

I spun around to face him. I pinched my forehead. "I'm sorry," I said, catching my breath. *That never even happened at the bell tower. It was just a dream.* His *dream.*

Horror spread across his face. "You're scared of me."

"I'm not scared of you. When you touched my neck, I just saw a flash of you—of your dream. It wasn't real."

His face flushed. "What did you see?"

"Y-you know what I saw—that night. You pushed me out of it."

"*What* did you see?"

My teeth gnashed together, not really wanting to articulate his private thoughts out loud. "We were in the bell tower, the night Emilio killed the Wolfman."

"And?"

"You kissed me."

"And?"

My face burned. "And you bit me—drank from me—"

"*And?*"

"To death."

"And?" he yelled.

"*And?*" I yelled back. "What do you mean *and?* That's it! You killed me!"

A hint of relief tugged his face.

"Then you pushed me out of your head!"

"There are things worse than death," he hissed and grabbed my elbow. He began walking me back toward the exit. "We shouldn't have come here. I don't know what I was thinking. You should be with your witch friends."

I'd never seen him this worked up before.

"You should be with Isaac."

I ripped my arm back. "You are my witch friend, Nicco, and I'm *not* scared of you."

"You should be! I'm a vampire!"

"But you were born *a witch*—"

"That person is dead."

"You are standing right in front of me!"

"I am not a witch—*I have no magic*!"

"Well, then I guess I'm not a witch either! I'm not scared of you, and I'm not leaving just because you're freaking out!" I turned and made a beeline for the Ferris wheel.

Nicco's footsteps followed behind, but I ignored him.

At the base of the ride, I started to climb the rusty ladder.

"Adele!"

I climbed faster. When I got to the cage in the center of the wheel, pure adrenaline hoisted me into it.

"Adele, what are you doing?" he shouted from below.

I glanced down, but I didn't have anything more to say to him on this topic.

"I'm sorry I yelled at you," he called out.

Sets of long metal spokes extended from the center of the ride to hold the passenger carriages, with thinner bars adjoining each set. They looked like monkey bars. I eyed a spoke that held one of the carriages out to the moon.

"Adele, don't!"

I jumped up, reaching for the first bar and caught it with a grunt, inching myself higher, just like I'd done on the playground as a kid. Only, you couldn't plummet to death at Cabrini Park.

"Adele! It's too dangerous!"

The fear in his voice would have been enough to make any rational person stop, but I swung to the second bar. Only then did I realize how tired my arms were from scaling the tower. I swung again, nearly missing the next bar but grabbed it just in time. But then the humidity-slicked metal began slipping from my fingers. I reestablished my grip and hung still for a second, focusing on my breathing. The buzz of cicadas rose up around me in waves. The weight of my body began stretching my wrists. *It's just one more bar.*

I looked down, through all the rusting metal that could skewer me on the fall, and my heart dropped into the pit of my stomach.

"Adele!" Nicco paced toward the ladder and back out, as if torn over whether to stay down and catch me if I fell, or run up and get me.

Stop looking down, Adele.

Sweat beaded my brow. I let go with my right hand and swung again, and made it to the last bar. But then, as I hung there, body violently shaking, I realized the gap was too large . . . I needed another bar or two to reach the carriage. *Shit.*

"I'm coming to get you!"

It was just a couple of feet. I rocked my body back and forth, gradually building up a longer swing.

"Adele, don't!" Nicco yelled as I swung.

I let go, flinging myself through mid-air—and crashed through the carriage door. Metal screeched as the Ferris wheel shifted under the weight of the impact. I clutched the inside of the cage, scared the wheel was going to completely fall apart and bury me under crunching metal. Death by steel. Ironic for a witch with my powers. *My former powers.*

The cage lurched again, and I screamed, my eyes squeezing shut; but then I felt Nicco cocooned over my back. The spoke dropped another notch and the whole wheel seemed to shudder, as if the Earth was opening up and sucking the machine into its core. We both froze, waiting to see if it was over.

When it seemed like the machine had stilled, Nicco helped me up and slid over to the seat. I sat on the opposite bench, unsure if we were still mid-argument.

He looked directly at me. "Please don't ever do anything like that again."

"Please don't ever tell me how I feel again." I met his gaze dead on. "I'm not scared of you."

He laughed gently. "Apparently you're not scared of anything."

I tried my best not to smile. A breeze blew my hair around my face, and I relaxed back into the seat. My shoulders burned, and my triceps ached in a way that was foreign to me. *Adele, that was the stupidest thing you've ever done in your life.* Yet, I didn't regret it. It had gotten us here. Just like the curse, and the attic, and . . .

"Why did it happen? The dreams?"

"I'm a *vampire*, Adele. My . . . *desires* might seem predatory to you, but I would never bite—"

"That's not what I meant!" My cheeks flamed. "Not why do you . . . *dream* about me." It's not like I'd never thought about him before I got together with Isaac. Although my fantasies never involved bloodshed. "I-I meant, why do our dreams connect?"

"Oh." He paused. "I don't know. It's never happened to me before."

His answer probably should have frightened me, remembering what Papa Olsin had said about dream-twinning and intertwined souls and . . . love. I prayed Nicco couldn't see my blush in the darkness.

"What?" he asked.

"Nothing."

"It's not nothing. Tell me what you were thinking about just then."

"Love . . ."

His eyes pulsed brighter.

"And magic."

Thump-thump.

Thump-thump.

"Two things that are unstoppable when combined . . . At least, that's how I imagine it." His gazed dropped to the floor. "The only thing I know about love is that your true enemies go after those you give your heart to, not you."

The way he looked at me, I'd have given anything for the power to stop time . . . to remain with him in that moment forever.

"Are you in love with Isaac?" he asked.

Invisible sandbags poured into my shoulders and chest, filling me with defensiveness. I nearly shouted that it was none of his business. Instead, I curled my knees into my chest. "I need my magic back, so I can protect the people I love."

"You didn't answer my question."

I know that. It was the question I'd been avoiding for the last three months, and now it was just here, floating around us in a decrepit Ferris wheel. "I-I don't know." It was the truth. I'm not even sure I knew what love was. "He killed my mother."

"He saved you."

"You saved me."

"From a vampire bite. He saved you from a vampire."

"You wouldn't have killed Brigitte."

"*Sì*. But he had no other choice. He could never have pulled her off, and if he'd tried, she'd have killed him instead. We both know you wouldn't have wanted that."

My eyes stung and my words came out a whisper. "I was just trying to protect Codi."

"I know, *bella*. Your mother was just too young of a vampire to handle the situation. She didn't mean to hurt you, I swear. She would have done anything for you."

I thought about Isaac lying in bed back in the shop. "I need my magic back."

"You'll get there."

I gave him a hard stare.

He leaned across the carriage, took my hand, and pulled me up. "Do you have one more daredevil move in you?"

"I'm not leaving this park until I know why Callis nearly burned us all."

"Who said anything about leaving?" He turned around. "All you have to do is get on my back."

I stepped onto the seat and looped my arms tightly around his neck, praying I had enough strength to hang on.

He pulled my legs up to his hips. "Tighter," he said.

I squeezed him with all four of my limbs, and instead of opening the carriage gate, he stepped on the rail and reached up the cage for the roof. Careful not to bump my head, he climbed out of the window. And then I was completely out of the carriage, clinging to his back. *Oh my God.* I hung on tighter, pinching my eyes shut.

I felt all the muscles in his core tighten as he reached up and hoisted us on to the metal roof. *We're going up?* The carriage rocked under his feet. He launched himself up again to grab at the side of the carriage above us, and I squeezed him so tight I could no longer feel my arms.

"Two more," he said, pulling us up the cage walls and onto the roof.

Each climb and jump was more dizzying, until we reached the highest carriage on the Ferris wheel. He climbed inside. My limbs were so locked that he had to help me off his back.

He sat on the bench, peering out. "*Perfetto.*"

My legs wobbled and I collapsed on the seat across from him.

He reached over for my hand and guided me to his bench. "The view is much better over here."

"Oh, is it?" I laughed gently.

He put his left arm around me. I pushed up the sleeve so I could see his Maleficium. I felt his body tense. I could tell it pained him to see it, but unlike the morning after the attack, he didn't try to yank his sleeve back down. If the loss I'd felt over the last few weeks was any indication of what he'd felt for the last four hundred years of not having his magic, I understood why it hurt him. Without my orbs, I felt like I was missing a part of myself.

He reached for my left arm and pushed up the sleeve of my dress, revealing the triangle. He lifted my arm to his lips, and I could hear his heartbeat as if it were my own as he kissed the center of the mark.

I exhaled, and the weight of the day went with it. When he looked at me, every impulse of my being made me want to twist into his lap. I wanted to feel him touch me. "Nicco?"

"*Sì, bella?*"

"I might not have moved your swing, but I moved a Ferris wheel."

His brow crooked. "*Sì?*"

"Why does Callis want to kill you? How is he still *alive*?"

He smiled. "*Bene, bella.* I will ruin this perfect moment by talking about Callisto Salazar."

I looked out over the twinkling park. "*Nothing* could ruin this moment."

His voice softened. "I'll tell you everything, but after, I want to know what happened while I was in the attic. Everything that he did to you. Every word that he ever said to you."

I nodded, slipped off my boots, and slid to the far end of the bench, stretching out my legs toward him. "So, Callis said the feud went back to the sixteenth century; you must have only been a few years old then."

"*Sì*, this feud nearly predates me. It certainly predates New Orleans." He untied his boots too, nudged them off, and stretched his legs out next to mine. "According to the Medicean archives, before that time, the West European Witches had lived mostly in peace with power fairly evenly distributed among five families: the Medici in Florence, the House of Norwood in England, the House of Monvoisin of France, the —What was that frown for?"

"Isaac's ancestors are Norwoods." *Annabelle's ancestors are Monvoisins.*

"New Orleans is a magical city," he said, almost able to hide the annoyance. "It's no surprise some of the great European lineages spread their tentacles here."

"Sorry. You were saying . . . Medici, Monvoisins, Norwoods, who else?"

"The Guldenmanns in Germany and, of course, House of Salazar in Spain."

Guldenmann? I know that name . . .

"My ancestors started collecting occult antiquities as soon as they first had coins to spare, so we had the greatest library in the world—and in the magical world, knowledge equals power, so we became the de facto leaders. We were also the closest to the Vatican, arguably the most powerful institution in the Western world at the time."

"Sword, cross, or coin," I said.

He looked startled for a moment, and I felt his heart skip before he recovered. "I was so terrified of having to wear that cardinal's hat." He smiled, shaking his head. "Little did I know then that my father already had plans for me . . ."

I wanted to ask him about every little detail from his dreams, but that would have to wait.

"Our grimoire contained more magical secrets than any other in the world, and family secrets were more protected than even the family jewels. It irked the Spanish that one family had more power than the other four. The Basque witches of Spain were the oldest in known European history, and they thought if anyone should lead, it ought to be them. They also believed that their magic, being oldest, was also the strongest. They thought of themselves as *the* Fire witches, and us as the bourgeoisie.

"Their elders were great healers and claimed the ability to bring life from death. Over time, they paralleled themselves to gods and became infatuated with the afterlife. It was rumored that they consorted with vampires and demonic creatures, and broke witch laws by tinkering in necromancy. My father said they became obsessed with the dead. All of this might have been overlooked, but they were ostentatious with their magic. They had such a great need to be revered that they pushed and pushed, testing the witching world's limits of secrecy by doing magic too close to the eyes and ears of the mundane.

"When the other witching households reprimanded them, they were infuriated and doubled down on their behavior. They truly believed their ancestral magic had become so great that they no longer had to abide by the rules of *il vecchio modo.*"

"The old world?"

He nodded. "Close. The old way. They were so blinded with arrogance and disillusioned by their power that when my family went on holiday in San Germano, the Basque witches formed a coup and tried to overthrow them."

The future rendezvous spot of León and Giovanna, I thought to myself. *Definitely* not saying it out loud.

"Many witches died in the battle—if you could even call it a battle—against the Royal Florentine Guard. Killing a fellow witch was enough to get your magic stripped back then, but striking against one of the Great Heads of House? And a Medici? You'd better have been sure to put a sword through his head.

"Grandfather knew that for a witch, there was one punishment worse than death, and he wanted Jakome Salazar to live to see his family fall. The Great Families decided excommunication was just punishment."

I was quite sure Isaac didn't know anything about his *Great Family.* I wondered if Annabelle did. *Was that why Callis was so interested in her?*

"The Salazar grimoire was confiscated so they could never pool their collective magic and use it against other witches again, and they were forced out of their ancient fortress in Basque territory. With all their family secrets confiscated, they barely earned enough to feed all of the children and were forced into a vagabond lifestyle. This poverty made them hate my family even more, and they blamed everything about their miserable lives on the Medici."

"Callis said your family destroyed his coven."

"His father destroyed their coven, and *he* nailed the coffin."

"Is this the buried alive part?"

He nodded. "They wandered Eastern Europe for a decade, where they were less recognizable to the local witches, and where the next generation of Salazars grew to become men and women."

"Let me guess: Callis?"

"*Esattamente.* He was the second son of his father and could easily remember the life they'd once had. He was supposedly the one who came up with the idea to go to the Archbishop of Toledo, a known witch-hunter and one of the founders of the Inquisition."

Sensing his tone darkening, I leaned in.

"Jakome Salazar confessed to the bishop that they were reformed witches and told him there were hundreds of witches across Europe—thousands of them! And that all witches were branded with a Maleficium—the mark of the Devil—which could only be seen by those who bore it. As an act of contrition, they said, it would be their honor to lead the righteous to all the diabolical ones so that they could be burned and sent back to Hell."

"Callis sold out all of the Great witches to the Inquisitors?"

"Worse, perhaps. The Salazars' true plan wasn't to burn *real witches.* This they knew would lead to their execution by the Council. Instead, they lied to the Inquisitors and pointed out dozens of innocent people in Spain, claiming that they bore the diabolical mark. Soon the frightened people began confessing to being witches just to avoid death by fire, but the confessions only solidified the Church's faith in the Jakome and his sons. Dozens of burned 'witches' became hundreds as the Inquisition swept through Europe on *La Caccia di Terrore*, the deadliest witch hunt in history."

"But *why*?" I asked, revolted by the thought. I could practically feel Callis's ropes burning against my skin. "What would the Salazars gain from having all of those innocent people killed?"

"In their twisted, acrimonious minds, they thought the Great families would bend to their threats. They sent ravens to Grandfather, saying that if he returned their grimoire, they would tell the bishop that Europe had been cleansed of the Devil. But Cosimo Lorenzo Medici did *not* bow to threats. And there was no way he'd hand them more power whilst they were on their murderous sweep. He burned their book of magic and sent back a raven's skull filled with the ashes.

"This, of course, directed Jakome Salazar's rage squarely at us. Callisto convinced the cardinals that we were heathens who hoarded sacrilegious artifacts in caverns beneath our libraries. Jakome made sure this information went all the way up to the Spanish throne, which occupied much of Italia at the time. Even the Vatican couldn't ignore such a public accusation of heresy when it came from the queen.

"The Church raided my childhood home in Florence. Mother and Father were prepared, of course, and everything important was hidden by magic beyond comprehension, just like it had been for centuries—but they also found the accusation very peculiar; the Salazars would have known this raid would be an exercise in futility.

"Their suspicion was valid. Jakome used the raid as their Trojan horse to get inside the Medici palazzo. Their plan was to kill my family and take our book of magic."

My back tensed.

"They did spill my grandfather's blood on the loggia of our own palazzo, but their eyes never saw a leaf of our grimoire before my father's blade cut straight through Jakome Salazar's throat. He delivered the rest of the Spanish witches to the Council, who unanimously agreed. Death. For what they had done to my family, we were to decide on the method. My grandmother sentenced them to be buried alive so that in their final minutes, they could feel the fear of execution they had instilled in others."

"But they're still roaming the streets of my city."

"Back then, I think not even the Salazars understood the extent of their Spektral powers. Had they not been given that particular sentence, maybe they never would have. Callisto, Celestina, and their family are still alive because they never died—all but Jakome. While entombed . . . they discovered their penchant for spirits. For over two hundred years, they drank the occupants of the cemetery, old and new. I guess it was just enough to keep their hearts beating and stave off decay, but never enough to give them the strength to break free."

"*What*? I thought you were going to tell me they found a spell to keep them alive . . . the *Elisir di Vita*?"

His eyes darkened. "Like the Salazars would be able to—"

"Wait. What do you mean, *drank the occupants*? Like people's *souls*?"

"Not souls. Spirits—your supernatural fingerprint, and everything else that makes up your ethereal form: your intellect, your individuality, and, for witches, their Elemental magic. Your spirit manifests physically in your head, while your soul manifests in your heart. Succubae consume spirits, but they can't drink souls—they could never steal your love, or, in your case, your Spektral magic—that's why I know a part of it's still inside your soul, *bella*."

"You mean, in *our* case?"

He smirked but didn't argue.

"So how did they get out?"

"Callisto would have to tell you that. Maybe plague, maybe war. Some atrocity where bodies were buried en masse, bringing hundreds of ghosts to them at once. All I know is, eventually Callisto gained enough strength to dig himself out inch by inch, and then he dug up the rest of his relatives. Their Fire had flamed out but not their Spektral magic. They reburied Jakome Salazar in the Basque family plot, idolizing him as a martyr, and then Callisto took over as the leader of their Fireless, grimoireless, unbound coven: the Animarum Praedators—Ghost Drinkers. We are lucky the ghost-drinking drains so much of their magic, so there's not much left for anything else." His voice trailed.

"Until I basically handed Callis a grimoire and my Fire, you mean?" My pulse raced. "I almost got you killed . . ."

"Callisto Salazar is *never* going to kill me, Adele."

The terror that had engulfed me when I was tied to the statue came back. The witches chanting, pulling my Fire. The fear that Nicco was going to be burned alive. I don't even know when I got up or launched myself into his arms, my own circled tightly around his neck. "I'm sorry! I just needed our dreams to connect so I could see for myself—I led him right to you." I pulled in a breath.

He held me close. "It's *not* your fault, Adele. If he hadn't been after me and Emilio, he never would have ended up in New Orleans in the first place."

"I'm glad that you did . . . end up in New Orleans."

A tremor ran through him, and he lay back with me his arms, keeping me close.

All the candles in the park burned out, until it was just us beneath the moon in the black sky, the carriage gently rocking in the breeze over the dark swamp. I realized there was only one thing I ever thought about more than my magic, and it was him.

Thump-thump.

"Adele . . . ?"

"*Oui?*"

"We can never be together."

I shot up, burning with embarrassment. "I-I know that!"

There was a little hurt in his expression. "You do?"

"Of course I do. You– you're immortal!"

The smile that spread across his face was the most humanlike emotion I'd seen him wear outside of his dreams when he was with his family.

"What are you smiling at?"

"Nothing . . ."

"Oh, no, no, no. Tell me."

"It's just that . . . you went straight to the immortal part."

"Well, it's true—"

"Rather than the blood-sucking-monster part."

"I refuse to believe you're a monster, Niccolò."

The glint momentarily outshone the permanent sadness hidden behind his crystalline eyes. "I'm giving you total amnesty to change your mind later."

"I'm not going to change my mind later."

He pulled me back. "Can we stay like this a little longer . . . please?"

"*Sì,*" I barely managed as I sank back against him. I wasn't ready to let go of him either.

As I gazed out at the glowing speck of Jupiter, reflecting on everything he'd told me, three things became clear.

The first was that Callis needed to go up in flames. What he'd done to all those innocent people was unfathomable. I didn't care if we had to trek to the Arctic to find him.

The second was that I could never let Nicco kill León— not because León didn't deserve it, especially not if everything Nicco suspected was true, but because I knew Nicco would never forgive himself if he did. I needed to protect León because it was the only way to protect Nicco from himself.

I might not know the truth about León, but I knew that Nicco was not a monster, and I wasn't going to let *Le Comte Saint-Germain* or anyone else turn him into one.

Nicco's hand grazed mine, and the touch of his skin felt like a kiss from the stars. I wove my fingers through his, and my heart walloped against my chest as if it was trying to reach the moon.

The third thing I knew was that he was never going to hold me like this again . . . I hung on to each little moment. "So which of Jupiter's moons was yours?"

His finger curled around mine. "Fourth child of my father, so the fourth moon . . . In his dedication to 'The Starry Messenger' Galileo said: *'Behold therefore, four stars reserved for your famous name, round the planet Jupiter, the most glorious of all the planets, as if they were his own children. The immortal graves of your souls have begun to shine on earth, when the bright stars present themselves in the heavens like tongues to tell and celebrate your most surpassing virtues to all time.'* One year later, my father was dead, and his four children became immortal. Galileo was always on the prophetic side. The only thing he got wrong was that we would roam the Earth and not the sky for eternity."

"What was it renamed?" I asked.

He laughed. "*Callisto.*"

"Yeah, *right.*"

"Look it up, I swear. Although, it was named after the daughter of Lycaon, not the succubus witch."

I smiled, and he began telling me another story about Galileo, his accent becoming thicker as he spoke.

The whole time, I could only wonder how all of this felt so normal . . . lying in a vampire's arms, listening to his stories about a magical time long past. Just two Fire witches with no flames, in a decrepit, swamp-filled amusement park in the middle of the night.

Everything was wrong and nothing felt off.

I thought I'd feel sad leaving the park, letting go of that perfect moment in the Ferris wheel, but I didn't. The moment carried with us on the ride home. Not the star-swept feeling of being entwined in each other's arms but something much more vast—the future was no longer about him or me; it was about us, and how our lives were twisted together in the cosmos.

I had an unexplainable feeling that tomorrow was going to be better than today, which, despite burying Brigitte, had been fractionally better than yesterday. I'd thought that burying my mother would be the worst night of them all, but . . . the dead-inside feeling had lifted, and there was something else there instead: a tingle of magic, a flicker of hope. And I wanted more of it.

I didn't have my Fire, but something about knowing Nicco would be a part of my tomorrow made me glow from the inside.

He walked me the few short blocks home. It was still dark, but I was ready for the sun. I should have been tired, but I wasn't. I was ready to start the day, even as a magicless, motherless witch.

He hung in the gateway as I unlocked the front door.

When I turned back, he was gazing up at the wrought-iron gas lamp hanging above us. "One more time," he said. "Try to use your magic."

My head fell back as I softly groaned. "And I thought nothing could ruin this night."

"Just try for me, please?"

"Fine."

This exercise was designed to fail if I had to stare into his twinkling peridot eyes. I shut my eyes and, instead of focusing the light fixture just above him, I focused on the gate behind him—something I'd opened and closed a hundred times telekinetically.

I felt for the bars.

Nothing.

I felt for the handle. *Brass. Brass. Brass. It's cool touch in the palm of my hand.* I visualized it swinging closed. I imagined myself reaching out and pulling it toward me. *Move.* Positive space moving into negative space, that's all it was. *Just. Positive. Space. Come here!*

I gasped and opened my eyes.

The gate hadn't budged.

I sighed, defeated, but Nicco was looking at me in surprise.

"What?" I asked.

"Nothing."

"I told you it wouldn't work. You don't have to look so shocked."

"Um . . . you shouldn't be so hard on yourself."

Um? Nicco doesn't say "um." He looked tense, even for him. "What? What's wrong?"

He shook his head.

"*Nicco.*"

"It worked," he said, blushing in a way I didn't know was possible for a vampire—or a Medici.

I peered over his shoulder again just to double check.

In a blur of motion, he moved his hands below his belt, and a tiny metallic noise zipped through the otherwise silent night.

"What was—?" My hands flew to my mouth. "Oh my God," I mumbled into my palms.

"This is good!" he said, trying to tug my hands away. "It's a sign! Your magic is in there somewhere."

"*It's a sign*?"

"Good to know you had a goal this time."

"I wasn't even thinking about your— *You.* I wasn't even thinking about you!" my voice squeaked as he pulled my hands away from my face.

"Maybe tomorrow, I'll wear more metal?"

"Stop talking about it, please!"

He wrapped his hands around mine. "It's only fair that I get a tiny glimpse into your head, after everything you've seen in mine."

"Adele?" Mac called from the street. We jumped apart as he stepped up to the gate.

"Dad? What are you—?"

"Good evening, Mr. Le Moyne."

But he didn't answer Nicco; he just stared at me with a perplexed expression.

Shit. Shit. Shit. It's way past my curfew. The city's curfew.

"You're . . . smiling?" He tilted his head. "I think?"

"I'm sorry! I know it's late. I was just. We were—"

"It's okay . . ." I think my mere presence outside of the house, in a dress and shoes, had caught him so off guard, he didn't know what to think. "Just be inside in five minutes." He nodded hello to Nicco as he passed between us, still with the perplexed look. "*Alone.*"

I nodded as he shut the door, and when I looked back at Nicco, the night became silently awkward for the first time. Neither of us seemed to know how to part ways. I thought about the candles and the car and all the metal at the park. "How long have you been planning this excursion?"

"You threw me out and didn't speak to me for nearly three months. I had a lot of time to think."

"Sorry about that."

He came up the next step. "It was worth it."

"It was," I echoed.

He leaned in and kissed my cheek. "*Buonanotte, bella.*"

"*Buonanotte, Niccolò.*" He stepped down to the street, and I closed the gate behind him. "Nicco?"

He turned back.

"*Grazie.*"

"For what?"

"For believing in me. And in my magic."

"Only a fool wouldn't."

The glow inside of me grew until I felt like I was beaming light as I watched him disappear down the street into the darkness.

PART II
THE GHEDE

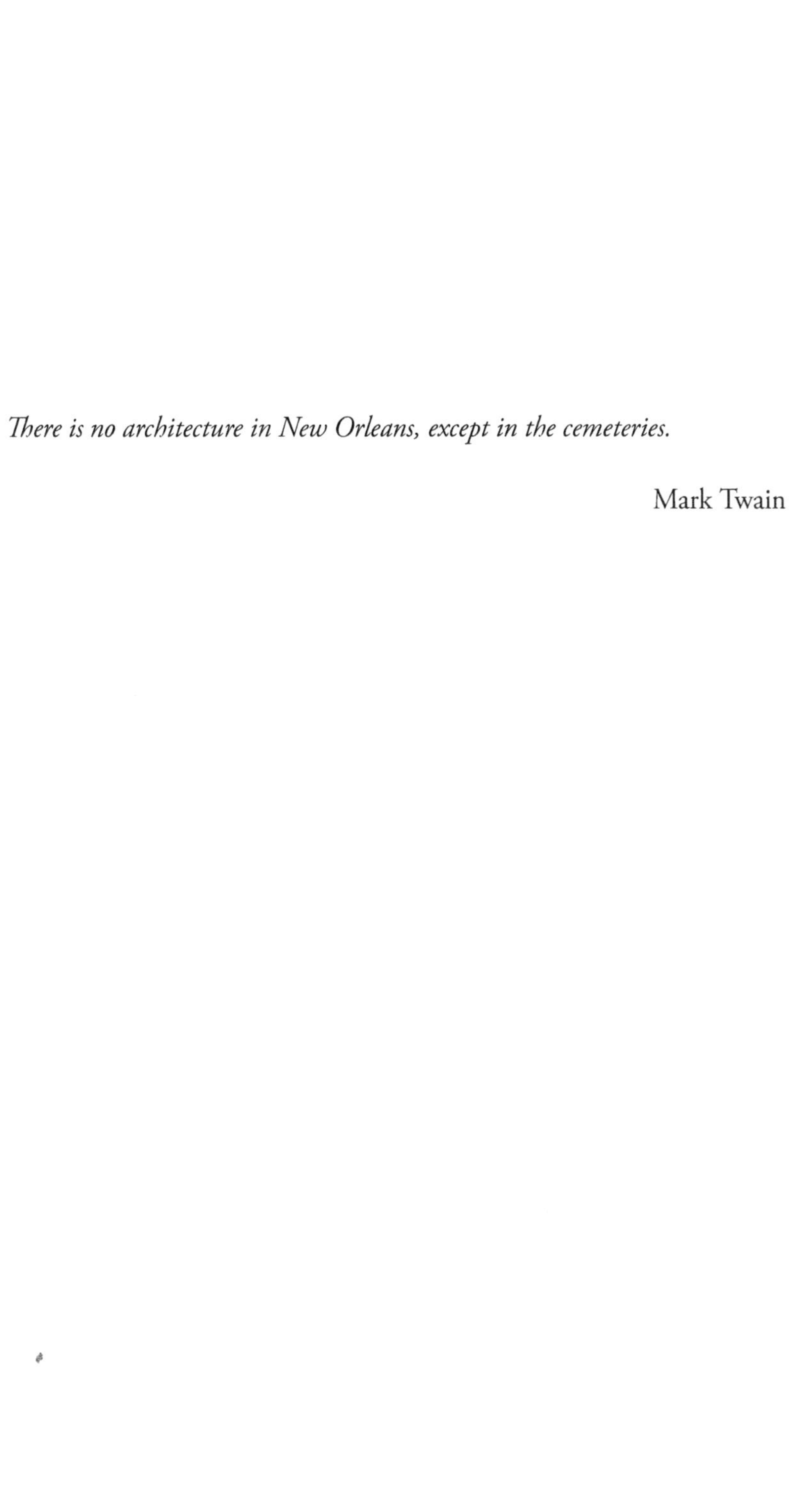

There is no architecture in New Orleans, except in the cemeteries.

Mark Twain

CHAPTER 17

POISONED DREAMS

April 20th

I shiver so violently, I wake up.

A clean white T-shirt clings to my chest with sweat. I feel around in the darkness, despite knowing I wouldn't be this cold if someone else was in the bed. The movement makes every muscle from my head to my hip ache—my neck feels like I pulled some kind of Linda Blair move in my sleep. I strip away a piece of fabric tying a poultice and lightly press the skin underneath. It's tender, but there's no wound.

My head's foggy. I rub my eyes.

Dee and Codi are in chairs next to the bed, their heads knocked together, looking like they fell asleep mid-watch.

Movement comes from the other side of the room. The silhouette of a man. When did he get—? *But then he disappears into the floor, dissolving in a* whoosh *like grains of black sand.*

A shadow slinks across the floor, thinner and longer until it stretches all the way to the door.

"What the—?"

I swing my legs over the side of the bed. My head spins, and I grab onto the bedpost.

The shadow slides out of the room, and I push myself up and stumble after it, bracing myself on the walls as I make my way down the hallway and into the taxidermy studio.

The shadow begins to morph, becoming paler but more opaque, as if flickering into being, solidifying into a snake-like shape, ten or twelve feet long. A thick, slithering muscle. White. Alive, like it has a pulse. Blooms of yellow spread over the white flesh like drips of watercolor from a paintbrush.

Hissing, the pale python slithers out the back door.

I blink several times, staring, and then I follow. A snake is hardly the most bizarre thing I've ever seen at Vodou Pourvoyeur after all. Hell, maybe it's one of Dee's relatives.

It slinks across the balcony, all the way over the courtyard, and turns the corner into the guesthouse door. So do I. Flames in the sconces guide me as the route begins to feel familiar, but my energy's depleting; I bump into the wall, knocking over a picture frame. Indiscernible mutterings come from behind the closed doors. The Possessed. *I make the final hallway turn to the master bedroom and follow the yellow slithering mass as it hisses across the floor, but I can't keep up.*

In the room, at the end, I can see Ren sitting on the floor, leaning against the bed, a despondent expression on his face and his mouth hanging open, like he's been drugged up. The snake glides through the invisible barricade.

"Ren?" My voice is scratchy, my throat dry.

He doesn't so much as blink.

"Ren," I yell, tottering forward.

The snake slithers over his legs and slowly coils around his hips and up to his chest, its tongue flicking out. "Ren!" Something about this isn't right.

The python slides around his shoulders, looks straight back at me, hisses, and turns back to Ren.

"No!" I slam into the invisible bars at the door as it slithers straight into his open mouth. "No!"

Ren finally wakes and begins choking.

"Ritha!" I scream, shaking the magical barricade. Why isn't it letting me in? Someone must have changed the spell! *The snake slides down his throat, forcing his jaw wider.*

"Ritha!"

His jaw widens and widens, until the snake has passed . . . the tip of its tail flicks behind it, and it's gone.

"Ren!" I shake the invisible bars with all the energy I have left.

He slumps over on the ground.

"Ritha, help! It's Ren!"

His eyes pop open and roll to stare directly at me—they're filled with a purple hue that almost glows.

"Ritha!"

I gasped awake, "*Ritha*!"

"I'm right here, baby," she said, a cold towel pressed to my head as I struggled for air.

My entire body shook in the sweat-drenched clothes. Bright morning light shone through the edges of the drawn curtains, stinging my eyes. Dee and Codi were asleep in the chair.

"Your fever's breaking." She removed the cloth, rewet it in the basin, and brought it back to my head.

The scent of rosewater chased the dream from my thoughts. Pain radiated from every part of my body, like I'd been round and round in a bullring. I groaned, trying to move my arm.

"Bad dream?" she asked. "One might expect as much after such a climactic night."

Each word was like a piece of a puzzle I had to put together to understand what she was saying.

"Ren," I mustered, my throat so dry, even the single syllable was difficult to produce.

She reached for a clay cup on the nightstand and helped me lean up just enough to take a sip. The warm drink tasted like cinnamon and licorice in a medicinal way and was probably no ordinary tea.

I leaned back, still in a daze, as bits and pieces of the night came and went. My gaze rested on the empty spot in the bed. "Was . . . she here? Or was that a dream too?"

Ritha patted my face with the towel. "She was here."

I sucked in a shallow breath. Just talking about her made my heart beat painfully.

"That little girl is very broken right now." She pressed the towel against the side of my face. "But she cares about you deeply. She saved your life."

I took another breath, and this time it hurt a tiny bit less.

"You're going to be fine," she said.

It felt like she was speaking directly to my heart and not my injuries. But I didn't want to hear that I was going to be fine; I wanted to hear that Adele was going to be fine—and that we were going to be fine.

"You're a strong witch and a hell of a fighter." She rested the cloth in the basin and smoothed back my hair. "And you're going to stop chasing after the Possessed, or I'm going to lock you in the room with Ren, do you hear me?" She leaned down with a questioning gaze.

"Yes, ma'am." I didn't remind her that this wound was from a vampire, not the Possessed.

"Good." She began unwrapping the dressing from around my neck. "It's not completely healed, but you wouldn't want to have seen it last night." I tried my best not to wince. "Tell me about your dream." I knew she was trying to distract me.

"I was here." I clutched fistfuls of bedding, hissing as she peeled away the last layer of cotton from the wound. "It was just like this. Dee and Codi were sleeping—" She poured something that felt like liquid fire over my neck, and my leg involuntarily kicked out. "There was a man, I think, but he turned into a shadow and then into a snake."

She paused. "What kind of snake?"

"A yellow and white python."

Her lips flattened with concern. "You're very in tune with the spirits, child. You need to embrace your Spektral magic more."

My eyes fell shut as she wrapped a fresh bandage around my neck. I didn't want to think about spirits right now.

"If it's your calling, you can't turn it off." She rested her hand over the mark on my forearm and gave me a squeeze. "Not at this point. Now, rest. There's something I need to attend to." She kissed the top of my head, just like she always did with Désirée, and excused herself.

I stared into the dim corner, eyes avoiding the bright light, riding out the waves of pain, trying to remember Adele being here in the bed with me, the weight of her body pressing against my aching chest.

The night was a shattered mirror of memories. *Adele was here. She doesn't hate me.* In my swarm of recollections, I heard Stormy barking. Birds screeching. Julie crying. Adele's voice screaming. She was scared. Bickering in French. A wave of white blonde hair.

What did Adele do to get Lisette here in a room full of witches?

As I dozed, I imagined the dangling shards of mirror in the room down the hall, gently swaying in the breeze like a chime. Soothing. *Sliding. Hissing.*

I woke up with a start.

Dee and Codi were still in their chairs, looking like they hadn't moved. I sat up, tugging the blanket off, and eased off the bed, holding my side. I felt the rug beneath my feet—this time it wasn't a dream. I swallowed the wave of pain as I stepped forward, not wanting to wake them; they'd already done enough for me.

I slowly passed a bathroom and then a bedroom. The next door was ajar. Energy pulsed from inside the room, encasing me with ghostly licks to my spine. I paused at the door, gripping the frame, and glanced into the tiny room. It was empty except for a huge altar along the back wall, with Ritha seated on the floor in front of it. Candles glowed bright in the darkness all around her, illuminating an assortment of skulls, flower cuttings, and bottles covered in beads. An enormous taxidermied owl with expanded wings cradled it all from above.

Ritha whispered something about it being "*too soon to take him.*" I wasn't ready to move, but I didn't want to eavesdrop. I pushed myself forward, down the hall and out the back door, to check on Ren.

Blinded by the daylight, I grabbed the balcony rail, covering my eyes, and clutched the banister all the way across to the guesthouse, before collapsing against the door on the other side.

The panic of the dream still ached inside my bones. *Come on, Isaac.* My breathing was heavy, but I pushed on, stumbling down the dark halls, trying to ignore the voices of the Possessed.

From behind one door came the soothing sound of a lullaby, and through another, a storm of cursing, reeking of Landry Dempsey's distinct flavor of filth—or rather, of the soul he was possessed by. Another Possessed pounded the floor, a single continuous beat, making my pulse thump.

I made the final turn. Three more steps and Ren became more than just a silhouette. He was sitting on the floor, facing out of the room, just like he had been in the dream. His dingy white shirt was open at the ruffles, and his curly hair hung like strings in his face. His expression was placid, and his lips moved as he muttered to himself.

I sank down against the wall right outside the invisible barrier.

He didn't move, but he also wasn't being choked by a snake.

"How's it going, Ren?"

"*Va bene caro.*"

"Good to know you're still kicking it too, Alessandro." I leaned my head back against the wall, and the movement sent fresh pangs of pain through the wound on my neck. "Julie will be glad to hear."

He twitched. "Have I ever told you the story about the Carter brothers?"

A laugh huffed from between my lips, and I held onto my side, trying to stabilize my ribs. Liquid oozed from my neck into the bandage. "Never heard of them."

And like that, Ren was back.

"The year was 1930, and John and Wayne Carter were a special kind of lads . . ."

"*Special.* That's one way of putting it," I murmured, my eyelids becoming too heavy to hold up.

I woke to a heavy pressure on my shoulder. Désirée's head. I glanced over and saw Codi on her other side, also sleeping against the wall. I tried to nudge her gently, so she'd lean on him, but she curled back my way in her sleep and her weight flopped back to my shoulder. "*Eff,*" I gasped with an exhale. Rather than push her away again, I adjusted myself beneath her, taking shallow breaths to try to lessen the pain. Désirée had, after all, saved my life—ten times over.

Murmurs came from the room. Ren was still awake, singing words so low they were barely audible.

I thought about that day on the street when he was possessed. "Ren, I don't know how, but I am going to find a way to save you. I swear to God."

He didn't respond, just continued to stare blankly ahead, murmuring the song a little louder now. "*Seven nights, seven moons, seven gates, seven tombs . . . follow the past, listen to lè mò, and the secrets of the dead you will know.*"

CHAPTER 18

GHOST DRINKER

I pulled the string, and the light—nothing more than a hanging bulb—clicked on. The estate attic was otherwise pitch black. A piece of fabric not-so-elegantly duct-taped over the small round window blocked both the sun and the moon, not allowing the witch to have the slightest sense of time. It had been several days since Emilio and I had captured the nameless Animarum Praedator, almost all of which he'd spent unconscious, thanks to Emilio's lack of self-control during the hunt.

His lips were cracking from dehydration, and each day the lines on his face aged him by a decade. Next would come the translucent paleness to his skin, and the contact lenses all the Animarum Praedators wore to hide their eyes would blink out, revealing his shiny, colorless irises. Silvery-white hairs would grow in, revealing the dark-chocolate dye job on the rest of his curls.

Over the years, I'd dissected the Animarum Praedators in the laboratory of my mind, trying to decipher how their magic worked, but that's the beauty of the magical world: its shroud of invisibility. There was no microscope, no x-ray, no injection of ink that would make the magic visible for examination. At an anatomical level, witches were exactly like the mundane. Knowing this didn't stop me from wanting to perform an autopsy on this witch as soon as his heart pumped its last chamber of blood.

The beat was already so faint, it was barely audible, despite my having drunk from him. I checked his pulse. It was a tight squeeze for my fingers between his wrist and the metal cuff that kept him chained to the wall.

Thump.

Thump.

Low but steady.

"It's not your time to go," I said, setting his hand down.

His eyes cracked open. "If you're so concerned about my healing, catch me a ghost with your demonic superspeed."

I smirked and inched to his right side. "Who needs a ghost?" I asked, running my fingers through his hair to the top of his head. "If I want you to heal"—I clutched a fistful of his curls and jerked his head back—"then you will heal."

Before he could blather another word, I pulled my wrist out of my mouth my wrist out of my mouth and jammed it between his lips.

After the night with Adele, I was tired of waiting.

He was going to pay for what he did to her.

They all were.

CHAPTER 19

LONE WITCH

"Moonage Daydream" scratched from the cone speaker of the old record player. I'd manually cranked the machine dozens of times while cleaning—not that I hadn't tried magically.

I'd spent the entire morning testing out my magic on every little thing, but all it'd done was fill me with frustration. At least now everything was sparkling. The entire house smelled like a meld of pine and lemon, and laundry detergent and ammonia. Everything that had happened at the amusement park felt like an ephemeral, star-dusted dream. Now it was just the day after my mother's funeral. The day after Isaac was brutally attacked by a vampire—who I'd let out of the attic.

Who I'd provoked.

I grabbed my phone and began typing.

Adele 3:39 p.m. Hi.

Is there any chance you could give me an update?

On Isaac?

Please answer, Codi. I removed a bundle of sage from the trunk where I stored all my witchy things. Throughout the day, I'd written at least eleven different messages to Désirée trying to explain why I hadn't stayed, but I never found the right words and had deleted them all before sending. I may have been deluding myself, but I felt like Isaac knew why I couldn't stay—whether my reason was right or wrong—and that he understood. Besides, I didn't owe Dee or anyone else an explanation. When I looked down, I realized my hand was cupped around the sage, waiting for it to light. I sighed with frustration and struck a match against the box, wondering if she'd really meant what she'd said. Désirée being that mad at me made me sick to my stomach.

The smoky sent of lavender-infused sage coiled into the air. I set the burning herbs into a seashell on the mantel, catching a glimpse of myself in the mirror above. The mint-green color of the crop-top sweater reminded me of Nicco's eyes.

I was more groomed than I had been in weeks. My skin glowed thanks to an exfoliant, a mud mask, and a slather of moisturizer. After I'd finished cleaning, I hadn't known what else to do. I didn't have any schoolwork left. No magic. My dad was sleeping, and I'd already eaten. Twice. So I'd just started on myself. Bubble bath. Tweezing. Eye creams. Face creams. Perfumes. My hair was so tamed I almost didn't believe the waves were mine. The blush on the apples of my cheeks made me look more lively, the mascara made my eyes look bigger, and the plum-colored lip gloss I'd bought in Paris made me look . . . pretty.

Like a doll.

And that's how I felt on the inside. Cold, and hard, and lifeless.

The girl staring back at me was some person I used to know who could produce flames from her hands and move metal with her mind. I *looked* like myself, but I didn't feel like myself.

Metal glinted behind a small stack of books on the mantel: the bronze Mardi Gras mask I'd taken off the statue Halloween night with the promise to return it. I picked it up, and purpose filled my bones.

Suddenly, I was moving out of the room, my long, black chiffon skirt fluttering up from my ankles. At the front door, I paused, hand wrapped around the metal knob, took a deep breath, and twisted it.

And then I was walking down the slate-stone sidewalk. Only . . . I felt like I didn't belong on my own street.

My pace increased to an unnatural speed as I imagined eyes staring at me through curtain slits and front-door peepholes and balcony-ferns, which I knew was insane. *How does something so familiar become so awkward? Why is the sunlight so bright?*

Clutching the mask, I ran down Chartres Street out of the Quarter, feeling the slight warble of Susannah's protection spell as I crossed Esplanade Avenue.

When I arrived on campus, I slowed. The street was in shambles, somehow worse than the last time I was here. Graffiti, mold, and wild foliage had taken over the warehouse buildings I used to call school. Houses with slumped roofs, beaten by sun and rain, lined both sides of the streets. They were too damaged even for looters to bother with, let alone for their owners to come home to and try to repair. I thought of all the people being screwed over by their insurance companies, and banks, and by all levels of government.

I spun around, searching. *Am I losing my mind?*

My bearings must be off, I reassured myself. Everything looked so different post-Storm.

I spotted the flagless flagpole a few yards away. *She is supposed to be here.* On a tuft of what used to be grass that was now a heap of wind-collected garbage.

I began pushing aside trash with my boot: a broken crate, a piece of wooden fencing. And slid away the pile of rain-sludge leaves, uncovering the metal anchor pole. *No.* Another swipe of my boot revealed the concrete pedestal it was cemented into. I'd held this piece of iron upright for my father when he'd poured the concrete.

"Where is she?" I twisted around. "Mom?" I yelled, as if a bronze statue might actually answer me.

How can she not be here? It's not like she could have just walked away! The ballerina had always been here with me, even after Brigitte had abandoned us. I was supposed to bring back her mask. "What the fuck?" I screamed, my voice echoing through the vacant buildings.

Brigitte had been taken from us twice, and now it was like she had never been in New Orleans at all. Like she'd never been in love with my father, never been my mother. Like I'd completely made her up, and the ballerina was just a figment of my imagination.

"No," I cried, picking up the crate. I hurled it into the building, smashing the remains of a window that had already met with a brick. I grabbed the piece of fence. *The mausoleum doesn't even have her name on it.* I slammed it against the corner of the building. "Why did Isaac have to kill her?" I screamed, slamming the board over and over again. "Why am I alive and she isn't?" I slammed the board so hard, pain shot up my arms to my shoulder.

I dropped the wooden post and clutched my knees, gasping for breath. I'd let the vampires back into the city. *I'd* killed my mother. *Have innocent people died because I'd opened the attic?* My gut twisted and I hugged my stomach, sure I was going throw up the meals I'd been so proud to have eaten.

Breathe.

The wave of nausea passed. I brushed off my palms, the skin now raw, and blotted the corners of my eyes where I could feel the makeup gathering.

I pulled out my phone to call my father and demand to know where the ballerina was, but then stopped myself. There was no way my father would remove her without telling me. Knowing his ballerina was gone would only hurt him.

When my breathing normalized, I started back down the street. And when a muumuu-clad elderly woman's gaze followed me as I walked past, I wasn't embarrassed. I didn't feel like a raging lunatic. I just felt like . . . a local.

My phone buzzed.

Codi 4:27 p.m. Where u at? You missed it. Insane. He went all vamp. Bloody nightmare. Pun intended.

I paused, staring at the phone like it had a disease. It buzzed again.

Codi 4:27 p.m. Just kidding. He's in good hands. The wound is gnarly, but a billion times better than yesterday.

My thumbs punched against the screen.

Adele 4:28 p.m. Have I ever told you that you are the least funny person on the planet, Codi Daure?

Codi 4:28 p.m. What, too soon?

Adele 4:28 p.m. WAY. TOO. SOON.

Codi 4:28 p.m. He's already trying to fix shit around the house. Driving Ritha nuts. He has a serious problem with sitting still. Dude is so not from around here. Zero chill.

When I laughed, a tear squirted from my eye. It was easy to imagine Isaac already wanting to go back to work one day after a near-death experience.

Codi 4:29 p.m. And hiiiiiiiiiii, BTW.

Adele 4:29 p.m. Hi.

Codi 4:29 p.m. Miss your face.

Adele 4:29 p.m. Ditto.

I kept walking, gazing around the neighborhood that I knew so well, but nothing felt familiar.

Isaac's crew worked not too far from here . . . Isaac, who spent every spare hour he had helping people. *That* was the Isaac I needed to remember now, not the one who put a stake through my mother's back.

A breeze floated through the layers of my black chiffon skirt, and I missed him. I missed the spark in the Air around him, and how he could twist my hair into crowns with his magic. I missed talking to him about everything.

I missed my best friend.

CHAPTER 20

GADJEN CIMITCHE

Désirée went from room to room in the Voodoo shop, plucking items that seemed random to me but were clearly meaningful to her. She dug through a basket of candles, pulling out only the ones that were black and purple, and dropped them into her bag. Then she selected a big silver piece of fabric with a metallic finish from a crate of scraps.

"Grab some Graveyard Dirt," she said, indicating the left-hand wall that was covered in floor-to-ceiling jars.

"Er . . . ?" I hobbled over to the wall.

"Top shelf in the middle."

I spotted an unmarked jar full of dirt and gravel. "Got it." I used a wooden barrel with a built-in step and reached for it very slowly. My left shoulder still ached, which sucked for flying.

I brought the jar to the counter and scooped some of the dirt-gravel mixture into a brown paper bag like it was granola at Whole Foods.

"*Dee*?" Codi's voice called from the front of the shop.

"In the back," she yelled. "I thought we were meeting at the brothel?"

"I just got a message from Chatham telling me to meet him here." He appeared in the doorway.

"Why?"

"Beats me. I thought you'd know." He flipped his phone around so we could see.

DAD1 3:15 p.m. Sorry for the last-min notice, son. Can you meet me at the Borges' shop in 20? There's something we need to discuss. Won't take long!

Désirée pulled her phone out of her bag and slid open the screen. "I have the same message from my gran. Without the encouraging exclamation point."

Confusion washed over both of their faces.

"They're probably negotiating your betrothal," I said. "You know, unite the two powerful witching families of New Orleans."

"Can you imagine them sitting across the table trying to negotiate that with their piles of bones and crystals?" Codi asked.

Désirée gave him a wry smile. "He'd need a crystal *palace* to negotiate that deal."

"Burn, Borges!" Codi motioned like she'd stabbed him in the heart.

"What? Like my gran would ever let me marry a non-Earth witch."

"Earth doesn't grow without Water," he said.

"*Désirée*?" Ritha called from deeper in the house. "Is that you?"

"Yes!" She hurried to stuff a fistful of dried chili peppers from a basket into her bag. "What's going on, Gran?"

The magenta curtain on the back wall opened, and Ritha entered, followed by Désirée's cousins, the duo from the Gran Bwa ceremony. Manon's braids were twisted into a big knot on top of her head. She and her brother, Remi, hung back behind the counter without a peep, but with subtle smirks. Désirée rolled her eyes at their presence.

"And how are you feeling today, my lovely granddaughter?" Ritha cupped Désirée's face in her wrinkled hand. "Any nausea? Soreness? Lapses in magic?"

"No, no, and I don't think so. I'm fine. The ride with Gran Bwa was two days ago."

"Yes, and in those forty-eight hours you've exerted yourself in exactly the manner I advised against!"

"But I feel *fine*. I've had hardly any side effects at all. Except that I couldn't heal Isaac when he— wait, do you think that's why?"

"You weren't able to heal Isaac because he was almost *killed by a vampire*. You can't bring back the dead, child!" She turned to me and removed the bandage from around my neck with the same ungentle touch as Dee. "After this, the three of you are going to *stop* tempting fate." She took a tin of ointment from her apron pocket and smeared it on the wound. "Let it air out."

"Nice to hear your voice, Ritha," Chatham said, coming through the doorway. Chatham, in his mint-green polo shirt and pressed jeans, appeared in stark contrast to the chaotic jumble of the Voodoo shop, but something about how comfortable he was, not giving a second glance to the burlap Voodoo dolls and cigarette-and-penny-adorned altars, made him seem like he fit right in. A small gold cross dangled from his ear, a match for his gold wire-frame glasses. Like Ritha, he hadn't come alone. Two fratty-looking guys with Codi's same dark hair and strong jaw were not far behind him. They both looked like they'd just come from the gym.

Dee and Codi's gazes went from the visitors back to each other.

"Is this a joint reprimand?" Dee asked Ritha, crossing her arms.

"Désirée, do not start or it will become one."

Chatham greeted the rest of the Borges, kissed his son's cheek warmly, and shook my hand. "Hello, Isaac."

Ritha lit a candle on the fireplace mantel and burned a small wooden stick, waving it around before setting it down.

"What are we all doing here?" Codi asked.

Chatham cleared his throat. "Ritha and I were talking this morning . . . Every coven from Dallas to Savannah has been alerted about the coven of succubae who can take another witch's magic. Both of our covens are scattered across the country, thanks to the Storm. Our magical resources are strained. And who knows how long it will be until we're all reunited. In the meantime, caring for the lost souls and trying to exorcise the Possessed is using a lot of magical energy that would otherwise be used to protect our covens, our families, and our legacies."

"A burden we are privileged to bear," Ritha added.

They exchanged a glance. "Until we've resolved this issue and can refocus our energy, Ritha and I have agreed that you all need to step up—"

"See," Codi said, "I *knew* we were helping! The Possessed need to be taken off the street!"

"You will *not* be tracking the Possessed anymore," Chatham nearly roared. "Caleb and Cameron are transferring to Tulane. With me, they'll handle finding the remaining Possessed while Fiona and her daughters track any roaming souls, although we hope there are none."

The shorter of the two guys grinned and gave Codi a little wave.

"Dad!"

"Codi! It's too dangerous. You don't even have your mark yet."

Codi's jaw clenched. Both of his brothers got their marks at eighteen, but he still didn't have his at nineteen.

The taller brother, Cameron, crossed his arms. "Stop stressing, baby bro. I'm sure Dad will let you come out once you get your mark."

"Yeah," Caleb said. "You should *really* be focusing on your magic right now."

"Remi and I will be joining them," said Manon, still behind the counter with Remi. Caleb crossed the room to give Remi some kind of hand-slap bro-bump.

"What?" Désirée yelled, turning to her grandmother. "Manon? She's barely even older than me!"

"Like my brothers are?" Codi said.

Manon smirked at Désirée. "Maybe you should have thought about that before dissing your *family* coven."

The voices in the room rose, and I was so used to not having a family around, I could barely keep up with the quibble.

"Enough," Ritha yelled, "before I change my mind about this."

"About what?" Dee asked, her tone flat. "We get to sit home and make memory powder for the rest of our lives?"

Ritha sucked in a breath with a face that said not to test her. "Since you three will have so much free time on your hands staying off the trails of the Possessed, we have another job for you—and I can't stress the importance of how serious this is. You're going to *gadjen cimitche*."

Désirée's eyes narrowed. "*Guard* the cemeteries?"

"It's more important now than ever to protect the spirits of those who came before us, and I *don't* need to remind you how important protecting our ancestors is to our magical line."

Protect the binding, protect the magic. I'd heard Ritha say it a hundred times. The spirits of our ancestors were the binding between witches and their magic.

"But why?" Désirée asked. "Are the Ghost Drinkers back?"

"I didn't say that."

"But you think it." Codi turned to his dad.

"We just want to be extra safe until they've been located," Chatham answered. "It's not worth taking any chances."

Ritha strode to the wooden counter, removed a pamphlet from a drawer, and handed it to Dee.

"Gran, I know where our family is buried. I don't need a city map."

"Oh, not just our family. You must protect all of the ancestors of La Nouvelle-Orléans."

"All?" Désirée asked.

"*All.* The very foundation of this city is built on the spirits who came before us. They survived fire and flood. Slave traders. Yellow fever epidemics. Segregation. Gentrification. And now the Storm of the centuries. We aren't about to lose the mystique of our grounds to these pests."

"But how do we protect *the dead*?" I asked.

"Protection spells. The Celts were quite renowned for them." She turned to Codi. "And the Choctaw."

Désirée unfolded the map like an accordion. "This is just a mundane Parish map."

"Start with the oldest cities of the dead, as they hold the most power."

Confusion twisted Désirée's face, like she couldn't tell whether this was a trick or something to be excited about.

Ritha stepped closer and smoothed down Dee's already straight hair. "Our ancestors have protected our family for the last three hundred years in this town; it's time to show them all we've learned from their grace."

"Don't worry," Désirée said, folding the map back up. "We've got this. The spirits are in good hands."

"I know they are." Ritha kissed the top of her head and then walked over to me. "Do you understand?"

"Yes, ma'am."

And when she kissed the top of my head too, a rush of warmth made me wish that my mother was here.

"You three better get started," she said. "You have a lot of ground to cover."

She nodded to the rest of the Daures. "Follow me upstairs, and I'll show you the processing room." Manon held the curtain open for her as she passed through. "It's imperative that anyone you bring in is taken straight there. The containing wards are . . ." Her voice faded beyond the curtain, and they left the way they came, with Caleb and Cameron following behind.

"I have faith in you, son," Chatham said, squeezing Codi's biceps.

Once they'd all left, the room became so quiet we heard a rodent-like scuffle in the wall. It was the kind of thing that usually made Désirée shudder, but she was too deep in thought to pay it any attention. Her eyes got squintier and squintier. "They're putting us at the kiddy table, aren't they?"

"Don't look at it that way, Borges," Codi said.

"We're on cemetery-babysitting duty, just because they don't want us to help round up the Possessed!"

He grabbed her free hand. *Brave man.*

"*Or* . . . they're giving us our own magical task. Our parents are finally acknowledging that we're our own coven—our own *mixed-magic* coven. There's probably never been one in New Orleans since Morning Star's group."

Her brow furrowed, and she glanced at me. "What do you think?"

I shrugged. "I know I'd beat Callis's ass before I'd let him touch Susannah or the spirits of any of my ancestors, or any of yours."

She nodded. "Amen."

"Damn straight," Codi said, swiping the map. "Now how the hell do we find *all* the cemeteries in the city?"

"I think I have an idea . . ." I said, and tossed Désirée the little brown sack of graveyard dirt before heading to the curtain. "Fingers crossed he's lucid."

Ren jumped up from the bed. "Did you know that there are more than *forty-five* cemeteries in the city of New Orleans?"

Forty-five? I mouthed to Désirée. How the hell were three of us going to guard forty-five cemeteries?

"We've got dead pirates! We've got dead Voodoo Queens! We've got everything in between!" He pranced to the fireplace. The glowing embers back-lit him like he was the concert headliner. "Thirty-one of our cemeteries are considered historical," he said, his volume rising. "Seven hold the Gates to Guinée. Five are officially listed on the National Register of Historic Places. Three are named for the King of France. And one was kept especially for the heathens!"

"There's a cemetery for witches?" That seemed a little on-display for our kind.

"Oh, no, son. Protestants." He laughed at his own joke.

"And that doesn't even take into account my people," Codi added. "The entire French Quarter was said to have been built on a Native burial grou—"

"Trying to take my job, Daure?" Ren yelled, as if he were the commander of a life-saving platoon. He shoved Codi's shoulder hard enough to topple him to the floor.

We tried to restrain ourselves but laughs rippled from Dee and me. This time was funny, but Ren's unnatural aggression wasn't a good thing.

Codi stayed on the floor and spread out the map. "I think we've come to the right place," he said, shaking his head. "Never has there been a person so excited about cemeteries."

I took my pen from behind my ear and tossed it to Codi.

He uncapped it. "Okay, Ren, lay 'em on us. Forty-five cemeteries. *Go*."

"Well, there's St. Louis No. 1, of course. And No. 2 and No. 3."

Codi drew little crosses on the map, marking the three French Quarter cemeteries.

"Valence . . ."

"Um?" Codi said.

"Uptown," Dee said. "Valence Street, near Napoleon."

Codi had barely marked the spot before Ren started again.

"Then there's Lafayette No. 1 and No. 2."

Codi made two marks in the same area.

"Cypress Grove. St. Vincent De Paul—three of those."

Désirée scavenged her bag for a pen as Codi scribbled, trying to keep up as Ren knelt and pointed wildly all around the map.

"Holt, St. Roch—"

"Jesus, slow down!"

"Greenwood, Carrollton, Mandeville. Then you have the Tomb of the Unknown Slave, the whole gosh darn Chalmette Battlefield, although neither of those are official cities of dead."

Désirée put stars next to those.

"Odd Fellows Rest." He pointed to an area at the top of Canal Street where several other markings were. "St. Joseph. Girod Street. Gates of Prayer. The Masonic. Hebrew Rest." He took a deep breath and rattled off a dozen more.

Codi and Dee's hands swept across the map in a frenzy of ink, trying to follow Ren's as it zigzagged across the page.

"Seven nights, seven moons, seven gates, seven tooooooooombs!" Ren sung at the top of his lungs, jumping up.

I clapped as he took a bow. Codi and Dee both leaned back, admiring their handiwork.

We all stared at the map—there were markings everywhere.

"How the hell are we going to do this?" Codi asked.

Dee licked her finger and wiped the ink off the side of her hand. "Divide and conquer?"

"Ugh," I groaned. "Having to creep around cemeteries at night with the two of you is already bad enough. I don't really want to do it on my own."

Ren paused from his song. "Oh, you won't be on your own . . . You'll be with the dead!" he roared.

Dee burst out laughing.

"Very comforting."

"Don't worry, bro." Codi hunched over, examining the map. "Julie and Stormy will protect you from the big bad ghosts."

"*Ha.*"

Désirée's lips formed a tight-pressed smile as she looked down at the map.

Ren flopped onto the bed, lying back, hands cradling his head. "Seven nights, seven moons, seven gates, seven tombs. *Sette. Sette. Sette!* You kids shouldn't be playing in the cemeteries at night! You know what they say."

"What is he going on about?" I asked.

"An old wives' tale," Codi said.

"To keep us from playing in cemeteries when we were kids." Désirée folded the map. "Basically, it says that if you ever get to a cemetery at night and the gate is open, you better turn around and run, otherwise the Baron might take you to Guinée and you'll be stuck there forever."

"What's Guinée?"

"A part of the Afterworld that goes back to the slave days. In the Natural World, Guinée was the old Slave Coast of Africa." Her tone softened. "The place where people were torn away from each other. Voodoo practitioners believed that upon death, they'd be reunited with their families in the homeland—so part of the Afterworld became known as Guinée, the meeting place of the ancestors."

"*Jesus . . .*"

The room became quiet, and it was impossible not to think about all those families all those years ago. I knew how traumatic it was for families to have loved ones disappear during natural disasters, but that was nothing compared to being forcibly separated and sold into slavery. I didn't know about my pop, but I knew that Ritha, Chatham, or Mac would have spent the rest of their lives trying to be reunited with their kids. My mom would have.

I imagined Marassa and her brother in that sugarcane field, when Makandal had let go of his sister because he was scared they'd kill her after he rose up. "Do you think Marassa and Makandal found each other in Guinée?"

"I like to think so." Her eyes became glossy. "I know it's stupid, but I have this fantasy in my head where they actually found each other in this world. That he escaped Saint-Domingue too, and made it to La Nouvelle-Orléans after the rebellions."

"It's not stupid. It's hope," Codi said. "And no rebellion would ever start if it didn't exist."

"Yeah ," she said. "That's what Guinée is . . . a lifetime of Natural-World-transcending hope."

"And in New Orleans," I added, "it's also a bedtime story for kids."

"Not a bedtime story," Codi said. "More like a warning to keep us out of the cemeteries at night."

"Because in New Orleans, kids would want to play in cemeteries at night." I slid the pen behind my ear. "The story doesn't seem so scary. Guinée seems kind of magical."

"Trust me, dude" Codi said, "when you're a kid, you don't want a bone-man taking you anywhere."

"What bone-man?"

"The Ghede." Désirée stepped to the fireplace mantel and picked up two small statuettes. She held them out to me with a little shake. "Baron Samedi and his wife Maman Brijit."

I inspected the fancily dressed skeleton figurines. "I don't think, as an adult, I want a bone-man taking me anywhere."

"Or bone-woman." She smiled, and I laughed the same uncomfortable laugh I usually reserved for Ritha. She glanced at Ren, who seemed to be in another world, and lowered her voice. "So now we just need a protection spell for forty-five cemeteries?"

"HQ?" I asked.

Codi led the way. "Tearoom. I'm not allowed to bring our grimoires off the property."

CHAPTER 21

DISCO WITCH

Codi untwisted the lock on the door and let us into the dark tearoom. "This way." He nodded to a passage behind the counter, where a light in the very back of the house beckoned.

The velvet drapes of the empty psychic booths swayed as we passed. It felt eerie. I wasn't sure if it was just because the shop was closed or because the last time I'd been there was the night Julie wrote her S.O.S on the steamy bathroom mirror.

Cold whirled around my torso and then up and around my chest. "*Bonjour*," she said, as if we had some kind of ESP. Maybe everyone in this place was psychic, including the ghosts.

"*Bonjour*," I replied.

She appeared next to me. "You are looking much better today. *Très bien.*"

"*Merci beaucoup.*" I tried and failed to mimic Adele's accent.

"There was a soul spotted," she reported. "Poppy, Lilly, and Dahlia are out chasing it. Fiona's daughters are quick on their feet, but they aren't as quick with their magic as Codi is, even without his Maleficium." She whirled past Dee, who jumped a little, and then around Codi.

"*Salut, Julie, comment ça va?*" he said.

Codi couldn't see ghosts like I could thanks to my Spektral magic, but he could sense Julie. Chatham said witch-children sometimes kept sight of certain specters they grew up with.

We followed up the back staircase, past the second-floor residential quarters—*where Callis had stayed*—and entered a long dimly lit hallway on the third floor. We walked all the way to the door at the end.

Codi threaded a set of keys through his fingers, selected a slender antique one, and slipped it in. He seemed nervous. "*Willkommen* to our humble abode." He pushed the door open to reveal a parlor room.

A fire was crackling on the opposite end of the room. The flames licked at the darkness, casting deeper shadows on the walls. He stepped inside.

As Dee and I entered, a whoosh of cold energy pushed back so fiercely that Désirée fell into me, and I had to grab the doorframe with both hands to keep us from falling.

"Sorry!" Codi said, reaching for her hand and helping her through. "Should have warned you about the threshold spell."

He reached over and clicked on a lamp, rustling the rose-colored beads that dripped from the shade. Oil paintings and black-and-white photographs in Victorian frames hung on the wine-colored walls. I looked back for Julie, but she was nowhere to be found.

Codi moved around the room, clicking on several more lamps: a floor lamp in the corner with a soft golden light, a couple on the walls and mantel, and three lampshades that hung from the ceiling like blossoming flowers. Each had strings of crystal beads dangling down from its shade, creating pockets of muted colored light. While the room remained shadowy, it felt like we were surrounded by a rainbow of lilac, amber, olive, and periwinkle.

The walls were peppered with Native American artifacts: pipes, necklaces, a bow with a matching sheath of arrows, clay plates with detailed artwork. But the centerpiece was magnificent: a ceremonial hide-skin dress, or cloak spread out in the middle of the wall, the wide sleeves pinned open, leather fringes hanging three feet long. It was threaded with colorful ribbons and silver discs like coins and covered in pictorials that looked like embroidery but were finely detailed paintings. It radiated magic.

"Family room?" Désirée asked in the way that most people would refer to a room with a flat screen and deep couch.

"Yup." He set his bag on a slate-colored rug in front of the fireplace.

The surrounding inset bookcases contained a collection that would be an occultist historian's wet dream. Geodes sparkled across the mantel. "It's so weird," Codi said. "I never thought there'd be a day when I'd be able to bring friends in here." He gestured to the plethora of large, plush pillows stacked neatly against the walls. "Make yourselves at home."

As I sat, I wondered if my family had ever had a room like this, or still did . . . *Is there anyone magical left in my bloodline?*

Dee sat across from me and set Marassa's book on the rug, still gazing around the room, while Codi went to a podium on the wall opposite the dress and removed a large tome. It was black leather with patches of dark green where the sheen had worn away. The edges were scalloped, giving it a dark femininity.

"Wow," Désirée said as he handed it to her. Enchantment emanated even from the binding. "This is not at all how I imagined Morning Star's grimoire. I wasn't sure she had one at all, given that books were more of a European thing back then."

Codi tried to respond, but she kept talking. He watched her with a half-smile.

"Unless maybe she started it? Like how Marassa created our family's book of magic. Do you want to know something cool? In her author note, Marassa said that she wrote the early pages with a bone brought over from Africa and passed down to her, which had been wrapped in a piece of bark *hidden in her grandmother's hair* when she was captured. We still have it."

"That's wicked," Codi said—and then his eyes bulged. "I mean, the bone dipped in ink slash defiance part, not the being captured part."

"*Obviously.*" She tried not to laugh.

"Anyway, you're right," he said. "This isn't Morning Star's grimoire; *That's* her grimoire." He nodded to the intricate hide-skin dress. "The pictorials tell our tribe's magical traditions. My dads would *kill me* if I brought it out of the house."

"Holy shit," I said, getting up for a closer look.

"Ritha would totally off me if I took her grimoire from the shop. Her coven uses the Borges book of shadows. Marassa was my mom's side." She gently patted her grimoire. "That's the only reason I escaped with my life when I took it."

The dress looked like something you'd find in a magical wing of the

Smithsonian. "You can touch the dress," Codi said to me. "Adele was obsessed with it when we were kids. When she was little, she used to braid her hair into pigtails, come in here, and sit on the floor and just stare at it. Eventually, Philly taught her how to sew and helped her make herself a similar one. We painted all over it, together, and she's been sewing ever since."

"I guess you've been bringing your friends in here for longer than you thought," I said, returning to my seat.

"Yeah. I never really thought about it that way before. Adele was always just a part of this place when we were kids. The rules never applied to her like they would have with non-family."

"The psychics had a hunch," Désirée said with a laugh.

I imagined Adele as a little girl looking at the dress with awe and wonder and thought about how her eyes still lit up when she saw a piece of art she was truly mesmerized by. I blinked away tears. *Christ, Isaac.*

"So what's this, then?" Dee gestured at Codi's grimoire.

"*This* beauty is from my Germanic side."

"The Daures?" I asked.

"Yep. Although, pre-Daure, we were the Guldenmanns. At least, that's what the book says inside."

Désirée scooted closer to him and skimmed her hand over the leather cover. "That's so cool." There was a softness in her voice I swear I'd never heard before. "The two grimoires in my family are so similar to each other: both Earthen, both African magic via Haiti. You have two completely different kinds of magic in your blood."

"They don't call it mixed-magic for nothing." His fingers softly tapped the cover. "You, uh, think it's cool?"

She nodded, and when he looked up their eyes locked, and suddenly the room got weirdly quiet. But then she sat up straight and switched into her usual take-charge mode. "Okay, we need a spell that can cover roughly a square city block."

What the hell was that?

"And one that doesn't require too many crazy ingredients," she added, "because we have to do it forty-five times."

I leaned back against a leather armchair, Susannah's grimoire propped on my knees, ready to find our family's best spell to guard the dead. As I flipped through the pages, I tried not to catch every time the other two casually glanced at each other.

I quickly realized that when it came to protection spells, there were loads of different kinds. Protection from demonic forces. Protection from jilted lovers. Unwanted advances. Neighboring witches. Protection for crops, houses, and ships. Various spells to keep away plague and a plethora of other archaic diseases. It was through the protection spells in each of our grimoires that you could tell what kind of lives our ancestors had lived.

The spells on the oldest leaves of the Norwood book of magic protected against the dangers and troubles of medieval life in England, while Susannah's spells were all tied to island life in Bermuda and seafaring. There were spells to protect from storm surges, gales and rain, and spells to mend sails and conjure high winds. There were protections from pirates and *for* pirates, and spells to find treasure or protect treasure. The spells morphed once Susannah arrived in New England.

Dee's pages weren't as old, but the information was. The earliest pages described bone-work for a multitude of purposes, dolls that looked more like statues, spell bags, and totems—all used for protections. It started out with similar themes as the Norwood grimoire—protections from weather, neighboring tribes, wild beasts in the night—but from there it just got more and more fucked up. There were protections from slave traders and slave masters, and spells to keep families together and to protect lost siblings. While mine had waves of protection spells against the mundane and to protect from the persecution of witches, Dee's had protections against the persecution of her entire race. When we'd learned about this stuff in history class, it had seemed so long ago it barely felt real; but I felt like I *knew* Susannah, Marassa, and Morning Star, and now the fears they'd lived with didn't seem very long ago at all.

I stopped on a meticulous drawing of a ship. I'd never seen sails like these in all the summers we'd gone sailing in Cape Cod. Each of the main masts was crowned with pockets. I read the notes pointing to them and figured out why: *Air*. They were pockets for magical air. *I guess we were sailors before we were pilots.*

A drawing of a bottle covered the next page, top to bottom—it had a long, slender neck and looked like the kind of bottle that would wash up on a sandy shore with the preserved scroll of a love note inside. The title made me sit up:

PROTECTION ON THE HIGH SEAS:
VVitch Bottle
Ile Saint-Marie

I quickly read through the list of ingredients: ginger root, dark rum, pins, needles, and beeswax. Simple enough.

At the bottom of the page there was a note in curly Old English that looked like it had been written by someone who wasn't the original spell-writer:

Draw map of route.
Drop scroll into bottle to cast protection net.

I grabbed my sketchbook and slid my pencil over a fresh page, drawing a replica.

Dee looked up from scribbling notes in her journal with an intrigued but competitive smile. "What did you find?"

"You'll see." I playfully turned up the edge of my pad. "I need to scavenge a bottle."

"What kind?" Codi asked. He must have discovered something too. He was already working on some kind of prototype.

"I don't think it really matters."

"I need a small square of fabric, ribbons," Désirée said, "and a bell if you have it."

"Roger that." He hustled out the door.

Just as I finished the sketch, he came back with a shoebox full of objects including a translucent turquoise bottle with a curvy bottom and long stem neck. The sides had burn marks and remnants of wax drippings. I pulled my bandana from my back pocket and wiped it down.

"Make sure to smudge it before you use it for spellwork," Codi said, and tossed me a bundle of sage from the box. "God only knows what it's been used for."

"Right." I imagined an old ghost or a love spell—or bubonic plague—floating out of the bottle upon opening.

Désirée capped her pen and crossed her legs under her knees.

"Okay, what have you got, Borges?" Codi asked.

She removed a square of neon-pink fabric from the box, took a couple of miniature jingle bells and some smaller crystal fragments, and put them in the center of the cloth. Then she gathered the fabric into a little pouch, twisted it, and tied it off with a ribbon. "Mojo bags," she said, holding it out in the palm of her hand. "Of course, we'd need obsidian to ward off any negative energy that comes in contact with the bag—"

"We've got tons downstairs."

"And amber—"

"At least a crateful."

"And a potpourri of other herbs to do the actual protecting. I'm thinking white sage, thistle, and anise."

"Easy enough."

"They're simple to construct, and if we make them in, er, more earthy tones—" She gave the neon-colored fabric an unforgiving look. "—they'll be easy to hide."

"You're on your own there. We're not exactly an *earthy tone* kind of household. But if you want multi-colored glitter, we've got you covered."

She snickered.

"Buuuut," I asked, "how big of an area do they cover? Would we have to make one for every grave?"

"Yeah, that's the part I'm still working out. Maybe we seal all of the gateways with red brick dust?"

"I was thinking red brick dust too," Codi said.

"I don't know anything about red brick dust, but this"—I turned my diagram around—"is a witch's bottle. An old sailor's spell to ward off enemy ships." *And by sailor's, I mean pirate's.* "Only five ingredients needed: a finger-length of ginger root, a cup of dark rum, six pins, six needles, and some beeswax to seal the bottles. The bottle traps the unwanted magic, the pins and needles impale it, the rum drowns it, and the ginger sends it away." I pushed Susannah's open grimoire toward Dee. "Check out the part about drawing a map to cast a protection net. I say we write down the coordinates of the cemetery, drop them into the bottles, and bury the bottles in the center of each cemetery. No one will ever even know they're there."

"That's pretty dope," Codi said. He looked at Dee. "Do you think we'd be able to find enough ginger root for forty-five bottles?"

"Longshot. The grocery stores barely have apples, much less ginger. We've got a bunch of powder at the shop, if that would work."

I shrugged. "No clue. So what did you find, Daure?"

He opened the German grimoire to a spot marked with a thick, dark-green ribbon and a loose page covered in his own notes. His handwriting was rigid and precise, unlike the swooping Gothic letters at the top of the grimoire page:

Hexenspiegel Zauber

"It means witch's mirror, and this protection spell turns any ordinary mirror into one. I say we hang one in each cemetery."

"How does it work?" Désirée asked.

"It traps negative energy in the glass, but get this—this is where it gets badass—it traps the energy and then reflects it back to the sender times *three*. It's like an *offensive* protection shield. If a Ghost Drinker lets their succubus powers rip on our people, the mirror is going to reflect back their own Spektral magic, draining them instead."

"Shit." I stared down at the old German words, which had been translated in the margins. "What about blind spots? If mirrors are only as good as the reflections they catch, people can sneak past them."

"That's exactly why we aren't going to use any ordinary mirrors." He tossed a golf-ball-size Styrofoam sphere at each of us and then uncupped his other hand, revealing the piece he'd been working on. The Styrofoam was covered in mirror fractals like a psychotic disco ball. "We put one of these in the center of each cemetery and bind the corners of the property to the hexenspeigel. It reflects from all angles so we have a perfect little cemetery-sized shield."

Désirée nodded, looking it over.

"That's cool, but won't it be kind of conspicuous, a disco ball hanging in the middle of the cemetery?"

They both let out a little laugh.

"What?"

Codi flicked the ball up in the air. "Dude, a disco ball is not even close to weirdest thing someone's going to find in a New Orleans cemetery."

I wondered what other weird activities went on in the cemeteries but stopped myself from asking. Some things are best left unknown.

"So we're in on the hexenspeigels?" Codi asked.

"In," I said.

Désirée was already sliding her finger down the page, noting needed ingredients.

"Yes! See? You want me and my mixed-magic in the coven!"

Dee and I looked at each other, shaking our heads. We'd already told him a hundred times that he didn't have to prove himself to us. He'd almost *died* trying to help Adele against Callis.

"So." I tossed up the ball. "Should we raid an abandoned craft store?"

"Why would we do that?" Codi asked.

"You just happen to have forty-two more of these Styrofoam balls lying around?"

"*Pfft*. Forty-two? Come with me, lady and gent."

We followed him across the hall to another room, where he flicked on a dramatic overhead chandelier, revealing a room with ironing boards, a drafting table, two different types of sewing machines, and plastic bins stacked taller than us in the corners. Bolts of fabric—velvets, sequins, holographic vinyl—stood two and three deep against the back wall. The wooden floor sparkled like a layer of glitter had been pounded into it over the years.

"Costume room?" Désirée asked flatly, as if that were a totally normal thing.

"Yeah, my dads are riding lieutenants in Bacchus . . ." He opened the door to a shallow closet lined with built-in shelves and brushed his hand over a stack of bins. "When we were kids, Edgar used to pay me and Adele a dime for every ball we painted purple so he could make grape-cluster arrangements." He tipped the top bin, and dozens of the Styrofoam balls poured out over us.

I started scooping them up as they bounced all over the wooden floor, not even pretending to know what the hell he was talking about, but made a mental note to ask Adele.

My pulse skipped. It was the first time in weeks I'd thought of her like that . . . like I'd just be able to ask her a question in the future. The bloom of hope made me feel lighter.

As I stood, I was almost dizzy. A whoosh of tingles ran from my fingertips to my palms, and I dropped the balls, taking a couple steps toward the door. My pulse thumped as if it were pulling me toward something. The sensation traveled up my arms as I entered the hallway.

"You okay?" Codi asked, following me out.

I walked to another door and twisted the crystal knob. It was locked. A chill flooded my veins. I whipped around. "What's in here?"

"Calm down. I'll let you in." He used another antique key to unlock the door. "Don't turn the light on. They don't like the light."

Huh?

The door moaned open, and I stepped in, another wave of cold coating my insides.

Just enough moonlight flooded in through the parlor window to reveal Julie sitting in a leather chair, Stormy in her lap. One hand stroked the dog's back, and the other rested on top of a Mason jar of milky water sitting on a small round side table. She looked . . . pale, if that was possible for a ghost. Maybe translucent was a better word. She didn't look as bad as the night the Salazars attacked her, but something was definitely wrong.

"Don't look at me when I am like *zhis, mon chérie*," she said, exactly like my mother had always said during chemo, with the same weak smile and weak voice.

"What the hell is going on?" I dropped to the floor by her chair. "What is this?" I grabbed the jar, raising it to the moonlight.

"Isaac, no!" she yelled, trying to snatch it back, but her hand went straight through it.

I tilted it over, and Stormy yelped as milky water sloshed through a small hole I hadn't noticed in the lid. I quickly turned it right side up. Something inside the sloshing water glowed, slamming itself into the top hole, blowing out water.

"*Jesus*!" Codi yelled. "Are you *trying* to become possessed?" He jammed a cork in the lid and slammed it tight. "You do have a death wish."

"Well, why the fuck was it uncorked in the first place?" I peered through the glass into the murky liquid. The glow became less diffuse as the water stilled, but even so, it was difficult to make out the outline of the orb.

"Because Julie was feeding it."

"*What?*"

"It's dying," Julie said. "We've already lost two of them."

"See how faint this soul is?" Codi said. "It doesn't have much longer. It's going to blink out soon."

"Wha-at?" Particles of shiny sediment sank to the bottom of the jar as the milkiness rose to the top, leaving the water in the middle clearer.

"*Zha* Possessed aren't *zha* only ones in danger," Julie said, her accent heavier, exhaustion in her voice.

"What happens to a soul after it blinks out?" I turned back to Julie. "And what does this have to do with you?"

"She's letting it leech on her spirit."

Désirée gasped from the doorway.

"I will be better in a couple days," Julie said, her eyelids drooping. "*Zha* other Royal Street spirits are taking turns too. It doesn't hurt much. It's . . . draining." Stormy licked her fingers.

"This is insane," I said.

Codi walked to a wall draped with a pair of long navy-blue damask curtains. He pulled a cord, revealing a library with a rolling ladder. Only the shelves weren't lined with books; they were lined with more Mason jars. All kinds of bottles, all with varying degrees of glow.

"Whoa," Désirée said, walking over to us, craning her neck.

Some of the jars were as bright as pulsing stars, and others looked like they contained thick clouds.

"It's insane," Codi said, placing the jar back on the shelf, "but we have to keep them pulsing while we figure out what to do with them permanently. We can't just let them blink out forever."

Forever?

Julie's chill pressed up against my back. "All these souls are someone's daughter, brother, teacher. Lover." Her chin rested on my shoulder. "Alessandro might soon be in one of these jars."

"Fuck," I whispered, under my breath. "*Ren.*" The mark on my arm was pulsing. I looked at the others. "We have to figure out how to save the Possessed. The souls. We can't keep them alive in jars forever!"

"Figuring that out is the golden plan." Codi closed the curtains. "So let's focus on protecting our ancestors, because without our magic, we're no help to anyone."

"Witchy disco balls it is," Dee said, following him out.

"They're called hexenspiegels," Codi said.

As we walked down the hallway, my fingers slipped into Julie's hand, or at least they tried to, but they fell right through.

"It's okay, *mon chéri*," she whispered. "I'm going to be fine." I felt the wisp of her lips on my cheek, and my heart pounded at the thought of losing her.

CHAPTER 22

CEMETERY DUTY

Codi stopped short in front of a Bourbon Street club whose neon light was off but had somehow survived the Storm. "Hold up." He peered at the substantial mound of garbage and broken furniture on the curb.

Désirée flicked on her phone's flashlight.

"It's perfect!" He handed me his bags and began climbing the pile of broken chairs, bar cabinets, and ten-foot-tall plastic martini glasses that I assumed were once stage props. His clambering knocked loose a long metal pole, which rolled halfway down the mound before sliding to a stop.

"Is that a stripper pole?" I asked.

"Want me to get it for you? Probably a good core workout—not that you need it." Plaster dust puffed up as chunks of drywall broke beneath his feet. When he coughed, he nearly slipped on a garbage bag coated in gunk. Désirée cringed. I wasn't sure if she was worried he might hurt himself or was appalled that he was climbing a strip club's garbage mountain.

He steadied himself, grasped the purple-painted wooden frame of a huge mirror, and gave it a couple of heaves, but he got a little more momentum than he bargained for and started to topple.

Désirée's magic grabbed the frame. "*Ew*, don't let it touch the street. This is Bourbon, for Goddess's sake."

Codi jumped down. "It came from a pile of garbage, not Saks." He grabbed the mirror from both sides, testing its weight.

"Still."

"I'll smudge it for you when we get back, princess." Codi heaved the heavy antique up and over, using his head to help balance it, and we started to walk.

"I'm less worried about bad juju and more worried about venereal diseases."

I picked up the bags. "I'm sure with all of the protection spells between the three of us, we have something for both."

"*Gross.*"

"I'm sure there's a spare mirror or ten in the brothel if you don't want to carry that beast," I said to Codi.

"No, this one's perfect. It's been outside all night."

"What does that matter?"

"Because," Désirée said, "if we're going to smash the mirror, it needs to be charged by the moonlight so we don't get bad luck."

He turned back and smiled. "Exactly, Borges."

She tried to angle her head so I wouldn't see, but I caught the little twitch of her lips.

When we got to the brothel, Codi kept his promise and took the mirror straight to the backyard for a cleaning-slash-smudging while Dee and I went to the blue room and plugged in glitter-covered glue guns.

Désirée inspected the altar she'd been building in the corner, and I flopped back onto the couch to wait for Codi. I stretched my legs, trying to relax. I wasn't exactly looking forward to creeping into the French Quarter cemeteries, and especially not the one I'd seen Adele and Nicco in. I didn't need a Magic 8-Ball to guess her mother was now buried there. Her mother, who I had killed.

My thumb rapped against my knee. I didn't want to step foot or feather in that place.

It's for Susannah, Isaac. And for the Casquette Girls' Coven. And for Brigitte's spirit . . .

I wanted to message Adele. She'd want to be part of this, especially if she thought Adeline might be in danger, or Ren. Or any of those souls back there in Mason jars. She'd felt bad about locking up vampires, for fuck's sake. *Now I knew why.* I thought about how she came to the Voodoo shop last night with Lisette to help me—*Why the hell would a vampire help her save me?* I went over to Désirée and watched over her shoulder as she twisted twine around sticks and burlap.

"Spit it out," she said, sensing me hovering.

"I was just wondering . . . When Adele—"

She sighed loudly.

"When Adele brought Lisette to the house. Do you think Lisette wanted to help because I was so bad off?"

Her eyes slanted up to mine. "Do I think a vampire helped the witch who trapped and starved her in an attic because the vampire has a heart of gold?"

"She used to be a witch too. And she was coven members with Susannah. Maybe she felt some kind of magical obligation?"

"No."

"How can you be so sure?"

"Because you didn't see the look in her eyes when she glared at Adele. Put my death-stare to shame."

"Well, then how do you think Adele got her to do it?"

"Oh, I don't know. Probably traded her own blood . . ."

I popped my thumb knuckles.

"Or her mortality . . . Or swore her allegiance to the Medici—"

"You don't really think that?"

"Or promised to be Nicco's eternal sex slave."

I scowled. "I know you don't thi—"

"Of course I don't think that!" Her tone turned sharp. "I don't know what she did or how she did it! She didn't bring me. She didn't tell me anything. *As usual!*"

"Who didn't tell you anything?" Codi asked, walking into the room.

We both turned. The mirror was now in two buckets, shattered into a million pieces.

"*Adele*," she answered.

"She texted me earlier," he said.

I froze.

"What?" Dee asked, taking the words out of my mouth. "She texted *you*?"

"What's so surprising about that? She's practically my baby sister."

"Nothing," Désirée said, dropping the sticks, holding her hands up in surrender. "This really isn't altar-building energy."

He set the buckets down at the coffee table. Every second that passed felt like an hour.

"*Well?*" I asked.

"Well, what?" He wiped the sweat off his face with the bottom of his T-shirt.

"What did she say?" I nearly shouted.

"Oh," he paused—and in that pause, my heart pounded, and I imagined beating it out of him. "She wanted to know if you were okay."

I sank onto the chair beside us in pure relief, fully aware of the dopey smile on my face. We had a plan, a bucket of glass shards fully charged by the moon, and Adele had texted asking about me.

"Isaac?" Dee said, sharing a glance with Codi. "Are you okay?"

"Obviously." My lips pressed together in a smirk. "Are we making these witch mirrors or what?"

We gathered around the coffee table and went to work gluing mirror fractals onto the Styrofoam spheres, excitement seeping from my pores, making my usually steady hands jittery.

"Shit," I yelped, burning myself for what felt like the hundredth time.

"Aren't you the one trying to go to art school?" Codi asked.

Désirée snickered, and I flicked the pearl of glue from my skin at her. "Crafting wasn't exactly an application requirement." I sucked the tip of my finger. The jagged shards made my creation look less like a miniature disco ball from the Studio 54 archives and more like a cruel torture device from a horror flick. We'd completed a dozen, four for each of us.

"Now that I think about it." Désirée held up one of the hexenspeigles. "We should do this together. Protecting the spirits of the Casquette Girls Coven, plus Codi's German witch ancestors, at least deserves the power of three, right?"

"Yeah, totally," Codi agreed. "What were we thinking?"

I leaned back against the couch, arms overhead, letting out a huge exhale.

That was the best news I'd heard all night . . . well, almost.

The three of us stared up at the iron arch of Louis No. 1's triple chain-locked gate. It was the dead of night and cool enough for the wrought-iron bars to glisten with dew, but I was still coated in a thin layer of sweat.

We weren't even inside the cemetery yet, but I could already feel my Spektral powers starting to go berserk. The pads of my toes tingled like the magic was waking up from a winter-sleep, traveling to the surface of my skin. In any other circumstance, feeling my magic enlivening was a cool thing, but when it was the dead calling it forward, it was next-level freaky.

"Adele's powers would be good right about now," Désirée said.

Codi slyly smiled at me, disappeared into a furry shadow, and slipped through to the other side. Before Désirée could scold him for turning on the open street, I pitched my arm and a gust of wind twisted her up and over the wrought-iron fleur-de-lis-shaped spikes. She shrieked with glee.

Codi popped back up to human form just as the twister touched down, and he reached out to steady her landing. I soared over the gate, spreading my wings out fully, pretending not to notice how she held onto him briefly before flinging him away.

"Don't do that again!" She turned to me, excitement still in her voice. "And aren't you supposed to not fly for a week?"

I landed back on my own two feet and stood upright. "It was ten feet."

"How did it feel? I could probably heal it the rest of the way now."

"Sore." I pulled our knapsacks through the gate and tossed Codi his. "But not too bad. You should save your energy for the spell."

"I agree," he said, opening up his knapsack. He removed two huge plastic bags and passed them to me. "The north corner gets the lavender, and the east corner gets the white rice."

Désirée opened her bag and pulled out her jar of pink salt and another with red brick dust. "South and west." She secured her bag on her back and the jars at her hips.

"Perfect," Codi said, practically bouncing on his toes as he went down the middle path. "I'll set up the circle in the center of the cemetery. Meet you there in a few."

Dee turned and headed down the left-hand path.

"You scared, Thompson?" Codi yelled, turning around.

I flipped him off and took the path to my right.

Gravel crunched under my feet. Despite the moon hanging overhead, the mausoleums on either side darkened the path. Houses of the dead, row after row, formed little streets between them: a little city of dead, as the locals called them. Algae covered the exposed bricks where cement and plaster had chipped away from some of them. At the first sight of a broken tomb entrance, I pulled out my flashlight and clicked it on, no longer comforted solely by the light of the moon.

The mausoleums all looked old, but their sizes and levels of grandeur varied. Some were six feet tall, others seven, eight, or twelve; some were topped with iron crosses, others with cement crosses, chipped cherubs, or weeping angels frozen in marble. Some were surrounded by miniature wrought-iron fences as intricate as French Quarter balconies and adorned with wilted roses or silk flowers faded from the sun.

I walked lightly, as if not to wake the residents of Louis No. 1, but as I passed row after row of looming mausoleums, my pace picked up. I tried not to think about the leathered corpses and arm-crossed skeletons inside them. I tried not to think about my mother's decaying body . . . worms crawling out of her eye sockets. And definitely not about Adele's mom being here, freshly rotting: the newest resident of this city of dead. My pace increased to a jog.

The beam of my flashlight illuminated the corner of the cemetery: two tall brick walls of what the locals referred to as oven tombs. Compartments of skeletons, stacks on stacks, each pushed to the back after a year and a day to make room for more dead.

How many ghosts live in this square block? I thought of all their spirits being sucked away, their souls released to become parasites or to blink out into oblivion, and a chill ripped up my spine. I'd never imagined there'd be something sicker than a vampire preying on a human, but somehow there was. *Souls are supposed to be forever.*

When I stopped near the oven tombs, cold wrapped around my ankles. I swung the flashlight to my feet, half-expecting to see ghostly fingers reaching out from the soft ground. There was just my sneakers, a pair of cracked purple beads, and a cigarette butt in the pool of light surrounded by darkness.

I set down the light and opened the first plastic bag. The scent of lavender billowed out from the mix of dried seeds and flower petals, and it made me miss Adele. I spread a handful amongst the weeds bursting through crevices in the brick path in the corner between the oven tomb walls, then twisted the bag closed and hurried on, wishing she was here, her hand in mine. She wouldn't think this was weird. None of these French Quarter kids thought cemeteries were weird.

Instead, I squeezed the bag of rice in one hand and the flashlight in the other and hustled down the wall of tombs, toward the next corner, shells crunching beneath my feet, telling myself that I was imagining the sweeps of cold brushing my ankles. I paused at the second corner and scooped my hand into the bag of rice. This time, cold fingers reached up the back of my shirt, and I jerked upright with a yelp, spilling rice everywhere and dropping the flashlight.

A chorus of faint giggles erupted.

I clutched the edge of the nearest mausoleum, sucking in air. Julie appeared with Stormy, whose tail was wagging.

"*Mon, chéri,* I thought you knew the feel of my touch?" Julie chirped with laughter.

"It's a little difficult to pinpoint your touch in this sea of spine-chills!"

Codi and Désirée howled with laughter from across the cemetery grounds.

"Very funny!" I yelled back to them.

Julie smiled, swirling around me in a supernatural hug.

I picked up the flashlight and headed down a row that led back to the center, wisps of giggles and chirps of ghostly laughter coming from each of the mausoleums as I passed.

"*Isaaaaac.*"

"*No need to be afraid of us, Isaac.*"

"*Isaac, we're not going to hurt you.*"

"*We're already dead, Isaac. No need to worry!*"

"*Nous sommes de ton côté!*"

I didn't want to ignore the ghosts, but interacting with them was something I needed to ease into. Just walking down the path was making me sweat again.

A phone-glow appeared ahead of me through the tombs. It was Codi, nearly finished pouring a salt circle around a tall obelisk.

"Since when are you afraid of Julie?" he asked with a wry smile.

"Yeah, I thought she was your spiritual BFF?" Désirée appeared from the darkness.

"I doubt you guys would think it was so funny if you could hear a chorus of voices calling your name as you walked through the rows of the dead."

Désirée gave an exaggerated shudder and knelt down inside the salt circle, digging through her bag.

Codi had placed three unlit white candles within the outline of the circle to form a triangle and was scattering salt, brick dust, lavender, and rice at the base of the statue. Dee poured some of the fiery rum into a tarnished metal chalice then pulled out a purple scarf and a cigar. "An offering for the Baron," she said when she saw us watching.

"Good call," said Codi. "We definitely want the Ghede on our side."

They spoke about these death lwa as if they were cousins coming over for Thanksgiving.

She placed the scarf on the ground then ripped the cigar in half and spread the tobacco leaves out, whispering words under her breath. When she lit a small candle, I thought I heard the deep, resonant voice of a man shake with laughter. And then came the slow, deep beats of a palm slapping leather—a drum somewhere out in the cemetery. I stepped out a few feet, looking into the darkness. Feathers rustled as a group of crows landed on the closest tombs, as if they were getting front-row seats to the magical performance about to go down.

I stepped back to the circle and a breeze rushed around us, fluttering my insides, just the way it always did right before we did group magic. We turned off flashlights and phone-lights, and it was just us and the moon and the one little votive lit for the Baron.

Codi rested the hexenspiegel on the purple scarf.

"All right, the moment of truth," he said, stepping back.

With each of us between the triangular points made by the candles, our hands locked together, Codi led the first verse of the spell.

Shards of glass, broken mirror, keep a watchful eye
See all, hear all, of those trying to get by.

The candles burst into flame, casting just enough light to see the shadowy smiles on Codi and Dee's faces. My pulse sped up; it was impossible not to get excited. Désirée and I joined the second verse.

Against thy enemies, you shall protect.
Reflect. Protect. Reflect. Protect.
Catch their faces, catch their spells. Magic, hexes,
see their tells,
Use their power for our gain,
Send it back, not once, not twice, three times
the pain.

The little witch's mirror began to tremble. It lifted a few inches off the ground, hovering, reflecting the candle flames. Grips tightened with anticipation.

No harm will come under your mighty shield,
To the people, to the witches, to the spirits of
this field.
Reflect. Protect. Reflect. Protect.

The witchy disco ball rose higher, and my heart pounded as the rush of magic pulsed stronger around the circle.

"Reflect. Protect. Reflect. Protect!"

A beam of filmy purple light shot up in the distance: it was one of Désirée's corners. We twisted around without breaking our grips, watching similar beams rise in the other three corners. The ground shook, and the voices in the cemetery coiled from the graves, wispy and willowy and ghostly.

Codi yelled the last line, and the mirror-ball snapped to the top of the obelisk as if locking into supernatural place. The hearty laugh returned, and the silhouette of a man with a top hat appeared, sitting on the roof of a mausoleum. My hands smashed theirs.

"Reflect. Protect. Reflect. Protect!"

A burst of light exploded from the hexenspiegel, fracturing out to the four corners of the cemetery, connecting with a loud *crack,* and we all went flying backward. I hit the gravel, skidded a couple feet down the path, and crashed into a palm tree.

I swallowed a groan and sat up halfway; the other two were smashed against mausoleums, sitting up, looking dazed but okay. The man with the top hat was gone.

"Oh my Goddess," Désirée yelled, both exhaustion and satisfaction in her voice.

I lay back down, catching my breath; I knew exactly how she felt. There was almost no better feeling in the world than doing group magic. *Only one thing really.* I blinked a few times at the sky. At first it was hard to sort the stars from the enchantment—but there was definitely a net stretching from one end of the cemetery to the other, tightly woven with magical threads of light.

I stood, swept away by the ethereal haze, twisting around to view the entire thing.

"It's sooooo pretty," Désirée said.

"Nice job, Daure."

He tried to shrug it off, but he beamed with pride as bright as the spell.

The luminescent threads slowly faded until they were almost invisible, like a spider's web against the nighttime sky, but a hint of iridescence catching the right angle of starlight confirmed its presence.

On the mausoleum to my right, swirls of shadow moved around a statue of the Virgin Mary, flowing up to her shoulders and crown. *What the?* I squinted, stepping closer, but then realized my focus was just fine —there *was* a swirl of black moving over the whole tomb. *Ants.* Thousands of them, all moving in sync. The top half of the tomb was covered in an array of "***XXX***" markings, as if someone had written all over it with a host of permanent markers, crayons, and pencils. The bottom half was covered in Storm sludge. The ants flooded over the entire tomb in a swirling, lacy pattern.

In the shadows between the tomb and its neighbor, two small purple dots glowed. The eyes grew bigger as a small black shape moved toward me. I quickly looked back at Codi to make sure it wasn't Onyx.

"*Whoa.*" Désirée stepped next to me.

It emerged out of the darkness, pecking. "Is that a . . . rooster?" I asked. Its purple glowing eyes were just like in the dream with Ren.

"Yes. And no."

What a perfectly Borges answer.

"It's Maman Brijit," she said.

"One of your relatives?" I asked, laughing uncomfortably. "Do you think she's checking up on our spell?"

"Maman is not a relative of mine. She's Baron Samedi's wife, the mother of the Ghede nation. Remember, the bone-woman?"

It clucked as it drew closer.

"Aren't roosters male?" I asked.

"Ha. Gender is pretty fluid with the Ghede lwa. Natural world societal norms are not their concern as they rule the dead."

"What is she doing here? We didn't call on any Ghede."

Codi began packing up the candles. "Well, you wouldn't put cookies out for Santa and expect him not to eat them."

"Yeah, actually, I would."

"*Pfft.* Don't compare the Ghede to Santa." Désirée turned to me, shaking her head. "The Ghede *nachon* aren't like the rest of the lwa. They don't need invitations, and they don't need Papa Legba to cross over. They do as they please and are notorious for gate-crashing. It's why you really shouldn't do rituals in cemeteries."

"Désirée!" I said. "No wonder Ritha was pissed when we did that séance—"

"Oh, hush. You got your mark. Trust me, if we'd offended the Barons, *we'd know.*"

I was unable to take my eyes off the rooster, clucking through the tobacco leaves. "There's more than one Baron?"

"Yes. And no." She walked back to the circle and began rolling up the scarf. "Baron Samedi is the patriarch of the Ghede *nachon*, the ruler of Guinée and all of the dead, and the father of New Orleans Voodoo, but he manifests in three other aspects: Baron Cimitère, who represents the grave and the bones, the transition from human form to spirit form. Baron La Croix, who represents the cross, or the intersection of the Spirit and Natural worlds, and Baron Kriminel, the manifestation of death itself."

Codi sat on a step in front of a mausoleum that had crumbled so badly it wasn't much more than a slab and a smattering of old bricks. "The Baron is the only one who decides whether it's someone's time to join the Afterworld or not—if the Baron tells you to dig your grave, you're basically toast."

I edged away from the rooster.

"*But,*" Désirée said, "as the Ghede represent death, they represent life, and the Baron and all his family are great healers and protectors. Especially for those going through transitions."

I thought about Ren's eyes in my dream and their matching purple glow. Was that what Ritha had been saying at the altar? Telling the Baron that it was too soon to take him? *Does Ren already have one foot in the grave?* My palms began to sweat.

"Like the rest of the lwa, each Ghede has a specialty. There are lwa you serve in times of sickness, and lwa you serve for fertility. Some Ghede protect kids, and others lead children to a special place in Guinée. There's a Ghede for criminals and murderers. It's not their job to judge. And their family never stops growing—"

"Yeah," Codi said, "we have a Ghede altar for those who died from queer-hate crimes."

"Exactly, there are Ghede for those who died from gunshots, cancer, AIDS. Pretty much anything."

An image of one of these Ghede lwa coming for my cancer-stricken mother painted my mind. It morphed to Julie letting the orb leech from her finger. "Is there a Ghede for parasitic souls?" I half-joked.

Dee's head snapped my way.

"What?" I asked.

She turned to Codi. "That's it! We're going to need more cigars. And coffee. And purple candles." She started pacing.

"Désirée?" I asked.

"And piman. A lot of piman."

"Dee!"

She looked back at me. "Tomorrow night. We're doing a séance to ask the Ghede what to do with the souls! Surely they'd know how to save them! Or how to take them back to the Afterworld! Like you said, we have to do *something*."

"That's like Voodoo level ten," Codi said. "I know you had a spin with Gran Bwa, but are you sure you can handle carrying a *Ghede?*"

I crossed my arms. "What would Ritha say?"

"You know what she'd say, but we don't have any more time to waste. You heard her and Chatham: their covens are *maxed* trying to protect the living. Someone's got to focus on the dead."

"My family is looking after the souls," Codi said.

"Yeah, they're finding them, keeping them alive and away from the mundane, but what's next for them?" She looked up at the sky. "*We're ready*. Our protection spell kicks ass."

"Hopefully." I said. "We won't know if it works until something trips it."

She turned to the rooster, who was teetering back to the shadows. "If Maman Brijit came to check it out, I'm sure it's on track." She slung on her mini-backpack. "Where are the Daures buried?"

"St. Roch."

"Let's go get my car. We've got eleven more hexenspiegels to activate."

CHAPTER 23

A STANDING OFFER

It took us hours to activate the rest of the witch mirrors, so I should have been exhausted afterward, but I was so worked up by all the group magic and Désirée's nonstop talking about conjuring death lwa, I couldn't sit still. I wound up in one of the rooms at the bar at two a.m., ripping out the termite-destroyed floor. I didn't really mind; I was behind on the project and didn't want Mac to think I was a slacker.

As I worked, my thoughts about magic and the Ghede and cemeteries floated away, and thoughts about Adele and her text to Codi floated in. With every pull of the crowbar, I debated messaging her. I wanted to fly over to her house and check on her like she'd checked on me. *Just be patient, Isaac.*

If she wanted you there, she'd call you.

I thought about her at the cemetery with Nicco, and I flung the crowbar down to the ground and pushed my dirty hair from my dirty face with my dirty hands.

I'd had enough for one night.

I went in search of a shower, and then a beer.

A solo pianist belted out an Elton John request from the audience.

The place was still bumping despite the late hour. I guess there still weren't that many options after curfew. Mac was behind the bar. There was something about being warm and clean and not smelling like mold that gave me a more positive outlook. I took a deep breath and walked over, sketchbook in hand.

He was helping customers down the other end as I took a seat on a stool, but he tipped a finger to me. I opened a half-finished sketch of the yellow python slithering down a row of mausoleums, pulled the pencil from my ear, and made long strokes, drawing the arch of the gate.

I felt his gaze when he came over, collecting the glasses from the bar and dumping the abandoned sips of drinks into the sink on his way. "Making progress?"

"Yeah, I'll finish it up tonight."

"Well, that's the fastest renovation project in New Orleans history."

I looked up. "Oh! I thought you meant . . ." I looked down at the sketchbook, flustered. *Of course he wasn't asking about the drawing.* "I got a pretty good chunk of floor out in one of the rooms tonight. Sorry for the delayed start. I had a pretty bad, um, fall at work and I was out of commission for a couple days."

"Don't put yourself out. It's been sitting empty for years." He reached under the counter where he kept his stash and pulled out a beer. "I moved an old twin bed into one of the rooms. It's nothing fancy—"

"I'm sure it's better than a sleeping bag," I said, trying to act casual. "And thanks, I really appreciate it."

He flipped the cap into the bin, pushed the beer across the bar to me, and then grabbed another for himself. "What are you working on there?"

I sat up taller, letting the sketchbook rest on the bar.

He slid a small candle over and turned it around. "Well, damn, son, you can draw." He flipped back to the previous page, to an image of Julie and Stormy, and I internally panicked.

My mind raced back through the sketches. A crow, then a page of skulls, then Jade, and then *Adele*. And Adele. And Adele. He flipped more of the pages. As he paused at Jade, my brain spun in New York hyperdrive, trying to think of what I could say when he flipped it again.

Oh, she's your daughter? I met her at a coffee shop. And then what, Isaac? You met her and now you obsessively draw her?

He flipped back to the current work-in-progress, and I released a breath. "You've got a real talent for capturing movement."

I took a sip of the beer, mumbling thanks. *You taught me.*

He looked up, his eyes catching someone behind me, his gaze following them across the room. I turned.

Nicco was walking in front of the stage to the corner where Gabe and the girls were sitting. I turned back.

Mac nodded to him. "You know that guy?"

I wanted to seize the opportunity to put a bad taste in Mac's mouth, but the way his eyes were slightly squinted made me think he could figure it out for himself. He'd been a bartender for a long time; I'm sure he had good instincts when it came to people.

"He's been hanging around my daughter," Mac added.

My leg jerked. *More like stalking your family for centuries.*

"He's hard to get a read on."

He's a manipulative, bloodsucking bastard.

"How *old* is he?"

"Ancient," I said, through my clamped jaw.

He laughed. "Well, then I must be a dinosaur. What's ancient to you? Nineteen?" When I didn't immediately respond, a flick of concern hit his words. "*Twenty*?" I sensed him panicking a little, probably wondering how old was too old for his almost seventeen-year-old daughter. If I lied and said he was twenty-eight, would Adele be banned from seeing him?

"I-I don't know," I said, suddenly feeling nauseous. "I don't know too many people in New Orleans." My fingers picked away at the label on the bottle.

"He's not around as much as his brothers, and he rarely ever drinks, but I don't know . . ."

He drinks blood. *Trust your gut. This guy is* bad news.

"You know when you can just feel that someone has something to hide?"

Yes.

"Something makes me want to go over there right now and grab him, put him in a cannon, and send him to the moon." He leaned on the counter, eyes still glued on Nicco. "But I can't get this image of Adele out of my head—"

"What image?"

"Standing on our stoop last night, with him. Smiling . . . It's been so long since I've seen her smile."

The breath sucked out of me. *Last night?*

He sipped his beer and looked at me like he owed me some kind of explanation. "Her mother . . . passed a couple months ago. It's been a dark time. I've barely been able to get her to eat, much less smile." He pushed his hands over his face, rubbing his forehead.

I no longer felt like I was in my own body. *I killed this man's wife.*

He leaned back down on the bar, a bemused expression softening the lines in his forehead. "Beh, he's probably just nervous around me, and that's what I'm picking up on."

"Why would he be nervous around you?"

"He likes her."

I took a long pull on the beer, wishing there was enough to drown myself.

"Trust me, when you have a kid, you'll always know when someone's into her. This primal thing happens inside you that makes you want to sprout tiger claws so you can slash and drive 'em away."

My thumb swirled through the condensation on the bottle. Had he ever thought that about me?

"I shouldn't say that. I trust my daughter. She has a good head on her shoulders, and she's a good judge of character." He paused. "It just kills me seeing this much darkness hanging over her. She has this beautiful sensitivity—"

I know she does. It feels like beams of sunshine.

"Just like her mother did—"

I clenched the bottle and blinked hard.

"And I hope nothing ever changes that inside her," he said with a sigh.

Did I change that inside her?

He looked back down at the sketchbook, and I let my eyes shut, pushing back the tears as they formed.

"There's something familiar here," he said.

"It's not one of my best." Words came out of my mouth despite feeling completely detached from my body. "I was just messing around. I have stuff that's edgier."

"Son, I'm not saying your work's pedestrian, just that I find it easy to connect with. *Hmm* . . . I can't put my finger on the feeling." His gaze traveled back to the corner behind me, but this time a small smile painted his mouth.

"What?"

He nodded. "Look for yourself. She's been staring over here ever since you sat down."

I turned around and instantly met Lisette's gaze from across the room. She sat up straighter. Her long, wavy blonde hair cascaded over her arms, draping her pale cleavage, which was barely contained by her pale-pink shirt—er, vest? There was still something about her that made her look like she'd stepped out of the eighteenth century.

She smiled, and I turned back around.

Mac let out a little laugh. "You have a girlfriend?"

"Huh?" I broke an instant sweat.

"A girlfriend. Do you have one?"

I tried to hide the hesitation in my voice, but I couldn't look him in the eye as I lied. "No."

"You gay?"

"What?"

"It's okay, son. It's New Orleans. You're free to be whoever you want."

"Yeah, but—I'm not gay."

"Hmm. Well, you're something, because I've never seen a young man scowl when a girl that pretty smiles at him."

She's not a girl. She's a monster who once clawed your daughter's throat like a savage animal.

He looked at me like he was still waiting for an explanation.

God, get me out of here, please. Anyone. I looked back at Lisette, pretending to be interested, watching as the people around her stole glances. She was easily the most beautiful girl in the room.

Martine saw me staring and raised an eyebrow.

I faced forward again. "She just doesn't do it for me."

He held his hands up in surrender. "All right. I can't fault a man for knowing what he wants." His gaze dropped to the drawing one more time. "I've got an idea. Tomorrow afternoon, come by my house. I do a mentorship with my daughter in my art studio. She's working on her fashion illustration portfolio."

My pulse charged like a hit of drugs was rushing into my bloodstream.

"You don't know many people in town. You could work on your drawings, and I'll give you some feedback. And you can meet Adele. She could use a little human interaction. You look like you could use a friend."

This was it. An in. *This is everything I wanted.* But then I imagined walking into the studio and Adele freaking out when she saw me. I didn't want to invade her life. I imagined Nicco making her smile, leaning in to kiss her.

I slid the pencil behind my ear and closed my sketchpad. "This is just a hobby."

"Well, you should take it more seriously. There's a lot of raw talent on that page."

"Thanks. I appreciate it, but I'm going to Colombia in the fall." *What the fuck, Isaac?* "I've got FEMA work. And the reno here. I don't want to waste your time."

He scribbled something down on a napkin and handed it to me. "It won't be a waste. If you change your mind, it's a standing offer."

It was their address and a time. It was the invitation back into his life.

Back into Adele's life.

"Thanks," I stuffed it in my pocket. I swigged the last sip of beer, left a tip on the bar after he refused to let me pay, and hustled back to the crowbar in the garçonnière.

Soon, I was coated in a thin layer of debris dust.

But this time, ripping out the rotten wood wasn't enough. I took the sledgehammer to the more stubborn boards. The two candles on the fireplace mantel gave me just enough light to punch through the right things.

Every other swing was at Callis.

Every other swing was at Nicco.

"Isaac?" a soft French voice called from behind.

A bolt of supernatural sensation went up my spine and I spun around, gripping the sledgehammer.

She hopped back a small step. In the dark, Lisette looked like a pale, innocent doll: a wraith in a long white skirt and pink vest.

"What do you want?" I asked, tossing down the tool.

"I . . . I just wanted to see if you were okay."

"Why did you do it?"

"Do what?"

"*Save me.*"

She didn't say anything. I crossed my arms, waiting.

"Adele didn't tell you?"

"I'm asking you." It was none of her business what Adele did or didn't tell me.

"It doesn't matter."

"*What* did Adele promise you?"

"It's between me and her."

"Get lost."

She didn't budge.

I picked the sledgehammer back up and turned back to the floorboards.

"Isaac?"

I strode straight over, tool in hand, and got in her face. I didn't care if she was a girl; she was a vampire. "I am *never* going to forget what you did to her. I am *never* going to forget that Annabelle is a traitorous monster, just like you. Maybe it's your Aether blood?"

Her gaze edged up to mine, and all I saw was the sadness in her eyes. A need to comfort her rushed me from inside, an overwhelming urge to apologize for being an asshole.

The corners of her lips perked up. I could feel the blood pulsing through my veins.

Her blood, I suddenly realized. It was her blood pulsing through my veins.

I pulled back, and she sucked in a breath through her nose.

"Thanks for saving me," I said. "Now get the hell out."

Her face hardened.

"You're a traitor." I pushed against every impulse pumping through my blood. "To your coven, your magic, and your sisters."

Her fangs snapped out with a hiss.

"You can't play both sides, Lisette. Go back to your clan of monsters."

She whipped away, her long white skirt blowing behind her.

CHAPTER 24

SLEEPLESS

A feeling of normalcy blanketed the warmly-lit parlor room—the kind that could only be sparked by those who shared your blood.

Across from my brocade armchair, Gabriel and Martine lounged on the green velvet couch, her legs draped over his lap, his hand draped over her legs. They were conversing in French, him trying to convince her that learning English was a worthwhile endeavor. They were so engaged with each other, it seemed they'd forgotten the witch slumped over in the chair to my left, unconscious from blood loss. But Lisette had not . . . she stood in the far corner by a window, brooding in the dark, her gaze shifting between the moon and the witch.

To my right, Emilio was leaning back in the armchair nearest the fireplace, soaking up its warmth, his legs outstretched and ankles crossed. He was utterly still, except for thumbing a gilded page of *Moby Dick* now and again as he read. It was the calmest I'd seen him since Brigitte's death, thanks mostly to the large quantity of magical blood he'd drunk—two witches in one week.

I studied the witch's sharp jawline and prominent nose. His mop of curly brown hair hung down to his shut eyes. It wasn't a face I recalled seeing in our home before. We'd tied them up back then, but this time there was no need for restraints. There was only one of him and five of us, all but one of whom had taken a drink.

Had he been in this parlor room before, back in the 30's when Emilio and I had nearly rid the world of the Animarum Praedators for good?

During the Depression, the Vieux Carré was destitute—death lurked on every corner, and fresh ghosts were abundant. We'd starved them for weeks but were still unable to drain them completely of the spirits they'd drunk so that they might meet final death. But this wasn't 1930. After the most recent attack, even with their magic regained, Callisto and his coven members were weak and destined to spend the rest of their existence—which would be short—seeking out sustenance.

It was almost serendipitous that Callisto had dove into the middle of everything here in New Orleans: we'd be able to eradicate all our oldest enemies in one whirl.

Sì, Adeline's curse would be broken, the Salazars would be taken out, and then we would find León and avenge our father. The tips of my fingers tingled with phantom magic. Every week was becoming a tiny bit more surreal. Every day, every night felt a step closer to realizing the string of images that had been crystalizing in my imagination throughout the years. They were all versions of the same fantasy, one that involved my family being back together, León being dead, and us returning to Italia with the *Elixir della Vita* to live in peace. Nothing more, nothing less. Giovanna used to be a part of this fantasy, but I was fairly certain I knew exactly where she was. *Riposi in pace, mio angelo.*

Now I just had to orchestrate it all in such a way that I kept Adele unscathed—without anyone knowing I was protecting her.

Thump-thump.

I gazed slowly around the room, taking notice of whether anyone was surreptitiously watching me. I tried not to even think about her unless I was alone, as if my brothers might be able to just pluck the thoughts from my mind.

The key to a successful deception was living it—thinking it, breathing it, believing it yourself—but now, as I sat with my family in the house we'd acquired centuries ago to stalk Saint-Germain, I imagined myself back in the attic, lying in the darkness, her cheek pressed to the other side of the wooden door. Her magic unhinging the locks. Unhinging me.

Thump-thump. Thump-thump.

I wiped my sweatless palms over my dark denim pants, pushing the image out of my mind and locking it away with all the other fantasies I'd never speak of. *It's just the residual effect of the blood exchange.*

I refocused on my family and on how remarkably different the house felt compared to the previous three hundred years of visits, when it had been just me and Emilio. Even as a cold-blooded, half-cursed vampire, Gabriel brought a warmth to every room he entered. Vampirism made him no less magnetic than when he was a human, which perhaps made him all the more dangerous. I smiled inwardly, wondering whether he even had to use his thrall to hunt or if everyone just naturally did anything he asked of them. If I didn't know better, I'd have thought he was once an Aether.

Martine wore the smile I'd seen so many girls wear as my brother's fingers strummed their waists. And he seemed equally infatuated with her.

I'd found Martine to be a nuisance at first, but beneath those pouty lips, perfectly placed finger curls, and delicate French words was a cunning woman who knew exactly what she was doing, no matter how playful or innocent she seemed. She would have gotten along famously with my sister.

Gabriel's arms closed around her, bringing her closer so his nose could tease hers.

I wondered if he loved her.

I wondered what it would be like awakening to a world that had cured the plague but where vampires still hid in the shadows; where men had been to the moon but hadn't cared enough to reinforce their antiquated levees; where men had merely looked on as Mother Nature obliterated the inhabitants of a cultural epicenter.

Lisette shifted in the corner. At first I thought it was Gabriel touching Martine that drew her from the shadows, but then I saw the twitch in her fingers, how the tip of her tongue grazed her bottom lip ever so slightly. Her gaze swept one last time from the moon to the witch.

Lisette and Martine were from the same era, both French, blonde, and bound to my brother, but I guessed Martine must have been closer to Gabriel's age upon human death and Lisette closer to mine —or younger, perhaps. She was the exact opposite of Martine. Under her cool and hardened exterior and her wild, wavy white hair, she was scared and lost, still trying to figure out if this life was something she could survive. Martine, my brothers, and Giovanna had never seemed afflicted by such feelings, but I recognized it in Lisette's eyes as she padded over to the warm-blooded creature in the room. I remembered that feeling—it had probably taken me a century to overcome it.

She leaned close to the witch, and his head fell to the side, his lashes fluttering, giving me a glimpse of his faux-mahogany-brown eyes. His foot kicked out when he saw me. *Panic.* But then she brushed a curl of hair from his face and tilted his chin up to her.

He relaxed back in the chair, his fear melting away as he focused on the angelic girl standing over him, her soft curves and delicate smile a distraction from the engorged fangs hiding beneath her lips. The way her fingers caressed his face drew the attention of the room.

"Please help me," he begged.

She slid onto his lap, straddling him, and I wasn't sure who was more aroused, the man beneath her skirts or the pair on the couch across from me.

As her mouth drew closer to the witch's neck, his hand found her hip, and I fought the compulsion to bind him to the chair. I'd warned him to remain still, but the closer the Animarum Praedators came to death, the less effective our thrall. His fingers curled into the fabric at her sides, but before I could stand, her teeth sank into his neck, her grip so tight on his shoulder that his arms fell back. As she fed, pulling his body closer to hers, Martine relaxed into Gabriel's chest so they could both watch, views unobstructed.

As the witch began to whimper, even Emilio looked up from Ishmael and Captain Ahab.

The witch's head fell to the other side, his gaze landing on Gabriel. "She's going to kill me," he pleaded, mistakenly thinking Gabe was the soft one in the room.

There were no soft ones in a room of vampires.

Gabriel moved Martine aside, rose from the couch, and stepped behind Lisette. He placed his hands on her shoulders, as if feeling each movement of her muscles as she swallowed, and then he brushed her hair from her eyes and gently coaxed her in French not to stop until she was satisfied.

"She's . . . she's going to kill me," the witch whimpered.

"Tell us where Callisto is," Gabriel said, his voice calm but without any promise that the witch would be spared by the exchange of information.

“You’re all going to die,” he choked out.

Lisette unlatched her jaw and sucked in a gasping breath, her mind still not having fully processed that she no longer needed air to live. “How is he still alive?”

Gabriel pulled her up, making sure she was steady after feeding from the magical blood, and led her to the couch.

“Both the frustrating thing,” I said to her, “*e il fantastico* thing about the Animarum Praedators is that they take forever to die.”

Gabriel resumed his position beside Martine, who pulled Lisette down to the cushion. She tugged the sleeve of Lisette’s dress and kissed her bare shoulder. “How long?” Lisette asked, trying to hide the resulting shiver.

“It’s hard to say.” My fingers steepled together. “It depends on how old they are and how healthy they are.” And by “healthy,” I meant how saturated they were with the spirits of the dead.

She settled into Martine’s chest, and Martine settled back into Gabriel as if they’d been together for centuries. Technically, they had been.

The witch tried to sit up, but the numbing effects of Lisette’s venom had kicked in and his head rolled back instead. “Callisto and Celestina are *very old*,” he said. “Older than even you hellions.”

The older the Animarum Praedators were, the stronger, meaning the longer they could go without feeding. Each spirit they consumed increased their lifespan a few weeks—each was a piece of gauzy duct tape stringing together their current moment to their next, creating a strange form of temporary life that both held the potential for immortality and yet, ironically, balanced on the edge of oblivion. My hypothesis was that the remnants of all the spirits they drank had some kind of regenerative effect on their vital organs.

“And what decade did they pick you up?” I asked him.

“Wouldn’t you like to know.”

“You still don’t seem to understand that death is your fate.”

“You still don’t seem to understand anything about our coven.”

“If you think Callisto is going to storm a vampire compound to save your pathetic life, you have no idea who you’re doing magic with. Or is it that Callisto has convinced you that you’re truly immortal?”

The look in his eyes told me just how far his delusions ran. And *that* was Callisto Salazar's true gift: that of the orator. A magical quality seemed to encase his words, convincing people to follow him. To join him. To believe their magic would be something the world had never seen. His words were more enchanting than his magic.

The witch's head rolled, but the hint of a smile on his lips told me that not only was Callisto's coven in town but that they were planning something. "As soon as everyone gets a little ghost in their belly," he whispered, drunk on delusion, "we're going to be the most powerful coven the world has ever seen."

"I don't care if we have to watch over every grave in this city until you all starve," I said. "We will."

He smirked. "Have fun playing in the cemeteries. When we're through, the mundane will worship us, the magical will bow down before us, and the dead will rise from the ashes to follow us."

Emilio peered up from his book. Our eyes locked for a brief moment before he returned to the whale waters.

"Spoken like a true Salazar," I said. "Delusional hyperbole."

The witch forced himself to sit back up. I was beginning to place him. Not from New Orleans, but from Europe. *Vecchio Modo.* He was a Salazar by blood. A cousin perhaps.

"*You,*" he said, "*all* of you will be dead. You'd already have faced final death, if it weren't for that witch-girl."

The threats to my family breezed past my ears; all my focus was on his last words. I felt all four pairs of vampire eyes turn to me.

Not a single muscle in my face stirred.

"Her magic is marvelous," the witch continued.

A plan began forming in my head, one of the abandoned warehouses down by the river being the perfect spot to interrogate him freely without arousing my brothers' suspicion. I needed to know if all Callisto wanted with Adele was her magic and our location. *Or does he want something more?* I mentally strummed the chair. *Don't say anything, Niccolò.*

"The feeling of her Fire flowing though my veins," the witch said.

My jaw clamped.

"If I let myself feel it too much, it's orgasmic."

Screw the warehouse—

"Well," Gabriel said. "I guess Callisto got everything he wanted from her?" It was as if he was pulling the words from my throat. "He took her magic, and he knows where my brothers are. That girl is useless to him now." He smirked. "He's free to come and get us."

"*That girl?*" the witch said. "Didn't she rescue you all from eternal entrapment? She should feel blessed Callisto has taken such a keen interest in her. Someone has to cleanse her mind of your brainwashing. He'll get through to her."

My nails dug into the arms of the leather chair. "What does he want with her?"

Gabriel turned a slow smile to me, which was echoed from the girls—taunting, teasing smiles. Only then did I realize I'd asked the question out loud. I glanced at Emilio, hoping he was so deep into Ishmael soliloquies he'd missed it. He was staring straight at me. *I've made my first mistake.*

"I don't give a shit what Callis wants with her," the witch said. "All I know is she's valuable to him alive. You, on the other hand, are more valuable dead. There's a big reward for bringing him a Medicean head."

Emilio's book closed with a loud *thud*, and in an instant he was directly behind the witch, one hand on the top of his head and the other beneath his chin. "I'm trying to read," he said, and snapped the man's neck.

He'd said the words with such sincerity, I could believe he'd really just broken a man's spine for interrupting the seafaring adventures of *Moby Dick*. Knowing Emilio's history of erratic behavior, it was quite possible.

He pressed down on the witch's shoulder. "I hope you enjoy that perverse immortality now."

The witch's head lolled my way in agony. "What's it to you what he does with the witch-girl?"

Emilio turned in my direction too. "Yes, Niccolò, what's it to you?" he asked me in Italian.

Gabriel looked at me with a playful expression.

This was the exact moment I'd been desperately trying to avoid with my brothers.

"You know what she is to me." I pushed my nervousness down into the pit of my feet. "León's descendant."

"Oh, okay," Emilio said. "Just León's descendant then . . ." He moved from around the witch. "I wonder if she's much like her mother?"

My face tensed into a curt smile as he stepped toward me.

"I wonder," he said, "if she smells like her mother?"

Don't give in, Niccolò. It's Emilio. This is what he does.

"Does she too smell like lavender, *fratellino*?"

I stood, my lips pinched as the smile became increasingly difficult to hold, and we met in the middle of the room.

He leaned closer as if to share a secret and lowered his voice. "I wonder if she *feels* like her mother?" His breath dampened my ear. "I wonder if she tastes like her?"

I fought against giving him exactly what he wanted, and let the rage pulse through my blood instead, focusing on the breaths streaming in and out of my nose.

His pale-green eyes matched my own with the same shiny glint. Our mother used to say that the glint in our eyes meant different things: Gabriel's eyes shone brighter when he was up to mischief, the sparkle in Giovanna's gave away her love, and mine was all the Medicean wonderment. *"Niccolò,"* she used to say, *"your curiosity will one day change the world!"* In Emilio's eyes, that glint showed he was brave and fearless. It was a mother's way of saying "psychotic."

I looked straight into that glint and with the steadiest of Italian, said, "If you touch Adele, I will rip your heart out of your chest with my bare hand, *fratello*."

His eyes pulsed bright.

We'd barely gotten along as humans, and as vampires we'd learned that the best way to co-exist was to stay away from each other. Emilio was erratic, impulsive, and vengeful. Everything I hated about being a vampire, he loved. The power. The lack of regret. The gluttony and the blood.

The corners of his mouth turned upward. "There's my baby brother," he said in a lighthearted tone. But the flare in his eyes told me he knew I was serious.

And I was. Deadly. None of them were going to touch her.

Gabriel folded his arms across his chest. "Is our baby brother in love? Should we have a party?"

"I'm not in love with her," I snapped.

"Invite her over?" His tone was warm and playful, but still it set me alight with concern. "Get to know her family?"

Emilio glowered at him.

"Oh," Gabriel frowned and made the sign of the cross. "*Riposi in pace, Brigitte.*"

"We have not been this close to finding León or the Medici grimoire since Adeline Saint-Germain was alive!"

All four of them stared at me with surprised expressions, little smiles peeking out, but the room remained silent. No one argued with me.

"I'm not in love with her," I repeated.

"Of course you aren't, Niccolò," Emilio said, stepping closer. "Love is about happiness. Joy. Ecstasy." He twisted behind me. "Lust."

"You," I scoffed as his arms draped over my shoulders, "lecturing me on love?"

"We all know you don't allow yourself to feel any such things—"

"Emilio, enough," Gabriel said.

"We all know that your heart is so mummified by centuries of self-loathing, you'd never be so indulgent as to allow yourself even the tiniest little pleasure." His fingertips tickled up the crook of my neck and I swatted them, stepping away, but he hugged me closer.

"Other than to feed . . . when *was* the last time you've touched a woman? Or a man? A vampiress? Anything with a pulse?" His hand traipsed my hip. "Do you even remember how—" Just as I went to knock him away, he grabbed my crotch with a forceful squeeze; I froze. "To use it?"

My jaw clenched. "Emilio, *get off of me.*"

"Of course you aren't in love. You wouldn't. Even. Know. How. To be."

"I just want to get our family's magic back," I said, swallowing the threats on my tongue.

He released me with a brotherly shove. "You're not a witch, Niccolò. You're a vampire. Get over it. It's been over four hundred years."

"You're a prick, Emilio." I grabbed my jacket from the chair and headed for the door.

"At least I still know how to use mine." He laughed. "I'm sure I could get León's whereabouts out of her faster than you could, so if that's all you're after, why don't I pay her a vis—"

I spun to grab him, but Gabe leaped between us just like when we were children; the only difference now was that I wasn't scared of Emilio anymore.

"We're all just teasing," Gabe said. "Save it for the Salazars. Let's all just go to bed and continue the search tomorrow night. It's nearly daybreak."

"*Buonanotte.*" On my way out, I shot Emilio a glare and slammed the door behind me.

"Leave him be," Gabe said in our native tongue.

I started to take off, but then I paused, listening through the wood.

"And you stop getting his hopes up. The girl is nothing. The Elixir is nothing. Just because Callisto got his magic back, doesn't mean we can too. We're *vampires*. It's *not* possible."

"Yet it's all he's cared about for the last four hundred years. You are *not* going to take this away from him."

"What do you know about Niccolò? You've been locked up in an attic for the last three centuries, thanks to your little fling with a Saint-Germain."

A compulsion to check on Adele washed over me, and I turned and hurried on, through the parlors and down the stairs. What the hell would Callis still want with her? Could he know about her connection to León? Could he be after our grimoire? *L'elisir di vita?* Another possibility made my heart knock violently against my chest: what if he wanted to hurt her for no other reason but to get to me? *He knows she saved me. Protected me.*

I shoved the front door open and whipped out to the street, pacing off in the last darkness before dawn.

"Nicco!" Gabriel's voice called out from the gate. I turned and waited for him to catch up. "You can go to sleep if you'd prefer," he said. "I'll stay up and make sure nothing happens to your precious *bella*."

He knew exactly where I was going.

I studied his face, his breath, looking for any sign of deception. He wasn't mocking me. I inherently trusted Gabriel. I also knew how much he wanted this curse broken.

"*Grazie*, but I'll take some air." I kissed his cheeks.

Little did he know that simply by staying awake, I was protecting her—from seeing too much. Ever since she'd rescued me that night, every time we slumbered, I wanted to sink into the dreams and give myself over to her. Give everything. All of our family secrets.

All of *my* secrets.

But I couldn't.

It was too hard to fight the connection in my sleep, so I went out and walked until the sun rose, until I could feel a tiny pulse beating inside my chest, next to my heart—a lingering effect of giving her my blood. Unless it was . . . the magic. All I knew was that the tiny pulse faded to almost nothing when she slept.

So I walked until she rose.

CHAPTER 25

PSYCHIC SANDWICH

April 21st

I twisted the lock closed and leaned against the inside of the door, inhaling a huge breath of coffee-bean air at Café Orléans. I'd made it. *And without running into anyone.*

The midday sun poured through the windows, and the stress of leaving the house melted off my shoulders like warm butter.

Someone walked past the shop window—a stranger—and I hurried behind the counter, leaving the lights off.

I hadn't spoken to any of my friends or regained my old life, but I'd gotten up at a decent hour, showered, and eaten, and now I was packing a perfect pull of espresso, as if it hadn't been months since I'd last been in the café. Waiting for the coffee to drip, I found myself staring at the corner table, as if expecting to see Isaac sitting there with his sketchpad. How many pages had he filled in the last couple months? How many sugar-free vanilla lattes would it take for Désirée to stop hating me?

I poured the espresso into a cup of steaming water, snapped a photo, and messaged it to my father, as if I deserved a medal for leaving the house.

He sent back the sunglasses smiley.

As I sipped the fresh cup of coffee, my phone buzzed again.

Dad 12:16 p.m. Don't forget. Studio session this afternoon. I'll show you the next step with your chainmaille dress. We'll get some of the bulk out.

Adele 12:17 p.m. Maybe you could go to work a little later and we could eat dinner together?

Dad 12:18 p.m. It's a date. I'll take the chicken out of the freezer.

Maybe spending some time in the studio would help me with my Spektral magic?

The back door to the courtyard shook open, and Sébastien hurried through. "Mon petit chou!" he said. "What are you doing here?"

It was strange seeing him in a suit jacket with his jeans. I guessed he was trying to make a good impression at the new job. "Just getting some coffee."

He leaned over the counter and kissed both of my cheeks.

"And . . . I was thinking, I could really use a job. Maybe I could re-open the café?" He of all people would understand the desire for employment. "I don't care about the money," I added.

"Adele." He took the coffee out of my hands. "You already have a job."

"I— But I don't—"

"Nope," he said, taking a sip. "If you don't go over there right now, I'm going to message Codi and tell him you're here."

"You wouldn't!"

He pulled his phone from his pocket and dangled it. "Do you want to tempt fate?"

"You don't even believe in fate."

"But you do." He smiled. "I'm so sorry, but I have to run. Going to be late." He took my coffee with him as he walked toward the front door. "À bientôt!" He twisted back and held up his phone one more time.

I sighed and began making myself a new coffee to go, nerves already jittering even without the caffeine.

Breathe.

⚜

The familiar bells jingled as I opened the door at Bottom of the Cup.

I stood there, staring at everyone, wondering how something that used to be so humdrum was now making my hand holding the coffee cup shake. Chatham was dusting the bookcase near the fireplace, and Edgar was rearranging merchandise on the opposite wall of glass shelves: balls, wands, and other items made of crystal that sparkled under the track lighting. Chatham's sister, Fiona, was at one of the zodiac tables, absorbed in flipping through tarot cards.

Codi, who was reading a schoolbook behind the counter, looked up. "Adele!" The attention shifted to me like dominos falling. He jumped from around the counter and had almost reached me before he stopped, as if he'd suddenly remembered I was made of fragile glass.

"Hi." I nervously shifted my weight. "How is everyone?"

If they were trying to hide their shock, no one was succeeding. I felt like an alien beneath their gazes. I figured it was best to get straight to the point. "I was hoping . . . to get my job back?"

Edgar's hand went to his hip. "Baby, you cannot have your job *back;* it never went anywhere. It was yours. It is yours. It will be yours until you don't want it."

"It will probably still be yours even after that," Codi said with a grin.

Edgar fluttered past him and scooped me into a hug.

"Hot coffee," I cried, holding the cup out as far as I could as he pulled me tightly to his flabby chest.

Chatham and Fiona bustled over, and before I knew it, I was in the middle of a psychic-sandwich. Their energy felt like warm honey, and the buzz of bees, and velvety flower petals.

"You look marvelous, Addie," Fiona said, stroking my hair. "Did you make that dress? Love the cerulean; it brings out your eyes."

"*Merci,*" I squeaked, nodding. Not that I had been so productive lately.

"Our little girl is back," Edgar said.

"I'm not a little girl," I groaned.

"Our young lady is back."

Codi's hand wrapped into mine, and he tugged me out of the witch-pile.

I set my coffee on a table, along with my bag, totally fine, but then when I looked back at him, emotion struck me and I jumped into his arms, suddenly having to blink back tears.

He lifted me off the ground with his hug. "I'm so sorry, Adele."

"For what?" I choked out.

"For not being able to do more that night."

My arms tightened around him. "It wasn't your fault."

"I know, but still . . ." He hugged me tighter, and I didn't understand how we weren't still little kids anymore, leaving out drinks of water on leaves for fairies. He set me down. "Thank you for saving my life."

I nodded, wiping my eyes. "I was really trying not to cry today."

"Sorry," he said, blinking his own tears away.

A sniffle came from the peanut gallery. Based on the lack of questions being thrown at me, I assumed he'd told his parents everything that had happened.

"Thank you, Adele," Edgar said, cheeks wet. "Our little boy."

Codi's face scrunched. "I'm five-eleven and a hundred and eighty-six pounds."

"Our big boy."

"Adele," Chatham said, and then gazed at me tenderly. "Your mother loved you so very much."

My lungs pinched. I really didn't want to talk about her. "*Merci,*" I whispered. "*Milles mercis.*"

Fiona looked shaky, like she was holding it all in for me, and Edgar began dusting a perfectly clean table, trying to hide his eyes.

I sucked back a huge breath with a smile. "Okay. That's enough for today. I'm sure there's important metaphysical work to be done."

"Right," Codi said, "let's all get back to those emergency dream interpretations."

Fiona hiccupped a laugh and moved back to the table.

"I'll put on some tea!" Edgar's kimono kicked up as he walked behind the counter to the massive selection of Mason jars filled with loose teas.

The huddle dispersed, and I followed Codi behind the counter. Papa Olsin was leaning on his cane in the dark hallway, watching us. I paused to greet the Daure patriarch, and he took my hand in between his, which were dry and rough from decades of shuffling cards and whittling the pipes sold in the shop. "This event may have ended in tragedy, Addie, but we will always do everything we can to protect you, like our own."

"Thank you, Papa." I squeezed his hand back.

His dark brown eyes shone as he grinned and then turned around with his cane and shuffled back down the hallway, behind the curtain, to his booth.

And then, as much as I asked everyone not to fuss, they did. There were tea and cookies and cakes, and little chocolates in the shape of mermaids that they were thinking about selling, each one with pink hair and crystalized-ginger shell-bras. They were so pretty that at first I didn't want to bite into them, but I hadn't tasted sugar in so long, I gobbled them up like a piglet.

"How has business been?" I asked.

"We can't complain, given the circumstances," Chatham said. "They've finally managed to reopen the airport, so there's been a trickle of tourists."

"*Disaster-spectators*," Edgar added, aghast.

I sipped my tea. "Disaster-spectators or not, I bet Ren is glad."

Everyone's movements slowed to a stop.

"What?"

Chatham stepped closer. "Baby, Ren is . . . sick."

"Like, he has the flu?"

"*Hmm.* Something like that."

"What do you mean? Is he okay?"

"He's going to be fine; we're making sure he's taken care of. No need to worry. Codi will take you to see him later, okay? For now, let's just try to have a normal afternoon."

"Says the witch in the psychic shop eating sparkly mermaid boobs," I said, and everyone laughed. It was the first time I'd ever acknowledged the witch-factor with them—it felt strange and invigorating and normal all at the same time.

"Exactly." He kissed the side of my head. "A normal day. We'll leave you two alone. I'm sure you have a lot of catching up to do."

The adults filed down the hallway and dispersed, leaving me alone with Codi for the first time since I'd dragged him into the convent the night of the attack.

"How's your leg?" I asked.

"Oh, totally fine." He gave it a good slap. "Désirée's Spektral magic is tiiiiight."

"Dee got her mark?"

"Yeah, she— It's— It's healing. I forgot you weren't . . . you know." He bit off the head of a mermaid. "Do you have yours?"

I nodded, lifting my sleeve to show him. "It was that night at the convent. Maybe even thanks to you. They say being around other witches can help bring out your magic, right?"

"I . . . uh . . . I can't see it."

I angled my arm closer.

"No, I don't have . . ." His voice deflated.

"Oh!" I quickly rolled down my dress sleeve. "I'm sorry."

"Don't be. I'm suuuper excited for you." He let his head fall back and groaned. "But that means I'm officially last. My brothers are never going to let me live this down. The baby of the group has her Maleficium before me."

"I'm not the baby of the group! I'm the same age as Dee." *And Annabelle.*

"You're the baby of our original group of French Quarter rats." He was referring to his family, me, and the Michels.

"Fine," I said, giving it to him.

"So, what's your Spektral?"

"Telekinesis. I guess I'd had signs of it all along, but I wasn't using it correctly. I'd always thought it was limited to metal, but then that night at the convent when we were tied up, and I removed the sleeping spell from the vampires . . . I think that's when it happened. I didn't even realize it had appeared until the next morning. I should have figured it out when I saw Nicco's mark, but I guess I was too out of it from the vampire bite."

"Whoa. Whoa. Whoa. *What?* Nicco's what?"

"*Oh* . . ." I'd somehow forgotten I hadn't spoken to any of my friends since the attack. "Nicco . . . is a witch." My heart thumped.

"Nicco, as in the Medici vampire? The one Isaac hates? The one who's into you?"

My face pinched. "He's not *into me.*"

"He better not be."

"*Don't* you start with me too. Nicco is just my friend."

"What kind of friend?"

"The kind who saves you from his savage family," I said sharply.

"Calm down, killah. How can he be a witch if he's a vampire? And what kind of witch?"

"Fire. And he doesn't have his powers anymore." My tone softened. "But it doesn't mean he isn't magical."

"He's not really a witch if he doesn't have any powers."

My eyes dropped to the counter.

"Oh, *shit,* I'm sorry. I didn't mean that. Not about you. You're a witch, in every aspect of magical." He grabbed my hand. "You're more of a witch than I am. I'm the only one without a Maleficium."

I sighed, trying to put aside my own magical frustrations. "You'll get your mark. Look around this place. How could you not?"

We both gazed out. All three of the Daure boys had worked in the shop growing up; it was a rite of passage, but for Codi it had always been different. He'd been attached to his grandmother's hip.

"So . . ." he said, "you don't have any magic left at all?"

I shook my head.

"No Fire?"

"No Fire, no telekinesis, no dream-magic. Nothing." *Not unless you count unzipping pants.* My cheeks flushed. "So if it makes you feel better, you have way more magic than me."

"That does not make me feel better. And it's bullshit." He pounded the counter, shaking the contents in the case.

"Dude, *glass.*"

"I'm sorry. It's just so messed up." He leaned down.

"Agreed, but we don't need to break all of Edgar's beautiful crystal wands because of it."

He snorted. "I want to break Callis's skull."

Same. Times a hundred.

I leaned down next to him. "You know . . . he's still out there."

"What? Did he contact you—"

"No. No. Nothing like that. Nicco thinks he's been here all along. He's been hunting him, and the rest of his coven." For such a dark thing to say, my tone sounded strangely placid, but knowing Callis had massacred all those innocent people just to get his grimoire back, I truly didn't care if Nicco and Emilio dragged Callis through the streets. I wanted my magic, but I'd never kill for it.

"Adele! How could you not tell me Callis was still here, after everything we went through?"

"*Calm down, killah.* I just found out last night."

"Wait 'til we tell Dee and Isaac."

My stomach twisted into a knot. "How . . . How is he?"

"Fine. He's like an ox. Ritha said he can start flying by the end of the week, but of course, secretly he's already trying. Thanks to you."

I exhaled in relief.

"You know," he continued, "it's none of my business—and you're like my sister and all so I'd do anything for you, including kick his ass—but, for what it's worth, he really cares about you."

I struggled to hold his gaze.

"He's been really worried about you. Like, *really* worried. He didn't know about Brig—"

"*I know*," I snapped, gripping the edge of the counter. "I'm sorry."

"Shit. No. I'm sorry. It's none of my business." He hugged me from the side.

"When did you get so gigantic?"

"Senior year. Some puberty-crew team combo. And now with the anthropomorphic powers . . . you should see my quads; they're like steel."

"I'll pass, thanks." I picked up my teacup and took a sip. "But thanks for the offer, *Onyx*."

"Sorry. I should have told you."

"Either way, it's so cool."

"I really did want to tell you, but my dads . . . they wanted you to come to us first. They suspected you were magical, but they say in witchery, you're supposed to always let a markless witchling come to you first. Never approach them in case you're wrong, or they're not ready, or some other BS. But that should haven't mattered with you. You're family."

"So is that why you didn't tell me about Callis?"

"Yeah. Well, that and we didn't know what the hell was going on with him and his little weirdo sister—and he seemed to be opening up to you."

"You used me as bait?"

"No! I mean . . . kind of? Not really. My dads knew he was a witch and that there was something off about him, but that's all. So when he asked for a job, they just figured it was easier to keep an eye on him under their noses. But we never left you alone with him! Me or Dad or Julie were always here. They'd never even heard of these Animarum Praedators before."

I let out an exasperated sigh. "How did we not figure it out sooner?"

"After the attack, Olsin and Ritha started digging and found something from the 1930s—some complaints in an old record book the NOLA witches kept. Nothing formal, just like a log of supernatural disturbances. There was a note about European witches in town at the same time as some cemetery break-ins, but then it stopped, so everyone went about their business."

"The Carter brothers," I said. "They stopped it."

Codi stared out at the tea room floor, as if lost in thought. "You mean the vampires from the legend?" he said.

"I mean, Nicco and—"

He was squinting at something on the shop floor, near one of the shelving cases. He slipped out from behind the counter, walked over to the case, and knelt down to retrieve something from underneath it. When he sat back up, he had a silver ring in his hand. "I don't remember this one from inventory," he said, examining it.

My eye for metal—I am my father's daughter—drew me nearer. I tipped his hand into the tracking light to see it better and brushed my fingers over the piece. "It's silver." A feeling of familiarity washed over me. *I know this ring.*

"Adele, I don't feel so—" He had a strange look on his face and his eyes fluttered.

"Codi?" I reached out for his shoulder.

Everything went black, and my stomach plummeted as if I were falling. I felt an impact to the back of my head, but then there was only cold.

A full moon shines over the stone castle nestled in the mountains. The castle isn't the most lavish in España, but its gargantuan stone bones are older

than most, and the family who bore its name treasured their history more than emerald-studded sconces and gilded-cherub fountains.

A little boy of about five years of age, in an impressive black gown quilted with silver threads and constructed especially for tonight's occasion, wanders out onto the circular rotunda of the northern tower. A guard posted sentry keeps a faithful eye as the boy wanders about, looking at the moon.

The boy's belly is full of goose pies and burnt custard and two entire bunches of grapes, and his raven-colored curls fall into his sleepy eyes. He brushes them away and yawns. He wants to go to sleep, but he can't find his nursemaid amongst the guests at the party. Everyone is too tall and too drunk and dancing too fast for him to meander in search of her. The music and merriment of the night's celebration floods out the windows of the old stone walls, and he wonders if the gargoyles can hear the music through their stone ears. He cranes his neck, looking up at the sky.

"Why are you out here by yourself, my little boy?" asks his father, who has followed him out. His moustache is thick in the middle and curls upward at the thinner edges, and his cloak is black with the same silver threads.

The little boy shrugs. "It's quiet out here, Papá. I like the moon. And I like the stars."

"They are magnificent, aren't they?" He scoops up the boy, rests him on his shoulder, and walks out to the ledge of the balcony wall. "One day, I promise, you will like the music and the wine and the chatter and all of the beautiful women in their costumes with their bosoms on display. One day they will fawn over you as they fawn over your brother now."

"The stars?"

The man's laugh is hearty. "No, mi cielito, *the women—although, with the right one it can be cosmic."*

The little boy's arm curls around his father's head as he grows sleepier.

"Look out there, son. See the forest and the mountains; hear the birds through the darkness. Antton will be the one to inherit the castillo and the title and the guard, but for you, I know it, mijo, there will be something much more important. Much more magical."

The boy's eyes light up. "Magic like the fire-breathers at carnival?"

"For you, mijo, it will undoubtedly involve Fire."

The little boy turns to his Papá and smiles his brightest smile. "I want it now, Papá. I don't want parties and parades and talking to so many people. I want the moon and the stars. I want to touch fire." The resolve shining through the boy's blue eyes, which are dark as the midnight sky, makes his father pause with pride.

He looks at him tenderly. "Maybe I was wrong, mijo. Maybe the cosmos will fawn over you."

He points out to the sky, at one star brighter than the rest, "It's called the King Star, and stands at the mighty Lion's breast. If you gaze just a tiny bit higher, you see his neck. And head. And this way . . ." His father points down. "Is his tail."

But the boy's gaze is affixed not on Leo, but on his father's finger, which bears a thick silver ring. A medallion, as simply adorned as the stone castillo, with a carving of a triangle in the center. The young boy sees for the first time that it isn't a triangle, but a flame. And he wants to breathe fire one day.

"Julie!" a distant voice boomed.

My head throbbed. I squinted, trying to open my eyes. The brick floor was cold. *Where am—?*

Bells on the front door jingled. "What the hell?" a voice cried.

"Caleb?" I asked, trying to sit up.

Codi's brother rushed into the shop, dropping his bag next to me. "What the heck are you two— Adele, are you bleeding?"

"Huh?"

I touched the side of my face. A dribble of liquid turned my fingers red. "What hap—?" Codi was lying on the floor beside me. A wave of panic rocked me. "Codi!" I shook his leg.

He grumbled awake.

"What happened?" Caleb asked, offering to help me up. "Did you guys get robbed?"

"Huh?" I took his hand and stood, a little woozy. "No. I don't think so."

"What the hell happened?" Codi asked, brushing off his pants.

"I think you passed out. And took me down with you."

"Is anyone hurt?" Chatham yelled, footsteps pounding down the staircase in the back of the house.

"I'm trying to do a phone reading here!" Edgar peeked out from behind one of the hallway curtains and saw me holding my head.

"What in God's name?" He rushed into the room and pulled my hand away, examining my scalp. "Is that blood?"

"Did you say blood?" Chatham asked.

The room tilted like it was off its axle, and I held onto the glass counter as Chatham ran water over a tea towel. A metal vase was spilled onto the brick floor, scattering a couple dozen long-stem roses—also made of metal, and the distinct work of my father—along with a hundred marble-like stones that had been holding them in an arrangement. *Was that Julie's S.O.S.? Is that what she was doing with the moon mugs when Callis was getting too close?*

I tried not to wince as Chatham patted the towel onto the sore spot on my head. "That's quite a bump, young lady, but nothing a bag of ice and a little healing salve won't take care of."

Caleb turned to his brother, crossing his arms. "I knew I overworked you at the gym this morning."

"You didn't overwo—" Codi tried to say as Edgar felt his forehead with the back of his hand. "I'm fine."

Caleb jerked up Codi's left hoodie sleeve.

Codi sighed. "Nothing."

"Patience, son," Chatham said, "It will come when it's the right time—"

"It better." Caleb kissed my cheek. "Good to see you, Addie."

"Welcome home," I said as he grabbed his bag and headed down the hallway.

Codi yanked his sleeve back down.

"Why's Caleb so concerned with your mark?" I asked.

"*Pfft.*"

Chatham handed me the towel to wipe my fingers. "In magical families, it's usually the youngest child who takes over the coven when the time comes for the next generation to lead, and let's just say that my eldest two sons are more of the linebacker-type than quarterback."

"I don't know what that means," I whispered to Codi.

"It means they're dumbasses."

"Codi Daure, that is *not* what I meant."

Edgar leaned my way. "Thank the universe for athletic scholarships."

I smiled and rested on the glass counter. Directly below me was a tray of zodiac necklaces—tiny gold posts connecting crystals to form constellations. One in particular caught my attention. *The lion.* "Leo," I whispered, a picture coming back to my mind. A starry night. A forest.

Edgar took out the necklace and held it up for me to see. "It's your star-sign."

"It's beautiful," I said, rubbing my head. "I had the weirdest dream about a little boy and a castle—"

"And a party?" Codi asked, confusion on his face.

I gave him a funny look. "Do you have your own psychic booth now?"

"When I passed out, I had a dream about a little boy and his father in this big stone fortress. In like medieval times or something, but that's all I really remember."

Edgar spun around in a kimono-whirl. "Dream-twinning?"

We both groaned.

"I always knew the two of you had a maaaagical connection."

"*Gross*, Dad. It's never going to happen." Codi turned to me. "No offense."

I looked at Edgar. "See, I told you so. Never going to happen."

He slipped the constellation necklace around my neck.

"Oh!" I yelped. "You don't have to. I didn't mean—"

He kissed my cheek. "It's beautiful on you. Besides, we missed your last birthday thanks to the Storm."

"*Merci beaucoup.*"

"And never say never," he replied, eliciting another double groan.

"It wasn't dream-twinning—" I said.

Codi turned to me. "How do you know?"

The room became silent as they all stared at me.

"*Dream-twinning*?" Codi asked. "You and Isaac *dream-twin*?"

"No! I mean, it's not—"

"That's so hardcore! I didn't even know it was possible for people our age."

My cheeks flushed so hard, I was certain I was part-beetroot. I didn't know what was worse, that I'd openly admitted something so personal, or that it wasn't with who they thought.

Chatham and Edgar went into full-blown witch-parent mode. "If I had realized," Chatham said, "when I gave you that book—"

"It's really not that big of a deal."

"It *is* a big deal!" Edgar said, beaming at his husband. "I'll never forget the first time our dreams touched—"

"Oh, *God*!" Codi yelled. "I do not want to hear—"

"I'm not doing it anymore," I stuttered. "My dream magic is gone with the rest of it, so we don't have to discuss this any—"

"It's not gone," said a voice from the hallway. Papa Olsin stood in the doorway, leaning on his cane. "There's nothing wrong with your dreams."

I wanted to tell him that there absolutely was, but I really just wanted this conversation to end.

"It's not the magic or the lack thereof blocking your connection; it's your twin-flame." There was something in his tone that hinted that this might not be a bad thing. *Could his psychic-witch brain see who I was dream-twinning with—or not dream-twinning with?*

The moon clock on the wall struck the hour.

"You've all got phone readings now," Codi said, shuffling everyone into the hallway.

I began scooping up the glass stones, dropping them back into the metal vase. *Does Papa Olsin mean that Nicco has been blocking me from his dreamscape?*

Codi reached for a stone. "Don't stress about it. Maybe the vampire bite broke the connection?"

"Huh?"

"I mean, he almost died."

"What? He's been dead for four—" *Oh God, he's still talking about Isaac.*

Codi examined the stone. When he moved, the light shifted, and I realized it wasn't a stone; it was the ring. He opened the glass case and placed it back with the other jewelry. "Speaking of witches," he said.

"We weren't really . . ."

"I know a couple of them who would love to see you."

If you walk out of that door, Adele, don't ever come back. My fingers found a twirl of hair and threaded it around and around as Désirée's words swirled in my head. "I don't think that's a great—"

"We're all meeting at the brothel tonight."

"The brothel?"

"Hell, we can go right now. I'll get Caleb to cover."

I paused. Here was my chance. An invitation back to my old life, and I wouldn't even have to go by myself. I pictured myself in the room with Isaac, and a crack of anxiety thundered in my stomach. *Could I really be with the person who killed my mother? Would that make me a horrible daughter?* The anger started to roil. *What if he asks me about her? I wouldn't even know what to say.* "I'm sorry," I snapped, "I can't." I took in a breath. "I don't have any magic. I'm sorry." Blaming it on that was just easier.

"Adele, we don't care about your magic."

"I care about my magic."

"That's not what I meant. Of course we *care* about it. But we don't care about you any less either way." His arm slid over my shoulder.

"*Merci beaucoup.*" I leaned my head against him.

"*Avec plaisir.*"

I think I'd taught him the French response when I was five.

He rocked me side to side in a silly way, but then stopped suddenly. "Uh, Adele? Who's that guy?"

I looked up at the smoky bay window.

Thump-thump.

"Oh. It's . . . Nicco."

Codi's hand dropped from my shoulder to the counter, caging me next to him. "*That's* the infamous Nicco?"

I sucked in a breath. "The one and only."

"He's . . . pretty hot."

My cheeks burned and I was glad Codi was still staring him down and not looking my way.

I knocked Codi's arm out of my way and waved for Nicco to enter.

He opened the door just enough to peer in. "Hi," he said gently. "Your father told me you might be here. I don't want to interrupt. I just wanted to see if I could walk you home . . . whenever."

I glanced at the moon clock and grabbed my bag. "Sure."

"I thought we were going to HQ?" Codi asked.

"No, you were going to HQ." I kissed his cheek. "I've got my mentorship with my dad now anyway. See you tomorrow?"

"I'll be here."

Nicco nodded to Codi, and we let the door swing shut behind us.

"I didn't mean to pull you away." He extended his elbow.

I took it as if it was the most normal move in the world, and we began walking in the direction of my house. "No, it's perfect timing actually."

"Why is that?"

"Codi was trying to get me to go with him to meet up with Désirée and Isaac."

Nicco's eyebrow crooked. "You don't want to see your friends?"

"No. Yes. I do, I mean. It's complicated. Our magic is what brought us all together, and I know it's not the reason we're all friends, but it's so weird for me—"

"Is that really why?"

I knew he was asking about Isaac. I didn't reply.

"*Je comprends*," he said. "I know what it's like to have to watch from a distance as all your friends grow into their magical positions. All your schoolmates go on to become renowned physicians, and not only can you not be at their side, but they can't even know you're alive, cheering them on from the sidelines and sneaking into their labs in the middle of the night to progress their work while they sleep."

I looked up at him and didn't know what to say. *Of course he understood.*

"On the other hand, maybe it would be good for your magic to be around other witches. Around your coven," he added, before I could remind him that I *was* in the company of a witch. "And not just that. It will be good for you. All this seclusion—it's almost vampiric." He smiled.

"Hey, I went out of the house two days in a row." But I couldn't really argue with him. The way my hand had gradually coiled deeper around his arm, you'd think I hadn't had human contact in a year. "And it was totally of my own accord and without meltdown."

We stopped in front of an art gallery. "And you'll get your magic back, totally of your own accord." His faith in me filled me with warmth that was almost as good as my Fire. "So, are you up for round two at Jazzland to work on your magic? Or are you sick of me by now?"

"*Sì*," I replied. "*Sì* that I'm up for round two, not that I'm sick of you."

"*Buono*. I think we have some chains in the attic."

"For what?"

"So I can wear them, of course."

As I groaned, a gentle breeze swept down the street. Nicco twitched upright, fangs snapping out. "What's that?" He reached for my head. "Are you bleeding?"

I lurched back. "It's nothing!" I yelped, covering it. "Just a bump."

"Adele, I'm not Lisette. I'm over four hundred years old. I can control myself around a scrape." That doctoral tone rose in his voice. "Let me look at it."

I nodded and angled my head down. His fingertips pushed away my hair. "It's shallow. No need for stitches. How did this happen?"

"Codi passed out on me—he's fine, I think, he just went too hard on his workout—and he knocked me down. I guess I hit my head, and then I had this weird dream . . . or vision . . . that connected with his."

He stood up straighter, hands pulling away. "Oh."

"It *wasn't* dream-twinning. I didn't get that feeling."

His eyebrow lifted. "What feeling?"

Like being intertwined in a way that made me think I'd die if we were pulled apart. "The connection," I barely choked out. "It felt magical, but it wasn't the same kind of connection. This was foreign to me."

"Magical. That's . . . good." His voice dropped, and his gaze was on my head again, his jaw tightening.

Every synapse in my body fired, telling me to flee. *Don't show it, Adele. There's nothing to fear. You trust Nicco.*

"I'm going"—his throat sounded pinched—"to go now."

I nodded vigorously.

He casually turned, took two steps down the sidewalk, and then disappeared in a blur.

A trapped breath escaped my lungs, and my leg bones felt like they'd turned to pudding.

And then it was just me, alone on the street, the realities of Nicco's nature setting in. *He's a vampire, Adele. A vampire.*

The further I walked from the shop, the more I missed that warm feeling of being around the Daures. I couldn't help but think about what it must have been like for Codi, growing up in a magical family, and before I knew it, I was walking down Désirée's street, approaching Vodou Pourvoyeur.

The block was full of parked cars, and warm light shone through the shop windows. A vèvè had been chalked on the sidewalk in front of the shop, and chicken bones littered the walk outside the courtyard gate. Clearly, something was going on. I could almost smell the cinnamon in the air and feel the bustle of Borges family members warmly bickering.

I fought the invisible thread of loneliness compelling me to the door —I wasn't sure I could handle Désirée telling me off again. A solitude flooded me that I hadn't felt in all those weeks by myself.

I walked the last few blocks, feeling a little jealous of Codi and Désirée. I hated the feeling. In that moment, I realized I'd never missed having magical family because Isaac and I had always had each other. Without him, the loneliness rushed me tenfold.

When I arrived, the house was still and quiet. "Dad!" I called, flipping on the hallway light.

I got nothing back but the tick-tock of the grandfather clock's pendulum. I dropped my keys on the foyer table and put down my bag.

The house was completely dark. *Is he sleeping?* I glanced into each of the rooms, but the house was empty. I checked my phone for messages. Nothing.

The chicken he'd promised was defrosting in the sink, but he wasn't here. As I manually turned on the oven, I once again tried not to think about the comforting feeling of the Daures' home. *How could he have forgotten our dinner plans?*

I opened the chicken, seasoned it the way we both liked, and began scrubbing some red potatoes, trying not to look at my phone every five minutes.

Half an hour later, I heard the front door open, and I tried to prepare myself for the disappointment of hearing how he'd forgotten about our plans.

"Hey baby," he said, putting his stuff on the counter. "I'm so sorry I'm late." He kissed my cheek. "I drove all the way across the damn river, but I found them."

"Found what?"

He nodded to the bags on the counter.

I wiped my hands on a towel and peered inside. A familiar blue tin: the butter ring cookies I used to eat when I was a kid. Not only that, there was a bag of Blue Eyes tea.

"That's the kind you and your mother used to drink, right? Pink tea?"

I sucked in a big breath, turned, and threw my arms around his neck. I didn't care if my dad didn't have powers; he was magical to me

CHAPTER 26

FIRE WITCH

My shoulder still throbbed as I hot-glued mirror fragments. The dining room table was covered in shiny shards. And books. Lots of books. Some were half-opened to specific pages marked with hand-scribbled notes or scraps of paper. Evidently, I wasn't the only one who'd had a late night. Désirée had stayed up scouring all our magical texts trying to find anything about Guinée, souls crossing over, and serving the Ghede lwa.

She leaned over her mini-cauldron, across the table from me, inhaling steam from the twenty-one habanero peppers she'd been soaking. Not twenty-three or twenty. Twenty-one. Apparently this number was significant and the reason my eyes were stinging, and why the whole brothel smelled like a perfumery—if that perfumery were in India or Mexico or someplace where chili peppers and nutmeg drenched the air.

"How's your shoulder?" she asked.

"Fine," I said, despite it feeling like the glass shards on the table had been pulled directly from it. But I wasn't going to tell Dee that I'd spent the remainder of my night ripping out a floor because it was the only thing that had prevented me from banging Nicco's door down and telling him to stay the hell away from Adele. "Have you figured out which Ghede you want to contact?"

As she told me about her findings, all I could think about was Nicco on Adele's stoop, and her smiling—*at him.*

Jesus Christ. Why the hell had she been out with him?

I'd tried to convince myself he'd just been dropping her off after the cemetery, but that didn't compute with the smiling part. There was no smiling after mother burials. Yet that was all I could imagine. Her smiling. Him inching closer. Touching her face.

"*Holy Goddess,*" Désirée said, fanning the air. "This will clear your sinuses."

"No shit." I rubbed my eyes with the back of my hand, wishing the steam would burn the image out of my head.

"I hope it's to Plumaj's taste."

"Who's Plumaj?"

"I just told you . . . Clearly someone wasn't paying attention."

"Sorry."

She nodded to her open grimoire. "Meet our frontrunner for tonight."

GHEDE PLUMAJ

– Zombi Collector –

PSYCHOPOMP

There was a drawing of a bone woman who looked not unlike the statue of the Baron, only she wore a fancy cape of feathers.

"Some Ghede remain always and forever in the Afterworld and others can go between the worlds: those are the psychopomps. Plumaj is a daughter of the Baron and Maman Brijit. It's her job to round up stray souls from the cemeteries, hence the nickname."

"*Zombi collector?*"

"Yep. She collects stray souls and brings them back to Guinée so fresh corpses aren't at risk of reanimation." She put on rubber gloves, unscrewed the lid from the unmarked bottle of booze she'd swiped, and added the mix of chili water into the bottle. A waft of rum mixed into the peppery air. "It's called piman. It's the favorite drink of the Ghede, and we'll need it for the séance tonight."

"It looks even more lethal than Ren's moonshine."

"Precisely. The Ghede are already dead, so it takes a lot more to fire them up. Which is why witches sometimes use it to test those who claim to have been taken by a lwa."

"They make them drink it?"

"That, or they have them rub it on . . . *sensitive* parts of their bodies. If they are a true *cheval* for the lwa, they won't feel a thing. If they're faking it, the piman reveals all."

"*Yo*!" Codi yelled as he came through the front door.

"Dining room!" Désirée yelled back.

I plugged in another glue gun.

His footsteps became louder, and then he came through the pocket doors with a white paper bag stamped with *The Bottom of the Cup Tea Room.* "Moonstone and pyrite for you," he said, holding the bag out to Dee.

"Thank you. I want to add this to the grout." She pulled out a mortar and pestle and dumped the contents into the bowl. "I think the opalescence will bind the mirror fragments even tighter once the spell is active."

As Désirée began grinding, he swung out the chair next to me and slid onto it, leaning over the wooden back. "And boy do I have news for you: Adele came by the shop today."

The plastic gun slipped over the slick piece of mirror directly into my finger, but I hardly noticed the burn.

"She wants her job back."

Désirée pushed down harder, grinding the moonstone.

"And, get this," he said, totally oblivious to the shift in energy in the room. "She thinks Callis is still alive."

"*What*? Did something hap—?"

"No. She just said Nicco and his brothers were tracking his coven."

Of course they were.

"Did you guys know that Nicco's a witch?" he asked.

A snort slipped from my throat.

Désirée stopped grinding. "Excuse me?"

"Or *was* a witch? That's what Adele said— And did you know she got her mark?"

"Oh, my Goddess!" She dropped the pestle with a clatter. "What's her Spektral?"

My head spun. "*Wait.* Go back to Nicco."

"I don't know, man. She didn't say much else about it. Fire witch before he got vamped. Anyway, she asked about you."

My fingers rapped the table. *They're both Fire witches? Is that how he was weaseling his way back into her life?*

"So he's like Lisette?" Désirée asked. "A witch with no powers?"

"I guess." He turned to me. "I tried to get her to come back here with me, but she's really down about the magic-loss thing. Then *he* showed up to walk her home and the conversation was over."

Désirée looked at me with one eyebrow raised before going back to the mortar and pestle.

"You should have seen the way her eyes lit up when I mentioned the brothel. I swear, she almost said yes."

My mouth went dry. A breeze rushed through an open window, fluttering the curtains. I forced the words out. "She doesn't want to come here because of me."

"Dude, she saved your life."

"And then she left me . . ." *After I told her I loved her.*

"And she's asked about you two days in a row."

Désirée stuck to grinding the moonstone, clearly not going to weigh in.

I shook my head. "I don't know . . ."

She sighed and lowered the pestle to the table, her eyes rising to the ceiling.

"What?" I asked.

"I— We— The night of the attack, when she left, we might have gotten into a little . . . tiff. And I might have told her to never come back." She picked up her coffee mug and took a sip.

"Désirée!"

"What?" she yelled. "You almost died! I was pissed she was leaving! I wanted her to be there for you. And I was scared! She should be here *with us*!"

"So you kicked her out of the coven?"

"In hindsight, my logic was a little faulty. I'm not used to being so emotional."

I pushed the hair that had fallen in my face behind my ears. *Is this why Adele isn't here with us right now? Not because she hates me?*

I got up and squeezed my arms around Désirée.

"Okay, this really isn't a hugging-level occasion."

"Let me work on her," Codi said, starting a fresh hexenspiegle. "She took a shift tomorrow. I know I can get her back here, as long as Mr. Dark-and-Dreamy doesn't show up. I don't know if I can compete with that."

Why the hell was Nicco walking Adele home from work? Mac's napkin invitation was suddenly burning a hole in my pocket. I grabbed my sketchbook and stuffed it into my bag. "I gotta go— I'll be back in a couple hours. Maybe sooner." *Maybe immediately, depending on how this goes.*

"Don't be late for the séance tonight!" Désirée yelled. "We can't do it without you!"

"What am I?" Codi asked.

"Can you see dead people?"

"I won't be late," I reassured her, and then raced all the way up to the third floor, to Cosette's room. I hastily dug through my clothes to the bottom of my duffel. I had two Hail Marys.

It was time to use one of them.

CHAPTER 27

INADVERTENT MATCHMAKER

I opened up a window to let in some fresh air; the breeze had the scent of rain as it rushed into the metal shop. The chicken and potatoes were roasting in the oven, and my father was hunched over my sketchbook looking at the designs I'd drawn months ago. It was the first time things had felt normal since the night of the attack. I don't know if it was the studio, or being there with him, or the distraction of the project, but it felt nice.

"All right," he said, studying the silhouette. "Why don't you go get Claire, and we'll attempt to drape your chainmaille."

"Sounds good," I said, and ran up to my room to get my dress form.

When I tried to lift Claire, I remembered how heavy she was. She was an antique, with a base and a center rod made of iron. Chatham had given her to me after his mother passed away. He said I'd been the one who named her Claire when I was little, when Philly began teaching me to sew.

I gave up trying to lift her and took a couple steps back to focus on the metal. I imagined her being easy to lift. *Light,* I thought. *Light as cotton, or tulle, or chiffon.* I pictured her rising a couple of inches.

I took a deep breath and focused on my intention.

I can do this. Up. Up. Up.

Claire stared back at me as if I was crazy, her expression almost mocking.

"I will not let you get me down," I told her. "I unzipped a zipper last night." I bent over and grabbed the base of the pole. "There *is* magic somewhere inside me. Even if I can't feel it, Nicco can." *Or so he says.*

I hoisted her up into my arms and carried her awkwardly down the stairs and through the kitchen, my fingers straining. *You seriously need to invest some time in strength training.*

"Dad!" I called out at the studio door, "help me set her—" I froze, seeing that he wasn't alone; but before I could shrink back into the hallway with my giant passenger, they both looked up.

Fear washed over Isaac's face, but then he leapt over to help me. *Because Isaac's reflex is to help.*

My arms circled tighter, clutching Claire, her weight no longer an issue. *Because my reflex was to turtle.* I tried wiping the stunned look off my face, but it felt like I was made of marble.

"Can I— Can I help you with that?" he asked. I could tell from the unsteadiness of his voice that he was trying not to panic.

My head bobbed, and I released Claire to him.

"Sweetheart," my father said, "do you remember when we went to that award ceremony in St. Claude for that photographer?"

Isaac had hated everything about that ceremony—well, everything except what had happened after: it was the first time we'd ever slept together.

I nodded.

"This is the infamous Isaac Thompson."

I knew being called infamous was probably making him cringe inside. We barely made eye contact as he carried Claire over to my side of the table. "Is here good?"

My head bobbed once more, and he put Claire down.

I couldn't stop staring as he pushed his hair behind his ears and straightened his pale blue short-sleeve shirt. It had little green whales embroidered on it and was unbuttoned with a plain white T-shirt underneath, but for some reason it felt awfully formal for the occasion. I didn't remember him having it. It looked more like something Codi would wear.

"I figured you could use a classmate," my father said, setting some of his tools on the table.

"This was your idea?" I was only able to cut the accusatory tone in my voice by half as I continued. "How do the two of you even know each other?"

My father gave me a funny look, like, *I thought you were ready to be around other humans.* "The bar." He gestured for Isaac to take the stool on my right. *His old seat.* "Make yourself at home."

"I'm helping renovate some of the back rooms," Isaac said to me, the concern showing through his expression, as if he might detonate a bomb by choosing the wrong words.

The bomb being me.

I wondered how long all of this had been going on, and my brain felt like it was going into nuclear meltdown.

Rain pattered against the house, and we all looked to the window. "You should see his sketchbook, hon," Mac said. A breeze blew droplets inside, and he got up to close the window.

I wondered if it was Isaac's doing. He turned to me, not nearly as confident as the first time he'd pulled this stunt, and all of our memories rushed me: all the good ones I'd locked in the secret magical safe underneath my closet floorboards so it was easier to forget he existed, and easier to forget he'd killed my—

"I can leave," he whispered.

I stared. It was like I'd forgotten how to speak.

He picked up his sketchpad, but I reached over and touched his arm. When his eyes met mine, I shook my head.

Are you sure? he mouthed.

I nodded.

He settled in his seat and opened his sketchbook to a fresh page.

This is happening.

"Adele is finishing up a dress for a school project," my father said, "so I thought I could give you a few tips on perspective."

He already knows about perspective . . . You taught it to us.

"Sounds good," Isaac said. I could tell he was consciously trying not to look my way. "Lay it on me."

I tried to focus on draping Claire with the chainmaille, which took ten times the number of pins as the heaviest fabric I'd ever worked with, but it was impossible not to steal glances at him. He was listening to Mac as if it were the first time he'd heard the lesson.

How could he still care about me after everything that had

happened? My hands trembled. *I still care about him, even after everything that's happened.*

I suddenly had a definite concern that tears were going to pour down my face, and I shot up in the seat. "I think I hear the kettle," I mumbled and ran off to the kitchen before my dad could realize I'd never put on the water.

Once I was alone in the kitchen, where my neuroses could roam free, I paced. *Kettle. Water.* If I didn't go back with tea, I'd look crazy.

I fired up the burner.

As the water boiled, I retrieved a tray from the top of the refrigerator and laid out three teacups and saucers. I spread the butter ring cookies on a plate and fumbled through the drawers for a tea strainer. Then I paced around the kitchen some more.

The kettle whistled. Usually it felt like an eternity waiting for the water to boil, but now it was like we had some kind of superstove.

I gathered more items for the tray—sugar cubes, a jar of honey, napkins, and spoons—for no other reason than to take up time. And then the only thing left to do was to place the kettle on a towel in the center.

Gripping the tray, I walked carefully back, hoping they didn't notice my unsteady hands rattling the tea cups.

They were both sitting at the worktable, Isaac practically curled around his sketchpad—as inward as he could possibly be. The vibe was noticeably more awkward than when I'd left.

When I set the tray down on the table, I saw her: the ballerina. The miniature version of the NOSA statue, upside down, just like the exercise we'd done in our first lesson together. A lump swelled in my throat. *My father is making Isaac draw my mother.* Isaac looked like he was internally collapsing. Without thinking, I snatched up the ballerina and hurried across the room. I threw her onto the sofa and covered her with a pillow like an absolute psycho.

My father jumped up. "Adele, I'm sorry—"

"It's fine." I felt both of them watching as my gaze darted around the studio, looking for a suitable replacement. The dirty old Care Bear on a shelf that hadn't been touched in a decade? *No, not enough detail.* A Joan of Arc helmet he'd made me two Mardi Gras ago? *Too easy.* I settled for the framed replica of a John Lavery painting. The scene depicted two women, a child, a dog, and a servant with a platter of fruit. There was a mirror reflection, varied lighting, and lots of other elements to draw. I grabbed it, took it back to the table, and propped it up between two cans of paintbrushes, upside down. Isaac's gaze was even wider than my father's.

"Sweetheart, I'm sorry. I wasn't thinking— We always draw your—"

"We don't have to talk about her!"

"Adele—"

"I'm fine, Dad." I placed the strainer over one of the teacups and poured a stream of pink into it, their gazes still coursing over me.

I served them each tea and then sat back with my cup, looking at the upside-down painting. I'd always loved the mix of flapper and Victorian dresses contrasted with the servant's Indian garments.

I blew on my tea and took a sip. "It's probably more your skill level anyway." I looked at Isaac. The golden flecks in his eyes glimmered and the corners of his mouth turned up meekly.

I reflected his smile and turned back to Claire.

"Yeah, probably," Mac said, giving me a questioning look as he came over.

I played oblivious. If he'd thought anything else was weird about the situation, besides me freaking out over the statue of my mother, he let it go.

Isaac flipped the page in his sketchbook and settled into the new assignment, and my father began showing me how to taper the silhouette by unhooking specific rings of chainmaille, reattaching them to others, and removing everything in between. For the next hour, Isaac sketched Lady Hazel and her daughters upside down, and I transformed two straight lines of chainmaille into a curve for a waist and a hip. My father gave Isaac occasional instructions and asked him questions about his life in New York and what his time as a first responder had been like. All of which Isaac answered with warmth and courteousness, trying not to overdo it or underdo it, his pencil never leaving his paper for more than a moment.

As we worked, there were metal clips from pliers, the rattles of teacups, and the munch of cookies, mostly from me; but for the most part, it was the silent concentration of artists. I couldn't help but watch Isaac's every movement from my peripheral vision. The longer we sat at the workbench in such quiet, close proximity, the stronger the urge grew to wrap my arms around his shoulders and apologize for leaving his side the other night. To beg him to forgive me for everything that had happened.

When the timer went off, he turned his sketchpad around and seemed genuinely in awe of how closely it matched the painting. The trick never got old.

"It's all about perspective," Mac said. "Sometimes it's best to turn things upside down and examine your subject from another point of view. It's a handy exercise to abandon your biases."

Isaac hadn't completed the entire painting in the allotted time, but the part he had finished was amazing.

From this view, *he* was amazing.

My father instructed him to go at it again, but now with less time on the clock. "Really try to look at it as just lines and shapes. Negative and positive space. Forget all your preconceived notions and just let go."

My father spoke about art the way Nicco spoke about magic.

The scent of rosemary grew stronger from the kitchen as we got closer to evening, and when Mac announced the end of the lesson, the sadness I felt became more pronounced. As did the normalcy of Isaac being there with us in the house.

"Would you like to stay for dinner, Isaac?" Mac asked as he polished a bracelet.

My back tensed. I tried to hide it, but Isaac had already noticed.

"Is it okay if I take a raincheck?" He looked back at me with an expression that reassured me he wasn't going to push his luck. "I've got a prior commitment."

My father accepted the raincheck and began telling him about the type of wood he'd salvaged for the garçonniere floor, and I found myself hoping the conversation would keep going. I realized *I wanted him to stay*. I wanted to him to eat chicken and then, after leaving through the front door, fly up to my bedroom window, which I'd leave open for him like I used to. I wanted to pull him under my blanket and whisper everything I hadn't been able to tell him in the last couple months: how scared I was of never getting my magic back, and how I daydreamed about killing Callis in the most violent ways I could think of, and how that scared me too.

I blinked and Isaac was already packed up.

He slid his pencil behind his ear. "It was nice meeting you." He extended his hand, and my palm floated into his as I nodded. I heard the words in my head, insisting that he stay, but they didn't come out of my mouth. "I like your dress—the whole concept, the metal. It's badass. It suits you."

"*Merci*," I said, not much more than a whisper. The feeling of his rough hand was sending shock waves of familiarity through my system.

"Would it be okay if I came again, Mr. LeMoyne?" The question was directed at my father, but his eyes were locked with mine.

"Anytime, son."

I nodded, and Isaac smiled.

"But call me . . . Mac." The tone of his voice shifted a little, almost like he was trying to figure out if keeping some formality was a better idea.

I turned to him and realized he was looking at us, specifically at my hand still in Isaac's. I pulled it back, trying to be natural, but my nervousness filled up the room.

Isaac stuffed his hands in his pockets and rocked back on his feet. "Thanks again, Mac."

"My pleasure." My father walked him out of the room.

I caught Isaac trying to steal one more look back without making my father suspicious, and it made me smile. From the kitchen, I could hear him insisting on seeing himself out.

His footsteps softened into nothingness, and the room somehow felt chillier without them—without Isaac's warmth.

I walked into the kitchen. My father was lifting the chicken out of the oven. I wrapped my arms around him before he even had it set on the stove.

"Two hugs in one day?"

"*Merci mille fois, Papa*."

"For what, sweetheart?"

For inadvertently playing matchmaker. *Again.* "For being my dad."

"I love you, baby."

"I know. *Je t'aime aussi, Papa*."

After we had eaten the chicken and washed the plates, my father whisked himself off to the bar. Practicing my Spektral powers so I didn't have any more accidental strip-magic with Nicco seemed like the smartest way to fill the time. I don't know if it was the unexpected afternoon with Isaac or the anticipation of the night to come, but I found myself pacing. I suddenly felt claustrophobic in the house I'd just spent so many weeks in. I needed to get out.

I'd only planned to get some air, not go for a run, but when my steps touched the path on the Moonwalk, they quickened all by themselves. I was gasping for breath after just six blocks. *How is it possible to be this out of shape?* But it didn't matter; I'd made it to the river, and the setting sun was throwing pinks and oranges into the sky, as if trying to outdo the moon's performance last night.

I pushed my muscles and gradually fell into a rhythm, hypnotized by the sparkly glare on the surface of the Mississippi, as I mulled over everything that had happened between me and Isaac over the last year. I thought about the moonlight on Nicco's face, and about how much Isaac hated him. How much he thought Nicco was a monster. My mind drifted back to Halloween night in the attic. A comment Emilio made to me had ticked in the back of my mind ever since: *"It really wasn't the brightest plan, trapping yourself in an attic with the most brutal vampire I've ever known . . . and me."*

Based on all the Medicean history I'd been privy to, *Emilio* was the most brutal vampire I could imagine. He'd wanted to feed Maddalena to Séraphine, for Christ's sake! Brutal wasn't a word I'd associate with Nicco. Dangerous? Fine. Threatening? Sure. He was predatory by nature—he was a vampire, after all. But *brutal* was something different. Brutal was unnecessary, and I couldn't imagine Nicco being unnecessarily violent.

There *was* a difference between him and Emilio, who'd killed the Michels and the Wolfman just to scare us into doing his bidding. I didn't care what anyone else—including Isaac—said.

I trusted Nicco.

The skin on my arms pricked, and a shadow passed over the sparkling water in my periphery, as if someone was approaching from behind. My defenses kicked in and I sped up, pumping my legs, but a pair of arms wrapped around me.

"Get off!" I screamed, bucking forward as he pinned me against his chest.

"*Ma petite Fée Verte.*" The voice was perfectly seductive without trying to be. *Gabe.*

"Put me down!" I jerked my shoulders, trying to twist away.

"Stop panicking and drop your weight—"

"Let me go!" I flailed again.

He shook me hard. "*Drop. Your. Weight.*"

It took me a second to realize he was instructing me. Against my better judgement, I stopped panicking and went dead in his arms.

"Now, if I was a real assailant, you would ground your right foot and then stomp my left on your exhale. Then without pause you'd send your left foot back into the crown jewels."

His grip loosened, and I planted my right foot and stomped down hard on his left.

"*Sì*, like tha—"

I sent my heel sailing back, straight between his legs.

"*Adel*—!"

He fell forward, and I twisted around.

"I thought we were role-playing?" he said, a slightly higher pitch to his tone, his face pinched tight as he gripped his knees.

"Do not *touch* me," I spat. I breathed heavily, my heart still racing. Other than at the funeral, the last time I'd seen Gabe had been when I'd drugged him with enchanted absinthe and locked him in chains—not a memory that comforted me with Nicco nowhere in sight, me with no magic, and just the two of us next to the turbulent river.

I backed further away from him. "What do you want?"

He stood upright. He looked like he'd raided the Nike store on Canal, and yet somehow still made athletic wear look sophisticated. "I was hoping for a peaceful sunset run."

"Then why did you attack me?"

"I didn't attack you! I was just testing your vulnerability, which clearly has room for improvement. Niccolò told me about your magical dilemma."

"The last time I saw you," I said in French, "you were yelling things at me that would make a Parisian prostitute join a convent to get away from you." I turned away and began jogging again.

He fell into place at my side. "Lock me up in chains again, and I promise to repeat them." I didn't like being sandwiched between him and the river. "Unless there's a bed involved. In that case, I'll still say them, but with a tone you'll like."

My eyes slanted his way. "I will *not* like it."

"I'm just kidding, *bella*! *Madonna mia,* loosen up."

I kept my gaze straight ahead.

"You're so serious . . ."

I continued to ignore him.

"I see why my brother likes you."

A mini explosion happened inside my chest, and I could sense him smiling, radiating mischievous joy and confirmation. I tried to take unnoticeably big breaths to temper my heart rate, but nothing was going to escape his vampiric senses. *Freakin' pulse!*

"Why are you running?" I asked, attempting a diversion. "Don't you have perfect vampire health?"

"Why are *you* running?"

"I needed some air."

"I needed some sunset. Look at how magnificent it is."

It was, but his grabbing me had left an invisible imprint, and it was all I could think about: how weak I was and how helpless I felt without my magic. Unlike the Medici brothers, who'd had years of sword practice even before they were magical or vampiric. The promise I'd made to myself when Callis attacked me that night—about learning how to fight sans magic—echoed in my head. A promise I'd done nothing to uphold.

I looked up at him. "You know, I heard a rumor about you."

"Oh?" He smiled slyly. "Do tell."

"That you used to be the best fighter of your time."

"I know my way around with a sword."

"Will you teach me to fight?"

He raised an eyebrow.

"What?"

He lifted my arm. "You don't possess the strength to swing a sword, much less fight with one."

I yanked it away. "I'll train. I'll do anything. It doesn't have to be a sword. I just don't want to be captured and tied up to a statue again!" I stopped running. "And for the record. I'm *going* to get my magic back. And then I'll be able to wield any piece of metal I want."

He smiled, but not in a mocking way; in a way that showed he had a lot of experience being an older brother. "Why don't you ask Niccolò? He loves imposing regiment. Especially," he added under his breath, "on everyone around him."

"Because I know Nicco would never hurt me. I want to feel it—the fear. I want to train it away."

"*Bella*?" he asked, with melodramatic shock. "You trust me with your fragile little self?"

I sucked in a heavy breath. "No." I started running again. "That's the point."

He followed. "I'm beginning to think I was wrong that night in the attic, *signorina*."

"About what?"

His smile deepened. "You do remind me of Adeline. Very much so."

A feeling of pride emanated from my chest and I ran a little taller, but I kept my poker face.

He peeled off the path.

"Wait, where are you going?"

He looked back, jogging in place. "I thought you were ready to train?"

"What's wrong with here?" I looked to the grassy areas that once would have been kept impeccable for tourists but were now littered with garbage. "Can't we just start with some basics?"

"Not here. Someone will see us, and they'll think I'm trying to hurt you and cause a scene, and then I'll end up taking their blood to erase their memories, and Nicco will be irate because I bit someone in front of you, et cetera, et cetera."

"Then where?"

"My place."

Something about this felt like a bad idea, especially given that the last time I was in the Medici house, I'd threatened two of its residents. And Gabe was cunning; he was the diplomat of the group . . . and the snake in the weeds. *You're the one who asked him for help, Adele.*

"What happened to wanting to feel the fear?"

I sucked in a big breath. I didn't know if I wanted to feel *that* much fear.

Even so, something inside me told me to go with him. The Medici were always the key to getting answers about my family's past.

"Aren't you and Nicco going out tonight, anyway?"

Sweat broke across my brow. *Nicco told him?* I knew he and Gabe were close, but . . .

Gabe grinned, and I realized Nicco hadn't told him. I just had.

"My little Niccolò, secretly rendezvousing."

My cheeks flamed, and I looked over my shoulder at the last sliver of sun sinking below the horizon. My instincts screamed at me to run . . . but my intuition told me something different: that Gabe loved Nicco, and that's what would protect me; he wouldn't hurt his brother by hurting me. I didn't trust Gabe, but I trusted my intuition.

As I stepped forward, I remembered an old warning from Nicco: "*Intuition is muddled with emotion—emotion will get you killed.*"

I pushed it away.

"Adele," he said, sensing my hesitation, "if I was going to kill you, I'd have already taken you behind a tree and sucked you dry."

"There are things worse than death, I hear."

"So dark." He laughed. "Now I really know you've been spending time with Niccolò.

CHAPTER 28

EN GARDE

"Wait here, I'll be right back," Gabriel said, leaving me in the middle of a long room on the second floor.

The old French Quarter home was cool and damp despite it being April, and it smelled like freshly burned candle wax. A row of heavy drapes, such a dark red they almost looked black in the lamplit room, lined the wall to my right. A grand fireplace was to my left, whose shadowy coals begged for flames. Big crystal tears dangled from a chandelier that hung from an intricate wooden medallion, but other than a gilded mirror over the fireplace and a few oil paintings of countryside landscapes, the only other furnishings were a couple of ancient Louis XIV benches against the adjacent walls. The rest of the room was completely empty. A floorboard creaked above my head, and the chandelier crystals swayed.

This is a trap, Adele.

My instincts urged me to know my exits. I peeked behind one of the drapes: the tall floor-to-ceiling windows led out to a balcony. I pressed my nose to the glass, trying to think about the Gabe who had taught his younger brother to fight, not the one who'd forced Lisette to kill her own sister.

I'd only ever been inside the Medici house twice before—both times looking for Lisette and on neither occasion invited—but now I found myself pulling back the curtains and letting in the moonlight, as if the house were my own. I peered back down below. The courtyard was overgrown, not in a post-Storm way, but as if Mother Nature had been given full reign over the last few centuries. Wild rosebushes had overtaken the perimeter, setting traps for anyone who dared try to enter the house while the Medici were away. I hugged myself in my thin, pink sweater, the dampness and the sheen of sweat from the run making me shiver.

I spotted the old metal fireplace key and a box of matches on the mantel. Still behaving as if I owned the place, I inserted it into the gas pipe, struck a match, and a few seconds later flames were crackling through the fake metal coals.

The fire warmed me as I waited, but my shoulders tightened as I tried to convince myself that Gabe wasn't upstairs, right now, telling his family that supper had arrived. *What is taking him so long?*

A loud crash came from above, and I jumped, half-expecting something—or someone—to come pummeling through the ceiling. In the quiet aftershock, I became very aware of the beating of my own heart. Something was wrong.

This was a bad idea.

My fingers stretched and unstretched, as if warming up for a fight—as if my hands still couldn't comprehend that my Fire was gone.

Footsteps and muffled voices shuffled from the third floor.

I should call Nicco, so someone knows I'm here.

I fumbled with my phone in my pocket, but then a foot swung the door open and Gabe came through, carrying a huge traveling trunk that looked like it hadn't been opened in a million years.

"Where's Nicco?" I asked.

He set down the trunk. I recognized the Medici coat of arms from Nicco's dreams.

"Out." He pressed his thumbs on the two main latches, releasing metal locks, and the trunk creaked as he pried it open. "With Lisette. He's teaching her the *proper* way for a vampire to co-exist with twenty-first-century society."

I stood on my toes, peering over his shoulder as he removed a velvet-lined panel, and then another.

"My brother is very particular about our lifestyle."

It took me a second to realize he meant they were out *feeding.* "I'm sure he has your best interests at heart."

"No doubt." Metal clanked as he dug through the trunk's contents: a swath of medieval weapons.

"I thought you said I was too weak to learn how to use a blade?"

"You are." He grasped something. "*Found it.*"

He turned around to toss me a long bundle of leather, which nearly made me topple over as I caught it against my chest.

"But then I wondered if *that* was still in La Nouvelle-Orléans." He nodded to the bundle. "Open it."

I unwound the leather wrapping, only to find another thick layer of fabric wound around some kind of sword. Beneath the fabric, a tight-woven mesh encased the blade.

"I started teaching my sister how to use her first rapier when she was eleven—when all my friends began staring at her breasts. As much as we'd have liked to, the three of us couldn't always be at her side."

When I slipped the mesh off, the sword felt dramatically lighter. "It hardly weighs anything."

"I had this one especially made for her wedding gift. Seeing her move out of the palazzo and in with that rat-faced viceroy was horrifying and heartbreaking for all of us."

"This was Giovanna's?" I studied the cage-like handle: a thin serpent, twisting back and around, eating its own tail. My father would love the detailing in the snake scales.

"The Ouroboros," he said. "The symbol for eternity. I wanted her to live forever. Ironic in retrospect."

"It's beautiful." It felt like a funny thing to say about a sword. "I wouldn't have taken her for the sword-fighting type."

He gave me a look, like, *How would you know?*

"O-oh," I stumbled, as if I'd been caught spying, not just on Nicco but on all their lives. "Nicco's told me a lot about her."

"Has he?"

I didn't say anything more. If Nicco hadn't told Gabe that we'd been hanging out, then he certainly hadn't told him we'd been dream-twinning.

I lifted the rapier, examining the thin blade. I wondered what

Adeline would think about me being here. How close had she gotten to Gabe before she knew she had to lock him up forever? The image of Adeline sending the stake through Giovanna's chest rose in my mind. Standing in this room, with a Medici blade in my hand, made them both seem so vivid. Giovanna, I realized, had died twice in this feud. I turned the rapier around. "How is it so . . . ?"

"Light?" he asked.

"*Oui*."

"Venetian witches with a propensity for metal. The finest bladesmiths I've ever known."

Ah. I knew it couldn't possibly have been natural.

He stepped in front of me, stuck his shoe in between my feet, and spread my legs into a wider stance. It felt awkward. He nudged my toes so that they pointed out slightly, giving me flashbacks to dance classes when I was four years old. Other than the costumes, I'd hated every single thing about ballet. I'd always cried on the way to the studio and begged my mom not to leave me there. After she left us for good, I was so scared it was my tantrums that drove her away—that I was a horrible little girl for telling her I didn't want to be a ballerina like her. I practiced the poses over and over when I was alone, telling her in my head that I was sorry, begging her to come back. I took a deep inhale. I'd forgotten about that until this moment.

His hands gently touched my hips, pressing down so that my knees bent. It only took a few seconds before my quads started to burn. "Now," he said, "you are *en garde*."

"Oh, I've been on guard since the moment I stepped into this house."

"*Buono*!" The sparkle in his eyes lit up. "Are you always this honest?"

"What's the point of lying if you can hear my heart accelerate?"

He smiled. The expression was not unlike Nicco's.

"*Cosa*?" I asked, trying out the simple Italian word I'd heard them say so many times.

"You know all about my legendary sword fighting, our vampiric senses, Giovanna's disposition. How much exactly has Nicco told you about us?"

My shoulders stiffened. "It's not a big deal."

"No, not at all. Niccolò loves opening up to people. It's not at all like seeing *una stella canendte*."

"What does that mean?"

His forehead pinched, like he was trying to remember the translation. The words rolled off his tongue in French, and my heart skipped.

"A shooting star?"

"*Sì*! *Shooting.* It's not at all like seeing a shooting star."

And there went my pulse, and there came his smile. There was no point in trying to argue, because when Nicco opened up to me, that's exactly what it felt like: a cosmic phenomenon.

He lightly smacked the side of my quad. "One of the most important things in any fight, be it sword or fist, is staying grounded. You're a witch. You get your power from the earth. Feel it." He pushed my shoulder back.

I wobbled, the rapier flailing in my hand, but my wide stance prevented my fall.

He slipped the handle from my fingers. "*Grazie,* I don't want to have to reattach any of my body parts, *bella*."

I was happy to release it to him. I didn't want to admit that even with the magically-light metal, my triceps were burning. I bent over to stretch my arms over my head and when I stood back upright, he was gone.

His arm curled around my throat from behind, and he yanked me backward.

I grasped at his arm, trying to pull him away. "I wasn't ready!" I choked.

"You must always be ready!" His grip tightened.

I can't bre—"

"I've already told you how to get out of this one!"

"Gabe! It's too tigh—"

He pulled me up. *No. No. I need the ground.* My toes pointed, stretching for the floor. *Adele, do not pass out in a vampire house!* I had one move before blackout. I swung my legs out as high as I could and threw all my weight to the floor, scooping back down, landing hard on my ass, but the momentum pulled him down with me. I scratched at his arms; I still couldn't breathe.

"*Torsion*!" he yelled, shaking me. "Twist! Twist!"

No more air. Spots of light.

"Twist, *dannazione*!"

I threw my weight to the right, twisting my shoulder underneath him, forcing him to fall forward and release me to brace himself. I scrambled away, choking on the air as I gasped it in too quickly.

"Now if this was a real fight," he started to say, but I was already swinging my leg straight at his chest. His arm thrust out, grabbing my calf with such force I fell back to the floor, my hip cracking against the wood. "*Ugh.*"

"*Sì!* Exactly like that, *bella!*" He hovered over me. "You would have kicked me exactly like that, but don't aim for the chest. Go straight for the head."

I swallowed a groan as his eyes lit up with pride.

"Now, let's see how hard you can hit." He pulled me to my feet and grabbed a striped pillow from one of the benches. "The best defensive conditioning is not about training away the fear. The right amount of fear keeps you alive. Defense is about reflex. It's about practice and repetition until your movements become instinctual. The less time you waste thinking, the quicker you get a step ahead of your opponent." He backed away a couple of feet. "Heel of the hand. Open palm strike. Lean into it when you come at me."

I drew back my arm and lunged for his nose just as he raised the pillow. My fist smashed into the soft shield.

"*Buono,*" he said, voice muffled. "Again."

I aimed for one of the other five pain-points Brooke and I had learned at summer camp freshman year. He blocked it again with the pillow. We hopped around, repeating the exercise over and over.

"Can I ask you something?" I sucked in a breath. "And you'll tell me the truth, even though I can't hear your heart rate?"

"Do we get to dare each other after? I like this game. I saw it on a film playing at your father's establishment." He moved the pillow over his solar plexus just as I hit his chest.

"The night in the attic . . . Halloween." My pulse climbed, and I wasn't sure if it was the physical activity or the subject I was broaching. "Why did Emilio refer to Nicco as the most brutal vampire he knew?"

Something in his demeanor changed. He was watching me even more intently. Part of me wanted to take it back, to tell him that it was none of my business.

"Niccolò . . ." He lifted the pillow a few inches, encouraging me to hit again. ". . . is the only vampire in known history to have ever"—my hand slammed into the pillow—"killed their Maker."

I stopped, letting my arms drop to my sides. "Nicco killed Séraphine?"

"Nicco told you about Séraphine?"

"Not in so many words," I said, realizing that Nicco hadn't really told me anything about her, other than suspecting León of letting her go. Everything I knew, I'd seen in his dreams. Unlike the rest of his past, she was not something we'd ever discussed. Now I knew why.

I made another play for his head; he blocked it with ease.

"Maybe I'm becoming jaded," I said, "but killing the vampire who murdered you—who murdered your whole family and forced you to kill your lover—doesn't exactly seem brutal to me, especially not in that time; it seems vengeful. And the accusation coming from Emilio, isn't it a bit hypocritical?"

"That's because you're human; you could never fathom the relationship between vampire and progeny, never understand how impossible defying even the smallest request from your Maker is, much less hide a murderous revenge plot from her, much less train your reflexes to be quicker than hers to execute it. It's *unimaginable.* Niccolò Giovanni Battista Medici was the first to sever the bond for himself—for all of us."

He moved the pillow down as I aimed for his gut.

"Emilio thinks him brutal because he loved Séraphine. We all loved her." He barely flinched as my hand butted the cushion. "Your eyes are *giving away your moves*!" he yelled, stepping forward, forcing me back. "Envision your strategy on a parallel plane, but not in this room—not in this universe!"

I had to actively concentrate on not stepping on my own feet as he moved me around so forcefully.

"Our baby brother might be the most brutal vampire to Emilio, but to me, he's simply the most patient man I have ever known in my four hundred years." The tone of his voice changed; he was no longer the jovial big brother but the slick diplomat, closing in at the end of a negotiation.

"Why is that?" I took two more steps back as he closed in on me.

"She loved all of us as her children, but she was *in love* with Niccolò. They jaunted around Europe in an affair so torrid it made me look like a schoolboy."

My pulse jolted hearing something so intimate about Nicco's past.

He thrust the pillow forward, meeting my hand. "Forty-one years."

"For what?"

He forced me back another step and smiled. "That's how long it took my sweet baby brother to truly win her trust. To trick us. Isolating her from us so we wouldn't stop him. It took him just over four decades to find the perfect, flawless moment to pull her into his arms with enough speed, strength, and confidence"—my back touched the wall —"to ram a stake through her spine and pierce her heart." I glimpsed his fangs. "*He took her from us!*"

I screamed as he leaned in, shut my eyes and thrust my fist forward. The bridge of his nose cracked as the heel of my hand smashed into it.

"And for breaking those shackles . . . !" His nose spewed blood down on me like a bursting balloon.

I screamed again, wincing under the shower of blood.

"We will always be indebted to him."

What? In the silence that followed, I opened my eyes.

The bones crunched as he re-adjusted his nose, but he was unfazed by the fresh gush of blood. "Did you just *close your eyes* when you hit me?"

A door slammed open with a surprised shout. In a blur, something came between us. *Leather and soap.*

"Nicco!" I yelled.

But he'd already hurled Gabe across the room, into one of the benches, smashing the antique like it was made of Popsicle sticks. Then I was in the air, and we were out the window, down the balcony stairs, standing in the middle of the crown of wild rosebushes.

"Where are you hurt?" he asked, frantically moving my hair, yanking the collar of my sweater, blood smearing across my neck.

"I'm fine!"

"She's fine," Gabe echoed from the balcony above, stretching his back.

Nicco whipped back up the stairs and grabbed his brother's collar.

"Calm down!" Gabe said in English, before a waterfall of Italian went back and forth between them.

I ran back up as Nicco shoved him into the house. The anger in Nicco's face deepened as Gabe, speaking wildly in Italian, gestured at the pillow and to me, and then shrugged like it was no big deal. The other three vampires had also come down. Lisette looked startled and even worried, but Martine was alert, like she might pounce on Nicco if this escalated any further. Emilio watched with calm interest. He crossed his arms, an almost nostalgic smile tugging the corners of his lips.

Nicco's gaze landed on the trunk. He stormed over to the sword, muttering what sounded like curses in Italian, picked it up off the floor, and turned to Emilio with a questioning look.

Emilio shrugged. "I've been upstairs with"—he glanced at me —"our houseguests."

Nicco looked to me for confirmation. Suddenly I felt like I'd completely invaded his life. If I knew one thing about Nicco, it was that he hated being left in the dark.

"*Désolée.*" I moved toward him. "*C'est ma faute.* I was running on the Moonwalk, waiting for you, and Gabe attacked me—" He turned a rage-filled glare on his brother, but I grabbed his arm. "Wait! It's fine. I *asked* him to train me to fight, and I accidentally broke his nose. It's his blood!"

He looked at the sheaths on the floor and then back to his brother. "She's barely experienced enough to touch a blade, let alone fight with one!"

"Yes, we established that," I said.

"She'd just end up hurting herself!"

"Not if she learned to use the Ouroboros properly."

Emilio's back stiffened, and he peered over at the rapier.

"I mean," Gabe said, "at her level it would take years, but—"

"You gave her Giovanna's sword?" Emilio roared.

Gabe threw his hands in the air. "It's been collecting dust for centuries!"

"So what! It's Giovanna's!"

"Giovanna is a vampire," Nicco said. "She doesn't need a weapon. She *is* a weapon."

Was. "Gabe didn't give it to me," I reassured him. "He just showed it to me."

They all turned to me.

I shrugged, echoing words from Nicco's dreams: "It's . . . *è magnifico.* And magical. Made by Venetian metal witches, like me. I mean, like I used to be. The witch part, not the Venetian part."

Nicco's frown was so tight it took a moment for his half-smile to form, and even then, he still just looked confused. I'd caught him off guard, which was not something I thought possible.

Emilio swiped the small rapier and its sheath from the floor, as if my mere presence was tainting it, and Gabe adjusted his nose again.

Nicco pulled me aside, and for the first time he didn't seem to care whose eyes were on us. He touched my face. "Are you sure you're okay?"

I nodded, following his gaze to the blood spatter all over my sweater. "All Gabe's."

"I'll take you home."

"Niccolò!" Gabe yelled. "When's the last time *you* swung a blade?"

"If you haven't noticed, brother, swordplay has gone out of fashion."

"*Eccellente*! *Di guardia*."

Nicco had just enough time to turn and catch the sword Gabe vamp-hurled at us. "Gabriel, I don't want—"

Before he could finish, Gabe's sword was slamming into his, and his free hand pushed me away so forcefully I fell to the floor and slid backward.

Emilio looked down at me. "You're going to want to move."

I scrambled away as the swords clanked and the brothers danced across the room. As I hurried to them, the other three vampires in the room all leaned in.

Gabe said something in Italian in a mocking voice, which made Emilio smirk with delight.

I don't know what it was—the fraternal bond, the physical exertion, or the adrenaline—but the mood in the room shifted. Gabe was more focused than I'd ever seen him, his usually perfect hair flopping messily into his eyes, but his joviality was back as he forced Nicco closer to the window.

Nicco wasn't close to jovial, but his brow had unfurled a bit.

Gabe swung his sword in an arc, straight at Nicco's torso, and I yelped, but Nicco leapt sideways so inhumanly fast, the blade missed him completely and swished through the velvet curtain instead. Gabe lunged toward him, keeping the offensive position, but Nicco blocked. Grunts expelled from their lips, and each slam of the blade became deafening. Gabe's earlier comment about having to reattach body parts suddenly felt like a very real possibility. Smiles crossed all the vampires' faces, but the thought of Nicco getting struck was making me nauseous.

I glanced at Emilio, whose enjoyment seemed to have soured slightly; his eyes were zeroed in on Nicco, scrutinizing his every move.

Gabe whipped around, his sword hitting Nicco's so hard the force twisted Nicco with it.

Emilio shook his head with brotherly disappointment, which for some reason made me extra nervous—and then I realized why. Gabe thrust his foot into Nicco's turn, and Nicco went down to the floor hard. Gabe's sword zipped to his throat, and I sprang forward, only to find Lisette at my side, her hand around my arm, keeping me from going farther.

"*Complementi*," Nicco said, looking up at his brother, still gripping his sword.

Gabe's eyes darkened as he looked down, emanating the same vibe I was getting from Emilio: annoyance and disappointment. Something in his posture indicated this was not over. "Niccolò Giovanni Battista Medici, if you think for *un secondo* that I believe your sword-skills have not outpaced mine in the *three hundred years* I slept in that attic, then you have forgotten that I am the brains of this family."

Nicco's smile widened, and with a move that made me wonder whether he'd spent part of his very long existence training as an immortal samurai, he threw his sword up to the ceiling, hooked Gabe's leg with his own, slamming him to the floor, and caught his own blade as he sprang back to his feet. Gabe leapt back up too, and their blades whipped through the air again, no longer just clicking and clanking but crashing like thunder.

Emilio's face unsoured, and he murmured to me, "He let Gabriel win the first time. Now it will actually be interesting."

As they moved around the room, my eyes could barely follow them, only catching pieces when they slowed each other with shows of pure strength. Gabe looked like a warrior, masterful and brave and relentless; but there was something about Nicco's level of training that made him look . . . otherworldly. The way he twisted and jumped and flipped through the air like he was flying. He easily regained the offensive position with a single move any time Gabe took the lead. He had a fearlessness in his eyes that I'd only ever seen in . . . Emilio.

Nicco struck so hard that Gabe planted his feet to better meet the swings—a succession of three. When the sequence didn't force Gabe's blade to the ground, Nicco leapt into the air and twisted, *a complete rotation*, throwing his full momentum behind his sword as it crashed into his brother's. The crack pierced my ears and sent Gabe's blade skidding across the floor. Only when I looked back did I realize Gabe's sword was still in hand—it had broken in half.

Nicco examined his own bent blade, and then tossed the weapon down to the wooden floor. He strode over to Emilio. "And that," he said, "is why vampires do not need swords." He yanked the leather-wrapped Ouroboros from Emilio's grip, took my hand with his other, and calmly walked us out of the room.

Thump-thump.

Thump-thump.

His fingers threaded through mine, and I knew he wasn't about to throw me out of the house for coming here without him.

And I was grateful.

Thump.

Thump.

We didn't speak as we walked down the sconce-lit hallway, but he was still breathing heavily. He led us into another dark room and closed the door behind us.

As he lit an oil lamp on the desk, a bed and some of the other furnishings came into view. *We're in his bedroom.*

As he gently set the Ouroboros down in the corner, my heart beat so hard I was sure it must be audible. *Why does this feel so bizarre to me?* I'd seen his old Florentine bedroom . . . but that was Nicco as a human; I'd never thought about the Nicco I knew as having something as normal as a bedroom. I don't know why. He was just this enigmatic creature to me, one who could twist through the air and scale Ferris wheels and look beautiful even in a dark shadow. But here we were next to a four-poster bed carved fantastically from a dark cherry wood. The book on the nightstand looked to be a hundred years old, resting underneath a pair of headphones. I wondered what he listened to. Rock 'n' roll? Podcasts? Operas?

He tugged my wrist, leading me across the room. On the way he paused to retrieve a plum-colored towel from the armoire and a black sweater from the dresser.

He opened another door and flipped the light on. A bathroom. Nicco's bathroom. *Nicco has a toothbrush and pomade and towels.* It was all so normal, it felt abnormal.

He tipped my chin up. "Are you sure you're okay?"

I nodded. And even though there was something in his eyes that told me he wanted to strip off my clothes and examine me for himself, he let out a breath and seemed to let it go.

He set down the towel and handed me the sweater, which I knew was cashmere as soon as it touched my fingertips. "You can wear this if you'd like. Or I could go ask Lise to lend you— Or, there's really no rush, I could take you home to change before we go out."

I was so caught off guard being in his intimate space that I didn't respond.

"If you still want to go after all this?" he added.

"This is fine." I quickly nodded. "*Grazie.*"

"Feel free to use anything here to clean up. I'm going to shower . . . Lisette and I were out . . ."

Thump-thump.

"There's another washroom down the hallway. I'll be there."

I nodded again.

"Will you lock the door behind me? I know it doesn't really matter in the grand scheme of things, but it will make me feel better about leaving you alone."

"D'accord."

We walked back into the bedroom, and he grabbed a few more things for himself. And then still stunned by the progression of the night, I followed him to the door.

He stepped out into the hallway and then looked back.

"I'll be fine," I said, and closed it as he stood watching me. I knew he was still on the other side, waiting to hear the lock. I twisted the key and leaned back against the wooden door, taking a few deep breaths, staring at Nicco's bed, contemplating for the first time everything Gabe had revealed.

I imagined Nicco in his bed with Séraphine, making love to her—twisting her around and plunging a stake through her back. Holding it in place as she fought for her last breath.

Then it wasn't Séraphine I was imagining.

It was me.

Bleeding out. Just like in Nicco's fantasies.
Thump-thump.
Thump-thump.
Never trust a vampire.
Never trust a Medici.

CHAPTER 29

THE GO-BETWEEN'ERS

After spending the afternoon in the studio with Adele, I felt a level of optimism that was unnatural for a New Yorker. Something had *finally* gone right between us. I was so protective of the moment, I hadn't told Dee or Codi. I'd needed something that was just ours, and now I felt more grounded than I had in weeks.

That optimism faded as the wheels of Désirée's SUV turned slowly over the broken street, crunching over months of debris. The solemnness of the neighborhood crept in. No one had bothered to clear the streets, because no one had returned to this part of the Ninth Ward yet. The neighborhood was blighted and desolate and felt like despair.

The electric grid was still defunct, so it was hard to see anything past the vehicle's headlights, especially on a night like tonight, when a low-forming fog was rolling through the streets from the river, but I was familiar enough with the area: the spray-painted *X's*, the water-marks. Every house told a story with the string of belongings that had floated out into the streets and into the trees. As Désirée crawled over potholes that stretched the width of the street, bouncing us in our seats, our mission rolled around in my head. Not only were we about to do a séance, but we were going to ask Ghede-Plumaj, aka *the zombi collector*, for assistance saving the library of souls.

Until tonight, I'd never had an issue fathoming any of it, not the witchery or magic or even the vampires, ghosts, and possessions . . . but *this*. Something about doing a séance to conjure a Ghede felt very next level. The Gran Bwa ritual had been badass, but I wasn't sure I wanted to encounter a death lwa. A death-anything. And so, the closer we got, the more the pre-séance anxiety began to consume me.

But I wanted to help.

Désirée stopped at the gate, cut the engine, and killed the lights. Codi leaned between us from the back seat, and we all gazed through the window up at the hexenspiegel's net, whose sparkles were only visible to the magical eye. We'd chosen St. Roch Cemetery with the idea that since so many of Codi's ancestors were buried here, it might help juice our magic.

The iron gates coiled into swirling patterns, strong and protective delicate frills. Beneath the sheen of the netting, the letters of the iron archway gleamed in the moonlight.

SAINT ROCH'S
CAMPOS SANTOS

"Just remember," Désirée said, "the Ghede are notorious tricksters."

I turned back to look at her. The glow of the dashboard lights underlit her face in a grim, blueish way. "What does that mean?"

"Nothing. Just tell the truth. The more you try to hide, the more they mess with you. They hate liars, hypocrisy—that sort of thing." She opened her car door and stepped out. "They're dead. They have no need to mince words or stroke delicate egos."

"So, they're basically New Yorkers," Codi said as we exited the car. "You should totally relate."

"Funny." I didn't slam the door, but it sounded like it in the pin-drop silent night.

Two huge brick pillars flanked the gate, each shouldering a limestone lady in prayer, giving the entrance a graceful feel.

Désirée popped a button to release the trunk.

I slung on my knapsack and grabbed two brown bags that contained a meal of hot coffee, herring, and black rice balls, all cooked in a sauce so spicy it would wake the dead. I guess that was kind of the point. Wake them. Warm them. Invite them for a ride.

Codi dropped to the ground, morphing into Onyx, and with a flick of his tail, hopped through the iron bars. I waited as Dee crossed the street to the neutral ground where a giant oak tree stretched out to both sides. She lifted her arm and a branch swooped down and raised her up. Then she ran across the branch to one of the brick pillars, and I flew over the arch, felt the weight of the sacred grounds—the energy of those who came before us.

As soon as my feet touched down, I heard the voices of the dead billowing through the invisible curtains that shrouded their unseen world.

Désirée lowered herself from the pillar and dropped to the ground. "Let's go," she said, picking up her bags.

I clicked on my flashlight.

Codi and I followed her down the center path as she scoped the grounds for the perfect place to set up. Purple flecks flickered across the grids of mausoleums, the walls of oven tombs, and the faces of Virgin Mary statues in grottos: the remnants of the protection spell we'd done last night.

"The crucifix might make a good *potomitan*," Désirée said, nodding down the path to the huge cross-bearing Jesus, on top of which was where we'd placed the hexenspiegel.

"A what?" I asked.

"A *potomitan.* A pole for the lwa to descend from the Spirit World into ours and then ascend again."

"Whatever works," Codi said.

I set my bags down and craned my neck to look up at it, picturing this death lwa appearing from the sky and crawling down Jesus to Désirée. I had no idea if that was how it actually happened, but my palms broke into a sweat.

Désirée fluffed out a black silk scarf with silver metallic fringe, cleansed the air, and unloaded the witchy picnic spread, the air around us absorbing the pungent aromas of sage, hot sauce, and coffee. In addition to the meal for the dead and the usual magical supplies, she'd brought a neon-pink feather boa, a box of Camels, a handful of pennies so shiny they looked freshly minted, some roasted pistachios, and several extra purple and black candles. And of course, the homemade piman.

Last, Désirée placed a clay pot with a matching lid on the scarf. I'd seen it before . . . the night of Ritha's circle. She handed me the heavy leather bag, its contents clanking together, and I went behind Codi, adding the glass-encased sanctuary candles as he poured the salt circle.

"*Isaac*?"

"What?" I stopped and looked at each of them when they didn't answer, but they both just looked at me like *huh?*

I shrugged, and they turned back to their tasks.

"Isaac? What's that?" "What's that smell?" "What are all of those things?" "An offering for the Baron. And it isn't even Saturday."

A whirl of cool air circled my neck.

"Something's going on."

"A fête."

"A fête. A fête. A fête."

I wondered where Julie was. It was easier to ignore the others when she was here—or maybe it's just that they felt less ominous with her and Stormy as their ambassadors.

"Oui, something's going on."

"Maybe it has to do with that sparkling net."

The air was thick and wet and even stickier than usual, which made it easier to feel another cool touch to my neck as the voices continued to swirl around me.

"Isaac, we're already dead. There's nothing to worry about."

"I'll be the judge of that," I said, resulting in side-eye from Dee.

Codi looked up. "It's going to rain."

The sky lit up with a flash of lightning, and instantly droplets of water began falling.

"*Shit*!" Désirée threw herself over her grimoire, and we scrambled to gather everything as the rain came down faster.

"*Hurry*!" With her arms full, she began running deeper into the cemetery.

"Should we just come back tomorrow night?" I yelled, but a crack of thunder drowned out my words, as if someone in the storm clouds differed in opinion.

"Don't you want to save Ren?" she yelled back.

"Yes! I'd also like to not get electrocuted!"

"Then run faster!"

The sky opened up in a way that it only did in New Orleans, with curtains of rain that swept the streets with intention, drenching anything that dared remain in the path of its cleanse.

We didn't stop until we got to the chapel, where we crammed together under the small overhang, backs flat against the arched wooden door.

"Shit," she said again, defeated, her wet hair sticking to her face. She tugged at the bag hanging from my elbow and with a huff, transferred some of the candles she was holding. Désirée did not like to deviate from the plan once it was set in motion.

"It's going to pass," Codi said. And then, as if he had a direct line with Mother Nature herself, the rain eased, and stopped. But the grounds were completely soaked, puddles covering the bricked paths in every direction.

A shiver ripped up my spine as something creaked behind us. We turned, and the chapel door opened wide with an answering groan. We stared into the pitch black beyond the threshold, and then at each other.

"Maybe it was Plumaj," Désirée said. "Maybe the Ghede know we're here, and they're waiting for us. Come on."

I smeared water off my eyes. "Do you really think it's a good idea to do a séance in a church?"

"Why not? It's dry, and the Ghede love hanging out in Catholic churches. The Baron is syncretic with St. Expédit, and Maman Brijit with St. Brigid. It's really not that weird. And it's literally offering itself to us." Désirée stepped inside, disappearing into the darkness.

I followed them in, and the door slammed shut behind us.

Goosebumps pricked the back of my neck.

"It wasn't the Ghede; it was me," came a soft, French-accented voice next to my ear.

My spine snapped straight, and I dropped one of the sanctuary candles, shattering the glass all over the marble floor. "Jesus, Julie!"

"Why are you so jumpy tonight, *mon chéri*?"

Codi and Désirée snickered.

"Oh, I don't know? Because we're trespassing in a cemetery chapel on a stormy night so we can conjure up a death lwa?"

"God," Désirée said, striking a match, "you really need to get laid or something." She leaned over a rack of small candles, lighting a row of them one by one. "I don't remember you being this uptight when Adele was around—"

"Gross," Codi said. "Not an image I want in my head."

"Maybe you should light a votive." She looked back at me. "Do a little banda to Ghede-Nibo so he'll bless your near future with orgas—"

"Okay, *okay*," Codi yelled, dipping his hand into the basin of holy water and blessing himself. "Thinking about Adele having sex is bad enough. I do not want to think about her having orgasms."

"I wasn't talking about her having one." She dipped her fingers. "I was talking about her giving one to—"

"*Désirée*!" My voice echoed up to the dome ceiling. "What is your deal?"

"Sorry!" She inhaled a deep breath through her nose. "I just want to make sure they don't think I'm a prude."

"Who?" Codi asked.

"The Ghede."

I slid the broken glass over to a corner with the side of my boot. "What does that matter?"

"Because they're erotic. Perverse. You know, sex, life, death, and the circle continues? They're dead. They have no reason to be reserved, and they especially like to pick on those who are more . . . prim. Or so I hear."

"Well, then talk about your own orgasms." I clicked on my flashlight and moseyed to the far-right aisle, thinking about Adele and the night on the S.S. *Hope*: how warm her body had felt against mine, how her orbs pulsed brighter the closer she got to peaking. *Ugh.* I wanted to kick the wooden pew in frustration. *What would have happened if I hadn't fallen asleep that night?* If we hadn't gotten separated?

I shone my flashlight through an iron gate that led to an adjoining room with medieval dungeon vibes. *Maybe she'd still have her magic. Maybe she wouldn't have been attacked by Brigitte—* The whites of a pair of eyes stared at me through the darkness. I jerked back hard, and the flashlight blinked out.

I shook it back on, searching for the eyes. "Who's there?"

"What's wrong?" Désirée asked, and both of them hurried up behind me.

I swept the light across the room and found the eyes again. And that's all they were: a pair of perfectly sculpted glass eyes, resting on a ceramic dish, staring back at us.

"St. Lucy," Codi said, as if no further explanation was required. He shined his phone on the statue holding the dish in front of her: a saintly woman in a purple robe with two shadowy eye sockets.

Dee opened the gate and we followed her in. "I remember my Auntie Cherise bringing me here once when I was a kid. My cousin was hit by a car, riding her bike, and they thought she was never going to walk again."

Codi struck a match, and a warm halo of light unmasked the dilapidated chamber. The right wall was covered with foot braces, leg braces, and old metal neck braces that looked straight out of a medical history textbook. Some of the contraptions were so antiquated I couldn't guess what they'd been used for. Boots, crutches, silk flowers, strands of pearls, and gold crosses were littered among them.

On the back wall, a large window made of many tiny panes of glass diffused the moonlight. "What is this place?" I was unsure whether to be completely freaked out or whether to memorize every inch of the space as inspiration for a future art project.

"The Healing Room," Codi said, lighting the dust-coated candles in a cobweb-encrusted iron rack below the window. The flickering flames gradually revealed the altar it stood on, which was covered with paper notes, prayer cards, and drawings of different body parts from kidneys to brains to hearts. Somehow it had all been spared by the floods—there was no waterline inside the church.

"What's a healing room?" I walked over, examining the antique anatomical curios and bric-a-brac, my gaze drawing to a yellowed piece of loose-leaf paper—a picture of a set of lungs drawn with red crayon.

"St. Roch was a great healer when the plague was raging in Europe. So when we had a yellow fever epidemic in the 1800s, the priest here prayed to him for a miracle: that his parishioners be spared. Tens of thousands of people died across the city, but here? Zero. Afterward, he built a shrine to St. Roch, and people have been leaving *ex-votos* asking for healing prayers ever since."

I gazed up at the wall beside me: a Dr. Frankenstein's gallery of body parts: plaster-cast feet, legs, hands, and arms hanging from crude iron hooks. They seemed to wriggle with the motion of the flickering candlelight. And hearts. So many plaster hearts. Some anatomical and others better resembling mammoth Valentine candies with the word "*MERCI*" etched on them.

"We should do the ritual here," Désirée said, setting down her bags. "The Ghede are great healers too. The energy is perfect."

"I'm into it," Codi said.

I shrugged, warming up to the idea of the chapel, one step removed from the graves and the voices.

"Good." Désirée dug through her bag. "Catch." She tossed me a burlap sack. It was heavy, like a small bag of flour.

"What's this?"

"Cornmeal. The Ghede vèvès are marked with a black ribbon in my grimoire. You're the artist; draw them outside the door while we finish. The Baron and Maman's, since we want to talk to one of their children."

I grabbed her book of magic from her bag and settled on the marble floor right outside the gate to the Healing Room. The page marked with the ribbon was entitled: **L E S G U E D E**.

The base of the Baron's vèvè was a cross, and the base of Maman's was a heart.

I dipped my fingers into the grains, which had been turned a dark color somewhere between purple and charcoal. As I sprinkled the cornmeal in the intricate patterns shown in the grimoire, Dee and Codi went out into the church to scavenge some kind of *potomitan*.

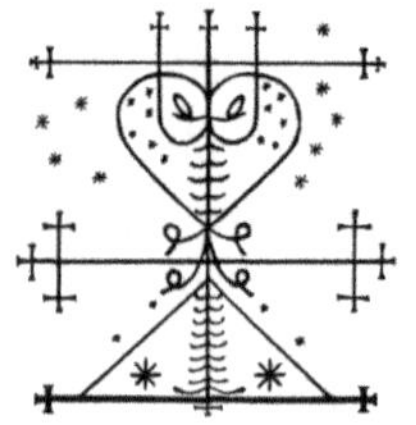

They came back with a giant sacramental candle that almost touched the ceiling of the Healing Room, and then began recreating the circle we'd started outside. Working on the vèvès was so soothing that by the time I'd finished, my jittery nerves were settling, despite the scents of spicy food and piman wafting out of the room, hinting at the events to come.

I went back into the chamber and gazed up at the huge candle. "Ghede stripper pole?"

Désirée glanced up, unamused.

The Ghede cornucopia, the pack of Camels, and the little clay pot were resting at the foot of the *potomitan* along with all of the other offerings. She opened a big brown paper bag that had barely survived the rain and removed two chains of a plant with blueish leaves.

"Herb of grace?" Codi's tone was sharp—almost accusatory—as she draped one over his shoulders. "What do we need that for?"

She slipped one around her own neck. "*Ruta graveolens* has a strong connection to all of the Invisibles, and it will help draw out the positive spirits like the Ghede while protecting you from *les morts*." She grabbed fistfuls of leaves from the bag, spreading them in the corners of the room.

"*Les morts*? Désirée, you didn't say anything about *les morts*!" Codi crossed his arms. "Are you sure this is a good idea?"

"Yes. Everyone just needs to have a little more faith."

"What are *les morts*?" I asked.

She turned to me, pulled one more herb chain from the bag, and placed it around my neck. "You know, like, malevolent spirits that could harm you."

My nerves went back to skillet-sizzling level. I could practically hear Ritha Hulking-out because we'd unleashed evil spirits into the city.

"We are *not* going to let any morts escape. I researched everything on how to close the ceremony properly this time." She pulled a tiny perfume vial from her pocket, popped the lid, and dabbed her finger. "But just in case." She rubbed the oil on my forehead in the shape of a cross.

Jesus Christ. What are we doing?

She repeated the ritual on Codi and then herself before slipping the vial back into her pocket. "Okay. You know what to do, right?" She took off her shoes and tied a white scarf around her head. "I probably won't be able to help you once I'm Plumaj's *cheval*."

Codi and I both nodded. "We ask her what to do with the souls," he answered.

"Don't let her distract you from the mission. And don't forget to give her the offering," she said, nodding to the spread of food, the spicy scent of which was filling the building. She took the bottle of piman and dribbled a stream from the door to the *potomitan* and handed me a bottle of water to do the same. Then she laid her grimoire open on the floor and took a deep breath. "We're ready."

Flashlights and phone-lights went off, and we gathered around the *potomitan*. The candles lit up the engorged plaster hearts on the wall, creating flickering shadows behind them. Désirée lit one more: a thick black candle. When the wax started to run, she dribbled it at the base of the *potomitan*, whispering words in Creole.

I pushed down the waves of nervousness washing over me. We linked hands, and the incantation rolled off Désirée's tongue like she was born to say it. I guess, technically, she was.

Baron Samedi bel garçon
Maman Brijit belle fille
We need you, we ask you
To send us your child.
She squeezed our hands: the cue to join in.
Ghede Plumaj's attention we seek
We need you, we ask you, we serve you
We've brought her a feast

My mouth bent awkwardly to form the foreign words, but as the air snapped around us, the words came stronger and louder, in a singsong rhythm that echoed out of the room and up to the dome of the church. The metal braces and hearts and feet and hands began to clap and tap against the walls. *Clap, tap. Clap, tap.*

"Ghede Plumaj's attention we seek."

A drumbeat sounded—staccato slaps—but there were no drummers here. A throb of energy pulled my gaze to the corner near the window, where an elderly black man was sitting on a stool, a silhouette nearly as dark as the shadows, slapping his long hand down on his drum. His skin looked like it had been brushed with a thick layer of talc, all but the hollows around his eyes and the button of his nose, which were pitch black, making his face resemble a skull. A corpse. The beat rose, a whole circle of drumming. A rattle. A hiss. Next came the voices.

"Don't be afraid to move, Isaac." "Don't you like to dance?" "Just move your hips. Don't Yankees dance the banda?" "Why so serious, sugar puddin'?"

And then I knew who was drumming and whose voices were filling the church. Filling my head.

"Zwazo a ti kras se pè."

"Don't be scared, little bird."

"We're here with you."
"Always, Isaac."
"Always."

Ghede Plumaj's attention we seek
We need you, we ask you, we serve you

Codi squeezed my hand harder.

Désirée's eyes locked with mine, and her voice rose over the symphony of spirits. "Whatever I do, just . . . go with it until you get the answers, okay?"

I nodded, but a last minute worry slipped out: "But what about the piman? Won't it make you sick?"

She didn't answer. Her eyes were on the little clay pot on the floor.

"What's it for?" I asked.

"To contain *my ti-bon-age*."

"To contain your what?"

"My—"

In a *whoosh*, every candle flame blew out.

"Her soul," she said in the darkness, but her voice sounded thick and strange.

"Whose soul?" My pulse pounded in my ears.

I could hear breaths in the silence as a tiny glow came from a single candle at the bottom of the altar—the thick black candle Désirée had bound the ritual to. It grew brighter and brighter, and then there was a distant *ding*.

Ding.

Ding.

Coming from the main chapel.

A sliver of moonlight shone through the window onto Désirée's face. She grabbed the bottle of piman from our cornucopia of offerings and headed into the darkness of the church.

"Did it work?" I whispered to Codi. "Is she Plumaj?"

When he didn't answer, I looked back. He was relighting the rack of votives, his back to me.

"Come on!" I said, nervous about Désirée being out there on her own.

"Where are you taking me?" The softness of his voice was strange.

He looked up. His eyes were black. No color. No whites.

"Codi . . . ?"

He rocked his hips to the side, and then in a figure-eight motion. His arms bent behind his head as he stepped closer, hips still rocking. I glanced down and jumped back.

"Codi!" He was erect—and not some kind of hallway-brush half-boner: he had a fully pitched tent.

He wagged closer, and I backed into the shelf, scattering glass eyeballs all over the bricks. He thrust again.

All I could do was gape at him—not because he was swinging his dick around, humping the air, but because the tent he was pitching was now some kind of sparkly black fabric. His sweats were gone.

"What the hell? How did you . . . ?" It was a dress. I think. On a man. I think? Who was definitely not Codi. *I think.*

He ran his hands up the sides of his face. His stubble had disappeared. His nose was widening and cheekbones sharpening, his bone structure morphing beneath his skin, which was darkening into a deep mahogany.

What the fuuuuu . . . ?

His lips plumped into a pout. His body became thinner, and the black sparkling dress laid flatter against his now birdish chest, the V-neckline plunging nearly to his navel.

"Désirée!" I called.

Codi gave an exaggerated twirl, and a swirl of mauve-colored fabric appeared from thin air around him: a long, form-fitting jacket with a line of small black buttons that looked like it could have belonged to a passenger on the *Titanic*. He went up on his tiptoes, as if some magical force was drawing him up, and long, soft dreadlocks decorated with ribbons and jewelry cascaded out of a mauve headscarf.

He thrust again.

"Désirée, we have a problem!" I yelled, leaning away.

"I can solve your problems," he said, going back to the figure eights.

"A really *big* problem!"

I scrambled out into the church. Codi—or Plumaj—followed me, pressing intimately against my back, his arms circling my shoulders as he began grinding against me.

"Codi!" I yelled, trying to twist away. "Come on—!"

His arms locked tighter; a shriek came from up above.

"I have titttttttties!"

We both paused to look up. Twenty feet above the altar, Désirée was sitting on the right arm of the giant crucifix . . . feeling herself up. *What the?*

"Désirée?" I shouted, searching around for a ladder. "How the hell did you get up there?"

She looked at me. "Isaac, I have titties!" Her accent sounded slightly off: less NOLA and more French or islander or something. She arched against the wall, squeezing her breasts, marveling at her own anatomy.

What the fuck? Was Désirée being molested by a Ghede? Does it count if it's with her own hands? "Dee, I'm getting you down!"

Ghede-Codi grabbed my hips, pulling me against him, egging her on. I twisted, trying to peel him off, but he only gyrated faster.

"Oussou!" she screamed, her eyes lighting up. She jumped to her feet, and the big wooden cross tilted beneath her weight, about to topple over.

"Shit!" I ripped away from Codi.

He howled with laughter. "Cursing in da Lawd's house!"

I pulled a gust of wind to catch Dee, but she opened her arms wide, and the cross just glided down for her. The arm tipped to the ground, and she leaped off.

As soon as her toes touched the floor, her floral blouse transformed into a black netted croptop, her breasts morphing into firm pecs. Her jeans dissolved into white leather pants, and a matching jacket covered her arms. Her long hair was gone, practically buzzed underneath a white leather bowler hat. When she smiled, she had a young man's face, with lips painted a deep shade of orchid and eyelids packed with purple glitter that extended out into a dramatic cat's-eye.

"Masaka!" Ghede-Codi yelled.

"Oussou, feel my tits!" Ghede-Dee said, poking out Désirée's chest and giving it a shake.

Codi's hands reached out, and I leapt between them."No way, man! Don't touch."

"Okay," he said, hooking his arms through mine, pinning me closer. And then Ghede-Dee's icy hands were underneath my shirt, tracing from my abs to my chest.

"Whoa!" I leaned back, only to feel a tongue against the base of my neck. My spine jumped. "Codi!"

As I tried to pull away, Ghede-Dee's orchid mouth crept closer to my collar, bringing me to a panic as I oscillated between breaking away and trying to keep them from touching each other. I felt like this was some kind of karmic retribution for having fantasized about threesomes which may have involved coven members, but where Adele had always been a key player. *And this was not at all how it went down!* Dee-whoever's lips puckered against my skin. "*No*!" I cried and rammed out from between them.

Ghede-Dee grabbed Ghede-Codi's hands and pulled them to her chest, and everything Dee had said earlier about prudish behavior suddenly made sense.

"Yes, Désirée, you have tits!" I yelled. "Nothing me and half the witches in this city haven't seen before."

They both turned to me with half-pout, half-smiles, like some kind of Death-Court jesters, and laughed wildly like this had all been a game and I'd finally figured out how to play.

"Very funny," I said, bent over my knees, breathing heavily.

"Just admit that you liked it," Ghede-Codi said, his finger tracing his stomach, pulling the very short dress up even higher.

"Well, what we gonna do now?" Ghede-Dee asked with a glittery pout.

I spied the bottle of piman on the floor, grabbed it, and hopped up to the altar. As soon as I uncorked the bottle, they scrambled to the altar and positioned themselves at the table across from me. Ghede-Codi leaned over and swiped it from my hand.

"Watch out, that's very hot! I don't think you want to—" But he was already downing a giant glug.

He howled from the burn, and for the first time since his Ghede had entered him, his hips stopped circling. Not that he'd *completely* calmed down. He shook off the extra piman from his chin and licked his lips. The waft from his breath alone stung my eyes. Any human would be puking all over the floor after one sip of what was essentially pepper spray on steroids.

I stole back the bottle, worried for Codi's stomach lining. "I'm guessing that neither of you are Ghede-Plumaj?"

"Plumaj?" Ghede-Codi screeched, slapping his knees like it was the funniest thing he'd ever heard.

"Silly boy," Ghede-Dee said slyly, pulling the pack of Camels out of her suit-jacket pocket. *How did she get those?* She slid a cigarette out and placed it between her now masculine lips.

"Oh." I reached out. "I don't think that's a good—"

She snapped her fingers, and with a *whoosh* every candle in the church ignited along with the cigarette. The end crackled as she took a long drag. "I am Masaka." She blew the smoke into my face. "And this is Oussou."

I fanned it away as Oussou-Codi twirled, his mauve-colored coat spinning out. When he came to a stop, there was a pickax hanging over his shoulder. "Pleased to make your acquaintance." He leaned over to kiss my hand.

"Likewise," I said.

He stepped back to rest on Masaka-Désirée's shoulder, his perfect cheekbones dangerously close to the shiny four-inch spikes her shoulders were studded with. Masaka took another drag of the cigarette. They looked like a couple of drag-queen models who'd worked a Chelsea club stage all night, only with a graveyard hue. Like the drumming man, they were also both dusted in a thin layer of whitish-gray powder.

"I'm Isaac."

"An island-witch with wings," Oussou-Codi said.

"Um, New Yorker-witch."

"And the Fire witch's lover—"

"Glad to hear someone still thinks I have a chance."

"New York, New Shmork," said Masaka-Dee, cigarette dangling from a sly glittering smile. "You an island witch, child."

"Right. Bermuda." I wondered if Susannah was watching me through some supernatural peephole. "Is it okay if I ask you a few questions?"

Masaka-Dee crossed her arms, and a thin leather cord floated in front of her face out of nowhere, with a thick sewing needle attached to one end. The needle whirled through the air like a worm. She snapped two fingers, and the cord disappeared. A droplet of red splashed onto the white altar cloth.

When I looked back up, blood was dripping down her stubbly chin, and the cord was threaded through her lips. *Dee's lips? Fuck, fuck, fuck.*

Oussou murmured something, and I glanced over to see that a metal zipper had closed Codi's mouth. *Holy shit.*

I paced along the backside of the altar. "*Ohhhh,* this is bad." How mad would Désirée be if I abandoned ship? But then again, how mad would she be to find part of her body mutilated?

Masaka didn't seem to be in pain . . . and Désirée could heal herself if need be. *Right*? And that was definitely Dee's death-stare burning through, as if telling me to get on with it.

Oussou-Codi uncrossed his arms and unzipped his lips. "You give me no love and no food. This fête is—" He pinched his nose and let out a long snore sound. Then he held his elbow out to Masaka, who took it, and they both turned to leave, hopping down the altar steps in sync.

"No, no, no, you can't go. We aren't finished!"

They both raised their free arms and simultaneously flipped me off.

"Oh, just because I didn't want to have some kind of freaky death-lwa orgy?"

Suddenly, Oussou's words registered. *Shit.* "Wait! I have food!" I ran down the steps to the healing room and quickly re-emerged with the plate of herring and Tabasco.

They were already opening the chapel door.

"Please, look! It's especially for you!" I uncapped the bottle of Tabasco and began shaking it wildly over the plate.

They both paused mid-step.

With a *whoosh*, they were back at the altar, gripping the table, staring down at the plate. The cord began unthreading from Masaka's lips, inch-by-inch. Oussou smacked his unzipped mouth.

"And there's more," I said. "I'll be right back."

As they dug into the first plate, I grabbed the other dishes of rice and herring and coffee and pistachios served on the altar. They sprinkled hot sauce over every bite. I'd also grabbed the big black candle, which had already burned halfway down.

Each time I started to ask a question, they stuffed more food in their mouths.

Dominate, Isaac. Don't fuck this up. My Pop's voice rumbled through my head: *Take control of the situation.*

I opened the tabernacle behind me and found two chalices and two crystal carafes, one with water, the other with wine. I hooked the two cups with my fingers and placed them on the altar. Their conversation had escalated to mimicking sexual positions. I turned back for the carafe, choking back a swig of cheap gross wine, wishing for a shot of moonshine.

"*Okay*!" I yelled.

They looked up, mid-banda.

"Let's play a game." I wiggled the bottle of piman. "I'm going to ask you a question, and whoever is the first to answer gets a shot."

"*Oui. Oui. Oui*," they both hissed, twirling the boas.

"First, an easy one," I said. "Can souls live apart from their spirits in Guinée?"

"Nuthin's *alive* in Guinée, boy," Masaka said. "It's the *After*world."

"Well, can they exist? Without blinking out into oblivion."

"*Oui*," they both said at once.

"Great." I breathed a sigh of relief. "Second question."

They both raised their eyebrows and slid their cups across the altar.

"Right." I poured a shot into each. The piman was swallowed up before I had the bottle back on the table. "My friends and I have a . . . situation."

"What kind of situation, baby?" Oussou yelled and hopped onto the altar to sit on the edge next to me, legs crossed sexily, leaning in.

"A soul-situation."

"Ooooo," Masaka cooed, springing onto the table, shiny black loafers crunching over top of the feast, until she was perched on my other side in a squat. "Love a good soul-catching."

"Well, that's great to hear." I poured two more shots even though I hadn't asked the question yet. "So there are these—"

"Succubi—?" Masaka asked.

"Yes! And they're wreaking havoc—"

"*Havoc*!" Oussou squeed.

"You need a grave dug?" Masaka stood tall and a long shovel appeared in her hand, like a staff, with a burlap sack tied to the handle with twine.

I remembered what Codi had said about the Baron digging graves, Grim Reaper-style, and was suddenly nervous. "No, no." I steadied my voice. "Nothing like that."

"You wanna gad?" Oussou asked, tilting my chin his way.

"What's a gad?"

"You wanna make a deal for protection?" He wagged his eyebrows.

"Um, no. I just need to get loose souls to the Afterworld so they can stop leeching off the Royal Street ghosts." It sounded harsher than I meant it, but that image of Julie weak in the chair, fading, freaked me the hell out. "They aren't going to last here. They need some peace."

"*Oh, Oui, Oui, Oui!*" said Masaka. "Ghede-Houson will want those souls."

"Who's Ghede-Houson?"

"The soul-keeper."

"There's a soul-keeper?" *That's promising, right?*

"Of course there's a soul-keeper. You think loose souls just get to run amuck?"

"I-I don't know." Dee had wanted Plumaj because she transported souls, right? "What's the difference between a soul keeper and a soul collector?"

They both looked at each other like I was a clown that they might have been taking too seriously.

"Plumaj," Masaka said, "roams the Natural World with her net collecting souls to trade."

"Trade for what?"

"A crown of teeth. I dunno! Whateva her dead heart desires. Houson is her biggest client. He watches over all of the loose ones, along with his brother, the medicine man."

So Houson would be going straight to the source? *Does the middleman really matter?*

I looked to Masaka. "So how would this happen? We'll bring them back here, and you'll—?"

"Us?" they both cackled.

"*Noooooooo*, not us," said Masaka. "We dig graves, not collect souls!"

"Well, that's why we called on the soul collector, but you gate-crashed! No offense, you're both lovely, but maybe this would just be easier if you left, so we can call on Plumaj?"

"*Plumaj*?" They hooted again.

"Plumaj don't want your trash-souls," Oussou said. "Plumaj only deals in healthy souls."

"Rare souls," Masaka added. "You know what Plumaj'd say 'bout your nasty souls?"

"What?"

They both slowly lifted their middle fingers at me and blew out their tongues.

"They aren't nasty souls," I pleaded. "They've been ripped from their spirits and are just trying to survive."

"*Nasty*," they both said, shuddering. The word echoed around the church, rippling in a chorus of ghostly voices. "*Nasty. Nasty souls.*"

"But you said the soul-keeper would want the souls."

"He would." Oussou drug a herring bone from a plate and picked at his teeth. "Houson isn't particular."

"Yes, fo sho. Might even give you a reward. Might even give you a gad."

"I don't want a reward; I just want to save them. And to keep them from hurting anyone else." I brushed my hair behind my ears, trying not to get anxious. "Look, can we just skip the middleman then and call for Ghede-Houson?"

They burst into more fits of laughter, and I heard the beat of the drum again in the distance. The air fluttered around us, making the flame of the black candle dance.

"Ghede-Houson doesn't leave Guinée," Masaka said.

"Nope. Nope. Never," echoed Oussou. The drumming rippled around the room, circling faster and faster. "The soul-keeper doesn't leave Guinée. He ain't no psychopomp."

"Guinée." "Guinée." "Guinée." "Seven nights, seven moons." Cold swirled around my neck as the graveyard voices flooded into the church. Only this time it wasn't just voices. I could see the spirits floating in through the rows of stained-glass windows: men and women, ghostly and evanescent, old and young, all in whimsical clothes from different times. "*Seven nights, seven moons.*" My pulse pounded in time with the drumbeat. Echoing up to the dome ceiling. The chanting picked up. Faster and faster.

"*Seven gates, seven tombs.*"

Oussou picked up the bottle of piman and waved it all around as if blessing us with its fiery contents. Masaka brought the shovel over her head, arching her back until she was lying back on the table in a provocative way, listening to the drums and chanting along as all of the voices shrieked in my head.

"*Seven keys will let you enter.*"

Her hand slid down her chest to her stomach. The voices grew louder. The drums rippled through my bloodstream. Fiery piman almost splashed in my face, and I tried to grab the bottle away from Oussou, but he leapt out of reach. Masaka's hand begin to dip into her pants.

"*Nibo's axe, Plumaj's feather.*"

"No!" I yelled, and without thinking, I drew in a breath and blew out the black candle-flame. My eyes smashed shut—and all the sounds stopped.

Shit.

I felt for the person next to me and touched a leg. It was slim and wrapped in denim.

"Isaac!" Désirée gasped, sitting up so quickly, she almost fell off the table.

I grabbed her arm, steadying her. "I got you."

She breathed heavily, her face beading with sweat and her floral blouse plastered to her skin. "What ha—?" she tried to ask, her voice scratchy. I grabbed the water from the tabernacle.

As she tipped the carafe back, I lit the black candle again. Her lips looked unmarred. *Thank God.* The halo of light warmed Codi's face, and his eyes went wide. He locked both hands over his crotch, his gaze snapping to Dee and back to me.

After swallowing the last gulp of water, she turned to him. "What's wrong?"

When Codi didn't say anything, I replied for him. "I think this whole experience has been a little *hard on* Codi."

She scooted closer to him, and he angled himself away.

"Are you okay?" She touched his shoulder, and he bolted off the table, holding himself as he ran through the dark to the Healing Room and swung the gate closed behind him.

After everything that had happened tonight, I couldn't help but laugh.

"Isaac?" Désirée's voice wobbled. "I don't feel—"

I grabbed her as she fell forward, and black spew hosed out of her mouth.

"*Fuck.*"

CHAPTER 30

SCENT OF MAGIC

Thump.

Thump-thump.

I held onto the faint beats of her heart as the steam filled the shower around me.

Adele is in my bedroom just down the hall. In my house. With my family. It was such a simple thing but it felt so . . . surreal.

Thump-thump.

As the warm water beat against my back, I imagined her walking softly around my room, hesitantly examining the furnishings and textiles. Touching the delicately carved wood of the wardrobe and the buttery velvet bench at the foot of the bed. I imagined her taking off her sweater, unafraid of the blood spattered across the fibers, washing the crimson smears from her neck, and patting her collar dry. I shuddered beneath the hot stream.

The fantasy morphed . . .

She walks out of my room and into the hallway, careful not to make a peep as she tiptoes down the hall and through the bathroom door, parting the shower curtain just enough to slip in next to me. She's soft and warm and lithe, and a hint of lavender imbues the steam as her lips touch mine.

Thump-thump.

Thump-thump.

Thump-thump.

My fangs engorged, and for a moment I couldn't distinguish whether the speeding heart rate was in my head or coming from my bedroom.

The fantasy burst, and all I could think about were my brothers. *What were you thinking, leaving her alone?* Four centuries had taught me patience, but now seconds felt like minutes—minutes would be all the time needed to drain Adele of every drop of blood.

She'd been here, sparring with Gabe, *alone*, and was fine.

I scrubbed the suds into my scalp, wondering if they suspected, yet, that I'd locked us all in the attic and saved her.

The soap had barely been rinsed before I shut off the water, a different scene unfolding in my mind: me walking downstairs to find her tied to a chair, just like the Ghost Drinker now in the attic was, all of my family waiting for me so I could witness their act of revenge.

Gabriel wouldn't. And he wouldn't let Emilio.

I grabbed the towel from the rack and ripped it across my back so quickly it burned the skin on my shoulders. It would take only seconds to heal since I had fed so recently. As I pulled on my pants, I felt for the beat of her heart.

It was faint, but there. The denim stuck to my damp legs as I sped through lacing my boots.

Stop freaking out.

I yanked the charcoal-colored T-shirt over my head, and barely had the sweater pulled on when I stepped out the door. *You're overreacting.* Being "overly sensitive" as Giovanna would have said.

I swore I could smell her spilled blood. My steps quickened down the hallway.

Thump-thump. Her pulse or mine, I wasn't sure.

No one was watching, but I felt like centuries of eyes were on me. *Get a grip, Niccolò.* I rapped the door lightly, but it creaked open—it had been left ajar.

Thump-thump-thump-thump.

The chamber was dark; I couldn't sense movement.

I darted to the washroom. Steam still coated the mirror, but she was gone. I whipped around the bed, looking for her crumpled body, signs of foul play, then ran out the door and down the hall, my senses grasping for her heartbeat as I entered the old dining room where we'd sparred. *No one.* I sped back into the hallway and turned the corner, momentarily losing the pulse to the sound of Martine's voice. And Lisette's. And Gabriel's, in the drawing room. I stopped myself in the doorway.

He was on the sofa, fangs retracted, reading a book and hardly paying attention to the girls, or at least that's how he appeared. There was never a room in which Gabriel wasn't catching every minute detail of its occupants. Lisette, Martine, and Adele were standing in front of the crackling fireplace. Martine was braiding Adele's hair into a crown.

She wasn't wearing the sweater I'd given her, but a long black dress. The silk curved delicately at her waist and over her hips. Small black buttons fastened at the bust and trailed down the flowing fabric nearly to the floor. She was noticeably taller—patent leather boots that were surely Martine's but looked made for a witch. Lisette was closing the dainty buttons on the lace at her wrists. None of it was practical for our plans this evening, but she looked so beautiful, I didn't say anything. I didn't move. I hardly breathed, watching her there with . . . my family.

Thump-thump.

The ache for some other life, where I walked into the room and wrapped my arms around her waist, and kissed her neck without being enraptured by the scent of her blood, became so overwhelming it bruised my insides.

"She smells like lavender," Emilio said, standing next to me. The fantasy dissolved. "And your soap." I felt him look at me. "Do you like that she smells of your soap, brother?" There was something in his tone that suggested threat.

I turned to him. "*Sì.*" The simple admittance seemed a stronger protection than any warning I could impose on him at this juncture.

His gaze lingered on her, and the way the glint in his eyes shone made me want to put an ocean between the two of them.

"Are you ready?" I asked softly, stepping into the room.

Her eyes caught mine in the mirror above the fireplace and she blushed. "Hi." She turned around with a meek shrug. "I told them I didn't need anything."

I suspected she wasn't used to this much attention.

"*Madonna Mia, Niccolò*. Stop being such an imbecile," Gabe said, closing the book. "You're an embarrassment to the Medici name. Tell her how beautiful she looks."

Warmth rushed my cheeks like I was eighteen years old again, and the words rolled off my tongue. *"Più del sole. Più della luna. Più delle stelle."*

Her gaze dropped to the floor, despite not understanding the words. Martine's lips pursed and I wondered how much Italian she'd learned in her opera days. I was relieved when she didn't whisper a translation of the celestials I'd just compared Adele to.

"Much better," Gabe said, resting back with the book. "You can stay in the family."

As I approached, Lisette chastised me in French, "I can't believe you were going to make her wear your clothes, Niccolò."

Even though the familial scene was woven with innocence, I tracked every finger touching Adele. There were so many pairs of fangs ready to snap out, just inches from her veins. I reached for her hand so we could leave.

"*Non*," Martine said, pulling her away.

My eyes darted to hers.

"*Ne pas toucher.*" She nodded to one last section of loose hair. "I'm not finished."

Adele leaned close and whispered in my ear, "I can't really walk in these boots, but I didn't want to offend her. She's a *vampire*."

Warmth nested somewhere deep inside me, and I smiled. "I'll go get your shoes."

When I returned with her things, I remained in the doorway, watching as Adele kissed each of their cheeks, thanking them in delicate French. My chest swelled in a way I thought only ever possible in my dreams. In my fantasies . . . which is exactly where she looked to have stepped from.

In the old silk dress, patent leather boots, and intricate braid, she looked somewhere in between her world and ours.

"Are you ready?" she asked.

I nodded, unable to recall the last time I'd felt so very unready.

⚜

The moonlight shone through the passenger window, highlighting her cheeks and the tip of her nose. Her energy was so noticeably different from the first ride out to the park—more at ease and less despondent. The further we got from the house, the deeper I was able to relax, one hand on the wheel. *She's fine, Nicco.* An evening at your house and she not only lived to tell the tale, she's completely unscathed.

"Can you please go over everything that happened?" I asked as we rolled through the miles of dark swamp. "How exactly you ended up at the house, and everything that Gabriel did."

"Are you going to freak out about this all night?"

"Did Emilio say anything to you?"

"Nicco, there's nothing to analyze."

"You don't know my brothers."

"Okay." She curled into her seat. "I'll go over everything, but only because I know if I don't, you'll obsess, and you won't be paying attention to me."

It's not vampirically possible for me to pay more attention to you. "You want me to pay attention to you?"

She nodded, smiling. "How else am I going to get my magic back without you breathing down my neck?"

Her smile was contagious. "Oh, I'm sure you'd find a way on your own."

"Thanks for the vote of confidence."

"Simple, really. You'd just envision stripping me over and over again until your magic breaks through."

"You wish . . ."

I did. I wished this car was fifty years older and I could slide her across the long leather seat and keep my arm around her. Instead, I peered out the window into the darkness. The clouds were rolling away, revealing the stars. I hoped the rain was done for the night. I thought about the view from the Ferris wheel, and looked over to the passenger seat. I hadn't told her everything that night, but it hadn't been since the days of the laboratory with León that I'd told someone so much about my family. Willingly, at least.

A memory of Séraphine tugged at my consciousness . . . her fingers tracing the line up the center of my stomach, taking anything she wanted from my mind with her Maker-thrall.

I shifted the car into fifth gear, glancing down at the speedometer and back to her. The draw was starting to feel impossible to mask, and that . . . was worrisome. "Adele?"

She turned to me.

I was sure she could read my pulse and hear my breathing. *Nicco, she's not a vampire.* My hands clenched the wheel. "What I said the other night . . . in the Ferris wheel . . ."

"*Sì?*"

"I meant it. You should be with Isaac." *Someone who isn't a predator.* "He loves you."

She looked away, wrapping her arms around herself.

"You belong together—"

"*Okay*, Nicco, I got it the first time."

I'd embarrassed her.

"I'm not—" I started to say, but I worried it was something I could be argued out of. That if she said the right words, touched me in the right way, I'd give in.

I rolled the window down, fighting the compulsion to glance her way to make sure she was okay. I wanted to know what she was thinking. I wanted to touch her hand. I wanted her to climb onto my lap and brush her lips against mine. *Fuck, Niccolò.*

"He came over this afternoon."

"Who?"

"Isaac."

The warmth that had nestled in my gut crackled into frost.

"Him and my dad . . . re-met, I guess, and Mac invited him to the studio during my mentorship. It's weird, because it's something we used to do together every day."

The frost froze into a heavy block of ice. "Oh," I steadied my voice. "How was that?"

"I don't know. Nice. Calm, mostly."

"Mostly?"

Her energy shifted inward. "I don't know if I'll ever get the image of him killing Brigitte out of my head." She paused, as if deep in thought. "I could feel it . . . the exact moment life left her. I can still feel it when I think about her."

As a vampire, I was more familiar with that moment than she could ever realize. There were years, decades, where I lived for those moments.

I released the window button and leaned slightly out, feeling the wind on my face. I wanted to ask her why she never told him about her mother. I knew I should tell her again that it wasn't his fault.

"I didn't take you for a wind-blowing-through-my-hair kind of guy," she said, and a smile formed on my lips.

But then a prickle to the back of my neck stiffened my spine. With a steady hand on the wheel, I leaned further out the window, taking a deep inhale.

"Nicco, what's wrong?"

I glanced at the seatbelt across her chest, making sure it was fastened, and slammed on the brakes, cutting the wheel hard. The car lurched, skidding to a stop on the side of the road. I'd barely killed the engine before I was out the door and on top of the roof.

Turning toward the dark forest, I opened up my senses.

I felt it again: an almost subsonic vibration that passed through my body, enlivening my skin: the scent of magic.

"Nicco, what's wrong?"

I looked down at her on the other side of the car. "I'm sorry, but we might have to take a raincheck on the magical training tonight." I jumped down next to her. "We can come back tomorrow night." I opened her door.

"No," she said, shaking her head. "What did you see? Who's out there?"

"I can't be certain from the road. Something magical," I said, despite being fairly sure I knew.

"We can't leave. What if it's the Ghost Drinkers?"

"That's precisely why I'm going to drop you off at home and come back."

"No *way*, Nicco. I'm coming with you."

"It's too dangerous for you without your magic."

"No, it's not." She looked straight at me. "I'll be with you."

The fearlessness in her eyes clouded my judgment, and in three strides, I was opening the trunk. I wondered how many of them were out there.

She paced back to her seat, pulled out her boots, and yanked off Martine's. "Nicco," she said, her tone more severe. "I'm *coming with* you."

I unzipped the duffel bag, searching . . . On one hand, I didn't know enough about the Ghost Drinkers' newfound magic, bound by Adele's Fire, to say with absolute certainty that this was safe; but I did know the Salazars were still too weakened by the fight and their ghost hunting to be a real threat. If they weren't, Callisto would have retaliated by now. Instead, they were hiding in swamps like the rats and snakes they were.

Ah, ha. I grabbed the heavy handle of the flashlight and shut the trunk.

"Nicco—" She stood, boots laced.

"Stay close." I placed the flashlight in her right hand, taking her left in my own. "And try not to make any noise."

"Right."

The woods were dense and foggy and smelled of damp moss and rain-soaked foliage.

She clicked on the light, and I covered it, shaking my head. "We don't need it."

"Why did you hand it to me, then?"

"If you can't activate your magic and someone gets too close, bash their head in with it."

Her fingers coiled tighter around mine. "Um . . . I know you're used to Lisette and Martine, but I don't know if I can do that."

I pulled her closer. "Then you better start trying harder with your magic."

As long as unneeded-immortal breath passed between my lips, nothing would happen to her, but I wanted her to feel the fear. It was the only way she'd harness the strength to access her Spektral magic. Just like our first night in the bell tower when she found her Fire. *I know it's inside her.* I could sense it now, just like I could feel the scent of magic in these woods.

"This way." I turned us farther north. Damp leaves and brambles crunched softly under her feet as she hurried to keep up, and I no longer cared about keeping quiet. I wanted to feel the alarm beneath their sternums; their pulses would betray their hiding spot, which likely wouldn't be too far from the cinders I could now smell nearby. Someone had lit a campfire, and I don't think it was for roasting marshmallows.

Adele took a deep inhale through her nose.

Good, bella.

She inhaled again, and my teeth sank onto my bottom lip watching her instincts take control. *She's caught the whiff of smoke.* I squeezed her hand and pulled her along, dodging tall, narrow cypress trees, weaving through the beating pulses of wildlife that were cloaked by the night and the swamp and the fog. We were almost there.

I shielded her face from the sticky silk strings as we crept through a dense thicket of palmetto leaves woven together with spiderwebs. A baby deer sprang awake from a bed of wet leaves, and Adele lurched back. I steadied her so she didn't fall.

"I'm sorry," she whispered, her pulse still rapid-firing.

"It's okay. We're here." I drew back a thin branch covered with Spanish moss that drooped down to the ground. "Let me go first," I said, making sure she was right behind me as we passed under.

The air was clearer on the other side, and the hum of cicadas swelled in a wave around a perimeter. We were in a small clearing that appeared to be empty.

I nodded to the flashlight in her hand. *Let it give us away.* We'll see if they dare to show themselves or if they only attack girls when they are tied to statues.

She clicked it on, shining the light over the grassy area, both of us taking cautious steps forward. "Nicco." She rotated the light in a clockwise motion over a patch of blackened grass in the center. *A burnt circle.* "It's practically still smoking."

"Only magic would light earth this wet." We walked closer. "Two of them," I guessed, based on the size of the circle. Three at the most.

More sweeps of the light revealed a pile of supplies they'd abandoned before scattering: a sack of salt, an ivory athame, a brass chalice, and a tarnished silver necklace with dangles of fluorite. Adele moved closer to the pile.

"Don't touch anything," I said. Who knew what kind of magic they were practicing, hidden by the canopy of the swamp? Surely they were now just beyond the trees, watching us, trying and failing to get a look at the strangers who'd stumbled upon their ritual. Were we hunters? Fishermen? Young lovers just giddily looking for a place to camp for the night? The light of the moon in the foggy night wasn't enough to give us away to them—they were witches, not vampires. I slowly turned as a hum of energy pulsed north.

"What is it?" Adele asked, taking a few steps back, as if she could feel it too.

A pulse of magical energy exploded from the woods, and something darted across the clearing, making me pull Adele closer as it rushed past. Before I could get a look, it whipped back in the direction it came from. The necklace was gone from the pile of belongings.

I cracked my knuckles. "A *speedster.*" Every nerve in my heels was ready to go after it. "I haven't seen one in years."

"What's a speedster?" Adele asked as it whipped through again, this time tugging her hair.

My fangs snapped out. "A witch with the power of celerity."

It whipped back through the clearing. The chalice was gone, but I knew it was using each swipe as an opportunity to get a better view of us. I hunched, ready to catch it when it came back for the athame, but it stayed due north, its pulse fading along with its footsteps.

Had it recognized us? I bounced up on my toes, inhaling to grasp for their scents. "There's another witch here. It's using an invisibility shield." I fought the impulse to go after it and instead took Adele's hand, pulling her in the direction of the car. "I'm taking you home. I'll come back with Emilio. We'll call him on the way so he can get a head start." I could easily take five of them at human speed before they could lay a hand on her, but I wasn't letting a speedster separate us.

She ripped her arm away. "*We're* here now, Nicco. What if the speedster leads you to Callis?" Her imploring eyes lit up every predatory compulsion inside me.

They'd all been commanded not to hurt her according to the witch chained to my attic wall, and unless there was a second speedster, no one could take her far before I could return. Speedsters were rare among witches.

"Here," I said, my hand on her back to guide her to the center of the circle. My gaze remained locked on her as I dipped my fingers into the sack of salt and darted around the circle, spreading it evenly.

"What are you doing?"

"You are going to protect yourself from this witch. *With* magic."

"I don't have my powers, Nicco, and neither do you—stop wasting time and go after the speedster. You could be back by now!"

"You might not have all of your powers, Adele, but you are still a witch. You are still bound to your coven. *You are still magical.*" My voice raised. "Do not focus on your powers. No Fire. No metal. Focus on a shield. You are not going to let *anyone* past this line." I started to back away. "Repeat after me: *Dammi forza, o, possenti antenati. Dammi fuoco. Proteggimi.*" My heart raced, hearing the first verse of the spell come out of my lips. It was my voice. My accent. My family's medieval magic.

Fear shone behind her eyes, but she nodded. *"Il fuoco dei miei antenati mi guida."*

I watched her lips move with the words as I said them. *"Il fuoco dei miei antenati mi protegge."* Medicean witching words—I had never cherished them more. And never had my love for my family and my need to restore our legacy ignited so brightly.

"Il fuoco dei miei antenati mi protegge." She repeated back the Italian, nodding rapidly. Encouraging me to go.

Instinct demanded I stay and protect her, but I knew with every shred of my Medicean intuition that she was going to be okay, and that was the only reason I turned my back and whipped away.

My lips mouthing the words, over and over. *"Il fuoco dei miei antenati distrugge coloro che cercano di portarmi del male, così che io possa servirti."*

I have always believed in *la magia della mia famiglia.*

And I believed in her.

And never in my life had my need to kill been so strong.

A predatory surge ripped through my limbs, carrying me through the trees, my heels barely touching the ground. The wind blew, and the scent of the witch penetrated my pores. *Female. Elementare Aria. Scandinavian blood. And the distinct pheromone of the Animarum Praedators.*

Her pulse grew stronger and the pull exponentiated—a desire I couldn't remember feeling since my first decades as a vampire.

And now . . . *She's summoning her magic.*

I adjusted my course slightly northeast, feeling her calling the wind inward. And then, in a blur of swirling, blonde curls, she shot through the air like a twisting cannon, and I launched myself into the trees with a hiss, arms outstretched, colliding with her head-on. She writhed in my grip, trying to use her magical Air to force me off, but my legs locked around hers, and we smashed onto the ground, rolling through the damp forest floor, gaining momentum until her back slammed into a tree stump, vertebrae cracking. Her blood poured into my throat, swallow after swallow of the metallic-tasting ambrosia. I knew I needed to stop, to interrogate her on Callis's whereabouts, but I could taste the magic flowing through her veins, and I wanted her to feel pain for what they had done to Adele. My fingers squeezed into her arms, and the crush of her bones was dizzying. I detached from her throat, stumbling up, wiping my mouth on the back of my hand, licking the blood off with a single stroke of my tongue.

I wanted more. *I want all of it.*

But why had she turned back when she could have just kept running north? Our captive witch must have been telling the truth about there being a price for the head of a Medici. Unless . . . My thoughts swirled into place as the dizziness settled . . . Unless she was drawing me away?

Thump-thump.

What if I'd been wrong? What if there had been more than I thought?

I tore back through the woods, knocking branches out of the way, my panic shattering the blood-high.

A shriek pierced my ears just before an explosion of light mushroomed through the dogwood silhouettes, washing back the inky dark.

"*Adele!*" I shouldn't have left her.

I burst into the edge of the clearing and picked up the scent of the second witch. *Male. Elementare Acqua. Slavic blood.*

Adele, still in the circle, screamed my name as he rocketed back toward her, athame in hand.

"*Adele!*"

Another explosion of light burst—a bright lucent dome radiating around the circle—and I slid down to the ground to stop myself from pummeling into the shield, heels digging into the dirt, my arm flinging over my eyes to block the light.

"*Nicco!*"

The dome fizzled. I clambered up and darted into the circle to see if she was okay, ready to annihilate the second witch. But once her arms were wrapped around me, and I was holding her against my chest, I didn't go anywhere.

Thump-thump. Thump-thump.

I wasn't even sure whether it was her heart or mine. She shook and her pulse of magic permeated me. I could always feel it, but this was . . . empyreal.

"Nicco, w-wh-at was that?"

I cupped her face so I could see her eyes. "You did it." *Adele used my family's spell to protect herself.* "I knew you still had your magic, that you could take back your Fire from them."

She gazed up at me. "Nicco, that was not my Fire."

"Of course it was, *mia bella*."

"No. It wasn't even a flame. It was more like . . . lightning."

I stepped back, looking out at the circle. "*Non è possibile.*" Patches of grass were on fire, illuminating a scorched ring that encapsulated the original salt-circle. "*Non ci piove.*" My fingers felt for her hands, dipping into the lace cuffs of her dress, the ache for the magic flowing through her veins billowing inside me.

But then her shaking became harder. "Is-is-is he dead?" she said, gazing over my shoulder. "He was coming into the circle for me."

I twisted around, and she stepped close behind me. The witch was facedown on the ground, charred to a crisp.

"Nicco, did I *kill* him?"

My hand reached back for hers, and her fingers twined into mine. I walked her over to the witch. "*No, mia bella.*" I grabbed the back of his still smoldering neck with my other hand, and starting walking back toward the car, dragging his body. "It takes a lot more than a little electricity to kill a Ghost Drinker."

CHAPTER 31

AMICI MAGICI

I couldn't even feel the leather seat beneath me; it was like I was hovering. Floating. Buzzing. And the car wasn't even moving yet. The magic reeled through my system like thousands of fireflies, wings beating and tails aglow. My chest moved heavily as I breathed.

Outside the car, metal purred as Nicco zipped the duffel bag in the trunk—which now contained the body of a witch.

A witch I'd *roasted.*

The car shook as he shut the trunk. I twisted in my seat, my eyes locked on him as he came around. I don't know why, but I wanted him to be back in the car . . . the separation was making me anxious.

Breathe.

But I couldn't. The Medici magic careened through my blood, sparking my nerves. I scratched my left arm, the long silk sleeves of Lisette's dress and the humidity not a great combo. Instead of opening the driver's door, Nicco paused to take out his phone. Rapid Italian followed. The conversation was brief.

He got in the car and started the engine. "I gave Emilio the coordinates. He's going to come and pick up the other one and search the area."

I nodded, not arguing this time about Emilio's assistance. I didn't want to go back into the woods to pick up another body, and I didn't want to stay in the car by myself with one zipped up in the trunk—one that could supposedly reanimate with the right meal of specter. Nicco started to shift the car out of park, but then turned to me. I felt like I was going to burst, just like the lightning dome.

His brow furrowed. "Are you okay?"

I shook my head rapidly.

He shifted closer. "He's not dead." He leaned away to cut the engine. "You didn't ki—

I wrapped my arms around his shoulders. "I'm not *okay*, Nicco; I'm exhilarated." The words scared me as much as the witch in the woods had. "I can feel magic."

Surprise softened his voice. "*Buono.* Your magic's in there. I told you."

I shook my head again. "I can feel it *in you*, Nicco. In the air around you. In the earth underneath you. You *are* magical."

A small smile drew from his lips. "You are just internalizing the spell, *mia bella.* My family's magic is powerful."

It's not his family's—it's his.

The lingering magic filled my soul with bravery. "It's yours," I whispered, coming so close, my nose brushed his. "Your magic is powerful."

When his lips parted, my heart thundered. And when his arm snaked around the small of my back and his hand slipped up my jaw, I felt like I was dreaming. I was sure he'd stop me when I came closer, but he scooped me into his lap. I wanted him to touch me. I wanted him to feel his magic. I tugged my dress higher, and his hand followed, sliding all the way up to my hip, lightning crackling beneath my skin to meet his fingertips. I wanted him to recognize the magic as his own as it swirled around my waist and over my ribs to the tips of my breasts.

I felt electrified.

My eyes slipped shut as his hands glided around me. He inched down in the seat, anchoring me close, and I gasped, feeling him beneath me. My entire body tightened. I no longer felt like I was floating—I felt every ounce of myself that was pressed into him as the magical rush began to peak. And peak. *And peak.*

I fell against him, and he held me as the magical rush released.

The moment passed, but it still took every ounce of my focus not to kiss his face. His lips. I wanted to kiss every part of him. My eyes opened to his crystalline gaze, just inches from mine: part-enraptured, part-astonished.

And then I froze, stunned. At myself.

What did I . . . ? "I'm— I'm sorry!"

"It's okay," he said, before I could panic. "It's just the magic." He touched my jaw. And even though the intensity of the connection was rippling off him in waves, there was nothing relenting about his stare.

Breathe.

It's just the magic.

"Could you feel it?" I asked.

A huff escaped his lips as he tried not to laugh. He leaned back against the seat, and I saw the tips of his fangs. "I'm sorry," I whispered. "I didn't mean to be so—"

"Please, don't be sorry," he said, still gazing deeply into my eyes. "I haven't felt my family's magic in centuries." He pulled down my skirt and rested his hand on my leg. "*Grazie infinite, bella.*"

"It's your magic, Niccolò."

He smiled an appeasing smile, and for the first time that night, I saw the red stains on his lips. He caught me looking, and for a second, he let me. I knew he was testing me again, seeing if I'd jump out of the car running.

I didn't know how to make him believe that I wasn't going anywhere.

A lingering tickle of magic prickled my spine, pushing me closer, and I actually contemplated kissing the corner of his mouth to show him. "Nicco . . . we're in this—whatever it is—together."

His expression morphed from appeasing to something more real. "I know." He touched his knuckle to my cheek, and I wondered if he was contemplating kissing me too.

"Friends?" he asked, and I guess I had my answer.

But I slowly shook my head, no.

The shimmer in his eyes pulsed brighter.

"What's the Italian word for friends?" I asked.

"*Amici.*"

"*Amici.* Magical friends."

And his lips curved into his not-so-innocent smile.

I meant the words, but I ached when he released me back to the seat.

As he drove, I curled into the window and got lost in the hazy moon, letting the imprint of both his magic and his touch permanently burn into my memory, my mind trying to process how anything could feel so gentle and searing at the same time. *Nicco and I have done magic together.*

As we sped down the highway, an eagerness brewed in my belly. I didn't have my powers, but I was magical. I wanted my old life back. One with friends and art and covens and psychic tea rooms. One with magic careening through my veins. And I was going to get my Fire back, if it was the last thing I ever did.

As the remnants of Nicco's magic rippled through me, all I could think about now was telling Dee and Codi . . . and Isaac.

I waited for the flood of guilt, but it didn't come.

I curled back into the seat, turning Nicco's way. "Can I still ask you anything?"

"Of course."

"Are you purposefully blocking our dreams from connecting?"

He sat up straighter. "Did Gabriel tell you tha—?"

"No. Papa Olsin said that my dream magic isn't gone, that my twin-flame is just shutting me out."

"Does he know you're dream-twinning with . . . me?"

"I've never told him, but I'm pretty sure he knows it's you. Psychic and all."

"And?"

"And what?"

"And are they coming after me with pitchforks?"

"*Nicco*. They aren't like that. And I would never let anyone hurt you."

He smirked. "I'm not worried about them hurting me, *bella.*"

"So, it's true, then?"

He sighed, nodding.

"You don't like me being so close?"

"*No*. Adele, I want the connection, believe me. I just . . . don't want to risk . . . "

"Risk what?"

"Us." He paused. "I'm not ready to let you go." He looked out his window. Out of all the things he'd ever told me, it somehow felt like the most honest thing he'd said.

"Nicco, you aren't going to lose me because of your past. I know monstrous things have happened but it— It wasn't your fault what happened with Maddalena."

His eyes lit up, and I wondered if I shouldn't have brought it up.

He took another breath before speaking. "Adele, you can ask me anything about my past, and I promise to tell you the truth, but you don't need to see all of my . . . transgressions at once."

Thump-thump.

"*Je comprends* . . . I just wish that you trusted me with your heart the way you trust me with your head."

"You don't want my heart," he snapped.

"Don't tell me what I want," I snapped back.

"I'm sorry. It's just . . ." His grip tightened on the steering wheel. "Some things can never be unseen."

I wanted to see all of him.

Thump-thump-thump-thump.

I didn't say it out loud, but I also didn't try to temper my rising heart rate. I felt him release the accelerator, and for a moment I thought he was going to throw the car into park and give me his full attention like I wanted. Like I knew he wanted.

But he didn't.

The rest of the car ride was silent, just like the desolate neighborhoods we drove through, but my nerves fluttered as we rolled back into the Quarter, back to reality.

I knew the next thing I had to do was make up with Désirée. I contemplated asking him to drop me off at the Borges shop, but at the last second, I chickened out, and then we were turning onto my block. He put the car in park in front of my house and leaned back in his seat, looking at me. "*Grazie, bella.*"

"For what?"

"For being so enchanting."

My breath caught in my throat. Nicco, in all of his sophistication and otherworldliness, calling me—a magicless witch—enchanting was almost absurd. I mirrored him in my seat. "*Merci beaucoup,* Nicco. For sharing your family's ancient magic with me, and . . ."

"And?"

"For giving me hope."

He smiled, and I thought he might reach out to touch me, but he didn't.

"Just know . . . there's nothing from your past that would ever make me think lesser of you, Niccolò Giovanni Battista." Even as I said the words, a little voice in the back of my head warned me to be careful, to keep both eyes open. To never trust a vampire.

Or a Medici.

I breathed out the little voice, leaned over, and kissed his cheek.

"*Grazie, bella.*" But there was something in his voice that was sad, like he didn't believe it, and it was only just a matter of time before everything came crumbling down. "Sweet dreams."

"*Buona note*," I said and got out of the car, but before he could pull away, I turned back. "Nicco?"

"*Sì*?"

"You are magical. And one day I'm going to prove it to you."

"If you are able to do that, *bella*, you aren't magical; you're divine."

"Well, then I guess you are going to call me *mio angelo* one day."

"I look forward to it." He smiled and once again it felt like I'd produced alchemical gold.

As he sped away, I knew he was going straight back to the swamp.

And I hoped the hunt was fruitful.

I hopped up the stairs to my room, feeling oddly conflicted. A part of me wanted to call Nicco back so I could go out with him and Emilio, and a part of me was psyching myself up to call Désirée and do whatever I needed to do to get her to talk to me again.

A brown paper bag that looked like it contained something heavy was hanging from my bedroom doorknob. *What did Mac do?* I took the gift, flipped on the light, and sat on my bed.

I reached inside, and a tidal wave of familiarity rushed through me as my fingertips touched the leather binding. I slid the book out with a gasp.

Adeline Saint-Germain's diary.

I hugged it into my chest and leaned back in the bed, thanking the universe, the spirits, whoever and everyone. Thanking . . . Isaac.

So that's why he'd insisted on seeing himself out.

CHAPTER 32

THE GATES TO GUINÉE

The sky had cleared, and the raindrops made the mausoleums glisten in the starlight.

"How could you let me smoke a cigarette?" Désirée asked, uncorking a bottle of homemade antiseptic from her witch-bag and forcefully gargling.

"What happened to, 'Isaac, whatever I do, just go with it'?"

She spat the mouthwash down a drain outside the chapel. "Yeah, but a *cigarette*? Gross."

"Well, at least it kept your hands occupied."

"What's that supposed to mean?" she said and took another swig.

"You can never give me shit about hugs again. You owe me hugs for a lifetime."

The word "hugs" earned me a look of horror as she swished around the antiseptic. She spat it out. "You're from New York. Isn't hugging antithetical to your very nature?"

"Ghede gonna Ghede," Codi said, exiting the chapel with the last of the bags.

A high-pitched chortle slipped out of Désirée's mouth.

"Borges, giggling?" I strapped on my knapsack. "Are you sure you're not drunk from all that piman? Or maybe Masaka's still here after all?"

She smirked, and everything started to feel normal again. We'd packed up quickly and mostly in silence, I think each of us was trying to process all that had happened.

"So you guys really don't remember anything?" I asked.

"The last thing I remember," Désirée said, re-tying her ponytail, "is the old Ghede in the corner drumming."

"Same. Drumming. Désirée laughing. Then I woke up on the altar table in the darkness."

"With a Ghede-sized boner," she added.

"Dammit! I didn't think you saw!"

A chorus of hollow snickers echoed down the row of mausoleums and I looked at him. "I'm pretty sure even the ghosts in the last row of graves saw that."

"Well, in that case, I should go pay homage to my ancestors for their super DNA." He grabbed the bundle of flowers we'd brought and headed down a row of mausoleums.

"It's perfectly natural!" Dee said as we followed.

He flipped both of us off from behind, and the cycle of Ghede jokes continued.

There was a levity I'd never felt with them before, despite it being the middle of the night and being surrounded by the dead. There just hadn't been room for anything light in the last few months. Even though the ritual had been borderline-traumatizing, now that Dee and Codi were back, the whole experience felt weirdly special.

We stopped to decorate the Daure mausoleum, and then Désirée dug a hole into a patch of grass and instructed Codi to dump in all the remaining food from the Ghede feast in order to properly close out the ritual and ensure there'd be no lwa coming home with us. I wondered how many Ghede meals had been buried in cemeteries by the witches of New Orleans over the centuries. As we worked, I filled them in on everything that had happened in the church. Everything that I could remember, at least. Some of the specifics were a blur.

"I can't believe you could *see* them this time!" Désirée said, quickly bottling up some graveyard dirt for our altar back at the brothel. "Ritha is going to freak. I mean, she would if we were telling her, which we aren't." She stood, leaning on the shovel, wiping her brow, and I couldn't help getting Masaka vibes.

"Too bad it was all for nothing," I said.

"What do you mean?"

"I blew it. I didn't get anyone to take the souls back or figure out what to do with them otherwise."

"Isaac, you told us yourself: Ghede-Houson wants the souls!"

"How is that useful if he doesn't leave Guinée, and Plumaj won't collect our 'nasty' souls to take back?"

She looked at us like we were missing it completely. "We did the ritual to find out how to save the souls, and they told us exactly what to do! *Take the souls to the soul-keeper.* We need to go to Guinée!"

I glanced at Codi. "She's kidding, right?"

"I think so? Or she's lost it."

"The only problem is . . . how do we get to the Afterworld?"

"*The only problem*?" I asked. "Désirée, I would take a bullet for you, but leaving the Natural World is where I draw the line."

"Isaac, you of all people should be down for this given your Spektral. What if this is, like, your destiny?"

"My destiny is Adele, and art school, and magic. Not a voyage to the deadlands."

"What about all that pirate stuff in your grimoire? Where's your sense of adventure? And what about Ren? Where's the front page of the *New York Times* first responder?"

"You're not talking about going into some stricken area after a natural disaster; you're talking about going to *another world*."

She crossed her arms and turned to Codi.

"Dude, can the living even go to Guinée? Just because we grew up with an old wives' tale about the Ghede snatching kids—"

"Well, of course *that's* not true. It's just a myth!"

"Ha," I mumbled. "Like there's ever such a thing in this city."

They both looked at me.

"Let's go visit Ritha," Désirée said. "And let me do the talking."

A pungent aroma, much stronger than the usual lingering scent of incense, tickled my nose as we filed past the touristy love potions and Voodoo dolls into the back room.

"Hello, my dears," Ritha said. Several bottles of oil were uncorked on the counter around her, along with a wooden contraption that held a row of slim test tubes. She dipped a thin stick into one, then pulled it out, gave it a little shake, and dipped it into the next test tube, holding it there for a few seconds.

Désirée kissed her cheek, picked up a drying incense punk, and gave it a sniff. "Night blossoms, my favorite."

"And how are the protection spells going?" Ritha asked.

"Good. Great," she answered, casually moving behind her gran to the back wall, which was lined with shelves like the rest of the room. Although these shelves were each guarded by a rusted chain strung end to end, indicating they were off limits to customers. Two shelves contained books, and the other three held powders and oils. A python's shedded skin hung over a nail. "Everything's on track." Her fingers grazed the guarded books, her head tilting to the right to read the spines. "We're getting better with each one, not as drained."

"No signs of foul play at the cemeteries?" Ritha asked, looking at me.

"Not that we've seen," I answered.

Désirée removed a volume and stuck it in her bag.

"Dense reading for this hour," Ritha said, like she had eyes in the back of her head.

"Well, all of that energy from the group magic—I'll probably be up for a while."

"I can make you some chamomile?" She dipped another punk.

"No thanks, I want to read."

"A book on the dead? What's the sudden interest?"

"Nothing really . . ." Désirée had this very specific way of lying to Ritha, where everything she said was true, but she just left out key pieces of information. "Spending all of this time at the cemeteries just has me thinking a lot."

"About death?"

"Death. What happens after. The Ghede. Guinée. All of it."

"All important parts of one's journey both for the magical and the mundane."

"About that journey. To the Afterworld, Guinée," Codi asked, leaning on the counter. Désirée shot him a look, but he remained cool. "The old rhyme from when we were kids: *Seven nights, seven moons, seven gates, seven tombs.* I thought it was something y'all told us when we were kids so we'd stay out of the cemeteries, but you never hear the tours touting that story or see it in any of the guide books."

Ritha took a deep inhale from a freshly dipped stick. "Do you know the rest of the verses of the rhyme? The way to get to Guinée?" Her tone made it clear she already knew the answer.

I could see both Codi and Dee repeating the verse in their heads.

"I don't remember there being more," he said.

"Same," echoed Dee. "It was always just the one."

"That's because you're not meant to know the way to Guinée. And if any huckster or showman says otherwise, they are full of bull. The Natural World is for the living, and the Afterworld is for the dead. In our magical tradition, some of the lwa go between. If need be, Papa Legba can grant communication privileges with the spirits, so there's no need for people to go back and forth. Witches included."

As they debated about the gates being real versus metaphorical, my mind drifted back to the chapel . . . the drumming, the chanting, the thrusting hips and sprinkles of piman. And the words slipped out of my mouth: "*Seven keys will let you enter. Nibo's axe, Plumaj's feather.*"

Ritha's glare shot my way. "What did you say?"

"Um . . . nothing," I mumbled.

Her stare became more severe, so I repeated the line: "*Seven nights, seven moons, seven gates, seven tombs. Seven keys will let you enter. Nibo's axe, Plumaj's feather.*"

"How do you know that verse?"

Désirée's face tightened even more severely than Ritha's, and I fumbled for words. "Um . . . I-I don't know. I think I, um, probably just heard Ren mumbling it, or something."

She came around the counter and felt my face. "Have you been feeling okay?"

"Yeah, I'm fine."

"Have you had any more dreams?"

"No."

Désirée and Codi both gave me inquisitive looks.

"What else have you heard?"

"Nothing. That's it. What does it mean? Who's Nibo?" Then, not wanting her to think I knew anything at all about the Ghede, I added, "And Plumaj?"

"Children of Samedi and Brijit. You could say that Ghede Nibo is their eldest son, and his father's right hand. He was a handsome young man who had a violent human death, and he's the patron of all those who die young." The way she looked at me made my heart race. "Along with five of their siblings, they guard the gates to Guinée. The Baron and his children give the map only to those who need it. Only those with one foot in the grave. They will only unlock the gates for those ready to completely surrender their intention to the Ghede. And that intention is supposed to be resting in peace."

Désirée's forehead tightened, like she was trying to see through the blizzard of esoteric ideas.

"Many people who have seen the light spend the rest of their lives in the physical world searching for that path again, trying to decipher their otherworldly experience. Ironic, isn't it? But the mind—your spirit—will repress information that is unneeded for this world and release it again when you are ready."

"I didn't see any light! I don't know any more of the rhyme." *Right?* I must have heard it from one of the Ghede? Or one of the ghosts during all these cemetery rituals, or something, right?

"Whoa," Désirée said. "Can you imagine having the secrets to the Afterworld floating around in your subconscious?"

Ritha's expression hardened. "Many witches have dug their own graves attempting to get the map, brushing too close to death, looking for magic darker than they are ready for. Doors open for those who can open them, not for those who simply seek them. The same goes for gates."

Désirée nodded, strumming her fingers against the book she was holding tight against her chest.

"Wow," said Codi. "I never thought about the gates being physical. Like a *real* threshold."

"Curiosity is healthy," Ritha continued. "And I'm glad that you are all connecting so deeply with your experiences in the cemetery, but I don't think I have to remind you all that curiosity also killed the cat?"

"No ma'am," Codi said. "No cats dying here."

Désirée's smile betrayed Codi's lie. It was a smile that told me I was going to be a zombie tomorrow at work because we were going to be up all night. Lucky for her, Ritha was focused on dipping the incense. She hurried around the counter. "We should probably work on the next batch of hexenspiegels. Love you, Gran."

"German witch mirrors? Nice choice."

"Thanks!" Codi said as Désirée pulled him through the curtain. "We found them in the Guldenmann grimoire."

But then as I started to follow, Ritha spoke to me. "Isaac?"

I stopped, and she came out from behind the counter once again. She lingered for a moment, then brushed the hair from my eyes. "You'll let me know if you have any more dreams? I've told you once, but I'll tell you again: you have a strong connection with the spirits. I know it can take some getting used to, but there is nothing to be afraid of."

I nodded and attempted to smile.

"Nothing to be afraid of as long as you aren't getting yourself into trouble, of course."

I nodded again, wondering if I should tell her that tonight was different. That unlike with Gran Bwa, I could see the Ghede. But then a hand was wrapping around my arm. "Come on," Désirée said, pulling me through the curtain. I waved goodbye and followed her rapid footsteps out the back of the house to the courtyard.

"Isaac!" she shrieked. "I can't believe you got that close to the Afterworld. I mean, I can—I *totally* thought you were toast after the vampire bite. What's the rest of the verse?"

"I don't know! That's all I've got."

"The Ghede wouldn't have given you a partial map when you were lying on your deathbed staring into the light."

"I didn't hear it then; I heard it *tonight.* During the séance," I whispered. "The ghosts? The Ghede? I don't know. It was pandemonium toward the end."

"It wouldn't have been the ghosts," Codi said. "If they're still here, haunting the Natural World, then they haven't crossed over yet."

"And Masaka and Oussou wouldn't have given it to you tonight. You weren't dying. What if you did get the map after Emilio attacked you and your spirit suppressed it because you didn't die, and it just started to come out tonight during the ceremony because you were expanding your mind, pushing your magic? What if it's there in the back of your brain buried beneath all of your PTSD and disdain for vampires and daydreams about Adele?"

"What?"

"Maybe you just need to meditate, or drink some wormwood or ayahuasca—"

"Hypnosis?" Codi asked.

"Nice one." She turned to him.

I scowled. "I did not talk to any Ghede after Emilio attacked me!"

"How do you know? You were completely out of it!"

I started to respond, but Désirée's eyes lit up, like she had another idea.

"What?" I asked.

"You aren't the only person who's ever been out of it."

She turned and practically ran across the courtyard to the guesthouse, leaving us no choice but to follow.

As we all whisked down the hallway together, she whispered, "Ritha said, people with one foot in the grave."

"Désirée!" I whispered back.

Any excitement deflated as soon as we crossed the magical threshold to Ren's room. He was sitting in the corner, in an old beat-up leather chair whose arms had been scratched up like a cat had gone to war with it. He was completely still, other than his hands softly stroking the leather, fingernails long and yellowing. *He* was the culprit who'd scratched up the chair, I realized.

If he'd noticed us, he showed no sign of it. We sat next to him at the foot of the bed. "How you feeling, Ren?" I asked.

He turned his head to me and, without so much as a blink, looked back straight ahead. No Yankee crack, no anything.

"*Buonasera*?" I tried, for Alessandro. It was one of the three Italian words I knew, all of which were thanks to Georgie, the owner of the pizzeria on my corner in Brooklyn who insisted on greeting every customer in his grandfather's native tongue.

Once more he looked at me and turned back without a blink.

Shit. Between the bar and the cemeteries, I hadn't been spending as much time with him as I usually did. "What if he's taken a turn for the worse?"

"Ritha would have said something."

"Come on, Ren," Codi said. "I know you're in there somewhere."

Désirée's hands went to her hips. "Ren, we want to hear a story—"

"Dee!" I whispered. "He's clearly not up for it."

"There's this . . . *legend*. We're having trouble remembering it, so we came straight to you. The night you were helping us with the map, you were singing the old tale about Guinée—"

"We can come back when you're feeling better!" I said.

"Will you tell it to us again? Do you remember the whole thing?"

He looked at her again, expression stone-cold. And all I could think about was my dream. His dead expression and the python slithering into his mouth, stopping his words. His breath. The dream Ritha had been asking me about.

"The one that's said to be passed down from the Baron himself."

"Come on," Codi said, "we should let him rest. He probably doesn't even know it."

Désirée shot him a dirty look, but then her mouth opened like she was catching his drift. *Dammit, Codi.* "You're right. He probably *doesn't even know—*"

"Young lady!" Ren barked. "Get me my hat, if you will?"

Désirée smiled at me, got up, and retrieved his old top hat from a coat rack.

"*Merci beaucoup.*" He placed it on his head as she sat down on the bed. "And my spectacles, *s'il vous plaît.*"

"Sure." She got up again, looking around.

"Mantel," Codi said.

She returned with a pair of thin, wire-framed glasses with round, translucent purple lenses.

Ren slid them on as she sat back down. "And my cane."

Swallowing a huff, she got back up and went to the coat rack to get the black walking stick he used on his tours. The handle was topped with a clear crystal skull.

"Anything else?" she asked before handing it to him. "Do you want your jacket?"

"That'll do!" He jumped up.

She sat in his seat, and we all leaned in as he took center stage, backlit by the fireplace.

For a moment, he stood still, hands on cane, looking up as if sorting through the files in his head. Then he took one finger and flicked the right lens from his glasses. It *tinked* on the floor. "Much better," he said.

"One eye on the living, one on the dead?" Désirée smiled. "Should we call you Baron Simoneaux?"

"Well, I do have a foot in the grave, or so I hear."

Désirée laughed nervously. "Glad to see you haven't lost your flair for the dramatic, Ren."

"*Neverrrrr*," he said, shaking the cane, more vigor in his voice than I could remember even in his peak health days. "Now, where to begin." He slowly paced across the fireplace. "Guinée. Guinée. Guinée. *Seven nights, seven moons. Seven gates, seven tombs.*" He repeated the first verse several more times, tossing around the cane.

I looked at Codi. "What does it even mean? That first verse?"

"I don't know? How long it takes to do the ritual? Seven nights?"

Désirée leaned in. "Seven gates must mean seven different cemeteries. But seven tombs? I don't know. Maybe you have to pass through seven different tombs to get to Guinée? Open one each night?"

"Pass through tombs?" I whispered. "Jesus Christ."

"Like portals?" Codi asked Dee.

"Yeah, maybe?"

We all looked back up as he started again.

Seven keys will let you enter
Nibo's axe, Plumaj's feather.
Scent of night blossoms for Masaka,
Sip of piman, dance the banda.

"Masaka!" Dee's eyes lit up. "That's three Ghede. Three keys!"

Codi held his stomach. "I think even the smell of piman right now would make me hurl."

Ren's voice got louder and he whirled the cane in the air.

Leave your ego in a jar,
The Ghede family will take you far.
Through waves of chaos, rocky cliffs of Abysmal
waters . . .

"Sounds charming," I said.

A loud throat cleared, and we all looked to the doorway. "What's going on here?" Ritha asked.

"We're going to the Afterworld!" Ren shouted victoriously.

"*Excuse me*?" Ritha's arms crossed, and I swear everything in the room rippled.

"We're just telling stories—" Dee tried to say, but this time Ritha wasn't having it.

"Désirée Nanette Borges, do not get any ideas. Don't go looking. Don't go casting spells. Don't go calling upon any Ghede. Do you hear me?"

Too late. I turned to Codi, who looked like he wanted to crawl under the bed. I knew the feeling.

"Just because you have one experience with a lwa does not mean you are ready to—"

"I am ready!"

Ritha walked up to her. "And what makes you so sure of yourself, child?" It was a Borges standoff.

Désirée's face reddened, and for a second I actually thought she was going to tell Ritha what we'd done. "I-I I just know. It's a feeling."

"Well, tell that feeling that one day you'll be a powerful priestess, but for now you need to stay away from the Ghede, and especially from Guinée! Being a cheval to a lwa in this world is an entirely different thing from traveling to theirs."

"Gran, like I'd want to go to the Afterworld."

"Désirée, do you hear the moaning coming from down the hall? I don't have time to deal with this! There are people on the verge of dying left and right. We're in the business of keeping people from going to the Afterworld, not sending them."

"Why do you think we're trying to help!"

"*Seven nights, seven moons, seven gates, seven tombs!*" Ren sang at the top of his lungs. "*Eight silver rings for—*"

But before he could reveal the next Ghede, Ritha's hand dipped into her pocket and she blew a puff of teal-colored chamomile at him. The flower buds floated around his head, and he slowly walked to the bed, his knees getting closer to the ground with each step, and then he collapsed onto the mattress.

"Now scoot, and let this man get some sleep."

He was already snoring as we stepped out of the room.

Désirée's ponytail swung as we followed her through the maze of hallways back to her bedroom in the main house.

She plopped onto her bed and lay back, huffing at the ceiling. I walked to the window and stared out into the darkness. Frankly, I thought the Ritha interruption was a godsend. There was absolutely no way in hell I was taking a trip to the Afterworld.

"It's gonna be okay, Borges," Codi said. "We'll find another way."

"How? Like Ritha said, there's a reason there are no books on getting to Guinée, and why it's not written on the pages of any grimoire. No witch is stupid enough to tell us. Especially now. Ritha's probably texting every witch in the South!"

Codi sat next to her on the edge of the bed. "What if we just ask the Ghede?"

I sneered at him for giving her more ideas.

"Don't worry, Isaac," she snapped. "It wouldn't work. You heard Ritha: if you don't know the route to Guinée, you're not supposed to get in. Asking the Ghede will just get you false information for snooping. God only knows where we might end up."

"And *that* is precisely why we don't need to go there."

Désirée rolled her eyes, mumbling under her breath, "I'm sure if it was Adele's idea you wouldn't be such a wuss."

"What?" I asked.

"Oh, nothing." She looked straight at me.

I crossed my arms, letting the comment slide. And for a moment, everyone was silent. I wondered if what Ren had said was true: that he really did have one foot in the grave. "I can't believe Ren is that bad off," I said.

"Yeah," Désirée said. "I can't imagine the French Quarter without him."

Codi got up, stretching his back, limber like a cat. "Don't even say it. Ren's always been such an ally to the magical, I forget sometimes that he's mundane."

"I wouldn't even be surprised if he used to be magical," Désirée said. "You know, a witch who never got his Maleficium."

Codi started to pace.

"You're going to get your mark, Daure," she said. "You need to stop stressing over it; you're throwing your aura out of whack."

"Now you sound like my grandpa."

"You know what would practically guarantee your mark?"

"What?"

"Doing something extraordinary. Pushing your magic. Getting to Guinée to save hundreds of souls."

I groaned as he seemed to contemplate it.

Désirée turned to me. "We're going to figure out which of the forty-five are the gates to Guinée, and we're going to figure out the rest of the keys. We're going to find a cure for the Possessed. We're going to save Ren and the souls. We're going to Guinée."

"*No,* we aren't," I said. "I want to live to see our coven fully realized."

"Ditto," echoed Codi.

"And I want to be here when Adele is ready to come back to us."

"Ditto."

"Fine." She crossed her arms. "If the two of you don't want to go, I'll venture to the Afterworld by myself. Adele's not the only one who can break away for a mission."

"You are not breaking away," I said.

"Try me."

CHAPTER 33

EARTH WITCH

The fan spun around and around above me, making shadows on the ceiling. My chest pounded hard against the diary as I got lost in the whirls. How many times had Isaac tried to return it to me over the last couple months, but I'd refused to acknowledge him? I sat up and ran my hands over the soft leather, staring at the antique metal lock, imagining it opening. I focused until I was straining; a sweat broke across my forehead.

Nothing.

A folded page had been inserted into the center of the book. I carefully pulled it out.

It was a drawing of the blue room at HQ. *Isaac's.* The fireplace was roaring. A cauldron bubbling. Potion bottles and bundles of herbs and crystals were scattered all over the furniture and floor. We were both there, suspended in the air, high above it all, wearing pointy, conical witch hats. Isaac was twirling me, and I was laughing, and he was smiling.

My heart squeezed.

I jumped off my bed and headed straight to the pile of airplanes on the floor beneath the window. I scooped them up, scrambled back onto the bed, and then began unfolding each one. They were all drawn with the same dark pencil, with thick lines and careful strokes. One showed Dee healing Codi's leg at the convent. Another showed them clearing out the backyard at the brothel and planting an herb garden. Then they were at the shop, getting yelled at by Ritha. Isaac running on the street with Stormy. Ren, disheveled, sitting in an old chair. Dee building an altar. I began laying them all out on the bed. It was like a graphic novel of their lives.

He was showing me everything that was going on in my absence.

For the first time, I didn't feel left out. I felt like I was right there with them through it all. I hurried to open the next paper plane, and found an image of him, lying in a sleeping bag on the floor, hugging a leather-bound book against his chest—Adeline's diary. He was staring at the ceiling with the saddest eyes I'd ever seen. A thought bubble hung over his head, and there I was, alone in my bed, not in our Creole cottage, but in a castle tower with a giant padlock at the bottom. I had big welling eyes, and my tears were flooding the room, the water coming all the way up to the bed, trapping me.

I sucked in a breath, blinking back tears. There was a gap in the drawings between the day I'd shut the window and now, and I hated myself for closing it. I wanted to know everything.

I pulled the diary back into my chest and curled into my bed.

When I closed my eyes, I could imagine a future where I had my magic back: us with my dad in the studio in the afternoons and with the coven at night. Volunteering on weekends and applying for art schools. I could even imagine kissing him . . . I could almost feel the way his fingers pushed through my hair. But then I thought about visiting my mother's tomb, and the image erupted, my throat burning—anger and love and every emotion in between exploding inside me like a New Year's sky.

Breathe.

"No."

I got up. I didn't want to lie in bed and process. I'd been doing that for weeks.

Before I could touch the handle, the door creaked open at Vodou Pourvoyeur. It was just the house, letting me in. *Of course it was.* I took a deep breath and stepped over the threshold. *Adele, you've locked yourself in an attic full of vampires and fought against a coven of succubus witches, you can say hello to Désirée Borges.*

The scent of the cinnamon-sandalwood-vanilla-tinged air felt familiar as I walked through the front room, and then through the rows of Voodoo dolls, hundreds of eyes following me. I paused in the apothecary, peeking behind the curtain that hid the little altar room where the three of us used to spend all of our time pre-brothel, lying on the floor in the piles of pillows below the shrine to Marassa and the rest of the Borges-Makandal ancestors. I longed to be back in that place with my friends. I hurried upstairs.

The hallway walls seemed to pulse closer, and by the time I reached Désirée's bedroom door, my anxiety was tenfold just staring at the warm light glowing from beneath the crack. My fingers curled into a fist, but before I could knock, the door opened, and once again, there was no one behind it.

Désirée was sitting on her bed, legs crossed, surrounded by books, half of them opened and covered with neon highlighter markings, the other half stacked with notes sticking out of them. "So, you got my messages?" she asked without looking up from her grimoire.

"Oh, um—" I fumbled into my bag for my phone. "No." I flicked it open. *Three missed calls: Désirée.* There were also some texts demanding to know where I was. I started to panic. "What happened?"

"Are you going to stay? I don't want to waste my breath if you're going to run off again."

"I'm not going anywhere," I said through partly clenched teeth. *I didn't come here to fight.*

"Good, because I need your help." She still refused to even look at me.

"What is all of this? You look like you're on a mission."

She added a neon-green stickie to her current page. "A mission is exactly what I'm on: a solo mission. Apparently I'm the only one in our coven with any confidence in our abilities, or with the balls to fix everything Callis wrecked."

"What do you mean? I'll help."

"That's exactly what I was hoping you'd say." She finally looked up at me—with her uptown smile, which freaked me out. "What are you *wearing*?" she asked.

"Oh, um." I looked down. "I had to borrow a dress because I got . . . blood on my sweater."

"Is that a leaf? Why do you look like you've been for a tumble in the woods with your prom date?"

I plucked a greenish sprig from my braid, poker face intact. "Is . . . Isaac here?" I asked, not really knowing why; the words just kind of slipped out.

"No, he went with Codi to—"

"I did magic," I gushed.

She sat up. "You got back your powers?"

"No, but I did a spell."

"What spell? You don't even have a grimoire."

"Nicco's"—the pitch of my voice soared—"spell."

"*Nicco's*? You did magic with Nicco—?"

"A protection spell. A succubus attacked me, and I made this lightning shield, dome thing, and I fried him!"

"This is exactly why you're going to be my wing-woman on this mission." She hurriedly made room for me on the bed.

I slipped off my shoes and sat next to her.

"Tell me *everything*."

I backtracked to the night of the attack—to the last time I'd felt in control of my magic—and told her how I could feel our slumbering spell inside of Nicco just before I removed it from him. How he cut me down from the statue and saved me from the vampire bite. The story came out in a jumbled mess. I skipped anything that had to do with my mom because I just couldn't talk about it. Désirée didn't push it.

"I know that he's magical, Désirée."

She gave me a look. "Are you sure you aren't just projecting what you want him to be? He's a vampire, Adele. One whose brother almost killed Isaac. Remember him? Your *boyfriend*?"

My face burned. "He's not my boyfriend," I snapped. "He killed my mother."

Surprise lit her eyes. "I-I'm sorry."

I immediately felt horrible. I didn't know if was for snapping at her, or because she was right, or that it was just that the subject matter just made me so tense. "No, I'm sorry."

"I shouldn't have said anything. Besides, we have way more important things to discuss, like figuring out how the hell to get your magic back, and how to get to *Guinée.*" She whispered the last part.

"Guinée? Like West Africa, Guinea?"

"Shh!" She put her finger over her mouth, eyes pointing to the ceiling and the walls. And then she grabbed her notebook and wrote out two words:

The
Afterworld

"Huh?"

"The mission," she whispered.

"Why are we whispering?"

She scribbled in the notebook again.

I think the house is listening in for my Gran.

She rolled her eyes in frustration.

"Uhhh. You're going to have to start from the beginning. And can I, maybe, borrow some clothes?"

She got up and tossed me a pair of jeans from her closet and a fitted, light-blue T-shirt that felt expensive. I changed out of the beautiful dress as she told me about Ritha's asylum for the Possessed and Chatham's library of souls, and then, more cryptically, about her insane plan to go to the Afterworld, only saying some parts out loud and writing other parts of it down.

(~~We think~~ We're pretty sure) you have to pass
through 7 gates to get to Guinée.
I think these are cemetery gates (or tombs?),
just like the old legend says.

7 Ghede guard them (7 keys open them):
Nibo (axe)
Plumaj (feather)
Masaka (night blossoms)
? (8 silver rings)

Then she started furiously scribbling some thoughts under the label: **Outstanding Questions.**

Which gates?
Does the order matter?
Does the day/time matter?
How do you get back?
WTF happens if you get something wrong?

This idea was Otherworld-level insane. Literally. But she only knew three of the Ghede, four of the keys, and zero of the gates—there were still so many unknown variables it seemed kind of implausible, so I didn't see any harm in helping her with research. Plus, I'd never seen her this excited about anything, and I just wanted things to go back to normal as quickly as possible. A magical project seemed like a fast track.

"Where do we start?" I asked, trying to hide my hesitation.

"I'm so glad you're back." She leapt over the books, scooping me into a hug. "But we don't have to cry or get weepy or anything like that, okay? Isaac has maxed my weepy quota."

Isaac could be sensitive as much as he could be abrasive, which was something I always loved about him, but it was hard to imagine his New Yorky-self being *weepy*. "You're the one doing the hugging."

"And we're not going to tell anyone about that."

"Your secret's safe with me." I hung onto her.

"Come on, let's make tea in the altar room. Maybe if we light candles for Marassa and Adeline, they'll guide us."

The idea made me fuzzy, and I was glad she didn't immediately suggest going to the brothel. There was something about the Voodoo shop that was warm and familiar and didn't have quite so many memories of me and Isaac making out in every corner of it.

We descended the stairs rapidly, our words picking up pace as well, and it was amazing how quickly we were back in sync.

She went behind the counter and pulled out one of her mini-cauldrons. Her eyes flicked to me. "Are you sure you can't light it?"

I nodded, trying not to seem defeatist.

"No sweat. Why don't you grab some elderberries from the shelf? Good for healing."

I went to the shelf, wishing that my magic was something that could be fixed with a strong herbal tea. Just when I picked up the jar of dried berries, we heard the front door open and then a mumble of voices and footsteps came into the shop.

"Oh . . . shit," Désirée said. "That's probably Codi and . . ."

She didn't need to finish the sentence. I heard Isaac's voice, and my pulse exploded.

They both stopped short when they entered the room, and I just stood there with the jar in hand.

Be normal, Adele.

"Addie!" Codi yelled.

I rested the jar on the counter, feeling anything but normal, as he charged my way, and Isaac gave Désirée a very distinct *How did you not tell me this?* look. I wondered if it was because he would have stayed away or would have come sooner.

Codi rested his arms on my shoulders. "I knew it was in the cards for you to be with us tonight."

"Yeah, it's like you're psychic or something." I laughed nervously.

Désirée grabbed his arm. "I need your help with something in the room of mirrors."

No.

"Okay, but it can wait—"

"*It can't wait,*" she said through gritted teeth.

"I'm sure you could do that later!" my voice squeaked. I don't know why I'd been so confident about this back in my bedroom with Isaac's airplanes, because now I felt like I was going to throw up.

"*Ohhh,*" Codi said.

No. No, no. Please don't leave, Codi.

He nodded to Isaac, like he finally got it.

The hurt in Isaac's eyes cut at me, and I regretted my desperate attempts to make them stay. I wanted to see him, but I needed a buffer. I'd freaked out and said horrible things the last time we were alone. I didn't trust myself.

"You guys don't have to go," Isaac said, but they hurried out. Désirée turned back with a face that said, *You got this.*

He looked back to me. "I didn't plan any of thi—"

"I know."

He breathed a small sigh of relief.

"How was the rest of your day?" I asked, as if he were a customer at the café and not someone I had shared the most intimate parts of myself with.

"Fine. I have one room at the bar ripped out entirely and pretty cleaned up."

"Oh, that's good." The progress report sounded even weirder. Like I was one of his crew members. My fingers reached for a lock of my hair before remembering it was up in the braid.

"It got pretty weird after that," he continued when I didn't think of something else to ask, "even by New Orleans standards."

"Oh?"

"Even for witch stuff."

"Oh?" I thought about the Ouroboros, and Lisette dragging me to her closet, and the scent of charred flesh filling my nostrils. "My night's been pretty weird too." How did just looking at him bring tears to my eyes?

"Oh?"

I took a breath. "I'm sorry if I'm being weird now. I'm nervous—"

"Adele, I'm sorry." His eyes glistened. "I'm sorry about Brigitte."

My insides shredded, hearing her name, and he nervously began to blather.

"We don't have to talk about this," I said.

"Mac showed me a picture—"

I don't want to talk about this. "We don't—"

"I wish I'd seen her face, before that night." Tears threatened to spill out of his eyes.

The words felt like his talons scratching over me, and I just wanted them to stop, but I was too scared to open my mouth in case something hurtful was lurking, waiting to snap out.

"You look just alike—"

Please stop. I stepped closer.

"I can't believe I kill—"

Please stop. Please stop. I slipped into his arms, images from that night bombing my brain.

"You were covered in bloo—"

I felt myself standing up on my toes and pressing my lips onto his. Shock stiffened his shoulders. The words. Finally. Stopped.

He cupped my cheek, breaking the kiss. "Adele, we don't have to—" I kissed him again and he broke it again. "We can just talk."

"I don't want to talk about it." My eyes slipped shut. I was scared I'd cry if I looked at him.

I didn't want to hurt him anymore.

"*Please*, just kiss me, Isa—"

His lips collided with mine, starved and tameless, and I held onto him tighter as I fought off the images of my mother in the attic that were trying to break through. *How warm my blood had felt oozing out of my neck, but how cold the marble floor was.* I focused on his earthy scent —letting it transport me to the life I wanted to reclaim—and I locked everything else out of my mind. No more dead mothers or vampires or Ferris wheels. Just him and his warmth and his kindness. For a second, the storm of grief released me from its vice-grip.

"I miss you," he whispered.

I kissed him harder, stealing back any space where words could wedge, and a groan buried into the back of his throat. My eyes popped open—*we're in the middle of the Borges' shop*. The magenta curtain tugged my gaze. Without skipping a beat, he walked me to the little altar room and behind the cloak of the curtain, our bags dropped to the floor and our touches became just as needy as our kisses.

"I missed you so fucking mu—"

I lightly bit his bottom lip and that was all it took. His mouth found mine again, and his tongue went silent as we moved deeper into the room.

When my back hit the wall, I got a flash of déjà vu, but my head was already spinning too much to remember of what. *Is this a good idea or a bad idea*? His hands slunk around me into the band of my jeans, squeezing my hips, and it became difficult to think about anything other than wrapping my legs around him.

He lifted me against the wall, and my head knocked the brick as he kissed my jaw—the déjà vu came back much stronger. *Wait.* He tugged my collar, and I gasped as his mouth slid to my neck. "*Isaac . . .*" My breath caught in my closing throat. *Stop.* He pressed harder against me. "St-s—" He kissed my neck, *pinching*— "Stop!" I screamed, pushing him so far away, I slid down the wall and landed hard on my tailbone. *Ugh.*

"What's wro—? I'm sorry! Are you oka—?"

"I'm sorry," I said, crawling, scrambling away from him. "I don't know what I was thinking." I picked up my bag and hurried through the curtain, apologizing again. "I don't want this. I can't do this."

I was halfway across the room when he grabbed my shoulder. "Adele, I'm sorry. Please don't leave. Please don't shut me out. We don't have to do this—we can just talk!"

I turned around and screamed, "*I killed my mother! Is that what you want me to say*?"

His eyes widened.

"Is that what you want me to talk about? *I killed her!* I didn't tell you that she was in the attic."

He just stood there, solid as a soldier, taking it.

"It's all my fault! Is that what you need to hear so you can go on with your life?" My chest heaved.

His gaze dropped to my neck, which I didn't even realize I was clutching. "*Fuck,* Adele, I'm sorry." In a panic, he tried to take my hand.

I stumbled back, covering the phantom wound my mother had left and Nicco had healed. I knew it wasn't there anymore, but I could feel it now—bloody and numb and lethal. I felt insane. I was acting crazy, and I hated it.

"I'm so sorry. I wasn't thinking—"

"I can't do this," I croaked. "Coming here was a mistake. I don't belong here anymore." I stepped back. I needed to get out.

"You belong here!" He grabbed my hands.

I was about to hyperventilate. "I'm sorry." I ripped away and ran through the store, out onto the street. The door shut loudly behind me and all six locks snapped shut at once. I didn't want him to follow.

As soon as my feet turned the corner on the street, the tears spilled out. My heart felt so swollen that it was going to burst.

My phone began buzzing with messages. I pulled it out of my bag, tears dropping on the screen.

Isaac 12:46 a.m. It's OK, Adele, I understand… I just want to be there for you.

When my mom died, I hated everyone and everything. I hated all of the doctors and nurses who couldn't save her. I knew it was irrational.

She had an incurable disease. No one had given it to her, and everyone did everything possible to save her. But still I hated them. I hated my pop, and I even hated her for not telling me sooner.

I can't imagine what it would have been like to have had one person to direct all that rage toward. But you can scream at me and cry and curse. I can take it, Adele. I love you so much I don't even know how to tell you.

My crying became hysterical and my knees became weak, and I worried I'd collapse on the street and never get up again.

Please come back.

Or just tell me where you are, and I'll come to you.

I know we can figure it out together, if you'll just let me in. We don't have to talk about it. We can just sketch. Be in the same room. Anything. Just please come back. Please don't give up on us.

If you're still reading this, just breathe.

And I did.

Breathe.

Slowly. I didn't need the inhaler. I just needed him.

Isaac 12:48 a.m. If you don't come back, I'll still be here for you when you're ready. We all will be. I get it. Why I'm the last person you want to talk to about everything. Talk to Codi. Dee.

Just please...

Please. Don't run to him just because you're mad at me. They're dangerous, Adele. We're going to work this out. I promise. All I want is for you to be safe.

I mentally dismissed his comment. *Like I would just run into Nicco's arms because I was upset.*

As I slipped the phone into my pocket, I noted where I was on the street: not facing the direction of my house, or the bar. I was pointed squarely in the direction of someone else's house.

My shoulders burned with embarrassment. I was unconsciously running to Nicco.

I turned and walked, not back to Isaac, not home, and not to Nicco's. I walked until the tears stopped and I could breathe again, and I found myself directly in front of . . .

The brothel.

I crossed the street, and the vines slithered away. The gate opened just enough for me to slip through, just like it always had when I had my magic. *The house hasn't forgotten me.*

I belong here.

As I stepped inside the front door of the empty mansion, a part of me felt like it was wrong. Like I was trespassing, but not because it was private property, more like I was infringing on the privacy of my friends.

I strolled through the rooms, noticing every little thing that was different: the improvements to the house, the evidence of their magical doings in the blue room.

A shadow of jealousy cloaked me, seeing the cauldrons and smattering of botanicals. I was the one who had discovered this place, and I'd loved it from my very first steps inside. It was special. It was *our* place. Mine, Isaac's, and Dee's. Now there were way more crystals. Surely, witchy evidence of a Daure. The thought of Codi being in our coven warmed my shivering heart. Codi was my family. I could almost hear the three of them laughing. Practicing magic here without me and it hurt.

I picked up a candle from an altar that looked like it was dedicated to some kind of forest lwa and continued to the second floor, yearning for my orbs, as nostalgia pulled me through more of the rooms. I'd never been here before without them.

I twisted my phone around and around, wanting to text him back.

Goosebumps tore down the back of my neck—a hint of supernatural sensation. *Was he here?*

I hurried, following the trail, not back downstairs but upstairs to the third floor, straight through the woodland-carved door to Cosette's secret bedroom.

But when I got there, the room was empty and dark, save for the moonlight pouring in from the windows that led out to the balcony, and the subtle twinkle outlining everything in the room thanks to the revealing spell we'd done with Annabelle.

The sensation pulsed stronger.

My eye caught sight of a blue rim—a Mets hat on the floor. Definitely Isaac's. *Why would his hat be up here?*

I set down my bag and flipped on the screen of my phone, but then, in the glow, I noticed something else on the floor: a pile of blankets and pillows, and a large army-grade duffel bag stuffed with clothes, and . . . Isaac's skateboard. *What the hell?* I activated my phone-light.

Under a couple dirty T-shirts, I discovered his sneakers and a pair of dumbbells he'd scavenged. A collection of art supplies my dad had given him lined the window ledge directly above the bedding. Tin cans and Mason jars filled with pens, brushes, and pencils, a jar of loose charcoal. Isaac barely had any stuff in New Orleans; this had to be . . . all of it?

What the hell? Has he been living here? By himself?

Isaac's dad was so strict, I'd always worried that there might be fallout after he punched that photographer, not that the guy didn't deserve it.

Wouldn't Dee have told me?

What, when you were purposefully keeping your phone uncharged? I thought about all the paper airplanes Isaac had thrown through my window, and waves of guilt pummeled me. And when I thought about being in the car tonight with Nicco, I felt ill.

I knelt down on the bedding and gripped the window ledge. In the direct shimmer of the moonlight, something—a chain dangling over the edge of a jar of markers—seemed to vibrate. *What?* I blinked a couple of times at the object inside the glass. I grabbed the jar, dumping everything out, totally overstepping boundaries, but as soon as the metal was in my hand, I no longer cared. The supernatural sensation. It was *my medallion.*

I hung it around my neck, my heart racing. *When did he find it?* He'd repaired the chain. Adeline's opal was intact, and so was the sun charm my father had made, but the silver feather was missing. My heart dipped at the thought of it still being out there somewhere, tarnishing in a gutter.

I settled down on the pallet and kicked off my shoes. His scent was so strong, I shivered, familiarity rushing back. His sketchbook was tucked halfway underneath the pillow. Three months ago, I wouldn't have thought twice about looking inside. Throwing decorum completely out the window, I opened it up to a recent page.

An ink of Onyx. Then, on the next page, a girl on a rocky beach, who I was quite sure was Susannah Bowen. I loved seeing how he imagined her. Strong. Her long red hair flowing in the wind. Another where she was in a field surround by dandelions.

I leafed through the pages, fingers on autopilot. I'd looked at it a hundred times in the past. Deep down, I knew he wouldn't mind. He never hid anything from me. *Other than an encrypted metal note and the fact that Nicco wasn't trying to kill me when he threw me out the window—that they'd planned it together.* There were pages of crows and feathers. An entire spread of quickly sketched male figures. All nude. Some were casual. Others were fully erect. All with the sweeping hand of an artist in thought, studying proportion and perspective and muscular anatomy.

Then there was a girl—not Susannah—a beautiful girl with a long white nightgown, her long, jet-black hair and the silky fabric fluttering around her. A twinge of jealousy pinched me. I definitely didn't know who she was.

There was another image of her, this one with a dog.

And there was page after page of a little girl, and I knew exactly who she was. *Jade.*

I almost scoffed with surprise finding a portrait of Lisette, considering how much he hated vampires. Then were several of him, Dee, and Codi.

My eyes stung . . . I hated how much of his life I'd missed.

I turned the page one last time, and my spine straightened. I stared back at myself, or some version of myself. The sadness in my eyes was chilling. My collarbones jutted out of the giant sweater, and I looked frail and broken.

Whoever the girl on the page was staring at, it was clear that she was scared of him. I choked on my own breath trying not to cry. I knew it was from the day on the street. I imagined him lying right here that night, unable to sleep after I said those horrible things. A teardrop fell on the page.

Shit. I tried to blot it off. "I ruined his life, and now I'm ruining his art."

"You couldn't ruin my art . . . you're my muse."

I looked up.

The doorway was so dark, I could hardly see him standing there.

"And you didn't ruin my life," he said. "You showed me what life can be."

CHAPTER 34

AIR WITCH

She quickly closed the book and just looked up at me with those big blue eyes, sad and swollen. Her hair was sticking out of the braid in a million directions, but she still looked so beautiful bathed in the moonlight that it caught my breath.

"Is it okay if I come in?" I asked, not moving a muscle.

She nodded, silent tears dripping from her eyes. "It only seems fair considering I'm sitting on your bed?"

I nodded, slowly stepping into the room.

She stood up and met me halfway. "Fight with your pop?"

"Yeah."

"After the ceremony?"

"Yeah." I stopped right in front of her.

"I'm sorry."

I shrugged, not really knowing what to say about it. My dad was a dick. My eyes dropped to the medallion around her neck. *Shiiit. She found it.*

"It's okay," she said, before I could panic.

"I'm sorry. I just . . . needed something to hang onto. I was scared."

"Of what?"

"That if I gave it back, there'd be no reason for you to ever talk to me again. I k-killed your mother." Out of nowhere, tears streamed down my face. "*Fuck.* I won't talk about it." I wiped them away. "I swear. I'm sorry."

"It's okay." She took a step closer, but her gaze was wide and burning, and not meeting mine. "It's not your fault," she said. "I'm the one who . . . It's my fau . . ." Her words choked out, and I just wanted to hold her, but I didn't know if I should touch her. "Callis was going to burn her alive. With my magic. I couldn't get down from the statue. I let them out."

"This was *not* your fault," I said, infuriated with myself that I hadn't been with her that night—and that Callis had been able to dupe us all so hard.

"You saved m . . . she was going to . . . my mother was going to ki . . ." She looked up, her voice pinching. "Isaac, my mother was going to kill me." The noise that came out of her throat sounded like a bottle of nightmares breaking—tears thundering, boundless pain and infinite darkness.

I stepped closer, and she fell against me.

"My mother tried to kill me," she said, trembling.

I would have given my soul to take her pain away. I wrapped my arms around her, and I felt her shatter. Her sobs brought the sound of the stake cracking into her mother's back echoing into my ears. The screams and the blood and the chaos. I sucked back a breath so my voice wasn't cloudy. "It wasn't her fault, Adele. It was Emilio's. He's the one who turned her into a monster."

She cried harder.

"I'm sorry, Adele." I waited for her to pull away and yell at me again, words already forming in my head to convince her to stay—but she only cried harder and her arms circled my torso, and she held onto me like we were in the eye of a storm and she was going to be ripped away.

"Breathe," I said, softly.

I was terrified that I didn't know how to put her back together, but I held onto her, cradling her head until her tears dried up and she stopped shaking.

"I don't want to lose you." Her voice was raspy. "I don't know how to fix this, and I'm scared that I'm going to push you away forever . . . You're my best friend."

"What?" The idea of *her* being worried over losing *me* was so ludicrous a little laugh slipped from my throat. I leaned down so I could peer directly into her glossy eyes. "Adele, you have a million things to be worried about, but losing me is not one of them. I promise, we'll figure it all out. And I swear to God, I'm never going to let Callis touch you again."

She took a couple breaths, her eyes locked to mine.

"I'm sorry for not telling you about Brigitte. And I'm sorry for asking Nicco to erase Mac's memories of you." She sucked in another quick breath through her nose. "And I'm sorry for those horrible things I said on the street. And I'm sorry for mauling you at the Voodoo shop earlier."

"Okay, okay," I said, cupping her cheeks. "You don't have to go that far."

She laughed, and I wrapped my arms back around her. And when the last waves of the squall finally seemed to subside, I pressed my lips to her forehead. When I broke the kiss and she looked up at me, every part of my being longed to comfort her.

She held up the two charms on her chain, showing me that one was missing. "Will you come back to the studio and make me another feather?"

"I could," I said, elated by her invitation, but I pulled out the ball chain from underneath my shirt. "Or I could give you this one." I slid the piece of metal away from my Grandpop's dog tags and unhooked it. Her eyes lit up.

Then I suddenly remembered Codi telling us how she used the rough edge of metal to cut open her arm to draw her mother away from him. I saw the blood coating her arm, and my fingers curled around the metal, hiding it.

"I want this one," she said, her hand covering mine.

"Are you sure?"

She nodded. "One bad memory shouldn't cancel out all the good ones." She lifted her hair, and I unclipped her chain and slipped it on. She glanced down at it, then walked over to the vanity mirror. She somehow looked more like herself with the necklace hanging against her chest. Her fingers instantly gravitated toward it, feeling the metal, fiddling with the three charms. She gazed into the mirror at me. "Is it really okay if we just sketch for a while?"

"*Mm-hmm.*" I tugged the tips of her fingers and sat on the pallet where the moonlight was strongest, pulling her down next to me.

She smiled and slid the pencil out from behind my ear and it was so hard not to kiss her.

I opened my sketchbook and leaned it against my knees. She took the left page and I took the right, just like we always used to. I don't know how it was possible for two people to sit so close and not be touching, but I was never so glad to have her next to me.

Her strokes exposed the freshly opened wounds inside her, long and heavy, nearly to the edges of the pages before swooping back. Abstract, mostly just her re-familiarizing herself with the tool while I sketched a pair of plump lips. Wing-tipped eyeliner. Eyelashes for days and a curve for the bowler hat. I felt her gaze wandering to the tip of my pencil as I drew the mesh crop top on Masaka's chest, and soon she was leaning closer, waiting to see what was coming next. I added the skulls and dead roses that had decorated the brim of his hat, and then the spikes and studs to the shoulders of his white leather jacket.

She angled herself to better examine the outfit. "It's so McQueen."

"What, like the race car driver?" I asked, straight face intact.

"*No!* Like the *legendary* fashion designer," she answered, aghast.

"I know who Alexander McQueen is!" I said, laughing, refraining from tickling her. "Adele Le Moyne, meet Ghede Masaka, Désirée's death-lwa passenger." I moved the sketchpad back over.

"Désirée was a *cheval for a lwa*?"

"Ooooh. Not just one." I turned the page. "And not just Désirée."

"What?" she asked in disbelief. "What did you guys do without me?"

I drew Oussou's long coat and short disco dress and told her the whole wild story, including Désirée loving herself and Codi humping everything that was or wasn't nailed down. "Finally, someone to share the trauma with," I joked. "I had no clue what to do. You have no idea how much I wished you were there."

As I drew the Ghede-feast, she put her pencil down, knees curling into her chest. I don't know what had changed, but I sensed her becoming more and more withdrawn. I set the pad down. I could feel the fear that had taken over her.

"Hey," I said, touching her chin so she'd look at me. She didn't.

"What's the matter?" *Besides the eight million fucked-up things in your life?*

Her voice was tight. "Can I ask you something about the night at the convent?"

"Yeah. Anything."

"Did anyone else . . . die because I opened the attic? Did the vampires kill anyone? Did anyone else die because of me?"

"What? *No.*"

"They were starving," she said, curling tighter into a ball, her voice shrinking back into her throat.

"No one else died."

"Are you lying just to make me feel better?"

"No, I swear. They got some of Callis's goons, but no one else."

Her breathing became erratic. I tried to tell her again that no one else died, but she only seemed to get worse and I was afraid she was going to have a panic attack. She gasped for air and then the words just slipped out of my mouth, something I knew she'd believe: "Nicco kept them under control."

She looked at me. "He did?"

"Yeah," I managed to say without tightening my jaw. "Nicco kept them all in line."

Her grip loosened from her knees and a serenity washed over her.

I was glad she could breathe again, but I hated how just the idea of him could calm her down like that.

"*Désolée*," she whispered. A few residual tears slid out of her bloodshot eyes.

"Come here," I said, my hand grazing hers.

She curled underneath my arm. "*Merci beaucoup*."

"For what?"

"For the messages you sent me earlier. And for saving my life. Again."

It was absurd that she'd thank me for anything that happened that horrendous night. I nestled her closer. "*Merci beaucoup too*."

"For what?" She tried not to laugh at my accent, but her chest shook.

"For saving me . . . for whatever you did to get Lisette to detox me."

Her smile flattened. "Emilio's not going to come after you anymore."

The words were supposed to be comforting, but my pulse pounded. *What did she do?*

But then she looked up at me. "Will you keep drawing, please? I don't want to go home yet."

And with that, I let my question go. I'd draw forever if it meant her not going home.

With one arm still swooped around her, I sketched a girl, tall and slender with sky-high legs, naked as the day she was born. Antlers sprouted from the top of her head, parting her long straight hair that hung all the way down to her waistline. Her nipples peeked through the shiny strands. She had hooves for hands and feet, and chains of flowers crowning her antlers. And as I drew, I told her the story of Gran Bwa.

Eventually, her breaths became so gentle, I knew she was sleeping. I set aside the sketchpad and stroked her hair, resting back against the wall.

Goose pimples rippling over Adele's skin beneath my fingers wake me up. A curtain at the far end of the room flutters in the breeze. Without disturbing her slumber, I gently move out from under her, walk to the curtain, and quietly shut the window.

A breeze kisses my neck, making me shiver. The curtain to my right is fluttering.

"What the?"

I shut it too, but then the next curtain flutters.

"Seven nights, seven moons. Seven gates, seven tombs," comes a voice behind me.

I spin back around. Across the room, in my bedroll, Adele is gone. Ren is sitting there, legs outstretched in a V, wearing his tattered top hat and his tiny purple sunglasses hanging low on the tip of his nose. I step closer, fixated on a little black shadow on his lip. It wiggles and his words slur as he speaks again. I freeze, and another appears. The shadows are legs. *The furry body of a spider pops out, its eight legs tickling down his chin and across his face.*

"Ren!"

Another spider crawls out of his mouth. His words go from a slur to a gurgle as shadows pour from his lips. Dozens of spiders, rippling like waves of darkness. He begins to choke, and I hurry closer, feeling their soft, furry bodies crunch beneath my bare feet.

Big bunches of cotton are stuffed in his ears. I want to pull them out and stuff them in mine so I can't hear him heave. I shove my fingers into his mouth and pull out the spiders, throwing them as far as I can. The more I pull out, the more appear. My skin crawls, and my spine shudders. His eyes have a faint purple glow.

"You do dance the banda, Isaac?" a voice whispers in my ear. Creole accent. Unmistakably Ghede.

Fingers crawled up my chest, and I lurched back against the wall, a small shriek escaping my mouth.

"It was just a dream," Adele said, brushing the hair from my sweaty face. "You're okay."

I shivered. All the windows were open, curtains fluttering.

"Isaac?" she was gazing at my arm. My mark was glowing white—just like that night in the cemetery when it'd first appeared, only this time, she could actually see the mark. "Are you okay?"

I nodded, looking between the glowing triangle and her. I couldn't believe she was here. That we had actually weathered this storm. "Are you up for a little walk? There's something you should see."

CHAPTER 35

TOGETHER AT LAST

Earth-magic bloomed from botanical blends in the Borges' courtyard that would give even a beginner horticulturist pause. Hibiscuses as big as my face and sunflowers that stretched up to the moon decorated the path. I accidentally stepped too close to Isaac, and our hands brushed. In my peripheral vision, I saw him stretch his fingers to mine and then pull back, hesitant, like he didn't know if he should touch me. I folded my arms together.

"Hey," Désirée said, quietly coming out of the main house along with . . . *Codi*?

Isaac looked at his watch. "What are you still doing here?"

Codi half-yawned, half-groaned. "Helping her try to figure out who the seven lwa are who guard the gates."

Isaac's eyes were rolling hard before Codi even finished the sentence.

As we followed Désirée to the guesthouse, Codi paused to hold up an enormous banana leaf for us to walk under. He pulled me back, his expression suddenly serious. "Are you okay?"

Only then did I realize they'd probably heard me screaming at Isaac before we'd left—the entire post-Storm French Quarter probably had. A wave of guilt washed over me. "*Merci. Ça va*," I assured him, and he let the leaf fall back into place behind us.

I followed the others up the stairs, and through a maze of hallways they seemed to know well, my heart inching up my throat as I heard the voices. "What's going to happen to them?" I asked, but the words were lost in the moans, cries, and gibberish coming through the floorboards and ceilings all around us.

Isaac fell back next to me as we turned a corner. "You might want to prepare yourself. Some days are better than others."

I nodded, still unable to process the idea that Ren was so bad off he needed to be magically contained.

We stopped outside the final room. The wooden door had been removed, but I could feel the magic pulsing from the threshold like a cage. Ren was sitting, hunched over a desk, writing, or drawing, his stringy curls hanging over his eyes. Embers crackled in the fireplace, casting shadows on the profile of his pallid face. Papers with crude sketches and scribbles spilled all over the desk and onto the floor.

"Ren?" Isaac called out.

Ren didn't turn our way.

"We brought a surprise visitor."

He tapped his pencil against the pad.

"*Salut, Ren, c'est moi!*" Fake cheeriness chirped from my voice as I stepped inside.

Désirée frowned when he didn't respond to the French greeting. "Alessandro?"

Still nothing. He just continued to scribble away at whatever he was working on.

"Who's Alessandro?" I asked.

Désirée looked at Isaac. "Oh boy."

He turned to me. "Remember the fruit picker's son from his Royal Street ghost tour? The story with the Romeo catchers?"

Codi cringed.

"No way."

"Yes, way," Désirée whispered to me. "Do you know any Italian?"

I shook my head.

"Oh come on. I know you, Adele. You haven't picked up *anything* hanging out with loverboy—?"

"*Buonasera, Ren*! *Come stai?*" I blurted out, infinitely glad Isaac couldn't telepathically gauge the rate of my speeding heart.

Ren's head slowly turned our way, and I swallowed a gasp. It was him and it wasn't. It was his dingy ruffled shirt and heavy industrial-

Goth boots, but the look in his eyes was wild. And I'd never seen a face so pale and gaunt—Goth or not. His eyes were sunken and his nose taller and skinnier thanks to his face thinning out.

"*Come stai*?" he repeated back. "*Come stai*?!" A string of spitfire Italian shot from his lips, and his fingers curled around the loose papers on the desk, his voice getting louder and more on edge until it was practically a growl. Codi took a little step in front of us. I couldn't comprehend a word of what Ren was saying, but I didn't need a translator to know he was *freaking out* about something.

"Okay, we'll let you get some rest," Désirée said, guiding me out the door and out of view. "Come on, we need to leave before he gets too worked up. If he starts yelling, they'll all start yelling, and we don't need to wake up Ritha."

We didn't pause until we were halfway across the courtyard.

I looked up at Isaac. "How long has he been in that room?"

"More or less since he tried to sock your dad at that fundraiser."

"Three months?"

"Ritha persuaded Detective Matthews to release him to her care instead of locking him up in OPP. It started out that he just couldn't leave the property, then the guesthouse. Then the room. He's gotten out a couple times; he attacked Theis. It was bad."

"Jesus."

"Do you see why we have to do something?" Désirée whispered, urgency in her voice. "And he's not the only one. We've already lost one woman. A priest was here tonight reading another her last rites!"

"Someone died?"

"They're all going to die, Adele. That's what's going to happen to them!"

"Désirée, do we have to start with this right now?" Isaac asked. "It's nearly two in the morning."

"Yeah," Codi echoed. "Adele's been back for like fifteen minutes. Can we at least wait one night?"

She crossed her arms. "One night."

He slapped her back. "Way to prove wrong all those people who say a Borges can't compromise."

She rolled her eyes.

"What's he talking about?" Isaac whispered to me.

"Her father's political opponent is already running smear campaigns despite the election being months away. I heard them on the radio."

"That sucks."

We walked the few blocks back to the old pink mansion, and this time, when the vines parted and the door creaked open and I walked into the house without my orbs, I didn't feel like an intruder, because our steps were in sync. And soon their voices and laughter, and the warmth from the fireplace, and the coils of lavender-infused sage burning in seashells on the mantel all threaded together, quilting together parts of me I hadn't even realized were still torn.

Nothing would fill the void of my missing powers, but my friends replenished my soul in a way that only those tied by magic could.

I walked straight to the trunk behind the sofa in the blue room and was relieved to find it still filled with witchy things, just like always. I removed the sack of salt, all three of them watching.

"Do you have something in mind?" Désirée asked.

"Something very specific." I looked at Codi. "Only for *official* coven members, though."

"Hey! It's not my fault I'm not official."

"Which is precisely why we should do the binding ceremony."

He smiled, and Isaac moved the coffee table. I drew a circle big enough for us all to fit. Codi laid out the candles, and Désirée smudged the four corners of the room. Then we all sat down, Isaac on my left, Dee on my right, and Codi directly across. Everything felt right.

We all joined hands, and the lights snapped out. In the darkness, I couldn't help but joke: "Can you believe we almost did this with Annabelle Lee Drake?"

Codi scoffed, and both of my hands were squeezed. With that, flames grew from the wicks all around us. Excitement rushed into Codi's face.

Désirée led the chant.

Papa Legba, ouvrez la porte.
Papa Legba, ouvrez la porte, open the door.
Papa Legba, open the door to the other side.
Open the door and be our guide;
We come to you in perfect love and perfect trust.

Every candle in the room ignited, and every reflective surface in the room mirrored the flames, from the gilded picture frames to the vases on the mantel and the chandelier crystals hanging overhead. All three of their energies filled me with warmth, and our voices filled the room as we joined in the next verse. We repeated the lines until our voices trembled, the pictures on the walls vibrated, and the chandelier swayed.

Together as one, with the Earth, Water, Air, and
Fire inside us, guide us.
From our ancestors we seek protection. Guide us.
Our decisions. Our actions. Our powers. Guide us.
We come to you in perfect love and perfect trust.
Bind us.

Flames burst in the fireplace.

Our voices trailed, and the candles extinguished in a single whoosh.

Codi cheered and lunged straight toward Dee. He picked her up in a twirling hug as the overhead light came back on.

"Put me down!" she screeched.

Isaac looked at me and I smiled, and before I knew it, Codi was lifting me in the air next, twirling me around. I didn't fight him because I loved him like we were blood, and I couldn't imagine anyone who I'd rather be magically bound to. Isaac hurried to the china cabinet and began rummaging around, clinking glasses, and then returned to the circle with four little port glasses he'd scrounged. Dee uncorked an unmarked bottle of rum that smelled like it had come straight off the S.S. *Gironde* and filled the glasses to the brim.

"Cheers to our fourth," Isaac said, and we all toasted.

I squirmed as my mouth filled with the burning liquid, and then swallowed it with a gulp before I accidentally spat it back out. As I sucked in a breath, Désirée poured another round.

"Cheers to Morning Star!" she shouted, raising her glass.

"And Marassa!" I echoed.

"To Susannah!" Codi yelled.

"And to Adeline Saint-Germain." Isaac held his glass up to ours.

"And cheers to the lady of the house," I said, "Cosette Monvoisin."

"Cheers to Cosette!" they all repeated.

"And cheers to Minette. And cheers . . . to Lisette"—I looked at

Isaac—"without whom you wouldn't be here." I threw the shot back with a scream.

As soon as I set the glass down, his arms encircled me, and he twisted me around, resting his head on mine. "Without you, I wouldn't be here."

"I would do anything for you," I said, peering up into his eyes.

"Obviously," Désirée said, and they all laughed.

I kissed his spiky cheek, already feeling the booze rushing to my head, and was again in awe at how quickly we could slip back into our old selves.

We cleared away the circle and settled around the coffee table, Isaac and I on the couch, Dee and Codi on the floor. Codi broke out some packages he'd brought from the shop: more of the mermaid sweets, cookies, and at least a dozen tea-sandwiches that had gone unsold for the day. Apparently, this was a daily occurrence for the three of them. Then, instead of spellwork or research or magical plans, we each took turns telling the story of what had happened to us the night of the attack.

I told them how Nicco had showed me the memory of the Carter brothers—and then subsequently hurried past it before Codi or Dee could make the connection about us dream-twinning. Codi told me how he'd tracked Callis and Celestina to the convent, and I was overcome with gratitude again that he'd been there. Isaac told me how Julie had been attacked at the tearoom, and how Dee had cast the location spell on Annabelle, ultimately leading them to me. It was never clearer that we were supposed to be together. Without everyone contributing their part, it's possible that all of us wouldn't have made it through the night alive.

I told them about the great European witching families and how the Salazars had condemned thousands of people to be burnt at the stake.

"They're terrorists," Isaac spat. I'd rarely seen him so worked up.

Codi bit the head off a merman. "If those had been our ancestors, we wouldn't be here. And who knows, it could have even been the end of our magical lines."

A lump formed in my throat. I wondered if I'd destroyed our family line for all my future descendants by letting Callis steal my Fire. "We have to clean up the mess the Ghost Drinkers made," I choked out. "We can't let them hurt anyone else, magical, mundane, or otherwise."

Dee grabbed the bottle of rum and poured each of us another glass. "To finding the gates of Guinée," she said, holding up her glass.

Codi and I both took deep breaths and held up our glasses.

"To Guinée," I echoed.

"To the Ghede," he said.

We all turned to Isaac. He shook his head, but raised his glass. "To the dead."

Dee radiated excitement, and I could tell it was taking every ounce of her restraint not to crack open her research. Then as if she could sense me thinking about her, she looked at me. "There's something you said before . . ." I could see her mind ticking over. "About Nicco. Do you mean *your* ancestor is the one who killed him?"

"No," I said quickly. "It was Séraphine, but Nicco thinks León had something to do with it, because he escaped unscathed. And with the Medici grimoire. Allegedly." I looked up at each one of them, knowing how silly the next words were going to sound given my current magical abilities. "I'm going to get my powers back. I don't know how, but I am —and I'm going to find León. I need to know if it's true. If he really conspired to murder an entire witching family to steal all of their magic. If he has the Medici grimoire. It's the most powerful book of shadows from the Renaissance."

"You're not going to do that," Désirée said.

We all looked at her.

"*We're* going to find him."

I smiled.

"We're in this together," Isaac said. "In perfect love and perfect trust."

"I'm never going to let them separate us again," I said.

"Never," Codi said. "And oh, our coven needs a badass name to follow up our ancestors."

Everyone agreed, and we all took turns shouting out suggestions, each one more ridiculous than the next. My fingers had hardly left Adeline's medallion all night, and my gaze hardly left Isaac as my mind simultaneously tried to process everything that had happened between us and everything that had happened back in the swamp with Nicco just hours ago. There was no denying that Nicco's destiny was entwined with my own—but maybe that's all it was? Maybe I was meant to reunite Nicco with his family, and he was supposed to teach me to believe in my magic, so together we could defeat a greater enemy to the witching world. Somewhere along the way, we'd become friends. The kind of friends I didn't have words for.

As he'd once told me, we were magical together.

Amici magici.

Magical friends.

Dee finished tying off a gris-gris she'd made for Codi, and he placed it around his neck and under his shirt. "You should be wearing labradorite all the time," she said.

"You sound like my cousins."

"Well, maybe you should listen to them. You're in the coven now, you need to get your Mark. Labradorite helps bring out magical abilities."

"I know the healing properties of labradorite!"

Isaac smiled at me. I wasn't sure if it was a general smile or because of the way they were bickering over crystals, but he gazed at me from across the couch with a hope that could save the world from all its evils, and it was melting. I moved closer and circled my arms around his neck, not caring that Dee and Codi were right there. I needed to feel his heart beating against mine. And when the weight of his arms sank around me, the ropes of anxiety and guilt and depression snapped, and I felt freed from the grief. At least momentarily.

I hoped he knew how much I loved him.

Because I did.

I knew it would have been easier if I just said it; I guess I just wasn't ready.

But I held onto him tighter.

CHAPTER 36

FOCUS

April 22nd

My arm glided under the silky fabric into the welcoming cool crevice beneath the pillow, and I basked in the glow of deep rest, stretching my legs out wide. My toes didn't reach the edge of the mattress. I jolted up in the darkness—my bed was not this big. *Where am I?*

It took a few seconds for the twinkling to come into view all around me, outlining the bed, the fireplace, the vanity. I was in Cosette Monvoisin's room, but I had no memory of getting up here. The last thing I remembered was falling asleep on the couch next to Isaac. I threw off the blanket. All of my clothes were on, except for my boots. There were no signs of anyone else having slept in the bed with me, and no sign of my phone nor of my bag, but my boots were on the floor. Isaac's pallet was empty, except for the shirt he'd been wearing last night.

I inched off the bed and picked up the blanket—a black twinkling shadow, just like everything else—and wrapped it over my shoulders. It dragged along the floor as I walked to the tall dressing mirror. My face appeared to bob along in the air, the invisible blanket hiding the rest of my body, and the twinkles shimmered when I moved my shoulders. *So cool.* I danced around a little, an outline of sparkles, and I couldn't remember the last time I'd smiled this soon upon waking.

I drew open one of the curtains, and bright sunshine poured into the room. *Shit.* I hardcore missed my curfew last night. I spread the blanket back over the bed and tiptoed out of the room, toggling between the excitement of being out of my house and at HQ, and the slight terror that Mac was going to freak out.

But on my way downstairs, I couldn't help but take a moment to wander through the second floor, mesmerized by the time capsule, as if it was my first time going through the parlor rooms. It all felt surreal, like at any moment I was going to wake up back in my bed at home, groggy from Désirée's sleepytime potion.

I stopped at one of the new additions to the house, surely the mark of Désirée: an altar to La Sirene, the mermaid lwa. There were altars all over the house now. I imagined Isaac scavenging planks from Storm wreckage to build the base structures for her. Each of the lwa was represented by different colors, and this altar was painted blue and white and adorned with seashells, coral, and bottles of sand and river water.

I bounced down the staircase into the far back room we'd transformed into a greenhouse. Bright light streamed in through all the tiny windowpanes onto an altar for Gran Bwa, strung with green and red ribbons and Spanish moss and stacked with small succulents. It was crowned with a picture of a golden Saint Sebastian, who was pinned to a tree with an arrow through his neck and watched over by an angel from up above. *Intense.*

By the time I made it through the dining room, I hadn't found anyone and was panicking over what time it might be. My footsteps picked up. *Like I really need to be grounded the day after getting back together with my friends.*

Désirée was on the couch in the blue room, reading a thick tome, a highlighter dangling from between her lips.

"Hey," I said, "what time is it?"

"Two."

"PM?" I yelped. "How could you let me—?"

"Don't worry. I texted Mac from your phone and told him you were sleeping at my house."

"You did?" I moved a pillow to sit down next to her.

"He replied saying it was fine. But to text him sooner next time."

"Oh . . . thanks," I said, partially grateful, partially unsettled that she'd opened my phone. *It's just Dee.* "Wait, two o'clock? My shift!" I jumped up. It was so weird having my job back, I'd completely forgotten.

"Codi's covering for you. Don't worry."

"Oh . . . " I sat back down.

The distinct aroma of coffee and chicory wafted from a half-full French press on the coffee table, which was covered in scattered pieces of paper, mostly lists with dates next to them.

"Help yourself," she said, nodding to the extra cup.

I practically salivated as I poured it. I sat back with the cup, savoring the first sip. It tasted like the Voodoo shop smelled: a swirl of cinnamon and vanilla.

Dee glanced back and forth between a book about architecture and her phone, which she was using to look things up.

"One more question," I said. "How did I get—?"

"Isaac carried you."

"Up three flights of stairs?"

"Yep. Then he went to work. He didn't wake you. He *said* it was because you could use the rest . . ."

"But?"

"But he had this look in his eyes . . . like he was so relieved you were here, I think he just didn't want it to end. I don't think any of us did. So we just let you sleep."

The sentiment somehow made me feel simultaneously loved and guilty. "I'm not going to leave the coven. You don't have to babysit me, I promise."

She smiled a crooked smile, and I knew our fight was buried in the past. "I figured someone should be around when you woke up so you didn't freak out, alone."

"*Merci*. It's nice being out of the house."

"You got another text too." She nodded to the floor. My phone was on top of my bag, right where I'd left it. "He just wanted to make sure you were okay after your intense night."

"You read my messages?" I snatched up the phone and slid the screen open.

Thump-thump.

"I didn't *read* it. It was just there, and I saw it flash. It's not like I could stop my brain from processing the words."

> **Nicco 8:59 a.m.** Buongiorno. I just wanted to see how you're doing after last night. It was a lot at once. I knew you had it in you, but seeing you break through–the power, and beauty, and grace–it was something to get caught up in.

"Graceful" was not something I'd ever been called. My insides swirled, and it was suddenly like I was back in the woods, in the circle, Nicco's voice in my head as the Italian words slipped from my lips, and I could barely feel the couch. It was like I was hovering again, his magic coursing through my veins.

The phone buzzed. *Jesus!*

> **Nicco 2:11 p.m.** Also, Gabe wants to know when you're coming over to spar.
>
> If you come early, I'll secretly teach you all of his tells. - N

I did my best not to smile as I read the messages—Désirée was scrutinizing my every movement—but the coquettish feeling his words elicited was difficult to suppress.

> **Adele 2:12 p.m.** It was all thanks to you. You never stopped believing in me.

> **Nicco 2:12 p.m.** Well, I can't argue with the latter.

> **Adele 2:13 p.m.** And you were right about something else too.

> **Nicco 2:13 p.m.** Oh?

Adele 2:13 p.m. About my friends being good for me.

Nicco 2:13 p.m. Oh?

Adele 2:14 p.m. Sí. Even Isaac.

Nicco 2:14 p.m. Oh.

Adele 2:14 p.m. And tell Gabe that I accept his challenge. And Nicco…

Nicco 2:14 p.m. Sí, bella?

Adele 2:15 p.m. I'm half a cup of coffee in. I won't be breaking into your dreams. You can go to sleep now.

Nicco 2:15 p.m. Buonanotte, bella.

Adele 2:15 p.m. Buonanotte.

I stared at the screen.

There had always been a safety in our flirtation because it was like a dead-end road with an impenetrable steel wall.

But now something felt different. Was it possible for steel to chink?

It's just the remnants of his magic.

I sipped the coffee and squashed the feeling. The words on the screen were simple, harmless, but for some reason, I was almost scared to look up from the phone. My relationship with Nicco, whatever it was, had always been this private nook, coated in mystery and intrigue; now it felt like the locks on the door were slowly twisting open one by one.

When I finally looked up, Désirée was staring at me. She raised her left eyebrow.

"What?" I asked.

"You tell me."

"You already know. He was just checking on me after the incident in the woods."

Her eyebrow somehow inched higher.

"I mean, I want to ask him more—about what happened when he and Emilio went back, and about the witch—but that seems like a conversation that should happen only in person."

"Yes, please be careful. You've already had Detective Matthews on your back because of their criminal activity once before."

She was right. "What are all these dates?" I pointed to her pages of lists, eager to change the subject.

"I'm looking up what year each cemetery opened. I figured we should prioritize the oldest ones since they'll have a deeper history with the Ghede."

I nodded.

Adeline's journal was peeking out of my bag. I had practically every line of it memorized. There was nothing on the pages that would help me find León, and he was who I should be focused on right now, especially while Nicco was distracted looking for Callis. But where to start? *How am I going to find someone Nicco hasn't been able to find for centuries?* Then I remembered something Isaac had said a while back, in this very room, when we'd been looking for the other descendants: he'd said it was 'a magical dilemma.'

Magic.

León.

I twirled Adeline's medallion around my finger. Maybe the answers weren't in the pages of her diary; maybe they were with . . . Adeline.

CHAPTER 37

SECOND CHANCE

My phone vibrated in my pocket.

Adele 14:46 Hi.

Off work yet?

I took the stairs of the garçonnière two at a time, despite the eight-hour shift and having gotten almost zero sleep last night. The text was a bigger energy jolt than a gallon of coffee. It was evidence that last night wasn't all just some kind of post-Ghede fantasyscape.

Adele 14:46 I hope you didn't have to operate any power tools today.

My fingers fumbled across the screen as I took the turns through the hallways.

Isaac 14:47 Yes and nope, but nearly slipped off the roof twice.

Adele 14:47 !!!!!!!!!!!!!!!

I promise I won't keep you up all night again.

Isaac 14:47 Worth it. Just gonna grab a quick shower. Be there in a few.

Adele 14:47 HQ :)

And there it was—all I'd wanted for the last few months. To see her smile. Even if it was just an emoji. The faster I moved, the sooner I'd be able to see the real thing. I tossed the phone onto the bed, hoping I had a set of clean clothes here. I'd move the rest of my stuff over later. Everything was falling into place: Housing. Studio mentorship. The coven. And now Adele had fallen asleep in my arms.

I pulled the mold-dusted shirt over my head and kicked away the jeans as I hustled to the bathroom, already feeling cleaner just having the gross clothes off my skin. I was impatient to see her, but once I was standing beneath the hot stream, I lingered. My muscles ached from overwork and dehydration; I stretched against the wall, letting the water beat onto my shoulders. The old spigot was so built up with calcium deposits, the water spurted out like bullets—like amazing, meditative massage bullets. Hot water dribbled over my collar bones, and I twitched as the memory flashed: *blood, oozing down my neck from Emilio's bite.*

I shuddered as it all flickered back: the unadulterated hatred in his eyes, the pure rage in his bite. He'd never let go of what I'd done to Brigitte. If Adele thought any differently, she was being naïve. All of this being besties with Nicco and taking on Emilio. Each of them was more manipulative than the next, spinning a web around her until she gave them what they wanted, or until she was so twisted in their sticky threads she couldn't get out. My biggest fear was that when she finally realized it and tried to fight through, it would be too late. I could see it so clearly: Nicco's fangs sinking into her flesh, his venom overpowering her as he drained her blood and took her life—took whatever he wanted from her.

I imagined the smile on his face. His satisfaction after he'd finally gotten everything he'd been after for the last four hundred years.

Murdering León Saint-Germain, getting his grimoire back. I imagined him stroking Adele's lifeless cheek. Her naked body sprawled in his bed.

This whole time, I'd thought Nicco was in love with Adele, but maybe I was wrong. Maybe it was all just a part of his plan to get to Saint-Germain.

For some fucked-up reason, that made me a little less uneasy. His murderous plans felt like something I could actually protect her from. His shy smiles and glimmering eyes and casual romantic Renaissance air, I wasn't so sure.

I spun the knob, turning off the water. Nicco Medici was *not* who I wanted to be thinking about in the shower.

I dried, dressed, and soared out the window into the warm sunshine, stretching my wings wide, gliding on a magical Air current. The stress released as soon as I went back to thinking about the fact that I was going to HQ and that *finally* Adele was there waiting for me.

I swooped through the broken transom in the brothel attic, down to the second floor, past La Sirene, and all the way downstairs into the blue room, where the giant cemetery map was now pinned to the wall and covered in bright pink sticky notes.

Adele was examining the Ghede family altar. It was a work in progress, but there wasn't a day that went by where Désirée wasn't adding something to it: the pouch of graveyard dirt from our séance, the bottle of piman or what was left of it, cigars, sunglasses covered in lilac sequins, a can of chicory coffee. From the looks of the scraps of paper all over the floor, they'd been decoupaging rum bottles with pictures from magazines. *Is that a vintage* Playboy*?*

I cawed so I didn't scare her and landed right behind her, unable to wait before wrapping my arms around her waist.

She rested back against my chest, looking up at me with a smile. "Yay, you're here."

"Hi," I said, trying not to be too obvious with how much I wanted to kiss her.

She twirled a lock of her hair through her fingers, something she always did when she was nervous.

"What's up?" By the looks of the mess all over the coffee table, I had a distinct feeling it had something to do with Désirée's Guinée plan.

She took my hand and led me down the hallway into one of the formal sitting rooms where we never really did coven stuff but had on occasion done . . . other things.

Most of the curtains were closed, letting in only cracks of daylight that shone harsh bright lines onto the century-old furnishings. Something about the way the room seemed like it hadn't been disturbed in decades made me want to whisper. The darkness and silence and too many decorations gave the feeling of privacy, like we could blend into the mix of Victorian and Art Deco curios. Her eyes flicked to a maroon couch near the corner, and her fingers twisted through mine. I sensed her nervousness growing.

Only then did I realize how silent the rest of the house was. *Is she . . . ? Are we . . . ?* We were definitely heading to the couch.

"Where are Dee and Codi?" I asked, trying to sound casual.

"Both at work. Dee left me on decoupaging duty." She pulled me down to the cushion and all impulse control drained from my body. I leaned close, reaching out to touch her face.

"I have an idea, but I wanted to ask you first." Excitement tickled her voice, and I got the feeling her idea was not something that involved my hands all over her.

"Okay."

"In case you don't want to do it."

"Okay." There weren't many things I didn't want to do with her.

"Remember the séance before you got your Mark?"

"Yeah."

"Well, I was thinking that maybe we could try to contact Adeline, like we did with Marassa . . . but I know how you are with séances and stuff, so I didn't want to put you on the spot."

The simple gesture pulled all my feelings of missing her to the surface. Remembering how well she knew me, that she cared, that there were private things we'd shared outside of even the coven—it was almost better than kissing. *Almost.*

"Of course." I never wanted her to be nervous asking me anything. "Are you gonna ask her for help getting your magic back?"

"Not exactly. I figure if there's anyone who knows where the count is, it would be Adeline."

"Wait—what? Did Nicco ask you to do this? To use the coven's magic to help him find León?" *Is this why she really came back to us?*

"No!"

"Adele, he wants to find him so he can *kill* him. Your ancestor!"

"I am not going to let Nicco kill him. I want to help exonerate him!"

"If he's really still alive."

"Even more reason to talk to Adeline. If she and León are together in Guinée, that would end this wild chase between the Medici and the Saint-Germains."

"True."

She smiled.

And with that, Nicco's wish—to find León—had become Adele's wish, and Adele's wish had become mine. And even though doing more séances was at the bottom of the list of what I wanted more of in my life, right next to spending more time with the Medici, we needed to get this whole family of assholes out of the city. They'd come here three hundred years ago stalking Adeline, and they weren't going to leave Adele alone until they were either six feet under, hearts staked, or they got what they came here for: León and the grimoire.

"Let's do it," I said.

"Really?" she squeed.

"Of course, babe. There's nothing I wouldn't do to keep you safe. Including talking to your dead relatives."

"*Merci beaucoup.*" She smiled, and for a second I thought she might lean in and kiss me, but she didn't, and when the moment quickly passed and it became a little awkward, she blushed.

"It's okay." I pulled her close. "I'm just so glad that you're back."

"Me too," she said, smiling against my unshaven cheek.

And then, for the first time ever, I was happy to do a séance, as long as it meant doing magic with her.

CHAPTER 38

ASG

Isaac struck a match to light his mini-cauldron, and the scent of espresso saturated the air. My excitement for the ritual bloomed so bright, I didn't even lament that I couldn't light it with my magic.

We moved the coffee table against the wall and prepped the circle with salt and candles. Isaac moved quickly—I was pretty sure he was worried Dee or Codi would come through the door any minute and suddenly this would be a group ritual instead of a duet. I could have told him that it'd be at least a couple hours before either of them got off work, but instead I just smiled. His energy felt good. And it made everything feel just a little closer to being back to normal—everything except not having my orbs.

I laid out a pink scarf in the center of the circle and placed Adeline's diary on top, fighting the part of my brain that told me I didn't know what I was doing, that I was powerless and didn't have any business being in a coven or doing magic with Isaac.

I imagined the version of us from three months ago, the two of us alone in the house, and me asking for a magical favor. In between words, we'd have been falling onto the couch, lips locked, stealing all the moments we had to ourselves.

But then I remembered being with Nicco on the Ferris wheel,

gazing up at the stars. Maybe I didn't deserve Isaac ever kissing me again.

Focus on the ritual. Focus on Adeline.

He handed me the jar of loose charcoal I'd asked to borrow, and when our fingers brushed, my insides fluttered. "*Merci.*" I unscrewed the lid and set it next to the diary.

"Are we doing an art lesson or a séance?"

"You'll see," I said, trying not to smile.

"All right." He knelt across the diary from me and placed a corncob pipe, a cup of coffee, and a handful of peanuts on the scarf. "Let's call on ole Papa Legba."

A tinge of envy pinched me at how familiar he seemed with the lwa now, but I was also thankful he'd had Désirée during all of this, especially after what his father had done. After I'd pushed him away.

"Here." He handed me an empty crystal bowl and a bottle of homemade rosewater and settled in. He knew rosewater was my favorite to help me relax. The small things, the reminders of how bonded we used to be, made me miss him—miss us—even though he was so close.

I uncorked the bottle and held it under my nose, inhaling the soothing scent. The aroma brought me back to last winter, when practicing magic had been a regular part of my day. I poured the rosewater into the bowl and swirled it around with my finger, my thoughts morphing into an old daydream about a future time when I'd travel to lands afar to find León. I'd have my Fire, and he'd teach me magic beyond my wildest dreams, and then one day he'd pass the Saint-Germain grimoire down to me, and one day I'd pass it down to my own daughter.

I slid my hands into Isaac's and began the invocation. "*Papa Legba, ouvrez la porte.*" An unnatural darkness swallowed the room.

"*Papa Legba,* open the door."

The pungent scent of tobacco infused with the rosewater and coffee aromas, and I looked down to see a wisp of smoke curling up from the corncob pipe. I rocked forward. How did I ever feel I didn't belong here?

"*Papa Legba, ouvrez la porte.*"

Embers sprouted in the old fireplace, through crumbles of coals so old and damp, only something truly magical could ignite them. They blossomed into flames. I wasn't delusional. I knew it wasn't my Fire; it was the power of the coven.

Open the door to the other side. Be our guide.
A connection to my ancestors, I seek.
Adeline Saint-Germain, I wish to speak.
Questions are all I have, answers are all I need.
Papa Legba, open the door.
Papa Legba, ouvrez la porte.

One by one, small flames popped into the candles around us. We repeated the words.

"*Papa Legba, ouvrez la porte.*"

Isaac picked up the chant, and I shut my eyes and fell silent, listening . . . for what, I didn't know.

Soon, in the darkness, I found myself speaking to her. "*Si vous êtes là, Adeline . . . je suis désolée.*" I used to feel so close to her, but when my mother died and I shut out the world, I'd excluded her too. I continued in French, a little shy about being so open: "*I'm sorry I've been neglecting you, Adeline. Sometimes, when I think about how you protected your father, I feel like a failure. I failed my mother completely. I probably don't deserve to have my magic, but I want you to know that I'm going to do everything in my power to get it back. I'm not going to destroy our family's legacy.*"

Isaac squeezed my hands, and excitement rose in his voice as he continued the chant.

Then I realized why: a rush of warmth swirled around me, sending a wave of shivers up my spine. The familial energy that filled the room made me realize that part of the emptiness plaguing me was the break in our ancestral connection—our Saint-Germain connection.

"Adele!" Isaac whispered.

My eyes fluttered open, and I felt a slight tug against my neck. The medallion floated in front of me. It had been so long since I'd seen it move, tears pricked. I didn't need to ask if she was here. I could feel her. "*Bonjour, Adeline.*"

The fire crackled and sparked. The coffee tin on the Ghede altar began to rattle, and the crystals on the chandelier hanging above us shook.

I could feel the pull: her desperation to communicate pulsing through the air. A soft rasping sound, barely discernible under Isaac's chanting, drew my gaze down. The little lock on the diary was sliding apart. The mechanism unclicked, and the book flipped open to a blank page.

I picked up the jar and tipped some of the charcoal on it. The black dust shifted around as if magnetized, dispersing and reforming to shape letters. The familiar handwriting matched the script of all the previous journal entries.

Bonjour, Mademoiselle.

Warmth filled me as I stared at the words. Even though we'd done séances before, this was different: this was Adeline. It felt so personal. I didn't know what to say—I hadn't thought this far ahead. I looked up at Isaac, and he smiled, egging me on.

"*Bonjour*!" I yelped. "You came!"

The charcoal particles began to shift around the page again and excitement shivered in my bones.

Pourquoi ma colombe?

I smiled, translating the words in my head: *Why my dove?* The sentiment made her seem exactly how I'd always imagined her. Like the kick-ass older sister I never had. "I-I don't know . . . because you're Adeline Saint-Germain and I'm . . . me."

Tu es mon sang et tu as des ennuis.

I turned to Isaac, stumbling through the words: "She's saying, *You are my blood, and you are in trouble.* Of course I would come."

His brow crinkled. "Trouble?"

Of course I'm in trouble. I lost my magic. I focused back on the page. "Adeline, are you in Guinée now?"

Oui.

My pulse raced. Now was the moment of truth. I glanced at Isaac and took a deep breath. “Adeline, is your father, le Comte Saint-Germain, with you in Guinée?”

Non.
Mon père me manque.

“She says that she misses her father.” We exchanged wide-eyed looks through the candlelight.

He squeezed my hand. “Well, what are you waiting for? Ask her where he is!”

I nodded, nervously smiling, turning back to the charcoal. “Do you know where León Saint-Germain is?” I asked in French.

Oui.

This is it. We were going to find León, and if he had the grimoire, Nicco could have his family’s legacy back, and the feud would be over. I just knew that having his family’s book of magic would satiate his need for revenge.

“Adeline, where is he?” I leaned over the notebook eagerly awaiting her response.

Je ne peux pas te dire.

“But . . . why? Why can’t you tell me?”

Je dois le protéger.

“I’m trying to protect him too. Please!”

Reste loin de Niccolò Medici.

My heart froze solid.

Isaac looked up with a worried frown. He wouldn’t have been able to understand the message, but the last two words wouldn’t have escaped him either.

I felt her breath on my neck as she whispered, "*Sois en sécurité et ne faites jamais confiance à Niccolò Medici.*"

"Adeline! I'm going to find him, and I'm not going to let Nicco hurt him."

"*Adele, reste loin de Niccolò Medici*—!"

"I am going to end this feud for good!"

"*Ne fais pas confiance à Nicco*—!"

I slammed the book closed in a rush of panic—*My own family doesn't trust my judgement!* The sense of her presence disappeared along with her warmth, and the flames in the fireplace dulled. I stood up, fear pushing me away from the diary.

The chandelier lights winked back on one by one.

Isaac stood, his gaze fixed on me. "What did she say?"

"She said . . ." My instinct told me to lie—that he couldn't understand the French and so he'd never know—but the words whooshed out. "She said, 'Be safe and stay away from Niccolò Medici.'"

His eyes pulsed brighter.

I felt sick.

And so, I popped off before he could, "Of course Adeline would feel this way! The Medici were after her and her father. They stalked her and threatened her life when she wouldn't give him up!"

"She didn't say the Medici; she said Niccolò."

"It was three hundred years ago," I yelled, suddenly so worked up I was shaking. I couldn't believe I was now going against Adeline Saint-Germain, the last known witch in my line, who I practically worshipped, and who *I'd* made contact with, despite my lack of Elemental magic. Everything about going against her felt wrong. I didn't want to disagree with her on anything. But I'd already lost faith in Nicco once, and it hadn't worked out well for anyone. "I trust Nicco!" My chest tightened. "*I trust him*!"

The tin of coffee tipped off the Ghede altar and poured all over the floor, and the chandelier began to swing overhead, and then Isaac's arms were wrapped around me. "It's fine," he said, holding me against his chest. "We'll figure out another way to find León . . . And we're not going to let Nicco or any Medici get to you. Or any of your family."

My arms coiled around him. "Nicco isn't going to hurt me." I squeezed him tighter, scared that if I said anything good at all about Nicco he was going to walk out the door.

"I know you trust him. But you heard Adeline— she said to stay away from him. Please promise me you'll listen to her warning."

I thought about Nicco's texts, and Gabe's offer, and I knew it was a promise I couldn't keep. "You aren't going to want to hear this, but I'm going over there tonight to train."

I felt his biceps twitch, but he didn't say anything. He just stood there, holding me.

His voice was calm when he finally spoke. "Adele, Codi and I can help you train—"

"I know . . . and I appreciate that. And we can train together too, but I like going over there. I like talking to Gabe—he *knew* Adeline and León."

"But going into a vampire compound without your magic is—"

"Nicco would never let any of them hurt me—"

"How can you be so sure? You don't have your magic! Nicco could use his thrall to erase your memories. You'd never even know!"

"He would never," I said, shaking my head.

"How do you *know*?"

"Because I do! The same way I know you'd never use your magic against me while I'm defenseless."

"That's insane," he scoffed. "I would never use magic against you, *period.* And he's a vampire and your family's sworn enemy!"

"I trust him! Just like I trust you! Why don't you trust me? My intuition? My judgement? My decisions?"

"I do trust you, Adele. I *love* you. I just want to keep you safe."

"I don't need another father." My tone had an edge more jagged than I'd meant.

He sat down on the couch and became quiet before he looked back up at me. "That night . . . when Nicco took you . . . I really thought you were dead. I've never been that scared. Not even when my mom died." His gaze dropped to the floor.

My breath skipped.

"I know," I said, moving closer. I tugged his fingers so he'd look back at me. "I'm sorry."

He pulled me down next to him, and I curled against his chest. "We all got fooled by Callis . . . but I promise, you don't have to worry about my safety when I'm with Nicco. He'll always protect me."

And I'll always protect him.

It was hard going against someone I loved; it was even harder going against the witch I'd idolized since my very first witching days, whose magical essence coursed through my blood. But I didn't care what anyone—past, present, or future—said about Nicco.

Despite the two of us sharing so much last night, there were things I'd left out. He knew it. He hadn't asked, but I could tell that he was anxious about it. There was something unsettled in the air between us, and it wasn't fair for me to make him ask. I had to tell Isaac everything.

I moved to the far end of the couch, and he gave me a funny look. He knew something was coming. The distance somehow made it easier to start talking, like I was already casting myself aside before he could.

And then I spilled. I told him everything that had happened with Nicco—not anything that would betray Nicco's confidence, but all of the broad strokes: the funeral, thc amusement park, the Ouroboros. His face never softened, but he listened without interruption, and at some point I uncurled and stretched my legs out toward his end of the couch, and he did the same. I told him about the Italian protection spell and the lightning and how Nicco's magic had felt like a million fireflies beneath my skin.

"You mean his family's spell?" They were the first words he'd spoken throughout the confession. "Nicco doesn't have magic, Adele."

I knew he was trying to hold back his disdain for Nicco, but the shadow of his feelings darkened his voice. "Yeah, I guess," I said, unable to look at him. "That's what Nicco said a million times too."

"What do you mean, 'you guess'?"

"I don't know. It was just so intense. I've never felt anything like it. It's hard for me to believe that there's no magic left in him." My eyes dragged back up to his.

In the pregnant pause that followed, I wondered if he still believed what he'd said last night: that we'd be able to figure this all out.

"You don't need his spells or his magic. You have me and the coven, and Ritha, and the Daures. You have more magical resources now as a witchling than most witches have in a lifetime."

I twisted a lock of my hair. I didn't know how to tell him that Nicco's magic had felt greater than all of theirs combined. I was already worried he was going to think I'd completely crossed the line with Nicco, perhaps even past the point of no return.

A few moments of silence went by. Then his hand slipped around my calf, and he gently massaged the muscle through the denim. "Can I ask you something?"

I nodded, just knowing that he was going to ask if Nicco had ever tried anything with me.

"Do you regret being with me?"

"What?" I whispered. "*No.* Why would you even ask me that?" Maybe I had pushed him too far by telling him everything. The words choked out: "Do you . . . regret being with me?"

His mouth tugged to the side, and he looked at me like, *Really*?

I crawled to his end of the couch, rested my cheek in its familiar place on his chest, and coiled my arm around him. I needed him. I needed everything to be okay.

In the quiet moments that passed, his fingers slipped beneath the hem of my shirt, and he mindlessly drew delicate circles on the small of my back.

I wanted to stretch up and kiss his jaw, but I knew where that might lead . . . and I guess I just wasn't ready. Instead, I listened to the rain pattering against the window, and wondered if Adeline and Susannah could see us.

Adeline, I'm sorry I accidentally broke your curse, but now it's time to end this for good. I didn't want my future descendants to accidentally unleash monsters on the city, or for Emilio or Gabe or any Medicean enemies to be after them because of the count.

But it was neither his words nor Adeline's that rang in my head as the warning signs began to flare all around me; they were Gabe's: "*Niccolò is the most patient man I have ever encountered in my four hundred years.*"

The thought chilled my blood.

Adele, don't even go there. There was no way this was all a ruse, a long-play by Nicco just to get the Elixir. And yet, I could see him showing up at the tailor shop when Adeline was having her traveling cloak made. I imagined Gabe coming into her bedroom at night, drunk from absinthe, and them talking all night. And I thought about me and Nicco, tucked away in the Ferris wheel under the blanket of stars, him so concerned with my magic—my safety. I thought about how I'd run into Gabe on the river.

Thump-thump.

"I guess I don't have to go over there *tonight*," I said, aching with disappointment before I'd even finished the sentence. I wanted to see Nicco. I wanted to know what happened to the witch I'd burnt, and I wanted to work on my magic more, and to figure out a plan to end all of this.

"Really?" he asked, a shine in his golden-brown eyes.

And that's when I realized that maybe I was wrong about being so focused on the mission. I needed to focus on him. "If you wanted, maybe we could do something, just the two of us. Something normal like watch a movie?"

"Are you asking me on a date?"

I nodded, trying not to be embarrassed.

"You have no idea how much I would love to do something normal with you."

I smiled and the tension eased.

"Want to go for a walk first?" he asked. "That's totally normal."

"*Oui*." I nodded and stood, holding out my hand to help him up. He didn't let go through the French Quarter, nor all the way up Esplanade Avenue to City Park.

We didn't stop, even as the light drizzle came and went. We ran through the oaks at sunset, and he used his wind to lift me into the trees which shook with raindrops. I watched him fly through the branches, and soon the moon poked through the leaves, shining on his feathers and glimmering on the obsidian ponds. At some point between the mossy oaks, the nervousness went away and the butterflies came back in.

We sat on elephant ears like they were lily pads, and I leaned against him, listening to frogs, not thinking about anything at all.

He stroked the side of my arm. "Instead of watching a movie . . . do you want to go . . . ?"

My pulse erupted. I don't know why; I wanted to be alone with him. I did.

". . . visit Ren?"

"*Oh*."

He smiled coyly. "What did you think I was going to say?"

"Nothing."

"Nothing?" He pulled me back against him. "Are you sure?"

I bit my bottom lip, nodding.

"Okay." He leaned in and kissed my bare collar bone, making me shiver.

And for the first time, it felt like not so much time had passed since we'd been together.

CHAPTER 39

MUSINGS OF A MADMAN

I followed Isaac through the sea of courtyard botanicals, guesthouse stairs, and hallways of moaning voices until we reached Ren's room.

"Oh my God," I whispered, peering through the magical barricade.

Every inch of the walls was covered in his illustrations, which were nothing more than tangles of lines. Ren was hunched over the desk, furiously drawing, singing in Italian, or perhaps it was just the incoherent ramblings of a madman.

"Shit," Isaac said.

Ren grabbed two handfuls of drawings from his desk, tossed them over his shoulders, and went back to sketching.

I stepped inside. "Ren?"

He sketched faster and harder. "*En-en-en-en-encan. Tis-i-mo*!"

"Mind if we join you?" Isaac asked.

He turned to us with an incoherent roar and fell backwards off the chair.

"Okay, okay!" Isaac said as Ren scratched at the dozens of papers on the floor, crumpling them into his palms as if to prevent us from stealing them. "We'll stay right outside. If you need anything, just let us know." He reached for my hand, but I'd already stepped back behind the threshold. It was weird and heartbreaking to be scared of Ren. I wasn't sure he'd even be able to ask for something if he needed it. A part of me wondered if we should bring Nicco here to speak to Alessandro, to make sure he—they—were okay.

Isaac walked me to a spot against the wall.

As I slid down next to him, I couldn't help but feel like this was my fault, all of it—the vampires and Callis and everything else that had happened in the aftermath of the events at the convent.

Isaac reached into his bag and took out his sketchpad, like it was something he'd done here dozens of times before. I didn't have to ask to know that he had. He'd probably visited Ren every day since the attack; it's just the kind of person he was. I imagined him younger, going to visit his mother every day in the hospital with nothing but his sketchbook and the pencil behind his ear. I wondered what he sketched back then. He was so good at drawing feathers, something told me he'd been drawing birds since long before he'd ever taken flight.

I didn't have my sketchpad, but I pulled out my journal with all of my translations of Adeline's diary. I hadn't written in it in months. I opened it to a fresh page and began to sketch the rough shape of a girl, just enough of a figure to drape the dress. The garment was where I'd pay attention to the detail. As my pencil glided over the page, I thought about the diary entries. And then Adeline's séance messages. I tried to focus on the positive part—that León was alive—and not the warning about Nicco. I visualized the dress I'd borrowed from Lisette as I constructed the silhouette, but this version was velvet with a high neck and long sleeves, tapering at the waist and billowing out on the floor in the back. I imagined the shape of a bird burned into the velvet—and then a fawn, and a fox and squirrel. Soon there was an entire forest scene floating around the ebony dress covering the girl.

Isaac peered over, leaning close enough to rest his chin on my shoulder. "It's just like Cosette's bedroom door."

I smiled because that was precisely my inspiration.

"It's amazing," he said.

I looked at his drawing and wanted to chuckle. If mine was amazing, his was *magnifique.* At first glance it seemed to be a secret garden behind an extravagant wrought iron fence, vines and thorny roses twisting around the bars, all broken out in dewy sweats. But when you looked through the bars, you could see the tombstones. Not mausoleums. It was the kind of graveyard I'd only ever seen in movies, set in places where you could bury people in the earth without worrying about them popping back up if it rained too hard.

He saw me looking at it. "It's this tiny cemetery in Brook—"

"*Eeennnnncaaaaaannteesimo*!" came a cry from inside the room.

We both jumped up and went back to the doorway.

"*Siiilenzi! Silenziamento! Mento!*" he yelled, frantically stomping over to the fireplace and ripping off pages from the wall, kicking at others that were on the floor.

"Ren, what's wrong?" I asked, stepping inside.

"*Eencanteeseemo di silenziamento!*" he screamed at me, hissing so fiercely I stepped back through the magical barrier into the hallway.

He ran back to his desk, repeating the words over and over, scooped up a stack of drawings, turned with a roar and flung them at me. Isaac whipped out his hand and a gust of Air scattered them up to the ceiling before they could hit my face.

"He's out of paper," he said, as the sheets softly floated down around us. "I think that's what he's trying to tell us."

Ren snarled, and then ran back to the wall to rip more pages down.

Without hesitation, Isaac bent down for his sketchbook, strode into the room with it, and placed it on his desk. "It's late, Ren, I'll scavenge you some more paper tomorrow. This should hold you over. Use the blank pages in the back."

Ren immediately calmed down and went back to the desk. He took out a calligraphy pen with a giant cream-colored plume, dipped it into the ink, and scratched it across the page, ripping through the paper as the fit of rage coursed through him. Isaac tried to hide a wince.

My pulse raced as we resettled on the floor, Isaac's arm around my shoulders, guilt on his face, as if Ren's deteriorating condition was his fault. Ren's scratching grew relentless, and a ripping noise came from the room. Through the doorway, I saw the rose-entwined gate float through the air, and it broke my heart.

"Shit," Isaac said, his head knocking against the wall.

It was just a sketch—just ink and paper, and Isaac could do a thousand more—but I couldn't stand it. He'd been on his own for these past months, with not much more than the clothes on his back, all so he could stay in the broken city and help people. He could have gone back to his home in New York. Back to normal life. School. Graduation.

Parties. But he chose to stay here and fix homes and neighborhoods and give people hope.

Another ripping sound came from the room, and I jumped up, journal in hand.

"Adele—" he said, my fingers slipping through his as I walked straight over to Ren or Alessandro or whoever he was, and reclaimed Isaac's sketchbook. He howled, and I handed him my journal. He calmed instantly—mine or Isaac's, it was just paper to him.

I stalked back to Isaac.

"You didn't have to—"

"This is not up for debate." I slid back down next to him.

"You worked hard on those translations."

I shrugged, trying not to panic internally. "I can read the original French, or translate it again, but I can't just watch him destroy your art. It's too beautiful." I opened the sketchbook across both of our laps, smoothing out the ripped page.

"Not as beautiful as the muse."

I looked up.

"Nothing could ever be as beautiful as you."

The butterflies fluttered. I knew I was staring into the kindest eyes I was ever going to encounter in this life.

He leaned in and dusted my lips with his, light and sweet, and I thought I might stop breathing.

"Too much?" he asked.

I rapidly shook my head. "I'm sorry. I don't know why I'm so nervous."

"It's okay . . . I'm nervous too."

"You are?"

A laugh slipped, and he pulled my palm to his chest. His heart was racing.

"I don't want you to be nervous to kiss me," I said.

"You don't?"

I shook my head again. I hadn't fully processed everything that was going on between us, and even as I said the words, I felt a rush of fear. Trusting someone was terrifying, but there was one thing I knew above everything else: I never wanted to hurt him again.

I leaned closer. His lips were soft, like pillows of sunshine. I'd forgotten how gentle he could be, despite all of his abrasive qualities. I'd do anything possible to make up for the pain I'd caused him. Our lips barely parted before I kissed him again.

He pushed the sketchpad away and pulled me close, his warmth engulfing, and the part of me that was still holding onto the pain began to melt away. As he kissed me back, something slipped back into place —the thing that had felt so *off* all these months. It had nothing to do with my magic or my ancestors or my coven; it was us.

The rip of paper came from the room, and I cringed. Isaac started to get up, but I held on to him. "I don't need my journal. I need you."

He sank back down, a bit of elation in his eyes, and he pulled me into his lap. As I resettled against his chest, he reached for his sketchbook and propped it against my knees so we could both draw in it at once, and it felt just like things had always been before.

As I sketched, and he inked his own version of my chainmaille dress, Ren's singing became louder and his mood seemed jollier, scribbling all over the pages in my journal and tearing them away. I ignored it by drawing fashion illustrations all over Isaac's pages.

"You know," I said, "you're losing cool points by the drove the longer you let me do this."

"If that's the case I don't want any cool points."

"No more street cred? What will your boys back home think?"

"Don't know. Don't care. You can ask them yourself one day."

My pulse ticked. I'd never been to New York. Although he'd described it so vividly, I could easily imagine his neighborhood: the trees on the Brooklyn streets, the street art, and us, sitting on his stoop, eating bagels with *schmear.* I imagined him in Prospect Park, flying through the trees as I chased him, and on the shores of Rockaway Beach, him trying to teach me to surf, cradling me in his magical Air to help me stand on the board. It was the first time since the Storm that I'd thought about leaving New Orleans without feeling sick.

I nestled closer, and then uncontrollably shivered as his lip grazed my earlobe.

But then I looked up, feeling a looming presence, and stiffened. "Hi, Ren," I stuttered.

Isaac loosened his grip. "Hey, Ren."

Ren looked down at the two of us and smiled. For a second he seemed like his old self, like he was about to tell the story of how vampires came to America or how Pirate's Alley got its name, but instead he looked straight at us and started singing. "*Sette notti, sette lune. Sette porte, sette tombe.*" He tossed my journal, or what remained of it, into the hall, turned back around, and walked away, humming to himself. "*Sette lune! Sette lune! Sette lune!*"

"We'll get him some more paper tomorrow." I got up and gathered the loose papers from the hallway and stuffed them into my bag.

On our way out, tiptoeing down the hallway together and trying not to wake the tortured masses, Isaac's hand slipped over my hip.

When we got to my house, I couldn't stop yawning. "I'm sorry."

"Go to bed. We can spend the whole day tomorrow working on your magic."

I smiled. It was exactly what I wanted.

"And I'll train you until you can kick Codi's ass," he added.

I sensed him getting nervous, like he thought as soon as he left, I was heading straight to Nicco's.

I wrapped my arms around his neck, pulling him close. "Stop worrying," I said gently.

He blushed. "Okay."

"Promise?"

"You know that I can't promise to stop worrying about you."

"Will you try?"

He nodded, smiling.

I touched my lips to his, lingering in the soft embrace for a moment, not even caring if my dad caught us.

CHAPTER 40

GHOSTSTICK

April 29th

As promised, Isaac was back the next day, and every day for the next week, to drag me out of bed and make me run with him on the river. He made me do planks on the grass until I screamed and pull-ups on a tree branch until I fell and he had to catch me with his Air. He even went with my dad to the junkyard and scavenged a variety of metal objects to see if any of them inspired my magic. They didn't. And even though I'd unzipped his pants once, it wasn't with my mind.

He'd claimed to see some vibrations when we practiced, but I knew there hadn't been a single positive sign of my Spektral magic. He tried to make up for it in kisses, and it did make me feel better . . . for a little while.

I'd eaten three square meals a day—or as square as they got post-Storm—restarted my job at the tearoom, visited Ren every day, and spent the rest of my waking moments with the coven. The more I came out of my shell, the more people seemed to stop walking on eggshells around me, which encouraged me more than anything else. I was sick of people treating me like I was made of glass.

So now, everything was how it was supposed to be.

But I didn't have my magic. And I hadn't seen Nicco in seven days.

Every day that went by without seeing him made me feel a little crazier, like I'd made it all up. Every morning when I woke up and our dreams hadn't connected, I feared that they never had. The better everything else in my life got, the more he faded; and the more he faded, the more my mind obsessed over remembering every little detail: the sound of his accent when he got excited, the way the moonlight highlighted his cheekbones, and, most vividly, the way his magic had felt beneath my skin.

I didn't want to be separated from him.

But for a week I'd asked him for rainchecks.

For Isaac.

For us.

"When you say 'malevolent,'" Chatham asked loudly into the phone, as if the person on the other end was hard of hearing, "do you mean your garden-variety, parlor-trick spooks? Opening windows, rearranging furniture, flickering lights, that sort of thing?" The creases in his brow tensed. "*Mmm. Mmm.* I see. Ohhh, *I see.*"

Codi was filling the sink behind the counter with water. With a wave of his hand, the faucet stopped, and the water rose into a giant bubble. It bobbed across the counter to a bookcase with long tendrils of ivy draping from the top. The bubble floated up past hundreds of tarot decks, Codi not seeming the slightest bit concerned that it might burst all over them. When it reached the ivy, he poked his finger into the air, and the bubble sprung a leak, pouring directly into the pots.

Chatham covered the bottom of the phone. "Codi Daure, not during business hours."

He flicked his fingers, and the bubble whizzed across to the fountain at the front of the shop and burst into its trickling streams.

I ached for my orbs.

Chatham hung up the phone, shaking his head.

"How bad is it?" Codi asked, pulling out a tray of crystal wands from the jewelry case.

After crystal balls and tarot cards, wands were the most common item in the shop, and the Daures' family specialty. Some were made of wood, others of metal or colored glass. Each was different than the next, infused with feathers, insect casings, and dried flowers, decorated with gemstones, inscribed with sigils, runes, and vèvès. My absolute favorites had amethyst points bound to the ends.

I'd always thought they were kept in the jewelry case to prevent them from being stolen or broken, but when I'd started working behind the counter, Chatham told me it was because they didn't let just *anyone* handle the wands. Only recently did I understand that they were each charged with different magical energy.

Chatham shook his head at the tray and pulled the lever of the old cash register. It popped open with a *zing*.

"Oh, shit," Codi said. "That bad?"

Chatham lifted the drawer and fetched an ornate key hidden beneath. "Poltergeist activity, possibly a Schattengeist."

He walked across to the tall armoire at the opposite end of the counter. I'd never paid much attention to it. "What's a Schattengeist?"

"A shadow ghost," Codi answered as his father unlocked the armoire.

"They think it may have attached itself to a child. I'm going to have to make a little trip upstate." As one of *the* foremost experts on specters in the country, Chatham often received calls to help with ghostly situations.

He opened both doors and began examining the crystal-tipped wands inside, which were racked like rifles in a gun case. About half a dozen hung from each of the doors, ranging from one to four feet in length. Despite being locked away and out of sight, they didn't seem as fancy as the smaller ones in the jewelry case. The wand stems were more branch-like, and the gems on the ends were big and raw with jagged edges that better resembled arrowheads. Their energy had a strange juxtaposition of sparkly but deadly, which was kind of like New Orleans herself—mixed in with the glitter and revelry was crime and corruption and complete systemic failure. "They're so beautiful," I said. "Why keep them hidden?"

"These aren't just any wands," Chatham said. "They're the *Geisterstabs*—the perfect blend of Choctaw and Germanic magic."

"Ghoststicks," Codi said.

Chatham examined each of them, as if choosing carefully. "The branches are broken from a tree fertilized with Guldenmann Earth magic."

"Guldenmann?"

"My grandma's side," Codi answered.

"And then they're soaked in magical Water and enchanted with indigenous Louisiana magic."

"*Morning Star*," I whispered, and they both nodded.

"These wands are only used as an extreme measure—after all forms of banishing and exorcising have failed." He removed one and placed it in my hand. "The Ghost Drinkers aren't the only ones who can bring harm to a specter."

"But I thought you were in the business of communicating with ghosts," I said. "Protecting them, not harming them."

"We are, most of the time, but every group that roams this realm has their dark ones, and don't you ever forget that." He took the wand back and blew dust from the gemstones. "This will bring final death to those of the specter variety."

Gabe had once told Adeline, "every species has their monsters."

He was right. And Callis Salazar had proved that witches were no exception. He gave the magical a bad name. A wretched, wicked name. Witnessing Ren's violent mood swings all week had created just one more twist in the dark storm brewing inside me. I wanted to find Callis and the rest of his coven, *now*. I didn't know what I'd do when I found them, but they could not be allowed to hurt anyone else. Magical, mundane, or otherwise.

I handed Chatham a dust cloth. "It's still so weird to think about a ghost dying."

"Other than the divine, no one is immortal at the hands of the magical . . . not man nor monster nor spirit nor soul."

Souls were supposed to be forever. Then again, my mother was supposed to be immortal. I still refused to believe she was a monster. I didn't care that she'd bitten me—I'd trapped and starved her for months. A flash of the stake plunged through my mind, and I stiffened, trying not to flinch. Isaac's stake. *Isaac's magical Air.*

Chatham reached over to the glass hand attached to the wall and slid a silk scarf from the dozens it held, all different shades of midnight blue. He wrapped the ghoststick and slipped it into a pillowed velvet sheath. It reminded me of the Ouroboros. I'd now rescheduled my training session with Gabe three times out of guilt.

Chatham hurried around the room, gathering a few more magical items into a leather doctor's bag.

"Where's the incident?" Codi asked.

"Shreveport."

"I could go with you."

"Someone has to hold down the fort."

"Adele's here!"

"I've already got company. I told your—"

"Don't tell me you're letting Caleb or Cameron go with you."

"No, they have to stay in the city; there were two more Possessed brought in last night. I messaged your cousin."

Two more Possessed? In one night?

"Poppy? She's younger than me! It's because she already has her Mark, isn't it? What if my Spektral magic has something to do with ghosts and I'm missing my opportunity to embrace it?"

"And what if your Spektral magic has to do with reading tea leaves? You could embrace it right here in the shop."

"Dad!"

"Tell your father I had to leave right away. God only knows how long it will take me to get there with the post-Storm roads, and I'd like to beat sunset." He strapped the bag over his shoulder. "Addie, don't let him use his magic in the shop. I *do not* like having to use memory powder on the customers. This should be a safe place for them and their psyches."

I smiled. "I'll try. Good luck with the shadow ghost."

"I should be back tomorrow," Chatham said, "two days tops if things go awry." He kissed Codi goodbye, and once again I wished that my father was part of my magical upbringing.

I picked up one of the long-stem metal roses from Julie's favorite vase. The craftsmanship was flawless, each petal as thin as paper. If my father were magical, I bet he could make a sword even better than those Venetian Fire witches and their snake-sword.

I slid it back into the vase, trying to remember the way metal used to tingle my fingers. Every instance where I'd felt even a little close to getting my magic back had been with Nicco. I couldn't help but feel that without him, I'd never get it back. I didn't know what was worse: being separated from him or feeling like I had to hide the anxiety it gave me.

My fingers threaded the feather on my chain. The Leo constellation rested high on my throat, and a new gris-gris lay beneath my dress.

Something from each of my coven members. I thought about Annabelle's heart necklace and pictured myself choking her with it. Not using my hands, but *my magic*.

I promised myself I'd keep my training date with Gabe tonight. No matter what kind of look Dee gave me, no matter how tightly Codi crossed his arms, and no matter what alternative plan Isaac came up with. I wanted to see Nicco.

"So," Codi said, hurling a series of water bubbles from the fountain to the tops of the shelves, continuing to water the ivy, "what's going on with you and Isaac? Are you back together?"

I leaned down on my elbows against the glass jewelry case. I didn't know why I found the question a little startling. Maybe because Isaac and I were too busy trying to *be* together to talk about being together, so it was weird discussing it with someone else. Maybe it was also weird because labeling relationships didn't seem like something Codi would care about. "I don't know— Wait, did Isaac ask you to ask me?"

"No." He answered quickly as if not wanting to get Isaac in trouble. "Dee."

That seemed more like it. "Why does she care?"

"I don't know. She's really protective of him . . ."

Dee feeling like she had to protect Isaac from me made me feel a little nauseous.

"I think she just wants things to be settled."

"What does our relationship status have to do with things being settled? Maybe if I got my magic back, things would start to feel settled. Maybe if a coven of succubus witches wasn't lurking around town, things would start to feel settled. Or if this whole city wasn't like a post-apocalyptic nightmare, things would start to feel settled!"

"Damn, dude. All I did was ask you if Isaac was your boyfriend."

"Remember in ninth grade when you used to get *so* mad when we asked if Stephen was your boyfriend?"

"Totally different! You weren't going to get your ass kicked at school because of your boyfriend status."

He was right. I don't know why the conversation pricked my nerves. Everything in my life had flipped upside down so many times over the last few months, it was hard to ever really feel grounded. "I'm sorry. I just . . . sometimes I can't stop worrying about Isaac, and I feel guilty that I'm wasting time thinking about a boy when I should be getting my family's magic back. Or stopping Callis from whatever the hell he's planning."

"Why do you think he's planning something?"

"Because he told me, in this very room, that he was in town to kill Nicco and Emilio, and he's yet to do that!"

"So you're worried about Nicco?"

When I didn't answer, he continued. "Just out of curiosity, who are you worried about more? Isaac or Nicco?"

My eyes slanted toward him, and then I looked down, cheeks flaming. Movement came from beneath the glass, and I squinted at the tray of silver rings directly beneath me. Was one of them *vibrating?*

I slid open the door and pulled out the black velvet display tray. Most of the rings had jagged clusters of amethyst, smooth aqua tourmaline, or polished moonstone, but the ring that had caught my attention was simple: a flat disc with a braided silver rope border. I pulled it out.

Codi glanced over. "Doesn't seem like your style. Wait, isn't that the ring we found on the floor?"

No initials were engraved on the disc, no stone inset, just a crude carving of a triangle—*a flame.* It was old, heavy, and tarnished, and it dwarfed my finger when I slid it on. Our weird shared dream came back: the little boy and his father in the fortress in the stars. But then . . . something else. "I know this ring."

"Duh, you work here." He tugged the collar of his T-shirt.

Not from here, and not from the dream. My memories cycled through the swath of silver that had adorned each of Callis's fingers. "This ring didn't escape the case. It was never in the case to begin with."

He took my hand, examining it. "Now that you mention it." His fingers squeezed mine as his voice faded.

"It's . . ."—my eyes fluttered and tingles shot up my arms—"Calli . . ." And then I was in free fall again. The darkness.

My knees buckled and my head knocked something. The trickle of the fountain filled my ears.

Birds chirping.

The smell of damp forest.

The trickling became babbling. It was a beautiful winding river, not wide and brown like the muddy Mississippi but . . .

. . . a smoky turquoise so mysterious and beautiful, it's no wonder the songs and ballads of the ancient ones sing of the gods coming down to the Earth from the clouds to splash in its beauty.

Even though the boy is eleven years of age—old enough to carry a dagger at his waist—he has never been this deep in the forest and is fascinated by how the ancient trees bend and twist. Their leaves, the color of burnt sunsets, blanket the forest floor, and their branches outstretch into each other, allowing just enough sunlight through to guide the family along the winding brook.

For thousands of years, the waterfalls have echoed through the trees, vibrating through the dirt, energizing the feathers of every creature soaring through its breezes, the hooves of every animal on its grounds, the petal of every flower blooming within its magical lands.

But today, the sounds of the forest go unheard.

There are no babbles of the rippling river, no calls of the mating wild, for not even the thunderous crashes of the waterfalls can be heard over the cries of his wailing mother. The sun begins to set, but the family has been shrouded in darkness for nine days.

Dozens of hands reach up to hold the glass box, none ready to let go, but the coffin is small and can't accommodate everyone's fingers. The cries grow louder, and the tears flow faster, the closer the procession gets to the burial site. The men lift the casket higher as the women become hysterical, and each bump makes the ebony ringlets, which had been carefully swept back, fall in front of little Donato Salazar's eyes. They had once shone midnight blue, but now they would remain forever closed.

"Ten years old!" his mother cries. "My baby!" She turns to her husband, one arm cradling her swollen belly. "Jakome, we are cursed, mi amor. *We are cursed!"*

The iron chamber Jakome had locked around his heart begins to shake apart, hearing the utter defeat in his beloved's voice. He grips the shoulder of his son, who has grown so big they can nearly share boots. Watching his children grow tall and strong is the greatest joy of his life, perhaps even greater than leading the ancient Basque coven.

The boy hears the cries of his mother and his aunts and his grandmothers, but he is mesmerized by the knobby roots of the beeches at the riverbank, which are covered in bright green foliage. Even though he is the youngest Basque witch in six generations to receive his Fire, his father has strict rules about entering the forest, and he is distracted by its splendor. "One day," Jakome always says. "Be patient my son. One day you will command the course of the river and the song of the birds. Be patient my son." *The boy has heard it so often from his papá, he's come to hate the sound of the words.* "Se paciente, mio."

He feels the magical energy beneath his boots, and realizes, for the first time, why his father has always been so adamant about him inheriting the forest while his brothers would inherit their riches: Fire could produce riches, but riches could not produce magic.

The magic and the forest are one. And in that moment, he sees all that is destined for him.

His family's magic. Their power.

An opening in the trees leads to an alcove that for many has become all too familiar in recent years. The mourning sounds of his family become stronger and the footsteps of the procession slower.

In the past week, there was a ceremony for the town. A hilarri constructed near the hill behind the fortress and an epitaph chiseled. The Bishop's words cried out to the family and the townspeople who all came out to mourn in the street below, but the flowers that continue to pile up in the family cemetery decorate an empty tomb.

The procession stops in the alcove and the witches look like a web of black lace across the fire-colored leaves as everyone sets into motion: some dig, some string flowers into wreaths, others light candles in a circle, just like when the witches had been here eight months ago to bury the family's youngest daughter, Clara.

Not even the magic of the ancients could stop the Black Death.

Jakome carves another rosette onto the hilarri. Three rosettes have been etched into the stone, one for each of his children laid to rest before their tenth birthdays.

"What use are these powers if we can't keep our children safe?" his weeping wife screams to him. "It's a curse. They know our magic is the strongest no matter their wealth and their power, and they wish to extinguish it from the universe!"

"Medici," Jakome's father whispers and then spits on the ancient soil.

The name echoes around the circle, more condemnation with each added voice.

As he stares at the glass case, the boy traces the Mark on his left arm through his sleeve. "Papá?" he asks. "Will they kill me next?"

"He's too young to be here, Jakome," his grandfather says to his father.

"He has his Mark." Jakome wraps his son in his arms, hugging him so tight the thick metal ring on his finger digs into the bone of his son's shoulder. "I will battle Death himself before I let anyone take you from me, Callisto."

"I'm not scared of curses," the boy says. "Or Medici."

"Nor should you be." He kisses the top of his head. "Now go and console your mother."

*"*Sí, Papá.*"*

Callisto stands tall next to his mother, and she falls to the ground weeping. He holds her and strokes her hair, and she clings to him. She screams as his uncles lower the glass case into the earth.

"It will be okay, Mamá. I am here."

And as the first spray of dirt falls over the casket, Callisto watches his brother's face through the glass, and he smiles.

Weak men wait.

The smile sent a shiver through my soul.

A hand shook my shoulder.

"Adele?"

My shoulder shook harder.

"Are you okay?"

I pried my eyes open. Codi was peering up at me; I was sprawled across his torso. I sat up too quickly, and my head spun as a wave of supernatural sensation lurched up my arms.

What the hell?

I reached for the counter and pulled myself up, and then helped him up too. "Can you feel that?"

He gripped the counter with both hands. "Yeah. I kind of feel like I got . . . electrocuted." His forehead scrunched. "But also kind of like I want another hit."

It felt like my *magic.* I flung my hand out to the metal vase, focusing on the roses inside.

Nothing.

I strained, feeling for the metal. A sweat broke across my hairline. I could *feel* the roses trying to vibrate.

"Come on, Adele, do it!" Codi said, going into coach-mode.

For the first time in a long time, I could *feel my magic inside,* but it was barricaded by a thousand keyless locks. I wanted to scream.

I ripped up my sleeve. The Mark was there, but there was nothing special about it. No glow, no anything.

Codi stared at my skin blankly.

"*I want my cards read!*" a voice yelled from outside. The bells jingled over the door and a gaggle of women stumbled in, at least eight or nine of them, voices raised to obnoxious volumes thanks to the nuclear-green, foot-tall drinks they carried. Hand Grenades. Never a good sign.

"This is the place I saw on the Travel Channel!"

"I'm going first!" yelled a spray-tanned girl with straight, jet-black, box-dyed hair, a tiara, and a white sash across her chest designating her: the bride.

Codi and I looked at each other with the exact same expression, eyes cocked to the ceiling.

An autopilot smile spread across his face. "Welcome to the Bottom of the Cup Tea Room, ladies."

A girl with a cheap, neon-pink wig stroked a crystal ball in a way that made me think she was on something stronger than Hand Grenades. "It's sooo shiny," she said.

"Don't touch that!" Codi yelled, leaping toward her as the crystal ball rolled off its golden-talon pedestal and smashed on the floor with a loud crack.

"You're going to have seven years of bad luck," squawked a brunette with a Jamaican accent and glossy lips.

Pink-wig burst into tears.

"Don't worry," Codi said, trying to comfort her. "It's just quartz, not a mirror. You'll be fine."

I plugged in the electric kettle, grabbed the dustpan and broom, and hurried over.

"This place freaks me out," another girl yelled, her drink sloshing over the edge of the cup as she tilted on her wedges.

I grabbed her elbow and guided her to the table.

"This is against the Bible!" she said.

"Drinking tea?" I asked.

"Tarot cards! Crystal balls! That's why it fell on the floor. You aren't paying for that, Stephie; it's just a cheap trick!" She leaned back in the chair, the jersey fabric of her expensive sundress so low-cut and stretched out, from God only knows what, that she was in near-danger of a nip-slip.

"I'm *so* sorry," said a small blonde girl, who you could tell was used to being the designated driver.

"Who's the blushing bride?" boomed a voice from behind the counter. *Edgar to the rescue.*

"Me!" squeaked Tiara.

"Well, come on down, my dear, and I'll introduce you to Papa Olsin, our most renowned reader!" He guided her shoulder. "Taurus?" he asked.

"How did you—?"

"Virgo moon?"

"What's that?"

"*Mm-hmm.*"

Fiona came out from making soaps in the back and brought the next girl to her booth, and Edgar showed the still-sobbing crystal-ball-breaker back to his. I made tea for the rest—the strongest, most sobering elixir I could brew.

As I waited for it to steep, my hand slipped back around the medallion. It was warm, as if it had been lying out in the afternoon sun.

The girls continued their ditzy conversation at top volume, but I wasn't listening anymore. I was thinking about . . . the dream of the boy in the woods.

Callis.

The ring. Where did it go?

CHAPTER 41

THE BLACK DEATH

I lowered my head and peered under the ghoststick armoire. I couldn't see anything in the dark crevice, so I begrudgingly inserted my hand and patted around, cringing at the idea of coming into contact with something with beady eyes and tiny, sharp teeth. I felt nothing but cool, surprisingly undusty brick.

The bachelorette party had finally cleared out, but not before an overly animated bridesmaid had accidentally smashed a vase and subsequently cried, and another had vomited in the bathroom. I'd finished the dishes, swept up a vase, and cleaned the bathroom. Twice. At least she'd made it there.

This was the first chance I'd had to look for the ring. I pulled back and reached into my purse for my phone.

Codi placed his hand over the landline and mouthed at me: "*What are you doing?*"

I flicked on the phone-light and flattened myself to the brick floor.

"No, I'm here, ma'am," he said.

The light gleamed on the dingy hunk of metal, far back against the wall. I willed it to come my way. "*Come on*, stupid magic that doesn't work." A sweat broke at the back of my neck.

I needed something long to reach it. I scrambled up and went to the vase of metal roses, feeling Codi's curious gaze tracking me. I chose a long stem and returned to the floor. Clutching the head of the rose, I fished around until I felt the clink of metal, then I wriggled the stem until it hooked the ring. *Gotcha.*

I'd felt what I believed to be my Spektral magic twice here at the tearoom with Codi. Both times had involved this ring. I slid it into my palm, the foggy images of a boy in the forest alcove, surrounded by wailing witches, trying to reclaim my mind. Not just any boy—*Callis.* I desperately tried to hold on to the details as they slipped away.

I wiped the ring clean of dust with a rag. There was nothing remarkable about the piece: just the simply etched triangle-flame, the symbol of all the old Fire witches—just like mine, just like Nicco's. I twisted it between my palms, feeling for a supernatural sensation.

But I didn't get a single tingle.

"No, you don't have to drink the tea, but you can if you want," Codi said, scribbling a name into the appointment book. "Okay, see you tomorrow at three." He hung up the phone.

I set the ring on the glass counter. "I'm pretty sure it's Callis's, but he wore so many of them, I can't be sure."

He rolled the ring on its side, and I could tell the memory was coming back to him. "That little kid with the freak-ass smile . . ."

"Callis, right? You saw it too? The forest? The glass casket?"

"What the hell *was* that?"

"Has anything like that . . . dream, vision, or whatever it was, ever happened to you before?"

"Just that one other time, with you. And that ring." His voice grew harsh. "I wonder if he lost it when they were attacking Julie? If I ever see that guy again, I am going to break his face!"

I picked up the ring again. "Or he planted it here, and it's cursed, and we're all going to die."

"That's dark, dude."

I wasn't entirely joking.

"Here," he said, holding out his hand. "Let me see it."

As I placed the ring in his palm, I wobbled. He caught me. But then my head danced as I slumped forward onto the glass counter, cool beneath me just like a . . .

Glass.

Coffin.

Young Callisto waits until nightfall, until after his nursemaid—whom he adamantly insists he does not need anymore—has told him goodnight and shuts the old arched door to his bed chamber. He lies patiently under the covers, staring out the window at the moon until sounds cease to echo and silence blankets the castle. He slips out of the warm bed and out of his dressing gown, and quickly pulls on his stockings, breeches, a dingy linen shirt and the doublet he stole from one of the stable boys. He buckles the pair of boots he took from the cobbler; his own are far too shiny and almost gave away his disguise once. He brushes his hair in front of his face and then moves through the castle's secret passages, as unnoticeable as the ghosts of his ancestors.

In the stable, he extracts an additional set of garments he'd hidden beneath a season's worth of hay. They will keep him more hidden than a costume at carnival. He throws on the long goat-leather robe whose black hood fits snugly over his head and shoulders, and the white lace neck-ruff, then fastens on the black leather hat which has a short crown and a wide circular brim. He digs through the next bale until he feels the crooked beak of the mask: the real reason he'll be able to pass through the streets without notice.

With the mask secured at his hip, he rides through the trees and brambles until he gets halfway down the hill. This is his last chance to cover his face before the inevitable run-in with the guards posted at the gate.

He lifts the mask to his head, trying not to inhale too deeply of the camphor-mint-myrrh mix on the first breath, and fastens the leather strap behind his head—the potpourri stored in the curve of the beak is something one needs to ease into. Last, he removes a pair of leather gloves, not only to protect himself from the Black Death, but to hide the only evidence that bears his family's mark—the silver ring on his right hand. He hasn't removed the heirloom since his father gave it to him.

The guards are to open the gates for no one at this time of night, but, as always, as soon as they see his dark beak in the moonlight, they crank the chains to allow him passage. No one would dare interfere with an urgent health emergency of the Salazar family, unless they want to see their heads roll.

The sounds of the cobblestone street, once filled with the whistles of larks and the gongs of competing church bells, are now a cacophonic chorus of victims crying for death to come quicker, the tired voices of priests saying last rites, and the sobs of surviving family members. The churches dig ditches until they strike water so that the bodies can be buried en masse. A dark cloud hangs over the town of Basque as thousands fall victim to the buboes.

The townspeople have come to fear the scents of cloves, rose, and frankincense—the mask of infection—in homes, and they've started referring to the hospital as simply "La Morgue," because they all know that anyone who enters never walks the streets again.

The great Salazar family spends a fortune bringing plague doctors into the city. At its peak, there were fourteen men, with their long black robes, probing canes, and beaked masks. Each with their different treacles and different cures for the Black Death, from urine face washes to spoonfuls of crushed emeralds to mercury bakes. They worked endlessly to balance the four humors of the townspeople, letting their blood, rubbing their pus-filled buboes with the skins of frogs, snakes, and pigeons, and, most importantly, trying to save the Salazar children as one by one they were overtaken. Of the original fourteen doctors, now there are eight. Nine if you count the boy galloping into town.

Lingering late-night crowds clear the streets for the masked rider, as if he's death himself; but then, through the fog, a woman runs out from a shop and throws herself in the path of his horse. "Please!" she screams. "Please! My husband needs a doctor!"

The horse skids to a stop and rears up, narrowly avoiding trampling her. Callisto keeps a firm rein to retain control of the nervous animal, cursing at the woman. But then just before he takes off again, a new plan unfolds before him, and he dismounts. "Take me to him." His voice echoes inside the mask, making him sound older than his fourteen years.

She guides him through the carriageway, where he ties up the horse, and then all the way up to the attic room where her husband lies, face contorting, eyes staring through Callis as if he's hallucinating. Pustules larger than the boy's fist bulge from the man's neck and arms.

Callisto lifts a blanket that covers the man's legs just enough to see the black on the tops of his toes. Nothing short of a miracle could save this man. No remedy, no magic.

"Fetch some hot water," he says to the woman. He takes one more look at the engorged buboes and seizes the opportunity—he won't even have to make the trip all the way to the hospital tonight.

The man's coughs explode like cannon shots, and the boy produces a silken handkerchief from his pocket and offers it to him. Although the silk would be considered average by some of the finer European families, it is the most exquisite thing the man has ever touched.

A cough sputtered from my lips.

A sharp edge dug into my waist. The chill of glass touched my cheek, and a weight rested over my back. Heavy and warm. An arm fell over my face.

"Codi?" I yelled, realizing I was smashed between him and the counter, bent over in a very, er, compromising position. I pushed off the glass, trying to lift him up. "Co—!"

"What is God's name?" came Edgar's voice behind us.

"What?" Codi murmured. "Oh my God!" He sprang backward, his hands in the air, falling against the back counter, rattling all the Mason jars of tea that lined the rear wall. "What the heck?"

I twisted around, gripping the counter behind me. *What was that?*

"What are you two doing?" Edgar's arms crossed, just like Codi always stood. "In the middle of the afternoon! In the middle of the shop! If you need privacy—"

"We don't need privacy!" Codi yelled. "We were just doing magic—not anything else!"

"What was that?" I whispered with a violent shake. My knees softened, and I sank to the floor, hugging my legs.

That tingle . . . It was different from that night in the forest, different from the tingle of the million fireflies coursing under my skin. It was familiar. Warmer.

It was my magic. I knew it.

"Are you okay, baby?" Edgar's big hands wrapped around my arms and he lifted me up. "What *exactly* were the two of you up to?"

"We weren't up to anything," Codi said.

I looked up at Edgar. "I can feel it."

"You can feel what?"

I shut my eyes, trying to hang onto the sensation.

He pushed the fabric on my dress sleeve up. "Addie . . ." excitement grew in his voice. "Addie."

I looked down. The Mark wasn't glowing, but there was a glimmer.

Edgar gently turned my arm back and forth so I could see the effect. I sucked in a breath and glanced up at Codi.

He covered his left arm with a sheepish smile. "Nothing," he said.

I gave him a sympathetic look. He held on to my arms, steadying me. "I'm fine. Just a little lightheaded."

"A little lightheaded is *not* fine." Edgar settled me on a stool. "Codi, come keep Addie steady while I put on the kettle."

"Really, I'm fine."

But he didn't leave my side until Codi switched places with him.

Codi squinted down at me. "Do you remember . . . a mask?"

As he said the words, the sound of galloping hooves came back to me, and the scent of potent camphor. "Callis?"

He nodded. "Where's the ring?"

I stood up straight, and we both scanned the bricked floor.

"There!" He swooped to the area just below the cash register and picked it up.

He held it out between us in a wide-open palm, as if afraid to touch it with his fingers. "This is definitely Salazar's. And he's definitely up to something."

"Excuse me?" Edgar asked.

"We found Callis's ring—"

He snapped a tea towel and, using it as a glove, plucked it from Codi's hand. "I'll take that, young man."

"Dad, that's Callis's! It's . . . showing us weird things."

"It won't be showing you anything until your grandpa examines it." He crumpled it into the towel and crammed it into his kimono pocket. "Codi Daure, you know better than to bring things of his into this house."

"I didn't!"

"Even more reason to have it purified. We don't need any of his juju in the shop."

"But—"

"We'll discuss it with your father when he's back."

As they continued to argue, I shut my eyes. I could feel the lingering effect of the magic fading. I lifted my arm to the metal roses and pulled. A yelp expelled from my throat, but the flower didn't budge, and I fell back down to the stool.

"Whoa," Codi said, putting an arm around my shoulder and squeezing. "Don't overdo it."

I nodded. As disappointing as it was to feel it slip away, my insides glowed. I was going to get my magic back; it was just a matter of time. And in that moment, all I could think about was telling Nicco.

I looked at the clock, wondering if he was awake yet. "Maybe I could leave work a little early? I want to tell—"

"Yeah!" Codi said. "Dee and Isaac are going to freak."

Guilt pinched my stomach. "Right! Yeah, let's go find them."

"I'll close up for the two of you, but you aren't going anywhere until after you've eaten something, Addie."

I turned to Edgar, who was holding out a moon mug of tea and a plate of cookies.

"Thank you," I said, munching one of the sesame seed balls. I swallowed a sip of the warm tea, already imagining the look on Désirée's face when I told them.

I crammed the rest of the cookie in my mouth, promising myself that I'd go to Nicco's tonight no matter what.

He was my friend. I wanted to see him.

CHAPTER 42

FLY

The map had started out simple enough, with our inked stars marking all the cemeteries in the city, but now, in her hunt to find the gates of Guinée, Désirée had decorated it with all kinds of other markings: gold foil star stickers, chalked vèvès with question marks, green highlighter, blue highlighter, push-pins with charms dangling from them, neon-colored stickies with scribbled dates. It looked like something from an episode of *Law and Order: Occult Division.*

She stood in front of it, staring, like it was a Magic Eye poster and she was waiting for the 3-D image to pop out. Next to it, she'd hung a whiteboard and started a series of color-coded lists: GATE ORDER, CEMETERY, GHEDE, KEY.

She'd stopped harassing me about Guinée for the last few days. I couldn't tell if she was just giving me a break because Adele was back or just letting me bank up happiness so she could cash in on it later. I knew she was not-so-secretly working on the plan every spare hour she had, so I was starting to worry that one day we'd get to HQ and she wouldn't be here. In her place there'd just be a note saying, *I've taken the souls. Be back soon. Don't wait up. xo.* It completely freaked me out.

"You seem way more obsessed with the gates than the other lists?" I said casually. I didn't want her to think I was at all interested in this plan.

"Do you see the blanks under the Gates list? That's why. But don't worry, I have a plan to figure it out." She looked down to the book in her hand, and then marked off one of the cemeteries uptown. "Actually, it involves you—"

"*Guess what?*" Adele's voice cried as the front door creaked open.

"Is Codi with you?" Désirée yelled.

"Yes," he shouted.

"Guess what?" she asked again, dropping her stuff on the floor and running straight into my arms.

I was so surprised by the burst of public affection, I forgot she'd asked something.

She smiled. "Guess what?"

"What, babe?" I suppressed every urge to kiss her, fully aware that things weren't totally back to normal.

"I felt my magic."

"Shit! What happened?"

"I don't know really. I was with Codi and there was this ring."

Désirée, who was now setting up her mini-cauldron on the coffee table, paused. "What ring?"

Codi sunk into the armchair. "A Salazar ring."

"*What?*" I asked.

She unlatched from around me and pulled me to the couch next to her. "We found this ring that I'm pretty sure is Callis's, and every time I touched it—"

"Sometimes," Codi interjected.

"Right, a couple of times when I touched it, I saw these flashes of his past. And it happened to Codi too—"

"Dream-twinning?" Désirée asked, unable to hide the shock in her voice, which was precisely what I was feeling.

"No!" they both yelled.

Adele squeezed my hand and gave me a reassuring look. I knew about the dream magic with Nicco, but we'd never really talked about why it had been happening. I wasn't sure that she even knew. "What did you see?" I asked.

"First, it was just him as a little boy in Spain with his dad. Then it was a funeral . . . for one of his younger brothers, I think? And then . . ." She looked at Codi and he continued: "Plague took over their village . . ." They both seemed foggy on this part. "It seems that before

Callis was a total POS, he was a doctor's assistant, or something, stealing into town to help people with his knowledge of medicine, or magic. Unclear."

"That's a pretty generous interpretation," Adele said.

"What do you mean?" he asked.

"I don't know. I just don't trust Callis, not even as a fourteen-year-old."

"But you got your magic back?" I asked.

"And you really have a possession of Callis's?" Désirée asked.

"No. I didn't get it back, but I could *feel* it." She was practically jittering when she spoke, and the glow was infectious. "And my Mark, it didn't light up, but it shimmered." It had been so long since I'd seen her this happy, I wasn't really thinking when I pulled her closer, and then I didn't care who was in the room when I pressed my mouth to hers and kissed her. She gasped a tiny bit, but then her mouth turned up into a smile. And it was the best part of my day.

"Hello, did anyone hear me?" Désirée asked.

I kissed Adele deeper so she couldn't respond, and she smiled harder, trying not to laugh.

"If you have a possession of Callis's," Désirée said, raising her voice, "we can do the location spell on him."

Adele froze mid-kiss and twisted around to Dee.

"I mean, seriously, how did you not consider this right away?"

"Well," Codi said, "it's kind of hard to think about anything when you're out cold out on the floor or barely remembering what happened afterward."

"You passed out?" I asked Adele.

"Something like that."

"Where's the ring?" Désirée asked.

They both sighed.

"Edgar has it," Adele said.

"As soon as he found out it was Callis's," Codi added, "he confiscated it."

Désirée lit her cauldron. "And so? Can you get it back?"

"I can try. It's going to be tough, though. People are arriving at the house tonight to prep for Hexennacht."

"Hexennacht?" I asked.

"Zaka Day." Désirée pulled out a jar of brown liquid from her bag and gave it a good shake. "I almost forgot; I've been so busy with the Ghede." She poured it into the cauldron.

I looked at Adele, who shrugged. I nestled her closer, glad I was no longer the coven's only kid-who-grew-up-without-a-magical-family.

"It's like Beltane." Codi took a whiff from Dee's cauldron and made a face. "In German magical tradition, Hexennacht was the night all the witches traveled to the highest peak in the mountains."

"What did they do there?"

"You know . . . feasted, danced around fires naked, grew horns, flew on broomsticks. That sort of thing. By the way, you're all invited tomorrow night. Sorry, should have told you sooner. And yes, my parents will be completely offended if you don't come. Feasting required. Naked fire dancing optional."

"I'm always down to feast," I said.

"Sure," Désirée replied, "but no dancing, naked or otherwise."

"Unless you're a cheval to Gran Bwa. Then there are no promises."

She chucked a sticky pad at me, which I deflected, laughing.

"Tomorrow night, we celebrate," she said. "Tonight, we work."

And that was it. Désirée had officially told us that she'd given us a vacation and now we owed her. *I knew it.*

"Who's down for some group magic?" she asked.

"Me!" Adele said.

Codi whooped and got up to grab his bag.

"Always," I said.

Désirée looked at me. "I'm so glad you feel that way."

I glanced at Adele, and she gave me another innocent shrug.

"Codi," Désirée asked, "did you bring the crystals?"

"Yup." He unzipped his duffel and pulled out a midnight-blue velvet sack about the size of a grapefruit.

"Excellent. You guys smudge and prep the circle."

"I'll get the salt," Adele said, and I went to help.

"Isaac, wait." Désirée stirred the pot, ladled some of the mixture into a moon mug, and handed it to me.

"What is this?"

"Tea."

"I don't like tea."

"It will help you relax."

"I don't need to relax."

"Just take two sips, please!"

I took a sip and promptly spit it back into the cup. It tasted like boiled tree bark and perfumey gym socks. "What the—?"

"Two sips."

I chugged back a gulp, gave her the cup, and then grabbed a sage stick and matches from the coffee table, wishing I could smudge the taste from my tongue.

She shook her head. "Baby."

As Adele started pouring the circle, Désirée opened her grimoire to a page marked with a ribbon, and then looked up. "Oh, can you make the circle bigger than usual?"

"How much bigger?"

"Isaac's height."

Huh?

But apparently, I was the only one who seemed to think that my body length was a weird form of measurement.

We set about cleansing the room and then sat inside the oblong circle. Désirée tossed the box of matches to Codi, and he began lighting the candles. When she saw the flame, Adele's gaze dropped to the floor.

"Hey," I whispered, leaning over. I kissed her lightly on the lips, and she gave me a weak smile. I thought about the ring and the location spell, and wondered if it was possible for me to beat Adele's Fire out of him.

Désirée switched the lights off and the room went pitch black other than the flames. White candles of all sizes lined the windowsills and fireplace, and the candles in the circle glowed around us through their glass cases.

"So what's this all about?" Codi asked, his face lit by the flickering flames.

"I'm going to need a lot of concentration," Désirée said, coming back to the circle. "We all are." She poured out the contents of the velvet bag: seven different chunks of raw crystal, all the colors of the rainbow, and then another, smaller, eggplant-colored velvet bag.

"For what?" he asked.

"To hypnotize Isaac."

"What?" I asked.

Adele looked my way. "Why are we doing that?"

"*Désirée*," I said, "the map to Guinée is not floating around the back of my mind."

Adele scrunched her forehead. "*What*?"

"How do you know what's buried deep in your subconscious? That's why it's called your *sub*conscious."

Adele turned to Codi. "What is she talking about?"

"Ritha told us that sometimes people who've had near-death experiences were actually given directions from the Baron on how to cross over, but if they regain consciousness, they suppress the supernal memory. And since Isaac . . . ya know. So Désirée thinks . . ."

Adele twisted a lock of her hair. I knew she didn't like thinking about that night.

"I found a very gentle meditation spell that is supposed to help with repressed memories," Désirée said, like we were just taking a spa day. "It puts you into such a deep state of relaxation, you're able to access parts of your mind you don't consciously use. I read that in a lot of cases, it strengthens people's magic afterward."

"I don't want my magic strengthened."

Désirée folded her arms. "Who actually doesn't want more magic? Look, if you're scared of spilling about your porn collection or something, I can teach Adele the spell, and Codi and I can wait in the other room."

"I-I don't know how to hypnotize someone," Adele said.

"I don't have anything to hide!"

"Well then, what's the problem?"

The problem is that I don't want to advance this stupid plan!

Adele looked at me, and I was certain that this was the part where she was supposed to convince me that everything would be fine and that we wouldn't push it too far.

"You don't have to do this," she said, not even flinching when Désirée gave her the death stare.

"Look, man," Codi said, "even if we get the map, it doesn't mean we *have* to go." He knew exactly why I didn't want to do this: if it worked, it put us that much closer to potentially *going to the Afterworld.*

Désirée crawled over next to me and plopped down on her knees. "Isaac, *please*. I've exhausted all other resources."

Adele's face scrunched in confusion again—it was exactly how I felt. Désirée resorting to begging was weird.

"I'm at a dead end. I need your help if we're going to save all of those souls."

I saw the flicker in Adele's eyes, and I knew she was imagining all the Mason jars in the tearoom library.

"What if it was Julie in one of those jars? Would you do it?"

"Of course I'd do it," I snapped. "Can't you dig around Codi's brain? Callis's coven almost killed him at the convent."

"Codi's the last resort—"

Codi threw up his hands. "You don't think I can do it?"

"Isaac's closer to the spirits. And his magic is stronger. *Please.*"

I really didn't want to do this. I looked at Adele.

"Whatever you want to do, I'll support you. It's your call."

Dee looked like her brain was going to melt out of her ears with anticipation.

"Fine," I grumbled through my teeth.

"Yes!" Dee launched onto me with a hug.

"Now you owe me another lifetime of hugs."

"You're getting one hug. That's it." She pulled away. "Now take off your shirt and lie on your back in the middle of the circle."

"Excuse me?"

"The crystals will work faster with stone-to-skin contact." She looked at Codi for confirmation.

"It's true."

Adele gave me another meek shrug.

Christ. I pulled my T-shirt over my head. I was just glad she was here this time.

I stretched out on the floor, and Codi grabbed a pillow from a chair to put under my head. I felt all six of their eyes on me, like I was about to be operated on. I one-hundred-percent hated everything about this. *Does Désirée even know what the hell she's doing? What if I say something stupid? About my mom . . . or I don't know?*

The only thing that gave me the slightest reprieve from the questions pounding my head was when I caught Adele's gaze lingering on my abs. I brushed her arm with my knuckle and watched the warmth rise in her cheeks as she looked away.

"If you two need to go sow your oats before we start, we can wait."

Even in the darkness, I saw Adele's cheeks go from warm to flamed.

"*Désirée*!" I said.

"What?" she asked innocently. "I'm just saying. If it will help you be more relaxed—"

"He's relaxed!" Adele shouted.

Codi spurted out a laugh, and I put my hands over my face, not knowing whether to laugh or scream. This week had been full of milestones for Adele and me, but we definitely hadn't had sex yet. We were in a good place, and every passing day was better than the one before, but I'd still give anything to be back in the place we left off three months ago. She took my hand and rubbed the top of my thumb, and I hoped she was thinking the same thing.

I felt a little pressure near my groin. "Yo!" I jolted, and something clanked to the floor. Codi's hand moved away.

"You knocked away the stone," Désirée said. "You need to stay still."

"What stone?"

Codi picked it up from the floor. "Garnet, root chakra."

"Whatever. A little warning next time?" My gaze followed as he placed the stone back. "Do we really have to supercharge my nuts for a memory ritual?"

"It's all about balance, bro." He picked up a rough, jagged orange stone. "Carnelian. Sacral chakra." He slowly placed it a couple inches below my navel. The stone was cold against my skin. Moments later the rest of the rainbow went up my stomach, heart, throat, third eye, and crown.

"What are the crystals for?" I asked, trying not to shake when I spoke.

"They'll help deepen your state of relaxation."

"You might start to feel lighter," Codi said. "Even like you're floating. They were charged last night, and it's almost the full Flower Moon."

Adele gave my hand a squeeze. "I've heard New Yorkers love to relax."

"Don't make him laugh!" Désirée said as the piece of amethyst fell off my head.

Adele placed it back and lightly kissed my cheek, and I momentarily forgot to regret this decision.

"Look straight up," Désirée said, towering over my head. She emptied the small eggplant-colored pouch into her hand, and then dropped another crystal toward my face, but it caught on a chain before it could poke me. "Eyes on the pendulum. Feel your connection to the ground beneath you."

I stared at the swinging crystal as she told Codi and Adele to place their hands on my body. I could sense the connection of their energy: how they were unsure where to touch me, how much weight to rest on me.

Désirée wiped a salve above my lip. It smelled like burnt oranges.

"Okay, Isaac. Take a deep breath and imagine yourself flying through the air. Weightless. Soaring through the clouds. Wind blowing through your hair— er, feathers. If I say the word 'sleep,' let your eyelids droop closed; and if you hear the word 'fly,' wake up, and you'll be here with us. Safe. In HQ. In perfect love and perfect trust." Five hands squeezed me. "Nod if you understand."

I felt my neck move, but my body was already starting to feel detached from my mind.

"We're going back to the night you were attacked in the park," Désirée said. "Afterward, you were lying in bed in my Gran's guest room. Go back there, into the memories. We'll be with you the entire way. If you get scared, just remember that we're right here. Are you ready?"

I felt my lips move and heard the word 'yes' in the faint distance, somewhere in the clouds.

Their voices began to fill the room:

The moon is up, the night is full,
Peace be yours, we'll hold you still.
Your eyelids brushed with her silver-dust
sprinkles,
May your dreams be vivid, like the brightest stars'
twinkles.
Spirits of the night will guard your mind,
Through the good, through the bad, no matter
what they might find.
We'll be here listening. Waiting. Guiding.
Protecting.
Let your muscles unwind, and free your mind,
To find the one and only road to the sublime.

The crystals felt heavier and my body felt lighter, as if floating up from the wooden floor.

"*Désirée*?" Adele's voice trembled.

"It's fine. Just go with it. He is an Air witch, after all. Isaac, when you wake up, you'll be back there, in that night. Now, it's time to sleep."

I started to feel lightheaded. "Désirée, what was in that tea—?" My head dropped back to the floor. I heard the amethyst and quartz clank to the ground.

I gasp in pain. Pain from every direction. I can't breathe. Just burning. Burning. Burning. Like there's bleach in my veins. My body twists and writhes on the bed as hands hold me down. Why are there so many people here? The room spins. I close my eyes.

"Désirée, is this right?" someone yells.

Adele. It can't be Adele. She's not here. I killed her mother. She's never going to forgive me. The pain inflames, and I try to hold in the scream.

"He needs to ride out the memory. Just let him. Isaac, look for the Ghede. Look for the Baron. Do you see anyone like that?"

I peek through the slits of my eyelids, and the room stops spinning. Everyone is gone. A woman is sitting on the bed in the dark next to me. When I see her mint-green nail polish, my eyes well. "Baby," she says.

"Mom?" She doesn't look sick anymore. She's beautiful.

"I'm going to take away the pain." She pulls away the blanket and holds out her hand. "Come with me, Isaac."

A voice screams in the background, from somewhere far away, over a mountain. It sounds like Adele; she begs me not to go. She's lying against my chest. I can feel her tears on my shirt. I want to stay with her, but I'm in so much pain.

"Isaac. Find the way to Guinée," says a deep voice from above.

I get out of the bed and take my mother's hand. She leads me out of the room. Through the hall. Past the taxidermy studio. Out the back door.

"You'll need this, Isaac, for Zaranye." She places something metal in my hand, curls my fingers around it, turns and starts running across the balcony over the courtyard. I can't keep up; there's too much pain. Suddenly, she's all the way across at the guesthouse door. A spider hurries over the railing. I start to step forward but . . . the balcony's disappeared.

"Jump!" she cries. "Isaac, jump!"

I shake my head. There's no way. It's too far. The pain is too much. I squeeze the piece of metal she put in my hand. It's a ring.

"You can do it, Isaac. You're so strong!"

"Mom, don't leave me! Mom!" I back all the way to the wall to get a running start, and I jump—but I don't even make it halfway across. As I fall, I try to take crow form, but there's nothing but pain in my bones, and now I'm going to splatter onto the bricks below.

"Mom! I don't want to die!"

"Désirée, stop!"

"He's fine! Just let him keep going!"

Darkness swirls all around me

as I fall.

Down.

Down.

Down.

I land on my feet, crouched, fingertips touching the wooden floor, spry like a cat. Like a vampire.

The floor is wet.

Drip. Drip.

I hear the strike of the match just before the flame appears, lighting up the tiny room.

A man is kneeling, back to me, lighting a candle. No, lighting a pipe. He puffs a cloud of smoke.

Is he the Ghede? Maybe he knows how to get to Guinée.

He lights the candles. Two. Four. Five. The water soaks through my sneakers, making me shiver. Strands of beads decorate statues of the Virgin Mary next to conch shells and plastic flowers. It's an altar. A large unsheathed athame hangs from a hook on the wall between framed photos. Probably of his family. His ancestors. Those who came before him. It's the spirits that bind us. Rosary beads. The walls are bright red.

Wait, I know this place.

A fly buzzes past my ear. I swat at it. I step forward. More flies. Buzzing. Black flies. The water is past my ankles now.

I lean forward to touch the man's shoulder. "Sir? The water's rising. We need to get out of here."

The room is small. Tiny. A closet. An altar room. I feel the water reach my knees. The man's shirt floats out behind him.

"Sir?" I yell louder, and tiny wings touch my lips. I spit out flies. The water sloshes up the walls.

The man turns around. Black swarms pour out of his hollow eye sockets into the air around us. "Corpse Whissssperrrrrer." He chokes maggots out of his throat.

I yell. And he yells, and he gags, spitting them out—squirming, fat, white maggots—into the water. He reaches out, offering me the pipe. I shake my head. He pulls out the pocket of my T-shirt and tucks it in. The burning tobacco sizzles against the damp cloth.

The water's now up to my waist. I blink, and it's at my shoulders.

It lifts me from the floor. I'm bobbing with drowning maggots and flies.

We both float up, and I have to paddle. The ceiling comes closer, shrinking the room. My hands bang against the plaster, and I scream one last time before the water goes over my nose. Don't panic, Isaac. *I kick up to the ceiling to suck in a last breath, and then the water consumes me.*

Observe, adapt, dominate.

It's murky and dark. I panic and air bubbles quickly escape my lungs, back into the water.

I need to get out. I need to save the man.

You can't save the dead.

The man's a corpse. You can't save . . .

The dead.

Guinée.

We have to save the dead.

I try to punch through the water to the ceiling, but my knuckles slip off the plaster. I need my crew. I need my tools.

I dive down to the altar and feel around the wall, over the picture frames to the athame—I rip it from the hook and kick off the wall, sending myself back up.

I punch into the ceiling with the blade. Don't panic, son, *my father's voice echoes in my head. I punch again.* Dominate.

Again.

"Dominate, Isaac!"

My lungs feel like fire; my head swirls with dizziness. My knuckles cut open as I punch up with the knife, but I break through the plaster. I touch air. I pull for my magic, but nothing comes. I drop the athame and rip at the hole with my hands.

"Dominate, son!"

I push my face up to the hole and suck in air.

"Isaac!"

Pop?

"Help!" I frantically shove my hands through the hole to rip off more of the roof. A strong arm grasps mine.

"Son! I've got you!" He pulls hard, and I burst through the crumbling roof.

"Pop?" On my hands and knees, I gasp for air, feeling the tears coming. There are so many dead.

"Are you crying, son?"

"No!"

A boot hits my chest, and I roll all the way down to the edge of the roof. The pipe flings from my pocket and plops in the water along with the ring. I grip the gutter so the undertow doesn't pull me away. Water isn't supposed to reach roofs. An eel glides next to me, and I yelp, almost letting go.

"Mister! Mister!"

I hear her. I hear them.

"I'm coming!" I let go and start swimming toward the voices, kicking against the current.

Pink dress. Yellow dress.

"Get the ring!" Jade yells, gargling a mouthful of water.

"Isaac, you need the pipe for Oussou!" shouts Rosalyn's tiny voice.

I have them both—fistfuls of dresses, holding them above the water. But I'm sinking.

I kick harder, but there's nowhere to go: The house is gone. The truck isn't here. There's nothing but water. And screams.

My boots get heavier.

I can't feel my legs.

I can't hear them screaming anymore.

"Help!" I shriek, gurgling water. "Help!"

I hear her voice: "Fly! Fly, Isaac!" But I can't. My magic isn't working. I can't turn.

"Isaac, fly!"

My voice was raw, but I yelled the words anyway: "*Silken rings for Zaranye. Oussou's pipe will get you high*!" I didn't even know what they meant.

I panted for air and opened my eyes. Knees were digging into my chest—not mine, but Adele's. I was curled around her waist like a child.

"Fly," she whispered.

It had been her. She was there with me the night I almost died.

She gripped me tight, her eyes wide. "It's okay. You're in HQ. The Storm is over. You saved Rosalyn. You saved Jade."

"I didn't save Jade."

"You saved her soul." She struggled to keep her voice steady. She was shaking.

No, I was shaking. I was shaking her. I pulled away and turned around. The crystals were on the floor. Codi looked like he'd seen a ghost. But it was me who'd seen ghosts.

Désirée was trying to hide her glee. "You did it, Isaac."

"I did?"

"'Silken rings for Zaranye. Oussou's pipe will get you high?' That's one more key and two more Ghede! *Jesus Christ,* you really did almost die. The rest has got to be in there. But take a breather; we can wait until tomorrow night to do it again."

"Désirée!" Adele shrieked through a locked jaw. "We are never doing this to him again!" She pulled me back into her lap, and I didn't say anything. I just lay back against her for a minute, sucking in air. Staring at the ceiling, gripping her arms.

I should have saved Jade.

CHAPTER 43

THE CITIES OF DEAD

As Désirée stood at the whiteboard adding the new lwa and their keys to her lists, I sat on the couch, anxiously waiting for Isaac to return from the bathroom. I couldn't believe I'd agreed to that.

"Tea?" Codi asked, setting up his mini-cauldron on the coffee table.

"Good idea," I said. "Anything but what Désirée brewed for Isaac."

She turned to me and smirked.

"I'm thinking a nice calming chamomile?" he asked.

I nodded as he struck a match, lighting the burner.

When Isaac came through the pocket doors, his shirt was back on and his hair was slicked behind his ears like he'd splashed water on his face. He sat on the far end of the couch, avoiding eye contact with everyone as he dipped into his bag for his sketchbook.

I tried not to stare at him. "Are you o—?"

He stretched over and pecked my lips. "I'm fine." But then he moved away again, crossed his ankle over his knee, and started sketching something I couldn't see because he was so closed off.

"Isaac, what did you see in there?" Dee asked, and Codi widened his eyes at her. *I can't believe she's still prying!*

"Nothing," he said without looking up. "First responder stuff."

I scooted over and leaned into his ear, so they couldn't hear. "Are you sure you're okay?"

He nodded.

"We can leave if you want . . ."

He turned to me. "I'm fine. I swear."

"Okay." I kissed his jaw and moved down to the coffee table on the floor, letting him have some space.

Codi poured the tea, and as Désirée took her cup, I gave her a look that said I was going to pounce on her if she asked anything else.

Sorry! she said back with her eyes.

Give her a break, Adele.

I knew she was just trying to help, and that she always felt she had something to prove because she'd defied her family and not joined their coven. But still, it had taken months for Isaac's Storm-PTSD to settle down. I wasn't going to let her flare it back up.

She curled into one of the periwinkle-colored armchairs with the carved lion's feet, her grimoire in hand, and Codi settled back in the other, reading pages from the Daures' German book of shadows, which he'd taken photos of since his parents wouldn't let him leave the house with the real copy. As she read, Désirée retied her hair. And then adjusted her blouse a couple of times. All the while discreetly stealing glances at him. *Mm-hmm.*

Whenever she was working on her magic, be it writing an incantation, building an altar, or making a powder, she'd glance at him when she thought no one was looking, as if to see if he was noticing. I'd thought it was friendly competition, but now . . . I smiled to myself as I sipped my tea, wondering which of them would finally make the first move.

I glanced at Isaac and back to them . . . I loved the three of them so much, my heart swelled.

As they all drank their tea and read, I pulled out Adeline's diary from my bag. I'd been ignoring it because I didn't want to think about her warning. Or about how she refused to tell me where León is.

I guess that's what I get for fraternizing with the enemy.

I opened the antique dairy, and a pile of papers spilled out.

"What's that mess?" Codi asked.

"Oh, you mean the pages formerly known as my journal?"

"You must have had a reaaally angsty day."

"Ha. I let Ren borrow it . . . It's no big deal. He didn't mean to destroy it."

Seeing the pile was a little depressing—not because my pages were ruined, but because his erratic drawings really did look like the markings of a madman: all lines, squiggles, and rudimentary starbursts. I turned one of the pages around. In the corner was a tiny drawing that didn't look nearly as incoherent as the larger strokes. I leaned closer. It was a winged hourglass. It reminded me of the night of my mother's funeral—the symbol on the gate at Louis No. 1. I browsed more of the pages and found a small drawing of a dart. I couldn't quite place it, but it felt familiar too.

I looked through the rest of the sheets, putting aside any of the pages with symbols. Something about the precision he'd drawn them with gave me hope for him.

There were seven in total: the winged hour glass, the dart, a sacred heart, a shamrock, a sword and shield, a fleur-de-lis, and something that might have been a Voodoo doll. I strummed my fingers. I rarely saw shamrocks except on St. Patrick's Day, or maybe on one of the signs at the Irish pubs, but Désirée had drawn one too.

I squinted at the map and found the blue-ink shamrock up on Canal Street, where the streetcar line ended. My eye drew further uptown, to a fleur-de-lis drawn not far from the Academy. "Dee, what does the fleur-de-lis on your map represent?"

"Lafayette Cemetery No. 2," she said without looking up.

"And the shamrock?"

"St. Patrick's."

Hmm. I stood up with the handful of sketches, grabbed some pins from her tin of school supplies, and went to the map. *It's just a weird coincidence.* I matched up the shamrock symbols and the fleur-de-lis, and then pushed the hourglass into the wall at St. Louis despite Dee not having drawn one. The three papers hung like lifeless leaves, part translated journal entries, part musings of a madman.

Ren doesn't believe in coincidences.

The lines that ran off the edges of the pages marked with the shamrock and the fleur-de-lis had similar thickness and swoop. When I turned the two pages at opposite forty-five-degree angles, the lines met—not only the main line, but every other line running off the papers matched up. Every swirl and squiggle. *Weird.*

I pinned them each in place and stepped back. "Does anyone know what a dart symbolizes?"

"Plague," Codi answered. "Disease in general."

"What? How do you know that?"

"Because they're all over St. Roch."

Hmm. I pinned the sheet with the dart to St. Roch Cemetery. When I glanced over at them, they were all looking at me.

Désirée closed her grimoire. "What are you doing?"

"I'm not totally sure. Is there a cemetery associated with the symbol of the sacred heart?"

"Um, like all of the Catholic ones?" she answered.

"That's not really going to narrow it down."

Isaac's brow furrowed, and he started thumbing back through the pages of his sketchbook.

Codi folded his arms. "You said these drawings were Ren's?"

"Yeah, but I don't know what these other symbols represent."

"You don't need to know them," Isaac said, examining a page in his sketchbook.

He got up and came over to me, extending his hand for the remaining pages. I passed them over.

He studied them for a minute, twisting them around, and then turned to the map and pinned up each page at odd angles. When he was done, the lines spilling off the edges all matched up, and the four remaining symbols naturally fell over four more cemeteries.

"How did you do that so quickly?" I asked.

"Go stand further back," he said.

I moved behind the couch.

"What do you see?" he asked.

I stared at the map until the dominant lines appeared stronger amongst the squiggles and starbursts. An image started to form. "A cross?"

"A mausoleum?" Codi asked.

"Whose cross?" Isaac asked, looking straight at Désirée.

Her eyes widened. "*Holy shit.* It's Baron Samedi's vèvè!"

I looked over at Isaac's sketchbook on the coffee table. He was exactly right. In the chaos of tangled lines, the Baron's vèvè stood out like it had been overlaid on a Jackson Pollock.

Désirée turned to me, and I couldn't tell if she wanted to slap me or kiss me. "Adele! Baron Samedi's vèvè is the map to the gates to Guinée!"

We all ran over to the wall, studying exactly where the vèvè overlaid the map—each of the seven main starbursts lined up with a cemetery gate.

"It's the seven gates; you figured out the way to Guinée!" She threw her arms around me, jumping up and down.

But I hardly moved, my gaze locked on Isaac. I'd never seen fear in his eyes like I saw now. I wasn't sure if I'd ever seen fear in his eyes at all.

"Well," I said, "Isaac did really. I just figured out the code. Ren made the drawings. You guys said you asked him how to get there, right? Maybe this was his way of trying to answer you."

The room fell silent. It was undeniable: Ren had been given the directions to Guinée.

Isaac's eyes were wide. "So that's what all of my dreams were about."

"What dreams?" Désirée asked.

"The python. The spiders. It's the Ghede coming for Ren."

"Not just Ren," she said, "all of the Possessed. I've been . . . doing some digging. Ghede Hounsou, the soul-keeper, has a brother who's a witchdoctor—a healer. Maybe when we get there, we could ask him to help Ren."

Isaac barely refrained from rolling his eyes at her. I knew he didn't want to go to Guinée.

I turned to Dee. "Can't we just ask him from this side?"

"Neither brother is a psychopomp," Codi said.

"Adele, the Ghede *told* us how to fix everything. The crystal is in our court. If we don't pick it up and do something to help, we're part of the problem."

"I get what you're saying, but we're not talking about rebuilding houses or starting a fundraiser. We're talking about leaving the Natural World!"

"We each have a choice. I'm going." Désirée crossed her arms.

"We don't need to fight about this," Codi said. "Seven gates, seven Ghede, seven keys. We don't have them all, plus they need to be paired up correctly, or you know, we make a wrong turn and end up on some other astral plane."

"*What*?" I asked, turning to Dee. "He's joking, right?"

"Kind of. Maybe. Voodoo magic is precise. You really want to get it right." She looked to Isaac with pleading eyes. "Which is why we need to get—"

"Désirée!" I couldn't believe she was about to ask to open up his head again.

"It's okay," he said. "I'll do whatever we need to do to save Ren."

Désirée sucked in a big breath, doing her best to temper her excitement, went over to her chart, and wrote in the additional information: all seven cemetery gates. Only two Ghede were missing and two keys.

She turned back to us, capping the Sharpie. "We made *huge* progress. Let's take a break and pick it back up tomorrow."

I think she knew I was going to explode if she pushed Isaac anymore tonight.

On the walk home, the almost full moon watched over us with her bright nocturnal glow. Muted music hummed from Bourbon Street along with the usual sounds of Thursday-night drunken revelry. There were more locals than tourists in the Quarter post-Storm, but any people-noise washing out the eerie quiet made things feel more back to normal. Isaac didn't speak the entire way home, just held my hand.

When we got to my stoop, I hopped up the step and turned to him, but before I could say anything, he took my hands. "What if we actually make it to Guinée . . . but it's different for me there because of my Spektral? What if I freak out? When we did the séance at St. Roch, I could see *all of them*." His eyes glistened. "I could see Adeline during the séance last week. I could see the fear in her eyes when she was talking to you."

My heart thumped. "You could see her? Why didn't you tell me?" Had he been afraid to?

"I don't know . . . I guess I just kinda forgot you couldn't see her. And we'd just started talking again, and you were already freaked out afterward. I didn't want to scare you anymore."

"I want you to be able to tell me anything. Always. No matter what."

He nodded, peering into my eyes.

"Isaac, do you really want to go to Guinée? This is not a rescue mission. It's a total unknown. I am not your father. You don't have to do this."

"I have to help. I can't let them down."

I pulled him close. "Isaac, no one is going to be disappointed in you."

"Dee will be."

"No, she won't."

"Did you not see that look in her eyes?"

"She's not going to be disappointed in you, because I'm going to tell her that I'm not going. She's knows you're not going to leave me here with . . . everything as it is. It will be my fault. It will buy us time to figure something else out." Our eyes locked, and I hated that there was even the slightest bit of shock in his gaze that I would do something like that for him. "We're a team—"

Before I could say anything else, his lips crashed against mine, and he kissed me so deeply I stumbled back, but his arms wrapped tightly around me. I didn't understand how one kiss could make me feel so needed and so in need at the same time. He pulled me even closer, and I felt the tension finally release from his locked shoulders. And that made me feel better.

"I'll tell her tomorrow," I said when we stopped to breathe. "Don't worry about it. I can handle the wrath of Désirée."

He smiled and kissed me again. Softer than before.

"Can I ask you something?"

He rested his head against mine and nodded.

"You don't have to answer though, if you don't want to."

"*Hmm*?"

"During the ritual . . . what did you see?"

"Corpses. And my mom. And my pop. And Jade. Just stuff you already know about."

"Just because I already know doesn't mean you can't talk about it . . . I mean, if you ever want to."

"Thanks." His voice was tender. "But I don't like talking about it. It just brings the memories back stronger."

I nodded. "We don't have to talk about it."

"Just being with you makes it better."

"It does?"

He nodded.

"*Bien.*" My heart raced in the silence. I don't know why I was so terrified of the words coming out of his mouth, but I knew that if he told me he loved me again, and I didn't say it back, it was going to be bad.

But . . . he didn't say it, and my pulse tempered.

He didn't tell me goodnight either. I knew he was lingering to see if I'd invite him inside, like I had last night. We'd fallen asleep watching *The Dark Knight*, intertwined on the couch. When Mac came home, we'd woken to the kitchen door rattling, with barely enough time for us to get Isaac out a window.

I wanted to pull him inside, but knowing he was okay, I refused to go back on the promise I'd made myself earlier. "Isaac, you trust me, right?"

His forehead pinched. "Of course I trust you."

I took another breath.

"Why?"

"I'm . . . I'm going over to Nicco's later. It's been a week. I want to see him."

His grip loosened.

"Isaac—"

"Did Adeline's message really mean nothing to you?"

"Of course it meant something to me." My face burned. "But it doesn't change all that Nicco's done for me."

"Well, it seems like you've made up your mind."

"I have." I refused to let him guilt me out of this.

He stared at me hard, but my stare back didn't waver. I trusted Nicco. And I needed to see him.

I needed my magic. I needed him.

We're friends.

I'm going.

I stood up my tiptoes and kissed him on the cheek. "Goodnight, Isaac. It's going to be fine."

CHAPTER 44

NIGHTCAP

Before I came to New Orleans, I'd started having these dreams about a girl who could hold fire. I knew she was from a different time because she wore these big dresses with corsets and spoke with the French-accented formality of a bygone era. The first time I ever saw Adele, I knew, inexplicably, that we were supposed to meet—that all of those dreams about the girl with fire were meant to get me to her. The first time I saw Adele throw a flame, it was like watching the girl from my dreams in real life.

Leaning into the bar, I flipped back to some of my sketchbook pages that predated the Storm, and there she was staring back at me: Adeline Saint-Germain.

Ever since leaving Adele's stoop, she was all I could think about—Adeline and her warning.

"You ever sleep, son?"

I looked up. Mac took away the still full moonshine concoction that had been sitting, sweating, on the bar for an hour since Mia made it. He dumped it in the sink and replaced it with a beer.

"Thanks." I set the pen down and stretched my back. "I'm better at drawing than sleeping. I'm better at most things than sleeping."

"A lot of people have been singing that tune since the Storm. It's hard to keep your dreams calm when your daytime's a nightmare."

I nodded. There had been a time when Mac asked me about my nightmares; now that seemed like so long ago.

"So . . ." He cracked a beer for himself and flipped the cap into the trash. "You've been in a noticeably better mood lately."

"Oh . . . ?"

"You've been spending a lot of time with my daughter."

I twisted the bottle around. "Um—" I don't think he really had an idea of exactly how much time, but I hoped that meant Adele was mentioning me outside of the mentorship lessons. "Is that okay?"

He took a sip of his beer and then set the bottle back on the counter. "Well, that would be a question for her, don't ya think?"

"Oh, yeah. Of course."

"Unless you're into drugs, or anything like that. Then I'm going to break your fingers—"

"No. *No*, I don't do drugs."

He smiled, and I knew he was just messing with me. "So," he said, "I guess there is someone who 'does it for you' after all?"

Shit. Why'd I say that about Lisette? I pushed my hair behind my ears.

"Well . . ." I recalled how Adele had so quickly and selflessly said she'd stick by my decision not to go to Guinée. It was going to be hard for her to break the news to the others tomorrow, but I knew she'd meant it. "She's pretty amazing . . ."

His brow raised.

"I mean, artistically—her ideas!" I felt like I was stumbling through a pit of fire. "I always thought fashion was kind of dumb—"

His arms crossed.

"Before I met her! But her concepts are so thoughtful and . . . precise. It's like they have . . . *emotion*."

"All good art does." He tipped his head to acknowledge someone else. "The usual?" he asked.

"Two, *grazie*."

I almost jumped off my barstool at hearing Nicco's voice. *Fuck!* How long had he been standing there?

Mac shoveled ice into two metal canisters as Nicco turned to me, inhaling deeply through his nose like an animal sniffing out a kill. "So, your girlfriend's into fashion?"

"Girlfriend?" Mac said, slamming the lid on the first martini shaker.

"She's not my girlfriend." *Damnit!* Not words I ever wanted to say to Nicco Medici. But what else could I say in front of Mac?

"One day, you should take her to Milano."

There was something about the way he said it that felt like he really meant, 'One day, *I'm* going to take her to Milano. And teach her Italian. And personally take her to Miuccia Prada's villa, and then to meet all of her other fashion idols, and then to see my family's entire fucking museum in Florence.'

"Italy's the fashion capital of Europe, no matter what the French say," he added with a soft smile.

Mac shook the canisters loudly.

The sketch of Adeline pulled my attention, and her warning rang loudly in my ears. "I wonder if she'd beg to differ?" I said, gesturing to the drawing.

His gaze focused on the portrait, and he bent a little closer, but his poker face did not falter. "Surely, she'd have a strong Parisian opinion, but I'm confident she'd come around. Adeline always had impeccable taste."

Just hearing her name so casually roll off his tongue made anger seethe through me.

Mac finished straining the drinks into a pair of martini glasses, and Nicco picked them up with a nod of thanks.

He walked back to his family's usual corner down by the stage. A jazz pianist was playing. They were all here tonight, including Gabe. As much as I loathed their presence, I wondered if that meant Adele's late-night plans would be spoiled. Or if she'd just be walking into a house of drunk vampires? I turned back around.

"Niccolò seems to make you tense," Mac said.

"What? No." I looked down at my hands and relaxed my tight grip on my pen. "You know his name?"

"I make it my business to know the names of people interested in my daughter."

My knee accidentally banged the bar. "Yeah, especially ones ordering moonshine martinis, I bet."

"They're for his brothers; the kid's never drunk on my watch. How old *is* he?"

What the eff? All this time I've been hanging out with Adele, Nicco's been hanging out with Mac?

"So?" He spread his hands over the bar. "Who does *Adele* like?"

I fought the part of me that wanted to tell him how she looked at me, and saved my sketchbook, and worried about my dreams. "That's probably a question for her," I said.

"Of course it is. But I'm asking you."

"Um?" I thought about all of the good moments we'd shared recently, but I also couldn't help focusing on the time right after the séance, when we'd been arguing: the way she'd casually breezed over it when I told her I loved her. "Me, hopefully."

"You don't know?"

Well, I thought I did . . .

"I mean, I guess we haven't really talked about it, specifically." It took every ounce of restraint for me not to jump off the stool and fly over to her bedroom so I could ask her to *for sure* be my girlfriend. Would she think that was endearing or psychotic? Was love somewhere in the middle? Why hadn't I already asked her?

Because, Isaac, you needed to take it slow so she didn't freak out and run away. Probably straight to Nicco.

"You like Batman*?"* he asked.

Shit.

I'd been paranoid he'd seen me scrambling to leave their house last night, after Adele and I had fallen asleep on the couch watching *The Dark Knight*. He thinks we just met a week ago.

"Superman is more my speed."

He squinted inquisitively. "Why?"

"You know, flying. That'd be cool." A part of me nearly spilled that we weren't doing anything, just sleeping. I don't know what was worse: him thinking I'd been there, trying to get with his daughter after just meeting her, or him thinking it was someone else. Did he suspect it might have been Nicco?

The idea made me sick.

The crowd behind me applauded and then, luckily, a rush of people came up to the bar, bombarding Mac for drinks before I could say anything stupid.

I took a sip of the beer and looked back down at the portrait of Adeline. I'd never really understood why she'd appeared in my dreams instead of Susannah, but now I did. She wasn't just guiding me to my future coven members; she was guiding me to *her descendant*, to help protect Adele from the predators who had stalked her and her father, and who'd killed Adele's mother and were now obsessed with her. Just like Susannah had once protected Adeline from the very same vampires.

This week, for the first time since the dreams, I'd seen her face—not in a dream, not in my sketchbook, but her spirit. I'd seen the anger in her eyes when she said Nicco's name.

Nicco had already made it clear that he wasn't leaving town until Adele was safe, whatever the fuck that meant coming from a vampire. *He* was the reason she wasn't safe. His effed-up family and his centuries-old grudges and feuds and enemies. She didn't need any of this shit. We didn't need it. New Orleans didn't need it.

I had to get him out of her life.

Now.

I picked up my phone without even checking the time and punched out a message:

Isaac 01:12 u awake?

Dee 01:13 That depends. How bad u injured?

Isaac 01:13 Ha. I'm coming over.

Dee 01:13 Altar room.

There were a surprising number of lights on in the Borges' place when I arrived, and freshly burnt vanilla incense still lingered in the air along with a trace of magic.

"Ritha's circle just finish up?" I asked, stepping through the curtain of the little altar room.

Désirée was lying in the pile of pillows, scanning a book with a highlighter. "No. She got an emergency call and had to put together some ointments."

I plopped down next to her. "Possession-related?"

"No, a sick cousin in the Delta."

"Where's that?"

"Mississippi. She just left with Remi and Manon." She looked up. "What's up?"

"Magic-related question."

She capped the highlighter.

"Do you think the two of us would be able to contact Adeline Saint-Germain on our own? Maybe Codi too, if he could keep his trap shut."

"Why would we contact Adeline—if that's even possible—without Adele?"

I exhaled and told her about the séance and Adeline's warning, and how Adele had freaked out. "She cut the connection before Adeline could tell her why. It was like she didn't even want to know!"

"So, you guys did a séance without me."

"Please don't give me shit. I'm trying to get close to her again."

"Even if we could make contact with Adeline, did you suddenly learn French?"

"Julie could translate."

"Oh, Goddess, you're serious . . ."

"All we need to ask is one question. I just need to know why she thinks Nicco is dangerous, besides the hundred obvious reasons."

"So, all week you've been trying to get closer to Adele, and now you want to go behind her back and contact her dead ancestor with your ghost-girl bestie?"

"I just want to protect her. Don't you?"

"Of course I want to protect her. But look at my lips when I speak to you. This. Is. A. Terrible. Idea. Do not, I repeat, *do not* do this."

"But—"

"No *buts*. Do you realize how pissed she's going to be when she finds out? She already has trust issues. And she's *so* sensitive when it comes to him."

I flopped back into the pillows, grumbling, "She doesn't have trust issues when it comes to *him*." But Désirée was right. This was the dumbest idea I'd ever had.

"What happened? Did you guys get into a fight?"

"No."

"Then why are you acting insane?"

The words huffed out: "I ran into Nicco."

"Well, that explains it. Wait, did he kick your ass again?"

"He did not 'kick my ass' the first time."

"I passed out when I healed you."

"And I thank you."

"For healing you, or for keeping you from destroying the last chance you have with the love of your life?"

"Both."

"You're welcome."

"Dee." I pulled her hand to my chest. "Julie's not my bestie; you are."

"I know."

I thought about the night Nicco launched me into the dumpster and that smug smile on his face tonight. "Do you remember that supercharged potion from Marassa's grimoire you made on Halloween night?"

"The heightening elixir?"

"Yeah. Can you make some for me?"

Her eyes slanted down. "Why?"

"No reason, really. It just seems like a good idea to have some around."

She crossed her arms. "Do I have stupid written across my face? I just bring up Nicco kicking your ass and then you ask me for a heightening elixir?"

"They've been stalking her family for four hundred years, Désirée. One of them almost killed me!"

"That's exactly why I don't want to make it for you! I know you! You aren't going to save it in case of an emergency; you're going to get pissed off and go after him!"

"I did your stupid hypnosis thing! Just make me the elixir."

She looked at me sternly and sucked in a breath before she got up and stalked into the shop.

I followed her.

"We're supposed to be protecting each other, not enabling each other to make asinine decisions."

"What, like you going to Guinée?"

She went behind the counter, pulled the cauldron out from the shelf below, and slammed it down. "I'm just trying to protect the city."

"What do you think I'm trying to do?"

"I know . . . but . . ."

"But what?"

"But I want to protect you too."

"You had a funny way of showing that earlier."

She looked at me apologetically. "I guess I didn't really think about all the Storm stuff you've been through. It's not like you ever talk about it. I was just thinking about the night the vampire attacked you, and I thought you could handle that—"

"I can," I snapped. "It's fine."

"Clearly."

We both knew we had bad ideas. But we were both sick of the people we loved being vulnerable to monsters.

"Grab the star anise from the shelf for me," she said. "It won't be ready until tomorrow night."

I scanned the shelf for the jar of little star-shaped seed pods and pulled it. "Thanks, Désirée."

"I'd say anytime, but I hope there's never a need."

"Me too."

She walked me to the front door. Before I took off, I turned to her. "Dee? Can we not tell Adele about my original idea?"

"I'm one step away from memory powdering myself so I don't have to remember that idea."

I smiled at her and then soared home. It took every ounce of strength not to stop at Adele's window to see if she was home, or out with the Medici.

CHAPTER 45

INCANTESIMO

The faint melody of an Italian aria rose through the attic floorboards from Martine's room. I clicked on the overhead light, and the three pairs of eyes of our captive witches pinched closed. The bulb glowed a dim amber in the pitch-black room. I'd taped black fabric to the windows a week ago.

Raúl Salazar, as we'd identified our original captive Ghost Drinker, a cousin from Old World Basque, was chained to the wall in the corner to my left. Josif, the lump of burned Balkan flesh who Adele had roasted, was slumped in the corner to my right. And Carina, the blonde Norwegian speedster, lay chained to the wall between them, with her cheek against the floor, her pale-blonde hair matted with blood.

Apparently, Callisto and Celestina had been collecting others of their soul-sucking kind from all over the world this past hundred years.

Raúl was able to sit up against the wall in his chains, thanks to my blood. Carina hadn't healed yet, and the patch of wood beneath her face was wet from drool and tears. The bones in her arms remained broken without the meal of specter, which she routinely begged for. All of Josif's fingers were blackened from where he'd tried to grab Adele, and a bone protruded from his pinky finger like a burnt piece of timber. There was hardly an inch of his flesh that wasn't blistered, swollen, or infected. He'd been burnt down to the muscle in patches, bone in others. If it weren't for his unique Spektral magic, he'd have died days ago. He could barely stay conscious more than a few minutes at a time. It was almost time to heal him, but I wanted him to live with that pain for as long as possible. I wanted him to remember her power.

She was going to be a greater witch than Adeline. I knew she'd eventually be able to find León, and I'd be able to reclaim my family's magic.

I thought about the portrait of Adeline Saint-Germain in Isaac's book. *Why the hell was he drawing her?* The resemblance was so remarkable I'd have sworn he'd been alive in the eighteenth century and known her.

I squatted down in front of Carina. Her exposed cheek was a deep shade of purple from when we'd collided in the forest. "Do you think Callisto has moved on and left you behind by now?"

Her eyelids floated open just enough to see me. I don't think she'd moved since yesterday, as her broken bones made her incapable of lifting the heavy chains. She was far better at giving me the silent treatment than Raúl, but she must have reached her pain threshold because today she answered without any issue. "Callisto hasn't left town."

Raúl gave her a warning look.

"I think you overestimate his commitment to saving you. We've had poor Raúl here for weeks."

She turned her head a few degrees to me. Her left eye was bloodshot, and her blue irises were starting to lose their color. "I don't overestimate his desire to save me. It's that I don't underestimate his desire to kill *you.*"

A groan came from the roasted witch. He tried to speak, but only wisps came out of his burnt throat.

I picked up the flask of water from the windowsill nearest him and slowly poured some in his mouth.

He lapped it up, wincing. When he'd finished, he asked in a pain-filled voice, "What . . . moon are we in?"

The eyes of the other two witches darted his way.

"Have you not been keeping track since you've arrived?" I asked.

"How could we?" Raúl growled. "Between the blacked-out windows and the actual blacking out from your delicate touches!"

I stepped in front of him. It had been a while since he'd popped off so aggressively. And over such a simple thing like the moon?

Though there was nothing simple about the moon when it came to witches. If a witch was concerned with *la luna*, it was not to simply count the calendar days. *So . . . whatever his coven is planning requires lunar strength.*

"But you're *una strega*," I said, running a finger down the side of his face. His pale-white irises were now almost as translucent as the spirits he consumed. A patch of hair was missing from where I'd ripped it from his head after he spat in my eye a few days ago. "A magnificent Salazar. Aren't you so in tune with the celestials that the journey of *la luna* courses through your veins?"

A doorbell chimed in the distance.

Thump-thump.

"Who's at the door?" Carina asked, a half-smile tugging her swollen lips.

"How would I know?"

"I think you do know," she said. "Your eyes flickered with hope."

"Must be the witch-girl," Raúl said.

I whipped to Carina and tied her gag.

"Definitely the witch," he echoed.

I secured his silence as well, and in a breath, I was out the attic door, twisting the locks and running down the stairs to the mezzanine.

She was standing in the foyer with my brother.

"I could have had ten bottles of moonshine," Gabriel said to her, "and you'd still be safer from the sword in my hand than I am from the sword in your hand, sober."

"True," she said, "but you're immortal."

"Touché."

"No drinking and sparring," I said.

When she looked up, I swore her eyes brightened. *You're being delusional.*

"Is everything okay?" I asked her, coming down the last set of stairs.

She nodded.

"Why do you assume something's wrong just because she's here?" Gabriel asked.

Because she only needs me when something is wrong.

"You're nothing but doom and gloom, Nicco." He turned back to Adele. "I don't know what you see in him."

Blood rose to her cheeks and she looked past him. "Nothing's wrong. I just wanted to see you."

Gabriel stepped aside, offering me his place with a dip of his hand. "She just wanted to see you, Niccolò."

Instead of taking his place, I nodded to the parlor room on my left.

"Hi," she said.

"*Ciao*." My hand grazed her back as I guided her inside.

She sat on the blue tufted sofa. Her lavender scent was stronger than usual; she'd freshly showered. Instead of sitting next to her, I opted for the chair to her right, trying not to think about Isaac touching her. Or even worse: her touching him. *It's clearly time for you to disengage from this situation, Niccolò.* To focus on Callis, and León, and the Elixir. And to get the hell out of here. I strummed the arms of the chair. "How's your magic coming?"

"Today . . . something happened at the tearoom with Codi. My Mark glimmered, or something."

"Being around other witches can—"

"I know, I know—can help bring out your magic. You were right." She smiled. "About everything."

I wasn't right about Isaac.

"We found this ring that we think is Callis's. It's a longshot, but we're going to try to do a location spell on it."

"If you get a hit, do not go after him without me."

"Of course not."

In the silence that followed, I wondered if she was going to tell me about Isaac. *Why did she shower before coming over?*

She recrossed her legs. "Oh! I have a question."

"*Sí, bella*?"

"What does *in-can-tee-zee-mo deeseelanzomento* mean in Italian?"

Suddenly the blood seemed to be coursing through my veins at a supersonic speed. "*Incantesimo di silenziamento*? How—? Where did you learn Italian magic? Did you find . . . ?"

Her eyes lit up. "Oh! No, I'm sorry! I haven't found anything of León's. Oh my God, if I had, I would have run straight here!"

"Then where?"

"It's Ren. He's possessed by an Italian boy's ghost who seems to have completely taken over Ren's mind. He keeps repeating that phrase over and over."

"It might not be that Ren's mind is completely gone, rather that someone doesn't want him talking. Someone magical, that is. It means Silencing Spell."

Her brow pinched in thought. "*Ritha,*" she whispered. "That makes total sense actually."

She paused as if giving me a chance to pick a new subject. I didn't, so she asked about our hunt and the condition of the witch she'd burnt, the whole time twirling a lock of her hair. I couldn't remember the last time she'd been this nervous around me. Even though they were all valid questions, it felt like small talk. I hated making fucking small talk with her.

She said something about her failed Spektral magic attempts with Isaac, and the words spilled out of my mouth. "You got back together with him . . ."

"How did you know?"

"We ran into each other."

"When?"

"Tonight."

She frowned. "What did he say about me?"

"He didn't have to say anything. Your scent was all over him."

Thump-thump. Thump-thump.

"I— He walked me— We did a ritual, so— I don't have anything to be ashamed of."

"I'm not trying to shame you."

Her gaze dropped. "I know."

"What made you change your mind about him?"

She dazedly fiddled with the feather on her chain, and I wanted to rip the arm off the chair. "I don't know. You were right: it wasn't his fault, about Brigitte. He cares about me. He makes me feel safe. And calm."

"You're a Fire witch," I snapped. "Maybe you don't need to feel calm, maybe you need to be impassioned!"

She crossed her arms and gave me a challenging look: a clear *And what are you going to do about it?*

We both knew the answer was nothing.

"Nicco . . . when I'm with you, I feel like I can take on the world because you believe in me. But you don't believe in *us.* Isaac believes in us more than he believes in anything."

"I'm sorry. I want to. I just know it's not—" I stood up. "I'm a . . ."

She stood too. "I know," she said softly.

She drew near, her eyes locked with mine, and I knew I was staring into my last chance. My last chance to kiss her.

When I didn't move, she leaned closer, until her lips pressed against my jaw. My spine released the slightest shiver at her touch.

"I know," she said again, and I swear I could physically feel her slipping away.

Thump-thump. Thump-thump. Thump-thump.

The feeling of pain was so foreign to me that for a second I said nothing. Then the fear of her leaving struck hard. "Can I ask you one question?"

She nodded.

"Why didn't you ever tell him about your mother?"

"I don't know . . ." Her eyes wandered away. "I guess I was scared."

"Why were you scared, Adele?"

All I got back were the thumps of her heart.

"Don't you . . . trust him?"

She looked back at me, her eyes glistening. "This isn't fair! *You* were the one who encouraged me. Pushed me to go back to him. To forgive him! Over and over, every time I tried to get close to you!"

"I know. I'm sorry." I took her hand between mine. "You deserve to be happy. He cares for you deeply. And for your father."

"Are you ready, Niccolò?" Emilio's voice asked from behind us.

We turned to see him standing in the doorway.

"*Sì, un minute, por favore.*" I turned back to Adele. "We're going back out to the swamp. There's so much ground to cover, and it's been raining so often, we've lost time."

She nodded and we stood. "Please, be safe."

"We will, *bella*."

I walked her out to the foyer. Just as I reached for the front door handle, she looked back up at me. "I almost forgot the reason I came over . . ."

"Oh?"

"We're having a party at the tearoom tomorrow, after closing. It's the last day of April."

Floralia.

"There will be a moon circle at midnight for Hexennacht."

"The Witch's Night."

She smiled gently. She was nervous about whatever she was going to ask. "I would really love it if you came."

I couldn't hide my surprise. "What?"

"You could meet the rest of my friends. I mean, meet them for real. It's nothing fancy, but it should be fun. And you know . . . being around other witches . . ."

"I'm a vampire."

"Yes, Nicco, I am acutely aware of that."

"I don't think it would be such a good idea, *bella*."

"Why not? You'll be my guest."

"You're being naïve," I snapped.

She looked startled. I'd never used that kind of tone with her.

"I know you would be very welcoming," I said in a softer voice, "but no one wants me dancing around their fire."

"I do."

I kissed her cheeks. "*Grazie* for the invitation."

"If you change your mind." She pulled a card from her pocket.

It was a handwritten note. *She made me an invitation.*

I nodded and thanked her again. "*Buonanotte*."

I watched her walk down the steps to the gate. I'd barely closed the door when Emilio's voice rang out from behind me: "What the hell was that?"

He was leaning on the doorframe to the parlor room, arms crossed. "A few days ago, you two were practically getting married."

I sucked a breath in through my nose. "You thought incorrectly."

"He did not!" Gabriel said from the mezzanine.

I groaned, throwing my head back.

He started down the stairs. "The girl you are in love with invites you to a party—on *Floralia*—and you say no?"

"Did you not see the feather around her neck?"

He stepped near. "Did you not see all of the other trinkets on her chain? Stop being an imbecile. I know you see the way she looks at you, Niccolò . . . because it's the same way you look at her."

"She's a distraction," I said.

"Agreed," Emilio echoed, staying in the shadows.

"So what?" Gabe sat on the bottom stair. "I like having her around. It reminds me of when Giovanna was with us."

There was something about the way he'd said *with us* that caught my attention. "Don't get too used to it. She's never going to be *with us.* We're never going to be together."

"Oh, stop acting like there isn't a way."

My fangs snapped out with a hiss. And then I was directly in front of him as he stood. "Gabriel, don't even think about it!" My pulse roiled, hearing the equal parts anger and desperation in my voice—I never lost control this badly.

"Stop pretending like you never think about her that way, Niccolò," Gabriel said.

I steadied my breathing, not allowing my heartbeat to rise and draw attention to my pulse.

"Strong," he continued. "Unbreakable. Beautiful. Someone to love for eternity. Someone to love you, so you can stop hating yourself."

"I can think of *nothing* that would make me hate myself more."

"Well, maybe you don't have to be involved in her transition. What if one night you wake up, and she's just . . . here."

Emilio snickered.

"Do not touch her, Gabriel. I don't want her! I want to find León. I want our grimoire. I want *l'elisir di vita!* It's the only way . . ." my voice trailed.

"It's the only way for what?" Emilio asked, coming toward us. "*L'elisir di vita* is not going to cure your vampirism. It's not going to bring your magic back."

"It made León immortal . . . You have no idea what the Elixir can do. I have eternity to figure things out if I just have—"

"I thought you would have learned after Maddalena," Gabriel said.

I took a step back. "What the hell is that supposed to mean?"

"It means do not take time for granted. You're obsessed with the Elixir now, just like you were back then in your laboratory, Niccolò, but there is more to life than magic—and Adele doesn't have forever." He stepped right in front of me, forcing my gaze an inch higher to meet his. "*Fratellino*, you might be able to temper your pulse, your breath, and every muscle in your being as if you were truly made of stone, but even you can't control your soul. And when that girl walks into the room, the glint in your eyes shines brighter than I have seen it in over four hundred years. And when she leaves, it dims like a dwindling star."

Thump-thump. Thump-thump.

"Take the night off, Nicco. Go to that party. I know you think you are the brains of this family, but you aren't." He touched my shoulder. "You are our heart."

I looked back up.

"*Go* get her."

PART III
THE GHOST DRINKERS

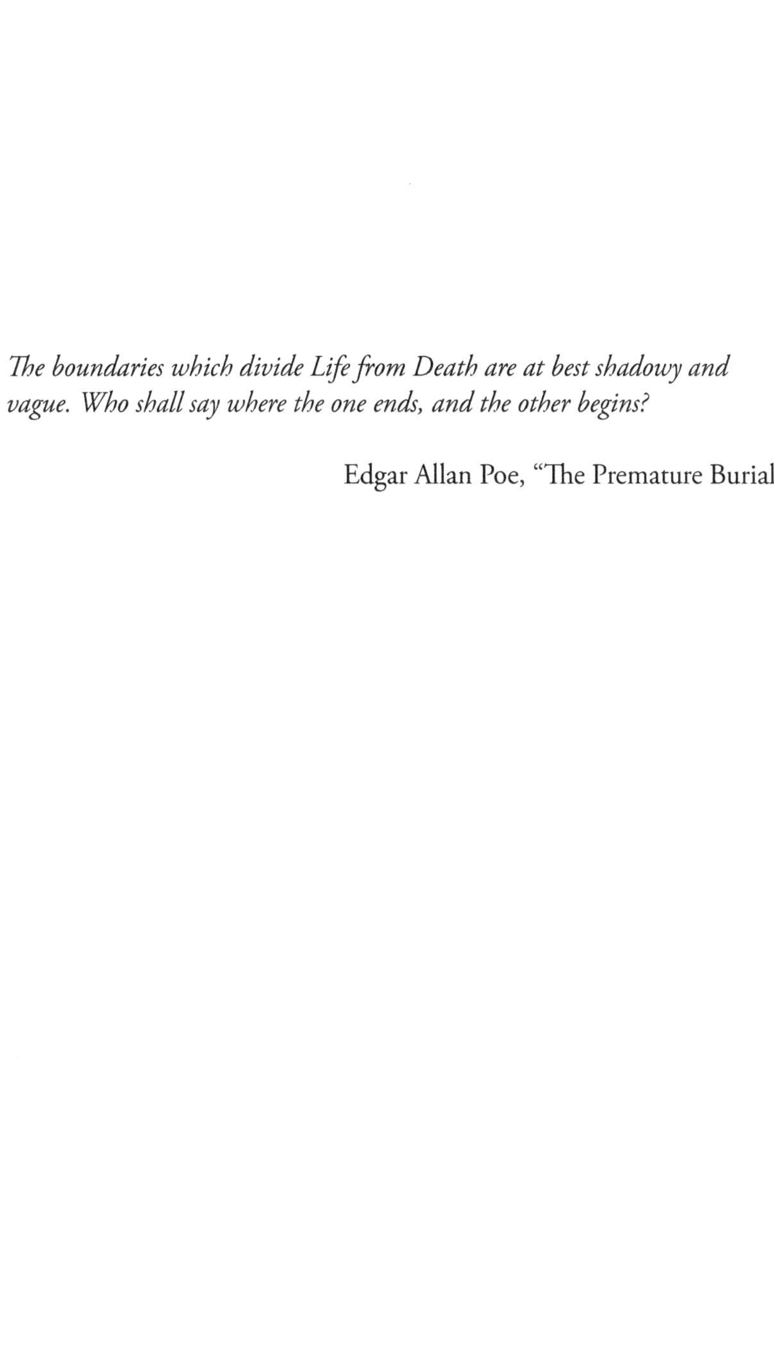

The boundaries which divide Life from Death are at best shadowy and vague. Who shall say where the one ends, and the other begins?

Edgar Allan Poe, "The Premature Burial"

CHAPTER 46

HEXENNACHT

April 30th

I put on one of my dad's Louis Armstrong records and sipped café-au-*not-faux*-lait from my strawberry mug, thumbing through hangers in my closet. It was the Eve of Beltane, as the night was described in Isaac's grimoire; or Hexennacht, as the Daures celebrated it; or Zaka Day, as the Borges called it, the midpoint between spring equinox and summer solstice. It meant a night off of coven duties, and it bought me a day to come up with the best way to tell Dee that I wasn't going to the Afterworld.

She'd texted me a dozen times this morning—if you could call noon morning—and only one message was about the Ghede; the rest were outfit planning. She'd never asked me about an outfit before. *Ever.* I wondered if it had something to do with tonight's host.

I flipped a hanger, trying to outfit plan myself, and not to think about how Nicco had pretty much shut the door in my face last night. *Nope, definitely not thinking about that.*

When I'd asked Fiona what one wears to such an event, she'd said, "Something that represents creation! Blossoming! Exuberance for life!" It sounded like something Madame Faucheux, the master seamstress at the Parisian atelier, would have said in my couture workshop last fall, leaving us all mulling over bolts of fabric and our naked dress forms. *Paris.*

I set the strawberry mug down on my nightstand, went to the little closet room, and dragged out the antique traveling trunk. I popped the latches.

Inside was the treasure trove of half-made garments from the workshop. I pulled them out, examining each. We'd constructed several different bodices, learning new techniques to structure garments so the delicate fabric could support elaborate embellishment. I set aside one that was covered in sequins and another made entirely of lace. I placed a navy-blue quilted satin that I *loved* in the "maybe" pile and kept looking for something more springish. Green was the color of the evening, and the only piece I'd made had been used for *la fée verte* costume, which now had bloodstains, thanks to Lisette slashing at my throat. *Fairies.*

I spun around and whisked over to the garment rack nestled between the windows.

For my mentorship last year, I'd worked for the costume department on a college production of *A Midsummer Night's Dream*, and I'd been so in love with one of Titania's dresses I'd assisted on, my mentor let me keep it after closing night. I pushed aside the other in-progress creations on the rack so I could view it fully.

The skirt was made of layers of sheer, pale-nude silk organza that matched my skin tone. And it had a rose-gold metallic shift that glimmered in the light. Two-inch-wide rainbow stripes were woven through the silk with terracotta, salmon, ochre, and mauve metallic threads, and they would have lined up in a chevron pattern, if the layers hadn't been purposefully cut out at random. Copper arcs bent toward the stripes, giving it extra dimension. The sleeveless bodice was nothing more than the sheer organza, dipping in a *V* all the way to the navel and plunging equally daringly in the back. The rainbow threads covered the right breast but not the left, and I remember being mesmerized by the actress who wore it—her utter confidence and commitment to the role. She'd been not at all fazed by how much of her body was visible.

I pulled it from the rack, lifted one side of the skirt out, and fell in love with it all over again. It was the fanciest thing I owned by a million. I remembered thinking that maybe one day I'd be invited to a

Mardi Gras ball I could wear it to. It wasn't exactly green, but I didn't care—I had an idea.

I tossed it on the bed and went back to the trunk. Hidden underneath the embellished bustiers was a simple bodice: a similar pale-nude organza, square neckline with a bias-cut ruffle, boxy crop at the waist. The organza straps lay so flat, they were hardly visible against the skin—it had been an exercise in creating a nude illusion.

I held it up to the skirt. It didn't have the same metallic shift, but I loved the pieces together anyway.

And so I spent the afternoon carefully removing the top of the dress and adding a waistband to the skirt out of scraps of gold metallic fabric.

It had been so long since I'd created a garment, I'd forgotten the sheer joy it brought me. With each stitch, I became more excited about just having the night off and being surrounded by the Daures' fervor for magic, dressing up, drinking punch, and spending time with my coven. And Isaac. I was glad Nicco knew we were working it out. It relieved a building pressure I hadn't realized was there.

I'd analyzed every detail of our conversation, going back and forth on whether Nicco simply didn't want to be my friend or only wanted to be my friend in the shadows. The former unnerved me completely, so I supposed the shadows were something I'd have to live with, if I wanted to continue working with him to find Callis and to end this feud between his family and mine. I couldn't force him to be a bigger part of my life.

But still . . . I had this fantasy where he was.

I knew it sounded ridiculous, inviting him to the party to be around all of my most beloved friends, but he was magical, just like them. He had his Mark, and I was certain they'd like him—that they wouldn't see him as a monster—if they just knew him. Even Isaac.

Sigh.

We'd stayed up late texting, so I knew Isaac had crashed the moment he got off work. I hoped he slept right up to the event, but I kept checking my phone as I showered, shaved, and prepped my hair to dry. There'd been messages from Codi and Dee; one from my dad, confirming receipt of my plans; one from Edgar, reminding me to bring the box of champagne flutes my dad had left for him; and one from Codi's cousin, Dahlia, asking to borrow a pair of sandals.

My phone buzzed.

Désirée 8:09 p.m. Too much?

A mirror-selfie popped up, showing her ensemble: a strapless dress, the bodice constructed of dark brown leather, and the asymmetrical multi-layered skirt cut from green and pink chiffon that tapered into points. All of her jewelry was gold: wrist cuffs, hoop earrings, a namesake necklace among tiered chains, but the coolest part of the look was the crown made of real ivy. She looked like an earthen goddess.

Adele 8:11 p.m. Love it. It's banjee meets wood-nymph.

Désirée 8:12 p.m. Totally what I was going for. See you soon.

I tossed the phone on my bed, picked up my bottle of lavender moisturizer, and coated every inch of my skin. *Well, I smell blossomy.* As my hair dried, the waves got bigger and bigger. I twisted the front into braids and secured them at the back of my head. Dewy blush on my cheeks. Golden shimmer across my eyelids. Mascara. And my favorite plum-colored lip gloss.

I slid on the skirt, secured the band high on my waist, and strapped on tan leather sandals. The skirt layers hung perfectly just above the floor. Last but not least, I delicately slipped my arms through the top and slid it down over my head, careful not to pop any stitches in the thin fabric.

I shook it out, remembering exactly how short the crop of the top was, just barely covering my stomach—thank God the skirt didn't sit low—but when I walked to the dressing mirror, I didn't care. It was perfect.

I twisted around, and both the skirt and the top puffed out. When the layers lay flat again, the skirt gave my hips a fullness that made me smile at myself. The jewelry I usually wore was all too much for the dainty top, so I wrapped the gris-gris around my wrist and opted for just the single Leo constellation necklace. It sparkled against my throat when I moved.

I grabbed my phone:

Adele 9:38 p.m. This is your wake-up text! I'm heading over a little early to bring some things. Xo

Isaac 9:38 p.m. Getting in the shower now. Then swinging by to pick up Dee. See you there.

Isaac 9:39 p.m. Wait. How dressed up are we supposed to be for this thing tonight? Codi just said he's wearing seersucker. What the hell is that?

I smiled as I typed out a response.

Adele 9:40 p.m. Something that represents creation! Blossoming! Exuberance for life!

Isaac 9:40 p.m. Uhhhhhh...............?

Adele 9:40 p.m. You'll be beautiful no matter what you wear. Just hurry! <3

I stuffed my phone into my bag, along with the shoes for Codi's cousin, and hustled down the stairs. Mac had left the case of champagne flutes and a bottle of Chartreuse by the front door so I wouldn't forget them. With the box and the bottle rested on each of my hips, I was off.

As I walked down the street into the twinkling night, I once again felt like Queen Titania.

It was strange to feel the eyes of people turning to look at me when I got to Bourbon, not just because they were gawking because I was overdressed, but because . . . there were people. The curfew had been lifted and it was Friday night. There were no tourists and not many venues had reopened, but music pumped out of the ones that had: the pounding of jazz piano, the bass of dance clubs, the disco beats of live karaoke. People were merry and drinking in the streets, the local colleges were on spring break, and it seemed like every other block had a sash-wearing bride-to-be. Apparently, we weren't the only ones celebrating under the full moon tonight.

The doorway and windowsills outside the tearoom were draped with strings of flowers, as if I really was about to enter a fairyland. The bell jingled as I opened the door.

Codi was on the phone, standing near his two brothers behind the counter. Cameron, seeing me juggling to keep hold of everything, swept over to help me with the box.

"I've got it, thanks, if you could just get the door."

"Whoa, Adele, I barely recognized you! When did you turn into such a babe?"

"Um? Thanks?"

Codi's nose scrunched; whether he was grossed out by the question or the thought was unclear.

Scents filled the shop from the back of the house, making my mouth water: the sweet aroma of cakes and the savory notes from something that might be roast with—I inhaled deeply, already loving Hexennacht—cloves? All three of them looked more cleaned up than usual, their customary athletic wear traded for pastel seersucker pants and white T-shirts. Codi and Caleb wore deck shoes, but Cameron was barefoot.

"No, sorry, Dad's out of town," Codi said into the phone. "But I can get you in with Olsin tomorrow afternoon."

"Chatham and Poppy are still in Shreveport?" I asked Cam.

"Apparently they're having a hard time getting the specter to come out and play. Dad only likes to use magical force when absolutely necessary."

The air around us shuddered, and I wondered if it was Julie.

Codi motioned to the hallway with his head. "Fiona and Edgar are in the back."

I carried the box down the hall, past the psychic booths and through the kitchen. The laughter and chattering grew louder as I neared the courtyard. And then I stepped outside, straight into a magical forest.

Every inch of the bricked walls that bordered the property was covered in flowers: bluebells, daisies, lilacs, marigolds, pansies, roses, and violets. They were everywhere, lit up by tiny tealights resting in small bird's nests scattered around the courtyard. A dozen or so people stood around with drinks in hand. A few I recognized from being around the shop over the years, though I'd had no idea they were witches. Some wore flower crowns, and others were dressed in modern Choctaw regalia; some wore both. To my left, a huge fire pit blazed, and the water in the fountain at the back, where the marble water-nymph was always bathing, was lavender-colored tonight. But the real centerpiece was the multi-tiered flower crown atop the fifteen-foot-high pole constructed in the middle of the yard, from which colorful streamers hung down to the ground.

Edgar bustled down the length of a table, focused on putting the final garnishes on plates. For a moment, I wished Mac was here, arriving with me, witchy goodies in hand.

I set the box on one of the many tables, each one displaying the most beautiful foods I'd ever seen: green-ombréd teacakes in the shape of hearts decorated with pink frosting and baby rose petals, a cheesecake covered with lilac crystals of rock candy, ginger cakes drizzled with honey and passion fruit. There were cheeses, meats, nuts. Fig truffles and elderflower lollipops. Pitchers of fizzy drinks filled with bobbing cherries and blueberries and blackberries and violets. I'd never seen anything so extravagant, not even in a movie. I did a double take at a bread basket. *Are those?* I lifted a towel to peer inside. *Yes. Yes, they are. Individual phallic-shaped breads, balls and all.* I secured the towel so they wouldn't get cold. No one wants cold balls. *Blossoming! Creation! Exuberance!*

Codi stepped out into the courtyard, leading two more couples. He showed them to the booze and then came over to greet me.

"Dad might have gone a little wild," he said. "This past year sucked so bad for everyone, Edgar wanted to go all out."

"Well, that he certainly did."

"I have a surprise for you."

"Nothing's going to top all of this."

"Oh, I think it might. I got . . . " His voice trailed off as his attention moved to the house. I turned around, sure that Désirée, in all of her earthen goddessness, had arrived and rendered him speechless.

But it wasn't.

Thump-thump.

Thump-thump.

Thump-thump.

Nicco was standing in the doorway with a brown wicker basket and paper bag in one hand, and a jug of something pink and frothy in the other.

"You got Nicco to come?" I asked under my breath. "Is he your surprise?"

"Hell no. I mean, he's definitely *a* surprise."

Nicco looked our way.

"Does Isaac know about this?" Codi whispered.

"No," I said, waving him over with a bright smile.

"You didn't think telling him would be a good idea?"

"Nicco declined my invitation. There was nothing to tell. Do you think I should text him?"

"Now?"

Nicco was already striding across the courtyard to greet us, the pink liquid sloshing and bubbling inside the jug. He was wearing a navy-blue button down, sleeves rolled up to his elbows, exposing the mark he usually kept so carefully hidden. I wondered if he felt like he had to prove he belonged here.

"Too late," Codi said.

"Hi." I tried not to burst with excitement.

CHAPTER 47

GREAT EXPECTATIONS

I entered the Voodoo Shop, feeling a little like I'd overreacted when I'd come here last night demanding the elixir from Désirée. Maybe it was the late-night marathon text messaging with Adele, or the intense day of manual labor, or the nap I'd taken after work, but I was calmer tonight.

Désirée, with a ring of green leaves on her head, was behind the counter, corking a small vial. "You ready?" I asked. She had on way more jewelry than usual and her arms and shoulders were shimmering bronze. "Wait, are we supposed to be dressed up for this thing?" I already felt formal wearing a new white shirt, pale-gray chinos instead of jeans, and Converse instead of work boots.

She glanced up. "You're fine. Just pull your hair back." She handed me a rubber band from her wrist.

I gathered my hair behind my head and tied it into a tiny nub. One little section fell in my face.

She leaned over and tucked it behind my ear. "There."

"I'm sorry about last night."

"So you've come to your senses about wanting this elixir."

"Well, I mean, you already made it. But don't worry. I'll save it for an emergency." I knocked on the wooden counter.

"Then why don't I hold onto it?"

I shrugged. "Fine."

"Really?"

"Sure. As long as it's activated."

"Why does that matter?"

"Well, if it's for emergencies, what good is it if we have to stop and do a ritual before drinking it?"

"True." She lit a candle, held a small palo santo stick over the flame, and quickly cleansed the air around us. With my hands in hers, she spoke the incantation. I joined in on the second verse, and silver sparkles rose from the bottom of the vial, shimmering through the viscous liquid like shards of glass.

"All right," I said, stepping back, but she squeezed my hands.

"*Not* that you are going to need this information right now, since you won't be taking the elixir, but I just want to remind you of a few things." She gave me a hard look, dead in the eyes.

"Okay."

"Heightening elixirs affect everyone differently. It depends on your size, health, hydration level, and your natural susceptibility to magic. It will heighten all of your natural abilities, physical, magical, and emotional. It will not—I repeat, *not*—make you as strong or as fast as a vampire. Do you understand me?" She held my hands even tighter.

I nodded, but she still didn't let go.

"And remember, the last time we took this elixir, we also drugged the vampires to slow them down. It won't be like that."

"I remember." I leaned over and kissed her cheek. "But thanks for being so concerned. Let's go."

"Why are you so anxious to get there?"

"I don't know. Tonight's the night."

"For what?"

"I'm going to ask Adele to . . . I don't know, to forgive me. To be my girlfriend or whatever. Don't let me wuss out."

"She's not your girlfriend already?"

"Maybe. I don't know. Do you think she is?"

"Guess I've just always thought of you guys as being together."

"I just want to be sure."

"Sounds reasonable." She slipped the little vial into the side pouch of her bag and zipped it closed.

As soon as we stepped out of the shop and began walking, butterflies tossed around the empty echo chamber of my stomach. I could envision the night ahead so clearly: witches, and moonlight rituals, and dancing, and then sneaking away with Adele, and the impossibly soft feeling of her skin.

CHAPTER 48

SOULS OF THINGS

"*Buonasera*," Nicco said, a hint of uncertainty behind his eyes.

I beamed as I awkwardly stepped forward, unsure how to greet him, especially in front of Codi. "You came."

He leaned in and kissed each of my cheeks. "If the invitation is still open?"

"Of course."

He glanced at Codi for affirmation, and Codi somehow managed to stumble over the word "sure."

"Your brothers let me in," Nicco said and handed him the jug. "And my brothers made this, so it's probably strong."

"Thanks." Codi looked at me and then back to him. "I guess I'll go put it with the rest of the booze."

As Codi walked away, Nicco set the basket down. "I'm sorry for the way I acted last night."

"It's okay. I'm just glad you're here." *Calm down, Adele.* "What made you change your mind?"

He smiled and uncrumpled the top of the brown bag, but he didn't answer the question. He lifted out what at first looked like a bouquet of flowers, but then I realized it was a wreath. "I brought you this."

"It's beautiful." Tiny white flowers had been woven throughout the masterful twists of marigolds, pansies, and pinkish-purple flowers shaped like bells. "Shall we put it on the front door?" I wanted him to know how truly welcome he was.

"It's not a wreath." He smiled again, set the bag down, and held out the flowers horizontally.

I blushed, realizing it was a crown.

"May I?"

I nodded and he placed it on my head. "Happy Floralia," he said softly, the reflections of tealights flickering in his eyes.

Thump-thump.

"What's Floralia?" I asked, feeling like my voice was detached from my person.

"Long before Beltane, there was a festival in ancient Rome to honor Flora, the goddess of blossoms. It was a favorite time of year for my family."

I imagined him in Florence with his family, dancing and drinking in the Mediterranean air, celebrating the turning of the seasons with his coven.

"There were six days of games and six nights of theatrical performances and circuses and sacrifices to please the goddess so in return she would bless the people throughout the year with hearty crops and fertility."

"Adele, is that you?" Fiona yelled joyously. The ribbons tied to her hair fluttered as she flounced across the courtyard from a group of people over to us. "Heavens, you look just like your moth—" She clapped her hand over her mouth. "You look like you just stepped out of a fairy tale." She took my hand and pulled me a couple steps closer, forcing me into a slow twirl. "Did you make this?"

"Most of it. Sorry, I didn't have anything green."

"Are you kidding? You look like the Beltane—"

"Fire," Nicco finished.

"Exactly." She smiled and eyed the crown. "Two-toned primrose, foxglove, sweet woodruff," she said, naming all the flowers I hadn't recognized. "A basket of sweets. Someone knows their traditions."

"Call me old-fashioned."

My abs twitched as I held in the laugh. He looked at me like, *What?*

"I'm Fiona Daure." She extended her hand. "And I thought I knew all the Fire witches in the state."

"Niccolò Medici."

Fiona chewed her lip, thinking. "Medici, as in the Great Fire witches of Florence?"

"Precisely."

I think we both held our breath as we waited for the next question.

"But where were you able to find fresh woodruff?" she asked. "Do you have a greenhouse?"

I slowly exhaled.

"It's incredible what you can discover if you go deep enough into the marshes of Acadiana," Nicco said.

She nodded, impressed, but her expression showed an underlying hint of skepticism.

He handed her the brown paper bag. "Shortbread."

She graciously accepted it and bowed away. That seemed to go okay.

I turned to him. "You spent the day picking wildflowers in Cajunland?"

"Not the whole day." He picked up the basket and handed it to me. "Some of it was spent picking strawberries, and some of it was spent baking."

I peeked into the basket. It was filled with wild strawberries and something I didn't immediately recognize as cookies because they were so beautiful: round shortbread with scalloped edges. Each had a large purple pansy pressed flat on top. A glaze made them shine like something from the fanciest of Parisian patisseries.

I took a small bite of one, petal and all. It was simple and buttery and sweet and lavendery.

"You bake?" I asked.

"Despite everything I've told you, and everything you've seen in my dreams, there are still things you don't know about me."

"I'd like to know them all." My eyes widened when I realized I had said it out loud.

He struggled not to smile. "I'd like that, *bella*."

Thump-thump.

Codi sauntered past, trying to be sly. I pulled him over. "Codi, this is Nicco. I don't think I properly introduced you before." I wondered if Dee and Isaac were close. I wanted them all to get to know each other.

Codi hesitated, as if eyeing him up, and then nodded. "What's up, man?"

"It's nice to finally meet you. Adele's told me a lot about you."

I had no idea if this was an appropriate level of awkwardness when trying to integrate a vampire into your life, or above average.

But then Codi extended his hand. "I never got to thank you for helping us that night at the convent. Pretty sure we almost got roasted alive."

Nicco shook his hand. "I can say the thanks goes both ways."

I exhaled.

Nicco nodded back to the tearoom. "It's hard to believe that it's been a hundred years since this place opened. Seems like yesterday."

Codi snorted, trying to not laugh. "So weird." He leaned closer to me. "Hey, remember that surprise?"

I nodded, and Nicco eyed us, curious.

"Hang on to this." Codi held out his hand to mine. "If my parents find out I swiped it, they'll wig."

He transferred a small metal object, pressing his palm to mine. I wavered forward . . .

And . . . was . . .

Out.

Light flashed across my eyelids.

And then everything went dark again.

My head was resting on stone. *The courtyard bricks?* The chill seeped through the organza skirt. I shivered forcefully as a breeze rushed over me, whirling and swirling away the fog above. A white light appeared overhead: the clouds parting from over the moon.

The silhouette of a looming winged creature came into focus. I scrambled back before realizing it was only the stone-cold expression of a gargoyle. *What the hell?*

The clattering of hooves echoed faintly in the night, rising up from beyond a surrounding stone wall. *Where am I?* I got up and looked over. Far below, torches flickered all the way down a hill to a medieval gate. I spun around: the stone tower. *I can't be in the fortress. It's in Spain!* I looked back just in time to see a horse charging up to the castle carrying a shadowy figure.

Callis?

I ran to the tower door but jolted back when a wall torch revealed a stern man standing guard. He had to have seen me, but he didn't so much as flinch. *What the hell?* I slowly moved past, tiptoeing right in front of him. His gaze didn't flicker.

What the hell? What the hell? I wound down the wide stone staircase to a giant hall big enough to hold hundreds of dancing couples. As I passed through, I imagined them twirling around me in lavish gowns and plume-topped hats. I didn't know where I was going or why, but something compelled me onward: a ghostly leash, pulling me through the cold, dark castle, room after room, at a speed that made me breathless. I entered an enormous medieval kitchen just in time to see a young man slip out through a door on the other side.

Fear pricked through my veins, a lurking feeling of doom that something bad would happen if I didn't keep up. I'd never felt an intuition so strong. I was supposed to be with the boy.

I crossed the room and reached for the door, but my hand went right through the latch. Panic arose, but I had a peculiar thought and reached out again. My hand passed through the wooden door. Holding my breath and pinching my eyes shut, I took a step forward—straight through the door—and gasped as darkness enveloped me. The freezing, damp air and pitch black pressed in all around me, and a sense of claustrophobia tightened my spine. I walked on, arms raised, until my fingertips scraped the jagged rock wall of a narrow corridor. This path was only for those who knew the way.

The compulsion grew stronger. I *needed* to catch up with the boy.

Footsteps echoed from up ahead.

I moved faster.

A small flame materialized on the stone floor, illuminating the confining passageway before me. I hurried along, and another flame appeared from the darkness, and another, like breadcrumbs on the stone floor until there were none. But it didn't matter; my feet didn't slow—a warm, pervasive halo lit the immediate area around me, guiding me. I glanced down, shocked to find the Mark on my arm glowing bright orange like embers burning through my skin.

Another light appeared farther down the corridor. "Adele!" called a familiar voice from up ahead.

"Codi?" The warmth of the compulsion grew with each step.

He was standing at a three-way fork of passages, a lit torch in his hand.

"What the hell is happening?" he asked, panting. "Something's . . . pulling me this way. Something warm."

"I don't know. I was following a boy. I think it's Callis."

"I haven't seen anyone but two guards getting it on in an armory room. I didn't know people could get so turned on by weap—"

"Codi! We have to keep going!" The urge to enter the tunnel to my left became so strong, I stumbled toward it involuntarily and fell, skinning my knees and palms on the stone.

"You okay?" he asked, helping me up. A braided silver ring on his middle finger glinted under the light of the torch. Each of his brothers wore them too.

The ring.

"Come on!" Still hanging onto his hand, I started to run down the tunnel. "I think we're supposed to be with the ring!"

A wooden door came into view. Codi dropped the torch, and the flame disappeared. My hand didn't go through this time. I fumbled it open, pushed it out, and we tumbled onto the floor of a dark room. We'd fallen straight out of . . . an armoire?

Codi pulled me closer as a shadowy figure moved in front of the faintly glowing embers in the fireplace. Metal scraped stone, and the embers coughed up tiny flames in the dark.

The figure added tinder, and the flames grew, illuminating the face of the boy crouching in front of it: young Callis. He still wore the gloves, but the rest of the costume was gone. He was back in the dingy shirt, stolen doublet and boots.

As the fire grew, a bed came into view. A boy of about ten or eleven was tucked in, asleep. The fire began to crackle, and Callis moved back to sit next to the boy. Without removing his gloves, he pulled a silk scarf from a pouch and wiped the sweat from the child's brow, cheeks, and neck.

The boy stirred awake.

"I just came to relight your fire, little brother, so your feet wouldn't be cold."

He smiled affectionately. "I got my Mark, Callisto."

"I know, little one."

"Papá said I'm even younger than you when you got yours. That we are destined for greatness."

"Of course we are." Callis tousled the boy's hair.

"I want to be just like you."

"And you will be, but now go back to sleep. You can show me your Mark again at breakfast, but don't forget, you can't tell Celestina, for she does not have hers yet."

"I know. I won't."

Callis waited until the boy's breaths purred and then reclaimed his place in front of the fire, standing and gazing into the flames. He tossed the scarf and the leather pouch it had come from into the fire, and then carefully removed the gloves and tossed them in too.

He turned around, his head backlit by the orange flames, and looked down at his hand. "I am destined for greatness." He straightened the ring on his finger, and then glanced over at us, as if something had just caught his attention.

He took two steps closer, and Codi's arm slipped firmly around my torso. My heart pounded.

Callis glanced down at the Mark on my arm, and then back into my eyes, reeling with confoundedness.

I gasped.

"Adele?" Codi asked. "Are you okay?"

I sucked in a huge gulp of air. Something cold trickled down my neck and chest.

"Adele, are you okay?" Nicco had an empty glass in his hand.

Water dripped from my chin. I wiped it away, looking at Codi. His face was soaking wet too.

"Dude," he said. "What *was* that?"

"Just water." Nicco held my wrist, checking my pulse. "You were unconscious."

"Not that." He looked at me. "Do you remember it?"

The rush of supernatural sensation railed through me, ten times stronger than either of the previous flashes. I sat up with excitement. "I can still *feel* it."

"Adele," Codi whispered. "Try to move something!"

I turned to Nicco, who gave me a concerned but encouraging shrug.

I focused on the nearest refreshment table. A jar of forks.

"Don't take my eye out, okay?" Nicco said, and I smiled, thinking how long ago that night in the diner now felt.

I ignored everyone as guests began coming our way trying to figure out what was going on. I could hear them murmuring about the girl who'd lost her magic. I pulled until my shoulders and neck strained and my head hurt, but it felt like I was pulling a gargantuan chain wrapped around a skyscraper and expecting it to move. *Ridiculous.*

"Do it again," Codi said, crouching next to Nicco. "You got this!"

I shot him a grateful smile—and froze. "C-Codi," I said, my breaths short. My heart sank, though I tried not to show it. "It's not my magic."

"Don't be like that. Positive attitudes yield positive results."

"Codi . . . It's yours." I nodded at his glowing seersucker jacket sleeve.

He ripped off his jacket. His Mark, a downward-pointing triangle, shone bright blue. "Dad!" He jumped up. "*Daaad!*"

"Thank God!" Caleb shouted.

Both his brothers ran over and sandwiched him, chest bumping him back and forth.

"What the heck is going on?" Edgar asked from the doorway.

"Codi got his Mark!" Dahlia yelled, and all of his cousins began surrounding him.

"Oh my!" Edgar and Fiona bustled over, trailing other party guests and beaming with pride.

The crowd swarmed over Codi, bubbling with questions about his Spektral and exclaiming how amazing it was that it had finally happened, and on Beltane.

I shook as I pushed the tears further inside me, into a tiny chest with a thousand locks, buried in the center of my soul. I tried to latch onto their joy, but all I felt was loneliness . . . a detachment from everything witchy. *Maybe I'll never get my magic back.*

"It's okay," Nicco whispered next to my ear for only me to hear. "Your magic's inside you, I swear."

I nodded quickly, not letting my eyes leave Codi, afraid that if I looked anywhere but at him, the smile I'd managed would break. I didn't know what made me feel worse: that all this time, the flashes hadn't been signs of my own magic coming back, or that I wasn't jumping with joy for one of my best friends who just got his Mark, out of fear that I might cry.

"What did he hand you before you both passed out?" Nicco asked, trying to pull my mind back from the dark hole it was teetering on.

"A ring." My voice shook in an embarrassing way.

"Did it show you something from a bygone time?"

I nodded.

"It's called psychometry. The ability to see the souls of things."

I tried to answer, but nothing came out. His fingertips stroked my back. The connection helped ground me. "What does that mean?"

"As objects cycle through existence, they have different owners, experiences, each one of those people and places leaving behind traces of energy embedded into the object. The magical are more in tune with this essence, which is why, as witches, we get so attached to our talismans. A funny Spektral power for the son of psychics, eh, *bella*? Seeing into the past . . ."

My smile became real, and I turned to him. "You said 'we.' We witches and our talismans."

He touched my cheek.

Voices chirped all around us. Codi's brothers, aunts, and cousins were all still tugging at his arm. Edgar managed to get Chatham on a video call and gushed tears as he told him the news, holding the screen up to show him the party, all of his family yelling into the phone. Fiona uncorked a bottle of champagne, and Lilly and Dahlia brought out a three-tiered cake that Edgar had made. A section was carved out and filled with turquoise rock candy that looked just like the geodes inside the shop. Frosting on top inscribed Codi's name and today's date. "How'd he know?" Lilly asked.

"Oh, I just had a feeling," Edgar said, patting his eyes.

"Dad, don't cry."

I felt Nicco watching me. "Are you ready to get up now?"

I nodded, and he helped me to my feet, gently brushing off my skirt.

A voice boomed from across the courtyard: "Get off of her, now!"

Everyone fell silent, turning to Papa Olsin, who stood in the doorway with his walking stick in one hand and a wand hanging at his side in the other. Heads turned to me like a wave of dominos, following the trajectory of his gaze.

"How did you get in here?" he asked, raising the wand our way.

Nicco released me, holding his hands in the air, a look hidden behind his eyes that said he knew this was going to happen.

"I know what you are," Papa Olsin said, more indignant with every word. "You're going to leave now. And you're going to stay away from her."

"You'd better point that thing away from me, old man," Nicco said, his voice calm.

In a blink, Papa Olsin was gone, and Nicco's fangs snapped out with a hiss. A snarl came from the ground, and I jumped back as a panther padded toward us. Yellow eyes narrowing, glossy black tail swishing behind.

Edgar pulled Lilly and Dahlia back. "Addie, step away."

"No. I invited Nicco. He's my guest! He's a Fire witch, like me!"

"It's okay, Adele." Nicco's eyes locked on the witches behind them. "I'll be going now," he said with a dignified glare.

"I'm coming with you."

The panther growled.

"*No, bella, è la Floralia.* You should be with your coven." Undaunted, he pressed his lips to my cheek. "*Grazie* for the invitation."

Growls came from the crowd and two more panthers stalked toward their grandfather, not exactly full-grown but not exactly kittens. Caleb and Cameron.

Nicco nodded to those gathered behind the bristling cats. "*Ciao.*" And then he was gone, over the wall of flowers so quickly that petals blew in his wake.

Everyone's breath released at once. The crowd turned away, whispering to one another, but the Daures all rushed over, surrounding me. "How did you meet him?" "When?" "Where's Isaac?"

I wished I could jump over the wall like he did.

"Adele, has he ever laid a hand on you?" Edgar asked.

"I can't believe you all!" I exploded, mortified that my friends, people I considered to be my family, could be so presumptuous. "He's important to me!"

I twisted through them.

"Adele—" Edgar stepped forward, but I ran through the courtyard, hands reaching out to grab me.

I stopped at the door and turned around. Olsin, Edgar, Fiona, and all of their children were standing in front of me. I looked at Codi.

"Congrats on getting your Mark. I am really proud of you." I felt genuinely horrible that this had happened on his special night. I glanced at Edgar. "If it weren't for Nicco, your son and I would both be dead."

"Addie, don't leave," Papa Olsin said. "He's more trouble than you know."

"Good night." I stormed away.

"Go with her," Olsin called out, panic shaking his voice.

"I don't need a bodyguard!" I ran into the shop.

"Adele!" Codi yelled, all three of them following me past the psychic booths, Edgar's kimono fluttering.

"She doesn't know what she needs!" Papa Olsin roared. I looked back, hurrying past the counter—the fear I caught in his eyes made my heart palpitate.

Codi yelled my name again, but it was too late. I slammed the front door, desperately wishing for magic so I could hold it while I got a head start.

I took a left, but then leapt into the nearest alley, hiding in the dark, flat against the brick wall. Onyx darted down the street past me. I peeked out, watching him until he turned onto Toulouse, then I slipped out, going the other way down Royal.

CHAPTER 49

MONSTER

As I charged down the street at a blurring speed, all I could hear were pulses thumping, floating out of houses through chimneys, doors, and windows, mixing with the images of the party still hanging in my mind. The pulses of all those sleeping, working, and dancing in the Vieux Carré.

The more I listened, the fainter the thumps of Adele's heart became; and the fainter her pulse became, the more I craved her and the more each door I passed almost became the one I broke down to rip into any throat masking a pulse. My fangs swelled, shooting pain through my gums, the urge begging to tear flesh and pierce veins to quell the thirst. I imagined the blood spurting so forcefully that it choked me as I gorged.

I blazed through the front door.

"Back so soon?" Emilio called from the front parlor, as I tore up the stairs to the second floor. I felt the presence of Gabriel, Martine, and Lisette in the piano room—all reading? *All waiting up for me.*

"Niccolò!" Lisette yelled. "Did she like the crown?"

I didn't stop.

"Qu'est-ce qu'il y a, Niccolò?" Lisette asked, running through the hallway after me.

"Nothing's wrong!" I flew up the stairs to the attic and slammed the door. Sliding, turning, twisting the locks. I didn't bother with the light.

"Prince Charming's back already?" Raúl asked. "Not much stamina? We can hear your brother going all night."

Maybe they'd be his last words. When I turned to him, I hoped my eyes gleamed bright enough that he saw his death in them.

I jerked him from the floor, ripping his shirt open, the pain of the pull almost unbearable. Carina's scream pierced through the pitch black as my jaw clamped onto his neck. He writhed beneath me as my fangs sank deeper, spilling his blood into my throat. I swallowed breathlessly, the darkness enlivening my olfactory sense, making his scent ever more intoxicating.

This is my life. She will never fit into mine. And I will never fit into hers. I bit harder and the witch cried out. He began to go limp in my arms, losing consciousness. I pulled away, fighting the need to take every last ounce.

I am in New Orleans to find Callis, León, and l'elisir della vita. Not to go to Beltane parties.

I lifted him against the wall with a slam. "Where is he, witch? Where is Callisto?" Blood shook from my lips.

"I'll nev—"

"Shh!" I hissed, straining to listen.

Thump-thump.

The doorbell rang. Followed by knocks on the door.

"I bet that hope is in your eyes again," Carina said, trying to be cute.

I dropped Raúl, and before he thudded to the floor, I had her by the throat. She choked as I lifted her, her chains rattling. "There is no hope," I spat.

Thump-thump.

I heard the front door creak open.

I whipped out of the room and down the stairs to the foyer mezzanine and peeked out from beside a wardrobe.

Emilio was casually hanging between the partially opened door and the frame. "*Ta beauté vient de ta mère, ma cherie.*"

"Don't call me that," she snipped.

"It's a compliment."

"Don't talk about my mother to me . . . I'm here to see Nicco."

"Obviously."

I stepped to the mezzanine, my hands sliding over the railing, as I imagined luring her into the house, not even making it to my room before plunging into her. *I want to taste her.*

"Can you let me in please?"

Emilio twisted around and looked up at me.

I shook my head.

His nose scrunched, but he turned back to her. "Not a good time."

I zipped next to him, keeping hidden behind the door.

"Emilio!" She pushed it, but he held it in place with ease.

"Adele, no." He glanced my way, and I shook my head again. He rolled his eyes but turned back to her. "Nicco's not even here. He's probably out feeding." I barely refrained from kicking his leg.

"Why didn't you just say that?"

"And miss this?" he yelled as she started to walk off.

I ached as she got farther away. I wanted to go after her. I wanted to show all of those witches that we *could* be together. That they couldn't stop us. That no one could stop us.

I slid down against the door, my brother staring at me, his lip curling. "This must be what León felt like all those years around Giovanna." My head fell back. "Watching her, knowing he could never have her."

Emilio crouched down in front of me. "Do not kid yourself, brother. León had Giovanna. It might not have been in the perfect way they wanted—in the perfect way you want everything to be—but she had him, and he had her. No prince, no title, no number of jewels or kingdom borders could have kept those two from giving themselves to each other."

I stared at him. I knew my brother. He wanted me to go after her. Not because he wanted me to be happy like Gabriel did, but because he wanted me to lose control. He wanted me to destroy her. He wanted me to see that he and I were the same. "Until he killed her, you mean?"

"Séraphine killed Giovanna," Gabriel said, stepping out of the parlor to my left.

"But *he* let her out of the cage."

I will never hurt Adele.

I stood, not looking at either of them, cracked my neck, and headed back up the stairs to the attic, completely composed. Once inside, I slammed my fists into the thick oak door. *I want her.*

I took a deep breath, twisted the lock closed, and pulled the string to click on the light. *I want to hurt every person who's hurt her.* I grabbed a chair from the corner, spun it in front of the three prisoners, and straddled it.

"Tonight, one of you is going to tell me where Callisto is, or you're all going to die."

CHAPTER 50

UNQUESTIONABLE

I stormed down Royal Street with no real idea where I was headed. I could think of a few places Isaac might go, but I had no idea where Nicco would go to blow off steam.

My nails dug into my palms. *You naïve dummy, Adele.* I'd set Nicco up for his worst fear—not being accepted as a witch—and made it come true. I turned down Toulouse. *It should have been fine!* Ritha I could imagine getting all angry mother bear-ish, but the Daures were the most open-minded people I knew. *They didn't even give him a chance!*

"Little Miss Addie Le Moyne?" Troy's voice called from the courtyard gate at Le Chat Noir. "Is that you?"

I veered his way, forcing a smile. "Hi, Troy."

"Why ya so dressed up? Is it prom or something?"

"No, Beltane."

"What's that? A Mardi Gras krewe?"

"Something like that."

"You here to visit your daddy?"

"Yeah . . . I think I am."

He patted my shoulder as I passed him by.

The volume of the music grew with intensity as I whisked through the courtyard, up the stairs, down the hallway to the ballroom in the garçonnière. It had been months since I'd been here.

As soon as I stepped into the secret cabaret, Mac did a double take all the way from behind the bar. He was talking to a customer, but his gaze stayed locked on me as I crossed through the crowd. When I stopped right in front of him, he still didn't say anything.

"Hi," I said.

His eyes tightened, almost like Emilio's had.

"Are you okay?"

He blinked a couple of times. "Whoa, whoa, whoa. *What* are you wearing?"

"What do you mean?"

"What do I mean? You look half-naked!"

I sat on the barstool. "That's why it's called a nude illusion."

"Well, I'm getting way more nude than illusion." He started unbuttoning his black outer shirt.

"Dad, I don't need your shirt."

"You do if you want to stay here." He came around the bar and held it behind me until I slid my arms through the sleeves. "Whatever this is," he gestured to my top, "it might be fine for a party at the Daures' but not for *anything* off Bourbon."

Something behind me had his attention; I turned around and saw a thirtysomething guy with curly blond hair staring at me. He creepily raised his eyebrow. *Ew.* I turned back around, tightening the shirt around me.

"Don't even think about walking home alone either." He looked back up at the guy. "In fact, I don't want you staying home alone tonight." He pulled out his phone. "I'm calling Chatham to see if you can—"

"No!"

He gave me a questioning look.

"I mean, you don't have to call. I'll ask them. I'm sure it's fine."

He shoveled ice into a glass, filled it with tonic, and slid a lime around the edge before tossing it in, just how I liked it. "Speaking of the Daures . . . why aren't you there? I thought you were going over at nine?"

"Oh . . . " I pushed the floating lime sliver around the top of the tonic. "I was. I am. We just finished setting up, and I thought I'd come visit you and show you my dress."

"I didn't mean that you shouldn't be proud of the dress. You just . . . caught me off guard. You look so much like your mother."

"Oh." I thought again about the way Emilio was looking lovingly at me. *Ugh.*

My phone buzzed. I glanced at it, hoping it was Nicco but sure it was Codi.

Isaac 10:19 p.m. Leaving Dee's. Be there in a few.

Shit. My stomach curdled thinking about Isaac showing up at the tearoom. I didn't want to hurt him; I just wanted him and Nicco to get along. *He's going to freak.* I picked up the drink and sucked half of it down.

"Whoa there," Mac said, as if it wasn't just fizzy water with minerals.

I thought about one of the last times Isaac and I had argued about Nicco, after the Adeline séance, when he'd said that he loved me.

Why didn't I say it back? More guilt ladled over me.

"Dad . . . how did you know when you were in love with Mom?" I never brought up my mother, so I surprised even myself with the question.

He looked at me, tapped his fingers on the bar a few times, then picked up a glass and started to dry it with a towel. "Tell me who you think you're in love with, and I'll tell you if you are."

"Ha. Nice try. I'm serious."

He refilled my glass. "Well, I knew it from the moment she first smiled at me."

I glanced up him.

"Just like that."

"Like what?"

"How you're smiling at me right now."

"I'm not smiling," I said, realizing I was.

"The first time I ever held you, you looked up and smiled at me, and I knew my heart would never be the same."

I smiled harder, trying not to be embarrassed.

"Yep, just like that." He leaned on the bar. "That's the thing about love . . ."

"What?"

"It's unquestionable."

"Right." His answer reminded me of a photo at our house. In it, my mom and dad were young and standing on the Seine in Paris. The way he was looking at her was exactly that: with unquestionable love.

My eyes pricked.

I tapped four words into my phone so Isaac wouldn't freak out worrying: *I'm at the bar.*

And then I shut it off.

CHAPTER 51

BUZZKILL

"You're practically skipping," Désirée said as we turned onto Royal Street.

"No, I'm not."

"You are. It's okay. It's kind of adorable."

I made a show of bouncing up the short steps at the tearoom and held open the door for her. "By the way," I said as she stepped through. "I'm sure Codi will love your dress."

She scoffed. "Why would that matter to me?"

"*Mm-hmm.*"

Other than the track lighting illuminating the glass shelves, the shop was dark, but voices and music came from the back.

"I don't know what you're talking about."

"Suuure you don't. You aren't blushing right now either."

"I don't blush." Her footsteps quickened, carrying her away from the conversation, and that was all the confirmation I needed.

I followed her down the hallway of psychic booths and sensed Julie swirl around me.

"Where have you been, *mon cher*?" she asked.

I glanced at my watch. "What? We're like fourteen minutes late."

Désirée turned back. "Well, if you hadn't insisted we activate the elix—"

"Not you. Julie."

"Oh." She looked up to the ceiling. "Do you think we'll all be able to see spirits in the Afterworld . . . ?" Her voice trailed off as we stepped outside into the courtyard.

"A lot can happen in fourteen minutes," Julie said, swirling up through long colorful streamers hanging down from a tall pole.

"Wow," Désirée said, gazing around at all the fancy decorations. But I was distracted by the way every single party guest had turned to us and stopped their conversation mid-sentence. A sparrow swooped down, chirping in the silence, and pecked at some fallen sesame seeds.

"Well, we know how to kill a vibe," Désirée said.

Codi strode over, a grim look on his face, pale and sweaty like he might be sick, but before he could say anything, Désirée dropped her bag on the ground and shrieked, "You got your Mark!"

"Oh, yeah, I almost forgot."

"You almost forgot?" I asked as he held out his arm to show the fresh turquoise glimmer.

"Thank Goddess! I was starting to worry that we bound you into the coven for no reason."

"Thanks, Borges."

"That's not what I meant! I just meant that if you didn't get status and then lost all your memories, it would, like, suck."

He crossed his arms. "You're totally into me."

Her back stiffened more than it usually was. "Can't I just be excited that our coven is finally living up to its potential?"

"So, what's your Spektral?" I asked, trying not to laugh.

"Psychometry. So lame. You see ghosts, she heals people, Adele gets to move things with her mind, and I get to see history lessons."

"History is knowledge," Désirée said. "And knowledge is power in the witching world."

"Congrats, man." We slapped hands and I brought him in for a half-hug.

When we were close, his fingers pushed something into my back pocket. "Callis's ring," he whispered.

I peered over his shoulder and couldn't help noticing that everyone was still staring at us . . . and not in a "We're *so* excited for Codi's magic" way; like, in a creepy, possibly overtaken by aliens kind of way.

Isn't this supposed to be a celebration? I scanned the sea of aliens, and someone was noticeably missing. "Where's Adele?"

"So, you, uh, haven't heard from her?"

I reached for my phone. "We were supposed to meet here."

"She was here."

"Was?" Désirée asked.

"So, uh, Nicco showed up."

"Why the hell would a vampire show up at a Beltane party?"

"Adele," his voice pinched, "invited him."

"*What*?"

"And there was a little confrontation. Papa Olsin saw him here and called him out. Let's just say his invitation was rescinded."

"Damn," Désirée said. "That sounds like a Ritha move."

"Ritha would kick someone out just for being a vampire?" I asked.

"Oh Goddess, yes."

I knew I liked her.

"It wasn't because he's a vampire," Codi said. "Not exactly."

"Well then, what exactly?" In my periphery, I saw people turning back around, pretending like they were laughing or chatting, or busying themselves with eating cake. "Codi, what the hell happened? Where is Adele?"

"Gramps got a little . . . threatening when he saw Nicco with Adele, because . . ."

"Because what?" The image of them together was making my heart pound so hard in my chest it felt like waves of energy were reverberating throughout my entire body.

He walked us away from the crowd, to a quiet corner near a wall of flowers. Petals were scattered all over the bricked ground. "You *can't* tell her . . . I'm not even supposed to tell you."

Désirée looked at me, concerned.

"Apparently, he saw something about Adele. The future. You know, psychic stuff."

"*And*?"

"He saw her . . . *die*," he whispered.

"*What*?" Désirée asked. "How?"

The heart reverb hit so hard, it was almost dizzying.

"Uh, it doesn't really work like that. No specifics. He just saw Nicco . . ."

"Just saw him what, Codi?"

"Kissing her. And then her dying. Nicco had the taste of her blood in his mouth."

"When?" I asked sharply.

"I don't know. Not too distant future? He said she didn't look too much older than she is now."

"Where is she?"

He nodded up. "Nicco took off over the wall, and she went after him—out the door, not over the wall. I tried to stop her, but she wasn't having it. I went to the bar first. Then her house. I was just about to go to HQ. Where else would she be?"

I bent down to Dee's bag and swiped the elixir from the side pouch, took off with a running start, popped the cork with my teeth and tilted the bottle into my mouth.

"Isaac!" she screamed as I leapt into the air.

But I was already soaring over the wall, the bitter elixir sliding down my throat.

All I could think about was Olsin's first prediction about Adele: that she was going to open the attic. And how she'd adamantly denied it was going to happen.

The elixir sent quakes through my feathers. Back on Halloween, we'd split the vial between the three of us. I'm pretty sure I chugged back the whole thing this time. I tried to remember how long it had taken for this stuff to kick in last time. With each pump of my wings, I got more pissed and more worried, and a little vindicated. I wanted to know everything the old man knew. The street sign up ahead warbled. I'd tried to be patient with this whole obsession Nicco had with Adele, but I was done. The air seemed to warble, too, but then . . . *whoa.*

I pumped my wings at triple speed, my vision became laser-sharp, and even the Air current that caught me ripped me down the street like I was blasting out of a rocket.

CHAPTER 52

PREMONITION

My mind felt like it was floating. Weightless. Carefree. Among a million shining stars where Pegasus galloped over Saturn's rings, and my lightning cracked like Zeus's bolts, and I could share shortbread cookies and strawberries with Adele without spitting them out.

It had been decades since I'd drunk so thoroughly. And magical blood at that. Two of the three witches were delirious from blood loss, and I was euphoric from the blood-high. I pulled off my shirt and cleaned the crimson stains from my chin and hands.

Carina rested back against the wall. I'd healed her first, so the bruising was gone from her cheek and she could move her arm, but there were still smears of blood and smudges of teary mascara across her face. Her throat was raw from screaming into my palm as I'd fed.

"No resting," I said, tossing my shirt to the floor. "We're just getting started."

But then the doorbell rang again. *She's back.*

Banging, forceful knocks. I listened for her heartbeat and couldn't find it. *Something's awry.*

I zipped out of the attic and down the stairs to my room, swished water over my face, fetched a new shirt, and barely had it on when I got down to the foyer. "What's wrong?" I asked, opening the door.

I'd barely registered who it was before I was flying backward, limbs flailing. The magical Air sent me crashing into the back wall; broken plaster showered around me when I landed. I sprang back up, feeling the fresh blood course through my system, enlivening my senses. "Have you lost your goddamn mind?"

"Where's Adele?" Isaac entered the house, coming straight for me. *Guess he found out about my party invite.*

Before he could make it halfway across the foyer, I was back in front of him. "Not here."

"Stay away from her," he yelled, trying to give me a shove, but I pushed him first—not enough to hurt him, just enough to swat him away.

"I'm not staying away from her unless she asks me to."

He stumbled back, but quickly steadied himself and came straight at me again. "When did asking ever keep you monsters away from the Saint-Germains?"

Something had changed. The anger in his eyes wasn't over a party.

"You're obsessed with Adele," he said, "just like you were obsessed with Adeline."

I shoved him harder this time, straight into the front door, smacking it closed. He knew something about Adeline. It was the second time he'd brought her up. I turned with him as he circled me. He was on some kind of magic. Probably a heightening elixir.

"Does it bother you when I spend time with her?" I asked, monitoring his every reaction. "When she confides in me?"

His heart sped up like a runaway freight train—definitely a heightening elixir.

"Does it bother you that she trusts me with her life more than she trusts you with even her secrets?"

He drew close, planting his feet. "Do you love her?"

Thump-thump.

He stared at me dead on.

"I'm surprised you think monsters are capable of love."

"I don't. I think you're a sick, fiendish freak, and I think you want to turn Adele into a sick freak like you, so you can live out eternity in some dark, sadistic fairy tale."

"And here I thought the people of this city were supposed to be so progressive."

"You think you know everything," he said. "Did Adele tell you that when you were stuck beneath that sleeping spell, Olsin Daure had a premonition that she'd open the attic?"

"It wouldn't have taken a master witch to figure that one out."

"She swore she wasn't going to do it."

"Well, we both know how that turned out." I smirked and crossed my arms, letting him think I didn't know what he was doing—but I could sense him pulling the Air almost as soon as he'd had the thought.

"Olsin Daure's had another premonition." He backed up a few steps, his right hand discreetly going behind his back.

I breathed in the fresh cut of cedar.

"Another vision of you and Adele." His wrist flicked, and the stake hurled toward me on supercharged Air. Before he could even register what I was doing, I'd snatched it and had him twisted in an armlock, pressing the point of the stake into his neck.

"Nicco!" Lisette screamed, running into the room, but she saw the look in my eyes and stopped halfway.

I inhaled the scent of his neck. There was no trace of her on him tonight. "That vision must have been pretty naughty to get everyone this worked up."

He didn't flinch. "She's dead in it. Thanks to you."

I felt the blood drain from my face, and my grip on the stake loosened.

"So if there is even a *sliver* of you that actually cares about her," he said, "get the hell out of this city."

I dropped him and the stake to the marble floor. "I'm not leaving until she's safe." I kicked the weapon across the floor to Lisette.

He stood up. "The only person she's not safe from is you."

"Callis has her Fire. Don't you care at all that she gets her magic back?"

"I think the real question is: why do you care so much about her magic?" He produced something from his pocket and flicked it to the ground at my feet. It clanked across the marble. "That's Callis's family ring. You want him? Go and get him."

"And what am I supposed to do with that bauble?"

He shrugged. "Location spell? Whatever you want. It's a full moon—maybe you can draw from it. You're a witch, right? One of the Greats?" He glanced at the Mark on my arm with a laugh, and I nearly put my fist through his throat. "Happy Flower Moon," he said, twisting the door open and taking flight.

"Love and light!" I yelled as he soared down the street. He was lucky I already had three witches in my possession. Otherwise, he'd be in chains, doing the spell under the threat of my fangs.

I shut the door, snapped the locks, and swiped the ring from the floor.

I waited, crossing my arms. "You can come out now."

Lisette moved sheepishly out of the shadow of an armoire. "When does it go away?" she asked quietly.

"When does what go away?"

"The need to know that he's okay."

"He was your first? Since your turning?"

She nodded.

"When he's dead."

Her eyes widened.

"You should be careful who you exchange blood with." My gaze dropped to the circle Marked on her arm. It wasn't something we'd ever spoken about. I knew it made her incredibly uncomfortable and, given that we had eternity, there had been no reason to push it. "When was the last time you did a spell?"

She huffed. "Seventeen-hundred-twenty-eight."

"Go get some salt and meet me in the attic."

She gave me an inquisitive look, but then in a blink she was gone through the front door.

I sped up to the mezzanine, pausing at the rail. I leaned over, gathering my thoughts, the adrenaline of a pending fight brewing in my veins. The cold stare in the old man's eyes came back to me: that fear mixed with anger when he'd told me to stay away from Adele. I imagined him sitting in his booth with his crystal ball, watching Adele and me together. He was going senile if he truly thought I was ever going to hurt her. *Or kill her.*

I thought about all the things she'd seen in my head while I was under the sleeping spell. My lips touching hers, the ecstasy I felt as my fangs slipped into her flesh and tasted her. Just as I began to ache, I jerked the railing, and it dislodged from the banister. Maybe Adele had been scared and said something to the old man. Or maybe he was just projecting his own fears into his magic.

Adele's not scared of you.

She trusts you.

Never trust a vampire.

There were many witches I was planning on killing—perhaps even tonight, by the light of the full moon—but Adele Le Moyne was not one of them.

I will always protect her.

From my family.

From myself.

I have to.

I tossed the railing aside. "Gabriel, find some sage!" I yelled. "And candles! Emilio, help me search the house for maps!"

"What kind of maps?" he shouted from somewhere deeper in the house.

"All you can find! Most likely the tristate area. We're going on a witch hunt."

CHAPTER 53

BOYFRIEND MATERIAL

My feet slapped down so quickly, thanks to the elixir, I stumbled forward with the momentum, nearly face-diving into the alleyway. I knew I should stop and take a breather; the elixir was taking my usual Nicco-rage from a ten to ninety. But when I pulled out my phone and saw the message from Adele—*I'm at the bar*—I took off running.

I'll cool down on the way.

Désirée wasn't wrong about this stuff jacking you up in every way imaginable. After the fight with Nicco, the adrenaline spike alone could have lifted me down the street to the bar.

As I passed through the gate to Le Chat Noir, Troy called out, "Your honey's inside."

"Thanks, man."

The band playing in the cabaret was a little more rock than the club's usual brass or piano vibe. I craned my neck, scanning the bar through the crowd, finding the usuals: a few people watching the band from afar; couples with hands on each other's laps, counting down the moments to getting laid; old regulars repeating the same political conversations every night, all drinking moonshine cocktails. In the farthest corner, a girl with a long skirt and a dark men's shirt twirled her drink with her finger. *Is that a flower crown?*

I hurried through the throng of people. "Hey." I touched her shoulder.

When she turned around, she looked relieved to see me.

"Well, look who it is," Mac said.

Panic struck her eyes, and I realized she hadn't really thought this through, either.

"Oh my God!" Mia shrieked, coming through the crowd with a bucket of ice. *Shit.* Before we could do anything, the ice was down and she had an arm around each of us. She seemed extra happy, like she'd had a couple shots with customers. "It's been so long, I was getting scared you guys broke up."

"Broke up?" Mac asked.

Mia let us go, picked up the bucket, and headed for the bar.

Adele turned to Mac and mouthed, "*Drunk.*"

He gave us both a questioning look. I wasn't sure he was buying it. Adele shrugged like she had no idea what Mia was taking about—but we needed to think of something quick, because she was going to be back around the bar in about twenty seconds.

Adele looked at me, her phone already in her hand, one leg inching from the stool. "So how's the renovation coming?"

"It's, uh, coming," I said, watching the train that was about to collide with our charade.

Adele looked at me more severely.

"Oh! One room's almost finished. I could show you!"

"Cool!" She hopped off the stool and grabbed her bag. "I want to see it." She headed for the door, pulling me along.

"Adele," Mac said loudly.

Fuck. We both stopped.

"Maybe Isaac could walk you back to the party after?"

"Oh. Yeah. Actually, maybe he could come with me." She looked at me and then back to him. "He'd probably like Codi. And Caleb and Cam."

"They're good kids," Mac said to me.

I nodded.

"And be careful out there with my daughter, okay?"

Adele's fingertips tugged mine, and I didn't even care if I was beaming like an idiot. "We will be!"

"Adele, keep that shirt on until you're at the party!"

"Dad!"

"Love you, sweetheart!"

"Love you!"

Once we were in the hallway, her hand slipped into mine, and we ran all the way to my room. The bass from the band coursed through my system along with the elixir. We barely had the door closed before we fell back against it.

"Did that really just happen?" she asked, the moonlight shining down on her excited smile— and I couldn't wait any longer. I kissed her.

Her mouth opened wider, and she kissed me back, pulling me closer. Fireworks lit up behind my eyes. *Jesus. What is in this stuff?*

"I'll take that as a yes," she said.

"*Definitely, yes.*" My head spun, remembering why we were here in the first place. "Wait. Are you okay?"

She nodded.

"Are you sure?"

She nodded again. "It's not me we should be asking. I'm not the one who got thrown out of the party for showing nothing but kindness . . . but I couldn't find Nicco."

As soon as she said his name, my heart felt like it was being physically squeezed. *Effing elixir.* Olsin's premonition flashed in my head, and I wondered if I should tell her now. She needed to stop hanging around him. Her life was at risk. "What happened? Why would you invite him to the tearoom?"

"Because it's Beltane, and he's a witch." The words rushed out. "Because he saved me from his family Halloween night, and from my mother's vampire bite. And I just . . . wanted the two of you to hang out."

"*Why?*"

"Because he's my friend, and you're my boyfriend." Frustration built in her voice. "And I don't want to have to have two different lives so you can each be in one."

"I'm your . . . ?"

Her eyes widened. "I th-o-ought . . . I mean, only if you wan—"

I kissed her, hard, and she relaxed again. "I want to."

She smiled. And as her lips inched back to mine, all of the pressure, weight, and stress of our broken relationship lifted off my shoulders. I could taste the limey tonic from her drink and I wanted to taste all of her. Her arms circled my neck.

"There's just one thing . . ."

"*Hmm?*"

"Nicco is my friend."

I swallowed a groan. *Why are we still talking about Nicco?*

"I care about him. Just as much as I care about Dee or Codi or anyone. Our lives are . . . entwined. He's the only key I have to ever finding out anything more about my family's magic. I'm not giving him up. If you can't handle that . . . this isn't going to work."

I paused, thinking again about Olsin's premonition, but as I opened my mouth to tell her the real reason he was thrown out, I understood why psychics didn't tell people this kind of grim stuff. I didn't want to scare her. I wanted to protect her. That was going to be impossible if I let Nicco drive a wedge between us. "I can handle it."

"Really?" Her expression brightened.

I internally growled. "I mean, I don't like it . . . but if it's this important to you."

She looked up at me with those big eyes. "Will you at least *try* to get along with him? I know you'll like him if you just get to know him. You're both so caring."

"Okay." I wondered if she'd still think so if she knew I just threw a stake at him. "I'll try."

Giddiness rushed through her kiss, and suddenly making her happy was all I cared about. Her palms slid down my chest, and she kissed me so deeply, I groaned into her mouth, starting to get hard—not something I ever thought a discussion about Nicco could lead to.

She let the dark shirt drop to the floor.

I wondered if it was his. It wasn't cold outside; why would he have given it to her? I pushed her hair away, fingers grazing a nearly invisible dress strap. I stepped back to check her out. "Jesus, Adele."

"What? What's wrong?"

"Nothing . . . you look amazing."

She raised her arms and did a slow twirl, showing me the dress. I tried not to laugh at her thinking I was talking about the garment. "Did you make it?"

She nodded, coming closer. "So be careful with it, okay?" Even in the pale moonlight, I could tell she was blushing.

"Was that an invitation to take it off?"

"*Mm-hmm.*" She stepped against me and slipped her hands beneath my T-shirt sleeves. I kissed her softly, and she kneaded into my muscles, wanting more. We stumbled across the floor to the bed, and I sat, pulling her into my lap. Every touch, every kiss was returned with greater strength. My hands slid beneath the silky shirt, straight for the clasp of her bra, and in a second it was off, and her breasts were in my palms. Soft and full and warm.

Her kisses became breathier, and I twisted her onto the bed, pushing her mouth open with mine, demanding more of her kisses.

I trailed down her jaw and over her collarbone, carefully avoiding her neck, lost in her flowery scent. Her fingers dipped into my hair, her chest rising and falling with her inhales, drawing my mouth to her curves. As I tasted her delicate skin, her breath stuttered, nearly sending me over the edge.

Calm down, Isaac.

But she clutched my hair, her hips pressing against me, and I couldn't. I imagined myself pushing inside her. The softest moan slipped from her throat, and I knew we should leave—go to her house or to HQ—but I didn't want to stop, and I didn't think she wanted to either.

"Can you lock the door?" I kissed between her breasts, smiling when I saw her eyes were shut. "Please?" She shuddered, trying to nod, and started to pull away, but I swept my tongue over the top of her breast, swirling the tip, and she gasped loudly.

"Adele, lock the door!" Anyone could walk in, *namely Mac.*

"Okay," she said hazily, pushing back my shoulders as she squirmed out from beneath me and off the bed.

Did I do something wrong? "Hey, we can go slower. We don't have to—"

She looked at me like I was losing it. "I want to."

My eyes widened. *Fuck.* "Oh my God, Adele. I forgot about . . ."

"Forgot what?"

"About your magic. I'm so sorry." I was so used to her telekinesis; the entire span of our relationship, she'd always been able to do something as simple as locking a door with her mind, even mid-kiss, or mid-other things. "I would never have barked at you like that if— I'd have gotten up myself. I'm so . . ."

But it was too late. Her face had sunk. "It's fine."

"I'm sorry." She came back, but she climbed over me to the empty side of the bed and lay down facing the window.

Shit. I blew out a breath.

"Hey . . ." I slid next to her and kissed her shoulder.

"It's fine," she murmured again. "I just need a second."

I spooned as close as I could, awkwardly, trying not to jab her with my still very erect dick.

"I was stupid to ever think I was getting my magic back," she said.

I nuzzled her closer. "Please don't call my best friend stupid."

"All those flashes—the whole time, it was Codi getting his Mark."

Oh. Shit. "Come here." I tugged her around to face me.

"I could feel it," she said, lying back down on her folded elbow. "I could *feel* magic. But I guess I was just getting the signals crossed, and it was his Spektral trying to break through. I'm happy for him, *I swear.* It just sucks."

"I'm sorry." I stroked her hair, thinking again about the premonition, and about what Nicco had said about not leaving town until she was safe. He'd never consider me protecting her to be safe enough. She *needed* her magic back. "Starting tomorrow, we will spend every hour of every day working on your magic. We can meditate and practice group spells. Hypnosis. Read every word of every grimoire in this town and raise every ancestor from the grave to help."

She looked up at me.

"We'll set Dee on it so she'll chill about Guinée."

She smiled.

"And when Ritha and Chatham are back in town, we can brainstorm. Hell, we can even talk to Nicco about it, if you think it will help."

Her eyes lit up. "Really?"

"Really." *If it's the thing that gets your magic back, so he gets the hell out of your life, then, yes.*

She stretched up and dusted my lips with hers. "*Merci.*"

And when she curled into my chest, and I wrapped an arm over her back, I felt the tension release.

We have to get her magic back.

CHAPTER 54

LOCATION IS KEY

I dropped the stack in the middle of the attic in front of the witches: a U.S. atlas from 1984, an original map of the Vieux Carré from the early eighteenth century, a brochure for a vampire tour with a hand-drawn French Quarter map, a Louisiana state map, and a globe of uncertain age but some time prior to the collapse of the Soviet Union.

My brothers stood at each of my shoulders, watching curiously. Lisette was near the door—she must have broken into the restaurant across the street, because she was hugging a thirty-pound sack of salt—and Martine had drifted over to the burned witch in the corner, drawn there by morbid curiosity perhaps mixed with hunger.

"How's everyone feeling?" I asked the witch trio.

Raúl's milky eyes brimmed with hatred for me. His veins had become visible beneath his ghostly translucent skin, and his jaw was locked so tight, he looked like glass about to crack under pressure. Carina's gaze went back and forth between us like a cornered fox.

"Anyone need a pick-me-up before we get started tonight?" I asked.

"Heal him," Carina yelled, pointing to Josif, who'd sunk into the corner, slumped down to the floor. I wondered if they were lovers. "Heal him like you healed me!" She jumped forward in her chains, pulling for her celerity as if she might be able to rip away.

The surge of adrenaline a prisoner gets when they think it's the end.

Josif's pulse was barely audible, even with my supercharged senses. I shrugged at Martine, who was nearest to him. "I suppose he is going to need to concentrate for tonight's opening act."

Before I could say anything else, she'd sprung forward and jammed her punctured wrist against his mouth, cradling him like a baby. "Drink up," she said in French. "It's time to play."

Josif whimpered, as the skin on his face sloughed off, new skin growing beneath.

"Not too much," Gabriel told her.

"Opening act?" Raúl snarled. "What were you doing in here earlier?"

"Preshow hors d'oeuvres, of course."

Emilio grasped my shoulder with a brotherly shake. "I really meant it when I said our Salazar years together are some of my fondest."

Raúl's head fell toward Carina. "He's not going to kill us. Flipping one of us is the only hope he has of finding our coven."

I smirked. "Again with the delusions . . . Lisette, pour the circle, please."

She came forward with the bag.

"What the hell is this?" Carina asked.

"Yes, what is this?" Martine chirped, pulling her wrist away from Josif. She was the only one of us who hadn't been a witch in her human years.

"They're forming a circle," Josif said, his rural Balkan accent thickening as the flesh on his neck regenerated.

"Look at them," Raúl howled. "Look at their meaningless Marks. What is more pathetic than a magicless witch?"

"One who has to suck ghost brains just to keep breathing," Lisette said, pouring a steady stream of salt onto the floor.

"And wrong again," I said. "We aren't forming a circle. *You* are forming a circle."

"Like hell we are!" Carina's ratty blonde hair shook into her face.

Raúl spat at my feet and went off with a slew of Spanish profanity.

I grabbed his ankle and jerked him into the circle so hard his chains snapped from the wall and his right shoulder cracked out of the socket with a loud pop.

"I thought you were the sane one in this group!" he cried.

"Your mistake." I roughly detached the other two witches from their chains and dragged them into the circle; they were slightly more cooperative, seeing Raúl's dangling arm.

"Is this really all because of the witch girl?" Raúl hissed. "How long ago did you lose your Fire, Medici? Can you taste her magic in my blood when you drink from me? Can you feel the power coursing through her when you fuck her? Does it make you feel magical again? All tingly inside?"

My brothers both looked at me as the room fell silent. I bit the insides of my cheeks. The floorboards creaked under my boots as I walked over to the window and tore off the blackout curtain, ripping the duct tape.

"Carina," I said, suppressing the rage as I tore off the next curtain with a quick whip. "Besides the charge of the full moon, what's the next best thing to help activate a spell?"

Her tone flattened with trepidation as her gaze followed me. "An eclipse."

I rolled my eyes as I tore off the next, letting the moon pour in throughout the room. "Other than a celestial event—what would almost guarantee the desired outcome, even if the witches performing the ritual were vile, truculent hacks?" I tore off another piece of fabric. When she didn't answer, I looked back, reeling. "Say the words, or it will be yours." My fangs bulged.

"*A blood sacrifice*," she said through locked jaw.

I whipped back to the circle, grabbed the Salazar witch's head, and twisted a complete three-sixty in the air, wrenching it off.

Carina screamed as blood sprayed from the stump of his neck.

The fangs of each vampire in the room snapped out.

"*You're all animals*!" she shrieked. "You always have been! *You don't deserve your magic*!"

I dumped his head into her lap. She shrieked again and flung it away, trembling, tears streaming down her blood-spattered face.

Martine stopped the rolling head with the tip of her boot. She picked it up, licked the blood from Raúl's cheek, and held him at her hip, unconcerned that blood from his neck-stump was soaking into her dress. One of his eyes drooped shut, but she popped it back open so he remained staring at his two surviving coven members.

Carina rapidly blinked back tears.

Emilio nudged the witch's body with his foot, spilling blood into the circle. "Are you ready to begin?" he asked her. "Or should my brother bathe you in his blood as well?" He nodded to the now only half-burnt witch. Josif's face and neck were red with fresh skin.

Carina's jaw clamped tighter.

"I'm going to take that as a yes," Gabriel said, stepping into the circle. He crouched next to them with a bundle of swamp sprigs, lit the herbs and slowly waved them over each of Carina's hands, the words of our family's cleansing ritual rolling off his tongue. Emilio placed the candles around the circle. When he was finished, Gabriel spoke calmly to the witches: "If you try anything other than the magic we instruct, I will dismember you, piece by piece, and slowly drain you for the next ten years."

"It's a marvel of magic and science," I said, "what the bodies of the Animarum Praedators can endure."

Carina looked at me with hate and determination, a combination that could make a person heroic. Too bad for her, it wouldn't be enough to survive.

"Join hands," I said.

Josif sneered.

Martine began to dance around the circle, singing a French requiem at an oddly chipper tempo.

"You will never defeat Callisto now that he has his Fire back," Carina gibed. "He's been planning this moment for centuries! To have his family back together—his coven. You Medici fools have spent so long brainwashing everyone into believing Salazar Fire is weak that you believe your own bullshit."

"Too bad his Fire isn't Salazar!" I was seething. "Join hands or be bound together."

Carina's hands slipped into Josif's pus-coated flesh. A section of skin slid off his palm, and she gagged.

"It's okay," he told her through gritted teeth, his gaze searing past her to me.

The maps were in a pile between them. I procured the ring from my front pocket, placed it on top, and watched the horror fill her eyes. I added two small candles inside the circle on either side of them, and struck a match, lighting each. "*Una per lo spirito di mio padre. Una per lo spirito di mia madre.*"

"May they forever rest in peace," Gabriel said of our parents, as he and Emilio crouched down on one side of the circle, Lisette and I on the other. Martine danced around us.

"Repeat after me," I said directly to the Ghost Drinkers. I spoke the first line of the Italian verse clearly, and they repeated it back. A ripple of magic went around the circle, setting the candles ablaze.

Gabriel led the next line, and on the repeat, the door blew open and a stream of air whirled around the room, blowing back Lisette's hair. She leaned into the circle, the power in the room undeniably growing.

The maps began slowly swirling on the floor. The globe spinning. The HAUNTED HISTORY TOURS brochure inched out from beneath the ring, tipping it onto the road map, before sailing over Carina's shoulder, into a dark corner. The road map slid out next and floated out of the circle too.

All eyes went to the atlas. Emilio inched closer, leading the next verse.

The ring rose, hovering in the air, forcibly shaking. The book slapped open, pages fanning out. My brothers masked their excitement well, but through the shadows cast on their cheeks, elation glinted in their eyes. Lisette's fangs dug so deeply into her lip, she drew blood.

The page showed the southeast corner of *La Louisiane*.

"*Mostralo a me*," everyone chanted. The ring rose higher. The four of us stood, all eyes on the piece of metal as it climbed, higher and higher, spinning in place. "*Show him to me*."

The atlas pages settled and the ring slammed back down. A burst of energy exploded from it, knocking everyone backward—everyone but me.

Darkness enveloped us as the candles extinguished, all but the two I'd lit for our parents, which shone bright. I could feel the spirit of my father compelling me to take down the Salazars. I stepped into the bloody circle, salt crunching beneath my boots, and crouched down, examining the spot under the talisman.

It was off I-10, east of the city, halfway between here and the amusement park. I pulled my phone from my jacket pocket and took a photo.

"There's nothing out there but swamp," Emilio said. "No cemeteries, no abandoned houses. It's nothing but Storm slabs."

We're missing something.

Callis needed strength before he could attack. But I'd searched every cemetery for him, every hospital morgue, every funeral home, and never found him or his Animarum Praedators. There was nothing out there in the wilderness. Emilio and I had searched every mile. I gazed at the blank area on the map. I'd driven right through it with Adele, and there had been nothing but darkness. *What would he be doing way out—*

A memory of something glowing in the dark jolted me. "There is something out there!"

Everyone looked at me.

"A place that thousands—tens of thousands—of dead have passed through."

Carina leapt up, garnering every bit of celerity power she had left, and zipped to the door. Lisette was on top of her before she made it past the threshold, fangs plunged into her neck.

"Carina!" Josif screamed, lurching after her, but Gabriel grabbed him. He thrashed as they shackled him back to the wall. "You got what you want! Let us go!"

"If she survives, perhaps." I turned to him. "But you? You should never have gone into that circle after Adele." I blew out the two remaining candles. "*Grazie, mamma e papà.*" I looked up at my brothers. "Let's go."

I sped out of the attic, each of them following, but when I got to the foyer, Gabriel cleared his throat, leaning down from the mezzanine. "Are you forgetting something curse-related?"

"*Dannazione*," I spat. I needed Gabriel tonight—everyone. We needed numbers.

His fangs snapped out. "Which one of those little witches holds the trapping spell?"

"Finally," Emilio said, rolling his eyes.

Lisette stood straight up, trying to mask her concern.

"You're *not* killing any of Adele's friends."

"You are not going out there by yourselves." Gabriel crossed his arms.

Emilio and I looked at each other with playful smirks.

"Brother," Emilio said, "have you forgotten that Niccolò and I have been tumbling with Callisto Salazar for centuries without you?"

"That was before he got his Elemental magic back," Gabriel said. "Before he was able to rebind his coven. Who knows what they will be capable of if they reach full strength. The magical world has never seen an Animarum Praedator at full power." He looked at me. "These witches have had enough time to break the curse."

We don't have time for this. We can't let the Animarum Praedators reach full strength.

"Give me a few minutes," I said and zipped out the door.

CHAPTER 55

HARD NO

I felt vibrations, but my eyelids were so heavy they seemed impossible to lift. I was warm and cozy. I cracked them open and saw Adele against my chest; I smiled, even though I'd never felt this tired in my life. I wondered if the elixir was also heightening my REM cycle. More vibrations. *My phone.* I dug it out of my pocket, trying not to disturb her.

I flicked the screen on.

There were a million messages, most of them from Désirée asking me whether I'd found Adele, was she okay, and were we coming back. I awkwardly typed, trying not to elbow her in the face:

Isaac 23:10 Found her... she's fine. Not sure about coming back. Probably, soon.

I looked at the clock. We hadn't missed the midnight moon circle yet.

The phone vibrated in my hand, but the next message wasn't from Dee; it was from . . . *Nicco*? I pushed it away, but then saw that I also had two missed calls from him. I opened the message.

Nicco 23:11 Where are you?

What the? I tried not to get annoyed. I didn't even want that kind of energy in the room with Adele and me in such a good place.

I quickly punched in two words and hit send:

Isaac 23:11 Fuck. Off.

Nicco 23:11 I went by the tearoom, but you weren't there. Not in the back, at least.

Isaac 23:12 See previous message.

Nicco 23:12 Meet me right now, or I'm coming to find you. You're only ever at four places. I've already been to two. Your call.

Goddammit, I mouthed, holding Adele steady so I didn't wake her as I lightly kicked the air. He'd nearly ruined this night once. I did *not* want him showing up here.

Isaac 23:13 Where?

Nicco 23:13 Same place as last time. Be there in five minutes.

I carefully moved from beneath her and gently placed her back on the pillow, praying she'd still be here when I got back. She'd said earlier that she couldn't find Nicco, and I wanted to keep it that way as long as possible. Olsin's premonition blazed in my mind. I locked the door so no one could get in, grabbed a piece of paper from my bag. *Be back in a few*, I scribbled, and drew a tiny crow. Set the note underneath her hand, kissed her cheek, and begrudgingly soared out the window.

Even though it only took a minute, by the time I got to the little park in Jackson Square, I was fuming. I spotted Nicco standing beneath the trees in the dark northeast corner, but I swept the perimeter anyway to see if he'd brought anyone else. I wondered if I should have brought Codi.

The park was clear.

An ambush didn't seem like Nicco's style, but I aimed for the most open area of the park just to be safe.

I landed hard, took a couple stumbling steps across the grass, and almost crashed into the dark figure that had practically materialized in front of me, he was so fast. I hated how he could do that.

"What do you want?" I asked, trying to temper my annoyance so we could get this over as quickly as possible and I could get back to Adele. "Couldn't get your location spell to work?"

"It worked perfectly," he said flatly. "*Grazie* for the ring."

"Uh, okay." Not what I was expecting him to say. How the fuck was he able to do a spell?

"We found him."

"Callis?"

"*Sì*. And, if I am correct, all of the Ghost Drinkers. They're planning something tonight, under the Flower Moon. We're going after them before they can gain more strength."

"Okay . . ."

"They're out past the parish line—"

"Good. Keep them the hell away from here."

"Indeed. There's only one problem . . ." His face kind of curdled. "I need your help."

I crossed my arms. *This ought to be good.*

"Break the rest of the curse on my family so they can come with me. Being seconds too late at the convent had massive consequences. We need to leave, *now*." He nodded up to the moon.

I shook my head, giving him back his own smug smile. "The last time we argued on the street, I offered to break the curse so you could take your family back to Italy. What did you tell me right before you slammed me into a dumpster?"

His jaw clenched.

"The offer still stands: I'll break the curse if you all leave."

"I'm not leaving her!" he said, voice raised.

"I'm not breaking the curse!" The elixir begged me to grab him by the collar. "*You* aren't contained here. Emilio isn't bound by the spell. The good ole Carter brothers? You're the reason she was in the attic that night. You're the reason Callis found her." I stepped closer. "You're the reason he was able to take her magic. This is your idiotic family's war." My hands slammed into his chest.

He stumbled two steps back and looked at me calmly. "Fine. You come with me then. Make sure that Callis and all of his disciples never touch Adele again. Never touch your coven. The rest of the town. Swoop in and be the hero. Your usual MO."

"What kind of idiot do you take me for? Things not on my Beltane list tonight: going into the swamp with the vampire who's in love with my girlfriend and his psychotic brother who almost killed me."

"You killed his child."

"Jesus, that is *sick*. I wouldn't care if Callis dropped you into a volcano. I would not waste a gust of wind to help you. He only came here to kill the two of you, no other reason. He told me himself—"

"Never mind!" he yelled, throwing up his hands, with a spit of ragey-sounding Italian. "Just tell me where Adele is."

"She can't help you. It's my part of the curse to break."

"Fuck the curse. Tell me where she is. Her phone's off."

"No."

"Why not?"

"Because! She'll want to go with you!"

"That's her choice."

"Not tonight."

His eyes narrowed.

"The last time I made a plan with you," I said, "she got hurled out of a third story window—"

"Would you rather she'd been locked in an attic with five vampires?"

"How many times are you going to almost get her killed?"

"I will protect her!"

"*I am* protecting her!" Olsin's premonition pulsed in my head: Nicco kissing her. The taste of her blood on his tongue as she died. The air around us began to swirl, picking up leaves and flowers and shaking rain from the trees.

"Where is she?"

"Whatever bullshit has happened between you and Callis has nothing to do with her. Leave her out of your feuds and stay out of our lives. Callis is not our problem!"

"You're a fool. The Animarum Praedators aren't a threat to the vampires, even with their Fire; we've swatted them away for centuries. The Salazars are a threat to witches, and especially to descendants of the

Greats, because after they have restored their health, their real quest for power will begin, starting with your *magia elementale*."

"He tried to take my Air once and that didn't work out for him."

"Forget I asked. We'll take care of it for you. I wouldn't want you to get your precious little hands dirty."

And with that he was gone, and only then did I realize how fast my pulse was charging. I quickly took flight, paranoid that he'd figured out where Adele was and would beat me there. But when I soared through my window, she was still in my bed, in the same exact position as when I'd left.

I sat on the mattress, contemplating Nicco's offer. Every pulse of magical energy within me wanted to go with him to find Callis and destroy him for everything he'd done: Brigitte's death, Mac's memories getting erased, Adele's Fire, Ren, Alessandro, all of the other Possessed, the souls. It all led back to him. But Olsin Daure's prediction flashed brighter than revenge, and I had no regrets; I would not charge ahead blindly or risk her life.

I pushed away my thoughts about the city, the souls, and the vampires. For once, I wanted to think only about her.

I crumpled up the note I'd left, kicked off my shoes, and slid down next to her. She stirred sleepily, and I scooped her into my arms. She kissed my jaw before burrowing back into the crook of my neck.

I loved her. And I'd promised her I'd never let Callis touch her again.

If Nicco and Emilio went after Callis, either he'd never be touching anyone ever again or, if they lost, the great enemy to Adele's family would be eliminated. Then our coven, along with the two great covens of New Orleans, could deal with the Ghost Drinkers, who'd be weakened from battling the vampires yet again. Who knows, maybe if they got what they originally came here for—the heads of Niccolò and Emilio Medici—they'd leave town.

I recalled the night of the last attack, before everything went haywire. It had been just the two of us in my dark room on the S.S. *Hope*. We were just like this. Only naked. The rain had been pattering against the ship, and her orbs hovering over us had dulled as she slept. She'd made me feel safe. If I hadn't fallen asleep that night, I'd have kept her safe.

Tonight, I would not make the same mistake.

"Your heart's racing," she said sleepily.

I hadn't realized she'd woken. I smiled down at her, stroking the back of her head. "I'm just happy you're here." There was nothing I'd rather do than lie in bed with her, but the thought of Nicco turning up here to look for her was gnawing at me. "Hey, do you want to go back to the party?"

"I would rather just celebrate with you."

I don't know if it was her smile or the softness of her voice, but her answer made the aggression that had been rising in me begin to deflate. Still, the need to get out of here grew with each passing moment. "What about HQ?" I asked. "I have something there I was saving for your birthday, but it could be a Beltane surprise instead."

"What surprise?"

"You do understand how surprises work, right?"

She pinched my side, and after a very long kiss, and a wish for teleportation magic that went unfulfilled, we peeled away from each other, straightened our clothes, grabbed my skateboard, and were off.

CHAPTER 56

FLOWER MOON

The wind blew my skirt back, and I held on to him tighter.

He didn't have to keep kicking us forward because his magical Air current kept us gliding down the bumpy street, but he did anyway and we went soaring over to the brothel.

I hopped off in front of the old mansion.

He kicked the board into his hand, and the vines on the gate slithered away to let us in.

I started to bounce up the porch steps, but he took my hand. "This way." He brought me back down and over to the side of the house.

"Where are we going?"

"I told you, it's a surprise." When we got to the back gate, he blocked the way. "You have to shut your eyes."

"Okay."

I took small steps as he guided me through the gate. The grass under my feet transitioned to brick. "Okay, stay right here, but don't open your eyes. *Promise.*"

"Promise."

He let go of my hand, and I fought the temptation to crack them open just the tiniest bit for a peek. Instead, I listened for sounds, but all I heard were the tree branches swaying in the wind and the trickle of water in the fountain. *Wait, since when does the fountain work?* Isaac knew I loved the fountain with the three girls dancing under the moon—I still liked to believe Cosette was the one who'd had it made, honoring her two dead sisters—but the last time I was back here, the girls were mired in algae and decades of black sludge. He must have gotten it working again. I smiled, completely impressed with myself for figuring it out.

"Okay, just a few steps more," he said, pulling me closer to the trickling. "Open them."

I looked up at the fountain. The triplets now glimmered under cascading water, hands to the sky, dancing under the moonlight, like they knew it was nearly the first of May and were celebrating with us. But before I could say anything, a twinkle caught my eye, and I looked around. Fairy lights had been strung throughout the backyard. The last time I'd been back here, the yard had been one giant vine-entwisted bramble, but now purple crepe myrtles, pink cherry blossoms, and cream-colored magnolias lined the walls. The dead trees, weed-infested flower beds, and broken trellises were gone. Bunches of bananas hung down from bright green leaves. There were dark green tomato plants and rose bushes—so many roses. It had been completely transformed into a magical garden. It reminded me of how things had been before the Storm.

"How . . . ?" I asked, turning around. "You . . . ?"

He smiled, watching me. "I can't take all the credit. Codi got the fountain working. Dee planted the gardens and we all nursed the plants back to life. I restored the pigeon house, or whatever it's called."

A swell of birds chirped, and I ran to the pigeonnier, but then paused, hand on the door.

"You can look inside. They aren't trapped in. I took out the glass in the windows up top, and put in feeders—"

I opened the door, and dozens of hummingbirds fluttered out. I backed into Isaac's chest as they flittered around us before dispersing around the garden, the lights reflecting off their iridescent green feathers.

"We thought having more wildlife around would be good for our magic."

"It's amazing . . . "

I whirled back to the fountain, taking it all in. We'd made plans for an herb garden to use for our spellwork, but this was extravagant. The flowerbeds were blooming like something from a Monet. "When did y'all do all of this?"

"Mostly right after . . . everything went down. I wasn't supposed to be on the streets because of Emilio, and I was so worried about you . . . I wanted you to have a place that seemed unaffected by the Storm. I know that nothing could ever be completely unaffected, but—"

"I don't want to be completely unaffected . . ." I peered up into his golden-brown eyes. "If it weren't for the Storm, we never would have met." I didn't know if it was a terrible thing to say, but it was true. The Storm was horrific, but I couldn't imagine my life without him. He came closer, and my heart swelled. When I kissed him, I didn't understand how it had been possible for me to not talk to him all that time.

He brushed his face against mine. "I'm glad you like it."

"I love it."

"Are you ready for your present?" He hesitated. "The surprise . . ."

The surprise?

He took my hand and led me down the brick path to the grove of willows in the far back corner. There was a small fountain with cherubs spurting water. It grew darker as we ducked under some trailing fronds of the largest willow.

"Wait right here for a sec." He disappeared. Something gleamed under the fractals of moonlight through the weeping branches.

Fairy lights suddenly lit up the grove, coiled around the tree trunk, and my eyes filled with tears.

There, beside the tree, the ballerina was mid-pirouette. Shining and completely intact and perfect. She hadn't been vandalized; she had been rescued. Isaac had rescued my mother.

A gentle breeze blew my hair back and the scent of lavender swirled around me.

I sucked in a breath, seeing pockets of the purple flowers around the trees and framing a beautifully carved bench under the tree, next to her.

When I turned back, his eyes were wide, watching me. "I hope it's okay that I—"

"*Merci,*" I said, trying not to cry. "*Merci mille fois.*"

He came to me. "Adele, I'm so sorry." His voice shook. "Can you please ever forgive—?"

I threw my arms around his neck. "I forgive you." I kissed his cheek. "I forgive you." I held him tight. "I'm sorry I didn't tell you about my mom."

He shook his head. "I love y—"

I kissed him.

And I felt happier than I had at any time since she'd died. The fairy lights behind him glowed bigger through my tears. "The lights . . . they look like my orbs."

"Does that make you sad?"

I shook my head. "It's all beautiful."

"It is now that you're here."

I smiled, and he kissed me slowly, and I stopped thinking about whether I deserved his love and just let it flood into me, and I felt lighter and lighter.

I cracked open my eyes and gasped.

His arms tightened around me. "I've got you."

Our feet were hanging in the air above the bench. "I've got you," he whispered. And I was never more grateful that he never let me go.

As we floated, the branches of the willow began to sway; loose crepe myrtles blossoms gently whirled around us; and flowers from the garden picked up into the billowing Air—roses, violets, azaleas—buds and petals every color of the rainbow swirled. The hummingbirds flitted through the wind along with blue jays and warblers, a beautiful medley of song and color, and suddenly everything felt like it was as it was meant to be. "It's just like the first time we kissed," I said. "In the Tremé."

"This is what it should have been, not inside a moldy Storm house. I'm sorry."

"I'm not," I said, peering up into his eyes. "It was raw and magical, like us. Being with you is always magical."

His lips swept mine, and we got so lost in the kiss, I hardly noticed when it started to drizzle. He raised his arm through the Air, and the twister tightened around us, lifting us higher into the swirl of flowers. I shrieked with glee as we went through the willows, and across the yard, and up over the rail of the third story balcony.

As soon as my feet were back on solid ground, I pulled his mouth back to mine. We hardly skipped a beat. I fell against the rail, and he fell against me, and I kissed him until I was lightheaded. Faint traces of supernatural sensation curled around me when I touched him. *His magic.* I thought of all those beautiful flower petals floating around us. I was never going to fit into that swirl of magic. He came from one of the *Great Witching families of Europe*! And I was the actual lamest witch on Earth. I held him back, and the words just came out: "What's going to happen to us if I don't get my powers back?"

He gripped my face. "What's going to happen? What's going to happen is we're going to go to school together in New York. And we're going to explore old abandoned buildings and lost subway tracks, and make love on the roof of the shitty Brooklyn building we live in. And we'll both have internships with crazy people. And you'll be a hot, up-and-coming designer, showing at some bleeding-cool place in the Lower East Side during Fashion Week, and the *New York Times* will profile you as 'one to watch.'"

I smiled hard at his fantasy, and he didn't stop. I didn't want him to.

"And I'll buy a thousand copies and clip out the article and wall-paper the apartment with them, and you'll"—his tone softened—"you'll come with me to visit my mom's grave, and you'll make daisy chains for her because she loved them. And you'll crack cheap champagne when I get my first gallery show. But then . . ."

"But then?"

He brushed a lock of hair from my face. "But then none of it will matter, because we'll move back here so we can be closer to your pop, and I'll convert the garçonnière into a house so we can live above the bar, which we take over, so Mac can finally retire and just make art like he's always wanted. And Dee and Codi will run this town, and our kids will all grow up together, and have their own coven, and we'll ride out every storm that comes our way because we love it here and we love each other."

I was speechless, lost in our future storybook, his dreams becoming my dreams. My hands twisted into his T-shirt and I pulled him close, kissing him so hard he moaned into my mouth. Pressed up against each other, it felt like we'd never been apart. Like none of the bad things had happened, and we'd always been at each other's sides. I wanted more. I broke away.

"What . . . ?" he asked, sucking in a breath.

"Inside," I said with a smile, and turned to step through the open window, already pulling my shirt up over my head.

CHAPTER 57

HEIGHTENED

I scanned the dark room, looking for Adele. Waiting for my eyes to adjust, I tried to catch my breath; the elixir had strengthened things that I hadn't even considered until her hands were all over me. Slowly, the twinkling outlines of the room came into focus.

On the middle of the rug, a glimmer of light in the form of a silhouette pulled my attention. "Adele?"

With a swish of fabric, a line of sparkles swept aside, revealing her standing there for a split second before she pulled it back and was gone again. *So cool . . . Wait, is she—?*

I stepped closer, and the invisible blanket whooshed open again, this time over my head. My hands answered my question, drifting down her bare back as her lips parted mine. She was completely naked down to her panties and flower crown. I felt like I was in a dream: the smell of the fresh flowers in her hair, the way her kisses deepened when I dipped into the silky fabric at the arch of her back, cupping her curves, each roam of my hand becoming more gripping. I let her go only long enough to pull my T-shirt over my head.

I fumbled with my pants, and then we were both pushing them down until there was nothing left between us but my need.

The more we kissed, the more everything else disappeared—any traces of guilt over not helping Nicco, my compulsion to destroy Callis, and all of the other bullshit around us—and when she took me in her hand, I was completely consumed with her. The sparkling blanket fell to the floor, and I struggled not to groan. I lifted her up, and her legs wrapped around me as I carried her to the bed.

When she pulled me down next to her, I felt closer and closer to that moment back on the ship, the one I still dreamt about every night, when I was certain she loved me and the rest of the world felt so far away. We tumbled over, the scent of embers and sage rising from the blankets. Magical energy prickled my skin. There was an honesty between us that made me want her more than I'd known was possible.

She tenderly kissed the back of my neck as I unrolled a condom, but when I turned back to her, I sensed hesitation . . . or something. "Are you okay?" I asked, tracing the curve of her hip.

"*Mm-hmm.*" But her gaze dropped to the bed. "I don't really know if I'm allowed to ask . . ."

"Ask me what?"

"Were you . . . with anyone else when we were broken up?"

I bit my lip so I wouldn't laugh. She was serious. "What? In between my working and gardening and ripping up your dad's bar?"

She blushed, and I kissed her cheek.

"Who would I have even slept with?"

"I don't know!" She lay back as I moved on top of her. "Some dumb drunk girl at the bar . . . Girls are always looking at you wherever we go!"

"Because I'm in the habit of picking up dumb drunk girls?"

"I didn't say habit."

I kissed the crook of her neck.

"I mean . . . if you did . . . I just want to know."

"Of course I didn't." I met her gaze. "Lisette's the only person who's touched me, and that was all you, unless you count attempts from lwa."

She smiled up at me.

"Wait, have you?" *Is that why she's asking? Nicco?*

She didn't even throw my own jokes back at me, just shook her head, and tilted her face the slightest bit so our lips touched. As I kissed her deeper, she shifted her leg to make more room for me, and I couldn't believe we were here. I couldn't believe we'd made it.

She held me tight as our bodies met, and I carefully felt for every time she pinched, every tiny wince, as I pressed deeper, scared I would hurt her.

She tensed.

"Breathe," I whispered.

I felt her inhale, and her arms unlocked a little from around me. "Are you okay?" I asked, doing my best to mask how badly I wanted her.

She nodded, looking up at me with heavy eyes. Her lips lingered against mine as she moved against me. She sucked in a breath as I met her. As I kissed her, my mind let go and I got lost in the salty taste of her skin, and the traces of her fingertips, and her warmth. And I met her over and over until she was clutching me again, and we were both trembling.

"I love you," I whispered.

She gazed back at me as if unable to speak and it made me infinitely happy.

The elixir swirled in my head, and I sank onto her as she held me close. "*I love you, Adele.*"

CHAPTER 58

GHOST DRINKING

I gasped and detached from the biker's neck. Feeding always made me a little ecstatic, but doing so with the image of Callisto Salazar on my mind exacerbated that feeling tenfold. Not even the sounds of Emilio slurping from the second biker could sour the moment, nor the acrid taste of the alcohol in this man's blood. I licked the wound on the man's neck, and the punctures started to close.

He wavered on his feet, and I pressed him up against the alley wall to keep him upright. "Give me your keys," I said.

He dug through his pocket, extracted them, and dropped them into my palm.

"Look at me."

He opened his drunken eyes a little wider.

"In the morning, you'll realize you got so loaded you forgot where you left your bike. You'll find it two blocks from the bar, and you won't remember me, my brother, or any of this."

Emilio snapped his fingers at the man he'd fed from. "You'll wake up with the worst hangover of your life and blame your friend here for giving you shots. Forget me." He ripped the key ring from the man's belt loop. "I'm taking your Iron."

"Who's taking my bike?" he asked gruffly.

"Go back to the bar with your friend."

I released his companion.

"Marty," the smaller man said. "How'd we get out here?"

He squeezed his buddy's shoulder. "Told you I brought the good stuff tonight."

They headed back toward the bar.

Emilio mounted one of the bikes. I swung my leg over the other, twisted the key, and nodded toward the river.

We rumbled down the street, wove our way through the broken roads of the neighboring wards, and then blazed down the old highway. I kept one eye on the dark road, the other on the dark sky as I maxed the throttle. The full Flower Moon was supposed to peak fourteen minutes after midnight, which left us about twenty minutes to get there. It would be a miracle if we made it before the witching hour.

The cool wind burned against my face, and my mind kept circling back to the fruitless meeting with Isaac in the square. After that encounter, I wasn't sure I cared whether Gabriel went after him. But there was also a part of me that was glad he'd decided to stay behind . . . he was keeping Adele out of the fray.

Of course, if Gabriel decided to take the curse into his own hands now, there was nothing I could do about it—the only hope for Isaac was that his connection with Lisette was still strong enough that she'd stop my brother.

I thought about what Gabriel had said about there being a way for Adele and me to be together. I pushed the bike faster as the old man's premonition swam through my thoughts. *I will never hurt her. Never.* I locked the image in the pit of my soul where I stored my darkest thoughts, memories, and desires, and leaned in, getting a waft of the tire burning against the road.

Then my attention pulled to the sky ahead.

It was a hazy night, but something sparkled in the near distance with a hue too indigo to be stars. I eased back on the throttle, squinting. *An invisibility shield.* Like the one they'd used that night at the convent to mask their ritual. I flashed my lights at Emilio.

We slowed to a stop and stashed the bikes in a palmetto thicket not far from the road, only a few miles from where FEMA had set up the Disaster Mortuary. The swampy, wooded area was close enough to be convenient to the city but far enough away from the prying eyes of civilians to bring in truckloads of dead as they stored them. Examined them. Organized them. Identified them and shipped off their remains to loved ones or disposed of them.

Idiota, Niccolò. You've been too distracted—by a girl. Thousands had been buried in the temporary graves while the city set aside the problems of the dead to deal with the problems of the living. The D-MORT burial sites would be the kingliest of feasts for the Animarum Praedators. Young, fresh spirits were easier to catch and consume. Rage kindled inside me for not thinking of it sooner.

We plowed into the woods that separated the interstate from the swamp and ran along the edge of the marsh where the ground was softest, our steps soundless. The air was thick and ghostly, blending the murky water into the night. Cicadas hummed in waves as we tore through their trees, following the glow of the stadium lights that shone hazily through the wilderness. The bright light in the middle of the woods signaled the kind of eeriness that could only be generated by government operations.

I stopped to listen. "Do you hear that?"

Emilio circled back, and I shut my eyes, pulling in the sounds, the scents, the traces of magic in the air.

"*O, Illargui Amandrea, eman zahuzu biziko eta hileko argia!*"

It had been at least two centuries since I'd heard their ancient dialect of the Basque language spoken. "'O, Lady Moon, give us the light of life and death,'" I said to my brother. "They've started the ritual. They're calling to Illargui—"

"The Basque moon goddess," he finished.

We raced onward, and the voices of the Animarum Praedators grew louder, billowing into the air like a chorus of nocturnal angels, seeming to come from multiple directions.

The moon is the light of the dead.
The moon is the light of the dead.
O, Lady Moon, Lady of the Dead,
Shine your light so that all may be seen.
Give us the light to see the dead.
Make the Invisible visible.
Keep the Visible invisible.

A dance of wading birds flapped out of the water, taking low flight in the direction we ran. The night sounds grew louder all around us: the groans of the frogs, the songs of crickets, and the heavy whoosh of an owl swooping low overhead. Two deer sprang from the grass and ran along with us rather than away. It was the pull of the Salazar spell. The distinct cry of a bear tore through the cypress trees, and Emilio looked my way. We both dug into the sprint, pulling ahead of the charging fauna, steps masked by the sounds of the wildlife. The creatures all knew something was wrong.

An indigo shadow appeared on the ground. Once, twice. Every few feet. *What the hell is he up to?*

"Fence," I said as the moonlight flickered on the chain-link, and we both launched onto it, scaled it, and hoisted ourselves over the looping barbed wire. I landed eye-to-eye with a doe still on the opposite side of the fence, a look in her eye as if warning me to be careful.

Give us the light to see the dead.
Make the Invisible visible.

The glimmering shield just up ahead formed a dome over the entire facility. I kicked a pine cone into it, wondering if the magic was simply to hide their activities or if it served some other purpose. The pine cone rolled through unscathed. I swatted a hand in it to test it again, and we stepped through, unaffected.

Emilio tipped his head to the right, signaling that he'd find a back way, and we split up.

A vast, mostly empty parking lot took up much of the corporate campus. The group of buildings in the rear looked too high tech for a FEMA budget, and the prison-like watchtowers dotted throughout the property made it feel like something secretive had gone on here before the Storm. Biotech, I guessed, judging by the hazardous waste disposal bins locked behind more chain-link.

The watchtowers' floodlights illuminated the federally sanctioned area with a sickly gray tint. I stayed in the shadows, weaving through the rows of military vehicles.

"*Make the Invisible visible*," the voices echoed up to the indigo dome, making it impossible to pinpoint their origin. The humming songs of the swamp rose through the chanting.

More indigo shadows materialized on the ground, popping up one by one, and I could sense the chill of something otherworldly.

I edged into the small group of civilian cars, my gaze fixated on the buildings ahead, looking for activity in the windows. A ventilation system on the roof of one of the back buildings released plumes of white into the air. My foot hit a dark form, and I stumbled trying to avoid stepping on the body of a woman in a lab coat.

I crouched to check her pulse. She was dead but still warm. There were two more bodies in the SUV next to us. These three had almost escaped.

"*Make the Invisible visible.*"

The shiny chip on the woman's plastic ID badge caught my eye. I unclipped it from her pocket and hurried on.

A line of government-issue trailers sat in front of the cluster of campus buildings with FEMA warehouses that seemed haphazardly built on either side. Probably storage for the dead. A sign on one of the trailers read,

REGION 3 DMORT

A small security camera was mounted near the sign. I pulled my hood over my head; it was dark, but still.

The generators and air-conditioning compressors hummed as I stalked past them to the main buildings: sleek white structures with glass doors, surrounded by areas for sculpted landscaping that were now overgrown with swamp weeds. I hopped up to the first building. A sign, nothing more than a piece of paper and black marker, had been taped to the inside of the glass door:

VICTIM IDENTIFICATION CENTER

A more formally printed one next to it warned,

CAUTION NOTICE
BIOHAZARD LEVEL II

I scanned the woman's badge over the little black security box. It beeped, and blinked red. I zipped to the next building and tried the card again. Access denied. I tried several more buildings, each of which was connected to a round edifice in the center via a glass walkway, as if the complex were a giant spiderweb. I guessed the round building in the middle was the morgue. There was another watchtower in the central yard, its two floodlights like the spider's watchful eyes.

At the last building I tried, the light blinked green, and I opened the door. The white hallway inside had a clinical cleanliness, but as soon as I stepped inside, my nose wrinkled. Gas.

A security guard lay on the floor, crumpled into a ball, a radio still clutched in his hand.

I whipped down the hallway, looking through the glass windows on each of the doors. They were all laboratories, all with people slumped over microscopes, beakers, and computers. A clock at the end of the corridor blinked **00:13**.

A loud electrical buzz hummed, and the lights went out. Far more would perish if Callisto and his coven were able to complete their ritual and unveil the dead. The emergency lights blinked on as I sped through a labyrinth of hallways, into the glass extension walkway, wondering if Emilio had found them yet.

The chanting grew louder. *The morgue.*

"*Make the Invisible visible.*"

Flames flickered all around me through the glass. I paused and peered out into the darkness to my left, but there were no candles or any flames outside, just the spotlights of the watchtower glowering over empty employee picnic tables.

A snarl came from my right, and I whipped around. On the other side of the glass, right outside, a bear bared its teeth in every direction, swiping as if cornered. Nothing but darkness surrounded the animal—and yet, in the glass, the ethereal flicker of flames appeared again: an arc of small lights outside and the faintest silhouettes of cloaked figures. They might have been invisible, but their reflections weren't. The glass revealed them. Their circle. *They're using some kind of cloaking spell.*

Make the Invisible visible.

Keep the Visible invisible.

I needed to get out there. The door to the morgue had a scanner next to it. I crept close and swiped the ID badge. Nothing. I tested the handle, but the door was locked.

Sticking to the shadows cast by the buildings, I ran back down the dark hallways, pausing at every glowing red exit sign to try each door. But the building was on lockdown.

A fire extinguisher in a red box jutted out from the wall. I smashed the emergency glass with my elbow, pulled out the extinguisher, and zipped back to the glass passageway.

"O, Lady Moon, Lady of the Dead," chanted the voices, muted by the glass wall.

I scanned the reflection of their circle. There were at least forty figures out there. "*Dannazione.*" How many Ghost Drinkers had Callisto found? I supposed this had been his life's mission for the last hundred years.

Their voices raised, calling to their ancestors, begging for the power of the moon, the light of the dead.

"Make the Invisible visible . . ."

It was a sight spell. Entry-level necromancy. The Salazars had always been obsessed with the dead. Even before they began drinking them.

My biceps twitched, and I nearly smashed the window, but giving myself away to forty witches was far from wise. *Where the hell is Emilio?*

"Make the Invisible visible. Bring them to me."

Cold swirled around me, chilling me to the core, and a woman, aglow like an icy firefly, floated up beside me. She wore a lab coat and had safety glasses hanging around her neck.

Outside, an animal cried out in pain, and blood sprayed across the glass. The bear, which had reared up on its hind legs, tipped and crashed to the ground. A pearlescent string of light formed out of darkness in its place. As it grew in length, swirling through the air, another string of light sprouted from it. Then they were forming by the dozen, sprouting from one another like invasive vines, shimmering with rainbow light like the schiller of moonstone.

The glowing rope of moon magic broke apart, and the witches began materializing in their circle around the bear corpse, each holding an individual shimmering rope.

The ghostly woman in the lab coat drifted closer to the glass wall. One of the pearly ropes was wrapped around her right wrist. "Help!" she yelled, scrabbling for something to hold.

I reached for her but couldn't grasp her ethereal form; my hand smacked into the glass wall.

She shrieked as she was pulled through the glass.

Just beyond the dead bear, a small, frail girl with swirls of black curls and a dainty mauve-colored dress tugged on the other end of the magic leash, reeling it in and dragging the woman across the garden. She gazed at her prey with an innocent expression. I should have killed her in 1930.

When the woman was close, Celestina Salazar fell to her knees, her face contorting with rabid starvation and excitement, mouth opening, tongue inching out. The woman screamed with fear. As Celestina sucked, the spirit's legs elongated, stretching toward her lips. The woman's feet slipped into her mouth, and Celestina's throat glowed icy blue. As she drank, the blue lit up her chest and then her stomach. The spirit coursed through her system until every inch, from her curls to her fingertips, shined icy blue.

Afterward, she hiccupped, the glowing soul popped out of her mouth, and the blue shimmer faded from her body.

She giggled and turned back to gaze at the moon rope in her hand with awe as it slithered through the air like a snake, and then turned around excitedly in search of her next drink.

They were everywhere—no longer invisible—indigo shadows transforming into ethereal human forms of blue light, floating out of the ground, the buildings, the roofs and the sky. Men, women, children, all aglow, all being pulled by magical leashes into the mouths of witches. The witches flickered into view: Ghost Drinkers in flowing black cloaks, charged by the beams of the Flower Moon, hands raised to the air, drawing in their prey.

I lifted the fire extinguisher, but before I could send it sailing through the window, a creak tore through the night, and the witches scattered, arms flailing, shrieking in fear. Overhead, the dark shape of a tree rose up against the sky, tilted, and then crashed to the ground with a showering of leaves and such a thud, the building shook. The half-crushed body of one of the women lay sprawled under its trunk.

Emilio. I smashed the extinguisher against the wall, and the glass spidered. One more hit shattered it, and I lunged through the shower of glass toward the nearest witch and tore into his neck, smashing him to the ground. He fumbled for the knife at his belt, but I grabbed it for him and rammed it into his side. He coughed blood over my shoulder, and I sprang up.

"See you on the other side, brother," Emilio yelled, racing after the witches who were making for the woods. He zipped between them like a wolf after chickens.

Hundreds, thousands, of spirits materialized in every direction. Blueish-gray outlines of people in despair, trying to figure out what was going on.

Many of the witches had reached a parking area and were already escaping. I scanned the chaos for their leader. The tires of a Humvee squealed as the driver swerved wildly, and two motorcycles revved out of the parking lot and howled into the night.

The shield began breaking apart into sweeping nets that fell, collecting swarms of spirits on their way. The witches used their moon-magic ropes to hastily attach the nets to their vehicles and then peeled off into the woods.

Something wrenched at my ankle. I jerked away, and the roots of a tree slithered farther out of the ground toward my legs. Not far away, an Earth witch twisted his hands in the air.

I yanked the root, and it rippled out of the earth for twenty feet. He commanded it again with his magic and it shot from my hand, around my neck. I gasped as the coil tightened. Then he jerked the root, snapping the opposite end from the ground. He pulled tighter, and I whipped it through the air and slapped it around him, crushing his ribs.

"Bastard!" he yelled in agony, tightening the root once more.

I slammed him into the base of the watchtower. He didn't get up, and the root slithered off my shoulders.

Loose souls hummed around me, buzzing. I swatted them away, my gaze darting from witch to witch as they fled. They were nearly impossible to distinguish from one another in their dark cloaks, but I spotted Celestina climbing into a sidecar. Callisto would never be far from his sister, but the witch starting the bike was a heavy-set blonde.

There. He was on the bike next to them. His hood slipped from his head as he stomped the bike alive, and the young woman seated behind him circled her arms around his torso. They took off, her long red hair cascading from her helmet.

I sped across the lawn after them. Callisto's bike shot to sixty, and I launched myself into the air, arms outstretched. I missed him but clamped onto the girl, pulling her down with me; we slid through the mud twisting and twisting until we slammed into a jagged boulder with a crack. The flare of pain told me it was my radius bone. She vanished from sight and tried to scramble away, but I didn't need to see her; the fear beating in her pulse was loud and clear. I gripped her throat with my good hand and removed her helmet with the other. I tossed it aside.

She reappeared. "You must be Nicco," she said, trying hard to bring out a seductive thrill in her voice. "I've heard so much about you."

"I can only imagine what Callisto has filled your head with." I glanced back to his bike, which was still heading toward the city.

"Maybe instead you should imagine everything Adele's told me about you."

I squeezed her throat tighter. I wasn't in the mood for games.

"God, she was *pathetic.* Wandering around in your leather jacket," she choked out.

I loosened my grip just enough so she could speak.

"Those big blue eyes glossing up over the poor vampire she couldn't get over. '*It felt magical.*' Barf."

Who is she? The watchtower light flooded over her face, but I didn't recognize her. Her Aether blood smelled familiar, but I couldn't immediately place it.

Callisto skidded to a stop and spun around, and several of his entourage came revving back from the woods at his sides.

"He's coming back for you. I didn't know Callisto had the capacity to care for anyone other than Salazars, not even pretty auburn-haired witches."

"I don't need him to save me. I'm not pathetic like Adele!"

"Looks to me like you do."

She smirked with the cultish delusion all of Callisto's disciples wore so proudly. "Sébastien!" she yelled.

I looked back, expecting to see a witch coming for me, or a snarling wolf familiar—but there was no one.

"Time to come out and play!" the girl called out.

I followed her gaze up to the watchtower. A young blond man in a lab coat stood on the lookout balcony. "*Is that*—?"

"My insurance plan," she said, as he climbed onto the rail. "Sébastien, *jump*!"

"*No*!" I slammed her shoulders into the ground.

Mud splashed over us as Callis's bike twisted to a stop, but I was already racing back toward Adele's friend who had sailed over the ledge, arms out. Motorcycles revved, coming after me. I skidded to the ground as I caught Sébastien, just barely, his vertebrae cracking against my arms —but I was going too fast to stop, and we crashed straight through one of the glass walkways and tumbled into the corridor.

"Stop wasting time here," Callis yelled over the rumble of idling bikes outside. "Go back to town and find Adele!"

I caught the whiff of Callisto's flame.

An explosion lifted us into the air, and all I could do was hang onto Sébastien as we were thrown down the hall and into one of the laboratories. My skull cracked against a concrete wall. I slid down, feeling a trickle of liquid into my hair. Dizziness dotted my vision, and heat rolled over us in waves.

Flames licked the walls, burning up the papers pinned to them; glass canisters began popping one by one. The air reeked of gas. We needed to get out of the lab, away from the chemicals. "Sébastien!" I yelled, looking around for him.

Pain flared from my thigh. A thick piece of window glass jutted out of it, the wound oozing dark-red blood. I grabbed the shard and tore it from my leg, letting out a roar. The sliced muscle bulged out of my flesh, releasing a river of blood. I pushed the muscle back in, my hands sliding, and pressed both sides together so muscle touched muscle and flesh touched flesh. I fought the dizziness, praying to the gods for the pieces to start mending.

A whoosh of gas ignited, and then everything went silent other than the ringing in my ears. The flames cradled me in a basket of warmth, lulling me to sleep. I told myself to fight the rising wave of darkness, but it crashed over me like a tsunami and pulled me under.

CHAPTER 59

FLORALIA

Sprawled over his chest, I gazed up at him as he slept. The twinkling blanket covered our legs, and the moonlight poured in through the windows across the rest of us.

The three little words echoed in my head.

Everything about Isaac was calming, but there was something about saying those three little words that made my stomach twist into knots. Not in an I-want-to-run-away way, just in a way that made me a level of nervous I'd never experienced before. And I was annoyed with myself because I didn't understand it.

His eyes blinked heavily, and I smiled.

"I didn't mean to fall asleep!" he said, slightly panicked.

"It's okay. You're beautiful when you sleep."

He laughed a little, adjusting his pillow, and then he looked at me as if with wonder. "You're still here."

"Of course I'm still here." I tried not to be hurt by his thinking I would actually skip out after all we'd been through.

He smiled and stroked my shoulder. "What were you thinking about before?"

My back tensed, and concern washed over his face.

"I-I . . ." I stuttered, trying to think of something else to say, but I was incapable of hiding anything from him after what happened with Brigitte. "I know that I love you."

His eyes widened.

"But I don't know why it's so hard for me to say it. Every time I try, I get so nervous, I feel like I'm going to throw up."

He held his expression still, as if trying to mask his confusion; I couldn't believe I'd said something so awful.

"Does it bother you when I say it?" he asked.

I thought about it and then shook my head. "No . . . it makes me feel good."

He smiled with nervous relief. "Well then, don't worry about it. I don't want you to feel pressured into anything, ever."

"But does it bother you when I don't say it?"

"Don't worry about me. Please, don't worry about anything right now." He smiled reassuringly and pulled me closer, his arms sliding around the small of my back. "Okay?"

"Okay." His smile made me smile, and when I kissed him, he rolled on top of me.

"Promise?" He brushed my neck with his lips. The tickle made my shoulders pinch.

"*Yes*," I said, trying to tug him back to my mouth, but he lowered himself down my body and kissed the roundest part of my stomach. "Do you feel better now?"

"*Mm-hmm*." My fingers floated into his hair, and I felt a little silly, like I'd been melodramatic, but I also felt a hundred times better, the pressure no longer weighing me down.

He kissed the crook of my waist, and my back arched a little from the bed. He moved lower, opening my leg, and kissed me again. "What about now?"

Just air came out of my throat, and he didn't stop until my fingers were twisting into the sheet.

This time when we finished, there was no stress. He wrapped me into his chest, and I clung to him, unable to stop gazing up at him.

He peered down and caught me staring, and I blushed hard, but I didn't care.

"We missed the moon circle," I said softly.

"This was way better, I promise."

I bit my bottom lip, trying not to laugh. "We're terrible witches. We missed all of Beltane."

"Pretty sure we celebrated the exuberance of life more than anyone."

I pinched his side, and he pulled me closer.

"The moon's still out there," he said.

"Want to have our own moon circle?"

"I want to do anything with you."

"*Bien.*" I kissed him.

"Want me to take you up to the roof? It's amazing up there, you can see all the way down to the river."

"*Oui!*"

"I think you have some shorts mixed in with my stuff."

I got up, dug through his clothes, and found the cutoffs I'd been missing for weeks, while he tugged on his jeans, a shawl of sparkles hiding his bare chest. I slipped on my dad's shirt and slid my phone into my back pocket.

"Ready?" he asked.

I nodded but first reached out for the blanket around his neck and pulled him close, unable to resist one more kiss before we left our perfect little nest.

We went up to the attic, climbed through one of the dormer windows, and walked across the roof's gentle slope to one of the chimneys. The electric grid to the east was still defunct, and the stars sprawled across the sky, shining brighter as if trying to make up for it.

He sat down, pulled me into his lap, and stretched the blanket out over us. I leaned into his chest.

"How's this?" he asked.

"It's perfect." The moon had been right above me every night of my life, but this felt like the first time I'd ever really taken the time to look at her. We were so high up, and she was so swollen, full and bright, it felt like we could reach up and touch her.

A breeze rolled off the river, carrying the sound of the waves crashing against the levee, and Isaac held me tighter.

"Happy Witches' Night," I said, craning my neck to see him.

"Happy Witches' Night, babe." He kissed me softly and I leaned back, basking in the beams of the Flower Moon and his calming aura.

At some point, my eyes slipped shut, and the river waves rolled my mind to another place. I smelled the faint scent of fire and wondered if it was the pit at the Daures' wafting up to us. The Beltane fire. Like what Nicco had called me.

I wanted my Fire.

A fire blazes beside us in the palazzo courtyard. The northern nighttime breeze in Venezia is cooler than it is back home, despite it being nearly spring.

"What brothers get their sister a rapier for her wedding gift?" Vittorio Barbargio asks.

Gabriel examines the blade Vittorio and his sister made for us. "Ones who hope she'll use it to slit her new husband's throat as he sleeps."

I look at León, who is lounging next to us near the fountain.

"It's beautiful," León says, and I am quite sure he's about to offer to deliver it himself and personally put it through the viceroy's neck.

I wonder if he's wearying of staying here. He surely hadn't expected to wait a whole month for my sister's wedding gift to be ready, but the Barbargio famiglia *had been gracious hosts, and León had seemed to enjoy trading spells and sharing circles with the maritime witches of the Adriatic.*

Gabriel hands me the sword so I can have a closer look. The magical metalsmithing has been passed down through the generations of Barbargios —one of the great patrician families of Venezia and one of the strongest allies of the Medici, both in the magical world and in the mundane—the craftsmanship of each descendant more remarkable than the one before. Legend has it, their propensity for metal, weaponry, and Venezia came from pirating gold on the Adriatic Sea before settling these ancient islands. However they came into their trade, I have never seen anyone produce more delicate and deadly weapons than Elena and Vittorio Barbargio, twins only a few years older than Gabriel.

I sheathe the blade and hand it back. As Gabriel sets it aside, I study the way Elena looks at my brother. I am quite sure she was Gabriel's first love and also the reason he'd made such a large investment in Veneziano silk, which gave him strong ties to the city and to her bed.

"Niccolò," she says, taking a sip of vino, "now that you have the sword, does this mean you'll be choosing the next stop on your sojourn?"

"Yes, it seems so. León and I will part ways with Tuviani, who travels

next to Bologna on his academic tour, and the big decision for us becomes: east to Dubrovnik or south to Sicilia."

"You can't leave yet," comes a voice from above, both assertive and angelic.

We all look up.

A young woman with long honey-colored curls steps from behind a column, watching over us from the mezzanine. The moonlight illuminates the pale skin beneath the sheer silk bodice of her dress, giving me a new appreciation for the female form, while her naked breasts give me a new appreciation for Veneziano fashion and our investment in silk.

"And why is that?" Gabriel asks.

Her eyes remain locked with mine as she speaks. "Because it's nearly Floralia. And there is nothing more beautiful than Venezia under the light of the spring moon. You wouldn't want to disappoint Flora by leaving so soon before her feast."

If my view of her beauty is any indication of the rest of Venezia in the moonlight, it is a point that cannot be argued. "Does your father know of your concern with ancient goddesses?" I ask, gazing at the stretch of her arm where her Mark would have been if she were magical.

"Of course he does." She drops down five small scrolls.

I reach for the one that lands in the fountain, rescuing it from the water before it can be damaged.

FLORALIA

Festa Romana di Primavera

28 aprile 1612

For six days and six nights,
We will celebrate spring
As the ancients once did.

I wonder what she'd say if she knew the witches of my acquaintance, many of whom still worship the old gods and goddesses on the major and even minor celestial events. Still, this from a mundane . . . it's positively beguiling.

I look back up, but she's gone.

Vittorio takes a sip from his glass. "She's a strange creature. Completely fascinated with the classics. Her father's spent a small fortune over the last few years hosting the festival just to please her, though by now it seems that most of the town is involved. Not that I am complaining. She is correct, there is nothing more beautiful than Venezia under the enchanting spring moon."

I find myself still looking up. "Who is—?"

"Maddalena Morosini," Elena says. "Her family lives in the corner palazzo on the adjacent canal."

"What's her relation to Marco Morosini?" Gabriel asks of the great swordsman.

"Younger sister," Vittorio says.

Elena continues: "We've watched her grow up like a wildcat ever since her mother died. Her father indulges all of her whims to distract her from the droves of men who come calling."

"Which are?" I ask.

"There was an English Duke and a Roman—"

"Not the men," I say. "Her whims. What are her whims?"

"Elaborate libraries. Elaborate swimming pools. She's rumored to have one pool so big she rows her own gondola in it. And of course, Floralia. This whim the entire town benefits from."

"How very donna strega," *Gabriel says.*

"Indeed. She grows a flower garden just to pick them for the festival. Her night blossoms are so bold, I sometimes use them for potions. She always delivers the invitations to the neighbors, but usually, she floats in like a goddess herself, dropping them down from the heavens without saying a word." She looks at her brother. "I can't remember her ever personally inviting either of us." A smile creeps over her face. "You should stay, Niccolò. We all know you have a passion for libraries."

I look at León, suddenly remembering the whole reason we started on this sojourn. "We couldn't. Now that we've parted ways with Tuviani, we can give our full attention to the goal of this trip: expanding our knowledge of the healing properties of Italian folk magic." And mending León's poor broken heart.

"I'm quite certain," Gabriel says, "that father approved of your deferment from university so that you could advance not only your magical acumen but also your knowledge of all the daughters of the Great families."

"The Morosini are not a Great family."

Vittorio dips his hand in the fountain. "Maybe not to the magical, but they are to Venezia."

"What they lack in magic, they make up for in fleets," Gabriel adds.

León stands, winking at my brother.

"Where are you going?" I ask.

"To accept the invitation on your behalf. My loveless future will not be the reason for yours."

"I am not worried about either of us having loveless futures."

"No need, León," Gabriel says, draining his cup and standing with a stretch. "I can go and accept on behalf of the family and get a tour of the garden. Maybe she—"

"I'll do it!" I spring up, scroll in hand, trying not to imagine my brother gaining a private audience with Maddalena Morosini. "I don't think you'll have any interest in libraries if she offers to show you her collection."

They all laugh, and he tries to tousle my hair as if I am still fifteen, but I easily escape his embrace.

"Please report back on her tomes," Vittorio says.

I shoot him a look as I throw on my cloak and hurriedly climb the stairs to the palazzo.

At the canal, I toss a coin to the gondolier to take me across.

"Where to, signore Medici?" he asks, twisting his dark moustache.

I name the place, and we push away from the dock.

As I sit back, I hear not the sounds of gently rocking waves but the crackling of flames. I smell fire: burning timber and the sharp scent of something like brimstone. "What can that be?" I twist around in the gondola. Flames are all around us, floating on top of the water. They grow closer with each stroke of the oar.

The gondolier looks at me. "Wake up," he says. "Wake up, Niccolò, or you'll never see her again."

If his words have meaning, they are lost on me.

Thump-thump.

"You're losing blood," he says. "We need to get out of here. The building is going to blow."

"You drunken fool," I say.

But then I look down at my leg and see my breeches are covered in crimson. I look once more to the gondolier and take a startled breath. His hair is now blond under the hat, and he has on the most unusual spectacles.

"I think I've changed my mind," I say. "I'm rather tired." I lay down in the boat, curling up, surrounded by warmth.

"No!" he yells, as if from a distance, but I am nodding off. I must have drunk too deeply of the wine tonight.

My head swirls with colors. Pinks. Purples. Oranges. Yellows.

Blossoms. Buds. And petals.

Twisted into crowns and masks and chains.

Both the high families of Venezia and the low families spare neither expense nor effort to cover the entire city in blossoms. By the time the sixth day of Floralia comes upon us, the canals are so covered in flowers, you would swear you could skip across them. I've spent every moment with León, going to games and circuses, all the while trying to be discreet with my glances at Maddalena, for anyone who comes within a stone's throw of him can sense his weeping heart, despite the best effort he puts forth to hide it. But as the days pass and the wine flows and the nights shorten, I find myself escaping more and more frequently to find her, until Elena and Vittorio and Gabriel and even León—whom I owe a lifetime of gratitude—are taking turns entertaining Marco Morosini, all so that Maddalena can escape his watchful eye, and I can escape the swing of his blade. Each night, we become closer; and each night, we become just a little more desperate, knowing that the festival is nearer to the end. Tonight, we flee to the square where, amongst the throngs of people, we don't need masks to steal kisses and touches as we dance in the crowds.

She catches me staring at the moon and asks me a peculiar question: "Do you like the forest, Niccolò?"

I kiss her hand and twirl her around, telling her exactly how much I adore the Natural World and all of its power to heal. I wish I could tell her that all witches love the forest.

My answer is apparently the one she wishes to hear, for she smiles a devious smile. "Can you keep a secret?" she asks. "I want to show you something."

There were days I felt like more of life was a secret than not. "I swear on my mother's grave."

She draws the hood of her cloak over her head so it shields her face from onlookers, and only after I do the same does she take my hand. She leads me all the way down to the river, but instead of paying the gondolier for a ride, she pays him to borrow his boat. I sense this isn't her first time doing so.

I pick up the long wooden oar, but she takes it from me, shaking her head. "We'll get there faster if I row," she says with a smile, and pushes the boat away from the shore, sending us into a steady glide.

"And what am I to do? Lie here and eat grapes?"

"Sì," she answers playfully. "And tell me a story."

And I do. I chose the Greek tale of the goddess Flora and the two brothers who fought over her heart: the aggressive, bitter North Wind, the bringer of cold, and the gentle West Wind, bringer of light and spring.

"Zephyr, the West Wind, made her blossom and won her heart," I say, "and together they bore a son, Karpos, the god of fruit, as Ovid told the tale . . ."

I am quite sure she knows the story, but she listens keenly as she pushes us out and across the widest part of the canal—not toward the neighboring streets or square but toward the forest to the North. Only when she starts to shake with fatigue does she let me slip the oar from her hands and paddle the rest of the way.

When we hit land, she hides the oar under some branches, and I wonder how many times she has done this before. She takes my hand and guides me through the untamed forest, led only by the light of the moon. The trees become denser, but we keep hiking. The deeper we go, the more astounded I am that she can navigate through the darkness—although I would not be devastated to be lost in the forest for days if it meant being alone with her. I revel in the magic of the trees, and before I even realize it, we've stumbled into an alcove, and she has already slipped off her cloak and let it drop to the forest floor.

She takes off her shoes. More pieces of her dress come off as she twirls under the stars, and I am so distracted by her beauty that at first I don't notice the ancient ruins she's brought me to see: an open-air temple lined with torches that once held great flames. The ruins are partially hidden beneath crawling vines and dipping tree branches, as if Mother Earth is reclaiming the broken stone columns.

While the temple might be a shambles, the energy is more alive than anything I've felt outside my father's circles. Fresh flowers have been scattered all over the forest floor, but most heavily condensed into an altar at the foot of the temple steps. Clearly, we are not the only ones to have come here tonight. Maddalena's eyes are ablaze with wonder, looking at the altar, for the magic is so powerful here under the full moon that it's impossible for it to go unnoticed, even by the mundane. I thank the northern Veneziano witches.

"Some still worship her," she tells me, a little nervousness in her voice.

Does she think I might run and alert her father—or worse, the bishop—that she is not only obsessed with the classics but is also a wild heathen who dances under the stars with the forest nymphs?

"We should have brought a sacrifice," I say, stepping close, my eyes on the cross dangling from her chain. I remove it from her neck, my knuckles skimming the chemise at her breasts, and let the necklace gently fall on top of her cloak on the forest floor, assuring her that her secret is safe and that from me she will get no judgment. I wish I could tell her why.

"I'm sure we'll find a way to please the gods," she says, and my lips ache to touch hers.

I step so close, our bodies brush. "How do you know about this place?"

"My mother used to take me here."

Is it possible her mother was a witch? I stroke her arm and gently lift it, turning it into the light.

"You are always glancing at it," she says. "Is it only my arm you are interested in?"

I slowly shake my head, and her defiant gaze locks with mine. I tug the last layer of her gown off her shoulders and let it slip to the forest floor.

Blossoms litter her long curls. I push back her hair, absorbing each of her shivers, and gaze at her, thoroughly mesmerized, and not just by her beauty but by the past days of conversations. Her inquisitive nature and her curiosity of my studies. And the way she cares for her father and brother. The longer I stare at the soft curves of her body, the more her beauty captivates me, and the more I yearn to make her blossom.

I bow my head to hers. "Is your mother a goddess? I am starting to have a hard time believing you aren't the daughter of Flora herself."

She fights a smile, and I can no longer resist. I kiss her lips—just barely. The gentle touch is a million times more sensational than all of our stolen kisses combined, for the cloak of the forest offers the chance for more, which I take, softly kissing her again and then more fully as her mouth opens to mine.

She pushes my doublet away from my arms, and I lift my shirt over my head. My desire builds as she removes each of my garments, until I'm as naked as she is and desperate for more of her shivers. Her lips return to mine, and I slide my hand between her legs. She falls against me, and I become enraptured by the sounds of her breath in the silent forest night.

I say a little devotion to Flora as I lay Maddalena on the bed of flowers. I lose myself to her touches, and the scent of the petals carves a permanent place in my memory, marking this moment of deepest pleasure. As we give ourselves to each other, the Flower Moon charges us with her bright beams of pale light, and despite the cool soil beneath us and the babbling of the nearby river, I feel as if I am barely on this Earth. My fingers twist into hers, and I pull her arms up over her head, deeper into the flora.

"Niccolò," she whispers, her voice unsteady. "Niccolò, il cielo notturno. Gaurdare!"

I twist us around, churning the blossoms. She whimpers as we come back together, and the sound makes me forget why we've moved. "We've pleased . . . the heavens."

Lightning flashes bright across the nocturnal sky, and I finally see past her nymphet beauty—my body stiffens as if I'd been struck. Monstrous flames blaze from the temple torches. I've never lost such control of my magic, ever. But I can't stop. I need her.

I need her completely.

I kiss her until long after we finish, and when I gaze upon her satisfied smile, I am so bewitched by it that I nearly tell her it wasn't Flora who she'd pleased, but me.

Maddalena Morosini might not have magic, but she has certainly enchanted me.

"Niccolò," she whispers. "Niccolò, my love. You have to wake up. Wake up, or you will never see her again."

Thump-thump.

"Nicco, wake up. For me."

I open my eyes to gaze at Adele, and I cannot remember the last time I was so happy to awaken. "The moonlight suits you, bella."

"The moon lights the dead, Nicco." She slides her hand up my chest, her touch drawing out my fangs, reminding me how starved I am.

Why am I so starved?

I peer into her eyes. "It will be best if we don't drag it out, my love."

She nods, and I twist on top of her, my fangs plunging into her neck. Her blood spills into my throat, sending me first into bliss and then into ecstasy when she bucks up against me, writhing.

Thump-thump.

Thump-thump.

Thump-thump.

Her body falls limp, and my venom takes her as I drink. Her pulse slows, and my euphoria rises, the taste of her magic making me come undone.

Thump.

Thump.

Thump.

"Il mio cuore è solo tuo," *she gasps with her last breath.*

"And my heart is yours," I say, sliding my teeth into my wrist, listening for the exact moment her heartbeat stops.

Thump.

I kiss her warm, dead lips, and then I hold out my wrist, letting my blood trickle over her mouth until her tongue draws to my skin. I pull away, just a bit, and she lifts her head to keep licking at the blood. She reaches out, wraps both hands around my arm, and settles back down to lap at my wrist.

I lay beside her, enthralled, as she drinks.

My blood. My life.

"You will blossom, bella."

Her naked body arches off the bed, and I dream about the moment I can touch her with her new vampiric sensitivity. The pleasure I can bring her. I gasp as her fangs dig into the wounds, opening them wider so she can drink deeper. And I let her until dizziness takes hold of my fantasy.

I remove my wrist and replace it with my lips. My tongue grazes her fangs, and I taste my own blood.

She pulls me close. "Nicco, I can taste your magic."

"It's just my blood."

"No, it's not, Nicco. I can taste it—your magic. Your lightning. I need more."

"And more you will get, but first we must find another, to complete your transition."

Thump-thump.

Thump-thump.

"I would never! Wake up, bella."

Thump-thump.

"Adele, wake up!"

"Stop, Nicco!" I yelled, bolting upright. I shrieked as an arm slid around my stomach.

"Adele, I've got you!"

I clutched onto Isaac, feeling a sense of vertigo as the city's rooftops swam into view below.

"What's wrong?" he asked, panicked.

Chest heaving, I shut my eyes. I could still feel the thumps of Nicco's heartbeat.

"Hey . . ." Isaac cocooned around me.

"*It was just a dream*," I told myself, trying to temper my trembles. "*Nicco would never.*"

"Nicco would never what?" He pulled my hand away from my neck. "Bite you? You're dreaming about Nicco biting you?"

"It wasn't my dream . . ." I was barely able to look at him. "It was Nicco's."

His teeth gnashed. "*Nicco*'s dreaming about biting you?"

"I think something's wrong."

"Of course something's wrong! A monster is fantasizing about killing you!"

"No. Something's wrong with Nicco. He never sleeps at night in case our dreams connect. He doesn't want me to see inside his head." Panic overtook me. "Something's wrong."

I stood up too quickly and wobbled. Again, Isaac caught me, this time with his Air. He gently pulled me back down. "Please don't go."

I patted myself, looking for my phone, and pulled it out of my shorts pocket.

When I turned it on, it lit up with missed calls and messages. Several were from Nicco, but the last one was from a couple hours ago.

I hit the call-back button.

It rang and rang, until a recording of an operator broke in to say, "The person you are calling is unavailable," and the line disconnected.

I punched in a message: *Sorry, my phone was off. Are you okay? I'm sorry about the party. I went to your house after, but you weren't there.*

My heart pounded as I stared at the screen, hoping for a sign that he was there on the other end.

Isaac slid the phone from my hand and set it down. "Nothing's wrong."

"How do you know?"

He pulled the blanket back over me. "I should have told you . . . but, before I got to the bar, Nicco and I got into it. I told him to stay the hell away from you."

"*Isaac.*"

"I wouldn't tell him where you were—only that we were together—

so he's just pissed off now and trying to show me that your connection with him is stronger."

I twisted around to look at him. "He already knew we were together. I told him last night."

"You did?"

"Why didn't you tell me you knew where he was? You knew I was looking for . . ." I trailed off, seeing the serious look on his face. "Isaac, what is it?"

"I'm not supposed to tell you."

"Tell me what?"

"Let's go back inside."

"No. Tell me now."

He sucked a breath through his nose and turned me completely around so he could see my face. He locked me between his legs so I wouldn't fall back. "Adele, I love you, and I'm not going to let anything happen to you." His Air swirled around us, strong and protective, as if ready to catch me.

"You're freaking me out."

"Earlier . . . Olsin Daure didn't throw Nicco out because he's vampire; he threw him out because . . ." He looked directly into my eyes. "He had a premonition . . ."

"Of?"

"Of . . . your death."

"What do you mean?"

"Nicco kil—"

"No." I shook my head, standing up.

"Adele—"

"What did he say?"

"Just that he saw the two of you kissing—"

I scoffed.

"Nicco had your *blood* in his mouth . . ."

I felt the tears coming. I twisted back around, blinking them away. His arms encased me. I could tell he was genuinely terrified. "I'm not going to let him take you," he said, trying to be gentle. We sat back down together.

"Nothing's going to happen. I'll be fine." My voice sounded strange, like I was somewhere else looking in. I imagined Nicco's fingers grazing my throat as he moved closer to my neck. His teeth on my skin. I sucked in a sharp breath.

Nicco would never hurt me.

I wasn't scared of Nicco. I hadn't been scared yesterday, I wasn't tonight, and I wouldn't be tomorrow. I knew from growing up around the Daures and working in the shop that psychics aren't perfect. That's why they don't tell people stuff like this. I knew in my heart, in my soul, that Nicco would never hurt me, but still, my hands trembled. I pulled Isaac's hand to my mouth and pressed my lips against it, hoping he wouldn't notice. "It's going to be fine, Isaac."

He leaned his head against mine and nuzzled my hair.

I gazed out toward the river, over the lower rooftops of the Quarter. The cathedral steeples, shining in the moonlight, towered above the rooftops, as if standing watch over the city as it slept. *Would he go to the bell tower if he was in distress?* It was our tower.

I didn't know if it was the big Flower Moon shining down on us or Isaac's arms around me or his magical Air, but there was a disturbing calmness. Like when the temperature eerily drops right before a storm and you know you're about to be in the hands of the hurricane.

"Did you tell Nicco about the premonition?"

"Yes."

And for the first time, I was scared. Not of Nicco, but that he'd left and I'd never see him again.

"I just want you to be safe."

"I know."

He held me tighter, and I gazed back out. The stars felt closer, blanketing us with their cosmic glow.

The moon's light shines on the dead.

Nicco's dream—his fantasy—slipped to the front of my mind. He hadn't been just biting me or killing me. He'd been turning me into a vampire. "*There are things worse than death.*" This was what he didn't want me to see.

"*Reste loin de Niccolò Medici*!" Adeline bellowed in my head.

Nicco would never hurt me.

"*Never trust a vampire.*"

The air whirled around us again, and from down in the garden behind us, the hummingbirds in the pigeonnier began to sing. However, the sweet chirping didn't match the ominous rustling of feathers that suddenly surrounded us. We glanced around. One by one, crows were landing on the roof, the chimney, the gables of the dormer windows—and everyone was looking out to the eastern sky.

"What are they doing?"

"I don't know," Isaac said, following their gazes.

A coyote howled in the distance, and the stars to the East seemed to pulse. I blinked, peering at the horizon. It looked as if the stars amassed there had fallen out of the sky, only . . . they were rising, not falling. Tiny bursts of light popping into the sky, like thousands of orbs.

Isaac's back stiffened.

"Do you see that?" I asked. "Is it fireworks?"

"Not like any I've ever seen."

The lights began clustering together, forming frenetic constellations, like the blinking tangles of Christmas lights going berserk.

The clusters merged, becoming clouds.

We both slowly stood up. I glanced at Isaac, and the look of horror on his face chilled me. His skin looked paler than the moonlight could account for.

The clouds were moving. Two huge storm clouds of blinking fire, lighting up the sky and rolling toward us. "We need to go," he said, grabbing my hand. "Those are souls! They're swarming."

CHAPTER 60

BETTER OFF

"*Wake up . . .*"

"*Wake up, Nicco.*"

I loved warmth: crackling fires, burning embers. When I was first turned into a vampire, I used to sit in front of the fireplace for hours each day, trying to forget the coldness of my being. But this warmth, this heat, was unbearable. The scent was toxic. And I was drenched in sweat. *I never sweat.*

"Nicco, wake up! Fire! The morgue is going to blow . . ." The voice trailed to nothingness.

I forced my eyes open, and the blurry room came into view, glowing orange everywhere. I shot up to my feet and then collapsed, holding my leg. It was soaked in blood and still not healed.

A cough came from the floor across the smoke-filled room. Adele's friend from the café was pinned beneath a metal shelving unit with broken jars of formaldehyde scattered all around him. I forced myself up again, pushing through the pain, and limped over to him.

I grasped the wall unit, the stainless steel sizzling into my skin, and heaved it aside.

His face and arm were charred where the metal had burned through skin and fat all the way to the bone in his cheek, and his arm was a blackened mess. My fangs pulsed as I inhaled the scent of his blood through the smoke, gas, and chemicals.

The flames around us had grown larger already. I needed his blood to heal me faster.

Glass panes in cabinets combusted in a series of sharp explosions.

My head spun from the pain.

He was unresponsive, and I couldn't get a read on his pulse through my dizziness. "Come on, Sébastien."

I surveyed the two exits: the glass window where we'd been thrown into the room, and the door. The small window was a raging inferno blasting heat into the room, but the doorway leading out to a dark hallway was barely visible behind the wall of bright flames and black coiling smoke. It was our best and only shot. I zipped around the room, snatching up towels and shaking glass from their folds, and then dragged an emergency hazmat shower over to Sébastien, ripped off his chemical-soaked lab coat and T-shirt, and slammed the button on the portable shower, soaking him and the towels. I pulled the wet material over his head and hoisted him up onto my shoulder.

"Hang on," I said to his deadweight.

The doorway, at least, was open, but its frame was already burning. I sped out into the hallway. It was black with toxic smoke, and fire crept up the left wall. An explosion of shattering glass echoed behind me as the heat blew open a walkway. The building moaned, and something cracked overhead. I dodged a collapsing support structure, reached an exit, and kicked it open.

My feet touched grass, and the air felt angelic. I sprinted toward the swamps. There was a great rumbling roar, and an epic wave of heat whooshed up from behind us as the building went up. I held onto Sébastien and threw us into the swamp, shoots of cane snapping all around as we crashed into the water.

I dragged him up a bank between some mossy trees, my leg repeatedly collapsing beneath us. *I can't let another person in her life die.*

I placed my fingers on his neck, and my fangs stretched when I felt the faint beats of his heart. I needed to heal faster. I needed to get back and find Adele before Callis did. *What the hell does he still want with her?*

I wiped away the smear of char from Sébastien's neck. Patches of his hair were burnt off and blotches of his skin were deep red and bubbling with chemical burns. *It's the only chance he has.* I sank straight into his artery, pulling, pulling, pulling, trying not to be intoxicated by the unusually warm temperature of his blood. My arm bone snapped back into place with a muted crack, and the muscle in my thigh twitched, regenerating rapidly. I monitored his pulse, and when it became faint, I tore my mouth away, hissing, wanting more. *No one would ever know.*

I drew my wrist to my mouth to heal him, but then the beat of his heart slipped from my senses.

I placed my ear to his chest and heard the muscle struggling to pump. He was barely hanging on. If I let him feed from me and he died, he'd start to turn.

He'd be better off dead.

His pulse slipped to nothingness. "*Merda.*"

I began performing chest compressions, fighting the urge to bolt—to find Adele, to check on my family, to go straight after Callisto and rip him limb from limb. I breathed into his mouth. Again.

"Come on, Sébastien!" I yelled, pressing on his chest. "We have to get back to Adele. To your sister. They need you!" An alarm screeched over the sound of burning, cracking timbers.

He gasped for air and made eye contact for a brief second before his head rolled back to the ground. His pulse was strengthening, but he was unconscious.

"It's better that way. This is going to hurt." I pulled him to a sitting position then hoisted him over my back and shoulders.

I took off toward the highway, my leg getting stronger with each passing minute. By the time we reached the road, it was nearly healed.

A pair of headlights approached down the dark strip. I waited until the car was close, and then leapt out in front of it.

Tires skidded to a stop on the slick road just before the hood of the car reached me.

"Are you okay?" a guy yelled as I moved to the driver's side door.

His eyes went wide, and I caught my own reflection in the window as I opened the door: clothes torn, charred, and swamp-sodden. A smear of blood across my chin.

"Get out."

CHAPTER 61

SOULS SEARCHING

I shoved my grimoire in my knapsack, keeping my eyes glued to Adele, as if a soul might burst through the window and dive straight into her. After she put on her sandals, I slipped the knapsack on her back.

I could tell she had a million questions, but I just took her hand. "Come on." And we bolted down the brothel hallway.

All I could think about was Nicco's plea. He'd said they were going to take down Callis somewhere outside of the parish lines, and those souls were definitely coming from the East. At the rate they were flooding across the sky, it wouldn't be long before they were here. *What the hell happened?*

"Isaac, what's going on?" Fear crept into her voice.

"I don't know . . . Let's just get to Ritha's." Maybe moving locations was a bad idea, but I'd been through enough natural disasters to know there was limited time to evacuate before you'd be trapped. The Voodoo shop was only a few blocks away.

We rushed down the stairs, but before we went out the front door, I turned to her. "Everything is going to be fine. Okay? We just need to get there before that swarm descends. Ritha will know what to do."

She nodded, and I kissed her, and we went back out into the world.

I pulled my phone out as we ran down the street and tapped Nicco's name.

"Who are you calling?"

"Désirée," I lied. *Fucking pick up, Nicco.*

The clicks of Stormy's nails were suddenly at my side, ghostly yelps vying for my attention.

"Isaac!" Adele yelled, pointing ahead. "Is that a . . . ?"

We both stopped. Just ahead of us, a stray soul shimmered, bright as a star plucked from the sky. It looked ethereal and beautiful bobbing down the street—not like a parasite hunting for a spirit to burrow into and suck the life out of.

"Shit." I backed us up a few steps. Maybe we should go back to the brothel, and I could go and get help. "Be as quiet as you can. They sense sound."

I stood in front of her and inched us back, monitoring its movements.

"There's another one!" she whispered, tugging at me. My gaze darted back in the other direction. *Fuck.* It was hovering between us and the brothel.

Observe.

Across the street, next to a house that looked like the residents hadn't returned, was an alleyway with a wrought-iron gate left ajar.

I gave Adele a look to signal my intention, and then directed the gentlest breeze against the bars, pushing it open to clear a path for us. She squeezed my hand, and we crept slowly across the street, trying not to make a sound.

A cat bolted out of the alley with a loud meow, and my pulse skipped. Both of the souls rotated as if to face us.

"Run!" I darted toward the gate, pulling Adele along with me. I glanced back just as we entered the alley to see both souls heading for us.

"It's a dead-end!" she said.

The brick wall at the other end of the alley glittered with shards of glass, fixed in place to keep out intruders.

"Don't slow down!" My voice echoed up the brick walls. "Don't stop!" I released her hand and pushed her on ahead of me. I stopped running and raised my hands, feeling the cool, damp air around me. *Adapt.*

She looked back. "Isaac!"

"Keep running!"

The glow of the souls approaching behind me lit up the alley walls. I spun the Air between my hands. She was almost there.

"Isaac!"

"Don't stop!"

When she neared the back wall, I hurled the Air down the alleyway and twisted her over, praying there weren't any mundane on the other side.

I soared over the glass shards and landed next to her. "Come on!" I said, grabbing her hand.

The souls were coming over the wall, lighting up the glass on top like a beautiful piece of art.

We set off running, heading in the opposite direction than we needed to go, but they were so close behind, we had no choice. The faster we ran, the louder her sandals slapped the pavement. We were almost out of the Quarter. There was only one place that would be as safe as the Borges' or the Daures' and it was just on the other side of Rampart.

"Isaac, they're getting closer!" she yelled, looking back as we ran.

"Keep running—straight to Louis No. 1! As fast as you can. Nothing can get you behind the gate!" I let go of her hand and leaped into the air.

"Isaac, no!" she screamed, and one of the orbs headed straight for her.

I dove at it, cawing and shrieking. My entire vision filled with its bright light as I came close enough to collide, but I swooped underneath, my head feathers nearly brushing it.

"Isaac!" The urgency in her voice told me the second one was on my tail.

I craned my head back to look. *Confirmed.*

The cemetery was only one more block away: she only had to cross Rampart, and Basin, and she'd be there. I just needed to keep them high enough in the air that they'd focus on me and not her. I sailed through third-floor balconies, through strings of ivy and coiled wrought iron, cawing and keeping one eye on Adele below.

She reached the cemetery gates. She'd need help getting over them—but she pushed on them and they swung open, and she ran through. *It was unlocked?*

I swooped down, landed outside the gate, and pulled it closed, securing her in.

"What are you doing?" she yelled, gripping the bars.

"Do not leave. I'll be right back."

"No! Get in here." She tried to open the gate, but I held it tight.

Cold air washed up from behind her, and gasps rippled through the rows of graves. Dozens of ghosts were floating out from their mausoleums and oven tombs, some with curiosity on their faces, others with fear. A little ghost boy with a pageboy hat neared the gate and poked his head through the bars.

"What are those things?" he asked in awe, and I knew the orbs were approaching.

I dipped my face to hers and kissed her. "*Stay here.*"

"Where are you—?"

"I have to catch the souls! They'll die if they touch the net!" I took off running along the cemetery perimeter, and she ran alongside me on the opposite side of the wall.

"Isaac!"

"Wake everyone up!"

"Isaac! I love you!"

I smiled in a way that made my insides swell and leapt back into the air, swooping on the currents. No matter what had happened now, I knew Adele loved me, and that was all I needed.

But what did happen?

Not knowing put me on edge. *Has Callis actually killed Nicco?* Somehow Nicco had convinced even me that he was invincible. I'd expected him to come back into the city wearing Callis's ring, with his head on a lance or some medieval bullshit like that. I'd expected to be dealing with him trying to court Adele for eternity. But maybe he wasn't invincible after all.

The souls stayed on my tail, but they slowed when a group of girls ran out of a Basin Street bar, loudly singing a pop song like their lives depended on it. I rammed into a potted plant on a balcony, sending the clay pot crashing into the street, and brought the souls' attention back to me.

I soared away, leading them farther from the French Quarter and into the Tremé where the Storm damage was so severe that hardly any of the residents had returned. I pumped my wings harder, ducking and swooping into the darkness, past one crumbling house after the next. There were no people, no dogs barking from back lawns, no jazz coming out of corner dive bars, just power lines that drooped down to the road like licorice sticks and a deep silence—the kind that made you want to turn around and run.

The energy of the souls came up behind me like ethereal beating pulses that could have zapped the power lines back to life. Now that I'd gotten them away from Adele, I had no idea what to do. I needed Dee and Codi.

Focus, Isaac. Adapt. Dominate.

I looked back again; they were gaining on me. *Shit.* I felt for the air and slipped into the current, gliding faster as I scanned the row of busted shops, cafés, and less recognizable buildings. A corner house, noticeably bigger than the others, was the only one that had a chimney. *Ugh.*

I angled downward, picking up speed with the decline. I imagined myself getting trapped in the chute with the spirit-sucking souls. Panic set in, but I dove in anyway. My feathers scraped the bricks, breaking up decades of impacted soot. I choked, trying to hold my breath, and descended into darkness.

The light of the first orb lit up the chimney passage from behind me. And then the second.

Fuck.

Nerves rattled my feathers. I aimed for the exit and swooped up and out, but my wing nicked the brick mantel, throwing me out of crow form. I tumbled to the floor, legs tangling, and slammed into a rotting, feculent couch. Tiny screeches erupted all around me and two black rats legged it across the hardwood floor, others skittered deeper into the house.

The room glowed an eerie greenish hue as the souls hovered among the dangling crystals of a chandelier, which, miraculously, hadn't been picked over by looters. They spun and turned on the spot, as if disoriented by the squeaking. I snapped back to crow form and froze, holding as still as the creatures in the Borges' taxidermy studio.

The souls hovered lower, as if listening for me.

My wings quivered.

One dipped toward me, and I froze again—but then a rodent that would have put any NYC subway rat to shame sprang out, screeching, and made a run for it. More rats scattered in every direction. The souls zoomed around, chasing them, and then followed them on into the next room. Its light faded as it disappeared deeper into the house.

I need to get back to Adele. I looked for an exit. The windows were still boarded up from the Storm, but from my vantage point I could see the front door in the next room. I hopped as quietly as I could across the floor and then took a low, gliding swoop to the door. I landed on my feet, one hand already reaching for the handle. The lock was busted and it opened easily. First responders.

I shut the door behind me and jumped down the porch steps, then turned to the house, walking away backwards, looking for souls exiting via the windows, chimneys, or otherwise.

My stomach dropped when I caught sight of the orange *X* on the exterior wall. It had the highest number I'd ever seen spray-painted: thirty-one bodies recovered here.

What is this place? It looked like just a run-down Victorian.

A sign lay face down in the grass, and I turned it over with my foot.

HOLY ANGELS ASSISTED LIVING

Stormy appeared a few feet ahead of me and barked. I looked to the one unboarded window on the second floor. A man was standing behind the glass. What the hell? Had I just trapped two souls in an occupied house? I blinked, and he was gone.

There was no way anyone was living in those conditions. Squatters? Stormy barked again, and a chill brushed past me. I caught a glimpse of a dress fluttering as Julie darted into the house.

"Julie, no!"

She disappeared through the front door, and Stormy bounded after her. *Shit.*

I ran back to the house, reminding myself that the protection spell at the cemetery would keep Adele safe.

There were no signs of life, natural or supernatural, as I went through the living rooms, the pungent Storm stench jerking my stomach. I had no idea what could or couldn't contain a soul, except that the Daures kept them in jars of water. I detoured to the kitchen. The fridge had been dragged across the room by the floodwater, but it was still upright. I opened the door.

It had been completely picked over. I thought back to the number painted outside. *They all stayed.* Or they'd been forced to, without the means to evacuate.

I grabbed an empty jar of . . . *pickled okra*? It was still half full of juice.

A swirl of cold pressed against the back of my neck, and the hairs on my arms stood straight up. I whirled around. "Julie?"

No one.

Okra jar in hand, I pressed deeper into the house, taking shallow breaths through my mouth. The air was rancid, unstirred, and moldy. The floor creaked as I stepped into a double ballroom where I imagined old people had once played games. I could feel them in the darkness. Hiding. In the walls. In the ceiling. Beneath the floorboards.

The dead.

Letting my Spektral guide me, I crossed the room to a staircase. I took the first stair and then stumbled back. A man was standing in front of me. His head was clean-shaven and his skin dark, arms covered in tatts, the portrait of a toddler girl on one, and a lion on the other. The plastic ID tag clipped to the pocket of his green medical scrubs read, "*Jamal Jenkins, Registered Nurse.*"

"I tried. I tried to save them." The gold cap on one of his front teeth shone as he spoke. "No one came."

Cold crept up from the floorboards, saturating my spine, crystalizing in my veins. *I trapped two souls in here with the spirits of thirty-one Storm victims.*

He stared at me with blank disbelief, waiting for an answer. So many people in this city, alive and dead, were still waiting for one.

"No one knew," I said, my throat closing. I wasn't even sure whether I believed it.

Tears slid down his cheeks. "No one came."

My gut tightened, as if it had been my personal responsibility. My pop's. Désirée's pop's. FEMA's? The president's? Lieutenant General DuPont's? *Who the fuck's responsibility had it been*? "I'm here, Jamal." *Nearly a year too late.* "Take me to them."

He turned away and walked up the dark stairs.

I followed him up to the second story and past a long stretch of doors, my gaze fixated on his shoulders, trying not to lose him in the darkness. The mermaid-green fabric of his scrubs had a translucent sheen in the obsidian hallway.

Scurrying sounds came from inside the walls. Claws scratching and teeth scraping. Rats, mice, and God knows what else. I imagined swarms of termites beneath the floorboards and wall beams, chewing and chewing, and the weight of my footsteps making the entire house collapse, burying the spirits in a pile of rubble.

I could feel their presences behind the doors: the grandpops and aunties who'd been scared of living their remaining years, months, days in this place, who'd become even more terrified when the Storm hit and the water rose to the second floor. The moldy wallpaper still shivered with the cold in their hearts when they'd made peace with knowing that no one was coming. They'd begged Jamal to leave them, but he wouldn't. He'd told each of them when they moved in that he'd be with them until the end, and he'd kept that promise, even when the Storm came. Even after he realized there were no more ambulances in the city. No more buses. No more gasoline to take anyone else out. And then, at last, when they'd said they were closing the roads. "*No one else in. No one else out*," he'd heard on the radio before the tower went down. And then the levees broke, and the water rose.

We went up another set of stairs. The air became warmer and thicker, making it easier to sense the chill of the spirits. They whispered curiously about the glowing orbs that had passed through.

"*Extraterrestrials.*"

"*They aren't aliens, Greta; it's someone coming to take us, finally!*"

"*The Lord and Savior, Jesus Christ. Amen.*"

"*We're finally getting out of here.*"

They began to emerge from the walls, and I sucked in a shallow breath of putrid air and looked away. I couldn't meet their eyes. I didn't want to be the one to tell them that their Savior wasn't coming.

A glow pulsed from underneath a door at the end of the hallway.

A woman materialized in front of me in a baggy yellow bathrobe, her gray hair hanging out of pink curlers. "What's going on here, young man? Where's Eunice?"

"*Eunice!*" Jamal said, and he rushed through the air to the closed door at the far end of the hall and vanished through it.

I hurried after him but the door was swollen shut in the frame. I slammed my shoulder against it and fell into the room.

The ethereal form of a woman sat at a table on the other side of the huge room, playing bingo alone. A soul was in the corner, poking through a wind chime that sang gently in the breeze from a broken window. "You always were a cheater," the woman said to no one, and the soul jolted around and zipped toward her.

"*Noooo*!" Jamal glided across the room, leaving a vaporous shadow in his trace, and hurled himself in front of her.

"Jamal, don't let it touch you!" I pitched a gust of wind at the soul, but I was too late. The soul went straight into his head.

His eyes rolled back, and he fell to the floor. I ran to his side. My okra jar rolled away, as useless first-responder protocol ran through my head. The orb bounced around inside his ghostly torso.

Julie and Stormy appeared beside us, and the wraithy residents came through the walls with gasps and cries and shivers.

"*He was a good boy*," a voice said, choking up.

"*Who will take care of us now?*"

"*We're dead, Vivian.*"

"*We're not dead. This isn't heaven.*"

A freezing hand wrapped around mine. Jamal's eyes were no longer full of fear. "You have to take care of them."

"They need you, Jamal," I said through gritted teeth.

"Promise me," he said, already fading into a thin outline of mermaid-green glow, leaving just the lines of his tats, the bling of his tooth.

"I prom—"

"*Mon cher*!" came a gasp, and Stormy yelped as Julie collapsed to the ground near Jamal's fading boots. Her back lit up.

"Julie!"

Ghosts hurried out of the way as I scrambled to her. She screamed. I turned her on her side. The second soul was burrowing into her back as she fought it.

"No. No. No!" I twirled my fingers, twisting the air with my magic, and sent the current straight into her ghostly body, trying to pull the soul out before it got any deeper.

Stormy barked, and the ghosts all around us gasped and chattered.

"You can't have Julie!" I shouted. I stood, pulling the line harder, and gave it a sharp yank. The Air slipped, and I fell back, crashing to the floor, and the soul entered her completely.

"No!" I screamed, scrambling to her side.

She crawled over to Jamal, the soul bouncing around her chest, and took his hand. "Isaac, get the jar ready."

"What?" I was unable to focus on anything through my tears but the glow from her chest.

"The jar! Jamal is about to release the soul."

I unscrewed the lid just as the soul released, and I was ready, not just for the parasite soul but for Jamal's as well. With a small stroke of Air, I pushed them both into the jar of okra juice.

I spun the lid. "Sorry, dude."

Julie pulled my hand to her face. She hadn't faded at all yet. If it weren't for the glow and the pinch in her forehead, I wouldn't have known anything was wrong. "Isaac, you have to go."

I shook my head.

"Isaac, go back to Adele. She needs you."

I choked on my breath, fighting the tears.

"Come back for me. He won't take me so easily. I'm—"

"Strong. I know." Suddenly, I imagined being at Adele's side, holding her cheek like this, and I was on my feet. "I'll come back."

She nodded. "I know you will."

"Stormy, stay with Julie."

Stormy whimpered and lifted Julie's arm, wedging herself beneath it.

I hurled a chair into the nearest window, shattering the glass, and backed up to get a running start.

"Be careful, *mon cheri*!" Julie yelled.

"I'm coming back! Chatham will know what to do. I'll get Adele to the others." *And then I'll find Callis and rip his soul out myself.*

"Be safe, Isaac!"

CHAPTER 62

WITCH'S MIRROR

I paced along the row of mausoleums, staring up at the sky, looking for any more stray orbs of light. The air was sticky like it was going to rain again. I fanned out my father's shirt, rolled the sleeves up to my elbows, and pinned my hair back into a messy nest on top of my head with a stick from the ground. At least it was off my neck.

I removed Isaac's knapsack from my shoulder and dug through it for my phone. My nerves jittered so hard they could have launched me into outer space. *If he's not back in two minutes, I'm going to freak out.* I didn't want souls to be chasing him, especially not when it was my fault that I couldn't defend myself. I didn't want to be stuck in a cemetery, not knowing what was going on. The more defenseless I felt, the more my rage for Callis kindled. I found my phone and grabbed Isaac's weapon-like flashlight too. Readjusting the bag on my back, I punched the speed dial for Codi, hoping he was still with Désirée.

He didn't answer.

I hung up and dialed Dee. As the phone rang, I watched the ethereal swarm in the distance blink brighter. *They're getting closer.* There were hundreds of souls in those clouds, if not more—hadn't Nicco said spirits were hard to catch? What had consuming so many spirits done for Callis and the rest of the Ghost Drinkers?

Dee's voicemail picked up, and I waited impatiently for the beep. "Désirée, call me back as soon as you get this. *Emergency*."

I hung up and punched in a message to both of them: *S.O.S.*

A woman's voice shrieked from somewhere deeper inside the Quarter. I ran back to the gate and pushed my face against the bars. A car alarm went off. The sounds of motorcycles roared from the east, then from uptown. Red and blue lights flashed somewhere down the street toward Canal.

I dialed Codi again. Voices from a crowd of people I couldn't see echoed through the side streets, but with the car alarm, sirens, and ambient sounds of Bourbon Street floating with the wind from the river, it was difficult to hear whether they were drunkenly laughing or freaking out about something—like, being possessed by parasitic souls. Turning down the center path, I hung up the call and dialed Dee, continually looking back out at the looming swarm. Shells crunched beneath my feet. I clicked on the flashlight and passed down rows of mausoleums, twisting deeper in the cemetery, searching all the tombs until I saw the one that said **Le Moyne**. Désirée's voicemail picked up.

What the hell, people?

I stuffed the phone in my pocket. The mausoleum was taller than me, but I made a running jump and grabbed hold of the top. Grunting, scraping my skin across the brick, I hoisted myself up and over the ledge. On the roof, two female angels guarded a large cross. The first stood tall, wings upright, looking into the sky with one hand shielding her eyes, like she knew they were coming too. The second angel was draped around her shoulders with grief, barely able to hold herself up. I wasn't going to be that girl.

I leaned against the pair of angels, searching the sky for Isaac. The protection spell, stretching like a net from the four corners to the central obelisk, shimmered purple where the moonlight hit it. I wondered if it was protecting my mother's spirit . . . Was she still here in this cemetery, or had she passed on? *I will never let anyone touch her again.*

More motorcycles hummed around the cemetery into the Quarter, creeping methodically, weaving back and forth up the streets.

The sky remained empty: no sign of a solitary crow heading my way. I hastily took out my phone again. It was nearly two in the morning, but maybe the others were still at the party, dancing under the moon. They probably wouldn't hear the phone ring, but I dialed the tearoom anyway.

Edgar's voice answered, and I spoke before realizing it was a recording.

I hung up and dialed Nicco.

Operator.

With each unanswered ring, each recorded voice, I imagined everyone I loved in a mountain of bodies, and Callis coming to get revenge on me for letting the vampires out of the attic, for the coven members he'd lost that night, for the witch I'd fried in the swamp. I scrolled through my contacts and, without thinking, punched *call* when it landed on Ritha Borges.

After two rings, she picked up, sleep in her voice.

"Mrs. Ritha!"

"Adele, baby, what's wrong?"

"They're coming!"

"Who's coming?"

"Souls! Hundreds of them!"

"Hundreds?" she asked, tone sharp as a blade.

"Maybe more? Go look out your attic window. Two huge swarms! They look like twinkling clouds, or something, but they're souls, I swear!"

"Put Désirée on."

"I'm-I'm not with Désirée. I haven't seen her since I left the party, and she's not answering. Isaac went to chase away two loose souls, and he hasn't come back. What if the Ghost Drinkers—?"

"Where are you?"

"St. Louis No. 1."

"Stay right there and keep calling Désirée. I'm with my cousins, three hours away in Vicksburg, but I'm calling Chatham and Ana Marie. Someone will come get you."

As soon as she hung up, I dialed Désirée back, and everything started crashing down around me. Ritha was three hours away with a *sick cousin*, and when she called Chatham, she'd realize he too was out of town, on a freak ghost-hunting trip. *There's no way this is a coincidence.* I didn't know how, but Callisto Salazar had planned this.

As the call rang, something Nicco had once told me rang in my head: *Your true enemies don't go after you; they go after those who have your heart.*

What if Callis has Nicco?

Callis has always been after Nicco.

"Hey!" Désirée's voice was so unexpected, I jumped. "Are you coming back to the party?"

"Désirée, listen to me—"

"Y'all missed the moon circle. It was amaaaazing." She sounded a little tipsy. "Is it possible to be drunk on moonbeams?"

"Désirée, get everyone inside. Go up to the attic and look out the window. Edgar and Fiona and everyone need to strengthen the protection wards on the house—"

"Adele, what are you talk—?"

"Désirée! Put me on speaker!"

"Happy Witch's Night!" Codi shouted.

"Callis is back!" I screamed, and more motorcycles revved nearby. They idled a moment and then sputtered off again. Chills darted up my spine, and I sat down on the ledge.

"Where are you?" Codi yelled.

I put the phone into the shirt pocket and lowered myself back to the ground. "Codi, souls are coming for the city—hundreds of them—right now! Callis tricked your dad!" My heart stopped. *Your true enemies don't come after you . . .* "Dad!"

"Adele!" Codi yelled.

I clutched the flashlight and took off running across the cemetery and straight out of the gate.

I crossed the first half of Basin Street to the neutral ground, feeling weirdly exposed. The wide-open street was still devoid of functioning street lights and traffic lights. When I got to Rampart, I slowed for a second, my gaze darting left and right. Something was wrong. A supernatural sensation rippled over me as a breeze carried voices from up ahead.

I slipped behind a tree and peered out around the trunk.

Two motorcycles were blocking the adjacent street into the Quarter, like the cops did during Mardi Gras. The riders, both in dark clothes, paced the street in front of a bar that looked like it had closed a hundred years ago. One was a college-aged guy with a thick dark-blond beard, his jeans ripped at the knees. I wondered if he was really that young or whether he could have patronized that bar in another century. The second man was enormous, like a barbarian from the old Conan movies, with a long dark ponytail and steel-toed boots—*I recognize those boots.* My heart thumped so hard in my chest I could swear they'd hear it. He was the brute from the convent who'd kicked Codi's leg so hard his bone split. Callis's right-hand witch. Undoubtedly a Salazar.

"She's here somewhere," he said. "My Fire can feel her."

My pulse erupted. *My* Fire.

"Stay alert," he said, a hunter's zeal in his voice. "She might be using a cloaking spell. But she's here."

I didn't move. Didn't breathe. I wished I knew a cloaking spell.

I looked back toward the cemetery. It was only a block and a half away, but it now felt like a million miles.

Their footsteps approached, their thick inhales and exhales loud in the silence.

Another motorcycle revved from a nearby street, and I nearly jumped out of my skin, giving myself away.

"I wonder if she can feel it?" the brute said.

They were close; I'd missed my chance to escape unnoticed, if I'd ever had one.

"Can you feel your Fire inside me, girlie?"

Yes. Yes, I can, you asshole. I broke cover and tore back toward Basin street.

"There!" the brute yelled.

Loud, quick stomps came up behind me. "Come 'ere," the bearded one said in what might have been an Irish accent. A gust of wind flung me back. *Freaking Air witch.* His arms wrapped around me. I screamed and flailed, losing my grip on the flashlight, which clattered away. *Don't flail.* I went limp, and his arms sank, nearly dropping me. I stomped his foot with my entire body weight and then sent my leg sailing back into his crotch. He howled, loosening his grip, and I broke away. But the knapsack lifted from my back, snatching me backwards with it.

"You little bitch," he squeaked.

I twisted out of the shoulder straps, and he cursed wildly, but I didn't look back—I just ran.

Sticks crunched under heavy boots behind me, and I sensed an enormous presence shadowing over me. I reached the neutral ground and kept sprinting. The brute's hand hit my back, and I screamed as the shove sent me crashing straight into a tree. I tried to grab the trunk but he slammed up behind me, crushing the breath from my lungs.

"Don't even think about doing anything like that with me." He kicked my feet apart and stood between them, his chest heaving into my back.

"Get off of me!" I pushed back against the tree, trying to get enough space to twist away.

"Keep it up," he said, heaving his full weight into me so my cheek scraped across the rough bark. "I'm going to make you regret letting that Medici out of the attic, little Fire witch."

"I don't have my Fire," I spat. "You already took it from me! Your coven's taken everything from me!"

"Not everything." His giant hand groped the front of my leg, sliding up my thigh. "Do you want to feel it? Maybe I can pound it back into you." His hand pushed up the denim.

"*Stop*!" I screamed, writhing into the tree. "Get off me!"

"I thought you wanted to play rough?" His hand shoved up to my hip and I shrieked. He grasped for the band of my panties, and my spine jolted, feeling his foreign fingers on my skin.

I clutched the tree, shaking uncontrollably. Then, it was if someone else took over my body—someone stronger than me. I found my voice. "*Not here. Not here. Not here*," I stuttered. "*Please, not on the street.*"

He breathed into my hair, but his hands pulled away from my shorts and slid up and down my arms. "See, Tommy, she knows how to behave."

My knees weakened.

"Let's go try out the backseat of that old Mustang across the street? You bang your big bad vampire boyfriend in the back of cars?"

I shook my head, tears falling from my eyes. "You're too big for that car."

He laughed a little. "I'm too big for all cars."

"The cemetery, where no one can see," I said, trying to control the tremble in my voice.

He looked at me a little hesitantly.

"Isn't that more your style? Won't you get off on all the ghosts watching?"

"I knew you were a freaky little one."

I forced a half-smile and imagined Adeline and Cosette next to me, telling me not to cry.

"*He's about to release you, ma fifille.*"

He backed away. My skin felt permanently stamped by the tree bark, but I could breathe again.

"Don't try anything stupid." He grabbed my arm and twisted it, keeping me right next to him.

As he jerked me across the street, I imagined Adeline and Cosette still next to me, and then Susannah and Marassa joining us on one side, and Morning Star and Minette on the other—a line of young women striding beside me.

The Air witch opened the gate and grabbed himself. "Yeah, I think I need to make sure all my parts are still working."

As soon as we stepped through, the gate slammed shut behind them. They turned to it, and I broke away and tore down the center path. My sandals were slippery against the broken shells and gravel, still slick from the earlier rain. I turned down a row of mausoleums to the right and let my sandals slide off without really stopping—I held my hands in front of me as I stumbled onward into the darkness, wincing as shells and broken brick pieces of graves cut into my feet.

"It was one of these rows," the brute said. "You take this one and I'll take the next."

I slowed down to be as silent as possible, swallowing my huffs; the only thing I had on my side was the darkness.

A warmth glowed from behind me—*shit.* The halo of light got closer with each of his heavy stomps. *Shit. The big one.* I glanced back down the row; flames were sprouting from the ground in front of him, lighting his way. *My own Fire's going to give me away.*

I pressed on the door of the nearest mausoleum, but it didn't budge. The light crept up behind me, nearly touching my back. I took a few more soundless steps and slipped into a tight grotto that displayed a Mary statue like a pearl in a shell. I huddled behind her, panting. I barely fit. The air was damp and her porcelain veil was cool and dewy against my heated skin.

I listened for his crunching steps. They slowed. The fire behind him cast a long dark shadow that peeked into view of the grotto entrance, pulsing with its light. He stopped just before the grotto—another step and he'd see me. *Why did he stop?*

He backed away a couple steps. He's leaving.

No. There was too much silence. Something was wrong. *He wants me to think he's leaving so I'll come out.* A shell crunched outside, and I held my breath. There was nothing else I could do but be ready. A giant hand reached into the grotto straight for my head. I shoved the statue with all of my might into his chest. He heaved it back with a menacing grunt, and I leapt out, hearing it smash into pieces behind me. He grabbed my leg, but it was slick with sweat and his hand slid off my skin. I scurried up as he blasted obscenities, and I tore back down the path the way we came, wondering where the other prick was. I tried to be silent, but it was impossible, struggling to catch my breath.

The sound of glass breaking came from the next row, and a slew of Irish profanity came with it. I ran faster. He was right there, running alongside me, just a depth of two mausoleums between us. I was almost back at the path. Maybe I could get out the gate. *Was I faster than him? What about his Air?* Noises came from behind. My arms pumped.

But then none of it mattered. I didn't even make it to the obelisk before the brute tackled me and I went flying, arms outstretched. My chin hit the ground and scraped across the shells. I tasted blood in my mouth. I dug my fingers into the ground, trying to claw out from beneath him.

"This secluded enough for you?" he grunted, crawling farther on top of me, sweating and panting and repulsive. "Or do you want me to chase you around some more?"

"Get the hell away from me!"

The Air witch ducked through the mausoleums toward us. "Y'er a little spitfire, aren't ya? I can see why Callis'd want to have ya for his collection." He came over right next to us. "Cemetery was a good idea. We can grab a snack after."

"Fuck you!" I screamed, and the Air witch's boot came hammering down on my hand. I felt the shells beneath my palm break even as my bones shattered. I shrieked, fractals of light exploding behind my eyes.

"That's the plan," the brute said. His heavy hand landed on my waist.

I shrieked louder, kicking up, but he slammed me back down, his arm in my back. My face hit the jagged shells again, but the sound of his belt buckle rattling open made me thrash harder.

"Keep it up," he said. "This is all just a little foreplay before I smash you into the Underworld."

A breeze swept voices over us. "*Against thy enemies, you shall protect . . .*"

"You'll know what a real Fire witch feels like. Not some pathetic magicless Medici!"

I flailed, twisting back and forth in his grip as he tried to tug my shorts over my hips. I felt the cold coming for us. I craned my neck, peering up, and saw them: dozens and dozens of people. Purple outlines, gathering all around the obelisk, whispering German. The whispers grew to a blunt chant.

"*Reflect. Protect. Reflect. Protect.*"

My eyes pinched as he threatened to rip open the denim if I didn't stop moving.

"*Send it back, not once, not twice, three times the pain.*"

"What was it you said that night at the convent?" he said. "How you'd never betray *Nicco*?"

A rusty wrought-iron mausoleum gate with an iron cross and spike-topped posts creaked open. The bars slipped apart and clanked to the ground.

"You think Nicco will still want you after this?"

My entire body pinched, and I wished the ground would swallow me up. The chanting grew. The Air witch began unbuckling his pants and cheering on his friend. *When I get my magic back, I'm going to choke both of them to death with their belts.*

Metal scraped metal.

The Air witch screamed.

Red splattered across my face.

I screamed.

"*No harm will come under your mighty shield.*"

The stub of the Air witch's arm was spraying blood everywhere; the rusty iron cross, along with his hand, were on the ground next to me. I shrieked.

Then the brute flailed on top of me with a roar. I clambered out from beneath him, cradling my arm. The decorative gate pole had impaled his left hand and driven itself into the ground. He clenched it, trying to pull it out, but it wouldn't budge.

I hobbled away, brushing bloody shell fragments from my rapidly swelling hand.

A gust of wind pulled me back a few feet, and I spun back to the Air witch. He yelled an incantation; his remaining hand was thrust toward me, his voice an octave higher than before. Broken vases and dead flowers swirled around us, but then a gale ripped from behind me and slammed him into an open, dilapidated crypt. The wind swirled, trapping him in.

I turned, expecting to find Isaac, but the Air was coming from above—reflecting from the hexenspiegel.

"*To the people, to the witches, to the spirits of this field.*"

The brute roared. His fingers were spread, digging into the shells, as if some great force was shoving him into the ground. Gusts of Air tugged at his pants. Another bar from the rusty gate rolled over the ground, straight for him.

"*Reflect. Protect. Reflect. Protect. We're going to smash you into the Underworld," the mirror mimicked his voice.*

I stomped on the pole before it reached him, and kicked it away, but then another rolled. I grabbed it. Ten more rolled to him, lifting in the air.

He looked up. "I thought you said you lost your magic?" He ripped the pole out of his hand like a wild madman and flung it at me, but I jumped and it crashed into a mausoleum. "You little vampire-loving whore!"

Rage exploded inside me, and I raised the pole over my head and slammed it across his back, screaming as his bones cracked. Pain shot up my arm. My chest heaved. "That wasn't my magic," I spat, "that was my coven's magic."

His eyes drooped shut. The other poles all clanked to the ground.

I shook so hard, I could barely hold the piece of metal. I threw it down.

I have to get to my dad.

The gates swung open. I picked up my shoes and stormed out.

I grabbed Isaac's knapsack from the neutral ground and then took the brute's helmet from his bike and slipped it over my head as I walked back into the Quarter. I had a feeling there were more of them here, and that they were all looking for me.

CHAPTER 63

TRUE ENEMIES

I shouldered through the crowds on Bourbon Street, the pain in my hand throbbing all the way to my ears. These people needed to be evacuated from the streets immediately, but the complete panic for my father had rendered me incapable of worrying about anyone else's safety. I dialed him with my good hand and slipped the phone under the helmet, unsure of what I'd even say. Be on the lookout for any Goth-looking biker-witch types? Would that even narrow it down much in the French Quarter? His voicemail picked up.

I kept calling back. I could hardly breathe by the time I got to the bar. A hundred people were pouring out of the courtyard, and I wondered what was creating the mass exodus. Floating orbs? Ghost Drinkers?

I shoved my way through the crowd, cradling my arm, and squeezed to the side entrance of the downstairs bar, but a hand reached out across my chest. "We're at capacity."

The bar looked sparse. I started to lift the helmet to tell the bouncer I was a VIP, but then I saw the Mark on her arm. I retreated instead, hustling through the throng of people to the stairs of the garçonnière.

When I passed Isaac's room, my chest tightened. Why hadn't he made it back to the cemetery? My anxiety sprouted horns as I raced down the hallway. What if a soul got him? Or a succubus? Or he fell out of the sky? *Where is he*? I took off the helmet and dropped it to the floor. The hallways were strangely quiet too. Usually the music and crowd noise grew louder as I neared the cabaret, but tonight it got quieter, until there were no noises but a faint melody on the . . . piano?

I opened the door to the back entrance, and there he was.

Callisto Salazar on the stage, hands tickling the keys, like this was all some elaborate performance for his entertainment.

The room had been cleared except for my father, who was sitting at one of the center cabaret tables: an audience of one. He lifted one shoulder, straining, and then the other. Ropes bound his wrists.

"Dad!"

His head turned. "Adele, get out of here! Now!"

I hurried between the tables, knocking over chairs. "Callis, let him go!" I screamed.

Callis didn't even look my way, but the lines in his forehead deepened as he punched the keys harder, the concerto becoming more dramatic.

Mac's eyes widened. "Baby, what happened to you?"

I could still taste blood and grit in my mouth and could only imagine what I looked like. "Dad, I'm sorry." My breath stuttered.

He thrashed in the rope binding. "Did he do this to you?"

I dropped to his side. "I'll be fine."

Callis paused from the song without taking his hands off the keys. "I knew if no one found you, you'd come running to your daddy eventually. Actually, I thought Mac and I would get to spend a little longer together before you turned up; I've barely gotten through the second movement."

"*Get* out of here," I said to Callis.

"Did you know that Mozart wrote his first symphony when he was just eleven?"

"I don't care about Mozart!" I tried to loosen the rope, but I had only one good hand.

"Don't bother," Callis said, turning on the bench to face us. "Magic."

But I didn't stop trying.

"Okay, fine, exhaust yourself." He wallowed in the bridge of the song, jet-black curls flopping into his eyes. He was in his usual getup: dark blue T-shirt, black leather vest, dark pants, boots. His fingers were adorned in silver. But there was something about him that looked different. He was still pale, but he didn't look so sickly. As he moved across the keys, he was . . . sprite.

"What the hell is wrong with you?" I asked him.

"Adele." Mac's eyes pleaded with me. "I can handle this," he said in a lowered voice. "He has more men all through the halls—just take the back alley and go straight to the tearoom. *Run.*"

"No." Callis stopped and moved to the edge of the stage. He sat on the lip, guarding my father like an agitated dog.

I stepped closer to him, fuming.

"Adele, get back here." Mac's chair stomped into the ground. "Don't you touch her!"

"What do you want from us?" I asked Callis.

"Oh, so many things . . ." He looked at me, his eyes piercing blue. "Being on your deathbed gives you a lot of time to think. A lot of time to read. A lot of time to catch up with old friends."

"You can save your existential crisis for your disciples. What do you want *with me*?"

"I want you to answer a question, or two. Maybe three."

"If you untie him. Now."

Callis whipped his hand to Mac, and the ropes unraveled.

Mac launched himself toward me, sending the table and chair flying, but a striped couch slid across from the wall into his path. Shock sprawled over his face as he crashed into it.

"Stay right there," Callis said, his hand raised in the air. "Don't move another step."

"How the hell did you do that?" Mac said, and slid down the back of the couch, pulling me down to him. I sucked in the wince from the pain that shot up my arm.

"Ask your daughter. She can do it too."

"No, I can't. You *ruined* my magic."

Mac turned and blinked at me like I'd just spoken an alien language.

"Ruined? You're so dramatic. It was just your Fire."

I jumped up, but Mac latched onto me. "What did this guy do to you?"

I turned to him, speaking in a low voice: "Dad, please, just do *whatever* he says. Everything will be fine, I promise."

He wrapped his arm tighter around me, looking at Callis with fire in his eyes. "I'll answer whatever questions you have, give you whatever you want—the register is full of cash, and I have a safe in the back—I won't even call the cops. Just let my daughter go."

"Not yet."

"What's your question, Callis?" I asked.

"You know, it's such a beautiful night out. I'd hate to miss even a minute of that gorgeous Flower Moon. Let's walk and talk." He hopped down from the stage and extended his elbow to me as if we were old chums going for a stroll in the garden.

I stood up, and Mac did too.

"My daughter isn't going anywhere with you. She's going to a hospital."

Callis looked at my hand, which had ballooned and parts of which had darkened to the color of an eggplant. "Were you uncooperative?"

I choked on my words and ended up just hissing at him.

"The moonbeams might put even you in a better mood." He sent a pair of Fire orbs hovering over his shoulder. "Let's go."

I glowered at him. Those were *my* Fire-orbs. "Unlikely," I said through gritted teeth. I glared at my orbs, pleading with them, pulling, pulling, *pulling*—until I gasped.

He gestured for me to lead the way out the door, and I wanted to burn his eyes right out of their sockets.

"She's not going," Mac said.

I grabbed his hand so he wouldn't try anything heroic.

"She is," Callis said, "and so are you."

"It's okay, Dad," I said, my voice begging. "Let's just go outside, and this will be done."

His forehead creased with trepidation, but he gave me a questioning look and then followed my lead.

We walked out the door and down the hall, side-by-side. Callis followed not more than a half-step behind us, bouncing down the stairs into the courtyard, which was now empty aside from his coven members standing in the bouncer's spot.

On the street, Callis stepped to my other side and led us down Pirate's Alley, along the side of the cathedral, and into Jackson Square, two of his sheep tailing us. They stayed back a block, guarding him but also giving him privacy as if he were some kind of dark prince.

With a wave of his hand, the iron gate to the park opened for us.

"What the hell?" Mac whispered under his breath.

We walked in.

"There she is." Callis craned his neck to the moon. "Is there anything more beautiful than the glow of raindrops under her beams?"

I refused to see any beauty in this situation.

"How's it been for you these months?" Callis asked. "Without your magic?"

"Delightful."

"I can help you."

"Don't act like you care."

He shook his head, looking bemused. "And this is why we need to spend more time together—"

"Like hell she does," Mac muttered.

"You clearly don't understand me," Callis said to me, feigning pity.

"Just because you can't brainwash me like you did to Annabelle doesn't mean I don't get you, Callis. *Je vous comprends parfaitement.* You want magic. And power. And you don't care who you have to destroy to get it. You didn't care in the sixteenth century and you don't now."

"I see Niccolò's gotten to you."

"Sixteenth century?" Mac asked. "What are you filling her head with? I've heard people spinning some bullshit in this town, but—"

"Well, despite the fact that you killed six of my coven members that last time we met, I'll re-extend my original offer to you: join us, and you can have your Fire back."

I looked at Mac. "I did not kill anyone, Dad." I turned back to Callis. "And I'm never joining your succubus cult."

"Christ, I should have known this was some kind of cult thing." Mac said. "My daughter isn't joining anything of yours."

I gazed up at the bell tower, and the bad feeling that coiled in my stomach was so intense I almost asked Callis where Nicco was. I clamped my jaws together.

"I know it was you who opened that attic," he said.

My heart flicked.

"I was so close to having them, but you had to go and save Nicco . . ."

"Niccolò from the bar?" Mac asked.

"Not to save Nicco," I told Callis. "My mother."

"*Brigitte*? Your mother get you involved in this? Did you meet this guy in Paris? I should never have—"

"You can save that spiel for Isaac," Callis said to me.

"Isaac's involved with this too?" Mac yelled.

I turned to my father with pleading eyes. "I swear, I'll explain later, Dad."

When I looked back at Callis, he smiled at me, like he knew everything about me. And again, I felt empowered as if by a greater force—by those who came before me. The delicate Ingénue was gone. I gazed back at him, unwavering. "I'm the one who locked them up," I said, my voice steady. "Why would I want to release the Medici?" The Tigress from the night at the convent was back.

"Good question. At one time, I thought it was because Niccolò had you under his thrall . . ."

"Nicco doesn't brainwash people; that's you."

"But when you told me about the dream-twinning, despite how sick it is, I had to consider that the two of you might really be in love."

We passed some shadowy bushes where a pair of eyes, low to the ground, glowed yellow in the foliage. I wondered how many anthropomorphic witches were in his coven.

"But now?" I asked.

"Now I have a theory." He paused. "The view is better at the river." He turned and started walking.

The witches who'd been trailing behind us stepped out from the trees, forcing us to follow him out the gate at the opposite end of the park. We crossed the street to the amphitheater and up the concrete stairs all the way to the lookout point.

It was probably one of the top postcard photographer spots in the world. Behind us was the perfect shot of the carriage-lined square and the cathedral, and before us, a view of the Mississippi, with the antique riverboats and the old streetcar line that ran right below us juxtaposed against the more modern steel bridge to the Westbank on the horizon. Neither the streetcar nor the riverboats had functioned since the Storm.

I stood between my father and Callis at the rail. "What's your theory, Callis?"

He nodded and leaned on the rail to peer out over the river. The moon glimmered on the gentle waves beyond the Moonwalk. "You once told me that your magic came from your father's side."

"It does."

Mac tensed and grasped the rail, but he didn't interrupt.

"And that before they were Le Moynes, your paternal side were the Saint-Germains."

The waves roiled in the darkness ahead. "So?"

"Well, I did a little digging into the *Saint-Germains*."

My pulse ticked. I was suddenly intrigued by whatever was coming next.

"I knew that your Fire was special from the very first time I saw you light a candle. It had hints of the Old World that I hadn't felt since . . . well, since my father was alive, when all of the Great families ruled. Since I had my Fire. So here was a Fire of European descent, and one so intoxicating I'd surely remember it, and yet I couldn't recall any Saint-Germains. So I went looking for info on the earliest European witches in La Nouvelle-Orléans, and I came across a witch in the mid-eighteenth century named Adeline Le Moyne, née Saint-Germain." He looked at me. "Lo and behold, you were telling the truth."

I fought to keep my expression hardened, wanting—*needing*—to know what else he might have discovered.

"But her ancestry was perplexing. I found no evidence of her mother. Just her father, the elusive Comte Saint-Germain, and from there, the family tree stopped. It was as if her father had materialized from thin air. Now, I know some powerful witches, but creating their own being into existence is something found in religious tomes." He glanced our way. "Dead ends can be so disheartening, but sometimes they're just what you need to set you on the right path. It forced me to go back to the Medici, trying to figure out the connection. What the hell would a clan of vampires want with a witchling who, as you said, has only budding telekinesis, no grimoire, no magical family, and no Mark?" He looked with a raised brow, letting me know that the question wasn't rhetorical.

Mac laughed. "Vampires?"

"They wanted me to break a trapping curse that Adeline's coven cast in 1728," I said.

"No. If it were so simple, they would have just killed you and your friends."

Mac scowled, moving closer to me.

"So, I thought about your magic," Callis continued. "I felt it in my blood, and then I wondered if Niccolò, even as a vampire, could sense it too: the Old World in your Fire. I wondered if it reminded him of the Fire he once possessed."

The pain radiated from my arm into every part of my body, but I no longer cared.

"The Medici claimed that we were obsessed with death, but they have always been just as obsessed with life. What is the difference, really, between raising the dead and prolonging the life of the living? Is one playing the hand of God more than the other? Nicco's father and grandfathers were obsessed with immortality. They didn't speak about it outside of their walls, but it was known among the inner circles. The *hypocrisy*," he spat.

"They weren't hurting anyone—brewing potions and tinctures. You've destroyed hundreds of people pushing your mortality past what it should be."

"It's natural selection."

"No, it's artificial selection. This is all on you, not nature."

"Let's call it supernatural selection then. Incomprehensible to the mere humans who defined the metaphorical food chain."

My gaze pulled to the orbs hovering over his shoulders—and I swear they pulsed brighter.

He noticed where my attention had gone, glanced up at them, and smiled. "Interesting how you've gotten past the idea of vampires feeding from the mundane but you can't accept our way of living."

"Drinking someone's blood is not the same as destroying t*heir soul*."

"We can't choose how our magic works."

"You can choose whether to die gracefully or—"

"Only the weak would *choose* to die. Would you not tell a young, terminally ill mother to fight the disease with everything she has?"

"Not if it was at someone else's expense."

"And if that person was your father?"

I wished I could light him on fire.

"We've gotten off track." He went to playfully strum my good arm, and I drew back, stumbling into Mac.

"Do not touch her," he growled, pulling me aside. "I've had enough of this shit." He grabbed Callis's collar with both hands, yanked him up off his feet, and held him out over the rail.

"Dad, don't!"

"If you don't stay the hell away from my daughter, your brains are going to end up splattered all over those train tracks, do you hear me?"

Before he'd even finished speaking, a dozen witches had us circled.

"Uh, uh, uh," Callis said, wagging his finger.

I grabbed Mac around the shoulders. "Dad, let him go."

"Listen to your daughter, Mac. She's wise in her youth."

Mac released him, and I pulled him away, stepping between them. His arm wrapped around me.

Callis's witch-sheep all stepped back into the shadows.

Callis took a breath and leaned back over the rail, staring out to the dark horizon. "I was entombed when the entire Medici empire was destroyed in one glorious night. The public thought the sons and daughters of Ferdinando de Medici were all simply murdered in their sleep, which they were, but the magical knew something far worse had happened to them. I was told that when the estate was parsed off, their Italian allies in Venice, Rome, and Sicily pillaged each of their palazzos, searching not for emeralds but for their magical possessions. Some said that the wards of Cosimo Medici could never be broken and nothing was found, not even the legendary Medicean book of shadows. Others believed that when the vampires rose, they raided the estate themselves. All of that I knew, but there was one other rumor that bubbled up among the magical . . ." He looked at me, as if for a sign that I knew what he was about to say.

I gave him nothing, but I had started to realize where this was leading.

"And this is what leads us here, under the Flower Moon, debating the morality of mortality."

I held my face solid as stone.

"When the bodies were collected for burial, there were five missing: all four of Ferdinando's legitimate children, plus a nephew or bastard named León, whom, it's said, he raised as his own."

Dizziness galloped over me.

"I've been chasing the Medici siblings for centuries, but there's never been a León in their clan."

"Your point?"

"León's body wasn't found, but if he wasn't made a vampire . . . maybe the Medici lineage didn't really end that day. Can it really be a coincidence that at the same time the Medici ended, this elusive Comte

Saint-Germain first appeared? Elusive and unremarkable, or perhaps just unmemorable? Perhaps purposefully so. Just a ghost of the greatest magical empire of the European Old World." He turned to me. "Is this why they're protecting you? Because you are the heir to the Medici magical legacy?"

I scoffed. "I'm not a Medici, and they aren't protecting me; they came here threatening to kill me. They've *killed* people I loved, and they were trying to kill Adeline back then too. That's why she locked them away, and why I did the same."

"Yet they saved you from me."

"An eye for an eye." Sweat broke across my hairline. I'd never been good at lying. "I saved them from you, and they did the same for me."

"If only I believed those three to be so noble."

"León Saint-Germain wasn't even a Medici by blood." Even though my knowledge of my ancestors was thin, I identified strongly as a Saint-Germain—my entire magical-self was built on our legacy—but I found the idea of being a Medici horrifying.

"So if you aren't in love with Nicco and you aren't a Medici, that means they need you for something. Something important."

I held his gaze so he wouldn't notice my shaking hand.

"Something magical. Why else wouldn't they have killed you yet—if they really want to do so? They love to kill. *That* didn't come with vampiric transition." His lips drew into a smile, as if all the pieces were fitting together for him.

I gripped the rail, and Mac's arms wrapped around me.

"Adele, when we met and I felt your Fire, I knew the universe had brought us together for something great. I thought it was for your Elemental magic and the Great Monvoisin book of shadows to bind my coven, but now I know it's for something much more important. The Medici stole our Salazar grimoire, and now the universe has brought us together so you can give me theirs. You are our karmic retribution."

"I am nothing to you—and I don't have a grimoire, or anything of the Medici's! If I did, I would have given it to them months ago, before anyone got hurt. All I had was my Fire."

"You have so much more than that. You have your coven. You have your father."

My back stiffened.

"But I know what it's like to feel empty. I carried that emptiness for centuries. I carried it for my family. For my coven. Now I know it will all have been worth it. For how many centuries did my Great family not understand how to use our Spektral magic to its fullest extent?" He took a few steps back. "And for how many centuries after that was I unable to access it to its fullest extent? But now that I am healthy . . . it's been only a couple of hours but look." He raised his arm toward us.

My father gasped, knocking my shoulder as he rose into the air.

"No!" I tried to grab him, but Callis flicked his wrist, and Mac floated up over the railing, out of my reach.

Words spit from Mac's mouth that I'd never heard him say as he tried to kick back to the rail, choking on incomprehension.

"Dad!" I stretched out my arm but couldn't reach him.

Callis pulled me back.

"Stop it!" I begged. "Put him back down. I'll do whatever you want!"

"I know you will. That's why I brought your papá with us." Callis lifted himself off the ground too. "I believe you, Adele, and I absolutely believe in your Fire. You will find that grimoire, and you will give it to me—not to Niccolò. If it really does contain the spell for the Medici's magnum opus, *l'elisir della vita*, what would a vampire need with it anyway? But us? The Animarum Praedators? With true immortality, we could stop living off the essence of others. Think of all the future spirits and souls you'd be saving."

The tears poured from my eyes. "I'll find it for you. Just put my dad down, safely. *Please.*"

He pouted. "*Oh, bella.*"

My spine jerked.

"That is what he calls you, isn't it, when he gets you to do what he wants?" He whooshed over the railing next to Mac. "Your papá is coming with me."

"No!"

"Just a little incentive to keep you focused."

"Adele," Mac shouted. "Go to the tearoom! Chatham and Edgar promised to take care of you if anything ever happened to me!"

Callis's expression darkened as he looked down at me. "If you betray me, Adele, I will kill your father, just as they killed mine. Only after his death, I'll drink his spirit and lock you up with his soul so he can destroy you—and then the Saint-Germains will blink out of existence just as mysteriously as they blinked into it only four hundred years ago." He pushed his arm forward, and they both floated out toward the river.

"No!" I screamed. "Stop!" I ran down the back staircase and across the train tracks as they glided through the nighttime sky.

"Adele, stay back!" Mac yelled.

"Dad!" I shrieked, kicking up rocks as I scrambled up the levee to the Moonwalk.

"Baby, I'm sorry."

They soared out over the water.

"*Dad*! I love you!"

I ran down to a lone rickety pier that had survived the Storm and kicked through a rusty chain-link fence. The pier led nowhere, but I kept running after the two small figures, begging.

"You keep your word, Adele, and I'll keep mine," Callis shouted.

"Adele, go back! I'll never stop loving you!"

On the other side of the river, an orange glow—some kind of ward —pulsed from a huge old plantation. I didn't think. I just sprinted across the shaky planks, screaming to my dad that I loved him, and when I got to the end, I hurled myself off into the water.

The water was colder than I expected, and the pain in my hand sliced all the way up to my shoulder.

For as long as I could remember, we'd always been told never to go in the river. But I was a strong swimmer.

Callis can't have my dad.

I didn't think about the pain. I didn't think about my magic, or my coven, or Nicco, or Isaac. Or any of the things that had consumed my mind for the last few months. All I thought about was my dad. I made it halfway across, but my arms were going numb, and the waves started pushing me downstream. The harder I fought the current, the more I panicked. I'd gotten my mother killed, and now I was getting my father killed. I hated being magical. As the water pulled me under, I wished I'd never gotten my Fire. Any of it. I wished I could go back in time to before the Storm and refuse to get on that plane to Paris. I'd stay there with him in Miami, and we'd build a new life. I'd enroll in school and be happy and he'd show at Art Basel and everyone would love him and we'd never come back to this shithole and I'd never open the attic.

Waves broke over my busted face as I continued to stroke.

I hate this town.

And all of its secrets and death and darkness.

I choked on muddy water, trying to break through the waves crashing over my head.

The undertow grabbed my ankle like a slithering python and pulled me under, twisting, roiling, squeezing the air out of my lungs. Thrashing me around like a rabbit. Pulling me farther under as I fought.

As a kid, I'd always wondered if I could make it across the river. The Westbank had never really seemed that far from the Moonwalk. I guess I had my answer.

The water rushed into my throat.

I hoped they never found my body; I didn't want Isaac to have nightmares about me drowning for the rest of his life.

CHAPTER 64

BLOODY HANDS

The wind zipped through my feathers as I glided high over the houses, struggling to hold the magical Air current. I was unnerved both over leaving Julie behind and over how long it had been since I'd left Adele. Had it been fifteen minutes? Twenty? I wanted to caw so she could hear me coming, but if I attracted any souls, it defeated the point of me leaving her to begin with.

Closer to the Quarter, the signs of chaos echoed up from the streets: cars peeled away, horns blared, cop lights flashed blue and red. As I soared over Armstrong Park, a girl ran through the trees, a soul chasing her like it was just a gleeful game of tag. *Shit.* I fought the first responder protocol ingrained in my system: *help the person nearest.*

A turquoise beam of light shot from the middle of the Quarter all the way up to the stars. Something told me it was a ward coming from the tearoom. That was a good sign. Adele got a hold of them, either that or the discord on the streets had alerted them to the swarms.

Just as I made it to the cemetery, a beam of dark green light shot up not too far from the blue one. *The Borges.* I flew through the hexen-spiegel net and circled the grounds from above, trying to find Adele, but it was too dark to see much.

I dropped to the ground near the obelisk, my sneakers pounding the path of shells as I came to a running stop.

"Adele?" I called, twisting around, starting to panic. I pulled out my phone. Dee and Codi probably came to get her; they were probably all back at one of the shops behind a protection ward. My phone lit up, illuminating the area around me, and I did a double take at the ground.

I directed my light at the pathway. A spattering of bright blood covered the white shells. "Adele?!"

A rush of cold swept up from behind me. Ghosts floated out of oven tombs and up from mausoleums. Men, women, all looking like they'd stepped out of different centuries. The little boy in the pageboy hat came forward. I kneeled in front of him. "Did you see a pretty girl here before? The one I came here with just a little while ago?"

He nodded.

"Was she hurt?"

He nodded again.

Fuck. "Where did she go?"

He pointed to the gates.

I bolted out of the cemetery, every worst-case scenario flashing through my mind. *I never should have left her. What was I thinking?* She had no magic. We'd been training, but she could still barely punch her way out of a paper bag.

When I crossed Basin into the neutral ground, the moonlight caught a glint of something in the grass. I stopped to pick it up. My flashlight. My heart pounded. It had been in my bag, with my grimoire.

I spun around, looking for any other signs of struggle, and then soared down the street, cawing, no longer worried if the souls heard.

In front of the Voodoo shop, two bikers straddled their Ninjas. They didn't seem like the type usually around; maybe Morgan was beefing up security in more ways than one. The entire Voodoo shop had a forest-green glow. As I flew into the alley, the protection ward warbled, nearly spinning me out. *Way stronger than usual.* The beating of drums came from the courtyard, and voices chanted.

Ana Marie was sitting in a circle with a couple of women, her sisters I think, working on the wards. The rippling magic in the air heightened my sense of danger. I dropped to the ground and raced into the house from the back.

Désirée, still in her fancy dress, jumped up from behind the counter. Dozens of open bottles of herbs and powders were spread out, and she had three different cauldrons bubbling.

"Where's Adele?" I asked.

"I thought she was with you?"

"She was, but then . . . She must be with Codi."

"Codi's out with his brothers on the street chasing souls. My mom came and got me, and she's making me stay home and brew potions—"

"Well, then she's probably at the tearoom with his parents." I spun around, heading for the door.

"Isaac, I *just* came from there. She's not with the Daures."

Someone pounded on the front door. "*Open up*! *Emergency*!"

"It's Nicco," I said. I never thought I'd be desperate to hear the sound of his voice.

We ran through the Voodoo dolls and tourist novelties, and Désirée pulled open the door.

He cradled a body in his arms, but it was too long and too male to be Adele. A burnt black jacket covered the figure like a blanket, mostly obscuring his face.

"Come in," Désirée said, and the ward let Nicco slip through the threshold. She shut the door behind him.

"What the hell is happening?" I asked.

"Oh, now you give a shit?" His hair was wet, and his perfect clothes were muddy. He maneuvered through the room with the body.

"What's that supposed to mean?" Désirée asked.

Nicco came straight to me. "He was too far gone. I couldn't heal him lest he turn into one of us." He dropped the guy into my arms so roughly, I stumbled back. "If he dies . . . this is on your hands, not mine."

"What?" The guy reeked of smoke and *chemicals*?

"Where's Adele?" Nicco asked, and without waiting for a response, he whipped out of the room into the next. The shop cat, who'd been nestled among the Voodoo dolls, sprang awake, knocking a tribal mask onto the floor.

"It's Sébastien!" Désirée shrieked.

I looked down. "*Shit*!"

We scrambled to lay him on the floor and carefully removed the jacket. He was almost unrecognizable without his glasses. A full thickness burn ran across the length of his left cheek and arm, where the skin and fat had melted away. The surrounding skin had charred and peeled back.

I pressed my fingers to his neck to check his pulse. "He's barely breathing." *Are those puncture . . . ?*

"Move out the way," Désirée said, her hands sliding over his swollen torso. His chest was black and blotchy from surfacing blood. Her eyes slipped shut.

I stood up, backing away a couple of steps. *What happened with Callis?* I laced my fingers on top of my head, trying to stop the shaking. *I should have gone with Nicco.*

"Where is she?" Nicco shouted, zipping back into the room. "Isaac!"

"She's . . . I left her at the cemetery. I led some souls away but when I got back, she was gone. I thought she came here. Th-th-there was blood."

Nicco's fangs snapped out, and he grabbed my throat. My arm flailed, knocking over a shelf of Florida Water and shattering one of the bottles. "All you had to do was stay with her, and you couldn't even do that!"

Ana Marie rushed out of the back room with her sisters in tow, muttering conjures. "Release him now!"

Nicco let go of me. The tchotchkes on the walls shook as the front door slammed open and he was gone.

"Isaac?" Désirée said. "*What* is he talking about?"

"I have to find her."

"Isaac, stay here," Ana Marie snapped. "We're getting everything under control."

I shook my head. Nothing was under control. I turned on my heel and spread my wings.

Dee jumped up.

"Désirée, don't even think about leaving this house!" her mother yelled.

I shot straight out the open door and heard it slam behind me with the *whack* of a witch-mother.

I have to find her.

CHAPTER 65

MOONSHINE

I screamed, trying to expel the water from my throat. As I tumbled through the cold, wet darkness, I imagined Mac's form, translucent and ghostly, disappearing past Callis's lips, until he was nothing but one of those glowing orbs destined to kill others. All because I never got my magic back and never found the Count. Never defeated Callis.

I am more than my magic.

I kicked harder against the undercurrent.

Callis can't have Mac.

He cannot have New Orleans.

But it was too late. I was too far under.

A glow pulsed through the darkness ahead. A bright light approaching. This was it. Would Brigitte float out of it to take me to the other side like Isaac's mom had? Or would Adeline? Probably not after the way I'd slammed the book in her face.

The glowing orb drew ever closer, shimmering turquoise until it was right in front of me. Once the orb took me, Mac would have no one left—if he even survived whatever Callis was doing to him. When I was gone, would anyone else try to save my dad? Would Callis have a need for him anymore?

I couldn't die and leave him alone. *I have to save him.*

I kicked away from the huge incandescent orb. The last bit of air coughed out from my lips and the Mississippi rushed into my throat. I tried to scream, but I just choked on the water rushing in. It shot up my nose, piercing my brain, setting my nerves on fire.

The river churned around me, iridescent ripples breaking up the roil of the natural current. I thrashed away from the light, but the ripples buffeted me back toward the glow.

I bounced inside the orb and heaved up water. *Air.* I desperately sucked it in, wheezing. I could breathe again. Or maybe I was just dead.

Above, the moon beamed through the murky river water. I was floating toward the surface. *To heaven? Guinée?* Was this the River Styx?

The orb rose, taking me up, up to the moon.

The moon lights the dead.

Dead people don't need air.

The iridescent ripples swirled the bubble through the black river water, twisting around it and then shooting it straight up through the surface, high into the starry sky. A roar came from the Moonwalk, then a dark shadow ripped down the pier. I screamed as the film burst and I fell back down, flailing. My gaze caught the fiery glow on the Westbank: Ghost Drinker HQ. I heard a giant splash right before I crashed back into the river. The water felt like glass shards against my broken bones. I kicked, fighting to stay at the surface, refusing to let the undertow pull me down. But then my arms stopped moving, my muscles defeated. My mind raced for survival, but my body was pushed past the brink of functioning, and I began to sink.

No, I have to save my dad!

Yellow eyes glowed in the dark water.

My shirt jerked up, pulling under my shoulders.

I rose closer to the surface again, higher and higher. I gasped as my face broke the water. An animal was pulling me. A panther. *Papa Olsin.*

I attempted to kick to shore, but my legs were as heavy as iron. But still, he paddled. A glowing blue current helped guide us through the black waves.

I squinted, and the cement river stairs that lead up to the Moonwalk came into view.

The panther clambered up, still dragging me. The algae-coated steps scraped my legs. We weren't allowed near the bottom steps when we were children because they were slippery. I collapsed against them, coughing. He roared, grabbed my shirt collar in his mouth again, and pulled me farther up the stairs. I crawled on one hand, hobbling to the top.

When we got to the running path, Papa Olsin turned back into his old wrinkly self, chest heaving, hair dripping. "Let's get you home, Addie."

I attempted to stand but teetered. He leapt behind me as I wheezed for air.

"Papa, they've got my—" My throat filled and I bent over, heaving up brown water.

He slapped my back. "Get it out, baby."

A motorbike ripped up the Moonwalk. There was something floating above the bike. *What the hell?* A translucent blue net, or balloon, tied to the back. I blinked, and the ghostly forms trapped inside came into view.

Two women, one with pink braids and the other wearing a red leather jacket, leapt off the bikes and threw down their helmets. Both had the same warm-taupe skin, forceful stride, and dark, determined eyes. Definitely sisters.

"That's not her," said the one with tight pink braids and spandex pink-camo pants.

"Move along." Papa Olsin stepped in front of me. "She's no concern of yours."

I should let them take me in. I needed to get across the river to that house with the fiery glow. I needed to save Mac. I took a step forward and my knees buckled. What would I do when I got there? *I need to go there with Nicco. Where is he? What happened to him?* I heaved for breath.

"No, it's her. Black shirt, cut-offs, scar on her face," said the other girl, like she was reading from a bounty hunter's assignment sheet. She flicked the collar of her red leather jacket. Her big windblown curls bounced when she walked.

"Callis already found me. You don't—"

"Nice try," she said.

Olsin mumbled words I couldn't understand—an incantation—and a ball of red light appeared in his palms. He stretched it once and then again in the opposite direction, and it morphed into a bow strung with an arrow that glowed red as blood. He shot it into the sky, and it exploded like a flare. Sparkles of light rained down around us.

I picked up a branch resting near us on the grass, brandishing it in front of me.

She laughed. "I guess Annabelle was right; you don't have any magic now."

Just hearing Annabelle's name made me nearly lunge at her.

The two women strode toward me, and Olsin twisted back into panther form with a humming growl. But the sisters weren't fazed. Camo-pants dropped to all fours, transforming into a lioness with a slight pink tint to her fur.

"Shit." I took small steps back. She was massive.

Olsin padded forward, lips curling back, teeth exposed, long and white.

As she circled, he stayed between us, circling me even more tightly.

I kept one eye on the other witch. She pulled a wand of sharpened bamboo from her leather jacket pocket.

The lioness leapt for me, and Olsin swiped her chest, drawing bloody slash marks. They tumbled into the grass, their growls turning into roars. Crimson flooded her fur. The other witch aimed her wand at him, yelling an incantation.

"Papa, look out!" I threw out my arm, pulling for the magical stick, imagining it leaving her palm and coming to mine.

Olsin turned, and the lioness leapt again, jaws open wide to clamp onto his side. He screeched, and she thrashed her neck, digging deeper into his him. The wand lit up.

"*No*!" I dug for my Spektral, fighting the incapacitating feeling of worthlessness.

The witch in red turned to me, and the bolt of coral-colored energy ripped from her wand. The magic hit my chest so hard, the force suspended me in the air for a second, freezing all of my muscles at once in a single explosion of pain before blasting me to the ground. I skidded across the stone and slammed into a park bench, landing wedged half underneath it.

Olsin jerked up, his mouth stretched open to show his enormous white teeth. He tore away from the lioness to charge at the other witch, and crashed into her, sending her wand clanking across the stone toward us. They tumbled down the river stairs.

The lioness turned back into her human form and stomped over to me. She grabbed my broken hand, bones crunching as they slid, and jerked me out from underneath the bench. I went blind from the pain. As she dragged me across the cement, I clawed for the wand—and reached it. With every ounce of adrenaline I had left, I stabbed it into the fleshy part of her calf.

Her cry was muffled by a boom from across the river.

We turned out to the water as fireworks lit up the sky. "I guess you were telling the truth," she said and leaned down to yank out the wand. "Nasha, let's go!" she yelled, hurrying toward her bike.

A deathly squawk shredded my ears as an albatross rose from the water and began soaring toward the house, her white feathers lined with red.

The lion witch looked back at me, her face lit with alarm. "You'd better hope my sister makes it home or I'm coming back for you."

Olsin sprang back up the levee. He gave himself a fierce shake, spraying reddened water from his fur. His eyes narrowed at the witch, and she took off, blasting through the puddles. He chased her down the Moonwalk until she jumped across the levee and revved down the street.

Olsin's footsteps slowed as he approached—as four of him approached. I tried to blink the dizziness away. My knees hit the stone hard.

He whimpered, padding closer. Blood dripped from his fur.

I reached out for him, and he crumpled. I pulled myself closer, scraping against the ground, muscles still spasming from the blow of magic.

"Get up," I said. "We just have to get you back to the tearoom, Papa."

I shoved myself up, grabbed around as much of him as I could with my good hand, and heaved. He hobbled up, but with each step we took, he pulled me closer to the ground again, until he collapsed.

I felt for the bite wound in his fur and pressed my hand into the bloody patch, trying to staunch the bleeding. That's when I realized how large the bite was—bigger than my hand. "You're going to be fine," I said, trembling. "Just hang on. We just have to stop the bleeding."

He pawed up my chest, his yellow eyes locked with mine, and filled with desperation. I knew it wasn't fear of death or even pain. It was his last effort to beg me to heed his warnings. He collapsed, and I fell back. His weight was crushing, but I hugged him tightly, still trying to keep pressure on the wound. He looked up at me, but then the light went out behind his flaxen eyes.

The waves crashed up the cement steps.

"*Help*!" I shrieked. I couldn't move. I could barely breathe from his weight. "Help!"

Motorcycles tore down the streets somewhere in the city behind me. Red sparkles still hung over us from the magical flare he'd sent up.

"*Help*," I croaked. Tears slid down my cheeks as I stared up to the Flower Moon, listening, feeling for the beat of his heart.

The moon shines down on the dead.

The moon shines down on the dead.

Thump.

Thump.

I need to save Mac before it's too late.

But all I could think about was telling Codi about his grandfather.

And for the first time, the pain was too much.

CHAPTER 66

LA PANTHÈRE

I cursed Isaac to hell and back as I tore down Bourbon, not giving a second thought to the crowds of mundane who might catch a glimpse of me at full speed. With all of the hysteria in the Quarter, I doubted anyone would notice anyway.

Why would he ever think Adele would stay inside a magical bubble while her father is out here, vulnerable to the Animarum Praedators?

Gabriel was waiting for me on the street in front of the bar with Lisette; he'd received my message.

"An arrow-flare just went up down by the river," she said, "like the ones the Native witches used to use."

"We'll check it out next. First search here. Split up," I said, leading them through the gate. "Gabriel, take the downstairs bar. We'll take the back."

Gabriel darted inside, and Lisette and I whipped up the stairs at the back of the courtyard. We broke apart in the dark hallway—she went off to check the residential quarters, and I went straight to the cabaret.

It was devoid of people, noise, merriment. Other than a few overturned chairs, there were no signs of a fight, but the fact that the place was unlocked and no one was here wasn't a good sign.

"*Mac*?" No answer. "*Adele*?" I zipped around, looking for blood, remnants of magic, bodies. Not a soul.

I smacked the register and the drawer opened. Full. And so was the tip jar. Mac had left in a hurry.

An unmanned bar just off Bourbon on a Friday night, and no takers? There was no doubt something magical was at work here.

"Isaac's room was empty," Lisette said in French, coming into the cabaret.

I nodded and walked over to the stage. I closed my eyes, opening up my senses, searching for the thumps of her heartbeat. I couldn't pick up her pulse, but through the meld of musty wallpaper, spilled booze, and sweat drips from horn players still sprinkled all over the stage, I picked up a hint of lavender.

I latched onto the scent. "Come with me."

I followed the trail, tearing back down the hall, out the door, and down the stairs, Lisette on my heels. Fireworks exploded toward the river, and a cacophony of motorcycles revved from the streets as if being conducted. Maybe they were. *He's calling his soldiers back in. Does that mean he got what he wanted? Fuck.*

Gabriel stepped back outside, looking at the sparks lighting up the sky. "The bar's empty."

"This way," I said, not wanting to lose the scent.

We blazed through Pirate's Alley to Jackson Square, and then up the amphitheater stairs to the lookout point.

I never should have left her with Isaac. I should have busted down his door and told Adele I'd found Callis. She'd have made him break the curse, and we could have gone after Callis together with my family. I would have protected her.

I didn't protect her.

The wind was stronger off the river, and I lost the lavender among the drifts of sulfur from the fireworks. But it didn't matter; the scent of magic hung in the air.

"*Regarde la panthère,*" Lisette said, and I turned to where she pointed up the Moonwalk.

There, under the spotlight of the Flower Moon, a red stain of water covered the running path where a huge panther lay still, and beneath him . . .

Thump-thump.

I leapt over the ledge, raced over the train tracks, and bounded up the levee.

Thump-thump.

No.

I dropped down, nearly grabbing her hand before I saw that it had been mangled, bones bent in unnatural directions. Olsin Daure was collapsed on top of her like a shield. Both of their eyes were shut. Her inhales softly stuttered—she had at least one broken rib. Her cheek was swollen and bruised, her chin gashed, lip puffed up. Blood pooled from her side.

Thump-thump.

Gabriel and Lisette appeared on her other side. He looked at me with alarm when he saw her face. He gestured toward the panther, and I nodded.

"Adele?" I asked, keeping my voice steady as he slipped his arms under the Daure patriarch and started to lift.

"*Wait!*" Her voice was just a wisp. Her eyes fluttered open, her embrace tightening around him. "Don't . . . move him. He's been . . . bit." Her right arm, still shaking, squeezed around the animal, covering his wound.

I didn't want to tell her that it was too late.

I leaned closer, so she'd look at me. "Gabriel's got him; you can let go," I said softly. "I need to check your injuries."

"B-ut . . . Gabe can't. The blood?"

I couldn't stand to lie to her. "Vampires don't drink the blood of the dead."

"Oh." She nodded, blinking back tears, and let Gabriel lift the panther away.

Gabriel set the panther down beside us, and Lisette's eyes got glossy.

"Adele, what happened?" I fought the impulse to scoop her into my arms and take her somewhere safe. Her legs were cut up, but none of the blood seemed to be hers.

She tried to speak, but no more words came out of her throat. She shook so hard, I lost the sound of her pulse. Her eyes shut again.

Thuuum . . .

She was starting to slip.

I bit down on my wrist and squeezed on my flesh, drawing the blood to the surface. As the first drop hit her lips, her eyes opened again. "Nicco?"

"*Sì, bella?*"

Her face tightened. “I need you.”

“I’m here. Just try to think about something more pleasant while I heal you. Think about something warm. It’s going to hurt, but I’ve got you now.”

She shook her head. “Not for me.” Her eyes pinched as she tried not to cry. “My—”

Cawing came from behind. Then flutters and stomping feet.

“Get off her!” Isaac yelled, palms pummeling my shoulders so hard, I nearly fell into her. Panic overtook him when he saw the blood. She tried to get the rest of her words out. Her throat was raw. From screams that had gone unheard.

“Don’t try to talk,” he said, kissing her forehead. “Dee’s coming behind me.”

I stepped back so I wouldn’t be tempted to rip him off her.

I wondered how she had ended up out here. Had she been to Mac’s bar; had they come here together? *Where is Mac?*

CHAPTER 67

SAVED

A breeze picked up from the river, and Adele shivered, soaking wet.

"I'm so sorry I left you," I said, huddling over her. I glanced over my shoulder for Désirée. She was running down the stairs from the lookout. Nicco was zipping around like a lunatic looking for something.

Only then did I notice the other giant animal on the ground beside Lisette. *What the fuck is going on?* Did it have a feather earring? *Is that . . . ?* "Désirée!" I shouted.

She was already sprinting up to the Moonwalk.

Nicco dumped something near us. *My knapsack.* He bent back down on her other side. "Adele?" he asked gently. "Where is your father?"

Her face pinched tighter as she wheezed. "Callis took him."

"Took him where?" he asked.

"What? *Mac*?"

"Across the river," she said to Nicco, trying to push herself up on one elbow. "He knows about the grimoire."

Nicco's eyes lit up.

"What grimoire?" Gabriel asked.

"Ours," Nicco spat. "*Lui vuole l'elisir.*"

I squinted, looking out over the river as they exchanged a few more words in Italian. A huge house on the other side had the distinct glow of magic.

Désirée arrived, breathing heavily. "*Oh my God!* Is that Olsin?"

"*Je vous présente toutes mes condoléances.*" Lisette said.

Her hand slipped over her mouth. "Does Codi know?"

Adele shook her head.

Dee turned to Adele. "What hurts the worst? I don't know if I can heal everything. Sébastien was bad off."

"*Sébastien*?" Adele yelped.

"He's going to be okay . . . I think. My mom's with him."

"Her hand," I said to Désirée.

Adele tried to hide her arm. "I'm fine. Don't waste your magic on me."

Désirée looked at it, and her eyes widened.

Nicco crouched down at Adele's other side again. And with barely a touch to her jaw, he had her full attention. "Listen to me. I am going to save your father. Do not worry about him or anyone else. Focus on Désirée's magic healing you."

She nodded, her gaze never leaving him.

Nicco eyed the other side of the river.

"*Niccolò*," Gabriel said.

He turned to his brother. "Stay with her. If she starts to slip . . ."

Gabe nodded.

Does Callis have Mac? I started to stand.

"Don't even think about leaving," Désirée snapped, and I knelt back down. "Focus your energy toward me."

She'd never asked for help to heal someone before. She linked her fingers with mine and drew our palms over Adele's broken hand. I tried to focus, but my attention pulled to Nicco as he took off straight into the river. Water sprayed up behind him as he *ran* over the surface.

A scream ripped from Adele's throat, and she lurched up. Lisette jumped over to help hold her down as her bones snapped into place.

Next came the rib. She writhed on the ground as Désirée chanted.

I couldn't stop watching the distant riverbank. Nicco was gone. He'd made it all the way across.

Mac couldn't get caught up in the magical crosshairs of this stupid feud. *He's an artist, for fuck's sake.* Why couldn't Callis have taken my dad? At least he had military training.

I was the one who'd killed Adele's mom; I couldn't get her dad killed too. She'd never forgive me after she found out I gave Nicco that ring.

If she didn't know already. *What does she know?*

My heart beat so hard in my chest, I felt it in my ears, my gut, my fingertips. Everyone became blurry as we chanted. As Adele screamed. Dee's eyes rolled back in her head, and I barely felt the usual panic when the recoil took her down. I was already too far past panic.

Now it was something deeper . . . a constant lurking dread fogging my consciousness.

Adele sat up and wrapped her arms tightly around my neck. *"I thought you were dead."*

I barely heard her, but when she started to cry, I told her that I loved her over and over again. I didn't know any other words.

In my head, she said it back.

I didn't know anything other than her. And Mac. And the coven. I didn't have anything else. They were all going to hate me when they found out.

She kissed my cheek and then tried to stand. "I want to go with Nicco."

That I heard.

"You need to rest," Gabe said.

"I'm fine." Her knees buckled.

He caught her. "I'll carry you back to the shop."

"Don't touch her," I said sharply. It all felt like a dream, a nightmare.

Désirée awoke groggily, and I helped her to her feet.

"Is your hand okay?" Dee asked Adele. "I can heal you more in a little while."

"*Merci*." Adele wrapped her arms around her.

"What hap—?" Dee asked

"Souls," Lisette said, pointing down river.

We all turned. Two orbs were glowing in the dark, cruising along the Moonwalk. They hadn't noticed us yet.

"You need to get behind a protection ward, all of you," Gabe said.

"I'm not leaving until Nicco's back," Adele said.

"Nicco would want you to be behind a magical wall right now, resting, restoring your energy."

She shook her head.

"Adele," he said, touching her shoulders. "I've got him."

"We can't leave Papa . . ." She started to waver again, and I gripped her arm to support her, even as she insisted that she could walk.

"I'll bring him," Lisette said, and carefully picked up the giant animal as if he was only the weight of a housecat. She rested him over her shoulder, cradling him like he was sacred, and whispered something in French—I caught the name *Morning Star*.

Désirée led the way.

I looked back over my shoulder at Gabe. He was still staring into the horizon, to the spot where Nicco had disappeared into under the Flower Moon.

"Dee," I said, and she turned around.

I led Adele close, and settled her arm over Désirée's shoulder.

"*Isaac*," Désirée said as I stepped backward. "Don't!"

"Isaac!" Adele screamed.

But I was already soaring past the vampire, out over the Mississippi.

CHAPTER 68

SNATCHED

Torches dotted the property, bringing me back to America's worst point in history—to a time of hoop skirts, steamboats, and sugar cane—only now, the chanting rising from the property wasn't coming from African slaves in the fields but from European witches who had no business being in New Orleans. At least, not under the current pretext.

The house, surely once magnificent, appeared to have been abandoned decades before the Storm. Its once-white columns were dingy, and the turquoise shutters were peeling. It was an antebellum plantation-type: three stories plus an octagonal cupola on the roof that looked fitted for a trapped damsel in a southern storybook. Tall rectangular windows lined the first two stories every few feet, and the third story—the attic—had six dormers in total. Lots of exits. The house was cloaked with cat's claw for additional privacy, and the thick air was drenched with wisteria and honeysuckle, as if to give off the immediate sense that something pleasant was happening within its walls.

The back of the house had been charred to a crisp at some point and the roof had wilted, beaten down from rain, but the edifice had that sense of sturdiness that came with Old World craftsmanship. No wind nor rain nor locust nor disease could take it down completely—a fitting place for the Animarum Praedators to claim as their own.

I circled the perimeter of the property, hidden by the hums of frogs and crickets and the mossy branches of live oaks that filtered the moonlight. The Westbank neighborhood had been decimated by the hurricane. There was nothing but darkness around for miles. No one to see their magic.

No one to hear their screams when I burned them all to ash.

The Salazars will *never* get my *magia della famiglia.*

Chanting billowed from the backyard where a group of Ghost Drinkers were channeling the energy of the full moon. The saffron glow of the protection ward extended over the house and the surrounding area. No one was getting in easily, and no mundane was getting out alive. Not tonight, anyway.

In the near distance, a pair of motorcycles flew down the main road, engines getting louder as they approached, until their headlights appeared when they turned onto the long dirt driveway to the house. I needed to make a move now before all his witches made it back.

Callisto's bike was parked on the side near a line of others, but he was nowhere to be seen—perhaps he was deep inside the house somewhere with his prized possession, ready to destroy Adele's family and steal from mine. Hiding like a sniveling weasel.

The magnolia branch above me shook, and my fangs snapped out. *A crow.*

Isaac swooped down and took human form right in front of me.

"*Dannazione.*" I could count on one hand the number of times I'd ever wished to replace someone with Emilio, and this was one of those times.

"What's the plan?" he asked.

"There is no plan. I had a plan earlier. You destroyed it."

"No." He shook his head. "If there's one thing I know about you, it's that you always have a plan. Whether it's to extend life with alchemy or steal my girlfriend, you always have a fucking plan. *What is the plan* to save Mac?"

"We're not saving Mac."

"You told Adele you would—"

"And I will. But right now there is no way for us to walk into a house full of who knows how many centuries-old witches of possibly unprecedented power and walk out with a mundane prisoner."

"But you were going to blow through their ritual in the swamp?"

"That was before I knew they'd drunk the spirits of a thousand ghosts."

"What the fu—?"

"D-MORT."

"*Shit.*"

"Then what are we doing here?"

"Getting leverage for the long-play." I bounded up the tree trunk and crouched in the branches, staying covered by the magnolia blossoms.

He flew up to perch on a neighboring branch and turned back to human form.

I nodded out to the yard where a dozen or so witches were in a circle, some loosely dancing with closed eyes, others sitting deep in concentration. "They took one of ours. We take one of theirs."

"What about the shield?"

"I'm going through it. Correction. You're launching me through it."

"*What?*"

"If you can handle that with your heightened Air—"

"I could throw you into the sun with my heightened Air."

"I'll settle for straight through there and into the river. I'll grab one of them on my way."

"You think he's really going to care if we take one of their witches?"

"He will if it's his sister."

He nodded. "But what will happen to you when you go through the shield? *If* you can even break through it."

"I guess we're about to find out. Callis is a Fire witch, so whatever it is, I'm sure it will burn."

"You really think this is a good idea?"

"We could launch you instead?"

"I'm sure you'll be fine."

"Follow me." I swung back to the ground and led him over to a patch that would give me enough open land for a run up and a perfect launching angle. I caught him watching me with a skeptical expression and turned to face him more fully, moving in close enough that I could smell Adele's scent still on him. "I am putting the safety of our plan in your hands. If you drop me into a circle of Ghost Drinkers, know that I will survive solely so that I can *hunt you down.* Am I clear?"

"Clear," he said, unflinching.

I grabbed a stick from the ground and quietly cracked off a six-inch piece. "And, Isaac, once I'm on the other side, you better fly out of here fast. You're on your own."

"Don't worry about me. I'll be gone."

I left him to move away from the wall, giving myself about a hundred meters. Isaac flittered up to a tree branch to give himself a better view, and stood back up in human form.

Adrenaline roiled through my bloodstream like ocean waves. This was the beginning of a battle that had been brewing for four hundred years. I placed the stick between my jaws, bit down, and said a little devotion to my grandfather.

Isaac nodded, and I took off, hitting my maximum speed just as I passed him. I jumped, and his Air lifted me up and over the surrounding brick wall. I clamped my eyes shut as I hit the shield. My skin seared like flaming acid, and I bit down harder on the stick. If his Air hadn't been forcing me through, I would have buckled and fallen to the ground. I covered my head, screams echoing in the back of my throat, and the stick dropped from my mouth. I swirled through the air, burning through the shield, and exploded into the circle, arms outstretched and eyes wide open. The witches startled out of their meditation, and Celestina flattened to the ground with an ear-splitting scream, but the red-headed Aether was within reach. She disappeared from view, but I snatched at where she'd been—and grasped her shoulders. As the Air rocketed me forward, I yanked her to my chest, arms latching around her and legs locking with hers.

Spells ricocheted off the twister, but Isaac's Air held us. The girl screamed for Callis.

"I thought you didn't need him to save you?" I shouted.

"You bastard!"

I clamped down around her, mentally preparing to take one more hit. I tried to cover my face as we propelled through the ward, a twisting, twirling rocket of fire, but my cheek bubbled and my lips burst, and the clothes on my back caught fire, burning hot. I yelled, shielding the witch from the flames as best I could—she'd be immune to the shield, but the flames in my hair and clothes would still burn her flesh. Halfway across the river, I let us drop, unable to wait any longer for the cool, quenching water.

My blistering wounds sizzled as we went under.

Even before we broke the surface, I plunged my fangs into her neck. The water curdled her screams.

Her body went limp in my arms as my venom overpowered her. I hooked an arm around her torso and swam, faster and faster, eager to reach the shore and drink from her more deeply. I needed to heal and get back to my brothers and to the rest of the New Orleans witches to make a plan. Back to Adele. This was no longer an age-old feud; it was a war for magical New Orleans.

Callisto had found a house and settled in.

I dragged the witch ashore a little farther east, just outside of the Quarter, where the park was more desolate. I barely had her up the levee before my teeth slid back into her neck, my wounds shrieking as the muscle and flesh regenerated. My venom had already taken hold of her, so this time there were no screams—only the look of future nightmares in her eyes as she stared at my fleshless face.

Her blood trickled down my throat along with the buttery taste of my own subcutaneous fat from my melted lips. Again, familiarity washed over me with her scent . . . but then I sensed another presence. I looked up. Isaac was standing fifty feet away, stunned, watching as I gorged.

"Leave!" I hissed. "Get away!"

He stumbled back.

"*Now!*"

He bolted into the night, soaring up toward the Flower Moon, back to the civilization that was getting increasingly less civil.

CHAPTER 69

STUNNED

I flew back to the Quarter, desperate to get back to Adele, the image of Nicco tearing into Annabelle's neck, the blood dripping from the bone of his blistered chin, shining bright in my mind. As I crossed Frenchman, it was pandemonium—and not the usual kind induced by gin and jazz. Souls were everywhere, chasing people out of clubs, into bushes, underneath cars. The two swarms were starting to descend.

I soared high. The noise below had attracted the orbs to the street level, so I only had to dodge a couple, but I stayed alert.

As the wind ripped through my feathers, I stressed over Nicco not getting Celestina. What if Callis didn't give a shit about Annabelle? What if he took it out on Mac? What was I going to tell Adele? I pumped my wings harder.

Things weren't any better once I crossed Esplanade into the Quarter. Witches I vaguely recognized from Chatham and Ritha's covens were chasing souls with magical Water nets, throwing calming powders onto the Possessed, protecting some and bringing others back to the asylum. The outlines of ghosts peeked from behind glass window panes. Pink puffs of memory powder dusted the slated streets and clouded the air.

I wanted to drop down and help, but as I wove over people and powders and bolts of whizzing magic, all I could think about was Nicco and keeping him away from Adele.

Papa Olsin might have passed, but I wouldn't forget him or his premonition—I still saw Nicco touching Adele's face, speaking gentle words to her, making her promises to save her father. Spinning his web around her, gaining her trust and her love and her kisses. And then I saw him on top of her, ripping into her throat like a savage monster, his true nature consuming her completely. I soared straight to Ritha's.

As I cut through the square, a wall of translucent white light shot up from Canal Street, pivoted over the tops of the tallest buildings, and connected to the iron cross extending from the center steeple of the cathedral. A blue wall shot up from Esplanade Avenue. Amber and green burst from the river and the cemetery, boxing in the Quarter. When they all connected at the steeple, sparks sprinkled down into the street and the shield settled, fading into the night until it was just a shimmer between us and the rest of the world, one that would go unnoticed by a mundane gazing up at the full moon.

A soul floating toward the river touched the shield and bounced back in. I'd assumed the ward was to keep the Ghost Drinkers out. *They're trapping everyone in. Controlling the chaos.*

I dropped into the Borges' courtyard. If I'd thought the streets were crazy, the chaos here was ten times greater. The shop often felt like a secret nook that had to be stumbled upon or known about, but now people were everywhere—dozens and dozens in a disoriented uproar, demanding to know what was happening, screaming in fright, crying over not knowing how they ended up here. People trampled through the gardens or sat in corners, holding their knees and rocking back and forth. Some were badly injured. Witches who were used to spending their days making night-blossom essential oils were now trying to wrangle drunk, angry partiers, many of whom were likely Possessed. Caleb and Cameron were trying to calm down some aggressive frat guys back near the guesthouse. I spotted Ritha on the second-story balcony with Remi and Manon. *Thank God she's back.* I flew up to land beside them and turned.

"Go down Royal and Chartres," she was saying to them, "into the closest restaurants and grocers. Find the biggest walk-in refrigeration system you can and clear it out." She nodded down to the courtyard. "May they rest in peace, but they can't stay here. We need to get them out quickly."

In the corner near the sunflowers, in between people nursing their injuries, crying, screaming for loved ones, three blankets hid human forms: a shape I'd dream about for the rest of my life.

"We've got it," Manon said, and they hurried off.

"Have you seen Adele?" I asked Ritha. "I'm ready to help, but I need to find her first."

"Yes, you do." Her voice was stern.

"What's wrong?"

"Nothing and everything. Just calm her down, Isaac. She needs you. We have too many crises at the moment to worry about any one missing person—even if it's her father."

Damn. I nodded. I knew she didn't mean it in as harsh a way as it sounded.

"We need to tackle one problem at a time. We need medical supplies. We need memory powder by the truckload."

"There's a FEMA warehouse down by the Esplanade pier. Wouldn't take too much to raid it."

"Smart thinking."

"What about the shield?"

"It will let our witches pass."

"Okay, I'll go, right after I find Ad—"

"No, not you. I need you on triage, and anyone else with any medic training. We can't magically heal everyone—there are too many, and we can't afford to be that vulnerable, given the current circumstances. I'll have Morgan handle the supplies. You get upstairs to help Désirée. And be careful. Don't take any chances of getting injured with anyone too out of their mind. The usual Bourbon Street intoxication level mixed with possession is an aggressive combo, and we're outnumbered here." She shoved a hand into her apron pocket and scooped a handful of assorted dried flower petals into my palm. "Keep this on you and don't be afraid to use it on anyone dangerous or getting out of control."

I nodded, and she hurried off, barking orders. I looked at the magic-laced plants in my palm and then shoved them into my pocket.

"And Isaac," she said, turning back. "Hurry upstairs. Don't let my granddaughter heal too many people and drain her magic."

"Okay."

I picked my way through the sea of folks and went into the house, looking into each room filled with people as I went by, getting flash-backs to every disaster site I'd ever been to with my Pop. It was the same look of terror on people's faces: the shock of witnessing something they'd never dreamed could happen. Some cried. Some prayed.

I checked Dee's room for Adele, but it was empty. Maybe she was with Ren or in the shop. I hurried downstairs.

When I parted the curtain to the backroom, I found her behind the counter, sorting herbs into cauldrons at Dee's usual post.

"Isaac!" She ran over and threw herself around my neck, fear in her grip. "Please don't ever fly off like that again."

"I'm fine . . ." I wrapped my arms around her. She was still damp. It was hard to look at her so battered and bruised, but at least her bones weren't broken. "I'm fine."

"What happened?" She pulled away, looking up at me. "Where's my dad?"

"Um."

Panic flooded her eyes.

"Callis . . . has the place seriously magically fortified. His coven attacked D-MORT and drank thousands of spirits—that's where all the souls came from."

"D-MORT? That's how Sébastien was attacked?"

I nodded. "He's got too much power now. Nicco got fried trying to break through the shield."

"What do you mean?" She backed away a step.

"He's fine. He's Nicco." I squeezed her shoulders. "He's a vampire. He was already healing when I left him."

"Where did you leave him?"

"He's *fine.*"

"I-I-I need to go across the river. We need a plan. A strategy. I need to talk to Callis. He has to let him go." Only then did I realize how wild she looked. Her eyes were bloodshot, and her hair was no longer in a knot but a huge mess, like she'd been scratching her head like crazy. Her feet were bare and the dark men's shirt swallowed her up.

She steepled her hands together and pushed them against her forehead. "I don't know how to find the Count or his grimoire. He has to settle for something else. I'll talk to Callis— I need a car."

"You don't drive."

"Or you can send me across with your Air."

"Adele," I said, holding her still. "Look at me!"

She did.

"Baby, you *cannot* go over there. No one can do anything right now. Ritha is back. Chatham will be here soon. We need to get the situation under control—people are *dying*—and then everyone will come up with a plan. Together. We will get Mac back. Do you hear me?"

She nodded, silent, but tears rolled out of her eyes.

My gut wrenched, and I pulled her against my chest. "I'm so sorry."

Her arms circled me. "I can't lose him."

"You're *not* going to lose him." I took a breath. "It's super late. Do you want to try to get some sleep?" I knew it was a stupid suggestion with things in such turmoil.

She shook her head. There was mud caked in her hair.

"Do you want to take a shower?"

She shook her head again. "I don't want to be alone."

She seemed afraid. I couldn't remember ever seeing her afraid before.

My forehead fell against hers, the images of her all cut up and broken permanently stamped behind my eyes, all because I left her. I kissed her brow. "I'm sorry for leaving you. I never should have—"

"It's not your fault; I just don't want to be alone."

"Ritha needs me to help upstairs. You can come up—"

"I don't need a babysitter."

"You said you didn't want to be alone."

"Oh . . . I just don't want to take a shower. There are too many people here." She wasn't making eye contact with me anymore. "I'm just going to stay and boil herbs and read through your grimoire—if that's okay?"

"Of course."

"Someone has to figure out a way to beat Callis while everyone else does damage control."

"Adele—"

The doorbell rang.

The back curtain flew open, and Ritha stormed past us, an irate look on her face.

We followed but kept some distance as she opened the door.

"Hello, Priestess Borges. I don't think we've been properly introduced." It was Gabe's voice.

"I know who you are. I know what you are."

"*Fantastico.* I'll skip the formalities. I've come to offer support on behalf of my family, the five of us here in New Orleans. Whatever we can do—"

"If it weren't for you, the Animarum Praedators wouldn't be here."

"Be that as it may, we'd like to help."

"You've done enough." She slammed the door in his face.

I instantly relaxed, but Adele cried out, "No! Ritha!"

I grabbed for her hand as she started for the door but missed.

Ritha met Adele and took both of her shoulders. She glanced at me. "Triage, Isaac." Then she turned her attention back to Adele. "Sugar, there is nothing we can do now. Once we know better what we're dealing with, and we have the means, we're going to do everything we can to help your father."

Adele smiled and nodded.

Ritha gave her a quick squeeze and said, "Everything will be okay." Then she hurried past me, giving me a *hurry it up look* on her way.

"See?" I said.

"Not everything. She's not going to do *everything* we can to help him."

"Why would you say that?"

"She just turned down help." Her expression went from perplexed to outraged. "We should be grateful to have their help!"

"They're the ones who started this in the first place."

"What? By stopping Callis's father from raising the dead? By stopping their witch hunt killing thousands of innocent people? Even so, Nicco was a child. He's no more responsible for his father's actions than I am for León's."

"They aren't trustworthy, Adele; they're *vampires!* No matter how much of a man Gabe looks or how beautiful Lisette is, no matter how gentle the words are that come out of Nicco's mouth, they are monsters."

The anger that had been brewing in her eyes boiled over. "I'm not going to just sit around making memory powder when my dad is out there being held hostage by a supernatural psychopath! You should stay and help everyone here. You have the training and the skills, and they need you." She pushed past me. "*I'm fine.* And I'll take Nicco's help even if Ritha won't. I'm going to take down Callis."

"Adele, stop!"

She turned back. "I'm sorry, Isaac. I'm going. I can't sit around here. I'm going."

"You can't leave!"

She stepped to the door, and in my mind I saw her dying. I heard a whisper of French in my ear. I saw the pool of blood around her as he ravished her in the woods. And before I knew what I was doing, the fistful of flowers was in my palm, and I blew them straight at her. "Calm down, Adele. Everything is going to be fine."

She froze mid-step, her hand on the doorknob.

My heart raced. I knew I'd completely crossed the line.

"Adele . . . I'm sorry!"

CHAPTER 70

GATES TO GUINÉE

An unnatural sense of calm waterfalled down my spine, releasing the built-up tension. I'd almost forgotten what I'd been so worked up about as I watched the cute little flowers float over me, draping me with serenity.

The doorknob was still in my palm, but when I tried to twist it, it wouldn't turn. No . . . it was my hand that wouldn't budge. *What the?* I wanted to open the door but . . . *I couldn't move.* My lungs pinched. The magic felt cold, seeping from my shoulders to the tips of my fingers and toes. I tried to shriek, but nothing came out.

"I'm so sorry," Isaac said, touching my shoulder. "I never should have done that."

I couldn't move away from his hand.

And that chilled me to the marrow.

He turned me around. My breath caught, and I shook, trying to get the words out. My brain was freaking the hell out, but my pulse was steady in a completely unnerving way.

I felt a tear sliding down my cheek.

"I-I'm sorry. I just wanted you to be safe."

Horror bloomed inside me like a thistle, pricking my organs, but I had no idea whether I was showing it on my face like I wanted. Getting each word out was like pushing a boulder over a cliff. "You . . . used . . . magic . . . against me."

"No!" He reached for my hand.

"Don't!"

"I'm sorry! I didn't know it would be so strong . . ."

I sucked in breaths, trying to push my feet forward, every muscle in my body straining, my mind ready to combust; yet still, my heart rate remained magically calm and steady. He reached out to help me again.

"Don't . . . touch me!"

"Tell me what to do," he said, fear creeping into his voice. "Do you want me to get Désirée?"

I didn't want her to see me like this. "*NnNnn.*" My head didn't shake like I wanted it to.

"Edgar?"

"No." The word squeaked out.

"It will wear off soon."

I looked anywhere but in his eyes. "Take . . . me . . . to Ren's. Please."

He nodded and cautiously took my hand. "Can you walk?"

I shook my head, or at least I think I did. He seemed to understand. "I'll carry you," he said softly, and then scooped me up and cradled me against his chest. "It's going to be okay," he said as he carefully maneuvered us through the shop, past the Voodoo dolls. Their eyes seemed to follow me with more movement than I was now capable of.

I let my face fall deeper into his chest as he stepped outside. I didn't want anyone to see me. I wouldn't know how to explain to anyone what Isaac had done. *He was supposed to love me.*

Of all the horrible things I'd encountered tonight—the souls, the cemetery, Callis, the undertow, the Ghost Drinkers—none had been able to disable me as completely as Isaac had.

I never got my magic back.

My dad was gone.

Papa Olsin was dead.

And Isaac had magically *drugged* me.

Everything. Was.

Wrong.

But the magic sang soothing lullabies in my ears. We went up the stairs of the guest house and down the halls, which echoed with the moans of the Possessed. When I saw the light from Ren's room, heard his voice, flickers of comfort hugged my shoulders.

As we entered, he was pacing the length of the room.

Isaac set me on his bed, glancing back at him. "I don't know if I should leave you in here with Ren like this, if you can't . . ."

I gazed at him. "Get. *Out.*" My heart had never felt so strained. My breath stuttered. I knew if it weren't for the magic, I'd be having a panic attack.

"We're a team." His voice croaked. "A coven. If you broke away, Adele, you might die. I need you. I didn't mean to."

"Get out!"

"Your dad would *not* want you coming after him."

"Don't tell me what my dad would want!" I screamed.

He stepped back.

The tears on his face killed me. Out of all the pain I'd felt tonight, this was the worst. But I still wanted to jump up and shove him out the door. If only I could move.

Ren started singing.

"Get out."

Isaac backed out of the room, his eyes locked with mine. I hated whoever had taken the doors off the hinges. I wanted to slam them; instead, I watched him until he was swallowed up by the darkness, and then I toppled over on my side, staring out from the bed.

My brain was foggy, and my muscles felt like they'd been filled with lead. I lay completely still, waiting for the drugs to wear off.

Ren paced back and forth from the fireplace to his desk, joyously singing, "*Sette notti, sette lune. Sette porte, sette tombe.*"

The words were close enough to French for me to translate in my head: seven nights, seven moons; seven gates, seven tombs. He was still going on about the gates to Guinée.

Focus on Mac. You need a plan for when this stuff wears off.

I wondered if Isaac was just around the corner in the hallway. I wondered if, when I could move again, I'd be able to squeeze out of Ren's tiny window.

Isaac had said that Callis had too much power now, and that the property was too fortified to break into. I tried to imagine what kind of plan Ritha and Chatham would come up with to attack Callis. Did the witches here even know how to fight? Callis was practically born with a sword in his hand. Jakome Salazar, his father, had been able to infiltrate the Medici palazzo and kill Nicco's grandfather. The witches of New Orleans might be great at protecting the people they loved, but they'd never be able to ambush a magical fortress and take down a coven of ancient, immortal witches—who could literally suck up magic. They were never going to get Mac back.

As soon as my pulse began charging, the magic swaddled it, and I began to calm again.

I don't want to be calmed.

If Callis had too much power for us to attack, then there was only one thing to do: we had to take away his power. But how to do that was not so simple . . .

"*Sette notti, sette lune,*" Ren sang as he tossed a handful of his drawings into the air and twirled in the falling papers. "*Sette porte, sette tombe.*"

Everything Ritha had taught me about magic raced through my mind, but I kept coming back to one thing. *The spirits are the binding.*

I looked at Ren, and an idea galloped across my heart. There *was* a way to take down Callis. To take away his power, we must destroy the tie that binds. *We have to break the Salazar family line!*

And Ren could help me . . . The ancestors of witches lived out eternity in Guinée.

Dizziness turned my head over, but I forced myself to sit up.

The night in the convent, when I'd been tied to the statue with the fire blazing around us, I'd felt Nicco above me, believing in me. But I'd believed in myself to save him and my mom. It wasn't just the night Callis had stolen my Fire; it was the night I got my Mark.

I'd removed the sleeping spell from the Medici.

I shut my eyes and focused. *It's just a sedative, Adele. It's not even a full-blown spell.* I imagined the light of the magic inside me, the tiny buds of magic-infused flower petals glowing like little fireflies. Only these fireflies made me loopy and tired and artificially calm. I imagined them coming out of my stomach and traveling up my throat. I pulled and pulled, and I toppled onto the floor and landed on my palms, choking, coughing up the invisible happiness, spitting, until something flew out of my mouth: six little buds of chamomile, rolled away, burnt to a crisp.

It all flooded back, the pain sending me lurching over to my side.

Isaac. My dad. Papa Olsin. The brute's breath and his sweaty stomach shoving into my back and his hand touching my waist. I shuddered.

Panting, I looked up at Ren, who was now staring at me. "I . . . can handle . . . the pain. I am stronger than everyone thinks."

Ren knelt on one knee next to me and nodded. "*Sì.*"

I shoved all the pain and betrayal to the black hole of my mind. *Focus on Mac. Nothing else.* And to save my father, I needed to take down Callis. I needed to go to Guinée.

The scent of citrus wafted my way. *Alessandro.*

I pointed to Ren. "*Incantesimo di silenziamento*?" I asked, mimicking Nicco's accent as best I could.

He nodded rapidly, eyes lighting up.

"I'm going to try to remove the spell from you. Is that okay?"

He nodded and stood, hand out to me.

I rose, and he hung onto me for a second longer. He could tell I was wobbly. "I'm okay," I said.

I can do this.

He spoke to me in rapid Italian. I was pretty sure he was cheering me on.

I held my hands out to his torso and let my eyes slip shut, feeling for the magic inside him. I felt his built-up aggression. His frustration. His loneliness. Fear. And then there it was, the supernatural sensation, buried like a little green glowworm. It wriggled as I reached for it.

I stepped back and twisted my hands together in the air, calling for it. Commanding it. Pulling it to me.

It's just positive space moving into negative space.

The worm loosened.

"Come on!" I planted my feet into the floor and pulled. I screamed with the effort and hoped the shouting of the Possessed down the hallway and the cacophony of chaos in the courtyard would mask my voice, and that Isaac wouldn't hear us and come busting in.

I gave one final yank and flew backward to the ground, sprawled out—but I didn't let go. I sat back on my knees, the glowing worm of energy in my hands. *The silencing spell.*

"*Bébé*!" he roared. "What in God's name?" He blew out his lips like a babe.

As we watched, the worm shrank until it completely fizzled out, no longer able to fulfill the intention of its caster.

He looked back at me. "That's quite a hairdo you've got there."

"Ren! It's so good to finally hear your voice!"

"I'm not sure anyone's ever said that to me, Addie."

"How do you feel?"

"Hmm . . . hard to say. Somewhere in between two and four Purple Dranks from Lafitte's."

"Ren! I need your help."

"*Oui, ma chère*?"

"I need you to tell me the story about the Gates to Guinée. You know it, right?"

"*Pfft*. Know it? Have you forgotten who you are speaking to?" He strutted to the coatrack, removed his Victorian-style velvet jacket, and swooped his arms through the sleeves, coattails wagging as he walked to the fireplace. He did a doubletake, seeing himself in the mirror. "That's quite a hairdo you have yourself, there, René."

He picked up his top hat off the mantel, covered his stringy curls, and then put on the thin wireframe glasses. One of the purple lenses was missing. His knees went a little wobbly, and I leapt up, holding him. "I'm fine! I'm fine! Just get me my walking stick, *s'il vous plaît*."

I hurried to his desk and grabbed the crystal-skull-adorned stick.

"Take a seat," he said as I handed it to him.

I sat back on the bed, hoping I wasn't pushing him too far.

He slid across the floor in his socks, cane in the air, and landed right in front of me. I swear the flames in the fireplace leapt higher, leaning in to listen as well.

He tossed the cane a couple of times and then pointed the skull my way, switching into full-drama mode. But there was something different this time, like he was so happy to talk, he was gliding on air. "Now you see, Miss Le Moyne, there are many theories all over the world about the entrances to the Afterworld. There are theories even here in our very own La Nouvelle-Orléans." He turned left and then right, as if making sure to give attention to the entire room. "There are those who believe that the seven gates to Guinée are here among our cities of dead."

I slipped my hand into my shirt pocket and hit the record button on my phone, just in case it was too much to remember.

"And those people would be exactly *correct*." I smiled despite wanting him to hurry it up. I needed to get out of there before Isaac came back. "But only those whose intentions are pure can know the way."

Was it really possible to go to the Afterworld? Nervousness began to bubble up inside of me.

"You see . . . there are:

Seven nights, seven moons,
Seven gates, seven tombs.

Seven keys will let you enter,
Nibo's axe, Plumaj's feather.
Scent of night blossoms for Masaka,
Sip of piman, dance the Banda.

Silken rings for Zaranye,
Oussou's pipe will get you high,
Leave your ego in a jar,
The family Ghede will take you far.

Through waves of chaos, rocky cliffs of Abysmal
waters
Where for a mirror, Doubye will steer you through
Truths, reflections, the bare depths of the real you.

Fields of poppies, whirls of pleasure,
will satisfy your every urge
And only when you're on the verge
of erotic doom
Will Ghede L'Oraille set you free so you can bloom.

He hopped around, wildly gesticulating with his cane, pointing to this and that.

The sanctimonious need not cross,
Your lies will only get you tossed.
Twisted words and veils of secrets,
turn to ash by licks from flaming tongues.
Only those who seek the truth will have any fun.

Follow the past, listen to lè mò,
And the secrets of the dead you will know.
Turn thrice and say the name of the one who
haunts you,
And find the Gates to Guinée beyond you.

"Doubye," I whispered, "and *L'Oraille."* The final two Ghede.

"A mirror and a poppy," he said.

"*Merci beaucoup*, Ren." I jumped up and hugged him. "I'm going to save Mac, thanks to you."

Now I just had to get the hell out of Ren's room without anyone noticing. I was sure the chaos would provide ample cover, but I didn't want to risk it—and if I ran into Dee, I didn't know if I could lie well enough to her. She'd want to come, but I couldn't risk anyone else's life. I wasn't letting anyone else I loved get hurt because this psycho-witch wanted something from my long-lost immortal ancestor!

I scanned the walls.

"You have to help me one more time, Ren," I whispered. "You have to help me get out of here." I dragged a chair over to the small window and stood on it. I was still barely tall enough to reach it.

"I've already tried that. Too small."

"Maybe for you." I unhooked the latch and pulled the window open. He was right. The space was minuscule. "All right, give me a boost, *s'il vous plaît.*"

He crouched down to let me step on his shoulders like I was five again and we were at a parade. "I don't think your Pa would like me pushing you out a window." He snugly held my bare feet and lifted me up.

"Well, he's going to have to get over it this one time." I reached my arms out the window and crumpled my shoulders inward. "I have to get out of here if I'm going to save him—and you."

There was a tree branch right outside. I grabbed it and prayed it would hold as I shimmied my hips through the window. Thank goodness for Earth witches and their powerhouse plants. I hugged the branch, and the latter half of my body gracelessly flopped out of the window.

I swung up to the tree branch, clutching it with all four limbs, and rested for a moment, feeling all of the fresh bruises.

"Good luck, *bébé*!" Ren yelled.

"*Shhh*! Quiet voice!" I doubted Isaac had gone very far.

If I ran into anyone, I'd be screwed. Luckily, I knew every back alley in the French Quarter, but I also had to make two stops first. Hopefully there would be a pair of shoes at one of them.

The tearoom was dark, and the scents of Hexennacht hung in the air, but the darkness surrounding the party décor was eerie and solemn. I could hear people in the back. Feet scrummaging upstairs. Girls sobbing. An image of Papa Olsin lying somewhere in this place made me freeze up. *I can't let anyone else I love die.* I walked across to the counter, keeping the lights off, guided only by the moonlight pouring in from the bay windows.

A sickly feeling hit the pit of my stomach. *I'm not stealing.* I pulled the lever on the cash register and it popped open with a zing. *Shit!* I held still for a second, listening for footsteps. I looked at the vase of roses, half expecting a ghostly chill to knock it over and alert everyone to my thieving.

I lifted the drawer and took out the ornate key hidden below, my heart pounding. I went to the armoire, slid the key into place, and twisted. The lock dropped.

I quickly examined the racks of ghoststicks inside. I had no idea what the difference was between them. My gaze landed on a dusty wand near the back, and I lifted it out. The branch was rough and damp, like it was still alive, soaking up water. Both ends were edged with huge rose quartz points that appeared to have swirls of smoke captured inside them. Words and symbols scrolled from each end of the wand and met in the middle, neither of which I could read: half were in German, and the other half in a language that must have been Choctaw. The slightest shift of my wrist caused prisms of rainbows to glow from the crystals.

"A ghoststick to kill the spirit of a Ghost Drinker," I whispered.

I locked up the armoire, scribbled out an IOU, and left the note in the drawer with the key.

The bell jingled as the door rattled open, and I froze in the darkness.

"Adele?"

Shit. Codi. I pushed the wand up the long sleeve of my shirt, clutching the crystal hidden in my palm, and turned around. I was barely able to look him in the face, and yet when our eyes locked, I couldn't look away despite feeling like the undertow was sweeping me away again.

"Désirée just told me that my gr— A-are you okay? Is it true?"

I slowly exhaled, my lungs on fire. I nodded. "I'm so sorry, Codi. He pulled me out of the river, and he sa— He savvv—" That was it. No more words would come out. I hurried from behind the counter as he came forward, and I pulled him into my arms.

He squeezed me tight. "I'm going to kill Callis," he whispered. "I'm going to kill that monster."

I held him close. I could feel the anger pulsing through his broad shoulders and heavy arms.

"I want to see him," Codi said.

"Of course, Codi. Go and be with your family. I'll make you some tea."

He nodded, let me go, and wiped his eyes.

I watched him as he walked to the hallway, thinking again about everything I had to do.

"Codi," I called out. He turned. "I love you."

"I love you too. We all do. You are our family."

I nodded and waited until he disappeared in the darkness, and then turned on the kettle and pulled out a tray. Cups, saucers, sugar, spoons. I put a soothing blend into the tea strainer and poured the steaming water into the pot, wondering if this was the last time I'd ever do this.

I carried it through the hallway and up the stairs, hearing the Daure's sobs growing louder with each step. When I got to the parlor on the third floor, I stopped outside the door, hidden in the shadows. *I can't go in. If I take one more step, I'll never leave.*

I set the tray down for them, turned, and walked away. I didn't run. Or cry like I wanted to. I just swiftly walked down the stairs and back through the shop.

On the way out, my eye caught a basket of moccasins that had been handmade by Papa Olsin. I imagined him constructing them, his gentle wrinkly hands sewing every last stitch so carefully, and my heart throbbed.

I remembered his warm smile.

And his warnings.

I took a deep breath, bent down, and swiped two moccasins that looked about my size.

My courage strengthened with each step as I hurried through the third floor of HQ. *This is for the best.*

It's the only way.

I ran down the stairs with my bag, not pausing, not thinking about all the memories I had here with Isaac and Désirée and Codi. I knew that if I paused, I might chicken out. I quickened my pace, running into the blue room.

I stopped in front of the map on the wall, gazing at it one last time in all of its glory. I held out my hand, focused on the nails holding it in place, and tried yanking them with my mind.

Nothing.

Freaking selective magic. I don't have time for this.

I began pulling the nails out, one by one, letting them clank to the floor. I rolled up the map, stuck it in my bag next to the ghoststick, and slung it on my back.

I turned to leave and froze.

Isaac stood in the doorway.

"What are you doing?" he asked, stepping closer.

"Get out of my way."

He stopped, pain filling his eyes.

The longer he stood staring at me, the closer I was to crumbling.

"Adele, I'm sorry. I didn't know the magic would have such a strong effect."

"Witchcraft 101: the strength of a spell lies within the intention of its caster. You used magic against me," I said, the words not much more than a wisp.

"I wasn't using it *against* you. I just wanted you to calm down so you wouldn't do anything stupid. I just wanted to keep you safe."

"I'm not something for you to keep safe—to put in a box so I don't break. I don't have my magic. I couldn't even defend myself!"

"You don't need to defend yourself against me! I love you!"

He stepped closer, and my arm instinctually flung out, trying to pull the chair between us. My magic failed me, once again.

"See! You can't even move a chair! How would you fare out there?"

"It's *my* choice."

The pain in his eyes deepened, but the words came out of my mouth anyway: "I know why it's so hard for me to say it . . ." My eyes welled. "I don't trust you, Isaac. I don't trust you to make decisions for me . . ." I sucked in a quick breath. "Or for my family. To know our secrets. How could I be in love with you?"

He didn't blink as the tears streamed from his eyes.

The lump in my throat was so big, I wasn't sure how I got the words past it. "I am going to save my father. And I am 'running' to Nicco. And I don't care what you think is best, or if you judge me or think I'm desperate. *I am desperate.*" I stormed past him.

"Adele!" He grabbed me, his strong fingers squeezing my shoulder, and I stiffened. "Just let me expl—"

"Get *off* of me," I said, not recognizing the cold fury in my own voice.

He released me, and I marched out the door. I felt him following behind me, out onto the porch. I turned and looked straight into his eyes. "If you follow me down that street, I'm going to scream for Nicco, and you better pray that he doesn't hear me."

"Adele, I just wanted to keep you safe."

"That's why I'm going to Nicco's. It's the only place I feel safe."

"Adele! We're going to get Mac back! Just stay! *Adele*!"

Every time he said my name, my heart fractured again, but I didn't look back as I strode down the lawn and out the gate. My heart might have been made of glass, but the rest of me was as strong as the wrought iron that decorated this town.

I was going to Guinée. I was going to kill the spirit of Jakome Salazar and put an end to their family's succubus magic.

And I was going to save my father.

CHAPTER 71

MAY DAY

I opened the gate at the Medici compound and walked up the steps to the front door.

Before I even knocked, even with the noisy bedlam on the streets behind me, I felt the thumps of his heart.

Nicco opened the door.

A look of relief washed over his face, and I somehow knew I'd made the right choice.

"We're going to get your father back, *bella*."

"I know . . . And we're going to avenge yours."

He moved aside, giving a welcoming wave of his hand, and I stepped over the threshold. He closed the door behind me.

Voices billowed from the library upstairs. A different kind of bustle filled the house. Not panic. It was an energy of those making plans. Preparations. By those who had done this kind of thing before.

We walked up the stairs together, steps in sync, and everything felt right.

I didn't feel safe here because Nicco was going to protect me. I felt safe here because Nicco made me feel strong.

Because I am strong.

THE EPIC CONCLUSION!

BOOK 4: THE GATES TO GUINÉE

To stay up to date on the latest news on the final book in *THE CASQUETTE GIRLS* series and other writing by Alys Arden, sign up for her mailing list at: www.alysarden.com.

ACKNOWLEDGMENTS

The Casquette Girls constellation has grown into a galaxy in the time since the second book was published. My brain swirls trying to figure out where to start.

From the bottom of my heart, I thank each and every one of you who has continued on the journey with Adele through the streets of New Orleans and now Basque. The joy from readers makes every five-a.m. morning, every re-write, every publishing-related tear worth it. The fans of this series are *magical.*

This novel transformed many times over, becoming stronger along the way thanks to a great number of people. First and foremost, my editor Marissa van Uden, who I believe loves Adele and company as much as I do. <3 <3 To Laura Perry, Monica S. Kuebler, Charlotte Ashley, Francesca Testaguzza, and Sarah LostButFound. Thank you to all the people in the occult world who answered my research questions (you know who you are.)

Eternal gratitude to Emilie Gagnet Leumas, archivist of the Archdiocese of New Orleans, for all of the shared cups of coffee, glasses of wine, and conversations that make strangers beg to know what we are talking about. To Amanda deLeon for encouraging me to go dark or die. And to Kami Garcia for getting me across the finish line.

Thank you to my agents extraordinaire: Alexandra Machinist and Zoë Sandler, at ICM Partners. A *massive* thank-you to Galen Dara for another magical and macabre cover illustration. And to Rachel Rivera for bearing with the printer through all the revisions.

Thank you to my parents for not blinking when I said I needed to build a mausoleum in my living room for an event.

And to all of these amazing people who continue to support me on my journey: The team at Skyscape for their continued love and support for this series. Marita Crandle, and the entire staff at Boutique du Vampyre. Jeanne Mullen and family at the Bottom of the Cup Tearoom. Ryan and Marcy Von Hesseling of One Eyed Jacks, and the entire staff at Fifi Mahony's. Russell Desmond, proprietor of Arcadian Books. Amy Lowery of Garden District Book Shop. Candice Detillier Huber of Tubby & Coo's Mid-City Book Shop and Veronica Brooks-Sigler at Octavia Books.

To all of my beta readers! And especially to Melissa Criswell Herman, Melanie Hogan, and Lindsey Clarke for carrying me through the journey when I couldn't see the light. To Melissa Lucas, Jackie Garlick, and Stormy Smith for being there during the early days of drafting. And to my friends who continue to support me in everything I do, but especially Alex Rosa, Lucas Stoffel, Jennifer Thurnau, Christy and Andrew Zolty.

To all of the amazing Bookstagrammers who bring me joy with your magical photos. And thank you to everyone in *The Attic*! (If you aren't a member of our group, you'll find us on Facebook.)

See you in the next one. xoxo

ABOUT THE AUTHOR

Alys Arden was raised by the street performers, tea-leaf readers, and glittering drag queens of the New Orleans French Quarter. She cut her teeth on the streets of New York and has worked all around the world since. She still dreams of running away with the circus one star-swept night. Follow her adventures on Twitter or Instagram at @alysarden.

CPSIA information can be obtained
at www.ICGtesting.com
Printed in the USA
LVHW091532050219
606471LV00003B/596/P